COUNTRY OF THE
BAD WOLFES

A Novel

BY JAMES CARLOS BLAKE

NO EXIT PRESS

First published in the UK in 2015 by No Exit Press,
an imprint of Oldcastle Books Ltd, PO Box 394,
Harpenden, Herts, AL5 1XJ, UK

noexit.co.uk

ISBN
978-1-84344-555-5 (print)
978-1-84344-556-2 (Epub)
978-1-84344-557-9 (Kindle)
978-1-84344-558-6 (pdf)

2 4 6 8 10 9 7 5 3 1

Book design by Blue Panda Design Studio
Printed in Great Britain by Clays Ltd, St Ives plc

IN MEMORY OF MY FATHER,

CARLOS SEBASTIÁN BLAKE
(1911-2002)

Therefore, since the world has still
Much good, but much less good than ill,
And while the sun and moon endure
Luck's a chance, but trouble's sure,
I'd face it as a wise man would,
And train for ill and not for good.

—A. E. HOUSMAN, *A Shropshire Lad*

We may be through with the past, but the past ain't through with us.

—PAUL THOMAS ANDERSON, *Magnolia*

What country more dear or defiant than that of our own blood?

—ANONYMOUS

No hay reglas fijas.

—A PRECEPT OF LONG STANDING ALONG THE LOWER RIO GRANDE

WOLFE
GENEALOGY

❧ HENRY MORGAN WOLFE *m* HEDDA JULIET BLAKE ❧

1 Roger Blake Wolfe ——————————— *2* Harrison Augustus
   m Mary Margaret Parham
      1 John Roger ——————————————— *w*/Alma Rodríguez
         m Elizabeth Anne Bartlett   ↓*1* Juana Merced
           1 John Samuel   *w*/Katrina Ávila
              m Victoria Clara Márquez   *1* Juan Lobo
                 1 Juan Sotero *m* Estér Leticia Hernandez
                    1 Juan Román
                    2 Carlos Sebastián
                 2 Roger Samuel
              2 James Sebastian *m* Marina Colmillo
                 1 Morgan James
                 2 Harry Sebastian
            3 Blake Cortéz
              m Remedios Marisól Delgallo
                 1 Jackson Ríos
                 2 César Augusto
                 3 Victoria Angélica
   2 Samuel Thomas
      m María Palomina Blanco
         1 Gloria Tomasina
            m Louis Welch Little
               1 Luis Charón Little *m* Rosario Monte DeLeón
                    1 Eduardo Luis Little
                    2 Sandra Rosario Little
                    3 Catalina Luisiana Little
         2 Bruno Tomás
            m Felicia Flor Méndez
              1 Javier Tomás
              2 Joaquín Félix
         3 Sofía Reina
            m Melchor Cervantes
            m Arturo Villaseñor
              1 Francisco Villaseñor
            m Jorge Cabaza
              1 Pieto Tomás Cabaza
              2 Samuel Palomino Cabaza
            m Diego Guzmán
            m Amos Bentley

PROLOGUE

The family landed in the Western Hemisphere in the person of Roger Blake Wolfe, who arrived with a price on his head. No likeness of him—a sketch, a painting, a daguerreotype—survived through the generations, and the accepted description of him as handsome was based solely on the family's penchant for romantic fancy and the genetic testament of their own good looks. Even his own sons never knew him in the flesh.

As a matter of record, Roger Blake Wolfe was born in London in 1797. His father was Henry Morgan Wolfe, an Irishman of murky lineage who triumphed over that disadvantage of birth to become a British naval officer and then managed the even more heroic achievement of marrying into a wealthy Knightsbridge family named Blake. Henry Wolfe had high ambitions for his son in the Royal Navy, but Roger, who loved the sea but abhorred regimentation, did not share them. When he ran away at age sixteen, absconding from a maritime academy, his father disinherited him through an announcement in the *Times*.

Thirteen years later Roger Blake Wolfe was a pirate captain of some notoriety, one of the last of a breed near to extinction by the early 19th century. His ship was named either the *Yorick* or the *York Witch*, the former name appearing in some reports and court documents, the latter in others. Although he restricted his freeboot to the waters off Iberia and West Africa and never attacked an English vessel, the British in 1826 acceded to diplomatic imperatives and joined with various aggrieved nations in posting a reward for his capture, dead or alive. Whereupon Captain Wolfe decided to distance himself from that part of the world. Three of the crew's Englishmen chose not to go with him and he put them ashore near Lisbon with enough money to make their way home. The first mate said he understood their feelings. He said it was a hard thing to say goodbye forever to one's home country. Captain Wolfe laughed at that and said it wasn't so hard when one's home country wanted to hang one. And set sail across the Atlantic.

Fifteen leagues shy of Nantucket the ship was struck by a ferocious storm and foundered. Only Roger and two of his crew survived the sinking, clutching to a spar in that plunging frigid sea. The storm at last abated during the night but one of the crewmen succumbed to the cold and slipped off into the darkness. Shortly afterward the spar suddenly shook in a phosphorescent agitation and the other crewman vanished, his scream lost to the depths. Roger did not see the shark that took him. Through the rest of the night he expected to be attacked too but was not. The following day broke clear and sun-bright on a calm sea, and by wondrous chance he was spotted by an American whaler bound for home. His fingers had to be pried from the spar and it was hours more before his shivering began to ease under a heavy cover of blankets and sizable doses of rum. He was landed in New Bedford and his adventure condensed to a newspaper item in which he claimed to be Morgan Blake and described the lost ship as a Dutch cargo carrier.

It is anyone's guess how he occupied himself during the next year or what took him to Portsmouth, New Hampshire, where in October of 1827 and under his true name he married Mary Margaret Parham, who at the time believed he was a merchant ship master. Six weeks later he sailed away to southward and she never heard from him again. Six months after his departure she bore his twin sons. The boys were a year old when she received notice of their father's execution in Mexico.

※

Archives in Veracruz contain a variety of documents pertaining to Roger Blake Wolfe's arrest in a waterfront cantina on Christmas Eve of 1828 and his ensuing trial and conviction on charges of piracy and murder in Mexican waters. In keeping with protocol, the British Consulate provided a Mexican attorney for his defense and afterward concurred with the court's verdict. For reasons unrecorded he was sentenced to be shot rather than hanged, the usual and more ignominious fate of condemned pirates.

The morning of his execution on the first day of February, 1829, was reported to be clear and mild. The central plaza raucous with parrots and marimba bands, with vendors hawking melon slices and coconut milk. The air tanged with the smell of the gulf. The large crowd was composed of every social class and in a mood even more festive than usual for an execution—perhaps, as one newspaper surmised, because of the novelty of the condemned man's Anglo nationality. When Roger was trundled to the plaza in a donkey cart amid the tolling of steeple bells and made to stand against the church wall in front of the firing squad, there were catcalls and whistles but also much comment on his undaunted demeanor and striking figure. His clothes were fresh-laundered, his beard in neat trim, his hatless black locks tied in a horse tail at his nape.

PROLOGUE

A diversion occurred when a pair of young women at the fore of the crowd, each claiming to be Captain Roger's true sweetheart, got into a skirt-hiking scuffle to the delight of the nearest male witnesses. It was said that the pirate himself seemed amused by this contest over his affections. In a valediction rendered through an interpreter, he assured the two girls that he loved them both to equal degree, a sentiment that stirred the crowd to murmurs of both grudging approbation and high skepticism. He gave one of the girls his gold earring and the other a finger ring set with a pearl in the shape of a skull. When he bequeathed his remaining credit at a cantina called Las Sirenas toward as many drinks as it would buy for the regular patrons of that establishment, there were loud cheers of "Viva el capitán!" from the corner of the plaza where that disreputable bunch was assembled.

He declined a blindfold and stood smoking a cigar, an insouciant thumb hooked in his belt, as the fusiliers took aim. At the muskets' discharge, a squall of birds burst from the trees and a slow blue cloud of powdersmoke ascended after them. The officer in charge of the execution—a young lieutenant named Montenegro—delivered the customary coup de grâce pistolshot to the head. Then unsheathed his saber and with an expert slash decapitated the corpse.

The head was taken at once to the yellow-rock fortress of San Juan de Ulúa at the mouth of the harbor and placed on a tower pike in warning to all the city and every passing ship. The body was borne off in the donkey cart, and onlookers made the sign of the cross as it passed them on its way to the graveyard. And the two women who had fought over him were not the only ones to dip their skirt hems in the blood puddled in the cobbles.

He was buried in the low-lying cemetery at the south end of the city. He had arranged for a marble headstone engraved with his name and *ad vivum praedo*. But within a week of his interment the marker was stolen by persons unknown.

On its high vantage over the harbor, the head blackened and was fed upon by birds and over time reduced to bare yellow bone with a .54-caliber hole in the parietal and an unremitting grin. The skull disappeared in the next hurricane, and the floodwaters forced open his grave and carried his bones to the sea.

PART ONE

꧁ HENRY MORGAN WOLFE *m* HEDDA JULIET BLAKE ꧂

1 Roger Blake Wolfe ————————— *2* Harrison Augustus

    m Mary Margaret Parham

        1 John Roger

            m Elizabeth Anne Bartlett

                1 John Samuel

        2 Samuel Thomas

            m María Palomina Blanco

                1 Gloria Tomasina

                2 Bruno Tomás

                3 Sofía Reina

MARY MARGARET
AND THE GEMINI

The twin sons of Roger Blake Wolfe were born in late May under the apt sign of Gemini. Mary Margaret named them Samuel Thomas—the elder by three minutes—and John Roger. She and the boys lived with her widower father, John Thomas Parham, in a flat above his Portsmouth tavern, where she tended tables every night. It was a waterfront pub catering to a seaman trade, Mr Parham himself having been thirteen years a merchant officer before a shipboard mishap left him crippled of foot and permanently dependent on a crutch. Except for the first six weeks of her marriage, during which she and Captain Wolfe lived in a rented cottage, the tavern was the only home Mary Margaret had ever known or would. Only nineteen years old when widowed, she would afterward not lack for suitors but she would not marry again. As in the case of Roger Blake Wolfe, no picture of her would pass down through the generations, but her sons would describe her to their children as blue-eyed and slender, with pale brown hair she liked to wear in a braid down her back.

❈

From the time of their early childhood the twins were curious about their father and now and again questioned Mary Margaret about him. Beyond telling them he had been a merchant ship captain and was lost at sea, she was disinclined to discuss him and was skilled at changing the subject. Both her reticence and her falsehoods were rooted in a sense of disgrace. She had not been able to surmount her angry shame over his desertion of her and their unborn children. A shame made all the worse after he had been gone for a year and a half and she received a letter from the British Embassy apprising her that her husband and British subject Roger Blake Wolfe, a captain of pirates and fugitive from justice, had been convicted of murder by the Mexican government and duly executed in the city of Veracruz. The letter did not relate the particulars of his crime or the means of his execution nor disclose the disposition of his remains, but she did not care to know any of those details. She wept for days in sorrowful and furious mortification. How could the man she loved so dearly have done such dreadful things? How was it possible she had loved a man so different in truth from what he had seemed to her? What other lies had he told her? The more she pondered these questions the more the very notion of love did baffle her.

She demanded her father's promise not to tell her sons of Roger's criminal occupation and ignoble death, and because he was sympathetic to her sentiments Mr Parham so promised. But although he did not say so, he believed she was in error to keep the truth from the twins. He was not so shocked as his daughter by the news about Captain Wolfe. He'd had his hunch about the man from the start, having been acquainted with a number of men disposed to outlawry and having at times even conspired in a bit of furtive business with some of them. This minor criminality was but one secret Mr Parham had kept from his wife and daughter. Another was that his father had been Red Ned Kennedy, the notorious mankiller and highwayman. Mr Parham himself had been unaware of his true paternity until after his mother died of the consumption when he was twelve and he was taken in by her old-maid sister. One day in a fit of meanness the aunt told him all about his nefarious father. "Hanged your pa was," she told him, "in the public square at Kittery in the glorious year of '76, not six months after your birth. Your poor mam so wanting to spare ye the dishonor of him, God pity her, that she quit his name and took back our own. Oh, she thought she had herself a prize, she did, when she married that one with his easy smile and blarney and his promises to be a lawful man. And just look what came of it. Heartbreak and shame and an early widowhood. I'd a thousand times choose to have no man a-tall than be wed to a blackguard like him." Young Mr Parham had affected a woeful disillusionment in his father in order to satisfy his aunt's righteousness and thereby ease the temper of his stay with her until he was of age to go to sea. But he would all his life harbor a secret pride in a sire who had been so feared in his time, and the only regret he'd ever had in being son to Red Ned Kennedy was that he himself was not more like him. He thought his grandsons might feel the same way to know their own pa had been a "gentleman of fortune," as the phrase of the day had it. Still, he knew better than to say so to Mary Margaret, who would certainly not agree nor even care to hear it.

But as the twins grew older their entreaties about their father became more insistent and difficult for Mary Margaret to deflect. She knew she could not go on refusing them but her heart remained a divided country in its feelings for her husband and she was uncertain of what to tell them. The boys were eleven when she at last capitulated to their appeals—and little by little, over the months, she acquainted them with Roger Blake Wolfe as she had known him. And in the process of so doing, she discovered that he yet held a greater claim on the sunny south of her heart than on its frosty north. Still, she never spoke of him to her sons by any name other than "your father," "Captain Wolfe," or simply "the captain." Nor did she soon recant her falsehoods about his true vocation and manner of demise. And her accounts to them omitted of course many private particulars.

❦

She met Roger Blake Wolfe on a summer eve when he came into the tavern for a mug of ale and dish of sausage. Dozens of sailors had wooed Mary Margaret in vain but with Captain Wolfe's first smile she was smitten. He was not tall but carried himself as a tall man. He wore a close pointed beard and his black hair and hazel eyes would be replicated in his sons. So too his cocky grin. He began showing up at the tavern every night and each time she caught sight of him her breath deepened. He gladdened her. Made her laugh. Made her blush and feel warm with his compliments. His speech was tinged with the brogue of his Irish da. He was the only one she ever permitted to call her Maggie. She had known him barely two weeks the first time she sneaked out her window late one night to rendezvous in a moonlit copse above the harbor. She was seventeen. He was her first lover and her last.

Mr Parham too had taken a shine to the captain and when Mary Margaret, after barely two months' society with the man, told her father they were in love and wanted to marry right away, he did not object. The next day he received Captain Wolfe at home and granted his request for his daughter's hand. Mary Margaret was pleased but had expected resistance. Ever since her childhood both her father and her mother, a comely and lettered woman who died when Mary Margaret was twelve, had many times warned her about sailors as a breed not prone to cleave close to the hearth. Her father's ready acceptance of the marriage convinced her he knew the real reason for her haste.

Her conviction was correct. Mr Parham had easily intuited Mary Margaret's compelling condition and knew it was not the less compelling for being as old as morality and as common as cliché. Given that the usual course of sailors in such a state of affairs was to abandon the girl to her shameful fate, the real surprise to Mr Parham was Captain Wolfe's willingness to marry Mary Margaret. It was testimony to the man's honor that he would not forsake mother and child to the disrepute of bastardy. But while Mr Parham had no doubt of his daughter's unreserved love for the captain, he knew the captain's love for her was of a different kind and that probably sooner rather than later the man could not help but break her heart.

On a crisp afternoon in early October they were wed in a maritime chapel overlooking Portsmouth Bay. The next six weeks were the happiest of Mary Margaret's life. The captain was only twice absent from home and for only a few days each time, once to Gloucester and once to Portland, on business which he did not confide and about which she did not inquire. He had told her little of his past, saying there was little enough to tell. His Irish father a boat builder by trade, his

English mother a beauty with a hearty laugh, both of them killed in a house fire when he was a child, and then a London orphanage until he ran away to sea. This bare synopsis was ample to her, as the man himself was her absorption. She liked to watch the play of his form as he axed cordwood, to see his enjoyment in meals of her making, to feel his fingers loosing her hair from its braid, to wake before him early of a morning and watch him still at sleep. To share in his love of dancing. Among her most joyful memories were those of high-stepping with him to the fiddles and pipes on a dancehall Saturday night. Sometimes when he was full of drink he would sing humorous bawdy songs and she would laugh even as she admonished him to mind his manners. He was a man of wit and easy laughter, she told her sons, and had a gift for telling a tale.

"Was he a good fighter?" Samuel Thomas once asked, his eyes avid. And was puzzled by the melancholic look his mother fixed upon him. Then she sighed and said yes, the captain could surely fight. She had witnessed the proof of it one busy evening in the tavern. There was a sudden commotion at the rear of the room and she looked over there to see a large man speaking angrily and pointing a finger in the captain's face, but she could not hear his words for the clamor of the crowd forming about them. Then she had to stand on a chair to see—and she nearly cried out at the sight of the man brandishing a long-bladed knife such as the shark-fishers used, and the captain barehanded. The circle of spectators moved across the floor with the two men as the sharker advanced on the captain with vicious swipes of the knife. She mimicked the sharker's action—*swish swish swish*—and how the captain hopped rearward with his arms outflinging at each pass of the blade. Her eyes were brighter than she knew as she reenacted the fight for her sons, who were spellbound. Then a heavy tankard came to the captain's hand, and in his next sidestep of the knife he struck the sharker a terrific blow to the head, staggering him. Then hit him again and knocked him stunned and bloody-faced to the floor. He kicked away the knife and stood over him with an easy smile and the room thundered with bellows to finish him, *finish him!* The man was on all fours when the captain clubbed him on the crown with the tankard and he buckled like a hammered beef. The walls shook with cheering. The unconscious sharker was dragged away by the heels to be deposited in the alley. The captain grinned whitely in the blackness of his beard and fired a cigar. Then his eyes found her still atop the chair and her hand to her mouth. And he winked.

"Yowwww. . . ." the twins said.

The more Mary Margaret told of him, the more vivid became her recollections—and more than once, as she described the captain's mischievous laugh or the cant of his sailor's walk or the distant cast of his eyes when he spoke of the open sea, she would be weeping before she was aware of it.

Came a cold November morning he told her he had been commissioned to transport a cargo out of Gloucester to Savannah and would be gone for perhaps three months. And that afternoon, carpetbag in hand, he kissed her goodbye and patted her haunch, said, "Fare ye well, Maggie darlin," and left her forever.

She of course did not divulge to her sons that she was already carrying them when she had stood at the altar with their father. She believed it was none of their affair and felt no qualm about keeping the secret. But her deliberate lies to them about the captain's true profession and mode of death troubled her and became ever harder to bear. They were nearly thirteen when she told them the truth. Indeed, let them read it for themselves, handing them the British Embassy's letter in evidence of the shameful facts. She was prepared for their shock and humiliation. Was prepared to tell them they had no call to feel disgrace, that their father's criminality was his own dishonor and in no way reflected on them. Their response was not what she was prepared for.

"A *pirate!*" Samuel Thomas said, turning to his brother. "A pirate *captain!*"

"Executed for *murder!*"

"I'll wager it *wasn't* murder! I'll wager it was self-defense but he couldn't prove it!"

"I'll wager that even if it *was* murder he had good cause and whoever the fella was had it coming."

Mr Parham, whom Mary Margaret had permitted to be present, chuckled at their exchange—then swallowed his smile and went mute under his daughter's furious scowl.

They begged to know more and were disappointed when she said she knew no more to tell. Did she at least know how he had been executed? Had he been hanged? Shot? Buried to his neck in the beach at low tide? She was appalled by their macabre questions and gesticulated in exasperation as she said she didn't *know* how he had met his end and didn't *care*, that it hardly mattered, after all.

The boys stared at her in wonder. How could such a thing not matter? They looked at each other and shrugged. They could not get enough of reading the letter and would henceforth handle it with the care of surgeons, lest it tear at the folds. Each wanted to be its keeper, so they tossed a coin that put it in John Roger's custody.

In days to follow, Mary Margaret would sometimes overhear them conversing about their father, speculating on his piratical prowess in comparison to the likes of William Kidd and Edward Teach the Blackbeard and other infamous sea raiders of the past, villains she'd many times heard mentioned in tavern discourse among grown men no less awed by them than were her sons. The twins wondered about his adventures, about duels he'd fought and ships he'd plundered and hapless captives he'd made to walk the plank. Mary Margaret rubbed her temples and sighed to hear them holding forth on keelhauling and how you had to be able to hold your breath a long time and be tough enough to endure the barnacle cuts and be lucky enough that the sharks didn't get you before you were hauled back out. And because there was no telling what trials their own fortunes held in store and keelhauling might be among them, they thought it wise to take turns timing each other in the practice of holding their breath.

⬥

They were keenly intelligent boys and under Mary Margaret's tutelage had learned to read and write and cipher even before she hired the best teachers in town for them. She instructed them too in basic etiquette and social decorum. They had a liking for music of various sorts but the only instrument to catch their fancy was the hornpipe their Grandfather John had given them on their tenth birthday. He taught them to play that simple flute and a patron showed them how to dance the sailor's jig its music had been made for. They composed a ditty they entitled "Good Jolly Roger" and Mary Margaret sometimes heard one or the other of them piping it in the late evening behind the closed door of their room. It would always make her want to cry but she never asked them to cease.

Through their early childhood they were so nearly identical in appearance that, except for their mother and grandfather, few could distinguish between them. But around age twelve Samuel Thomas became the slightly huskier, John Roger the slightly taller and more perceptibly serious of mien. They were strong and nimble athletes, especially fond of swimming and wrestling and footracing. When they could find no other competitors, they contended with each other, and sometimes one of them won and sometimes the other, but as they grew older Samuel Thomas more and more often prevailed.

They loved the sea. They taught themselves to sail, to navigate and read the weather. Without their mother's knowledge and long before she thought them old enough to sail outside the harbor, they were piloting their catboat all the way to the Isles of Shoals. They were on the return leg of one such excursion when the fickle weather of early spring took an abrupt turn and the sky darkened and the sun vanished and the wind came squalling off the open sea. They were a half mile from the harbor when the storm overtook them. The rain struck in a slashing torrent and the swells hove them so high they felt they might be sent flying—then dropped them into troughs so deep they could see nothing but walls of water the color of iron. They feared the sail would be ripped away. Samuel Thomas wrestled the tiller and John Roger bailed in a frenzy and both were wide-eyed with euphoric terror as time and again they were nearly capsized before at last making the harbor. When they got home and Mary Margaret saw their sodden state she scolded them for dunces and wondered aloud how they could do so well in their schooling when they didn't have sense enough to get out of the rain.

When they turned thirteen, Mary Margaret enrolled them in the Madison

School—a local day institution that claimed itself the academic equal of Phillips Exeter—paying for their tuition with money she'd saved over the years. And now a signal difference formed between them. John Roger grew to love academics above all else and gained recognition as the best student in the school. He read with omnivorous rapacity and phenomenal retention. He developed the habit of writing a critical summary of every book as soon as he finished reading it. He could with speed and accuracy solve arithmetic problems in his head. He had a natural aptitude for languages and by the age of fifteen was translating Cicero and could read French passably well. He developed an ardent interest in the law and hoped to matriculate at Dartmouth. Samuel Thomas, on the other hand, had become bored with schoolwork, though he continued to earn fair marks by dint of native intellect. The only books that still held his interest were atlases. He spent hours admiring the ships in the harbor. His main pleasures were now in prowling the waterfront alleys, in dicing, in fighting with his fists. Delivering fresh bedclothes to the boys' room one day while they were at school, Mary Margaret saw an atlas on Samuel Thomas's desk lying open to a map of the Gulf of Mexico. He had inked a circle around Veracruz and alongside it drawn a skull-and-crossbones with the notation, "Here lies Father."

On the threshold of young manhood, the brothers were beardless duplicates of their sire, but Mary Margaret could see that Samuel Thomas had inherited the larger measure of his father's soul, and he was hence her greater worry. She at times wondered if religion might have served to temper his wilder nature and fretted that she'd been wrong to deny such moral instruction to her children. But even in girlhood she had spurned the prevalent Christian view of carnal pleasure as a Deadly Sin, an irreverence that had incited many a loud row with her mother, a devout Catholic.

❦

The boys were sixteen when their Grandfather John made a misstep with his crutch near the top of the stairs and broke his neck in the tumble. Mary Margaret inherited the tavern and conscripted the twins as potboys. Each day after school they waited tables and swept the floor, washed mugs and rinsed out cuspidors and reset rat traps in the storeroom. She hired a girl to assist her in the later evenings so the boys could attend to their studies upstairs. But while John Roger was assiduous in his nightly schoolwork, Samuel Thomas more and more frequently slipped out their window to the sublunary enticements of the streets, particularly those at a quayside cathouse called the Blue Mermaid. It was there he had his first coitus, the news of which he gave to his brother with an affected casualness.

John Roger was enthralled. "What's it *like*?" he asked.

"Can't be described," Samuel Thomas said. "Go with me next time and find out."

John Roger said he would. But he did not own his brother's daring or disregard for the proprieties, and when the next time came he begged off, saying he had to study.

"Suit yourself. But if you ever change your mind, you're welcome to come along."

Samuel Thomas's evening rambles always lasted till the wee hours, and on each of his stealthy re-entries through their window, exuding the mingled odors of perfume and ale and sexual residue, he would find John Roger awake and waiting for him, insistent on hearing the details of his escapade before letting him go to sleep.

The vicarious excitement John Roger derived from his brother's exploits made the fact of his own inexperience increasingly intolerable, and one night he finally accompanied Samuel Thomas out the window and down the drainpipe and along the shadowed streets to the Blue Mermaid. He there drank his first full mug of ale and had the first dance of his life with a woman not his mother. When a sailor tripped him for a prank, his brother lashed into the man with a flurry of wicked punches that sent him crashing over a table and streaming blood from his broken nose. The girls cheered the entertainment and John Roger was agawk with admiration. "God almighty, Sammy! You settled his hash!" The bouncer decreed the sailor at fault and booted him from the premises. The girls had been tickled to learn Samuel Thomas had a twin, and when they learned he was virgin they squabbled over which of them would be his initiator. They each enticed John Roger to pick her over the others and he blushed furiously and could not decide until Sammy said, "Just pick one, for Christ's sake!" John Roger pointed at the youngest-looking, a plump genial girl named Megan who looked innocent as a choir girl and, as he soon discovered, had a spider tattoo on her tummy.

They sang on their way home and laughed at the imprecations from the windows of roused sleepers. When they drew near to home they shushed each other with warnings not to wake their mother, and they were furtive as burglars in climbing the pipe back up to their window. Samuel Thomas was asleep as soon as he put head to pillow but John Roger struggled to stay awake, to savor a while longer the heady feeling of having crossed over to the world of men.

The following morning his pleasure gave way to a chill anxiety that he might have contracted a horrid disease. He had read about venereal corruptions in a medical text and the symptomatic descriptions had induced a palpable cringing of his privates. He dared not mention his misgivings to Samuel Thomas who no doubt disdained such fears and would likely laugh at him. He berated himself for a reckless fool and cursed the erotic compulsion that had overwhelmed his good sense. For weeks afterward his every visit to the privy included a meticulous scrutiny of his member for some sign of encroaching infection. When he was finally sure he had come through unscathed, his relief was profound. He never again went on such a frisk with his brother and never told him why not. And swore to himself never again to engage with a whore.

On those occasions when Samuel Thomas came back from a night's cavort with facial bruises, he would explain them to his mother as a consequence of roughhouse with his brother, whom he accused of not knowing his own strength, and John Roger never failed to provide loyal perjuries of corroboration. But Mary Margaret knew a few things about sneaking through windows and was well aware of Samuel Thomas's nocturnal excursions. She feared his fondness for hazardous entertainments and gave him a warning lecture against them. He listened with due respect and said he would bear her counsel in mind. And then once again, in a pre-dawn hour of a subsequent morning, she woke to faint scrapings as he shinnied up the pipe at the far end of the roof overhang and stole back into his room. It was little consolation to remind herself it would have been as futile for her father to try keeping her from Captain Wolfe. She sensed Samuel Thomas's impatience to be out in the world, and though she could do nothing to dissuade him from his ramblings—she would not stoop to haranguing nor to weeping in plea—she implored him to at least complete his studies at the Madison School and receive his diploma. And he promised her he would.

❈

Two months before her sons' graduations Mary Margaret got sick for the first time in her life. She went to bed with a fever one night and in the morning was sheened with sweat and aching to the bone and too weak to rouse herself. She refused to send for a doctor, saying she would recover soon enough after a cup of broth and bit of rest. The next day she was worse. John Roger fetched a doctor who prescribed a physic and cold compresses and said he would return in the morning. That evening she was delirious. The twins sat at her bedside in the amber light of an oil lamp and took turns mopping her brow and neck. She tossed through the night, her eyes dark hollows, her nightdress pasted to her skin, the shadowed room malodorous with her sickly swelter. Just before dawn she startled them when she suddenly sat up and stared unblinking into a shadowy corner of the room. Then lay back and fixed Samuel Thomas with a stare that glowed like blown embers and said, "Do not be him or ye are damned." Then said, "The light is too bright." And closed her eyes and died. John Roger wept while Samuel Thomas straightened her nightdress and arranged the bedclothes and washed her face and brushed her hair and then sent for the doctor. For lack of a better guess the medico cited brain fever on the death certificate.

A number of longtime patrons of the pub attended the funeral, and flowers were heaped about the headstone.

Mary Parham Wolfe

1810 – 1845

Beloved Mother

of John and Samuel

In sorting through her belongings they found a loaded derringer in a drawer of her vanity. The handlegrips were of ivory and engraved with RBW. Both of them

23

wanted the gun and again resorted to the spin of a coin. And that antique agent of fate conferred the pistol on Samuel Thomas.

—✳—

They received their diplomas in June and that same day posed together in a Market Street studio for a pair of daguerreotype photographs, one for each of them. Standing side by side in their formal graduation dress they presented a double image of a single and somberly handsome seventeen-year-old self. Some weeks later they sold the tavern and took lodging at a sailors' hostel called the Yardarm Inn, where they would reside through the rest of the summer before taking leave of Portsmouth. John Roger was bound for Hanover and the freshman class at Dartmouth, having earned a scholarship by means of his superior academic record, a host of glowing letters of recommendation, and a fine application essay expounding on the nobility of the legal profession. Samuel Thomas had signed as a deck hand with a cargo ship scheduled to set sail five days after his brother left town. The *Atropos* would make several ports of call along the seaboard down to Jacksonville before reversing course back to Portsmouth.

John Roger had favored an equal division of the proceeds from the tavern sale but Samuel Thomas would accept only enough money to see him through until he shipped out. "You'll be needing a fat purse for college a lot more than I'll be needing one at sea."

They had never before been separated, and during the last hours before his departure for Hanover on the evening coach, John Roger's glumness was plain to see. Over a café supper, Samuel Thomas reminded him that the *Atropos* would be gone for only six months. He promised to go see him at Dartmouth as soon as he returned.

At the coach station, they embraced and wished each other well. Samuel Thomas said he would post a letter from every port of call. "Plan on me being back around the middle of winter," he said with a grin. "Whether you like it or not."

It is an ancient joke that to make God laugh you need only tell Him your plans.

—✳—

After seeing his brother off, Samuel Thomas returned to the Yardarm, but he was not sleepy and tried to pass the time with a small atlas. It was the only book he had packed in his carpetbag together with some clothes and toiletries, the graduation daguerreotype, his grandfather's hornpipe—which he had won by yet another coin toss—and the derringer. But he felt John Roger's absence like a great gap in his chest and the atlas could not hold his attention. He wished the *Atropos* were weighing anchor in the morning rather than in five days. Near midnight he was yet wide awake and decided a long walk and a pint might be of help. He was almost out the door when he remembered that some of the inn's rooms had been robbed the night before while their residents were away. The only thing in his bag of value to a thief was the derringer, so he retrieved it and put it in his jacket pocket.

He walked a long way down the waterfront with his collar turned up against a chill breeze. He did not desire conversation and so chose a saloon he had not patronized before and where no one knew him. He drank by himself at the end of the bar, downing three slow mugs of ale before taking his leave at just after two o'clock, a pleasant tingle on his lips. The wind had come up and carried a heavy smell of impending rain. The misty lamp-lit streets lay deserted to the late hour and the coming storm.

He had his head down against the wind as he turned a corner—and collided with a large man coming from the other direction, his forehead striking the man in the face, jarring him rearward and bringing blood from his nose. The man's instant reaction was to yell "Bastard!" and lash out with the truncheon in his hand, striking Samuel Thomas on the ear and knocking off his hat. Samuel Thomas yelped and punched at the man in reflex but missed, and the man rushed at him, flailing in a fury, driving him back against a wall. Then the derringer was in Samuel Thomas's hand and the pistol cracked with a yellow flash—the first time he'd fired a gun in his life—and the half-inch ball punched through the man's neck and rang off a lamppost. The man's head slumped like a puppet's snipped of its string and his hat rolled off and his body raced it to the ground. Staring at the sprawled figure and the black ribbons of blood unspooling along the cobblestone seams, Samuel Thomas knew the man was dead, and a chaos of sensations coursed through him. Then he saw the watchman brassard on the man's arm and was jolted with cold dread. He looked all about and saw no one. Then snatched up his hat and ran.

He'd gone two blocks before realizing he still had the gun in his hand and he flung it high onto a rooftop. His ear throbbed and felt to his fingers like a chunk of peeled fruit. He kept to the shadows as he hurried through the empty streets and without destination other than away from the harbor. He held his hat to his head against the strengthening wind and felt the first pricks of rain on his face—and then it was slapping into him in gusting swirls.

His thoughts were a turmoil. What if there were a witness, someone who had been looking on from the shadows? What if there were inquiries at the sailors' inns and it was learned at the Yardarm of a guest of his description, Samuel Wolfe by name, who had gone out and not returned even to retrieve his carpetbag? He remembered now that his carpetbag still held the photograph of himself and his brother and he had a moment's frantic impulse to return for it—then cursed himself for a fool and hastened on. To report to the *Atropos* was out of the question. Someone might check the crew rosters of all ships in harbor. The more he pondered his plight the worse it seemed. Homicide was in any instance a grave matter but the killing of a watchman always roused an outrage. He had once read a newspaper account of a Boston sailor who killed a watchman in a fight and then fled, fearing no one would believe his claim of self-defense. He was shortly run to ground by manhunters seeking the posted reward and his fear was borne out. Although none of the witnesses could say how the fight had started, and though he swore before God and jurymen that he had only been defending himself against a severe and unjustified attack, he was judged guilty of murder and hanged.

Samuel Thomas was sure the bountymen would soon be on his track. He thought to keep walking until he was clear of Portsmouth and into the woods. But then what? He turned at the next corner for no reason other than a fugitive's instinct to vary his course. And saw up ahead and across the street a handful of men huddled in their coats and standing against the wall in front of an office with a sign identifying it as a recruiting post for the Army of the United States.

⚜

It was still raining hard when the sergeant arrived and unlocked the office, giving merry praise to such patriotism as would abide a drenching in order to serve its country. They all went inside and formed a line in front of the sergeant's desk. When it was Samuel Thomas's turn before the sergeant and he was asked his name, he said, "Thomas, Samuel Thomas," believing the alias a clever one, false only in its lack of complete truth. The recruiter began to write it down. "And what's the middle initial, Mr Thomas?"

He was unprepared for that. "It's, ah . . . H." The first letter that came to mind.

The sergeant smiled and entered it. Then looked up again and studied Samuel Thomas's battered ear. "What was it she hit you with, lad, a fry pan? Well, it's off to a better mistress now, you can be sure. She'll clothe ye and feed ye and give ye a rifle. A goodly more than most will do, now aint it?"

Before noon he and seven other enlistees were on a recruiting wagon bound for Fort Hamilton in New York. He had decided he would not write to John Roger for a long while. He could not trust anyone to carry a letter to him without reading it—or worse, permitting it to fall into the wrong hands and be of help to manhunters.

His plan was to hide in the army for a year or so, long enough for the bountymen to give up their search. Then he would desert. He would go to the nearest port and under another name sign on with a ship for New England. He would seek out John Roger in Hanover and apologize for his long silence and explain everything to him.

Such, in any case, was his plan.

THE TURNCOAT'S TRIALS

In February of 1845 the United States annexed the nine-year-old Republic of Texas and six months later was still in diplomatic dispute with Mexico over the location of the border between the two countries. The U.S. insisted, as Texas always had, that the border was the Rio Grande. And as always, Mexico insisted it was at the Nueces River, more than a hundred miles north. But it had now become obvious that President James Knox Polk's greater ambition was to acquire the necessary territory to expand the Yankee republic all the way to the Pacific. Acquire it by whatever means necessary. Newspapers across the country carried heated opinions on both sides of the issue. At the same time that the president was proposing diplomatic resolutions to the border argument—all of them so unfavorable to Mexico that it could never agree to them— he dispatched the benignly named Army of Observation under the command of General Zachary Taylor to the mouth of the Nueces River. Taylor's ostensible purpose was to protect Texas against Mexican invasion, but as everyone knew, including the Mexicans, Mr Polk was in fact making ready an invasion of his own.

⚜

Even before taking refuge in the ranks, Samuel Thomas had been aware of the war talk. But the risk of combat in Mexico seemed a lesser one than facing a murder charge in Portsmouth. He was not the only one in the company on the run from legal complications, and there were of course patriots in the ranks, and no shortage of callow youths in quest of battlefield glory, but the majority of his comrades had enlisted for the ageless reason of escape from poverty. A number of them had arrived on immigrant ships, mostly Irishmen fled from the Famine. But the America they'd

27

landed in was predominantly Protestant and of English stock, and its larger cities were hotbeds of nativist loathing of the foreign tide staining its shores, especially of the Paddies and their slavish papist faith. It was a hatred no less virulent than what the Hibernians had endured in Britain and as much a barrier to any but the most abject jobs. Rather than dig privies or scrounge in the streets for survival, many of them enlisted in the army, believing it a lesser adversity.

In late winter their regiment at last received the order to join General Taylor in Texas. For most of the company, and certainly for Samuel Thomas, who had never been outside New Hampshire before his enlistment, the journey from New York to the Gulf of Mexico was an education in American geography and regional societies. Traversing a countryside early thawing to mud, they were transported by wagons to Pittsburgh and there put aboard a sternwheel steamboat that carried them west along the Ohio River and through country budding with incipient greenery. Where the Ohio joined the Mississippi they transferred onto a side-wheeler for the trip south. The Old Man, the boatmen called the great river, and Samuel Thomas was awestruck by its breadth. The country they passed through grew more distinct from that which they left behind. The dense woodlands along the banks occasionally gave way to verdant pasturelands and fields of black earth so fertile he could smell it from the railing. He saw turtles the size of saddlebags sunning themselves on mud banks and driftwood. Saw a bald eagle high on a pine eviscerating a limp panther cub in its talons. Saw a trio of boys hauling onto the bank a hooked catfish bigger than any of them.

They churned downriver through days of surpassing loveliness and then entered an unseasonable heat broken by sporadic rainfall. When they were not sopped with rain they were sodden with sweat. They passed by a sequence of port towns and made brief moorings at some of them for fuel and supplies. Towns loud and rough and seeming like foreign countries, so profuse were they with Negroes, with the drawling speech of blacks and whites alike. The river journey ended at New Orleans, where they passed two joyous days and nights and Samuel Thomas spent the best two dollars of his life for the pleasures of an octoroon girl with caramel skin and nipples dark as chocolate and a mouth like red fruit. It was said the city suffered from chronic afflictions of fire and flood and devastating storm, that it was notorious for yellow fever and murder and every sort of carnal delinquency. But Samuel Thomas fancied its bohemian character and exuberant wickedness, and he felt somehow more at home in his two days there than he'd ever felt in Portsmouth. He thought he might someday return to stay.

They shipped out on the steamship *Alabama*. His first view of the Gulf of Mexico was under a low morning sun that made an undulant gold of the water's surface. He was struck by the dissimilarity of smell from the North Atlantic, the squalling gulls of different cry and character from those of New England. The pelicans were a novel entertainment—graceful on the wing, but in repose so like comical, jowly, big-bottomed bureaucrats. The ship steamed into the gulf under high billowing clouds of dazzling white, and the mainland shrank from view off the starboard.

The weather held well. They were four days on the placid sea before sighting the dark line of the Texas coast. They moored that evening off the shallows of Corpus Christi Bay, the army campfires on the beach glimmering like a fallen rain of stars. In the morning they debarked onto lighters and were ferried ashore. The ship's crew had already told them much about this badland of winter northers sharp as razors and endless sweltering summers, about the hordes of insects and rattlesnakes, the scourge of cactus and thorny brush, the sand storms that could blind a man sure if he were not careful of his eyes. Considering that Taylor's army had been here since the previous summer, the new men were surprised to find the camp in high spirits and a flurry of activity. Then learned that Taylor had only an hour earlier received orders to march down to the Rio Grande, Mexican objections be damned. War had not yet been declared, but its imminence could be felt in the camp's excitement as the soldiers got ready to move out in the morning. "You're a right lucky bunch to be going straight to the elephant and not spend more than one night in this shithole," a red-eyed corporal told Samuel Thomas. "A right lucky bunch."

They set out well before sunrise, off to "see the elephant," the day's expression for novel adventure. An hour into the march, in the gray light of dawn, Samuel Thomas got his first look at General Taylor, Old Rough and Ready himself, as he rode his white horse past the column. Craggy-faced, clad in a checkered shirt and coarse pants held up by suspenders, shod in brogans and wearing a tattered straw hat. "Looks like a damned farmer, don't he?" said a grinning man marching next to Samuel Thomas. "But there aint no better general in the whole army."

Day after day they marched from dawn to just before sundown, trekking through sun and wind and rain, through sandy flatland covered with mesquites and bramble and thorny scrub brush of all sorts. Three weeks after departing Corpus Christi they arrived at the Rio Grande. Taylor ordered construction to begin at once on a fort directly across from Matamoros and its garrison of Mexican lancers. He christened it Fort Texas, though one of his officers said they should call it Dogtown in deference to all the scrawny mutts at large in the vicinity. It would be two years yet before that raw riparian ground gave rise to the hamlet of Brownsville, but thus was Samuel Thomas the first of the Wolfes to set foot there.

He was there only a short time. On the march from Corpus Christi he had cultivated a hatred of the army far exceeding that of most enlisted men. The root of his antipathy had been planted at Fort Hamilton when he was caught dicing in the wagon shed with two other trainees. All the next day, under guard and in full view of the camp, the three of them were made to stand atop upright barrels on a layer of shattered bricks. It was a constant strain to maintain balance on the unsteady barrelheads, and each man several times fell to the broken brick. At sunset they were helped off the barrels, bruised and aching, bloody of knees and hands, and would be stiff-jointed for days. The punishment made Samuel Thomas resentful, but its severity paled in contrast to what he witnessed on the way to Fort Texas and during his time there. While he understood that severe offenses called for severe punishments, he was enraged by the stark cruelty of some of the penalties inflicted for minor infractions. It was one thing to flog a man bloody for sleeping on guard, quite another to lash him for failure to salute an officer. Or to brand him on the forehead with the "HD" of the habitual drunkard because he stood too tipsy at morning muster. A rifle laxly carried or a tunic improperly buttoned, a surly glance at an officer, an insufficient alacrity in obeying a command—and a soldier could find himself straddling a sawhorse for hours with his hands tied behind him and weights attached to his ankles. Or lugging a ball and chain for a week. Or wearing a heavy iron collar affixed with spokes that made it impossible to lay his head down for sleep. Or passing a few hours sitting bucked and gagged on the ground—immobilized with his knees drawn up and his arms bound around them and a stout stick set crosswise under the knees and over the arms.

In an army whose officers were largely nativist and Protestant, it was only natural that the most maltreated in the ranks were Irishmen, three of whom—Jack Riley, John Little, and Lucas Malone—Samuel had become friends with during the southward march. Though he had no giveaway accent, he had at once been taken for Irish by Riley, and he admitted to an Irish grandfather. In keeping daily company with these men, Samuel Thomas began to assume a mild brogue, though he was unaware of it until they were almost to the Rio Grande and Lucas Malone said, "Listen to this lad, willya? Bedamn if he's not sounding like he was weaned in County Cork."

Malone and John Little hated the army with even greater fervor than Samuel Thomas did. Both of them had been punished harshly numerous times, for one offense or another. Both had undergone the buck and gag, and Little had once worn the spiked collar, and Malone had taken a ride on the sawhorse on their first day at the Rio Grande. And though he'd never yet been physically punished, Jack Riley was no less galled than either of them. He had served almost ten years in the British army and earned a sergeant's stripes even in the face of English bigotry, then had mustered out and migrated to America and joined the Yankee ranks, confident that his military experience would soon win him another sergeancy as well as the respect denied him in Her Majesty's service. But he found the Irish were as much scorned by the Yanks as by John Bull, and in the six months since his American enlistment he had grown convinced he would never become a sergeant. As a man of sizable self-esteem, it enraged him to be rebuked by college-boy officers not half the soldier he was. The injury to his pride cut deep as a whip.

They had been on the Rio Grande four days when the corporal in charge of Samuel Thomas's labor detail shot a nearby dog for no reason but boredom. The gut-wounded animal screamed and ran a short distance and fell down but kept trying to run, yowling and turning in a tight circle on the blood-muddying ground for an interminable half minute before John Little drove a pick through its head to end its misery. The corporal was recharging his pistol and didn't notice Samuel Thomas stalking toward him until too late to avoid the punch that knocked him sprawling with two dislodged teeth. It was Samuel Thomas's intention to kick the man to death but before he could commence he was subdued by others, including Malone, who hissed into his ear, "Hold enough, lad! Put the boot to him and you'll be fucked most truly."

That evening he was convicted of assault on a non-commissioned officer and was sentenced to the loss of six months' wages, disqualification for promotion for two years, and a week of the buck and gag from daybreak to sunset.

For much of the following week Fort Texas was pounded by rainstorms, and Samuel Thomas was soaked without respite as he sat trussed and gagged in the mud, seething in his fury. On the third day of his punishment, the camp woke to find its soggy grounds littered with leaflets strewn by infiltrators in the night. Printed in English and signed by the Mexican commander in Matamoros, the flyers exhorted immigrant Yankee soldiers, especially the Catholics, to reject the imperialistic mission of the slave-owning, Protestant United States and join with anti-slavery Mexico in defense of its sovereignty and national faith. They promised enlistment bonuses, good pay, and land grants of 320 acres to every Yankee who would fight for the righteous Mexican side. Before the end of the day, the first desertions were reported.

Zachary Taylor was irate. He increased the number of river sentries and ordered them to shoot any man trying to cross over who refused the command to turn back. Over the next days six men would be shot in the water and four others drowned, but thirty or so would make it to the other side. When Jack Riley ambled up to where Samuel Thomas sat bucked and gagged and asked him in low voice if he was for going across, Samuel Thomas did not hesitate to nod. But he was under tent arrest every night of his week of punishment, so they had to wait until he'd completed it. Each day of the buck drove the pain deeper into the roots of his back, and when he was freed of the restraints for the seventh time he could not get to his feet without assistance and it was an agony to straighten up. Still, he was with Riley and Little and Malone that night when they sneaked along the shadows past the fort guards and crawled through the brush down to the river and eased into the water with their boots tied together and hung around their necks.

The river was misty silver under a bright moon but smelled of rot and tasted of mud. The current was stronger than usual with the runoff of the recent rains and Samuel Thomas wasn't the only one of them close to panic as they were carried downstream while struggling to swim across. Their frenetic splashings alerted the sentries, who shouted a warning and then opened fire. Rifle balls smacked the water around them and John Little was hit in the calf and Lucas Malone nicked along the ribs but they all four made the opposing bank and clambered up through the cattails and into the cover of the trees. Mexican soldiers presently appeared, bayonets at the ready, but when the quartet declared their desire to fight for the Mexican cause, they were welcomed like brothers and taken to the garrison to have their wounds treated.

Thus began the band of Yankee army deserters known in Mexico as the gallant San Patricios—so named because most of them were Irish Catholics—and in the remoter pages of American history as the turncoat Saint Patrick Battalion. The unit's numbers grew as U.S. desertions continued, and they were formed into an artillery company under command of a Mexican captain, though Lieutenant Jack Riley was the executive officer and their true leader. In their first action against their former comrades, a week before the American declaration of war, the San Patricios bombarded Fort Texas and in the process killed one Major Jacob Brown, in whose honor the fort was renamed and Brownsville would be christened.

Everywhere they went this legion of foreigners pledged to Mexico's defense was honored by people of every social class. The Patricios were surprised to find that not all Mexicans were brownskinned, though the great mass of them were, being either Indian or, more likely, mestizo, the burgeoning Spanish-Indian caste that had over the past two centuries come to comprise the majority of the population. But the ruling native class, the peak of the social pyramid, was the Creole—the Spanish descendants whose Caucasian blood remained free of Indian taint. They were a courtly society, educated, formal of speech and manner, given to religious ostentation and devoted to European tradition. They were also passionate about their honor, both family and personal, and vehement in redressing injury to it.

In the course of their deployments over the following year, the San Patricios marched through sierra ranges of jagged peaks and thick timber, through deep canyons misted blue with the spray of booming rivers. They traversed broad plains of green and yellow grasses rippling in the wind like a restless sea. They crossed pale deserts flat as tables extending to the burning horizons and shimmering in the heat. They heard the roar of cougars in the mountain nights, their evenings in open country quivered with wolf howls and the high crying of coyotes. In Tampico they were granted two days of liberty and sported on the beach a few miles from town. Samuel Thomas had known only the cold cobalt water of the sharp-shelved North Atlantic coast and he reveled in the warm green clarity of the gulf shallows. They swam, lazed on the sand, got sunburned. They cut coconuts off the trees and hacked open the husks and punched holes in the eyes of the brown nut with their bayonets to get to the cool sweet milk, the most delectable drink Samuel Thomas had ever put tongue to. Where but in heaven might a man get milk from the trees? He relished the spicy native cooking and acquired a taste for the coppery sting of tequila and the smoky burn of mescal. He delighted in the skiffle music of the villages and learned a variety of rustic dances. He had an affinity for the Spanish language and gained swift fluency with it, a great advantage with the camp women who traveled with the army and cooked for it and tended its wounds. Most of these women were young and given to playful laughter and mischievous banter. Any camp woman could share herself with whomever she wished but also had the right to refuse anyone, and a man who tried to take her against her will risked a maiming from his comrades.

The Patricios were a formidable force, dealing heavy casualties in their every engagement and stoking ever higher the vengeful wrath of the Yankees—or "gringos," as the Americans were now known in Mexico, a newly-coined pejorative that would long outlast the war. But as the fighting progressed, the turncoats began to understand that Mexico could not win and that their own future was headed toward an ultimate choice of dying in battle or at the end of an American rope. Their desperation made them the more intrepid. General Lopez de Santa Ana, the supreme commander of the Mexican army, would later say that if he'd had but five hundred more men of the Patricios' mettle he could have won the war.

The Saint Patricks fought at Monterrey, at Saltillo, at Buena Vista, at Cerro Gordo. And then, in the war's decisive and bloodiest battle, on an infernal August afternoon at a place called Churubusco, at the very gates of Mexico City, they were done for. Some managed to escape but two-thirds of them were killed in that fight and the rest taken prisoner, many of them with severe wounds. Samuel Thomas's left hand was mutilated by shrapnel, his hipbone pierced by a bayonet. He would never again be able to sit a horse, and the thumb and remaining two fingers of his ruined hand would never come unclawed.

Seventy Saint Patricks stood trial for desertion. They were made to wear their unwashed and bloodied Mexican uniforms in court, exuding a reek that intensified the hateful grimaces in the room and seemed in keeping with the odiousness of their crime. Every man of them was convicted and sentenced to hang.

In his judicial review, however, General Winfield Scott pardoned five of the condemned outright on different legal bases, and he spared fifteen others on the ground that they had deserted prior to the declaration of war and so were exempt from the death penalty. Those fifteen—including Samuel Thomas, Jack Riley, and John Little—were sentenced instead to fifty lashes on the bare back and the "D" brand of the deserter burned into their right cheek. Because Lucas Malone's desertion had erroneously been recorded as occurring six weeks after it actually did, and because the court would give no credence to his comrades' attestations that he had deserted with them before the declaration of war, he remained among the condemned. "Aint it the shits?" Malone said. "I keep my skin through all the fightin and get done in by some jackass of a clerk."

Samuel Thomas was among those who received their punishment in front of hundreds of witnessing American soldiers in the main plaza of San Angel, a village on the outskirt of the capital. In the center of the plaza stood a newly erected gallows consisting of a single long crossbeam from which dangled sixteen noosed ropes—the others of the condemned would be executed over the next three days. Set in a row under the crossbeam were eight small mule-drawn carts, and in each one stood a pair of San Patricios with their hands bound behind them. The carts faced a line of trees along one side of the plaza where the men to be flogged were stripped bare to the waist and each one tied to a tree trunk. The officer in charge kept loud count as the whippings were laid on. Samuel Thomas locked his jaws to keep from crying out but he passed out on the thirty-ninth lash. After the fiftieth, he was revived with a pail of water so he would be conscious for his branding. Two men held his head fast while another applied the glowing iron directly below his eye and he smelled his own searing flesh and bone and screamed in violation of his vow that he would not. It went even worse for Riley, who was the most hated of the deserters for being their leader. His brand was applied upside down, purportedly by accident, and so, to the loud approval of the spectating troops, the officer in charge ordered that it be burned correctly into his other cheek. Riley had managed to hold silent the first time but could not stifle himself the second, and his screams roused a great and happy chorus of derision.

Then the hangings. White hoods were drawn over the heads of the condemned and the nooses snugged round their necks. At an officer's signal, the muleteers' whips cracked and the carts rumbled out from under the crossbeam and the plaza rang with cheers. A fortunate few of the gibbeted died instantly of snapped necks but most of them, including Lucas Malone, strangled to death, choking with awful sounds as their hysterical feet sought purchase on the empty air and their trousers darkened with piss and shit. The flogged and branded were then made to dig the hanged men's graves and bury them, Samuel Thomas scooping at the earth with a trowel in his one good hand.

⸙

With the fall of Mexico City, the war was over in every sense but officially. It was another five months before the signing in early 1848 of the Treaty of Guadalupe Hidalgo, by which compact Mexico ceded to the United States an enormous portion of land that extended the American border to the Pacific coast. But it was still another month before the treaty was accepted by the American Senate, and then another two and a half months before it was ratified by Mexico. And all that while, the captive Saint Patricks labored daily with picks and shovels in a garbage pit a quarter-mile wide at the edge of the city, a monstrous crater writhing with rats and swarming with flies and aflutter with great flocks of carrion birds. Into this pit were emptied daily wagonloads of every sort of refuse and organic rot, including carcasses of animals large and small, the discard of miscarriages and abortions. The fetor made

34

their eyes water and stung their throats even through the bandanas they wore over nose and mouth, and every man of them had bloodshot eyes and a chronic cough.

They were at first incarcerated in the Acordada Penitentiary, near the center of the capital, and every morning before going to the pit they unloaded dead bodies from the municipal wagons that each dawn collected them off the streets and alleyways, as many of them victims of murder as of exposure and malnutrition and alcohol poisoning and disease and total exhaustion of the will to live. These dead were displayed on the prison's front steps all day and night for anyone to claim. Those still there the next morning were then removed to make room for the new day's corpses and were taken for burial in the potter's field adjoining the garbage pit.

After two of the Patricios escaped from the city penitentiary—both breakouts abetted by visitors—the prisoners were moved to the nearby fortress of Chapultepec castle and visiting privileges were curtailed. One of the escapees had been a diminutive man named Duhan, who dressed himself in smuggled women's clothing and then simply walked out with the female visitors when they departed. The other to escape was John Little, who had spoken hardly at all since their capture at Churubusco. His liberation also entailed a disguise sneaked in to him by a woman visitor, a rich Mexican sympathetic to the Patricios, though none of them had any notion of why she had specifically chosen John Little to help escape. His disguise was designed to let him walk out in place of a servant who had accompanied her, but the guards became aware of the ruse just as the party was exiting the prison and was within sight of the carriage waiting at the curb. A gunfight ensued and the woman's two employees were killed and the woman herself arrested. But John Little made away, and none of his comrades would ever know what became of him.

On a day in late spring, less than two weeks before the last American troops withdrew from Mexico, the Saint Patricks were mustered into the central courtyard and there shorn of their hair, every man of them razored to the scalp, blood lacing down their heads, and then made to march in single file around the yard to a drum-and-fife rendition of "The Rogue's March" while they were vilified and spat upon by the troops. And were finally directed out the front gate and set free. Jack Riley and a few other stalwarts would return to the Mexican army, but the others had had enough of the soldier's life, and after sharing a common cell for nine months most of them had had enough of each other. As soon as they were into the park and out of view of the American soldiers they began drifting apart in different directions without words of farewell nor mentions of destination, and few of them would meet again. As for the promise of land grants, it had been made by a government anticipating victory over the Yankees and since then usurped many times over.

❦

Even if he'd had the use of both hands and could walk properly, Samuel Thomas would never have returned to the ranks. Nor would he go back to the U.S.

The brand on his face was a mark of Cain to Americans and he would be a despised pariah. He might have done as some of the other Patricios had and disfigured the "D" to an unrecognizable scar, but the scar would still attract notice and raise questions, as would his crippled hand and pronounced limp. To say the maimings were war wounds would oblige him to answer queries about the unit he had served with and of some of his officers and comrades. And what of his name? "Samuel H. Thomas" was on the official roster of punished deserters, so he would have to revert to his real one or assume another one altogether. There were any number of pitfalls to such deceits, just as there were to any personal history he might invent for the past two years that did not include the war but accounted for his maimings. Such were the arguments he gave himself and he accepted them as sound enough. But the main reason he would not go home was his brother. He could neither lie to John Roger nor face him with the truth. His twin—the collegian, the man of principle—would never understand his desertion and for sure not his turned coat. Better that Johnny should imagine him dead by whatever misadventure struck his fancy than to see what had become of him. And to learn why. So he stayed in Mexico City.

Through the rest of that summer he was frequently drunk, as much to blunt his memory as to ease his chronic pains. He kept to the heart of the city, which had been little damaged by the war and where the fashionable neighborhoods of the privileged flanked the Plaza de la Constitución, the vast central square and center of the federal government. This main plaza was more commonly called the zócalo— and the term had come to refer to any town's main square that contained a cathedral and municipal building.

He got money for liquor by stealing from church poor boxes, by robbing drunks on the late-night streets. He wrested bottles from weaker men. He occasionally encountered a bartender or patron who took his branded face for a badge of honor and stood him a few drinks. He fed at the alley doors of restaurants where a man might be meted leftovers when the dinner trade was done, or in whose garbage cans he might find something still edible, but on some days he ate nothing. A friendly vendor of old clothing provided him with a shirt and pants and a woolen poncho to replace his tattered uniform. He somehow obtained a sombrero. From a distance he looked like one more dispossessed peón at large on the capital's teeming streets. He slept in the parks. When the weather was inclement he took shelter in pulquerías, the most squalid of drinking places but where a man could sleep undisturbed in a corner among a litter of other homeless drunks. He spent his days ambling about the central city. He washed at public fountains. He sat on park benches and observed without curiosity the city's passing spectacle. He had lost all interest in the doings of the world and ignored even discarded newspapers and broadsheets except as insulation against cold nights. He one day saw a former Patricio comrade on the street, wearing a spanking new Mexican army uniform, and ducked into the crowd before the soldier caught sight of him.

His was a solitary existence and by now he could conceive of no other. But the streets were especially dangerous for a man alone. The capital was rife with rateros and brutos—thieves and roving gangs of young thugs—and the city's police force of the time was small and poorly trained. People of the better classes did not venture outside after dark except in groups and with hired bodyguards. The first time he was set upon was in the darkness of a park where he slept in the shrubbery, and he lost a front tooth and was robbed of his shoes. The episode clarified to him the severity of his handicaps and how dim-witted he was to be weaponless. From a marketplace meat stall he stole a boning knife and honed its curved seven-inch blade sharper still on the stone rim of a fountain. Two nights later when a trio of thugs swooped on him he slashed the throat of one and wounded both of the others before they scrabbled away in a cursing retreat. He stripped the sandals from the one he killed, took the few centavos in his pocket. In the months that followed he killed at least three more assailants and bloodied a number of others in driving them off. He gained a daunting reputation among the local street gangs. El Yanqui Feo, they called him, and most of them eventually let him be. But he remained a challenge to young street toughs wanting to make a name for themselves, and his clothes were rarely free of recent blood stains.

So did his days pass. Each the same as the one before. Each tomorrow his vague and only future. Every dawn's waking one more astonishment. He was twenty years old and felt decrepit.

—❀—

In the last days of September came a cold and chronic rain. He got sick, grew weak and dizzy, went about in a sweating chill. His body felt peculiar, as though its flesh was barely clinging to its bones. One morning he was nearly run over as he crossed a street, staggering back as the mule team clopped by. It was a municipal wagon with a load of corpses loosely covered with a tarp. He clearly saw the face of one at the bottom of the pile—eyes open and teeth bared in a grimace that might have passed for a maniacal grin. The face, Samuel Thomas was certain, winked at him.

On a raw dank night, walking in a small plaza of bright shops and restaurants a few blocks north of the zócalo, he was seized by a sudden sensation of being weightless and then the earth tipped under him and he fell unconscious on the sidewalk. But even in the better parts of town the prostrate forms of insensate drunks were a common sight, and passersby on their way to supper or the theater stepped around him with no more interest than if he had been a hole in the ground. The common sentiment about bodies on the central streets was that they would either revive and move on or be picked up in the morning by the collection wagons.

He came to awareness under a sky of iron gray. A young woman was crouched beside him, studying him with curiosity. She wore an apron and held a broom and had a white crescent scar at the outer corner of one eye. She asked if he were wounded. He said he didn't think so. His voice sounded to him like a stranger's. He tried to get up but fell back and nearly passed out again. She put the back of her hand to his cheek and then a palm to his forehead, then said she would be right back.

In her absence he was unsure whether she had been real or imagined. But then she returned, accompanied by a grayhaired man with a black eye patch. They helped him to stand and steered him a short way down the sidewalk and into a small café cast in soft yellow light and infused with the aromas of coffee and sausage and cinnamon. There were tables covered with white cloth and a small bar with a few stools. Samuel Thomas was unsure if he in fact apologized for his stink or if he only thought he did. Then nearly took the girl and old man down with him as he fell in a swoon.

He awoke on a cot in a dimly lighted storeroom. The sole window was small and high and the daylight in it was as gray as he'd last seen it. An oil lamp with its wick set low burned on a small table beside the cot. The air pungent with peppery odors. The walls were hung with cookware, the ceiling with strings of dried sausages and chiles, the shelves held condiments, sacks of sugar and salt and maize and wheat flour. There were casks of beer and cases of bottled wine. In a corner of the room, a rat lay with its neck under the sprung bail of the trap, its eyes like little pink balloons and the cheese white in its mouth. Samuel was under a blanket and wearing a night shirt. He only vaguely recalled someone undressing him, washing him with a warm cloth, holding a glass to his lips. A wonderful liquor of a kind he had never tasted before.

He'd been awake but a few minutes when the door opened slightly and the girl looked in and saw his open eyes, and smiled. She went away and a few minutes later came back with a tray of food and set it on the little bedside table. She said he had slept around the clock. He guessed her to be a few years older than himself.

She put a cool palm to his forehead and smiled. Your fever is nearly gone, she said, in the clearly enunciated Spanish of those educated in the capital.

She leaned down to take a look into the chamber pot under the bed. She said that she had at first feared he had eaten something spoiled or drunk bad water, but had since decided he was not poisoned, only malnourished. A few days of rest and proper feeding, she told him, and he should be fine.

She helped him to sit up. On the tray was a steaming bowl of the tripe stew called menudo, seasoned with lemon juice and chopped green chile, and a small plate of white rice topped with a fried egg. He felt he could feed himself but did not object when she sat on the edge of the cot and began spooning the menudo to him. She said her name was María Palomina Blanco Lobos. The one-eyed man was her grandfather Bruno Blanco. He owned the café, La Rosa Mariposa, and she had been helping him to operate it since she was a child. They lived in an apartment upstairs and had no family but each other.

The food was delicious but he could not finish half of it before he was sated. She said it was an excellent sign that he had any appetite at all. He asked if he might have some of whatever it was they had given him to drink before. A French brandy, she told him, then left the room and returned a minute later with a small glass of the reddish liquor. He sipped from it and felt its sweet burn down his throat.

He asked why they were being so kind to him. Did they take in every man they found lying on the sidewalk?

Of course not, she said. It was the mark on his face. She knew what it meant. She and her grandfather had read about the San Patricios in the newspapers. Bruno Blanco too had once been a brave fighter, in the long war for independence begun by the great Father Hidalgo. Even after he saw Hidalgo's severed head on display at Guanajuato, Bruno Blanco had continued to fight against the brute Spaniards until independence was won. That was how he lost his eye, in that war.

But I still do not know your name, she said. "Como se llama?"

"Samuel Tomás," he said.

Are you Irish?

No, he said.

"Ah pues, eres americano." She smiled.

Not anymore, he said.

She seemed puzzled by that but let it pass. "Tomás no es su apellido, verdad?"

No, he said, his family name was Wolfe.

"Wooolf," she said, trying it on her tongue. Then asked why he smiled.

He asked if she knew what the name meant.

No. What?

"Lobo."

"En verdad? Lo mismo como la familia de mi mamá?"

Well, not quite the same. For one thing, her mother's maiden name was in plural form—Lobos—but his name was not. Also, his surname had an "e" on the end. "En inglés no hay una 'e' en la palabra para el lobo."

Even so, she said, the coincidence of their family names was a little curious.

He said he supposed so.

Where had he learned to speak Spanish?

Everywhere between Matamoros and Mexico City.

Well, she said with a smile, she did not mean to be rude, but it sounded like it. His grammar was good, but that accent! It had to be the only one of its kind in Mexico.

He returned her smile. The brandy warmed him. He asked about the scar and she said she'd got it from a fight with a ratero who stole her purse on the street about a year ago. Some weeks after, she and her grandfather were shopping in the rowdy Volador Market behind the zócalo when she spotted the thief in a packed crowd in front of a kiosk, watching a puppet show. Bruno Blanco asked if she were absolutely sure, and she was. Her grandfather had then eased through the crowd and up alongside the thief and so neatly stabbed him in the heart from behind that he was dead without a cry. As her grandfather withdrew from the crowd, the man sank in the press of people around him without drawing more than a glance of irritation at one more drunk passing out in public.

Your grandfather is an honorable and capable man, but I would have made the bastard look at you before I killed him. So he would know why he was getting it.

She studied his eyes. I believe you.

You have beautiful skin.

She blushed even as she laughed at his sudden compliment. Then held out an arm for his inspection and said, "Leche teñida por un poquito de café." Her family had been Creole until Grandfather Bruno married a mestiza. It was that grandmother who put the trace of milk-and-coffee in her complexion.

Had she ever been married?

No, but she had been engaged to an army officer when she was sixteen. He was sent to Sonora to fight Yaquis, and a month before he was due to return for their wedding he took an arrow in the leg. The wound became infected and the leg had to be cut off. He wrote her a letter saying he would understand if she decided not to marry him now that he was an incomplete man. She wrote back to tell him not to be foolish, that she didn't care if he was without a leg. But the infection had poisoned his blood and by the time her letter got to the military hospital he had been dead almost a week.

Did you love him very much?

Yes. But now I cannot clearly remember his face.

You have no picture of him?

No. From her apron pocket she produced a black cigarillo and set it between her teeth, then rasped a lucifer into flame and put it to the end of the little cigar. The smoke was blue and sweet. The only women he'd ever seen smoke were some of the girls of the Blue Mermaid and some women of the Mexican outlands. He was taken with her easy confidence. She smiled and asked if he wanted a puff, then held the cigarillo to his lips. It was moist with the touch of her tongue. The act seemed to him somehow more intimate than any he had ever shared with even a naked woman.

She closed her fingers around his clawed hand and said, Listen. And told him that even after she saw the brand on his face she had been in doubt of what to do. She had thought to leave him on the sidewalk to recover on his own or to die, whichever way fate would have it.

It was like a little trial in my head, she said. One side argued that I should help you because you fought for my country and the other side said not to be foolish, life in this terrible time is dangerous enough without bringing a stranger under our roof, especially a foreigner. A man who has killed so many might choose to kill us too for whatever reason enters his head. And then you opened your eyes. When I saw them it was decided. You have true eyes.

He said he was glad the verdict went his way. He would have hated to become one more corpse for the dead wagon to collect.

You are luckier than you know, she said. I was decided before I saw you smile. I do not mean to insult you, but with that hole in your teeth and the way that scar pulls your face, it is not the kind of smile to make others smile back. If I had seen you smile before deciding about you . . . well, who knows what the verdict might have been.

She laughed. And his grimace of a grin widened.

❦

He accepted Bruno Blanco's offer of employment as the café's barman, a job he could do with one good hand and one bad one. He could live in the storeroom, old Bruno said. He had been there a week when she tiptoed down the stairs in the middle of the night and slipped into his cot. After a month of it, Bruno Blanco said they should stop thinking they were fooling anyone and might as well live together in her room with the larger and more comfortable bed. In the darkness of their trysts she had shed silent tears as her fingers traced the whip scars on his back, and when she saw them in the lamplight she cried harder yet and cursed the whoresons who had given them to him. Cursed all armies of the earth as gangs of barbarians.

They had been together only two months when she proposed marriage because she wanted children. But if you do not want to be a father, she said, we can continue as we are. You are my first importance. And because there was nothing he wished to do with his life other than what he was doing, nowhere he wished to be other than where he was, he could think of no objection to marriage or fatherhood and so said all right.

They never spoke of love. She would in time tell him that she had never had a better friend, but he knew it was not true, knew her grandfather had been a better friend to her than anyone else could ever be. But she did not know he told the same lie, for she was unaware of his brother. He had told her he was an orphaned only child. He lied for no reason but to keep things simple, and he assumed she did too.

But he had not lied about no longer regarding himself as an American. When they married in January he renounced his Anglo surname and took her family name for his own. María Palomina Blanco y Blanco was congratulated for her marriage to a gallant defender of Mexico, a man the more noble for his greater allegiance to justice than to birthplace. Old Bruno beamed with pride in his fine grandson-in-law.

So. He entered a life of daily routine that called for no hard decisions and required no plans and demanded no accounting of his past. He was an able bartender, efficient and circumspect, and as the job called for more listening than talking, it suited him well. The place catered to a respectable patronage, most of it neighborhood shopkeepers and residents, regular customers of long standing. Their gazes at his brand were mostly discreet, and he was never questioned about the war that gave it to him.

He had told María Palomina of his liking for the hornpipe and having been taught to play it by his grandfather, and she one day spied one in a pawnshop window and bought it for him. He found he could clutch it well enough with his clawed hand while the fingers of his good one worked the note holes. She clapped and shouted "Bravo!" when in spite of his bad hip he managed a few hobbling steps of a sailor's jig as he played a tweedling tune.

He acquired the habit of a daily walk around the neighborhood before lunch, but never went farther than three blocks in any direction. Whenever he approached that outer boundary he got a hollow feeling in his stomach, a peculiar sensation that if he went any farther he would have a hard time finding his way back. It was not something he could fully explain even to himself and he would never even try to explain it to anyone else.

His enduring pleasure was drink. Every night after the café closed he would sit at the bar with a bottle and glass for another few hours, on occasion until nearly dawn. María Palomina sometimes joined him for a drink or two and sometimes old Bruno as well, but usually they left him to imbibe by himself, as they sensed he preferred to do. He was a quiet drunk and a tidy one, never clumsy or impolite, and possessed a constitution that well tolerated hangover. If María Palomina ever wondered what thoughts he kept in those late inebriate nights, she never asked. Had she done so, and had he answered truthfully, he could only have said that he was fairly sure he thought of nothing at all, and when he did think about things, he could never remember them the morning after, nor tried very hard to.

Their first child, Gloria Tomasina, was born the next winter, and a year later came Bruno Tomás. The year after that saw the birth of Mariano, who lived but six days. A month after the infant's funeral their grief was enlarged when Old Bruno died in his sleep. Their last child, born in the summer of 1853, they christened Sofia Reina.

DARTMOUTH DAYS

John Roger had not really expected Samuel Thomas to post a letter to him from every port as he had promised, but as winter gave way to the first muddy thaw of spring he was sorely disappointed not to have received even a note from him in the six months since they'd last seen each other. He was expecting him to appear in Hanover any day now, perhaps with explanation for his lack of correspondence, perhaps with no reference to it whatever. In either case, he knew his brother would be smiling and full of confidence and have stories to tell, and knew that his pique toward Samuel Thomas would not withstand the pleasure of seeing him again.

Then the trees were greening and beginning to bloom, and he completed his freshman final examinations—and still there was no word from Samuel Thomas. And now he began to be worried.

He wrote to the Portsmouth harbormaster's office, inquiring after the *Atropos,* and was informed the ship had been delayed on its return voyage, incurring damage in a storm off Cape Hatteras. The vessel had been under repair for weeks before again setting sail, and it was now due to make Portsmouth in the middle of June. John Roger was relieved but also vexed. How much effort would it have taken for Samuel Thomas to write him a note about the delay? He had planned on going to Portsmouth to greet him at the dock but now thought he might rather accept the invitation of some college friends to spend a few weeks in Boston. Let that thoughtless blockhead do a little worrying of his own when he didn't find him in Hanover.

But on the sunny afternoon the *Atropos* landed in Portsmouth, John Roger was there to meet the ship. And found out from one of its officers that Samuel T Wolfe was not among the crew and had in fact not reported for duty before the ship left Portsmouth in August. All John Roger could think to say was, "I see."

COUNTRY OF THE BAD WOLFES

He walked along the waterfront for a time without a coherent thought, then halted and looked about him like a roused sleepwalker. Then made directly for the Yardarm Inn where he and Sammy had quartered the previous summer. The desk man consulted a register and said that a Samuel Wolfe had been living there at the end of August, all right, but had quit the premises in debt of a day's rent. The date of his arrears coincided with John Roger's departure for Hanover. If he'd left any possessions they had been sold or discarded.

John Roger then went to the office of the city graveyard and pored over its registries. Then to the local hospital, where an administrator carefully examined its record of patients. In none of those pages was entered his brother's name. Over the next weeks he went to every jail and prison fifty miles to the north and south of Portsmouth. In Boston the jail clerk ran his finger down the inmate ledger and stopped at a name and looked at it more closely. "Ah yah," he said, "Samuel Wolfe, right here he is. And don't I remember him now?" He peered over the rims of his spectacles at John Roger, whose pulse sped. "But grayhaired he was and black in the teeth with his sixty years and more, so I don't suppose he was your brother, now was he?" John Roger said, "*Damn* it!"—and received a severe look and stern reminder that he was in a Boston municipal office and not in some waterfront public house and such profanity could get him ten days in one of the cells down the hall.

He was at breakfast in a café when it occurred to him that Samuel Thomas may have contracted amnesia by some means and be wandering about with no inkling of his own identity. Perhaps right there in Boston. For the next three days he scoured the city streets before conceding the impossible odds of finding him by this haphazard means. Then admitted the desperate foolishness of thinking Sammy could be amnestic. Unable to think of what else he might do, he returned to Hanover.

He lived in a small and Spartan room near the campus, his scholarship not providing for dormitory lodging. He lay awake deep into the nights, his imagination amok and returning again and again to the grim possibility that Samuel Thomas had been killed in some hideous accident or taken fatally ill, his unidentified remains consigned to a pauper's grave. Or had been murdered while being robbed, or in some street affray, and his body pitched into the river or the sea or the city refuse pit to be burned with the waste. He could conceive of no other explanations for his brother's disappearance and lack of communication. He spent part of every day staring at their graduation picture.

The summer was waning into its last weeks when he awoke one morning with the sure conviction that Samuel Thomas was dead, and that he may have been dead since their first night apart. Dead all that time that he had so blithely thought of him as alive. He could hardly draw breath against the crushing sensation of his loss, his overwhelming aloneness. "Oh God, Sammy!" he said. Then wept with such force he ruptured a blood vessel in his throat. Which became infected, then worsened, then prostrated him with a raging fever.

He had not come out of his room for three days when his landlady, Mrs Burrows, who had doted on him through his freshman year, became concerned. She tapped at his door and asked if all was well. Then knocked louder but still received no reply. And so let herself into the shadowy quarters and discovered him abed and barely conscious, stewing in his own filth, unable to speak for the burning rawness of his throat.

"Merciful Jesus." She hastened to give him water, then opened the windows to air the room. Then cleaned him and dressed him in fresh nightclothes and helped him to sit in a chair so that she could change his bedding. Then fetched him a measure of whiskey and told him to sip it slowly. His eyes flooded at the burn of it.

Over the next week she several times a day gave him spoonings of various nostrums. Each morning she changed his bedding and bore away his slops, then brought a breakfast of honeyed tea and parboiled eggs and soft breads. She brought dinners of mashed and buttered vegetables, supper broths of mutton and beef. In the first low raspings of his returning voice he told her of the recent notification that his brother, the last of his living kin, had been lost at sea. Her commiseration was tearful. She well knew the pain of losing loved ones, the loneliness of being without family. She had buried her only child, a month-old daughter, twenty-three years ago, and it was eighteen years now she had been widowed.

⁕

He was physically recovered by the beginning of the academic year, though his voice had been permanently deepened to a raspy bass. His emotional recuperation took a while longer, but nothing else could have served it so well as the resumption of university life. His freshman year had been a notable triumph—he'd made the dean's list both semesters, and his essay on the merits of Hamiltonian economics was published in a university review.

His successes continued through the rest of his student years. He studied Spanish in ancillary courses and while still a sophomore became fluent enough to read *Don Quixote* in the original and write a monograph on it in Spanish. He had always enjoyed numbers but in college they became a passion and he dazzled his instructors in mathematics. Accounting was child's play. His studies came to him with such ease that he had time for extracurricular pursuits. He joined the debate club and became a redoubtable adversary, winning the annual New England competition with a rousing defense of President Polk's war in Mexico as essential to America's Manifest Destiny. At the urging of a professor who admired his forensic flair, he auditioned for a junior-year production of *Henry the Fourth* and won praise for his rendition of Hotspur, and then as a senior he played the lead in Marlowe's *Faustus*. On a dare, he enrolled in a fencing class and was as surprised as everyone else by his swiftly acquired proficiency with a foil. His style was unaggressive and lacked finesse but was marked by an impenetrable defense, relying on clockwork parries that inevitably frustrated his opponents into rash moves that left them open to counterthrust hits. He was recruited for the varsity team and within a year became its ace. In his junior year he was narrowly defeated by his Princeton opponent in the interscholastic finals, and then as a senior he beat the Brown University ace for the championship.

All the while, through careful observation of his classmates, he learned the bearing of a gentleman. In emulation of his favorite professor he took up smoking a calabash pipe. He was popular among his fellows, a convivial companion who relished political argument and an occasional wager on a horse race, who enjoyed a pint and a ribald joke as well as the next man.

And yet, for all his friends, he did not truly confide in any of them. He was amiably chary in all reference to family. The adventurous sire he'd admired as a boy had become a secret to guard against the social exclusion he was sure would befall him were it known he was son to a murderer. As far as anyone at Dartmouth knew, his parents had died when he was a young child and he and his brother had been raised in Portsmouth by a maiden aunt, the aunt now also deceased. He had admitted to a living brother only because he had expected Samuel Thomas sooner or later to show up in search of him, and he would have to introduce him to friends. He had told them Sammy was a junior officer on a merchant ship, an elevation in rank he was certain Sammy would enjoy simulating, just as he would surely understand why his classmates mustn't know the truth about their father—though Sammy would doubtless have chivvied him for his social fastidiousness. He had been sure, too, that his friends would enjoy the surprise of seeing that they were twins. When he sadly told his fellows, at the start of sophomore year, that his brother's ship had gone down in a storm off Hispaniola that summer and the entire crew with it, he was accorded the special sympathy reserved for those who have lost the last of their family.

His only confidant during his Dartmouth years was a leatherbound ledger that served as a journal in which he made random entries with no purpose but to clarify to himself his own thoughts and reflections. Whenever he was unclear about some idea or emotion, uncertain in his perception of someone or vague about a memory, he sat to his journal and wrote as precisely as he could what he thought or felt or remembered, and thereby gave those thoughts and feelings and memories the solidity and authority of words recorded on a page. And by that simple act made of them his abiding truth.

—✦—

He graduated summa cum laude but was bested by a whisker for valedictorian and so delivered the salutatory address. Then went to work as a legal assistant in the Concord office of Fletcher, McIntosh & Bartlett. He gained the position through the influence of his best friend and fencing teammate, James Davison Bartlett, son to one of the firm's partners and himself studying toward a legal career. A rakish sort, Jimmy Bartlett had once sneaked a young prostitute into his dormitory simply to prove he could do it, then was caught as he was trying to sneak her out again. It was one of numerous pranks for which he might have been expelled but for the might of his family name. The Bartletts had landed with the Pilgrims. They were among the first families of New Hampshire—and major benefactors of Dartmouth College. In addition to the builders of the paper mills on which the Bartlett fortune was founded and had continued to expand, the bloodline included a lieutenant governor, a state Supreme Court justice, and a state's attorney general. Jimmy's father, Sebastian, was one of the most highly respected contract lawyers in New England, and his Uncle Elliott was an administrator in the consular service. His mother, Alexandra Davison Bartlett, belonged to a prominent New York family long acquainted with the Sullivan County Van Burens, family of the former president of the United States.

It was the most pleasant spring John Roger had known since boyhood. He fulfilled his office duties with precision and could research and annotate a point of law with utter thoroughness and dispatch. On his own initiative he devised and proposed a simpler but more efficient accounting system for the company, an innovation that earned him a handsome bonus and the partners' unstinting praise. He kept a rented room on boisterous Center Street and gave his weekday evenings to reviewing Coke and Blackstone and other legal texts he'd been absorbing since his freshman year. But on almost every weekend he would be Jimmy's guest at the Bartlett estate on the Merrimack. Except for Jimmy's sister, who was away at school in Exeter, he made the acquaintance of all the Bartletts and enjoyed their company as much as they did his.

He and Jimmy liked to scull on the river, liked to saddle a pair of the thoroughbreds stabled on the grounds and race each other across the meadows. The Bartletts also owned a seaside cottage near Rockport, Massachusetts, and he sometimes went there with Jimmy for holiday stays. They would sail off rocky Cape Ann in the family ketch *Hecuba*. They went for long hikes in the hilly woods. They did much target-shooting with Jimmy's Colt Dragoon. The revolver was a graduation gift from his father, who'd received it from Samuel Colt himself in appreciation for his contractual expertise in establishing the Colt factory in Hartford. It was an imposing weapon, weighing above four pounds and firing a .44-caliber ball that would make hash of a man's heart. "Picture yourself a hundred years ago in command of a militia company armed with the only ones of these in existence," Jimmy said. "You would've been the lords of the earth."

Once a week they practiced their swordsmanship, usually with the foils they had competed with at Dartmouth, but sometimes with the cavalry sabers Jimmy's great-grandfather had acquired in the Revolutionary War. The first time John Roger hefted a saber he at once felt its difference from a fencing foil. This was no instrument of sport but a weapon of war. Its very heft evoked mortal menace. It was made for slashing as well as thrusting and its blade was grooved to allow for easier passage through a torso, for the run of blood. A saber contest called for greater strength and stamina than did rapier fencing, and its proper art entailed fighting with a two-handed grip when necessary. It was easy to get caught up in the flailing zeal of a saber match, and during one heated exchange John Roger inadvertently nicked Jimmy's arm. For a week after, his friend bore the bandaged wound as proudly as a war veteran.

SISTER OF FORTUNA

In mid-summer they passed their bar examinations, John Roger with ease, Jimmy by the skin of his teeth—a fact in which he seemed to take perverse pride—and they were hired as junior members at Fletcher, McIntosh & Bartlett. To mark the occasion, Sebastian Bartlett invited a host of friends to a Saturday picnic on his riverside lawn, to be followed by a ballroom dance that evening.

The day of the picnic was blessed with ideal weather, the turnout large and in festive spirit. A bandstand had been erected on the lawn and a brass ensemble played gaily through the afternoon. Jimmy's sister, Elizabeth Anne, would not arrive until later in the day, coming by coach from Exeter, where she had been spending the past weeks with friends, following her graduation from the Athenian Female Seminary. Her oil portrait hung on the parlor wall of the Merrimack house and John Roger had often paused to admire it. As pictured, she was truly beautiful. Hair the color of polished copper in green-ribboned ringlets to her bare shoulders, the ribbons matching the color of her eyes. An elegant throat necklaced with pearls. Full lips in a small smile suggestive of some secret amusement. John Roger suspected that the artist may have gilded the lily in gratitude for Mr Bartlett's no-doubt-hefty commission.

Jimmy told him the painting of Lizzie—as he and his father called her, while Mrs Bartlett referred to her by no name but Elizabeth—had been done less than a year before. "You'd never know by that picture what a tomboy she was," Jimmy said. All through girlhood she had been one for foot-racing, climbing trees, flying kites, chucking stones. She had badgered their father into teaching her to swim at a much younger age than Jimmy had learned, and then pestered Jimmy into instructing her how to sail his gaff-rigged pram. She was a constant fret to their mother, who was ever upbraiding her to behave herself as a respectable young lady ought. Even though Jimmy and his friends refused to let her join their Adventurers' Club, she persisted in swimming with them in the river. "We all wanted to dunk her," Jimmy said, "but none of us could catch her. She swims like an otter. I don't care to say how many times she beat me in races. She could beat all of us."

Their mother thought it unseemly that Lizzie was frisking in the river with the boys, but their father, who was proud of her aquatic superiority, believed it was simple innocent fun. Then came the family's first swim of the summer when she was fourteen and her sodden bathing costume clung to her in startling new ways. "You could see the fruit was getting ripe, if you know what I mean," Jimmy said. Her evident physical bloom effected an abrupt change in Mr Bartlett's outlook and he told her there would be no more swimming in company with boys. Lizzie alleged not to understand his objection and for days persisted in asking an explanation of him, and he would every time reiterate that it simply wasn't proper. But *how* was it improper, Lizzie would demand to know, and red-faced Mr Bartlett would sputter that she should ask her mother. "She didn't have to ask Mum," Jimmy said. "Lizzie knew very well what Father was talking about. She was just deviling him for the fun of it. It's how she's always been."

The same devilment was at the root of what Jimmy called the music scandal. His sister was a fine pianist, trained in the classics, but their parents had been unaware of the bohemian element in her repertoire until one evening when she was entertaining the family after supper and segued from "Für Elise" into a rousing dance-hall number of recent French import. Jimmy had heard her play the bawdy music once before, when their parents were away from the house, and had cautioned her against it, and she'd shown him her tongue in retort. But as he'd warned, their mother was dismayed by the lewd composition and she ordered Lizzie to desist from it at once. Very well, the girl said, and banged the fallboard over the keys and got up from the bench and—*humming* the sprightly tune—danced about the parlor with her skirts swirling to her knees. "Mum barely spoke to her for the next couple of days," Jimmy said.

Mrs Bartlett was finally pushed past her wit's end with her audacious daughter when the girl was seen mounted astride her stallion as she rode on the public road flanking their property. When Lizzie countered her mother's angry reprimand with the contention that it was the more sensible as well as more comfortable way to ride, Mrs Bartlett called upon Mr Bartlett to prohibit her from riding until she promised to do so in the proper, sidesaddle fashion. Lizzie was so cross, Jimmy said, that she threatened to run away and live among the Indians. Her parents never knew for sure when she was joking, but such impertinence was anyway the concluding proof to Mrs Bartlett that the girl was in critical need of social remediation before it was too late. "Do something, Sebastian," she told her husband.

Mr Bartlett dismissed Lizzie's private tutors and enrolled her at the Athenian

Seminary for her final year of schooling. Renowned for its instruction in the social graces as much as for its rigorous academic curriculum, the institution had molded more than one recalcitrant miss into a decorous young lady. When Elizabeth came home for Christmas holiday at the end of her first semester, she comported herself as the very model of refined femininity her mother had prayed for.

"That's when she sat for that picture on the wall," Jimmy said.

And now, as John Roger and Jimmy stood talking on the riverside lawn, Mrs Bartlett came up behind them, saying, "John, dear, here is someone you must meet." The happy matron was hugging the arm of the young woman she presented as her daughter, Elizabeth. In the dusky gold light of late afternoon the girl was smiling at him as in the painting. She was surprisingly tall, her eyes almost on a level with his, and both leaner and more buxom than her portrait suggested. He thought her even lovelier than her picture, and only by force of will kept his jaw from going slack.

"Mr Wolfe," she said, offering her hand, "Jimmy has written me so much about you, I feel as though we've long been acquainted."

He said the pleasure was entirely his and kissed her hand. Her eyes went brighter. Her mother tittered.

⁕

Before the end of their first dance that evening he knew he was in love, though she would later say that he may not have known it until then but she knew he had fallen in love the minute their eyes met. Directly on the heels of his dancefloor insight, however, he had the distressing thought that she might already have a beau—or worse, be betrothed. He could not muster the boldness to ask directly if she were spoken for, and as they waltzed about the floor he was frantic for some clever way to find out.

His worry was more evident than he knew, and she intuited its cause. "If it's of concern to anyone you know, Mr Wolfe," she said during a dance, "I'm under no obligation to any party whatever." He flushed in surprise at both her acuity and her candor. His relief was so manifest she nearly laughed aloud—and so endearing she had to resist the urge to kiss him right there on the dance floor.

Later in the evening they went out to the garden under an oblong ivory moon and followed a winding pathway to a low rock wall bordering the lawn. A mild breeze carried the scents of night flowers and the river, stirring the trees, swaying the shadows. The ballroom music was faint at this distance. Against the house lights filtering through the foliage she was mostly silhouette. An undulant wisp of moonlight played on her hair and glinted on an earring. He said he had heard many an interesting tale of her rowdy tomboy days with the gents of the Adventurers' Club.

"Oh, those rascals," she said. "They never did let me be a member, you know." She leaned closer and said in lowered voice, "But that club was never so interesting as the one I belong to at the seminary. It's a most clandestine association, so I mustn't tell you anything of it unless you promise absolutely never to repeat it to a living soul."

John Roger swore her secret was safe with him.

They were the Sisters of Fortuna, she said, and they performed such rituals as would have surely got them burned for witches not so long ago. He heard a timbre of mischief in her voice and suspected she was having sport with him, yet her daring insinuations at once amused and beguiled him. He asked what sorts of rituals.

She leaned closer still and told him the Sisters met only on nights of the full moon, in a meadow deep in the woods, even on the coldest nights. They would build a large bonfire and then remove their cloaks, under which they wore only thin white nightdresses and black woolen stockings. They would sing hymns to Fortuna and dance like dervishes in a circle round the fire, their loosed hair flinging and nightdresses awhirl.

He felt her perfumed warmth on his face, her breath at his ear as she whispered, "We dance faster and faster, and my heart just pounds against my ribs like . . . like some wild thing in a cage. And then . . ." she took a deep breath, "then we throw off our nightdresses and dance naked but for our stockings. *Naked.*"

She quickly drew back to look at his face—which felt to him on fire. In a bobbing shard of moonlight he glimpsed a bright eye and flash of grin. Then she kissed him full on the lips—and before he could even think to react she darted away toward the ballroom, glancing back over her shoulder and saying, "Close your mouth, Mr Wolfe, before an insect flies into it. And *hurry*, or we'll miss the last dance."

In the years ahead he would from time to time and with feigned casualness ask her if there had really been a Sisters of Fortuna sorority. And she would each time respond with no more than her smile of secret amusement.

❦

Through the rest of the summer they saw each other every day. They went for walks along the river. They went rowing. They went riding—and yes, she rode astraddle. They went swimming with Jimmy and his latest sweetheart, a girl named Madeline Groom, whose father was a federal judge. Even in her woolen neck-to-ankle bathing outfit Elizabeth Anne easily outdistanced John Roger in a race. "Told you so," Jimmy said. Out of earshot of the others, Elizabeth Anne said to John Roger, "How mush faster I could swim if I took off this foolish costume. Just imagine it." He imagined it—and she smiled at the look on his face.

It came as no surprise to him that she was a fine sailor, as he learned at the Rockport estate when they went out on the *Hecuba*. Or that she was an ace pistolshot, having learned to shoot from Jimmy when she was thirteen. At her suggestion, the three of them spent an afternoon firing the family caplocks at a variety of small targets set upon a fence rail. When she demolished a potato from forty paces, a shot John Roger had just missed, she smiled and blew the powdersmoke from the muzzle as she'd seen trickshooters do at county fairs, then slipped the pistol into the belt of her skirt and stood with hands on hips, grinning at him.

"Humiliating, isn't it?" Jimmy said. "Bad enough she can outswim us, but *outshoot*? It's more than shameful. I couldn't bring myself to say anything to you about it till she beat you too. It's the same with the Colt. She needs both hands just to aim that monster and still shoots it better than me. I tell you, chum, there's something supernatural about this wench."

She affected a ghostly apparition, wriggling the fingers of her raised hands and saying, "*Woooooooo.*"

※

They passed the evenings on the Bartlett's porch glider, holding hands and conversing in low voice, and the next day John Roger would have poor recollection of what they had talked about, so distracted had he been by the nearness of her—and even more so by the kisses they shared at every opportunity. The first time she eased her tongue into his mouth he nearly flinched in his astonishment before going lightheaded with the thrill of it and responding in kind. When they broke for breath, she said she had never kissed anyone that way before but had heard talk of it among some of the Sisters of Fortuna. It was said to be a French innovation. Some of the Sisters had thought the idea vile but most were curious about it. Elizabeth Anne said she herself had been intrigued by it and had made a secret vow to try it sometime.

"Now that you've tried it," he said, "what do you think of it?"

"What do you think I think of it?"

And they did it again. And found it was possible to smile, even giggle, while they were at it. But he was in such a state of arousal—and would be in every instance of such kissing—that he was reluctant to uncross his legs for fear that even in the dim light of the porch she might notice his condition and be repulsed by his baseness.

※

He proposed to her in early October, during a Bartlett dinner party on an Indian-summer evening. They went out along the moonlit riverbank and he got down on one knee. His heart heaving as much in terror that she would refuse him as with the bedazzling possibility of her acceptance. He stammered on the word "marry" and she covered her smile with her hand. Then lowered the hand to his hair and said, "Of course I will, my beloved."

He jumped up and they kissed for a time and then rushed hand in hand up the sloping yard and into the house to make the announcement—both of them breathless, Elizabeth Anne radiant, John Roger happy and red-faced and oblivious of her lip paint on his mouth and the mud caked on his knee. The Bartletts were jubilant at the news, so too their guests. Mrs Bartlett wept as she hugged her daughter and John Roger in turn. Elizabeth Anne later joked to him that she suspected her mother's tears were as much of relief that her errant daughter had managed to attract any husband at all as they were of joy that she had acquired such a prize as John Roger. Sebastian Bartlett pumped John Roger's hand and welcomed him to the family. Jimmy clapped him on the shoulder and wished him luck, saying that with his sister he would surely need it, and then laughed at Elizabeth Anne's slap to his arm. The dinner party became a celebration that lasted until dawn.

❦

They married in the First Congregational Church in Concord on a bright but chilly March morning, then were conveyed to the station by landau and boarded a coach for Boston, where they would spend a week's honeymoon in a fine hotel overlooking the Charles. The other passengers smiled on the happy newlyweds and wished them well.

Underlying John Roger's happiness, however, was a mounting apprehension as the wedding night drew near. He'd had no sexual mating other than his initiation by the tattooed whore in Portsmouth, and he was afraid he would prove a maladroit lover to his bride. Throughout their college days Jimmy Bartlett had favored occasional sprees in Portland's infamous brothels, and during the first year of their friendship he never failed to ask John Roger to go along. But he each time begged off with some excuse until Jimmy finally shrugged and said, "So be it, chum. Every man to his own foibles."

The truth was that throughout his college years John Roger had an ardent crave of sexual pleasure. But he had never wholly recovered from the wrenching dread of infection that had haunted him for weeks after his lark with the Blue Mermaid whore. Not only had he never again patronized a brothel, he had even shied from his opportunities with women who were neither whores nor models of virtue. He believed his sexual phobia was absurd but he had not been able to overcome it. Until the advent of Elizabeth Anne, he had feared he was doomed to a lonely and masturbatory bachelorhood. But while his desire for her was rooted in love and free of all fear of disease, he had begun to fret more and more that his lack of experience would render him inadequate in the marriage bed.

On their wedding night, as he lay abed in their room while she finished with her bath, his apprehension grew overwhelming and he was certain of impotence. She emerged with her face rosy from the bath and the heat of her own excitement, her hair a lustrous spill on the shoulders of her white gown. But as she approached the bed she sensed his tension and in the low candlelight saw the alarm in his eyes. An instinct she hadn't known she possessed prompted her to kiss a fingertip and put it to his lips, and then she stepped back and turned about and unbelted her gown and let it cascade to her feet. He gaped at her pale nakedness in the lampglow, the shadowed groove of spine and cleft of buttocks. She hummed a tune he did not recognize and slowly turned to face him, smiling her secret smile in the low light, one arm partially covering her breasts, her other hand over her sex. His anxiety gave way to a rush of desire. She flung her arms wide in a presentation of her stark nakedness, breasts upraised and nipples puckered and lean belly sloping to a rubric delta—then swooped down to kiss him, her tongue slicking into his mouth, her breasts pressing to his chest. He broke the kiss with a gasp and pulled her onto the bed and rolled up over her and clumsily positioned himself as her hand went under his nightshirt and found him ready and guided him into her. They cried out together and almost at once, he in the convulsive onset of his climax and she in a momentary twinge and ensuing flash of pleasure. He collapsed on her and rolled onto his side, breathless as one who's been saved from drowning.

After a time he raised up on an elbow to look at her. "Are you . . . all right?" And saw that she was smiling.

And then they were kissing and making bold explorations with their hands as their breath and eager blood quickened yet again. He broke for a moment to fling off his nightshirt and they joined once more. And this time were longer about it.

They did not fall asleep until nearly dawn, John Roger spooned against her from behind, his face in her hair. Not an hour later he woke to find her turned toward him and studying his face. "What?" he said. "This." She kissed him. Closed her hand on him. And they coupled again.

Such concupiscence on a wedding night is of course hardly uncommon—the wonder would be that their carnal appetite for one another would not abate over the years. Hugging him close in the early light of their first day as Mr and Mrs John Roger Wolfe, she told him she had not believed she would ever find a mate with whom she could be her true self. He said he never believed he would cease to envy other men for their amorous adventures. She kissed his ear and her smile was sly as she asked, "And now?" Now, he said, he knew that *she* was the quintessential amorous adventure. They laughed in their happiness at making believers of each other.

UNCLE REDBEARD

Although they made love almost nightly, Elizabeth Anne did not conceive in the first year of their marriage. Nor in the second. Nor the third. They concluded she was barren or his seed was lacking, and their disappointment ran deep. But they felt no less fortunate in their shared life. They sought no social entertainment outside of each other and rarely attended parties other than those of her parents. They lived in a lakeside bungalow off Rumford Street, a short walk from the offices of Fletcher, McIntosh & Bartlett. He undertook the study of maritime law and international port regulations and became so expert with them that the firm gained a number of new contracts with major shippers out of Boston. Sebastian Bartlett assured him of a full partnership within three years, which would make him the youngest partner in the firm. Jimmy wasn't jealous. "You're better at this game than everybody in the place except Father, so why shouldn't you be rewarded for it?" he said.

During the third Christmastide of their marriage, Richard Davison came to visit at the Bartlett home. He was the youngest of Alexandra Davison Bartlett's three brothers, and the family's black sheep, but he and Alexandra had always been each other's favorite. While his brothers pursued careers in New York state politics, Richard left home and roamed widely, mostly in the Southland, and tried his hand at different occupations, but he rarely let three months pass without a letter to his sister. He had been a canal boatman, a stagecoach driver, a town marshal, a river port manager. There were rumors, however, of darker undertakings. Of manhunting for bounty in the Carolinas. Of a fatal street fight in Savannah. Of making off with a man's wife in Mississippi. Of partnership in a Cincinnati bawdy house. Mrs Bartlett's veneration of her brother withstood all such gossip, and she would brook no aspersions toward him in her house. Six years earlier in Boston, Richard Davison had formed the Trade Wind Company to import commodities from Mexico and the Caribbean, and Mrs Bartlett took great satisfaction in informing her family of the firm's growing success. He had visited Concord only once before, in the summer when Elizabeth Anne was six years old, but she had not forgotten his fierce red beard and bright blue eyes, his stubby remnant of a ring finger which he told her had been bitten off by a mermaid. She called him Uncle Redbeard. He had carried her piggyback along the riverbank and made her laugh with his funny stories and vernacular mode of speech that contrasted so bluntly with the formal idiom of the Bartletts.

Alexandra Bartlett had not seen her brother since a Boston trip she'd made some years before, and she was overjoyed to have him under her roof, if for only three days. He was of medium height and sinewy build, his red beard closecropped and shot with gray, his eyes in permanent pinch from years in the sun. His handshake felt to John Roger like a clasp of dry leather. Though Richard's pleasure in his sister's company was apparent, he was reserved with the Bartlett men at the supper table, who in turn were tentative toward him. But he doted on Elizabeth Anne and took an easy liking to John Roger.

That evening, after the others retired, John Roger and Elizabeth Anne continued chatting with Richard over glasses of port in the parlor, seated before a blazing fireplace as moonlit snowfall drifted past the windows. Entreated by his niece to tell of his adventures, Richard recounted comical anecdotes relating to his sundry occupations, one tale after another, and John and Lizzie struggled to muffle their laughter in deference to those abed. So it went, until the hearth fire was reduced to red embers and the clock softly chimed midnight. By which time the conversation had taken various turns and Richard had learned of John Roger's fluency in Spanish and mastery of accounting.

"Bedamn, Johnny," he said, "if you might not be the very man I'm looking for."

He told John Roger that he had opened a branch office in New Orleans, where he was headed from here and where he now received all imports. He could cut his intermediary expenses even more if he had a company office in Mexico, from where he imported coffee and tobacco, his most profitable goods. If he had his own trusted man to run things down there he would no longer have to rely on the local Mexican broker who for almost six years had been working on commission as his middleman with the plantations. "Haciendas, the Mexies call them," Richard said. "They're like the plantations we got down South, only a far sight bigger and fancier, or so I've heard. And just like down South, the owners—hacendados, they're called— they live like kings and got the power of God over the slaves, except in Mexico the slaves are Indians and half-breeds on account of they aint got hardly any niggers. Slavery's supposed to be against their constitution—and who woulda thought they even had such a thing?—but they got slaves just the same, mostly by way of debt to hacienda stores and such. Curious folk, the Mexies. Call us gringos and Yankees and I can understand that, but when they call us North Americans I have to wonder what continent they think they're a part of. Anyhow, the point is, I got a hunch the Mexie broker's been cheating me from the start. Sends me a report every year of the coffee that gets stole from the warehouse before shipment, coffee I already paid for, you see. But for all I know he's the one stealing it."

After an extensive correspondence with a Mexican realty firm, he had negotiated a lease for a port office and warehouse, but he hadn't yet found the right man to put in charge of it. "I need somebody with a head on his shoulders and who can talk good Mexican, and you surely fit the bill, Johnny. But the man I'm looking for has got to have the sand to live down there. I won't lie to you, son, it's rough country. Aint been there myself and don't intend ever to go—it's the good ole U S of A for me and I aim to stay put—but I know lots who been there and they all tell me it's rough country, even where you'd be."

"And where is that?" John Roger said.

"Main port on the gulf. Place called Veracruz. Now, I'll tell you just two more things and I'm done selling. First, you'd have full authority to negotiate for the company down there, and I mean with everybody from the hacendados to the overland transporters to the shippers to the warehouse cleaners. It'd take forever to get anything done if you had to get my OK first on every decision. If after a year you're doing a bad job of it, I'll fire you without discussion. If you're doing a good one, I'll show my appreciation and you can count on that. The other thing is this. Whatever these legal bigwigs are paying you, I'll top it by thirty percent. And in case you don't know it, a Yankee dollar weighs even more down in Mexico. All right, then. What do you say, Johnny? Yay or nay?"

Except for his own brother, John Roger had never met a man less given to beating about the bush. And not until the moment Richard Davison presented him with this prospect did he realize that, even while he excelled as a New England lawyer and was content with the profession, he was not fully satisfied. He yearned for . . . he couldn't say what, exactly. . . . Something Other. A sally into the larger world. An Adventure. The realization was itself no less stunning than the possibility that he had been feeling this way for some time without even knowing it. He hadn't given Mexico a passing thought in years. But now the idea of going there was intoxicating. He turned to Elizabeth Anne to ask if she were amenable to at least discussing the subject, wondering how he might try to sway her. And saw that she was smiling, eyes bright.

"Oh Johnny," she said. "Do say yay."

***

Next morning, when they told her family, Sebastian Bartlett was aghast. He said it was beyond folly for John Roger to resign a secure and highly valued position for the sake of a whim. "Odds are you'll not be long in comprehending your error and wanting to return to the firm," Mr Bartlett said. "But I cannot promise that the partners will be willing to welcome you back into their employ, not in light of this irresponsible leave of it. And even if they should take you back, your bright prospect for a partnership will undoubtedly have dimmed, if not altogether expired."

John Roger said he understood the chance he was taking and thanked Mr Bartlett for his concerned advice.

Mrs Bartlett's concern was entirely with her daughter's well-being. Mexico was so far away. Everyone knew it was a place of political chaos, of disease and poverty and ignorance. Every veteran of the war down there described the people as half-caste brutes given to casual murder. Except for its capital city and a handful of colonial towns, the country was nothing but primitive villages dispersed over every sort of wilderness. How could Elizabeth even think of going there to live?

Elizabeth Anne took her mother's hands in her own and said, "Dearest Mother. I love you too. Very much. But I'm going."

Jimmy drew John Roger aside and wished him well and said he respected his pluck. "I sometimes think of giving up this easeful life and going off to some wild place to try my manly fortune and tomorrow be damned." He grinned. "But then I always sober up." He said he knew John Roger would take good care of Lizzie. "She's a pest, of course, but, just between us, I am somewhat fond of her." John Roger said he'd always had that suspicion. Later that evening, in the privacy of his room, Jimmy presented Elizabeth Anne with the Colt Dragoon as a parting gift. "For protection from those half-caste brutes that so worry Mother," he said.

Richard Davison gave John Roger a scrawled list of the regional haciendas with which the Trade Wind Company had contracts for coffee and tobacco and specifying the general terms of each of those agreements. He told John Roger it might be a good while before he could provide him with any other records of the company's coffee and tobacco dealings. He had always kept most business details in his head and been lax about organizing the paperwork, or even reviewing it beyond a quick look at the net income. Since he'd moved to New Orleans, his papers were in greater disorder than ever. John Roger said those records weren't important. "All I need to know is this," he said, tapping a finger on the list of haciendas.

Richard Davison slapped him on the back. "You're the man for the job, all right. Just the same, I promise I'll get you them other records soon as I can." And he departed for New Orleans.

——

The next two months sped by in a blur of planning and preparation. Elizabeth Anne hired a tutor in Spanish and worked hard at her daily lessons and was quizzed on them by John Roger every night. There was a farewell party at the Bartlett home in Concord, and then some days later yet another one at the family's Rockport estate. Dozens of well-wishers showed up at Boston Harbor to see them off on a raw, gray morning in late winter. Mrs Bartlett wept as if at a funeral. John Roger and Elizabeth Anne waved and waved from the deck rail, hugging close and smiling at the widening world as the ship drew away from the dock.

VILLA RICA
DE LA VERA CRUZ

The city was bright white under the morning sun when the steamer churned
past the yellowrock island prison of San Juan de Ulúa and into the harbor of
Villa Rica de la Vera Cruz, the name long since shortened to Veracruz. The steamer
eased up to the dock amid blasts of horns and whistles. The air heavy and tainted
with marine decay. A loud Babel of stevedores all along the wharf. Flocks of vultures
spiraling over the town, roosting on the rooftops. With their wrinkled red heads and
heavy cloaks of black feather they looked to John Roger like a hideous union of
undertakers in patient wait of work.

"My God, they're ugly," Elizabeth Anne said, holding to his arm at the deck rail.

"Not the most cheerful sight, are they? You're not sorry we came?"

"Sorry? Johnny, if I had a tail it would be wagging in a blur."

He bent to her ear and said she had a lovely tail, and she grinned and kissed his
cheek. She was feeling better than she had in days, having enjoyed the voyage until
rough waters in the Florida Strait afflicted her with a severe nausea. Her stomach
had not properly recovered since, and John Roger had gently teased her about the
lingering first-time seasickness of someone who had been sailing since she was a child.

Through his connections in the consular service, her Uncle Elliott had
arranged for them to be met at the dock by the American consul, a loquacious little
Texan named Charles Patterson. He stood but a couple of inches above five feet, his
eyes below the level of Elizabeth Anne's. His sizable mustache was as white as his
suit, and his coat flap bulged at the revolver on his hip. He had a team and wagon
standing by for their luggage, and as they waited for it to be offloaded he advised
them to favor of a wardrobe of light cottons and linen. He said that contrary to the
common wisdom, there were four seasons in the tropics—the hot-and-humid, the
hot-and-rainy, and very fine spring and fall seasons of about two weeks each.

"It's nice enough weather now," Patterson said, "but pretty soon the place'll turn into a damned caldron—beg pardon, mam. It's but one reason you don't find a lot of Americans here other than those passing through on the way to the capital and higher country. Me, I'm from Galveston, so wet heat's nothing new. Truth be told, I like it. Been here since the end of Mister Polk's War. Call me a odd duck."

In Spanish, John Roger said he was sure he would prefer the local climate over the winters of New England. Patterson smiled and with equal fluency told him it was a fine thing he could speak Spanish. He said it was shameful so many Americans who came to live and work in Mexico didn't know a word of the language and still didn't when they left. In Spanish more heavily accented than theirs, Elizabeth Anne said she must be an odd duck too—amusing them with her literal translation of the English idiom as "un pato extraño"—because she also liked the tropic heat.

"Truth to tell, the heat won't hardly be your biggest worry here," Patterson said. "I assume you folk been told how bad this place is for the yellow jack."

John Roger said they had indeed been apprised of the region's notorious susceptibility to yellow fever. "There was a lively debate at the captain's table one evening," he said, "as to whether garlic or quinine was the better prophylactic."

Patterson made a pained face. "I've known folk to eat enough garlic to knock over a buzzard with their breath and drink quinine till their ears rang like church bells, and Mister Jack still took them. Me, I had it when I was a kid, so it can't get me again. If you and the missus aint had it yet, well, I have to tell you the only thing that'll keep you safe from it is awful good luck."

"Well then," Elizabeth Anne said, "I'd say we are as well protected as can be, as we are certainly blessed with good luck."

"Glad to know it," Patterson said. "Best thing in the world, good luck. Except for sometimes. Like this gambler fella I knew. Wasn't all that skillful, actually, but just about always come out winners. Everbody at the card table always cussing him for a lucky so-and-so and he'd just smile and say he'd ruther be lucky than good. Said it an awful lot. Everbody knew what he meant by it and probly most of them agreed. But it's the sort of thing can start setting teeth on edge if it gets said too often, and no matter how lucky a fella is with the cards, the luck aint been invented that'll help much when some sore loser gets tired of hearing about your luck and takes a mind to lean across the table and shoot you in the eye. Which is what happened to this fella I'm talking about. Guess you could say he was a little too lucky for his own good."

Elizabeth Anne gave John Roger a sidelong frown. "An instructive parable, Mr Patterson," John Roger said. "But it seems to me that the fellow's failing was not so much an excess of good luck as an excess of talking about it."

"Yessir, that too," Patterson said. "The Mexicans say the quickest way to have your luck go bad is to talk about how good it is."

"I take your point, Mr Patterson," Elizabeth Anne said, "and I will make no further mention of our you-know-what."

"Call me Charley," Patterson said.

He had their baggage loaded onto the wagon and gave the driver delivery directions and sent him on his way. Then escorted the couple to the Trade Wind Company office near the far end of the wharf so John Roger could look it over. The place was infested with cockroaches but otherwise in good order, needing only a scrubbing and some new furniture. To keep the roaches in check, Patterson advised buying a couple of iguanas at the nearest market and setting them loose in the office. There was an adjoining warehouse for storing the coffee and tobacco before its export to New Orleans. Elizabeth Anne took two steps through its door before whirling right back out, sickened by the lingering stench of the fishmeal formerly stored there. Patterson said he could recommend a good crew to scour the room clean.

They went out onto the malecón—the seawall promenade fronting the harbor—then crossed over to the zócalo. The arcades were lined with shops and the handcarts of vendors. The square teemed with businessmen in pastel suits, peons in white cotton, beggar women in black head shawls asquat on the church steps, their skeletal brown hands extended to the passing world. There were spouting fountains, walkways flanked with wrought-iron benches and towering palms and broad shade trees shrilling with parrots. The redolence of flowers mingled with the aroma of coffee and the piquancy of cooking spices and the stinks of garbage and animal droppings and open privies. Marimba bands chiming at various points of the square. Patterson said he hoped they liked that sort of music because they would be hearing a great lot of it. They passed an alleyway where a pair of buzzards gorged on a dog carcass and Elizabeth Anne remarked on the scavengers' profusion. Patterson said to be grateful for them, they were the city's main means of street sanitation. In the shade of an arcade stood several lines of persons awaiting their turn at one of the tables manned by scribes who for a fee would write any sort of document from a government petition to a personal letter. "Love letters, mostly," Patterson said. "Lots of love letters. Somebody has to write them for the Romeos and somebody has to read them to the Juliets."

John Roger was surprised at the number of people with discernible Negroid features. According to Richard Davison the Spanish had brought Negro slaves to Mexico but they proved unnecessary in the face of so much available Indian labor. Patterson said that was so. "You'll find plenty enough niggers all over the Caribbean, Lord knows, but hardly any in Mexico except for some of the port towns, and the most of them right here in True Cross City. Way back when, they mixed with the Indians to make a breed called zambos. Pardos, some call them. Gave the mestizos and mulattos somebody to look down on. Whatever their race, all Veracruzanos are called jarochos. It's a word the old Spaniards used for insolent, profane people, and believe you me, you won't find a more foul-mouthed folk anywhere in the country. There's an old joke that if God banned cussing in Veracruz you'd have a city full of mutes."

At Elliott Bartlett's behest, Patterson had seen to the rental and readiness of their new home. It was only two blocks from the zócalo, a large two-story house in a well-tended neighborhood called Colonia Brisas. It fronted a street shaded by palms and was enclosed by high stone walls whose tops were lined with broken bottles affixed in cement. There were two front entryways—a heavy wooden door reinforced with iron bars, and a wide carriage gate of wood six inches thick. The gates opened onto a spacious cobblestone courtyard with a large circular fountain centered with a statue of Poseidon brandishing a trident and spouting water from his mouth. There were clusters of banana plants ten feet high, mango trees red-yellow with fruit. Clay pots of flowers hanging all along the portales. The smell was of florescence and mossy stone. The residence was staffed with an elderly female cook, a pair of teenage housemaids, and a young man with a game leg who lived in the carriage house and served as a general handyman. Patterson made the introductions all around and gave the Wolfes a tour of the place, then bid them good day and went back to the consulate.

That evening, they ascended the indoor stairway to the rooftop where there was wickerwork furniture under a sturdy ramada of vines and palm fronds. Up there was a sea breeze and they could view a greater span of the starry sky, could see the harbor lights and the glow of the central plaza through the trees.

Elizabeth Anne kissed him and said, "Thank you, dear man, for bringing me to this brave new world."

The nausea that had begun on the voyage continued to trouble Elizabeth Anne, and though she was sure it would eventually ease, it did not, and John Roger grew concerned. They had been in Mexico more than a month before she acceded to his urging that she have a medical examination. Patterson referred her to an expatriate English nurse, a lank horse-faced widow named Beckett whose husband, a doctor, had died of yellow fever a few years before. "She's good as any doc in town," Patterson said.

It took only a few minutes for Nurse Beckett to determine that Elizabeth Anne was pregnant. "Two months should be my guess, perhaps a bit more," she said.

Elizabeth Anne thought she must be mistaken. How could it be, after three years of fruitless effort? "But are you absolutely certain?" she said.

"Doubtless," Nurse Beckett said.

"There's no possibility of error?"

Nurse Beckett smiled. "Be assured, Mrs Wolfe, the only question is whether the child will be male or female."

John Roger's first reaction to Lizzie's report was also incredulity—and then he whooped in elation. That night they held each other close and talked till a late hour about their grand turn of fortune.

When he gave the news to Patterson the next noonday, the little man insisted they repair to a cantina for a congratulatory cup of rum. They ended up having several, over the course of which Patterson became wistful and his drawl more pronounced. He told John Roger he'd been a widower for sixteen years. Except for the loss of his wife, his greatest regret was their failure to have children. She miscarried their first two and had not conceived again.

"It's all we got to leave of ourselves in this world is children," Patterson said. "Man or woman without a child dies and it's like they never lived except to add a little more dust to the earth. The fella who said a wife and kids are like hostages to fortune and put an end to a man's adventuring days and so forth was probably right, but I'll tell you what—I'da quit my adventuring days long ago in trade for a living child. I'd give an arm today if Dame Fortune was willing to make the deal."

They took leave of each other as the city was rousing from the midday siesta. The shops reopening, the zócalo resuming its bustle. John Roger watched Patterson crossing the square with the precise stride of a man who knows he's drunk and wants not to let it show.

John Roger didn't know why—maybe because of all the talk about children— but his father had come to mind. Roger Blake Wolfe, the outlaw stranger. He had not often thought about him since his days at Dartmouth, but since coming to Mexico he'd occasionally dreamt of him. He could never recall much about the dreams except that his father's face was always indistinct and yet he seemed always to be smiling. Jimmy had told Elizabeth Anne of John Roger's having being orphaned in childhood and reared by an aunt and of the loss at sea of his mariner brother, Samuel, and John Roger had thanked her for her expression of sympathy. During their courtship he had frequently come very near to telling her the truth but had each time resisted the inclination, fearing that her love for him might be bruised by the fact of his outlaw father. It pained him to persist in the falsehood, but once they were married he felt he had let the lie go on for too long to rectify it, and so never had.

For reasons less explicable, ever since his arrival in Veracruz he had resisted the impulse to search in the local archives for information about his father. But now, standing outside the cantina and goaded by both the afternoon's rum and the fact of his own impending fatherhood, he more strongly than ever felt the urge to learn what he could about Roger Blake Wolfe. Across the plaza was the municipal building where the public records were archived. He consulted his pocketwatch. Then crossed the plaza and went into the building. In his brief time in Veracruz he had become well acquainted with the unruliness of Mexican recordkeeping and was not yet as adept as he would become at navigating its disorder, and it took him a while to uncover the sparse records pertaining to his father.

It was late afternoon when he came back out. He paused at the top step and gazed across the plaza at the cathedral. At the wall where the firing squad executions took place. Patterson had confided that during his first few years in Veracruz he had attended a number of public executions before losing interest. "I never did hear any last words worth remembering," he said, "and after a while the entertainment wasn't hardly worth the standing in the sun amongst all them people."

Right there's where he took his last breath, John Roger thought. He imagined his father against the wall and facing the muskets. Contained in the archival records was a newspaper report by an eyewitness journalist who included such details as the condemned man's neat grooming and fearless—even cheerful—attitude, and told of a scrap two young women got into over him. Told of his rejection of a blindfold and of his casual bearing to the very end. And told too of his decapitation, yet another detail absent from the British Embassy's letter to his widow.

He looked toward the harbor and the San Juan de Ulúa fortress where the head had been displayed from the tower. Where was it now, his father's skull? Was it yet intact somewhere? Did it lie at the bottom of the sea, little fish passing through the empty sockets and the casing that had housed his mind? Had it been blown into the mountains and reduced to shards? Pulverized to dust and scattered on the wind?

He took a mule trolley to the graveyard, where according to the records the headless remains had been interred. He searched all the crooked rows of vaults and gravestones as the tree shadows deepened and the air grew heavier, but he found no grave with the name of his father. He spied a gravedigger at work and told him of his search and was told that several hurricanes had hit the city since 1829 and the flood of each one had opened dozens of graves and carried their contents away and maybe that happened to the one he was looking for.

When he debarked from the return trolley to the zócalo, the red sun was almost down to the rooftops. He was crossing the square when he spotted a sketch artist, a white-haired old man, sitting under a tree alongside the arcade of the scribes. A sign attached to his easel said "RETRATOS." And he had an inspiration.

He sat down on the stool facing the old man, who smiled and said, "A su servicio, señor. Tinta o carboncillo? Grande o chico?" An ink drawing cost more than one of charcoal and took a little longer to make, but the detail was more faithful. A full-sheet sketch of course cost more than a half-sheet. John Roger chose a half-sheet ink portrait, and the old man set to work with deft flicks of his quill, the nib darting between ink pot and paper, his eyes cutting between John Roger's face and the sketch pad. He finished the drawing in minutes. John Roger looked it over and expressed admiration for the likeness. "Otra cosa más," he told the artist. And described the beard he wanted added to the face.

The old man shrugged and said, "Muy bien, señor." And went to work again, twice pausing to make sure John Roger was satisfied with the way the beard was shaping. When the alteration was complete, the old man handed him the drawing and John Roger stared hard at it. The finished face was exactly as his mother had many times described it to him and his brother.

Hello, father, he thought. Nice to see you.

The sketch became one more concealment in his life. Along the bottom of it, he wrote, "Roger Blake Wolfe (b ? - d 1829)" and stored it in the same document case containing the graduation daguerreotype of himself and his brother and the embassy letter about their father. He kept the case in his office at home, in the same desk drawer where under lock and key he stowed the journal he had begun in college and only once or twice put to use since. But on the evening he brought the sketch home, he entered into the journal all that he had learned about his father from the archives and noted his fruitless search for his grave.

He began a correspondence with a London genealogist who over the course of more than two years informed him that his father's parents were Henry Morgan Wolfe (died London 1835, age 67) of County Galway in Ireland, who'd had a distinguished career in the Royal Navy, and Hedda Juliet Blake (died London 1815, age 37), born to a London family of "inestimable fortune," in the genealogist's phrase. John Roger would learn too that Roger Blake Wolfe had been born in London in April of 1797 and had been publicly disinherited by his parents via newspaper promulgation in 1813. The researcher would uncover an 1825 *Times* report of an act of piracy attributed to the Englishmen Roger Blake Wolfe and the crew of his ship, the *York Witch*, against the Portuguese trader *Doralinda*, during the commission of which crime, according to testimony by the Portagee captain, five members of the *Doralinda* crew were murdered. A later item in the *Times* would report that several countries, including the United Kingdom, had posted an official bounty for the capture or proved killing of "the Pirate Wolfe." Insofar as the genealogist would be able to determine, Roger Blake Wolfe had but one sibling, a much younger brother, Harrison Augustus Wolfe, born in September, 1814. Except for the registry of birth, the genealogist would uncover no other documents pertaining to Harrison Augustus save his inclusion on a series of student rosters at the Runnymede Academy of London from 1824 through 1830.

He stored this correspondence in the document case and entered its chief points in his journal. He had no intention of ever revealing the journal's content to anyone and was not even sure why he recorded it. And then on learning of Lizzie's pregnancy, he'd suddenly had a reason. He thought it only proper that he leave to his child a factual record of the family ancestry. There would be times, however, when he would doubt the wisdom of this purpose and wonder if his offspring might not be better off never knowing about his criminal forebear. On several instances of such misgiving, he would come very near to pitching every word about Roger Blake Wolfe into the fire.

And too, over the years, he would every so often, and always late at night, sit at his desk behind closed doors and take out the ink portrait and study it intently. As though the face were in fact his father's and might yet reveal to him some vital secret shared between them.

Their first Veracruz summer was a model of Patterson's prediction. Steamy days and nights. Torrential rains. A haze of mosquitoes. But even in the increasing discomfort of her pregnancy, Elizabeth Anne loved the coastal summer in all its sultriness and birdsong and riot of colors, its babble of Spanish and incessant marimba tinklings, its mingled smells of tropical flora and saltine gulf and pungent cookery. She loved the thunderstorms that whipped the trees and clattered the shutters and lit the night in flashings of eerie blue, that left the city cool and fresh if only for a few blessed hours. At last did autumn begin to ease down the coast with its mornings of deeper blue and afternoons of longer shadows, its cooler nights and brighter stars. She could not tell John Roger enough how much she cherished this exotic place, its lushness and rhapsodic language, its paradoxical character of mania and melancholy.

Patterson was not the only one to tell them of the dangers at large outside their courtyard gates, to warn them that the town abounded with ruffians and was notorious for street fights and killings. John Roger took the little man's advice to carry a pocket pistol under his coat whenever he left the house. But they would be in Veracruz for nearly five years before they witnessed any violence greater than the frequent street grapplings between drunks. The most proximate case of murder in those early years occurred one morning at a residence a block from their own. Word of it had flown from the servants of one household to those of the next and within an hour the entire neighborhood knew the story. The man of the house, a jeweler who spent long days at his shop, had killed his wife in culmination of a shouting argument provoked by her pet parrot. The bird had mimicked sexually specific endearments familiar to the husband but which the parrot attached to the name Cristiano, the name of the household's young gardener, who fled the property at the sound of the first gunshot. That first report delivered a fatal bullet to the wife's head and was followed by five more shots in quick succession, each of them intended for the parrot, the husband no less enraged at the informer as at the informed upon. The parrot screeched and flapped about the room as bullets smashed glass and glanced off the walls and gouged the furniture and one round rang off a church bell a block away and the last one ricocheted off two walls before piercing the husband's buttock. The man screamed and fell to the floor as the parrot swooped out the window. Police were summoned, and a short time later husband and wife were carried out on stretchers to be placed in separate wagons, she with a sheet over her face and bound for the undertaker's, he facedown with a bandaged ass and off to the jail.

Elizabeth Anne got the story from the housemaids and in turn told it to John Roger. Who smiled and said, "We are without question among a mercurial people."

He had come to agree with Charley Patterson that the most salient traits of the Mexican character were its contradictions and volatilities. Mexicans were at once a people affable and suspicious, convivial and violent. No one was better-mannered than a Mexican or as quick to turn dangerous. One moment he might be laughing and joking, and the next in a murderous rage. In the midst of singing the joys of life or the glories of womanhood, he could abruptly give way to weeping over life's relentless sorrows or cursing women's eternal treacheries. There was a marked incongruity between the effusiveness of Mexican politeness and the stark fact of Mexican distrust. Between a Mexican's easy hospitality and his deliberate isolation. "Mi casa es su casa," a Mexican would aver with utmost earnestness, even as the barred gates of his house and the high broken-glass-topped walls surrounding it made clear his desire to keep the world without. "A su servicio," the Mexican would maintain, even as he stood ready to take umbrage at the first hint of being deemed subservient. While the Creoles were not exempt from these traits—perhaps even had them to greater degree but were better able to mask them behind the ornate and ritual civility of their class—they were most obvious in the mestizos, the country's principal caste, whose emotional and contradictory nature, Patterson professed, was the natural legacy of its origin.

"Just imagine coming from people of two different races that had not a blamed thing in common except a love of blood in every which way," Patterson said. "Imagine knowing your white daddy was a robber and killer just crazy with greed who raped your Indian momma who herself believed in cutting out people's hearts to please the gods and eating what was left of the victim. Hardly any wonder the Mexies are the way they are. Sad to say, but they pretty much acquired all the worst traits of both races and little of the good. It's an interesting subject but some of them can be a mite tender about it. Best not to bring it up in their company."

Elizabeth Anne was not as much interested in such ethnic generalities as she was fascinated by Mexican folk culture—its ubiquitous spiritualism, its widespread belief in witchcraft and sorcery, in necromancy and ghosts, its pervasive personification of Death, so widely depicted in broadside illustrations and wall posters and murals as an amiable and amused skeletal presence in the midst of the foolish living. Of the many ghost stories she heard from the maids and the old cook—whose name was Josefina Cortéz—none so captivated her as that of La Llorona, the Crying Woman. The way Josefina told it, the Crying Woman had been a Spanish aristocrat who was forsaken by her husband for another woman, a mestiza, and the betrayal so crazed her with fury that she murdered her children in order to punish her husband. On comprehending the horror she had committed, she was consumed with grief and killed herself, but her spirit was condemned to wander through the nights in everlasting search of the little ones' lost souls. It was a story told with variations in different parts of the country—in some she was not a Spaniard but a poor Indian, and the specific adultery that provoked her to murder the children varied from version to version. But almost every regional variation agreed that whoever had the bad fortune to come upon the Crying Woman and looked into her eyes would be afflicted with her anguish and kill themselves because of it. The young maids nodded in big-eyed accord as Josefina told Elizabeth Anne that to this day you might on some late nights hear La Llorona crying for her children in the streets—

"*Aaaayyy, mis hijos! Mis hiiiijos!*" Sometimes her cries came from a great distance in the countryside, sometimes from just across town, sometimes from the darkness just outside one's window. The tale prickled the fine hairs of Elizabeth Anne's nape even as her eyes welled in sympathy for the Crying Woman.

She learned about curanderismo—the primitive and magical healing arts—and of brujería, the practice of witchcraft, both beneficent and malign. Scattered in the back streets of town were a variety of shops where one could buy secret herbs and potions to effect almost any desire of the heart and soul. There were special candles and little books of cryptic incantations to gain favor from an importuned spirit. Charms and amulets and talismans against the evil eye. A curandera could cure ailments defiant of medical science, but a bruja possessed even greater and darker powers. A bruja could invoke hexes, cast spells, instill or cure dementia of every kind. Could commune with the spirits of the dead. And as for love—a dementia so commonplace that most brujas viewed it with the same bored scorn of doctors for the head cold—there were many rituals anyone could employ without the help of a sorceress. A dead hummingbird in a man's pocket made him irresistible to the opposite sex. A woman wishing to be loved by a particular man should wear a rooster feather next to her heart when she was in his presence, but if she wanted to be loved by many men she should carry the feather in her underwear. A man wanting to seduce a woman should put in her food the leg of a beetle or a pinch of bone dust from a human female skeleton. But he had to be very careful because too much of either ingredient would drive the woman insane past all hope of recovery. Insanity was also a risk if a woman wanting to gain dominance over her husband put an excess of jimson weed in his coffee. It was not hard to understand, Josefina told Elizabeth Anne, why there were so many crazy people in the world, especially lovers.

Elizabeth Anne could not get enough of such lore and superstition. John Roger teased her for her interest in such claptrap, as he termed it. He wondered aloud if maybe she had put a bit too much jimson weed in his coffee and then drunk it herself by mistake. She crossed her eyes and affected to babble as if mentally unhinged. Then beamed at his happy laughter.

As soon as she'd learned of her impending motherhood she had written her parents the news. They were elated—but her mother pleaded with Elizabeth Anne to come home to have the baby.

"Surely you wish the child to be born on American ground," Mrs Bartlett wrote. "And certainly you must be even more aware than I of the hazards of giving birth in that primitive land. Come home, darling daughter, for the safety of the child as well as your own."

John Roger saw the sadness in her eyes as she read the letter to him. Just as he was about to say that if she wanted to have the child in New Hampshire it would be all right with him, she said, "Poor Mother. She simply cannot comprehend that I *am* home."

—❦—

Through the offices of Charles Patterson, the Wolfes had become acquainted with a number of well-placed persons—British and American entrepreneurs, municipal officials, prominent Mexican businessmen, and several hacendados who kept a second residence in Veracruz. The city's mayor was a friend. So too the young captain of police, Ramón Mendoza, whose small force was almost exclusively employed in keeping order in the zócalo and patrolling the neighborhoods of the affluent. Although the Wolfes adhered to the protocols of their social class and hosted their share of formal dinner parties, they as always preferred their own company, and even before Elizabeth Anne's advancing pregnancy made it easy to beg off from party invitations, they took guilty pride in their finesse at fabricating plausible excuses.

They were, however, very curious about the hacienda world they had heard so much about, and when a hacendado friend invited them to attend his daughter's quinceañera—the traditional celebration of a girl's fifteenth birthday, marking her passage into womanhood—they happily accepted. Because of Elizabeth Anne's pregnancy, John Roger had at first been unsure if they should make the trip, but she was only in her fourth month and she assured him she felt quite up to it.

The hacienda was named Corazón de la Virgen and lay twenty-five miles southwest of the city. There was a special mass for the girl on the morning of her birthday, then a reception and a formal dinner, then a party with four hundred guests. The gala lasted until sunrise and then everyone departed for home except for a few special guests, including the Wolfes, who were hosted for another two days, until the birthday girl was taken to the port in Veracruz to embark on a chaperoned two-month stay in Paris, her parents' main gift to her.

As in the standard design of most haciendas, its hub was a high-walled compound that was a small town unto itself. While most of the hacienda's workers lived outside the compound, within it was a residential quarter for the most important employees. The compound contained a plaza with a communal well, a church, stables, corrals, stock pens, granaries, workshops, a store where the workers could purchase goods on credit. There was an armory sufficient to a military company, and next to it the quarters for the band of former soldiers the patrón employed to protect his property and, whenever necessary, enforce his will. The center of the compound was the family residence—the casa grande—itself walled off from the rest of the compound and sometimes also referred to as the hacienda. The casa grande enclave had its own well and stable, several patios, various flower and vegetable gardens, a small fruit orchard. The two-story house had more than enough bedrooms to accommodate the special guests. Its ballroom had mirrored walls and a lofty ceiling hung with chandeliers. It had a wide spiral staircase to the second floor. The lamplit and high-shadowed hallways were hung with ornate tapestries and oil portraits of an ancestral line predating the founding of New Spain. There were kitchens and bathing rooms, dining halls and drawing rooms and dens, two libraries, a billiard room, a chapel. Both the compound walls and the casa grande's rooftop were lined with battlements. "You could hold off the world from in here," John Roger told Elizabeth Anne.

Their host provided a buggy for them to explore the property as they wished, and on each morning of their visit they rose early and had breakfast while most of the other guests continued to sleep off the effects of the night before, and then they went for a long ride, each day ranging in a different direction to see another part of the sixty-square-mile estate.

"It's like a country of its own," Elizabeth Anne said. "The villages are its various towns and the compound is its capital city. The casa grande is the capitol building. If we owned such a place, you would be its president and I the vice-president. Our child would serve as our cabinet."

John Roger said it sounded rather a roguish government, especially if their child should be a girl and render the majority of its administration female. Elizabeth Anne slapped his arm in sham umbrage.

On the trip back to Veracruz they talked and talked about the splendors of hacienda life.

❧

The baby was born on the night of November the first, directly amid the Days of the Dead, the annual two-day celebration in honor of the deceased and of Death herself—and the date nearly proved prophetic for both mother and child. Awkwardly positioned, the baby could not come out. Elizabeth Anne screamed against her will while in an outer room John Roger paced, tormented by her suffering and enraged at his helplessness.

Nurse Beckett was blood to the wrists and dripping with sweat when she deferred in desperation to Josefina, who had much experience as a midwife and was assisting. The old woman reached into Elizabeth Anne and felt the baby and crooned to it as she tried to turn it. Elizabeth Anne screamed louder.

Josefina felt the child shift slightly and implored, "Empuje, hija! *Empuje!* Ya viene!"

Elizabeth Anne pushed with all her remaining strength and Josefina guided the child with her hand and a moment later it emerged into the larger world. Blood-coated and blue-skinned and unbreathing.

"O my dear God," Nurse Beckett said.

Josefina freed the infant of the cord round its neck and then alternately blew into its nose and mouth. In the other room John Roger stood arrested in dread at the sudden cessation of his wife's screams. Then nearly jumped at the first of the baby's squalls.

At length he was permitted to enter the room. It yet held a raw smell of pain and blood. Elizabeth Anne lay still and waxen and he knew with cold conviction that she was dead and seemed himself to forget how to breathe. Then her eyes opened and she saw him and managed a weak smile—and he grinned and brushed at his eyes and sat on the bed and put his hand to her face.

Nurse Beckett said it had been a near thing. The bleeding had been profuse and difficult to stem. But the baby was faring well and appeared to be free of defect, and Mrs Wolfe was young and strong and should recover satisfactorily. Josefina positioned the swaddled infant in John Roger's arms and he sat on the edge of the bed and held the baby for Elizabeth Anne to see. She smiled and her eyes shone.

The child was a boy. They named him John Samuel.

❦

By the end of the Wolfes' second year in Mexico the Trade Wind Company was earning higher revenues from coffee and tobacco imports than Richard Davison had ever dared to expect. John Roger had improved the logistics of the business, reducing the costs of transporting the commodities from the haciendas to the port and then shipping them on to New Orleans. And because not so much as a cupful of coffee had gone missing from the company's warehouse under John Roger's management, Richard was now convinced the Mexican broker had been pilfering the coffee he'd reported stolen every year. "But never mind that," he wrote to John Roger. "I doubt we could prove it and it wouldn't be worth the trouble nor expense to try. Its a business insult and that aint the same as a personal one. I anyway learned a long time ago to cut my losses and don't worry about yesterday. What counts is today and tomorrow." He was so pleased with John Roger's work that he not only raised his salary for the second year in a row but also put him on a commission. And John Roger prospered.

❦

He and Lizzie had sometimes talked about making a trip to Mexico City to acquaint themselves with that storied metropolis. But it would be nearly two decades yet before the rail line to the capital was completed, and the stagecoach trip was long and arduous, and they did not want to be away for so long from John Samuel, who for years yet would be too young for such a rugged journey. But they loved Veracruz and it was no hardship to keep to it. They often swam off the beach in the early sunrise before John Roger went to the Trade Wind office. They strolled the malecón in the late afternoons after his day's work, sometimes walking all the way to the outskirt of the foreboding Chinese district where outsiders rarely entered and from which its denizens rarely ventured. They had not even known of the Chinese quarter until Charles Patterson thought to warn them about it. "There's nothing in Chink Town you want to see up close," he told them. "Take my word for it and keep out of there." John Roger had assured him they would mind his caution, but as soon as they parted his company they went at once to see that foreign locale for themselves. They had neither one seen a Chinese before nor visited in such a foreign world. The streets here even narrower than in the rest of the city, labyrinthine and smoke-misted, devoid of wagons but crowded with pedestrians and pushcarts, with kiosks vending plucked ducks and shock-eyed pigs and the flensed and headless but unmistakable carcasses of dogs of every size. Where also were sold still other less-identifiable meats and curious vegetables and roots and herbs of tangy scents that mingled with the mélange of unfamiliar smells. Buyers and hawkers bartering loud in what sounded like the speech of cats. Elizabeth Anne held close to John Roger's arm. Their stares were unrequited, their presence unacknowledged by even a glance that they were aware of, yet no one in that throng so much as brushed against them. They felt like overlarge and ungainly ghosts remanded to some alien afterworld. On the way home John Roger cocked an eyebrow and asked if she would care to return sometime. "I'll let you know," she said, and never would.

They sometimes had dinner at a zócalo restaurant, then joined the spirited crowd of sweaty dancers by the park bandstand. On such nights they would come home at a late hour with their blood in high excitement and go up to the rooftop and make love under the winking stars. They desired more children, but despite their frequent attempts she did not conceive again. Not even after a double effort under the April full moon, which Josefina had assured Elizabeth Anne was the night most auspicious for the womb to accept a man's seed. Elizabeth Anne discussed their failing hopes with Nurse Beckett, who told her it was just as well, considering her ordeal in delivering John Samuel, whose conception had clearly been a case of lightning in a bottle.

❦

The good fortune of their first two years in Veracruz included the city's being spared from its chronic epidemics of yellow fever. El vómito negro, the Mexicans called it, because of its deadliest salient trait. There was a mild outbreak in their second year but the sickness inexplicably quit the city before its contagion could spread. Then late in their third summer the yellow jack struck again—hard—and once more Elizabeth Anne and John Samuel nearly died in each other's close company.

Both of the young maids were also stricken. The household's four victims lay under blankets in a shivering, soaking sweat, moaning with the pain in their heads and joints, soiling their beds, vomiting into chamber pots, eyes and skin going yellow. The house was a mephitic reek. Having contracted the disease in the past, Josefina and Beto the handyman were now immune, and by some blessing of genetics John Roger was among those naturally resistant to it. An understanding of the pathology of yellow fever was still a half century in the future, and there was little a doctor of the day could do for the afflicted beyond prescription of quinine, cold compresses for the forehead, mustard plasters for the feet, and quantities of hot tea. They advised the populace to keep their windows open to the fresh air day and night.

John Roger spent most of every day tending to Elizabeth Anne. When he was not drying her brow or spooning broth to her or holding the pot for her to vomit into or cleaning her and changing her sheets, he would be reading to her from her favored volume of Shakespeare's sonnets, suspecting that his words had little register in her fevered mind but hoping the sound of his voice was itself some comfort. Josefina sneaked a dead beetle called a crucifijo under Elizabeth Anne's pillow and another one under John Samuel's. Characterized by a thin red cross on its black back, the bug was a rare sort long regarded by the local Indians as a curative for the vómito negro. Josefina had found only those two crucifijos in the garden, else she would have put some under the pillows of the maids as well.

The plague worsened. The stench of the sickness carried through the narrow streets. So too the raspings and bangings of the coffin makers, the lachrymose wails of the bereaved. There were daily processions to the cemetery. Doors all over town were hung with black crepe. No one in the city dared to shake hands or even stand too close to another. The two young maids now bled from the mouth and nose and could not keep from screaming their pain. When their vomit began to look like black coffee grounds Josefina made the sign of the cross over them. They died within a few hours of each other, and their meager corteges were added to the succession of mourning parties trudging to the graveyard.

At length the epidemic diminished and then at last was gone and both Elizabeth Anne and John Samuel recovered. She would hereafter fatigue more easily than before and have to take greater care in the sun, but John Samuel's skirmish with the disease had no more lasting effect than did the desperate struggle of his birth. He was not yet three years old and his eyes were now green as his mother's, his hair the same coppery shade. He would grow into a hale, clever, polite boy and would earn the unanimous praise of his tutors. But he would always be a solitary soul, even after he married and became a father. He would never form a close friendship nor regret the lack of one, and nobody—not his parents, not his brothers, not his wife or children—would ever really know him. He would not shed a tear in his life until his final moments. And his happiest memories would forever be of his mother coming to his room in the evenings to sing him to sleep.

─❦─

Toward the end of their fourth year the news and public discourse was mostly of war. Since its humiliating defeat by the United States and the loss of half of its territory to the Yankees, Mexico had been fighting with itself more often than not. With rarely as much as a few months' peace between them, one uprising followed another, as first this political faction and then that one conceived a new plan of national government and declared itself in rebellion against the incumbent regime.

Even when a revolt succeeded for a brief time, nothing would change in the lives of the impoverished multitude, and the country's leadership would remain as autocratic and avaricious and unstable as ever. Now the nation was embroiled in its most brutal civil war yet—the War of the Reform, between the Liberals of Benito Juárez, whose principal objective was an end to Church power in Mexico, and the national Conservatives, an alliance of the ecclesiastical and the secular rich, who opposed any change to their privileged order.

As in most other wars, this one was largely fought in the interior of the country and had but small impact on Veracruz, which had not been badly damaged by warfare since the Yankee invasion. But Mexico was now of so little interest to its newly grown behemoth of a neighbor that news of its latest internecine bloodshed hardly carried beyond Texas, an unawareness reflected in Mrs Bartlett's letters to her daughter. They were always full of questions about her grandson but made only cursory inquiry of what else might be new and implied a total ignorance of Mexican affairs.

There was a federal garrison near the Veracruz port, but it was always quick to ally itself with any general who arrived with a larger force and declared himself in command of the city. In every such instance, pressgangs would scour the streets for recruits. Males of military age stayed out of sight until the occupiers departed, usually before long, and then the city would revert to its easy ways until the next time it was taken over.

Every war also prompted some among Mexico City's moneyed class to flee to Veracruz in readiness to take refuge outside the country if need be. The War of the Reform brought a greater number than usual of such affluent refugees. And as always, they sold jewelry at bargain prices in order to have ample hard money in hand. Even as John Roger was persuading Richard Davison to expand the company's range of imports to include a variety of exquisite ornamentation wrought by Spanish and Indian craftsmen of the past three centuries—necklaces and brooches and bracelets and rings—he was already buying all the refugee jewelry he could. Richard found a ready market for it and the company's profits rose to new heights. And John Roger grew richer still.

RECKONINGS

It was in the late summer of that fourth year that John Roger received a packet from New Orleans containing records of Trade Wind business in Mexico prior to his employment. Richard's enclosed note said, "Heres the stuff I promised, sorry it took so long to round it all up but you anyway didnt need it just like you said you didnt to do the good job youve done. Never much cared for working with papers my self. Do with them what you will." John Roger smiled at the thought that the man surely did keep a promise, no matter how long it might take. He was certain that by this time there could be nothing in the old records of use to him, and he thought of pitching them in the waste can, but it was not in his nature to get rid of any papers he had not at least scanned, so he emptied the packet's contents onto his desktop and began sorting through them.

Among the papers were the Mexican broker's annual invoices to the company for the coffee and tobacco he had received from the various haciendas and in turn shipped to the United States. For the past four years John Roger had sent similar invoices to Richard Davison. It was no surprise to see that the amounts of a commodity delivered to the broker by each of the haciendas had varied from one year to the next, some years more, some years less. With one exception. During the years of the broker's service, the annual delivery of coffee by a hacienda named La Sombra Verde was always the largest of any plantation. And always greater from year to year. It had by far earned more money from the Trade Wind Company than any of the other haciendas. It puzzled John Roger that the name of the company's most productive plantation for those years was only vaguely familiar to him. He referred to his own invoices and saw that La Sombra Verde had not only produced less coffee in each of the past four years than in any of the previous six, but less by far than all the other plantations. Either the hacienda had undergone a monumental reversal in productivity—coincident with John Roger's assumption of Trade Wind management in Mexico—or the broker had been inflating its figures. He shuffled through the papers and found the broker's annual theft records. The amount of coffee reported as stolen from the warehouse, after delivery by the haciendas, had grown greater every year, but always a little greater than the increase in La Sombra Verde's reported delivery. The broker hadn't been so foolish as to let the amounts match exactly.

Well now. Richard had been cheated, all right, but not in the way he'd thought. The broker hadn't been stealing coffee out of the warehouse. He'd been charging the company for coffee that didn't exist.

Had the owner of the hacienda conspired in the scheme? Every hacendado had to sign the delivery invoice from his own estate. It was not impossible that the broker had substituted forged invoices for the actual, but why do it for the same hacienda every year when it would have been more plausible to forge a different estate's invoice each time? The only answer was collusion between the broker and La Sombra Verde.

The question now was, So what? Richard had been right in his suspicion of being cheated, but he was also right that they could never prove it. And as Richard had also said, even if the broker had been cheating, it was over with—it had stopped with John Roger's takeover of the Mexican branch operations—and the company's only concern should be with the present and the future.

But the swindle was too irksome for John Roger to shrug off. He had heard that the broker, whose name was Guillermo Demarco, was still doing business in Veracruz, but he had never had occasion to meet him. Nor was he acquainted with the patrón of La Sombra Verde, one of only two or three hacendados under contract with the Trade Wind he'd not met, having dealt only with their agents who brought the commodities to port.

<hr />

The next day, during their weekly lunch date at a zócalo restaurant, he told Patterson all about it. The little Texan didn't know anything about Guillermo Demarco but said he would make discreet inquiries and let John Roger know what he found out. He did, however, know a good deal about La Sombra Verde. The hacienda was more than 250 years old. It encompassed an area of over forty square miles and its nearest boundary to Veracruz lay about thirty-five miles up the coast. But it was bordered in a very odd fashion, flanking the Río Perdido for a mile to either side at the estate's widest point and a half mile to either side at its narrowest, all the way from an upland coffee plantation down to the river's outlet at the Gulf of Mexico. A meandering property that spanned a diverse geography of foothills and pastureland, a portion of rain forest, and a mile of seacoast. The nearest town was

Jalapa, ten rugged miles from its westernmost border.

Originally established by a Spanish nobleman named Valledolid near the end of the sixteenth century, La Sombra Verde had by patrimony passed down through generations of eldest sons, all of them forceful men equal to the responsibilities and duties of a patrón. And then a generation ago it was inherited by twenty-one-year-old Martín Valledolid, an impetuous and romantic young man. He had been the patrón for only a year when he fell in desperate love with a beautiful but spiteful girl named Yasmina Montenegro, who took pleasure in toying with his affections. She lived in Veracruz with her widowed father, a former army officer named Claudio Montenegro. She had always been an exasperation to Claudio and he was as eager to marry her off as she was to be married and gone from him, but he had been hoping for a match of some benefit to himself. In Martin Valledolid's rapture with Yasmina, he recognized a singular opportunity. He denied him the girl's hand except in wager against the title to La Sombra Verde. Martín refused the proposition twice but was too addled by love to refuse it the third time, and in the presence of a dozen astounded witnesses he lost the hacienda on the turn of a card. His family reviled him for his monumental stupidity. His younger brother attacked him and broke his nose and jaw. After a futile series of legal efforts to retain the property, the family disavowed Martín and resettled in Córdoba.

For his part, Claudio said it seemed only fair to permit Martín to marry Yasmina anyway—though he insisted they would have to make their own way through life—and the young man was overcome with gratitude. The couple rented a house in Veracruz, where Martín secured employment as a customs officer at the port. But they had been wed only six months when he discovered Yasmina's cuckoldry. When he confronted her, she laughed and admitted to several lovers, whereupon he throttled her and then drowned himself in the harbor. He left a note accusing Claudio of having cheated him out of the hacienda and he put a curse on the place for as long as it was in Montenegro hands. Claudio made a proper show of public mourning for his daughter and son-in-law and said poor Martín had obviously and tragically become deranged. And in private said good riddance to them both and laughed at Martín's curse.

But no sooner had he gained ownership of La Sombra Verde than its fecund coffee farm, which had always kept the hacienda solvent, was ravaged by a blight that inexplicably exempted every other coffee plantation in the state. In the years since, the farm had never achieved even half of its former yield but had managed to bring in just enough money from year to year to maintain the hacienda's strained subsistence.

The coffee farm's setback was in keeping with the Montenegro family's long history of misfortune. Most of its males died in infancy and its females were disposed to early madness. It was whispered that such propensities were signs of incestuous breeding. A neighboring hacendado named Beltrán did not whisper it softly enough, however, and when Claudio got wind of what he'd said he rode directly to Beltrán's estate and gave him the choice of a duel or a public admission that he was a liar and a cowardly son of a whore. They met at a riverside meadow at sunrise and fought with pistols at forty paces. Claudio took a minor wound to the hip but his own ball lodged in Beltrán's gut and the man lay in agony for four days before dying. The episode inspired a greater caution among the local gossip-prone, and from then on, the Montenegros were as zealous in defense of their family honor as any Creole clan of classical lineage.

A few years after Claudio acquired La Sombra Verde, his health went into a swift and mystifying decline and he died of an undiagnosed illness. The hacienda then transferred to his son—and its current patrón—Hernán José Montenegro Velasquez. Like his father before him, Hernán had been an officer in the army, intending to make it his career, but upon inheritance of La Sombra Verde he resigned his commission in order to live the life of a hacendado. Also like his father, he had the temper of a red dog. It was said he had killed seven or eight or nine men in duels, some with sword, some with pistol. Hernán's only living son, Enrique, now 17, was reputed to be no less of a hothead but something of a dolt.

"It don't surprise me a bit Hernán would partner with the broker fella in hoodwinking your outfit," Patterson said. "He's always in bad need of money, and the way I heard it he aint too particular how he gets it. They say he cheats at cards something awful, same as his old daddy did. Mendoza played cards with Hernán once and said it was one time too many."

The next afternoon Patterson stopped by the Trade Wind office with the information that Guillermo Demarco, prior to going into business as a broker, had been employed as secretary to Hernán Montenegro.

⬥

John Roger deliberated for two days. Then wrote a letter to Montenegro, informing him that due to financial improprieties perpetrated against the Trade Wind Company by La Sombra Verde in concert with the brokerage service of Guillermo Demarco, the company was severing its contract with the hacienda.

He then went to Demarco's office on the third floor of a commercial building near the harbor. He introduced himself and told Demarco he was there to collect reimbursement for the substantial overpayments he had received from the company through fraudulent means over a period of six years. He handed him their disparate invoices and theft reports and an estimated bill for the total overpayment.

Guillermo Demarco, sitting behind a spacious desk with his back to a large window framing a view of the harbor, smiled as he scanned the papers. He was a small and tidy man, well seasoned in business dispute. He dropped the papers on the desk and pushed them away with a fingertip. Then leaned back in his chair and said John Roger's so-called evidence of fraud was worthless. Try to make a case in a Mexican

80

court with this and you will be laughed out of the room, he said. Unless you make the judge so angry for wasting his time that he locks *you* in San Juan de Ulúa.

I might not have much of a legal case, John Roger said, but you and I both know it's true you cheated the company.

Demarco said truth was a beautiful thing but of little significance in commerce or the law. It pained him that the Trade Wind Company was displeased with his former services, but, be that as it may, there was really nothing they could do about it.

I could pass the word around town of what a cheat you are.

Demarco grinned. Oh dear, he said.

John Roger had not expected to collect on the bill, only to let Demarco know that his fraud had not gone undiscovered and to shame him if he could. But as he now understood, the man was immune to shame. And his smugness was galling.

I guess you're right, John Roger said. There isn't much I can do about it legally. But what I most assuredly *can* do, Mr Demarco, is throw you out that window.

He surprised himself no less than he did Demarco. He'd made the threat with an easy confidence that he could make good on it—and with the unmistakable implication that he was leaning toward doing so.

The broker straightened in his chair and cleared his throat. But Mr Wolfe, he said, even if you were not joking, what could you gain from such a barbarity except many years in prison?

Maybe some personal satisfaction, John Roger said. And stood up. Demarco shoved back from the desk and sprang to his feet, eyes wide. Then realized he had put himself even closer to the window, and he sidled hurriedly over to the wall.

"Don't soil your pants, you low son of a bitch. You're not worth the trouble of killing."

"Como?" said Demarco, who did not speak English.

"Chinga tu madre, pendejo," John Roger said. His ready ear had familiarized him with the profanities of the street, and while he had always shied from such coarseness in English, in Spanish it came without qualm. He gathered up the papers and plucked out the bill and laid it back on Demarco's desk. Then left.

He was awed by the discovery he'd made about himself—his readiness to throw a man from a window—and yet also felt uneasy about it. It was disquieting to think there might be even other facets of himself with which he was unfamiliar.

When he told Patterson of his meeting with Demarco, the little man laughed and said, "Hellfire, I'da paid money to see his face when you threatened to pitch him. Bedamn, son, if you aint got a proper share of grit. You sure your people aint from Texas?"

A week later, a lawyer representing La Sombra Verde showed up at the office to warn him that Don Hernán Montenegro would sue for violation of contract unless the Trade Wind Company continued to buy his coffee. John Roger dared him to do it. If Montenegro should sue him, he said, he would in turn sue Montenegro for defrauding the Trade Wind in collusion with the brokerage of Guillermo Demarco. The lawyer, whose name was Herrera, scoffed that such a charge could never be legally proven.

John Roger said maybe not, but the accusation would anyway be of great interest to the newspapers and the printers of broadsides. As everyone knew, even an accusation unsustained in court could do public injury to a reputation.

Herrera's face was stiff with contempt. Only a man without honor would do such a thing, he said.

Nevertheless, John Roger said.

You disappoint me, sir.

How sad, John Roger said. Listen, Mr Herrera, I suggest it would be in the best interest of everyone concerned to forgo the unpleasantness of public allegations and courtroom procedures and simply agree to the termination of the contract.

Herrera said he would have to discuss it with Don Hernán, though it might be some time before he could meet with him, as the don had left for Mexico City just two days prior on urgent business that could detain him for some time.

John Roger said he understood perfectly. And that he hoped it was understood equally well that he would under no condition, including legal threat, do further business with La Sombra Verde.

He wrote to Richard to tell him of his rescission of the Montenegro contract and the reason for it and said he hoped Richard was not offended that he had done it without first consulting with him. Richard responded that he was glad John Roger had figured out the swindle, even though it had come to an end four years ago, and he agreed with the decision to cut ties with Montenegro. "And don't fret about making a decision on your own," Richard wrote. "I told you when I hired you Johnny, in Mexico *you're* the Trade Wind."

Nearly two months after Herrera's visit, John Roger had not heard from the man again but had learned that La Sombra Verde had begun selling its coffee to another export firm. He therefore concluded that there would be no legal action against the Trade Wind and that the entire matter was done with.

⸙

The following month, on the Day of the Dead, they hosted a lively party celebrating John Samuel's fourth birthday. After the festivities were done and the guests had gone home and Elizabeth Anne had sung the boy to sleep, as John Roger was discussing with her whether they should buy the house they had been renting for almost five years or look for one with a view of the sea, there was a pounding of the street door's iron knocker.

John Roger went to an open window and in the light of the patio lanterns saw lame Beto the handyman come out of his carriage-house quarters in his nightshirt and hobble toward the gate. It was a rarity for anyone to call uninvited at such a late hour for any reason other than an emergency. Beto opened the little peep window on the door and was loud about asking who was there. John Roger felt Elizabeth Anne come up beside him. The voice outside the gate was indistinct, and then Beto said, Yes, of course, of course, one moment. Then turned and saw John Roger at the window and called out that Don Hernán Montenegro Velásquez wished to speak with the master of the house.

John Roger felt a feathery stir in his stomach, gone before he could identify it. He reproached himself for the erroneous assumption that Montenegro had let the issue drop. Still, the cheek of the man! To come knocking at this hour. He was about to have Beto send him away with instruction to call at the office, but then thought no, if the business could be settled for good and all right now, so much the better.

"Déjalo pasar," he said.

Beto lifted the wooden crossbar and drew back the iron bolt latch and pulled open the door. Elizabeth Anne asked John Roger who it was. Her voice composed but her eyes intense. "Someone I must talk with," he said. He told her to stay inside while he met with the visitor in the patio. As he went out the door in his shirtsleeves he heard her hurrying up the stairs.

There were two of them. Of similar height and leanness, wearing expensive dark suits and cavalier hats. One carried a bundle shaped like a bedroll. They watched his approach as Beto shouldered the door closed behind them. "Bienvenidos, caballeros," John Roger said. "Yo soy el dueño, Juan Wolfe, a su servicio."

He was near enough now to see their similarity of features behind the pointed Spanish beards and to know them for father and son. The elder's aspect evinced a mix of curiosity and resolve, the younger's was bright and excited as a pup's.

Hernán Montenegro introduced himself and then Enrique, and then got directly to the point. Mr Wolfe had offended Montenegro honor. First in the letter terminating the contract between the Trade Wind and La Sombra Verde, and then twice more in direct assertions—to Guillermo Demarco and to Stephano Herrera, the attorney representing the Montenegro interests. I have been detained in Mexico City these past months, Montenegro said, else I would have answered these insults before now. His tone was of cool indignation and his bearing assured, but his Spanish lacked the Castilian inflections pervasive among the hacendados of John Roger's acquaintance.

I beg to differ, sir, John Roger said. I committed no offense against your name. You slighted yourself when you conspired with Demarco to cheat my employer.

Montenegro's face tightened. "Y otra insulta más," he said. Then looked at Beto and said, "Quítate." The handyman gave John Roger an apologetic look, then turned and hurried off to shut himself in the carriage house.

The hacendado nodded at his son. The young man squatted and lay the bundle on the cobbles and unrolled it to reveal two caplock pistols and a pair of unsheathed cavalry sabers. Then stood up and grinned at John Roger.

I demand satisfaction, Hernán Montenegro said, removing his jacket and handing it to his son. Pistols or blades. The choice is yours. He handed the boy his hat.

John Roger's eyes went from the man to the weapons and back up to the man. He smiled and felt inane for it. And then again felt the flutter in his belly. And this time knew it for fear. This is absurd, he said.

Pistols or blades, sir, Montenegro said.

No, John Roger said. *No*, of course not. I'm not going to fight a . . . a *duel* with you. Especially not in—

Montenegro's backhand slap knocked him rearward in a half turn. Its stinging surprise gave immediate way to fury and he whirled back around with his fists raised but the man had already snatched up both sabers and held one with its point only inches from John Roger's throat. He had to be fifty years old but was quick as a cat.

As you have declined the prerogative to choose, Montenegro said, I pick the sword. It allows for a more personal engagement, don't you agree?

He stepped back and lobbed the other saber at John Roger, who fumbled the catch and had to grab the sword blade with both hands, cutting his left palm.

The son sniggered. Montenegro smiled and said, Even before we begin I have drawn first blood. He told John Roger not to be concerned about Enrique, whose only warrant was to serve as his second. Or to bear away my body, should I not prevail, he said with a smile. Enrique grinned.

Listen, John Roger said, listen. This is ridiculous. Let's be reasonable. There are courtrooms, for God's sake. There are laws for—

"En garde!"

John Roger instinctively brought up his sword and the hacendado touched his own blade to it—and then attacked with a clear intention of making short work of him. But John Roger nimbly skipped rearward, parrying the thrusts, and Montenegro paused to stare at him in smiling surprise. And went at him again.

And now John Roger knew the fearsome difference between a college sporting contest and a mortal combat. He retreated around and around the fountain, keeping close to it in order to deny Montenegro a wider latitude of attack, fending against the man's furious onslaught. Their wavering shadows moved along the walls and over the cobbles to no sound save the ringing of blades and shufflings of feet, the heaves of their breath. After ten minutes that John Roger would have guessed at an hour, they were gasping and soaked in sweat. Both of them now gripping their saber with two hands, John Roger's bloody palm still the only wound in evidence.

Then he stumbled on a cobble and went sprawling—and received a grazing slash to the head as he rolled away from Montenegro and rose onto one knee. He caught a burning blow high on his shielding arm in the same instant that he swung his own blade sidearm and he felt its edge slice into Montenegro's leg, and the man let a yelping curse. Then was again on his feet and again giving ground as he warded Montenegro's resumed offensive. Both men now trailing blood as they circled the fountain. John Roger's left arm dangling useless. Montenegro limping after him, disposed of all finesse and hacking two-handed with the saber as if pursuing him through jungle. John Roger was only dimly aware of the pain of his wounds, his sword now heavy as stone and one eye blurred with blood from his gashed scalp. Yet he sensed Montenegro's desperation to end the fight before the failing leg quit him, and he readied himself for the rash move he knew was coming.

And it came. Montenegro bellowed and rushed at him with a manic sidelong slash of his sword meant to wound some part of him, any part, and create an opening for a thrust. John Roger dropped to a crouch and the blade flicked his hair as it whisked over his head and he thrust his own sword blade up into the man's lower belly and felt the point glance off the spine and pass through.

John Roger fell on his rump, still gripping the sword on which Montenegro, huge-eyed with disbelief, was impaled in an arrested stoop with six inches of blade jutting from his back. Then blood spouted from the man's mouth to sop John Roger's sleeve and his saber clattered onto the cobbles and his eyes lost their light like blown candles. He toppled sideways and the force of his weight twisted the sword from John Roger's grasp.

Enrique screamed.

John Roger, braced on his elbow, turned and saw the boy raising a pistol at him. Saw him cock the hammer.

There was a gunblast—and Enrique's head jerked sideways and his hat flew off together with fragments of bloody skull and his pistol discharged into the rim of the fountain and the ball ricocheted into the night as he collapsed in a lifeless heap.

John Roger looked up to the balcony to see Elizabeth Anne standing there, the smoking Dragoon gripped in both hands. And he keeled into unconsciousness.

❖

He woke in his bed. The window ashen with imminent dawn. His head and arm ponderous with bandages and pulsing with pain.

Elizabeth Anne dozed in a chair at his side. He stared at her and she came awake. He smiled. "Hello, darling. It appears I'm still among the quick."

Her eyes filled with tears and she leaned forward and placed her cheek on his chest with her face turned away from him and he felt the soft heaves of her weeping. He caressed her shoulder. "I'm all right, Lizzie." And then believed he understood her true distress and said, "I know. I know how you must feel. It was an awful thing to have to do, but if you hadn't shot—"

"*No!*" she cried, turning her head to look at him. "That's not—oh, God, no, don't you see? If I hadn't been so damned afraid I—"

"Shush, darling, it's all right, it's—"

"No, no it's not all right! What a worthless . . . *ninny* I was. I knew something wasn't right, I knew it by your face and your voice. I'd never known you to look that way. I ran upstairs without even knowing why and then I just . . . *stood* there for the longest time, not knowing what to do or think or anything. And then I heard the swords—I *heard* them, Johnny, and I was terrified. And that's when I thought to get the gun. But dear Jesus I couldn't find it. I was crying and throwing everything out of the wardrobe and the trunk and I was furious that I couldn't find it and that I had to keep wiping my eyes and. . . ." She paused for breath and better control of her voice. "And then there it *was*. And I grabbed it and ran to the balcony and I saw . . . oh God, I saw the blood on your face, all the dark blood, and then you ducked down and he was bending over you and I couldn't see what was happening and you were so close together I was afraid of shooting *you*, but then he fell over and I knew he was dead, the way he fell, I knew it, but then that other one screamed and I saw his gun and I didn't even think, I just . . . did it."

"It was some shot, Lizzie."

"But don't you see! If I hadn't been so afraid and crying like such a child I could have found the gun immediately and I could have shot them *both* before you were wounded. But I was so afraid and you're hurt because of it and you might have been. . . ." She put her head on his chest, facing away so he couldn't see her tears.

He stroked her hair. And couldn't suppress his small laugh.

She turned to him in red-eyed confusion. "*What?*"

"You're not at fault for my wounds, Lizzie. And they will heal."

"I am at fault! As soon as. . . . *why* are you smiling?"

"Because of my extreme good fortune in a wife. Or maybe I'm delirious. A kiss might help to restore my wit."

She gaped. Then smiled too, and being careful of his wounds, kissed him.

The light at the window paled as she laved his face with a damp cloth and told how she'd sent Beto as fast as he could hobble to fetch Nurse Beckett and Chief Mendoza and Charles Patterson. She put John Samuel in the care of a maid who took him to her room to sleep, and with the help of Josefina—who had witnessed the fight from the little window of her quarters—she stanched the bleeding from John Roger's arm. She was alarmed by his head wound but Josefina assured her it was not really very bad, that scalp cuts always bled profusely and often looked worse than they were. Then Nurse Beckett arrived with a surgeon she'd roused and the doctor applied a tourniquet to the wounded arm and the four of them carried John Roger to his bed. The surgeon was still suturing his wounds with Josefina's assistance when Captain Mendoza arrived at the courtyard gate with two subordinates, and as Elizabeth Anne went out to speak with him, Patterson showed up. Their immediate concern was John Roger's condition and they were relieved when she told them the surgeon's optimistic prognosis. Both police captain and consul seemed less troubled by the fact of the dead Montenegros than impressed by the state of them. When she explained that she'd shot one of them from the balcony, they gave her odd looks, as if suddenly unsure who she was—and then both men smiled and Mendoza told her she had done very well.

Mendoza deemed both killings clear cases of self-defense and then searched the dead men and laughed at his good luck in finding just enough money on them to cover the cost of his investigation. He sent for some men who came with a burro cart and he had them help Beto wash the blood from the patio stones before they bore away the bodies. Patterson offered to assign one of his best clerks to the Trade Wind office to take care of business during John Roger's recuperation, and Elizabeth Anne gratefully accepted. "I hope you approve," she said to John Roger. "I didn't know what else to do."

"You did . . . very well." He stroked her cheek with the back of his hand, then shut his eyes and was asleep again.

During the next three days he grew feverish and the wounded arm became so darkly and malodorously swollen that the surgeon saw no alternative but to amputate just below the shoulder.

It was an exemplary surgery. There was but minor infection and the fever soon gave way. In a week he was up and about the house, though yet in much pain, and began to learn the ways of a one-armed man.

In the first few days he tended to lean slightly sideways to offset a real or imagined sense of imbalance. He was mystified by the itching in a limb no longer extant. When the bandage came off his head, he fretted that the hair might not grow back where the surgeon had sewn the wound, but the doctor assured him the hair around the scar would grow out and cover it. Elizabeth Anne sewed the left arms of all his shirts and coats in a high fold. Dressing himself was not so hard, though she had to fasten his cuff button and knot his ties. When she first cut his meat for him at the table he made a joke about his need of John Samuel's former highchair. He would permit such assistance from her only when they ate by themselves at home. In days to come when they dined in public or among friends, he would eat nothing other than what he could manage with spoon or fork. It vexed him that he would no longer be able to do such things as load a gun or handle a rifle, saddle his own horse or properly pack his calabash. But he could still shoot a pistol and could mount up and ride and could light his own cigars. He could still shave himself but not as closely. He could still do most of the things he'd always enjoyed, albeit many of them required modification of technique, from the way he held a book or a dance partner to the way he rode a horse to the way he and Elizabeth Anne made love. Some of the standard positions were lost to them, some were not, and their experimentation with new configurations was nothing less than joy.

He was still in convalescence when Guillermo Demarco came calling. Elizabeth Anne led the broker into the drawing room, where John Roger greeted him with no more than a silent nod. They sat on facing armchairs and Demarco placed a valise on the low table between them and got directly to the point. He had made a careful review of his records and found that John Roger—whom he addressed throughout this meeting as Don Juan—had been right. There *had* been bookkeeping errors in his invoices to the Trade Wind Company. The mistakes of an incompetent clerk in his employ, who Don Juan could be sure had been both excoriated and dismissed. Demarco opened the valise and withdrew a small cloth sack and untied it and emptied a chittering rush of gold coins onto the table. He said there were five other such sacks in the valise for a total worth equal to the amount of the Trade Wind's bill of restitution plus five percent annual interest on that amount for six years. He hoped Don Juan found it satisfactory. John Roger said it seemed fair enough to him.

Yes, very well, yes, the broker said. But made no move to go. He wanted something more but did not know how to say it. John Roger guessed what it was. Proof of having settled the matter. Don't forget to have me sign a receipt, Mr Demarco, he said. You and I know a receipt is unnecessary between men of honor, but business has its rules, after all. Records are important.

Demarco's relief was evident. Yes, yes, he said, thank you for reminding me. A mere formality, of course, but, as you say. . . . His gesture bespoke the bothersome nature of such mundane detail. He withdrew the prepared paper from his coat and spread it on the table. John Roger signed it and Demarco put it back in his coat and then consulted his fob watch and expressed surprise at the hour. He apologized for his rudeness in departing in such haste, but he was late for an appointment and he anyway knew Don Juan was a busy man. Please don't get up, he said—though John Roger had made no move to rise—I can make my way out. And then was gone. In the entirety of the visit, he had met John Roger's eyes only in the briefest glances and had not once looked at his empty sleeve.

At dinner that evening, as she cut his beefsteak, Elizabeth Anne asked, "What did that oily little man want with you?"

"To clear up an overdue account."

She gave him an arch look. "I believe you have acquired a rather formidable reputation, Mr Wolfe. He was terrified of you."

He returned her look in kind. "How do you know it was *I* he was terrified of, Mrs Wolfe? I'm sure I'm not the only one in this house who has acquired something of a formidable reputation."

She blushed through her smile and stoppered his chuckle with a piece of beef on the end of her fork.

He wrote to Richard Davison to tell him what happened and assure him the office was in good hands, and concluded with the news of Demarco's reimbursement. The sum was sizable and he asked Richard if he wanted him to send it to New

Orleans via the consulate's courier service. In his answering letter, Richard wrote, "Dont think about getting back to work till youre all healed up good. Are you getting proper doctoring? They say theres American doctors to be found in Mexico City. Im truly heartsore about your arm Johnny but my hats off to you for making the son of a bitch pay the full freight. And sounds to me like you mightve scared Demarco enough to make him partly honest. Keep the money he gave you son, youve earned it."

❈

He had agreed with Elizabeth Anne that to tell her family the truth about his arm would only stoke their perpetual fear for her safety in Mexico. She hated to lie but hated even more to increase her family's worry. So she had written that John Roger had lost an arm in a carriage accident but was adjusting well and in good spirits. Mrs Bartlett wrote back—it was always she who wrote the letters, never Sebastian, never Jimmy—that they were all of them dismayed to learn of John Roger's severe mishap and wished him a sound recovery. But she could not refrain from adding that she had never known anyone to lose an arm in a carriage accident in New England.

❈

He returned to work in early January. The clerk Patterson had assigned to the office was a stocky twenty-year-old Charlestonian named Amos Bentley, moon-faced and sandy-haired, who had been grateful for the chance to do something other than sit around the consulate in wait of new files to shuffle. He welcomed John Roger back and complimented him on his scrupulous recordkeeping, which had made a simple task of serving as his surrogate. They reviewed the deliveries and shipments that had taken place in John Roger's absence, then the correspondence received and sent. John Roger commended Bentley's precise bookkeeping and the cogency of his prose. His dulcet Carolina accent imbued even his perfect Spanish, as John Roger heard when the young man read to him some key sections of the correspondence. Amos had greatly enjoyed dealing with the transport agents and the shipping officers, most of them earthier types than he was used to. He found the import-export trade enticing, in a way even adventurous, and was sorry to be going back to the dull duty of a consular assistant.

John Roger had been back to work only a few days and was attending to paperwork in the office when Patterson showed up unexpected and accompanied by a woman dressed in black and carrying a small portfolio. A large, rough-looking man in an ill-fitting suit started to come in with them but the woman gestured to him and he nodded and went back out into the hall and closed the door behind him.

In formal Spanish Patterson apologized to John Roger for the unannounced intrusion but said the concern was most important. John Roger had stood up when the woman entered, and he somehow knew who she was even before Patterson presented her as "la señora Consuelo Albéniz de Montenegro."

"Encantado, señora," John Roger said. And at once felt witless for conveying gladness to meet a woman he'd made a widow. He invited them to be seated and Patterson held a chair for her in front of the desk, then sat himself at a small remove and told John Roger that Mrs Albéniz, as she preferred to be called, had come to him at the consulate seeking to know where she might find Mr Wolfe. She explained to me her purpose in wishing to meet with you, Patterson said, and has asked that I be present during the proceedings, if you have no objection. I am to serve as, ah—he looked at Mrs Albéniz—an official witness?

"Solamente con el permiso del Señor Wolfe," Mrs Albéniz said.

"Como no," John Roger said. Whatever madam wishes.

Thank you, the woman said. Her gaze direct but difficult to read. She was visibly much younger than the man to whom she'd been married and clearly not the mother of Enrique. And pretty, irrespective of the small pink scar on her chin and a pale one of older vintage under her left eye.

She gestured at John Roger's coat sleeve, folded double and pinned up, and said, I wish you to know that I am very sorry for your terrible injury.

And I am very sorry for . . . about your husband, John Roger said. Please believe me, madam, it was not my preference to fight. He gave me no choice.

I do believe you, Mr Wolfe. My husband had no interest in anyone's preferences but his own. And please believe me when I say you have caused me no grief. The black dress is but a necessary convention. My marriage to Hernán Montenegro was arranged by my father when I was fourteen, in settlement of some bargain between them. Our family's social standing was superior to that of the Montenegros, but my father and my husband were men of the same character and I had no love for either of them. Nor did my husband love me, I assure you. He had been wed twice before and fathered God knows how many children, but neither wife survived, and by some bad joke of God the only male child who did was Enrique, who was as stupid as he was cruel. Hernán married me solely in hope of siring a worthier heir. I hope I do not offend you with my frankness.

You have no cause to make apology, madam, John Roger said. Please speak as frankly as you wish.

You are kind, she said. I have a daughter, Esmeralda, soon to be seven years old. She is the sole happiness of my marriage. I gave birth twice more, a son each time, but neither one lived even two months. May God forgive me, and you will think I am heartless, but I did not mourn their deaths. I feared they would have become their father. Or mine. I must again risk offending you, Mr Wolfe, in view of your severe suffering, but I am glad you had no choice except to fight, because the outcome of that fight has liberated me from Hernán Montenegro. And from his equal brute of a son. One reason I am here is to thank you.

I appreciate your sentiments, madam, John Roger said, but please understand that it gave me no pleasure to . . . I mean, I had no intention to, ah. . . .

I understand, she said. Although, if I have been correctly told, it is Mrs Wolfe who rid the world of Enrique.

Well, yes, that's true. But, ah. . . .

I am told she also had no choice.

No. She didn't.

She must be an exceptional woman.

She is, yes.

The fact remains, I have been liberated by your hand and hers. Partially liberated, I should say, because my emancipation is incomplete. That is the other reason I am here.

John Roger cut a look at Patterson, who smiled tightly and lifted a finger to indicate that he should simply listen.

There are no Montenegro men left alive, Mr Wolfe, Mrs Albéniz said, and I have inherited a hacienda on which I have no wish to live. The only family left to me is a widowed sister in Cuernavaca. I have decided to sell La Sombra Verde and buy a house in Cuernavaca large enough for her and my daughter and myself.

The sale of the estate should certainly make you financially comfortable, John Roger said. I am pleased for you.

Thank you, she said. But though I have my faults, greed is not one of them. I need only enough money to purchase a house and to maintain us in comfort. I have asked appraisals from three different advisors and they are in close agreement as to the worth of La Sombra Verde. I believe Mr Patterson is also not without knowledge about these things. She turned to Patterson and stated a sum. To John Roger's ears an immense sum.

I'm no assayer, Patterson said, but that sounds right.

The accountants with whom I consulted, Mrs Albéniz continued, have assured me that twenty percent of that amount would be more than adequate to provide for me and my sister for the rest of our lives. For my daughter, as well, if she should choose never to marry. The accountants believe I intend to invest the difference, and I did not disabuse them. The point, Mr Wolfe, is that I have thought about this quite carefully, and as I have no other means to repay you for the severe mutilation inflicted on you by my husband, I wish to offer you La Sombra Verde for twenty percent of its worth. You could then, if you so wish, sell it in turn and gain a very large profit. I know of course that no amount of money can make amends for—

Forgive me, madam, John Roger said. You are under no obligation to recompense me for anything.

I am not here to argue the point, Mr Wolfe. Mr Patterson told me you might be reluctant to accept my offer for fear of taking advantage, but I shall be very offended if you should turn it down. Besides, my motives are not entirely benevolent. While I certainly believe you should be compensated by Hernán Montenegro's estate, I have another reason for selling it to you for less than its full worth. Can you guess that reason?

They held stares for a moment, and then he said, Your husband would not like it.

She smiled. You understand everything. Nothing would enrage the man more. It pleases me to believe that even in hell he will learn of it and it will add to his misery.

Forgive my intrusion, madam, Patterson said, and turned to John Roger and said in English, "No offense, Johnny, but if it's a question of money, I can see to it that in less than an hour you have a loan of as much as—"

I have the money, John Roger said.

"Que bueno," the woman said. She leaned forward and placed the portfolio on the desk and opened it to reveal a small sheaf of legal documents. My attorneys have seen to the necessary paperwork, she said. It has all been certified and requires only our own signatures and that of Mr Patterson as witness before it is registered and becomes official.

John Roger looked at Patterson. "It's not right, Charley. She's giving it away."

"Como?" said Mrs Albéniz.

Maybe you want to talk it over with Lizzie, Patterson said.

"Leezee?" the woman said.

My wife.

You wish to ask for the opinion of your *wife*?

No. I don't have to.

I did not think so. It is the same with the men of this country.

That was not my meaning, John Roger said. My wife's opinion is of importance to me. I simply meant that I know what she will say. Because we have discussed our, ah, aspirations for the future, you see.

How extraordinary, the woman said. So tell me. What will she say?

John Roger cut a look at Patterson, looked back at the woman, cleared his throat. Yes. She will say yes.

Mrs Albéniz smiled. So we are agreed?

For thirty percent of the property's worth, John Rodger said.

The woman looked quizzical. Your wife will say for thirty percent?

No, I'm saying for thirty percent.

You are saying. . . ? Mr Wolfe, I do not know very much about business, but I know it is contrary to basic principle for a buyer to offer more than a seller asks.

Thirty percent. Agreed?

No, she said. She looked at Patterson and made a small gesture of perplexity.

I would be stealing it at thirty percent, John Roger said to her.

For the love of God, she said, you are stealing nothing. It is *my* price."

Thirty percent is—

"Ay, pero que terco!" Twenty-*five* percent, Mr Wolfe, and that is all. Not one penny more. Now please, sir, let us end this silliness.

He studied her face. She raised her brow in question. He smiled.

She smiled back. "Ah pues, estamos de acuerdo, no? We have, ah . . . como se dice? . . . make the busyness?"

Yes.

<hr />

He dispatched the news to Richard, who congratulated him for his good fortune but opposed his resignation from the company. He persuaded John Roger to stay on in the Trade Wind's employ as head bookkeeper, a duty he could fulfill from the hacienda. Twice a month Richard would send him the company's most recent paperwork for final accounting. The records would be relayed by Amos Bentley, whom, on John Roger's recommendation, Richard hired to manage the company's Mexican office.

PART TWO

❧ Henry Morgan Wolfe *m* Hedda Juliet Blake ❧

1 Roger Blake Wolfe ———————————— *2* Harrison Augustus

   m Mary Margaret Parham

      1 John Roger ——————————————— *w/*Alma Rodríguez

        m Elizabeth Anne Bartlett   ↓ *1* Juana Merced

          1 John Samuel   *w/*Katrina Ávila

            m Victoria Clara Márquez   *1* Juan Lobo

              1 Juan Sotero

              2 Roger Samuel

          2 James Sebastian

          3 Blake Cortéz

      2 Samuel Thomas

        m María Palomina Blanco

          1 Gloria Tomasina

          2 Bruno Tomás

          3 Sofía Reina

BUENAVENTURA

Sombra Verde was very different in geographical character from the hacienda Corazón de la Virgen that they had visited some years earlier, but the estates were similar in organization and amenities. It was a self-sustaining settlement, feeding off its cornfields and orchards, its pig farms and chicken roosts and dairy, its beef cattle that were processed into meat at the downriver slaughterhouse. The compound was centered by a plaza with a fountain and a church, a main store, a trio of stables with a large adjoining corral. Also fronting the plaza was the walled enclave containing the casa grande. Though it had three stories, the compact design of the house made it small by hacienda standards, but it was still larger than either of the mansions in which Elizabeth Anne had been reared. It boasted all the usual facilities, including an armory, though few of the arms had seen use since the days of the Valledolids, who had kept in hire a dozen pistoleros, while the Montenegros could scarcely afford to maintain half that many. John Roger told these men their service was no longer required and paid them a discharge bonus and they shrugged and left. At Elizabeth Anne's suggestion he renamed the estate Buenaventura de la Espada, which over time would be simplified in casual reference to Buenaventura. All of the casa grande's furniture had been shipped from Spain for the Valledolids, and the Wolfes chose to keep most of it. Elizabeth Anne was especially delighted by the piano in the salon, though it was in bad need of tuning. The only item of furniture they rejected was the bed in their private chamber. It was a mammoth thing of polished mahogany and a feather mattress, but they would not lie where Montenegro had lain. John Roger had the mattress burned and a bookcase made from the fine wood frame. The walls of the residence were cleared of Montenegro portraits and they too went into a fire. He had the bones in every Montenegro grave exhumed from the little cemetery adjoining the casa grande garden and reburied in the communal graveyard of the neighboring village of Santa Rosalba. As the Montenegros had done with the bones of the Valledolids.

❧

Every morning, before breakfast—always prepared for them by Josefina herself, though she now had several helpers in the kitchen—they took coffee on a third-floor balcony from which they could see the huts of Santa Rosalba and its cornfield and the orange sun swelling up from the far reach of the forest. The air cool and redolent of wet foliage. The cock crowings loud. Santa Rosalba was one of two villages on the estate. The other, Agua Negra, was up in the foothills, next to the coffee farm.

They liked to watch the hacienda plaza come to life. The workers from the village arriving at the gate. The head-scarfed women scurrying to the church bell's call to early mass. Storekeepers dampening and sweeping the sidewalk in front of their shops. Gardeners wheeling their barrows full of tools, the smithy stoking his furnace just inside the stable door, the wranglers at the corral rails. The rising odors of cookfires and dust. At day's end John Roger and Elizabeth Anne would sit on the other side of the house and watch the sun lower into the western sierras. This balcony overlooked the hacienda's main docks on the Río Perdido, the water the color of copper in the late afternoon light. Herons stalked the shallows along the bank. Roosting parrots screeched in the trees. Fishermen moored their dugouts and unloaded their night's catch of fish and eels and turtles.

After breakfast, it was John Roger's daily ritual to meet with his estate manager—the mayordomo, Reynaldo Espinosa de la Santa Cruz—and review the day's schedule and discuss any business of importance. While a patrón's authority was absolute, the chief administrator on most haciendas, the man to whom all lesser supervisors had to answer directly, was the mayordomo. A slim courtly man with a black spade beard and only three years John Roger's senior, Reynaldo had been the mayordomo for ten years, the latest in a continuous line of Espinosas to have administered the hacienda since its founding in the sixteenth century. His family had served many Valledolid patrones and two Montenegros. He and his wife and children lived in a spacious residence within the casa grande enclave. He had welcomed John Roger with such warm respect that it seemed needless to ask how he felt about the change in owners. Given the man's knowledge of the hacienda and his expertise in its operation, John Roger naturally wanted him to stay on as his mayordomo, and he was relieved when Reynaldo said, I would be honored to remain in your service, Don Juan.

They met every morning of the week but Sunday, and after their conference John Roger would usually devote himself to reviewing Trade Wind accounts. On Saturdays, after Reynaldo meted out the workers' weekly wages, paying them one-

98

fourth in silver specie and the rest in script redeemable at the hacienda store, John Roger would conduct the weekly court session in the compound plaza. He sat at a table in the shade of a tree and settled grievances large and small concerning hacienda residents. Most cases were trivial contentions of property between neighbors—a dispute over the rightful ownership of a stray pig, or of the eggs laid by someone's hen in someone else's yard. But at times he was presented with more serious issues. A petition for retribution by a man whose young son was mauled by another man's dog. A bridegroom's allegation of fraud whereby his bride in an arranged marriage proved not to be the virgin he had been assured she was. The judicial responsibility was one of the most important of a patrón, and John Roger fulfilled it well. He viewed the Saturday courts as a recurrent test of his reasoning and principles of justice, and his judgments earned him wide respect as a man both wise and fair. Elizabeth Anne greatly enjoyed these court sessions and never failed to attend them. It pleased her that in almost every case John Roger's ruling was such as she herself would have made. She confessed to him that back in their Concord days she'd had a covert hope he would one day run for mayor, as she was convinced he would make a fine one. But as patrón of Buenaventura, he had the full powers of an entire government—executive, legislative, and judicial. "Why, it's better than being governor of New Hampshire!" she said. He laughed and said he believed it was.

During their first months in residence at the hacienda, they sometimes made the daylong journey to Veracruz to spend a few days, but by the end of their first year as hacendados they rarely went to town, and the only times they saw their friends were when they came to Buenaventura. Charles Patterson and Amos Bentley would come to the hacienda on every other Friday for a visit of a day or two. They would bring the most recent editions of American newspapers and their own news of the city and of the country at large. Amos would deliver the latest Trade Wind paperwork for John Roger's review and collect the records he had examined over the previous fortnight. In the warmest weather they would all don bathing costumes and cool off in the shallow concrete pool in the garden arbor, and after dining in the company of Elizabeth Anne the men would repair to the den for whiskey and cigars and would converse into the night.

Also in that first year a strange and wondrous thing happened—the coffee farm rejuvenated and produced the largest harvest in its history. The next season's yield would be even greater. Such bountifulness would persist for a long time to come and earn John Roger yet another fortune. There was no rational explanation for the farm's robust revival after twenty years of meager output, but the villagers believed the farm's plight had been caused by the legendary curse of Martín Valledolid, and that the cessation of Montenegro proprietorship had ended the curse. But more than that, they believed Don Juan and Doña Isabel were favored by God, and so the hacienda was now divinely blessed.

When Reynaldo told the Wolfes of these popular explanations for the farm's renewed fertility, they were amused, although Elizabeth Anne thought the villagers could be right. How else explain such a miraculous turn of good fortune except by divine favor? Reynaldo smiled on her like a fond uncle and said that whatever the reason for such fecundity, it had even reached into his own house. His wife had informed him just the night before that she was in the family way.

The Wolfes were thrilled. They knew Reynaldo's sad history of parenthood. Of the twelve children his wife had born one after the other, nine had died of illness or by accident before their tenth birthday, leaving the family with a sole son, Mauricio, and two daughters. Though Reynaldo and his wife both wanted another son, she had not conceived for the past three years. Until now.

You see! Elizabeth Anne cried. You see how blessed we all are? She hugged Reynaldo in congratulations and said she knew he was hoping for a boy and asked what name he had chosen if it should be.

Alfredo, Reynaldo said.

ENSENADA DE ISABEL

They made a gradual acquaintance with the entire hacienda, exploring it by buggy, on horseback, in canoe, afoot, until they'd seen all of it except for a section of rain forest along the lower river—which, so far as anyone knew, had never been penetrated even by Indians—and no part of the estate was dearer to them than its little cove at the mouth of the Río Perdido some twelve miles below the compound as the crow flew. The route to get there, however, was hardly as direct as crow flight. And although the river snaked through the jungle all the way to the coast, it was of little use for downriver transport because of the rapids that began just four miles below the compound docks, a stretch of whitewater so daunting that not even the hacienda's most able boatmen would brave them. A few had tried it in years past and had never been seen again. It was supposed that the rapids ran for many miles, but no one knew for sure.

The first time John Roger and Elizabeth Anne went to the cove, they left the compound three hours before dawn and were conveyed by a lantern–lit raft through the river darkness to a small dockage about a half mile above the rapids. Even at that distance they could faintly hear the whitewater rush. From this lower landing they proceeded by ox wagon, with supplies and camping gear, on a narrow trail that had been hacked out many years before by the crew of fishermen whose periodic duty it had been to provide Hernán Montenegro with the oysters and crabs and shrimp he cherished. Reynaldo the mayordomo knew of no one who had ever been to the cove but those fishing crews. The fishermen had praised the prettiness and the bounty of the place, but said that if they had had a choice they would rather forgo the rigors of getting there, and they wished Don Hernán had not had such a liking for shellfish. They would scoop oysters and net crabs and shrimp until they had sackfuls of each, then smoke the entire catch to preserve it for the return trip. And then one night, about a year before his death, Don Hernán had become violently sick after a meal of the smoked oysters. The servants tending to him could hardly believe the quantities of vomit and horrifically stinking shit he produced on that interminable night, and they thought it a wonder that he survived it. At daybreak he looked like he'd lost twenty pounds and was as sickly pale as wax. He never again ate shellfish of any form, and so far as Reynaldo knew, no one had been to the hacienda's seashore since.

The track held close to the river's meander and in places was so narrow the foliage brushed against both sides of the wagon as they swayed and tilted over the uneven ground. Both the driver and their guard were Indians, the guard riding behind on a burro. Both men armed with machetes and shotguns. Although the disorder of the Reform War had worsened the national plague of banditry, robbers were most unlikely in this jungle—but jaguars and wild boars and poisonous snakes were not. Under his leather jacket John Roger carried a .36-caliber Colt in a shoulder holster, and in Elizabeth Anne's handbag was a .41-caliber derringer. To fend against the rage of mosquitoes they had covered their faces and necks and hands with an unguent of Josefina's concoction that smelled so foul they questioned whether the mosquitoes might not be the lesser torment.

Under a high shadowing canopy of trees shrill with birds and monkeys, the air grew hotter and wetter, riper in its smells of vegetation. The light was an eerie green. John Roger had been fretful of Elizabeth Anne risking her health in such close heat, but she assured him she felt fine. It was his guess that in some places they were hardly more than ten yards from the river and never farther than twenty, but the undergrowth was so heavy that at no point did they get so much as a glimpse of the water. They might not have known the river was there but for the rumble of the rapids, which grew louder and louder until they were abreast of them for several miles in which the green air was misty with vapor and they had to raise their voices to be heard. He wanted to have a look, but to get near enough to the riverbank would have required an hour or more of hacking with machetes by all three men, an expense of valuable time they could not afford. And too, there was the matter of jaguars and boars and snakes. They pressed on, the roar of the rapids gradually diminishing back to a rumble, and after a while longer they heard only the river's low hiss through the bankside reeds.

⚜

Near day's end they emerged from the closing darkness of the river into the last afternoon light of the cove. It was an oval some eighty yards wide from the landward to the seaward side and half again that long from north to south. The trailhead was near the cove's northwest end, within sight of the river mouth. The cove surface looked like a slightly warped mirror of green glass, much darker at this hour than it would be under the overhead sun. They could not see the inlet on the other side because it did not open directly to the gulf but lay between a pair of narrow and overlapping tongues of land parallel to the coastline and dense with coconut palms. The trees blocked their view of the ocean but they could hear the swash of small waves on the outer shore. On the cove's landward side the jungle ended on a small bluff that sloped down onto a smooth white beach. The beach curved all the way around the south end of the cove and was askitter with crabs of red-and-blue.

"My God, it's so beautiful," Elizabeth Anne said. She pointed to the bluff. "Up there, Johnny, up there's the place for a house."

John Roger told the guard and driver to relax, and the two men settled themselves under a tree and began to roll cigarettes. He and Elizabeth Anne then took off their shoes and walked barefoot out on the beach, crabs sidling out of the way ahead of them. They went up the slope to the little bluff and found that although it was not quite high enough for them to see the gulf on the other side of the palms, there was a steady breeze that kept off the mosquitoes. John Roger agreed it was a fine spot to build a house.

They went back down to the beach and walked around to the other side of the cove and went through the palms and there the gulf was. As far as they could see to north and south a high wall of palms leaning to landward was fronted by a sand-and-rock beach barely ten yards wide at any point at this hour of ebb tide. The gentle waves rolled in low and crested as small breakers, spraying on the rocky shore and rushing over it in a foaming sheet and then running back out again.

They backtracked through the palms to the cove beach and headed for the inlet and before they got there the sand under their feet became stony ground. The inlet formed a pass less than fifteen feet wide and about fifteen yards long from its outer mouth to its inner one, both banks craggy with rocks. It looked about four feet deep at the ebb and John Roger guessed it would rise close to two feet at high tide. On the inland side of the pass the bottom grass leaned toward the cove with the incoming current but on the outer side where they stood the grass was pulled the other way by the current going out.

"See how the current makes an easy circuit all the way around?" John Roger said, gesturing with his arm. "But through this pass it moves pretty fast coming in and going out." He picked up a coconut and dropped it into the water and it whipped away on the outgoing current and around the outer tongue of the inlet. It carried out into the gulf for about fifty feet before it slowed to an easy bobbing and began drifting toward the southward shore.

The outer mouth presented a difficult angle of approach from the open water. John Roger thought only expert hands might be able to sail a boat through this pass without either hitting the rocky projection of its outer tongue or veering into the leeward rocks. Elizabeth Anne grinned and said she was game whenever he was.

Because the inlet faced up the coast and its outer arm overlapped the inner one and was so thick with palms, it was impossible to see it from anywhere out on the gulf except if you were north of the inlet and very close to the shore, and even then you would have to be looking hard for it. "You could sail by within fifty yards and never see this opening," John Roger said.

"Our own secret harbor," Elizabeth Anne said. "I love it."

He christened the cove Ensenada de Isabel and rued the lack of a flag to plant.

Josefina had supplied them with an oilskin sack of food—a stack of tortillas bundled in a damp cloth, a pouch of dried beef, two jugs of cooked beans, and a bag of oranges. In the last red light of day John Roger made a fire on the bluff and Elizabeth Anne invited the driver and guard to come and sup with them. The men had brought their own provisions and had made a campfire near the wagon, but they accepted the Wolfes' invitation. After supper John Roger told them they could sleep in the wagon, and he and Elizabeth Anne went up on the bluff, up where the crabs did not go, and huddled on one blanket and covered themselves with another against the evening's cool breeze.

He woke twice in the night, savoring the sea breeze, the crush of stars, the bronze gibbous moon low in the east. The feel of Lizzie snugged against him. The second time, just as he was about to doze off again, he heard her murmur, "This is heaven." And next time woke to a radiant sunrise.

They got back to the compound after dark, and later that night, in the privacy of his office, John Roger took out the journal he had not opened in years and recorded his happy plans.

﹡

It took a year to build the house and improve the trail for getting to it. John Roger spent long periods encamped at the cove with the labor crews and supervising the construction. He had the wagon track lengthened from the river mouth to the landing at the hacienda compound and improved the trail the full length of its entire river-hugging wind through the jungle. Each time he came home for a visit he was leaner, harder of muscle, more darkly sunbrowned. After the first few months, he forwent shaving and his beard grew black and wild. Elizabeth Anne was roused by his brutish appearance. When she said he now looked more like a pirate than even her Uncle Richard, he affected a menacing leer and advanced on her, saying in low growl, "Arrgh, me captive beauty, it's yer sweet flesh I'll have for me sport"—and she let a gleeful cry as he tumbled her into bed. She loved the beard and asked him to keep it and she trimmed it for him. She missed him terribly in his absences and chafed at her long exclusion from her cherished cove. She pleaded to go back with him and swore she would not complain about living in a tent until the house was ready to move into. But he would not permit her to see it until it was completed.

In the long weeks without him, her sanctuary against loneliness was the company of Josefina and young John Samuel. The boy liked being the center of her attention while his father was away, but although he was not shy he did not talk very much, not even when he and his mother were alone together. Elizabeth Anne would love him dearly to the end of her life without comprehending him. Josefina, on the other hand, liked to talk and was a good listener in turn, and Elizabeth Anne took pleasure in their conversations. Everyone of the casa grande knew that Josefina was from the state of Chihuahua—her accent was irrefutable testament to her roots in that northern region. But Elizabeth Anne was the only one to know that Josefina's entire family except for herself and her younger brother Gonsalvo had been killed and her village razed when she was twelve years old.

Elizabeth Anne asked who killed them and Josefina shrugged and said, "Hombres con armas." It was a war, she said, there was always a war, always men with guns, and war was no less cruel to those who did not fight in it than to those who did. After losing their parents and home, she and Gonsalvo decided to go to Veracruz to live with the family of their maternal aunt. Besides the fact that their aunt lived there, they knew nothing of Veracruz except that it was far away to the southeast and was next to the sea. Not until afterward did they learn it was a journey of a thousand miles as the eagle flies but truly much farther, crossing every sort of terrain, including the eastern sierras. They sometimes got rides on passing wagons, but they walked more often than they rode. Many things happened and they saw much that was wonderful and much that was terrible and met many people and heard many strange languages. They crossed the mountains in the company of another displaced family and it seemed the crossing would never end and she would never be warm again. One of Gonsalvo's hands was badly frostbitten and two fingers had to be removed. Eleven years old, Josefina said, and you never saw a boy so brave. He never made a sound except to take a deep breath when the man chopped both fingers at once with a hatchet and then again when he closed the wounds with a hot knife. The trip took a year. Their aunt's family welcomed them and wept for their loss and marveled at their trek from Chihuahua. Gonsalvo fell in love with the gulf the moment he saw it, and he soon learned to swim in it and swam almost every day. But the sea frightened Josefina and she never went into it any deeper than her knees. In their second summer on the coast they both caught the yellow fever and she survived but Gonsalvo did not. She had lived in Veracruz state ever since.

Had she ever married?

Yes. Once. His name was Lotario Quito. He was a gentle man—*too* gentle, God forgive her for saying so, but it was the truth. There are times in a man's life when rashness is necessary but the capacity for rashness was not in Lotario. Still, one cannot help but love whom one loves, and they loved each other very much. He was a clerk in a bookstore and earned extra money by writing letters and other documents for illiterates who came to his little table at the zócalo. That she herself could not read was of no matter to him. He would have given her a reading lesson whenever she asked, but only when she asked, because he was afraid that if he should suggest a lesson to her she might think he was implying that she was dull and in need of education, but he did not think that and did not wish to offend her. Even after he told her this and she said she would not take offense, he would never ask if she wished a lesson, and because she did not want to disturb his own reading in the evening, she would not ask for lessons and so never did learn to read and write. They had been married almost two years—and had produced one child, who died in his sleep in his second month—when a pair of thugs accosted them on the street late one night after a dance. They were forced into an alley and the thugs took turns raping her while the other held a razor to Lotario's throat. They took his money and his father's pocketwatch and shattered his spectacles for the meanness of it. They were laughing when they walked away, not even running. Lotario's weeping was so piteous it broke her heart. He could not stop crying, even after they got home, and she held him close all night, crooning to him as to a child frighted by a bad dream.

Elizabeth Anne was tearful on hearing the story and Josefina chided her for it, saying that life was after all full of bad times as well as good ones, and even a bad time, if it did not cause unbearable pain, was better than being killed. In plain truth, she said, she was not without good luck on that night of the thugs, as they did not make her pregnant. As for Lotario, some months later a hurricane hit the city, and as was often the case the storm was followed by a typhoid epidemic, and he caught the disease and died.

Had she had any close gentlemen friends since then? That was how Elizabeth Anne phrased it—close gentlemen friends—and they both blushed a little at what she was really asking. Well, missus, Josefina answered, I can only say that some were closer than others and some more gentlemanly—and they laughed like schoolgirls.

⁂

There finally came the day when John Roger drove Elizabeth Anne in a mule wagon, just the two of them, along the improved trail to the cove, now a drive of ten hours from the compound—in fair weather, anyhow. And there he presented her with the house, lovely and bright with whitewash in the shade of the tall palms on the rise above the beach. Crafted of hardwoods and set ten feet off the ground on pilings two feet thick, it was as solid as an ark and would withstand every hurricane and flood. Its roof peaked and shingled with slate and fitted with a widow's walk. It had only four rooms, but the wide run-around verandah gave the house a sense of greater spaciousness. The gulf was visible from the verandah—and from up on the widow's walk it seemed to Elizabeth Anne that she could see all the way to the blue curve of the earth. The house had tall shuttered windows, a kitchen with a stove, a plumbing system piped from a pair of cisterns in the back of the building. There was a fireplace, a feature far more nostalgic than practical, which would see use but a few days a year. A small stable stood off to the side of the house, designed to keep out even the strongest of jaguars, and directly off the beach, in front of the house, a stout narrow dock extended fifteen yards into the water at low tide.

"For the sailboat we're going to get," John Roger said.

Elizabeth Anne flung herself on him, locking her legs around him and kissing him all over his face, and he couldn't balance himself against her weight with just one arm and they tumbled onto the sand in a laughing heap.

Over the following years it would be their custom to come out to this isolate world every couple of months with a store of supplies and spend a week or so in blissful privacy. He grew adept at one-armed swimming, and they would swim across to the inner mouth of the inlet and into the incoming current and let it carry them gently all the way around the cove and then swim out of it onto the beach just short of the rocky pass where the current accelerated and went whipping around the outer point of the inlet.

They scandalized themselves the first time they swam naked at sundown and then made love dog-fashion on the beach. They bathed together in the large wooden tub behind the house, washed each other's hair, dried each other off. Besides sandals, she wore only a sleeveless shirt of his that hung to her thighs and he but a pair of pants he'd cut off at the knees. They professed mock concern about reverting to a primitive state. They preferred to sleep in the big hammock on the verandah rather than on the indoor bed and liked to lie awake and watch the moon rise over the gulf and see the fiery sparklings of fish breaking the surface in the cove. The nights were raucous with the ringing of frogs, with sudden frantic splashings, with indefinable shrieks from the black wilderness behind the house. Nights of rain brought a darkness exceeding all imagination, in which only the force of gravity let them define up from down. They sometimes heard the low resonant growl of a jaguar—and sometimes a scream that never failed to make them flinch and clutch to each other even as they giggled at their own fright. They joked about slathering themselves with Josefina's salve to keep the jaguars from eating them in their sleep, and damn the risk of asphyxiation.

❧

At a Veracruz boatyard he bought a small fishing sloop and had the name *Lizzie* painted on the stern. It had a little cabin just fore of the fish hold and was very light and maneuverable, its draft so shallow that John Roger joked that they could sail it on the streets of Veracruz in the rainy season. They studied every navigational map available and were not surprised to see that their cove was marked on none of them. They pored over the charts and estimated where the inlet would be. He could manage the tiller with one arm, and with Elizabeth Anne working the sheets, her straw sombrero snugged down tight by a chin thong and its brim flapping in the wind, they set sail up the coast under a bright sky of dizzying blue and towering clouds in the distance.

The water was so clear they could see the grassy bottom far below them. Elizabeth Anne asked how deep he thought it was. "Four or five fathoms," he said.

And she recited:

> Full fathom five thy father lies;
> Of his bones are coral made;
> Those are pearls that were his eyes:
> Nothing of him that doth fade
> But doth suffer a sea-change
> Into something rich and strange.

She could not know the chilliness he'd felt on his first encounter with those lines in his Shakespeare studies at Dartmouth. Hearing her recite them, he felt the same chill, together with a sudden melancholy—and a rush of guilt for never having told her the truth of his father. Then upbraided himself for this turn of mind and pushed the thoughts away. "A fine recitation, young miss," he said. "It's top marks for you."

"Thank you, kind sir." She attempted a curtsy but lost her balance as the boat pitched on a swell and she just did manage to catch hold of a stay to keep from falling on her backside.

"That'll teach ye to try that la-de-da stuff on the briny, ye fancy-bred wench," he said in his best mariner growl.

She made a rude face at him.

When a band of dolphins surfaced within yards of the boat and frolicked alongside it, Elizabeth Anne waved to them and called hello and told them they were a fine-looking bunch. "Don't they have the happiest faces you've ever seen?" she yelled over the rush of the wind. He returned her grin and regarded her face and thought, No darling girl, they don't.

They were 150 yards off the coast as they approached that stretch of it where they thought the cove would be, and he tillered the boat to shoreward. The *Lizzie* rose and dipped on the easy swells, its mainsail and jib outslung and bright. They had set their course by dead reckoning and were confident it would get them near enough to the cove to see the house, which they would then use to get their bearing on the inlet. They had also calculated that the tide would be within four hours of its flood and high enough that they were in no danger of going aground in the shallow approach to the inlet. But the wind had been stronger than usual and the *Lizzie* even faster than they had expected. When John Roger observed that they would be going in when the tide had barely reversed its ebb, Elizabeth Anne grinned and said, "Good! We seafarers love a challenge!"

The house being white, they were sure it would be easy enough to spot it against the dark jungle. From out on the open sea, however, the jungle seemed even denser, its shadows deeper. Less than a hundred yards off the coast they still did not see it. Nor did they at sixty yards, with the bottom risen to fifteen feet and coming up fast. "Oh, good Christ," John Roger said. "Where *is* it?"

Elizabeth Anne snatched up the telescope and began to scan the jungle shoreline. The scope's view was so tightly compassed she had to scan swiftly and she feared she might overlook the house. The sloop rose and dipped and bore toward the rocky coast. They were now only forty yards offshore and in less than ten feet of water over a bottom fast becoming rock. They thought they'd made a mistake in their calculations. Then there was only four feet between them and the rushing bottom and he knew they were going to tear up the hull if he didn't come about in the next few seconds. And Lizzie yelled "*There!*" and pointed.

He looked hard and saw it. Nestled in the shadows of the trees and barely visible in the jungle canopy. And he knew where the inlet was. He yelled "Hard to port!" and yanked on the tiller. Holding to the mast, Elizabeth Anne ducked under the quick swipe of the boom as the boat turned sharply and they felt the keel's slight scrape against the bottom as the sails *whumped* tight as drumheads and the boat heeled hard to leeward in a broad reach and bolted forward.

They hurtled toward the small mouth of the cove and John Roger's tillering was nothing short of artful. With as much finesse as if they'd done it a hundred times before, they sped through the inlet with four feet to spare on the leeward side. The mainsail softened in the sudden fall of wind behind the palm trees and then they were clear of the passage and John Roger steered the boat to starboard and into the tranquility of Ensenada de Isabel.

"*Whooo-eee!*" Elizabeth Anne yelled.

The mainsail luffed and she loosed its sheet and let the sail drop, and the jib carried them most of the way across the cove before she freed its line too and the little sail fell slack. John Roger steered the *Lizzie*'s glide toward the outer end of the pier and when the bow lightly glanced it Elizabeth Anne leaped from the deck with a line in hand and made it fast to a mooring post.

And they were home. Happy as children.

-❦-

Although they revered their privacy at the beach house, the enjoyment of their retreats was diluted by guilt over leaving John Samuel at home in Josefina's care. The boy was now almost seven, and in fact he didn't mind staying home while they were gone, preferring as he did to be near his gray pony, John Roger's present to him on his sixth birthday. Horses were the boy's great joy, and he rode with admirable skill and confidence for one so young. He was five when his father one day leaned down from his stallion and whisked him up onto the saddle and against his chest and took him for a galloping ride that had the boy yelling with exhilaration. When John Roger jumped the horse over a high fence rail the boy whooped and Elizabeth Anne, watching, bit her lip. John Samuel afterward described the experience to his mother as feeling like he had ridden the wind.

Still, they felt derelict for excluding him from their trips to the cove, and during a spell of fine December weather they finally took him with them for a week's stay. They asked Josefina to go, too, but she declined, saying she had not lived to such an old age just to get eaten by a tiger.

They were surprised by John Samuel's indifference to the pleasures of the place. He had learned to swim in the river but did not really like it, even less in saltwater, and fishing held no allure for him. When they took him for a sail on the *Lizzie*—his first venture on a boat other than a river dugout—they had no sooner cleared the inlet, leaving the placid water of the cove for the mild rise and fall of the gulf's swells, than he sickened and threw up. John Roger told him it was nothing to be ashamed of, he would get his sea legs soon enough, he came from a family of born sailors, after all. John Samuel nodded and made no complaint, but the farther they sailed into open water the more forceful his stomach's rebellion, and at Elizabeth Anne's request John Roger turned back.

The next day, while John Roger reminisced to him about the times he and his brother had set trot lines in Portsmouth creeks, they rigged such a line between the river dock and the opposite bank, and the day after that John Samuel helped his father to collect the fish off the hooks. But his parents could see that his interest in these activities was less real than shammed for their sake, and so they left him to his preferred diversion of sitting on the verandah and reading books about horses. His mealtime conversation was almost wholly about his pony and his hope that it was getting proper care from the stable hand he'd left in charge of it.

John Samuel would not go to the cove again, not with them nor anyone else nor by himself. From then on, whenever they readied to go to the beach house, they would tell him he was welcome to come and he would pretend to mull the invitation before saying he thought he should stay and care for his horse, and they would say that was fine, they understood. This ritual would persist for a year before they eventually overcame their guilt and ceased to offer the dutiful invitation. From then on they simply let him know when they were going and for how long, leaving him in Josefina's custody, and he would always respond with a wish for them to have a good time. Which, in the primitive privacy of their haven, they always did.

SEASONS OF MARS
AND VENUS AND MORS

The American Civil War came as no shock to any of them, for they had long sensed it as inevitable. A letter from Mrs Bartlett reported that many of the state's young men had enlisted and gone off to fight the wretched secessionists, but Jimmy had been commissioned as an army captain and she thanked God her husband had the influence to get him posted in Washington as a records officer. Otherwise, she wrote, the war seemed as distant from New Hampshire as did Mexico. Its most conspicuous effect was a significant increase in profits for the Bartlett paper mills, as purchase orders poured in from the federal government.

Elizabeth Anne nearly wept in her anger at her mother's letter. She shared Patterson's convictions that it was a war between rich northern industrialists and rich southern planters and that the Confederacy's economic cause was no less compelling than the Union's and that the North's denunciation of slavery was rank hypocrisy. She asked John Roger's promise to stay out of "that criminal folly," as she phrased it. "I will not be made a widow or have my child left fatherless in the cause of any bigwig's greed, including my father's."

John Roger smiled and said that with one arm he could hardly do other than stay out of it. Then saw how near to enraged tears she was and gave his promise.

"Thank you," she said. "Besides, *this* is our country now."

He agreed it was. The notion that patriotic fidelity was irrevocably bound to birthplace had always seemed to him logically indefensible. You could not choose where you were born but you could choose where to make your home, and it was to homeland that you owed allegiance. She was right that Mexico had become their home. They had chosen it. They had borne a son who was native to it.

Charles Patterson made no secret of his Confederate sympathies but admitted his gladness at being too old for the ranks. He had fought for Texas in its war of independence and had been with Houston at San Jacinto, where they slaughtered the Mexican force and then committed a great many defilements of the dead and wounded, and he had seen enough of such mad carnage for one lifetime. He retained his post at the U.S. consulate, absent all hope it would ever fly the flag of the C.S.A. and not unaware of his underlings' jocular references to him as Colonel Dixie. Young Bentley, too, was a Southerner, but had been orphaned in Charleston when he was nine and then lived in a detested foster home until he went away to college on a scholarship, and the idea of risking his life for a cause in which he had no personal stake struck him as absurd.

The war boosted prices for the Trade Wind's coffee and tobacco, and in the first year of hostilities the company's profits boomed. But when Union forces took New Orleans in the spring of '62 they robbed the Trade Wind of its store of commodities and razed its warehouses and offices together with all its records. The bad news came to John Roger and Amos in a letter from Richard Davison, who gave them the name of a Yankee entrepreneur in New Orleans eager to assume the contract for Buenaventura's coffee. He himself did not know what he would do next but promised to write to them soon.

They heard nothing from or about him for the next eight months. Then Jimmy Bartlett sent a letter from Washington with the report that Richard Davison had tried to smuggle a shipment of arms past the Federal blockade off the Texas coast and was killed when a gunboat sank his vessel. His body had not been recovered and his kin might never have known what became of him except that his crew's only survivor named him as the captain. Mrs Bartlett, Jimmy wrote, was inconsolable.

On receiving the news about Richard, Elizabeth Anne said only "God *damn* war," then went up to her room and wept in private. She spoke barely a word during the next few days. She had never said so, but John Roger knew she favored her Uncle Redbeard over her own brother, her own father.

Even as the war in the United States intensified, Mexico got into another war of its own, though this time not with itself. The Reform War had ended in a Liberal victory but left the country bankrupt, forcing President Juárez to declare a two-year suspension of payments on the nation's foreign debt. The moratorium angered European creditors. In a united effort to exact payment, France and Britain and Spain sent troops. John Roger and Elizabeth Anne heard all about it from Patterson and Bentley when they came to visit Buenaventura—about the warships in the Veracruz harbor, the foreign uniforms in the plazas. The Brits and Spanish were soon placated and withdrew, but the French remained, no longer making any secret of their colonial intentions. They were all the more emboldened by the United States' incapacity to enforce its Monroe Doctrine against European incursion in the Western Hemisphere, distracted as the Americans were with a civil war that threatened their very nationhood. The Church, which had been pillaged by the Juárez liberals, was in vehement support of the French. So too were the majority of Creoles, who believed only a monarchy could both restore civic stability and preserve their economic advantage. Backed by these two powerful Mexican blocs, France sent more soldiers and the war was on. The Juárez republicans achieved some early victories, the most noteworthy in Puebla—where a firebrand young officer and devoted Juarista named José de la Cruz Porfirio Díaz gained renown for his battlefield valor. But only a year later the French were ensconced in the capital and Juárez was in refuge in Texas and Díaz was a prisoner of war—though he would soon escape and resume the fight. The year after that, the provisional government of conservatives and French interventionists declared Mexico a Catholic empire and persuaded Erzherzog Maximilian of Austria to accept the Mexican crown.

John Roger and Elizabeth Anne were among the witnesses on the fine day in May when Maximilian arrived in Veracruz on the SMS *Novarra*. In the company of Patterson and Bentley, peering through field glasses from the roof of the U.S. consulate, they had a good look at the lean blond emperor with the lush muttonchop beard as he debarked. On his arm was the Empress Carlotta, a blackhaired beauty with doleful eyes. Maximilian would swiftly come to love Mexico. He would become fluent in Spanish, prefer Mexican food, wear Mexican clothes, esteem Mexican customs and take part in Mexican festivities. But irrespective of his great love for the country, he was no less an invader of it, and the war went on. Veracruz was again spared major damage and the port remained in operation. John Roger contracted with the American agent who had been recommended by Richard Davison and continued to ship coffee to New Orleans. At such far remove from the war, Buenaventura continued to flourish.

Came the news of Appomattox. Shortly after which the reunited States of America warned the French to get out of Mexico. By then the tide had anyway turned against the monarchists in their war with Juárez, and the French—who had been losing battles to the forces of Porfirio Díaz—were swift to disengage, leaving Maximilian on his own. The abandoned emperor fled to Querétaro with the remnant of his imperial army and withstood siege by the Juaristas for one hundred days before surrendering. On a bright June morning in 1867, and notwithstanding the pleas of a number of European heads of state for Benito Juárez to spare him, Maximilian was stood before a firing squad and shouted "Viva Mexico!" before the rifles discharged into his heart. The following day, Porfirio Díaz liberated Mexico City from the last holdouts of the imperial army.

Thus was the Mexican republic restored. And thus did Porfirio Díaz become a national hero. In the course of the war he had twice been badly wounded and twice been captured and twice escaped. He had subsequently led his army in a series of spectacular victories, most of them against superior numbers. When he was told that

Juárez, his estimable mentor, was jealous of his growing fame, Díaz dismissed such talk as foolish rumor. But when he congratulated Juárez on his triumphant return to Mexico City to resume his presidency, the little Indian snubbed him. The insult pained Díaz as much as it angered him, and the two men were evermore estranged.

In the autumn of that year, Díaz unsuccessfully challenged Juárez for the presidency. He was publicly gracious about the defeat, but his pride seethed.

※

A few months earlier, Amos Bentley had begun courting a comely eighteen-year-old Creole named Teresa Serafina Nevada Marichál, whom he had met at the wedding of a mutual friend. She was the only child of Victor Mordecai Nevada Oquendo, who owned a number of silver mines in western Veracruz state as well as the most lucrative gold mine in eastern Mexico. In addition to his high-country hacienda called Las Nevadas, that overlooked the mines, Don Victor owned a house in Jalapa and another in the heart of Mexico City.

At first, the don gave little import to young Bentley's formal visits to his daughter in Jalapa. Teresa had been receiving suitors since the age of fifteen—the visits always conducted in the parlor and of course always overseen by her trio of dueñas, the watchful old women Teresa referred to as the Three Black Crows. Thus far no aspirant beau had managed even slight purchase on the girl's affections, and that had been fine with Don Victor. None of his sons had survived infancy and he was relying on his daughter to bear him a grandson to whom he would by one means or another bequeath legal title to the Nevada properties. But it was crucial that she choose her husband wisely, and he assumed that she shared his standards for a proper mate. As the beautiful and sole heir of an immensely rich man, she was an outstanding prize, and it was Don Victor's ambition to see her wed into a family no less wealthy than her own and with no heirs but her husband. The first criterion did much to narrow the field of possible candidates, and the second reduced it to a very rare few. Yet Don Victor was optimistic that the right suitor would soon enough present himself. That she entertained so many admirers who stood no chance of gaining her hand was not so much a puzzle to him as an irritation. She had always been a quirksome girl and he supposed it gratified her vanity to receive even the most hopeless of wooers. Whatever the case, she had been motherless since the age of seven and had grown up under his guidance and so could be as headstrong as himself. He knew better than to argue with her if he could help it.

But as the months passed and Amos Bentley's visits persisted, it became clear to Don Victor that Teresa was taking uncommon pleasure in the young gringo's company and he began to sense the seriousness of things. But he had kenned to it too late. Before he could decide what to do, Teresa announced at breakfast one day that Amos had asked her to marry him and she was giving the question serious thought. Don Victor masked his apprehension with a fatherly smile and said, Of course. You are too kind to break a heart in any way but with gentleness. To know that you have given serious thought to his proposal will soften his disappointment at least a little.

Actually, she said, I think I love him.

Don Victor's shock was exceeded only by his barely suppressed alarm. He did business with Yankees, yes, but business was a thing apart from personal emotions. He had in truth felt a great bitterness toward Americans ever since their invasion of his country. The only imaginable thing worse than an impoverished son-in-law was an impoverished gringo son-in-law. Over the next days he tried with calm logic to dissuade Teresa from accepting Amos's proposal. He said it would be the gravest of mistakes to marry any man beneath her social station, and worse still one from another culture. But the more he argued against the marriage the more he could see by the set of her face that he was losing ground.

Then one morning she was decided. She told Don Victor she was going to say yes to Amos. There followed a loud and heated argument in which Don Victor only just did manage to restrain himself from forbidding the marriage outright, fearing she would make good on her threat to elope—a threat that did not waver even in the face of his counterthreat to disinherit her if she should marry without his permission.

She confided the entire argument to Amos, who in turn confided it to John Roger, admitting to him that he had gone weak in the knees when Teresa told him of the don's warning of disinheritance. "I'm sure you can understand my concern, John," he said. "I mean, of course I love her very much and admire her passionate nature and willingness to place love above all and so on and so forth, but one should not permit one's emotions to supersede practical consideration entirely, should one?" John Roger smiled and said, "Not entirely, I shouldn't think." He understood the practical consideration Amos had in mind was the young lady's birthright, which through marriage would of course also become his.

Don Victor at last offered his daughter a compromise. He would consent to the marriage on condition that she agree to a courtship period of one year to be followed by a formal engagement of yet another year. If she still wanted to marry Mr Bentley after the year of betrothal, they would have his full blessing.

Teresa insisted to Amos that they should refuse her father's conditions. We must not permit him to make the rules for any part of our lives, she argued. If we do, we are no different from his peons, we are only better dressed and better fed. Please, my love, we don't need anything from him.

Amos gently but with equal insistence entreated her to agree to the don's terms. Her father was only trying to assure his only child's happiness, Amos told her in his most earnest manner. By agreeing to Don Victor's conditions, they would prove to him what she already knew—that he, Amos Bentley, loved her so much that he was willing to meet any stipulation to satisfy her father of the sincerity of his affection. Believe me, my love, said Amos, who had told her of his orphan childhood, I have long known the pain and loneliness of being without a family. You do not want to be estranged from the only family left to you. How much better if we can live in harmony with your father and preserve the family. Don't you see? Don't you agree? Isn't that more reasonable?

She finally gave in. But not without a woeful suspicion that, in some vital aspect, Amos might not be so different from her father. A suspicion that, like her father—perhaps like all men—Amos was not averse to using any tactic necessary, with anyone, in order to have his own way.

In addition to the certainty that young Bentley would persuade Teresa to accept his conditions for their marriage, Don Victor fully expected that, at some point before the elapse of the two years, his daughter's infatuation—he was certain it was no more than that—would come to an end and she would send the gringo packing. Not only did that not happen but, as the don became better acquainted with Amos, he found the young man to be quite pleasant and, even more important, possessed of a shrewd talent for business in general and bookkeeping in particular. In fact, Don Victor was so impressed with the young American's talents that, by the day of the wedding, Amos had already been the head bookkeeper of the Nevada Mining Company for almost a year.

※

The nuptials took place in the ballroom of the Hacienda de las Nevadas. The spring day was bright as a jewel, the air cool and sharp and seasoned with pine. John Roger and Elizabeth Anne were among the guests, as was Charles Patterson. Many of the attendees were from Mexico City, and nearly as many of them British or American as Mexican. Don Victor was effusive in his welcome of the Wolfes and said he had been looking forward to meeting them. After the ceremony, the party sat to a banquet in the central courtyard, followed by dancing to the music of a full orchestra. Spiders of special breed imported from Guatemala had spun canopies of connecting webs from tree to tree in the courtyard and the webs had been sown with gold dust, suffusing the courtyard with a lovely amber haze. At one point John Roger saw a young mestizo waiter gazing in open wonder at the enwebbed gold whose worth he could not have begun to estimate—then receiving a rap to the ear from his overseer who barked for him to get to work if he knew what was good for him.

When Don Victor joined the Wolfes and other guests for a glass of wine at the newlyweds' table, the topic under discussion was national politics. There was a chorus of loud approbation in response to someone's expressed hope that Porfirio Díaz would become the next president, and glasses were raised in tribute to the general. Don Victor took the opportunity to inform the Wolfes that he had been friends with Don Porfirio since the time of the Yankee invasion, when they were both fifteen. They had served together in a Oaxaca guard battalion composed of schoolboys like themselves, but much to their great disappointment they had not been sent into combat. At the end of the war Victor returned to his engineering education, but Porfirio, who had been studying for the priesthood prior to joining the ranks, had found his true calling as a soldier. Do you know, Don Victor said, that Porfirio's birthday is on the eve of Mexico's day of independence? It's the truth—and what could be more fitting? It was Don Victor's iron opinion that only General Díaz could end the antagonisms between Mexico's many political factions and unify the nation in a common cause. He is destined to be the president, Don Victor said. Take it for a fact.

John Roger had heard the same thing from almost every hacendado of his acquaintance. He thought it curious that so many Creoles held in such esteem a man whose own blood was mostly indigenous. It was no secret that Díaz's mother was a Mixtec Indian and his father a mestizo. Despite a warning look from Amos, John Roger said that Don Victor might be right that General Díaz would one day be president, but Benito Juárez was very popular with the masses and it should be as difficult for Díaz to beat him in the next election as in the last one.

Juárez! The don spoke the name as if it were a vile taste in his mouth. That heathen half-pint and his filthy Indian rabble are the ruin of the nation. It is long past time for the makers of Mexico to rescue the country from them. General Díaz is our greatest hope, and I assure you, sir, that one way or another he *will* become the president!

Before the don's fervor grew any hotter, Amos Bentley stepped up on a chair and called for everyone's attention and proposed a toast to his dear friend, John Wolfe. I owe my happiness to him, Amos told the assemblage. It was Don Juan who secured my employment with the Trade Wind Company, and it was through the Trade Wind that I was able to make the acquaintance of so many fine people, a series of acquaintances that led me to my darling Teresa Serafina. So here's to you, Don Juan, for your hand in the making of my great happiness. "Salud!"

The toast was cheered and—for the moment—the subject of Díaz set aside.

※

It was the finest spring they'd known in Mexico. The hacienda abloom with color, the air rich with the aromas of flowers and rain-ripened earth. As they took their post-dinner stroll in the garden one evening, admiring the beauty of the quarter moon, the brightest comet either of them had ever seen flashed across the sky. Elizabeth Anne shut her eyes and he knew she was making a wish, as she always did on spying a shooting star. Then she looked at him and said, "You too, quick!" He smiled and said there was nothing to wish for, that a man could not ask for better fortune than his.

Some months later, on a sultry summer night at Ensenada de Isabel, as they lay embraced in the big hammock of the cove house verandah and looked out at the stars over the gulf while the jungle blackness chirmed and screeched, Elizabeth Anne reminded him of that night in the garden and of the radiant shooting star and said that the wish she'd made had come true. They were going to have another child.

❋

"I don't know why *now* any more than I knew why last time," Nurse Beckett said. Her hair had gone grayer and the lines of her face deeper in the nearly fifteen years since John Samuel's birth. "But at this rate, you'll be sixty when you have your next one." Elizabeth Anne gave a gasp of mock shock, and they both burst into girlish giggles.

Underneath her levity, Nurse Beckett was apprehensive. She had not forgotten Elizabeth Anne's difficulty in bearing John Samuel at the age of twenty-one, and she was now thirty-six. And though he never said so, John Roger was worried too. As inexplicable as the pregnancy itself, however, was the easiness with which it progressed to term, an easiness that allayed their fears. During her carriage of John Samuel, Elizabeth Anne had been sick almost every morning, but this time did not have a single instance of nausea, or much discomfort of any sort other than the general nuisance of her swelling. The trouble-free pregnancy was the more notable because she bloated even larger this time and her quickening was more pronounced, the stirrings and kicks in her womb more insistent than John Samuel's had been. Nurse Beckett predicted a strapping boy.

Even the labor itself was easier than the time before—ensuing shortly after sundown on the eve of the vernal equinox. Josefina, that ageless grandam, was once again on hand to assist Nurse Beckett. John Roger again paced in an adjoining room with his fist in a ready clench to endure Elizabeth Anne's howls. But she this time made little outcry beyond a few sporadic yelps. Shortly before midnight John Samuel, incipient adulthood already evident in his face, came downstairs in his sleepshirt to ask if the baby had arrived. John Roger said not yet, and they paced together, father and son.

In the first minutes of the new season, Elizabeth Anne let her only piercing scream of the night, and John Samuel fixed wide eyes on his father. "It's only natural, son, don't worry," John Roger said. "Soon now. Soon."

They were still awaiting the baby's cries of arrival when the bedroom door opened and Nurse Beckett stood there staring at John Roger, unable to cohere into words the dejection on her face. He at once knew the child was dead.

He rushed past Nurse Beckett into the room with no thought but to embrace Lizzie in their shared bereavement. Her eyes were closed as before, her face as deathly pale. He sat on the edge of the bed and patted her hand and told her everything would all right, then bent to put his arm around her. And only then saw the prodigious soak of blood beneath her and in that same freezing moment felt the

118

uninhabited stillness of her. His breath stopped. He drew back from her and looked about, for a moment blind with shock. And then saw Josefina sitting across the room, her skeletal face the color of earth and hung with the weight of her woe. Holding a swaddled infant in each arm.

As their father's wrenching anguish rang through the house, the newborn twins held their unblinking stares on John Samuel at the door, his red glare raging, *You killed her! You killed her!*

THE SECOND TWINS

Even as Elizabeth Anne's body was being readied for the wake and her grave being dug in the casa grande graveyard and the spreading news of her death raising a collective lament that would for months hang over Buenaventura like a lingering sickness, Reynaldo the mayordomo was sending men to comply with Josefina's urgent requisition to round up every wet nurse to be found on the compound or in the villages of Santa Rosalba and Agua Negra. Of the thirteen young mestizas brought to her, Josefina dismissed eight out of hand because they were nursing their own infants and she wanted one who would feed only the twins. The other five had lost their babies shortly after birth and were still lactating. From each of them Josefina pinched a drop of milk from a nipple and tongued it off her finger, and by this cryptic assay decided on the youngest of them, Marina Colmillo, barely a month past her fourteenth birthday.

Only six days earlier Marina's baby son had been bitten by a poisonous spider and died within hours. She was a shapely thing of early bloom and had been impregnated when raped by a pair of strangers who came upon her washing clothes at a small riverside clearing—jaguar hunters, she believed, judging by their clothes and the guns they carried. She had fought them and clawed one of them blind in one eye and that he did not kill her for it was a wonder. But he wrecked her face in beating her insensible before spending himself in her. Her resultant disfigurement— the scars and missing front teeth and awkward knit of the facial bones—was like some primitive mask. Her only living brother had set out in pursuit of the violators with a machete in his hand but he did not return. Some weeks later, a party of parrot catchers in the jungle came upon his deliquescent corpse, boiling with insects but recognizable by the absent big toe lost in a childhood mishap, the skull bored front and back by the huge bullet of a jaguar gun. Marina had been motherless since age nine, the sole female in a family of violent men, all of them now dead, and ever since the loss of her brother she had been living with family friends. She had always been an isolate soul, even in childhood, and could not abide the company of a clutch of gossiping women, which was why she habitually shunned the communal wash point and did her laundry at a place well upriver from it—and why some in the village believed that what happened to the snooty girl was no less than she deserved. The combined facts of her rape and its consequent bastard and her disfigured face and her lack of shame in any of it—her refusal to turn away from stares, her habit of singing to herself while going about her chores—made for poor odds she would ever receive an offer of marriage.

She was quartered in a room across a small hallway from the kitchen. Whenever she was not nursing the infants she served as helper to Josefina. Even after the boys were weaned, Josefina would retain the girl as her assistant. And if it could be said that the twins were reared by anyone other than themselves, it was by these two women, one of them already old at the time of their birth and the other not much more than a child herself.

For planting the seed of them in her, John Roger would always place on himself the foremost blame for Elizabeth Anne's death. But he would for years carry a suppressed anger at them for being twins and demanding more effort of her to bear them than she could survive. He was aware of this resentment and knew it was irrational and it shamed him, but he could not rid himself of it. Nor of his anger at Nurse Beckett and the medical science she represented. Nor of his bitter sense of betrayal by the crone Josefina for not having saved Lizzie as she had done before. In days to come he would again and again order himself to stop assigning blame for what could not be helped and was no one's fault. And would time and again fail to obey his own enjoinder. And yet, regardless of his displeasure with Josefina, he would not put the babes into anyone's care but hers.

Neither would he ever do otherwise than as Elizabeth Anne had wished, and she had wanted to name the baby, if it should be a boy, Sebastian Cortéz, after her father and Josefina. "I've not always been entirely admiring of Father," Elizabeth Anne had said, "but I've always admired his name." And though he himself did not care for her father's name, John Roger christened the boys James Sebastian and Blake Cortéz. He had always been partial to "James," and his choice of "Blake" was a capricious and secret deference to his own father.

They came into the world, these twins, with an instinctive understanding that it was a treacherous place in which no one could be trusted except each other and

122

that secrecy was a valuable device. They had neither one cried out when Nurse Beckett slapped their bottom—a sure indication, Josefina would tell them, that they were masters of pain and that little could hurt them. And they had emerged from their mother with their eyes open wide, an unmistakable sign to Josefina that God had given them the gift of seeing the truth of things, and never mind those who would say it was more curse than gift because the truth was more often a despair than a comfort. No gypsy woman with her cards or bones or ball of glass could know the truth of someone so truly as the twins would know it with one good look in the person's eyes. It was a power granted them from birth and with no need of language, and in their first minutes of life they saw in the eyes of the women in the room that their mother was dead—and saw in their brother's glare that he held them at fault for it. And only a short time later, as they suckled at Marina Colmillo's breasts, their father loomed into view and they had their first close look at his face and even through the distortion of his grief they saw his accusation too. During their earliest years they would sometimes see in his eyes the question he would never speak aloud and was perhaps not even conscious of—Why not the two of you instead of her? John Samuel's opinion would never matter to them, but they would always place a secret value on their father's estimation, and his silent indictment and the distance he kept from them because of it would be the sole rue of their childhood.

Josefina herself had proficiency in the language of eyes and so from the start was aware of the twins' feelings about their father. They were still very young when she told them that they must not believe he did not love them. She had known him a long time and she knew he loved them very much. It was his loss no less than theirs that he could not tell them so. His loss that his own heart had become such a stranger to him. All men were confused by love, Josefina said, some in more terrible ways than others. Their father was confused because he could not help but relate their presence on the earth to their mother's enraging and sorrowful absence from it. It was unjust and unreasonable that he should hold them in any way responsible for her death and he probably knew it, but love cared nothing for justice or reason. The prisons and madhouses and graveyards were full of people put there by an unbearable loss of love to infidelity or death or some other misfortune. But as always and with all things, Josefina told them, what cannot be remedied must be endured. Their father was a man of many strengths but he did not endure well.

—❦—

They could never know how much their father differed from the man he was before their birth. Could never know it despite all that Josefina would tell them of him, she who had known him since his first day in Mexico, and despite what they would learn of him by other means. The father of their early childhood was aloof and unforthcoming and shared little of his company with them except at dinner, the evening meal, the only one to which the four Wolfes sat together, always in suits and ties. Even then, his conversation was usually with John Samuel and mainly about hacienda matters. The dinnertime attention he gave the twins was mostly to correct some deficiency in their table etiquette or reprimand them for some mischief of which they stood accused or interrogate them about some mischief of which they were suspected. John Samuel rarely addressed the twins at all, at the table or any other time, which was fine with them.

They were in fact very curious about their parents, but their father's unwillingness to tell of himself or of their mother was made clear to them when they were six years old and asked him what their mother was like. There was an odor about him in those years they would in time come to know as that of mescal. He stared at them with eyes like wet stones and said, "What does it matter?" And left the room. They had pledged to themselves never again to ask him a personal question or request anything of him. Nor would they give him a truthful answer to any question he should ask them—if they should deign to give him any answer at all other than a mute smiling shrug more defiant than words. They loved him, yes, but that did not mean he was the only one who could make rules about how things would be.

And so it was from Josefina that they got their early learning about their parents. When they asked her how their father lost his arm and she told them the story they grinned like wolf pups. *That* is your father, the old woman said, the man who killed that hacendado brute. Your father was a lawyer and a man of business before he became patrón of Buenaventura, but I tell you it is not lawyer's or merchant's blood in his veins. Or in yours.

She expected them to ask what kind of blood she believed they and their father possessed, and she could only have said she did not know, except that it was not that of lawyers or merchants. But they only asked, What about John Samuel? She made a gesture of uncertainty and said that Don Juanito was a clever young man and they should respect him as their older brother. But the greater part of his blood was of their mother's people, who were mostly bookkeepers and politicians, with the exception of her Uncle Richard—Uncle Redbeard, as their mother called him—whom she had loved the most of all her kin for the simple reason that he and she were the only two of their kind in the family. Josefina would over time pass on to the twins all the stories she'd heard from their mother about "Tío Barbarosa" and some of the things he was said to have done, including his attempt to smuggle guns to the rebels during the gringos' civil war. The boys loved those stories. It was clear enough to them that even though Uncle Redbeard had engaged in various legitimate businesses, he was at heart a rebel for sure and maybe even an outlaw. The way he died, they said, was proof of it.

Josefina commended their astuteness. It is a saying as old as Mexico, she said. Tell me how you died and I will tell you who you were.

❈

Their first view of their mother was a framed daguerreotype portrait that Josefina kept on the wall of her little room. Elizabeth Anne had seen her admiring it one day on its parlor shelf and had presented it to her. The photograph had been made in Concord ("*Cone*-core," Josefina pronounced it) when Elizabeth Anne was seventeen years old and only a few weeks before her wedding.

The twins thought she was beautiful. Josefina told them she was even more so in the flesh, that no picture could ever show how beautiful she truly was. When she told them of their mother shooting the younger Montenegro to save their father's life, their eyes shone. And they studied her picture all the more.

Of all that she knew about their parents, Josefina would withhold from the twins only the fact of their father's two bastard children—bastards in that he sired them by women he was not married to, though the children were officially legitimate in being born to married women. Both of those births, and the dire aftermath to one of them, had occurred before the twins were seven years old, and Josefina saw no need to burden them with the shameful fact of their illegitimate siblings.

But they were always better informed than she knew. They had the ears of cats and missed little of anything even whispered in their proximity, and from earliest childhood they were skilled eavesdroppers and peepers. They were nine when they discovered the cracks in the patio shutters through which they could spy on the maids at their bath—and coincidentally overhear much bathing room gossip. By age eleven they knew all about their baseborn kin but let no one know that they did, and they would soon enough dismiss them as trivial effects of their father's sporting, of which they were also aware and regarded as insignificant.

THE BASTARDS

The first child had preceded the second by a year and was born to Alma Rodríguez, an unmarried eighteen-year-old resident maid in the casa grande. John Roger had been having relations with her for three months when she told him of her condition. He remedied the problem in quick order by finding her a suitable husband, choosing a Veracruz police clerk named Pedro Altamonte, who'd been vouched for by Comandante Mendoza himself. Pedro was an intelligent and good-natured young man, but a birthmark that covered half his face like a brushstroke of purple paint had always made him self-conscious and timorous with women. John Roger had a talk with him, then bought him a new suit to wear and took him to Buenaventura to meet Alma. The clerk's eyes brightened at his first sight of her, in her best white dress and with a silver ribbon in her indigo hair. The three of them sat in a drawing room and had a frank discussion, and the couple agreed to the marriage. As John Roger had anticipated, knowing Alma for a sensible girl, she was appreciative of Pedro's manners and admired his education and bureaucratic position. She made light of the birthmark and said she would sew shirts for him of a color to match. Pedro was happy to gain such a pretty and congenial wife for the simple price of granting his name to the child she carried and swearing to cherish it as his own. He had been told whose it was and he felt honored. John Roger bought them a house for a wedding present.

Their marriage would be a good one and they would both live to a contented old age. In addition to the first child—a daughter they would name Juana Merced and whose actual father they would always keep secret from her—they would have three more children, all of them girls. They would all survive to adulthood and would be educated at the excellent school of the Sisters of Divine Mercy. After graduation Juana Merced would work for the school as its registrar. She would one day fall in love with a visiting director of a female academy in Barcelona, they would marry in Veracruz, and five months after their arrival in Spain she would give birth to the first of their seven children.

⚜

The matter of the second child was not so free of tribulation. The mother of this one was Katrina Llosa de Ávila. She was also a maid in the casa grande but did not reside in it. Like most of the household help, she lived in one of the little row-houses in the compound's residential quarter. She was without debate the prettiest woman on the casa grande staff—some, herself among them, would have said on the entire hacienda. The other women resented her for her vanity and because she had always been a flagrant flirt and had stolen the boyfriend of more than one girl. Since childhood she had entertained fantasies of being the wife of a hacendado and living a luxurious life in the manner of Doña Isabel, and she had long admired Don Juan from afar. But even after she had been working in the casa grande for six months, John Roger did not know she existed, as she was assigned to a lower-floor section of the house where he never had cause to go. Not until after the head maid reassigned Katrina to the bedrooms on the upper floors did John Roger take notice of her. On her third day of upstairs duty, he met her in a hallway as she was passing by with a large armload of fresh linen and towels. A pretty girl and a strong one, he said, and asked her name. "Katrina, mi patrón," she said, and gave him her best smile.

The next morning, after a swim in the garden pool, he returned to his bedroom just as she was making up his bed. Her back was to him and she had one knee up on the mattress and was reaching across the bed to adjust the covers. The thin cotton skirt molded itself to her fine rump, and the raised hem exposed almost all of one lean brown leg. He made a small sound he was unaware of making and startled her. She spun about and met his eyes. And smiled. He shut the door behind him and their clothes flew. He had not had a woman since his last time with Alma, more than eight months before, and he was so becrazed with desire he did not even wonder if she were married. He anyway would have assumed that, like most of the household girls, she was not. As for Katrina, she had decided beforehand that if he should ask if she were married she would tell him the truth. But he did not ask.

In fact, everyone in the house but John Roger knew she had been married for more than a year to Alfonso Ávila. He was an army corporal posted sixty miles away at the garrison in Orizaba and had not received leave to come home in over five months. He had been a mason at the hacienda when Katrina married him on a passionate impulse when they were both seventeen. He was handsome and strong but, unlike her, illiterate. They'd been married three months when they went to Veracruz one Sunday to attend the wedding of a friend and that night Alfonso got into a drunken street fight and beat a man to permanent paralysis. He was jailed overnight and then given the choice of enlisting in the army or facing a sure conviction for maiming and several years in prison.

No sexual escapade in the casa grande could be kept secret for very long, and within hours of its occurrence the don's dalliance with Katrina was known to the entire staff, just as they'd known of his intimacies with Alma Rodríguez. But the housemaids were proud of their trusted position, and it was a rule among them never to gossip of household affairs or of the don—except of course among themselves. They knew how much Don Juan had loved Doña Isabel and how desolate he had been since the loss of her, and they understood the respite, however illusory and short-lived, that sex could give to loneliness. They did not regard his sexual indulgence as disrespectful to la doña's memory, nor had they disapproved of Alma Rodríguez, who had been single when she comforted the don with her flesh. Katrina Ávila, on the other hand, they deemed a shameless wanton who had betrayed not only her absent husband but Don Juan as well—by withholding from him the fact that she was wed. They all knew the patrón was not one to take advantage ever of another man's wife, regardless of her willingness. His conduct in that respect was well established and in contrast to that of many hacendados, some of whom still exercised a patrón's ancient Right of First Night with the bride of any worker on their estate. When Josefina got word of John Roger's cavort with Katrina, she went to him and informed him the girl was a wife. He was furious, and ashamed of his own carelessness. The next day, in the privacy of his office, he rebuked Katrina for her lie of omission and demoted her from the casa grande staff to the compound dairy.

Had anyone asked her why she'd done it—which no one did or would—Katrina would have said she didn't know, or that it was just a foolish impulse of the moment. Had she pressed herself for a truthful answer, she might have admitted she'd done it for adventure. To enliven her dull life. But she hadn't figured on losing her position in the casa grande—nor on a far more serious consequence when two months later she realized she was carrying Don Juan's child. She bemoaned the wretched luck that would impregnate her on a single mating with the patrón, while all of her husband's tenacious efforts had thus far been fruitless, much to his disappointment. She debated with herself for days before deciding she would go to the curandera of Santa Rosalba, who was said to be highly skilled at relieving this sort of difficulty. The decision of course carried risks. Some girls had died in consequence of the procedure. And even if it went well, her visit to the curandera was sure to attract the notice of nosy villagers who would speculate about its purpose. What if such talk should make its way from the village into the compound and maybe even somehow become known to Alfonso? Still, what other choice did she have?

But bad fortune was not yet done with her, and on the morning of the day she intended to go to the curandera, Corporal Alfonso Ávila came rushing through the door with a great loud laugh and snatched her up in his arms and spun her around as he told her of the ten-day leave the army had granted him and wasn't this a wonderful surprise! He lofted her onto the bed and didn't even fully remove his pants in his rush to make love to the wife he had not seen in so long. For the whole week he was home they mated at least thrice daily—and thus was Katrina's course set. Maybe this time we will be lucky and make a baby, Alfonso said.

We can only hope and pray, she said.

A visit to the curandera was now out of the question. Should Alfonso learn of it, he would believe she had murdered his child. It was all she could do to wait a scant month before sending him the happy news of their baby in the making. In his response by dictated letter Alfonso proclaimed great joy but asked how she could be so sure so soon.

She wrote back that there are some things a woman just knows.

By then, some of the older women with whom she worked at the dairy had begun to suspect the truth, and their gossip reached the casa grande and Josefina's ear. When she told John Roger that he may have seeded a child in Katrina, he put his head in his hands. I do not mean to be disrespectful, Don Juan, the old woman said, but perhaps it would be best to do it only with courtesans from now on. They do not have such accidents. That was the word she used—"cortesanas." Her scolding sarcasm galled him, but she withstood his glare with equanimity until he looked away.

Katrina delivered a son in July, much earlier than she had claimed to expect him, and the child's complexion and facial features told the truth of his paternity to everyone who saw him. As the news made swift circulation of the hacienda, there was little faulting of Don Juan and much malicious derision of Katrina Ávila, who was mortified. On learning from Josefina that he was without doubt the father, John Roger cursed. Then sighed. Then sent a man to Katrina with a purse of silver specie. Beyond that, he could only wish her well.

Katrina kept to her house to care for the baby and lived in terror of the day Alfonso would know the truth. She waited for more than two months before sending him the news of the baby's birth, allowing him the assumption that it had just been born. Alfonso's response was full of joyous declarations of love but included also a profane tirade about the goddam army, which in the past month had reduced him to the rank of private and was restricting him to the post indefinitely, all because of a little fight with another soldier who happened to lose an eye.

The baby was nearly six months old before Private Avila at last received leave to go home and see him. And as Katrina had feared, he perceived the truth at once and flew into a rage. The neighbors too had expected him to know at first sight that the child was not his and they had debated among themselves whether he would kill Katrina or merely maim her. They in any event expected a loud and impassioned entertainment and they got it. But they were disappointed by its brevity. Alfonso had hit Katrina only a few times before she was able to divert him with the purse of silver. He sat at the table and counted it twice. It was more money than he'd ever thought he might hold in his hands.

Everyone would agree it should have ended there. Like everybody else, Alfonso knew that many a man's wife on many a hacienda had been obliged to attend a patrón's bed. It was a common humiliation of hacienda life, one against which hacienda workers had no legal recourse, which they could only endure. But it was a rare thing for a patrón to make any sort of recompense for an act he could by right exercise with impunity. Like everybody else, Alfonso knew that too. But Katrina was his *wife*, goddammit! *His* wife. Had he known John Roger had thought she was unmarried, his pain would not have been so sharp. You could not after all blame a man for enjoying a woman he supposed to be single. But he assumed that the don had known she was married, and he never thought to ask Katrina whether that was so.

Katrina had of course been afraid he would ask that very question. She knew how much worse it would go for her if Alfonso should learn that the full extent of her perfidy included having withheld from the don the fact of her wifehood. She had thought about lying if Alfonso should ask, but she knew the lie would not stand up to the patrón's denial, and so she determined to tell the truth. Tell it and hope to survive the consequence. But tell it only if Alfonso asked. And he didn't.

She would later say that Alfonso had seemed resigned to the situation. He sat at the table and toyed with the silver pieces and drank from a bottle of aguardiente. He did not say anything about the patrón that could be taken as a threat. His sole reference to the don seemed directed to himself as much as to her—that at least the father wasn't some stupid good-for-nothing. A neighbor woman looked in to see if Katrina was still alive, then took her and the baby to her house to treat the bruises on her face.

Alfonso counted the money once again, then drank the last swallow from the bottle. He was pleased about the money but felt in need of more drink to soothe his agitated soul. He could have bought another bottle in the hacienda store but he did not want to chance running into anyone he knew and having to converse, so instead decided to go to the cantina of Santa Rosalba. As he walked across the compound plaza toward the main gate, those who recognized him were surprised to see him and would later say he seemed disturbed by their smiles of welcome. Not until afterward did the possibility occur to them that he thought they were laughing at him for the horns on his head.

Earlier that day John Roger had gone out to the coffee farm, and that afternoon he happened to come riding back through the gate as Alfonso Ávila was crossing the plaza. According to witnesses, Private Ávila stopped in his tracks at the sight of the patrón on his trotting stallion. One observer would describe Alfonso as looking like he had just remembered something very important. John Roger was unaware of him but would not anyway have known who he was, never having met him. He reined up at a fruit stand and told the vendor the mangos looked delicious. As the vendor sought the best one for the patrón, Alfonso walked over to a gardener's wagon parked at the fountain and took a machete from it.

Cries of warning drew John Roger's attention to the soldier running at him with a machete raised to strike. He reined the horse around hard just as Alfonso swung at him and the blade sliced into the animal's neck. The horse screamed and reared and there was a fount of blood as Alfonso yanked the machete free and fell down. John Roger tumbled from the saddle and landed on his back amid an outburst of panicked shrieks. The screaming horse bolted and Alfonso barely managed to roll out of its way. Then got up and started toward the don again. Supine and breathless, John Roger drew his revolver from under his coat and shot Alfonso twice, the first bullet hitting his shoulder and jarring him half-about and the second punching through his side and knocking him down. Alfonso struggled to get up, still gripping the machete, lung-shot and streaming blood from his mouth. He was on all fours when John Roger shot him above the ear and the bullet exited the other side of his head in a scarlet spray and ricocheted off a stone wall and smacked the haunch of a tethered burro and the animal flinched and brayed.

John Roger's breath returned in a rush. The fruit vendor helped him up and people came out from behind the wagons and trees and walls where they had taken cover. Somewhere his horse was screaming without pause—and then a rifle shot silenced it.

He stood over the dead man and asked "Quién es?" and was told he was Alfonso Ávila. And then remembered Katrina's husband was a soldier, and understood why the man had wanted to kill him.

The flesh, he thought. The damnable flesh.

Take him to Santoso, he said. And headed for the casa grande as Alfonso was gathered up and borne away to the coffin-maker.

The six-year-old twins had been playing in a room at the rear of the house when they heard the faint screams and the first two gunshots and then the third. They ran through a series of hallways to the forward part of the house and out onto a shaded balcony from where they could see the plaza. A crowd was flanking their father, who held a pistol and stood beside a soldier sprawled in a puddle of blood, a machete in his hand. The twins would never speak of their witness of this scene except to each other and it would be a few years yet before they came to know the particulars of it. But observing unseen from the shadow of the balcony, they understood that their father had been attacked and had in retaliation killed the attacker. They grinned at each other, proud of a sire so adept at self-defense. And with but one arm.

John Samuel also saw the aftermath. He was working on some ledgers in his office when the sudden screams of the horse got his attention and then came the gunshots. He hurried from the office and across the hall into a room facing the plaza and from the window saw his father assisted to his feet and then stand over a fallen soldier as a throng gathered about them. There was a great deal of blood. It took

John Samuel a moment to comprehend that the soldier was dead, that his father had shot him, and he fought down the impulse to be sick. He stood unmoving until his father started toward the house, then he went to the main stairway and there waited until he heard him enter the main room. Then went down to him, saying, "Father! My God! Are you all right?"

John Roger saw his son's pale fright and assured him that he was unhurt. They went into the main office and John Roger poured drinks. John Samuel asked what happened, and John Roger said the attacker was a soldier married to a woman who'd once been a maid in the house. It seemed somebody of malicious intent lied to the soldier that the patrón had been taking advantage of his wife. "As I'm sure you know," John Roger said, "there are many false rumors about every patrón of every hacienda. It's unfortunate that sometimes the wrong men believe them."

John Samuel heard the tight timbre in his father's voice and knew it for the sound of a lie, the first he was ever aware of hearing from him. The lie saddened him even as the reason for it filled him with disgust. He had an urge to weep. How could you have been so weak, he thought. So unfaithful to your wife? To *my* mother? So disrespectful of her? And with a *housemaid*!

"I'm just . . . relieved that you're all right, Father."

John Roger was moved by the shimmer in John Samuel's eyes. He went to him and put a hand on his shoulder. "Everything's fine, son."

The next morning he telegraphed an account of Alfonso's death to the colonel in command of the Orizaba garrison. He explained that he had been obliged to shoot the soldier in self-defense when the man tried to kill him in a drunken fury and the mistaken conviction that he had violated his wife. The colonel wired back that the problem of drunken peón soldiers and their violent petty jealousies was nothing new to him and that he well understood what happened. Moreover, Private Ávila had always been a troublemaker. He thanked John Roger for the report and said he would greatly appreciate it if the don would see to the disposal of the remains. Alfonso was buried that afternoon.

Six weeks later he took Katrina and the baby to the train station in Veracruz, having arranged employment for her at a hacienda in Puebla. The rail line connecting Veracruz to Mexico City, with stations at towns in between, had been completed three years earlier, and shortly after its opening John Roger had commissioned his own rail track from Buenaventura to Veracruz for the transport of his coffee. The hacienda now had a depot with several side tracks and its own locomotive and freight cars, plus a passenger car by which John Roger had since made all his trips to Veracruz.

On their way there he asked Katrina if she had yet named her child. That was how he said it—"tu niño." The attribution did not escape her and she gave him a sharp look that made him curse himself for a stooge and wish he had said "el niño."

"Juan Lobo," she said. He said it was not amusing. She said it was not meant to be.

At the Veracruz station he escorted her to the platform for the Puebla train, together with the maid assigned to assist her on the trip and the armed man charged with protecting them. At the coach steps he gave her yet more money and entreated her to be careful and to take good care of the child.

You should be more careful too, Don Juan, she said.

He waited on the platform until the train at last lurched into motion with great reverberant clankings. Then raised his hand to wave goodbye, but she had already turned her face from the window.

ACCOUNT TO
THE COURTESAN

For a long time after the killing of Alfonso Ávila, John Roger was sick at soul. He was sworn not to father another child nor chance another gulling by a married woman or the wrath of another husband. He tried to work himself to a tiredness too great for much reflection. When he wasn't at the coffee farm he was at the horse ranch John Samuel had started on Buenaventura and named Rancho Isabela.

But there was no ignoring the crave of the flesh. He knew Josefina had been correct about the way to avoid such risks, but he had not forgotten his boyhood vow to abstain from prostitutes forevermore. A man was only as worthy as his word and no pledge he made was more important than one made to himself. A man who broke his word to himself would break it to anybody. Still, the more he thought about it, the more he began to construe his vow as a gesture of callow youth, as lacking the sanction of experience. In this fashion did his yearning grapple with his principles, off and on, for almost four years before he finally concluded that a grown man should not be ruled by an oath made as a boy. Besides, in a world of such fickle turnings, it seemed senseless to ever say never again.

He made his first visit to El Castillo de las Princesas on a starry November evening. A mansion that had once been the residence of a state governor, it was the most extravagant brothel on the Mexican gulf coast, an exclusive establishment whose members were all men of means and social station. It had a ballroom with a glass ceiling and a parquet floor. Every room was furnished with its own porcelain bathtub and canopied feather bed. All the girls of the house were young Creoles, none less than lovely, none without education or social poise. And all of them outcasts from landed families, disowned for one or another unforgivable transgression against the family honor, the details in each case known only—if known at all—to the madam and perhaps to some person who had guided the girl to her.

Ever a man of routine, John Roger began patronizing El Castillo on the first and third Tuesdays of every month. He chose a different girl on each of his first five visits, and the first four of them would have agreed that he seemed to take no true pleasure in the act but went about it in the way of a man who drinks only to be drunk. The fifth time, he chose a new girl, Margarita, who had come to El Castillo only the week before. She was pretty of course, but he could see she was older than the others. The others were girls, while she was a woman. She had claimed, with a wink, to be twenty-two, but even at that age would have been older than the next oldest girl in the house by three years. The general guess was that she was not younger than twenty-five and likely closer to thirty. She liked to joke about being the house senior. As she and John Roger ascended the stairs together, she said she was getting so old that before long she'd have to be carried up to the room.

After their coupling, they were lying side by side and gazing at the crescent moon framed in the black rectangle of the window when a shooting star described a bright streak just below the moon and was gone.

Quick, Margarita said, make a wish.

She shut her eyes to make her own wish. Then felt him sit up and looked to see him staring at the window.

What is it? she said, and put a hand on his arm. And he broke into tears.

"Ay, querido! Qué te pasa?" She sat up and put her arms around him and drew him to her. He heaved with sobs and she felt his breath hot against her neck, his tears on her shoulder. She rocked him as she would a frightened child. "Ya, mijo, ya. Todo será bien, mijito, ya lo verás." She rocked him and crooned to him and petted him, and after a time his sobs began to ease to a softer gasping.

She lay back, hugging him down alongside her, cradling his head in her arms, his cheek to her bosom. His nose was running and he snorted for breath, and she plucked her chemise from the bedpost and put it to his nostrils and said Blow, and he did, and she said Again, and he did. She wiped his nose and put the chemise aside, and again held him close. She felt his respiration begin to slow, the tension slackening in his muscles. "Dime, mi amor," she said. Whatever it is. You can tell me.

And he did. Beginning with Elizabeth Anne, of course, who had always made a wish at the sight of a falling star. Of whom he had spoken to no one since she had been taken from him. Nearly eleven years now and still there were moments of emotional ambush when he missed her so much he would forget to breathe. He told Margarita of their meeting and marriage and moving to Mexico. Told her of their first child, who was quiet and studious and dearly loved horses. Told of their two later ones, the identical twins she died giving birth to.

"Ay, pobrecita," Margarita said. "Que terrible. Que triste."

Yes, he said. And fell asleep in her arms.

From then on he wanted none of the other girls, only Margarita. He kept his account paid for months in advance to ensure her availability to him for the entire evening on his two Tuesdays every month. Each time he came to see her, they would first make love and then talk. Or rather he would talk, for the most part, and she would listen. She was a good listener, her interest unfeigned, and she did not hesitate to say so when he was unclear in anything he told. He would then try to clarify what he meant, realizing she hadn't understood because he hadn't been sure what he was trying to say. In this way did she help him to better understand himself. Sometimes he would pause in his discourse and stare at the ceiling or out the window and she would wait in silence for as long as he needed to ponder before he resumed, though sometimes he would first have to ask Where was I? and she would remind him.

He spoke to her of things he had kept to himself in a hard and solitary confinement for these eleven years. He was still troubled that he could not remember the last thing Elizabeth Anne had said to him. She had said something to him a minute or two before that but he had never been able to recall what it was. Josefina told him la doña had said that the pink sky in the window was lovely, that she wished she knew what kind of bird was singing in the patio, that her backside itched. Doña Isabel said many things before you left the room, Josefina told him, and whether she was saying them to you or to somebody else and which was the very last thing, well, who knows? You know she loved you, that is all that is important. Let her last words be whatever you would like them to be. He told the crone such reasoning was self-deluding and called her an old fool. She said it was even more foolish to put so much importance on memory, which was the greatest deluder of all.

He had tried every night for a week after Lizzie's funeral before he was able to compose a coherent letter to her parents and notify them of her death. The response was written by her father, the first letter he had ever posted to Mexico, and was terse and to the point. It advised John Roger that Mrs Bartlett was nearly mad with grief and excoriated him for his utter lack of judgment in having taken Lizzie to "that filthy, wretched place with its dearth of proper medical facility," a lack that had no doubt contributed to his daughter's death as much as had her husband's own recklessness. Mr Bartlett demanded that her body be shipped home for burial in the family plot and that her children be sent to Concord as well, so they could receive "a proper upbringing." John Roger wrote back to say Elizabeth Anne was already buried in her family's plot and that their children would receive "a proper enough upbringing, I assure you, right here at home."

Mr Bartlett's next letter began with "Damn you" and closed with "Should you ever again show yourself in Concord, I swear by the Eternal I shall pummel you in the street." In an accompanying note of two lines, Jimmy Bartlett, now a full partner in the firm, warned John Roger that if he did not ship Lizzie's body to New Hampshire "I will go there myself to retrieve my Dear Sister's bones by whatever means necessary." John Roger did not answer either missive, and no Bartlett wrote to him again. And Jimmy did not come to Mexico.

~※~

He took to drink, though he had enough force of will to do it only in the evenings, when he would shut himself in his room with a bottle of mescal and linger over her photographs. As always, each picture revived not only the occasion of its making but a rush of other memories as well. Random recollections of her in radiant animation. Working the sails of their sloop and grinning under her sombrero. Gesturing for emphasis as she told him of yet another superstition or ghost story she had recently heard from the maids or old Josefina. Savoring a mango, its juice dripping from her chin. Swimming with dolphin grace in the shimmering cove. Smiling at him in the vanity mirror while she brushed her hair and he watched from the bed. A chain of memory after memory.

His mornings were glazed with hangover, yet he never failed to make his daily meeting with Reynaldo the mayordomo or to oversee the business of the coffee farm or to preside over the hacienda's Saturday court, fulfilling his duties with a mechanical competence. As the days passed in rote sequence he told himself to cease his self-pity, that he was not the only man who had ever lost a wife. And each time would rebut himself that no, he was not, he was just the only one who ever lost *her*. Every visit to her grave in the enclave cemetery was a keener despair. Each day was a raw new regret.

The self-pity nearly undid him. She had been gone four months on the evening he once again spread her pictures on the desktop, but this time, sitting in the low light of the desk lamp, he lingered on his mental image of her standing at the balcony with the smoking Dragoon in her hands—and thought how simple it would be to end his pain. He finished the mescal bottle and opened a drawer and took out her Colt.

He sat for a time, cocking and uncocking the big revolver, watching the turns of the fully loaded cylinder. Take out all but one bullet and it was Russian Roulette. In Mexican Roulette, as he'd heard it defined, you took out only one. In Drunk Mexican Roulette you didn't take out any. He envisioned the muzzle at his temple. Imagined a white blaze in his brain and his obliterated memories a scarlet mess on the wall. He could not imagine the nothingness to follow. He cocked the Colt again.

Where was best? Surest? He touched the muzzle to his forehead. His temple. Placed it in his mouth. The taste of the oiled metal was a novel fright. You would not want to fail, to achieve no more than a bad wound. Or worse by far, end up crippled. Paralyzed. Mind-damaged. Imagine the talk.

His gaze fell on a portrait photograph of her taken in a Boston studio on their second day of marriage. As she smiled for the camera she suddenly puckered her lips and smacked a kiss at him where he stood behind the photographer, who implored, "Madam, please! You must be still." She'd made a contrite face toward the camera, then smiled again and looked at John Roger and winked—"*Maaadam!*"—and his breath had caught at the absolute wonder of her. An hour afterward they were eating oysters on the half shell at a window table overlooking the harbor. He recalled the briny savor of the oysters, the clean tartness of the wine. Recalled that same smile beaming at him as they touched glasses across the table and she said, "To you, Mr Wolfe. Till death do us part. Love's dearest pledge." So had they toasted, but he did not dwell on the remark, not until all those years later when he sat at the desk with her loaded gun cocked in his hand, staring at the picture of her taken on that day.

Love's dearest pledge. Till death did them part. And he had thought death had done so. But as he stared at her picture he saw the truth. They were not parted. Not yet. Not while he remembered her. While he lived, she lived too—in the selfsame memories that tormented him for the lack of her living presence. Till death did them part. The pledge implied a fealty to life, an understood promise to hold to the memory of the other and damn the pain of it. To end the pain by such means as Drunk Mexican Roulette was a brute betrayal of that promise. He was not unaware of the banal cast of his argument but its effect was no less persuasive for that. And he put up the gun. He did not tell Margarita how many times since then he'd wondered if he simply lacked the courage to pull the trigger.

Margarita's eyes were wide. I know, she said. The temptation of it. I know.

He asked how she knew, but she shook her head and looked away.

<hr />

For more than four years after the loss of Elizabeth Anne he did not make love to another woman. But there were occasional late nights when a sudden remembrance of her without clothes—in her bath, swimming in the cove, lying beside him in the hammock of the moonlit verandah—would incite him to a frenzied masturbation that each time climaxed with him in tears. The more he recalled their pleasure in each other's flesh, the more he wanted to yowl with the loneliness of his loss, his great aching yearn for the feel of her, the touch. That was when he began taking Alma Rodríguez to his bed. And though the trysts with Alma mauled his heart with the knowledge that the flesh he was relishing was not Lizzie's and never never never again would be, he could not stop himself from returning to it again and again.

Then Alma got pregnant and he married her off. And then, fool that he was—selfish, stupid, self-deceptive fool who even after his experience with Alma would not yet face the truth that he was as much in thrall to the desires of his own damnable flesh as to the memory of his beloved—he bedded Katrina and she conceived too. And this time his selfish indulgence not only produced another bastard but provoked a man to try to kill him, and so made of the mother a widow as well. In consequence of which there followed another four years of maddening celibacy before his arrival at El Castillo de las Princesas.

❧

His recounts to Margarita followed no order of chronology. Now he might speak of a thing that happened last month, now of a thing that took place when he was ten years old. But no matter the sequence, he told her many things he had never told anyone else. Told of his boyhood in Portsmouth and of his mother and his grandfather Thomas. Told her even of his pirate father. He told of his own twin brother Samuel Thomas and of the last time he'd seen him and of his mysterious disappearance and how the realization that Sammy was dead had almost killed him too. And told how—fool that he was, fool!—he thought he'd never again know such heartache as the loss of his brother. He told of his college days among an elite society of well-bred classmates and of keeping secret from them the truth about his father. When he said he had kept that truth even from Elizabeth Anne because he was afraid to jeopardize her love, Margarita sighed and her gaze on him was one of great pity.

She asked to know how he'd lost his arm and he told her, though he could no longer vouch for the truth of the particulars. It seemed to him he was describing something he had not done but dreamt. His memory of it was mostly an amalgam of blurry images and roiled sensations, of heavy sabers and ringing of steel, an antic play of torchlight shadows, a hardness of cobblestones under knees and hand. The indescribable feel of driving a sword blade through a man.

He told her of Richard Davison. Of Amos Bentley, that resourceful young fellow who had married into a rich and politically powerful Mexican family. Of his dear friend Charley Patterson, who had continued to make visits to the hacienda for years after Elizabeth Anne's death. But Charley had known her so well that John Roger could not bear to talk to him about her, so they conversed mostly about the national upheavals of the day. They spoke often of Porfirio Díaz, who had become an avowed anti-reelectionist, and the little Texan had predicted that if Díaz were to lose to Juárez again in the next election he would rebel against him—which was what happened. John Roger had then accepted Charley's wager of one dollar that Díaz's rebellion would fail. And lost the bet when the federals scattered the rebel forces and Díaz went into hiding, no one was sure where, though some said he'd gone all the way to Texas. When Juárez dropped dead of a heart attack—a death the more shocking to most Mexicans in that the attack on his heart did not involve a bullet or a knife—neither John Roger nor Charley had known what historical turn to bet on next until Juárez's successor, Sebastián Lerdo, offered amnesty to all rebels who would lay down their arms, and Patterson bet another dollar that Díaz would accept it. John Roger took the bet and lost again. Díaz's public proclamation of his retirement from politics in order to devote himself to growing sugar cane on the gulf coast produced no bet between them because neither one believed him. They were sure Díaz was planning another revolt and were proved right when he pronounced against Lerdo in the spring. This time Díaz was triumphant. He took Mexico City in November of 1876 and only a few weeks later was duly elected president. One of his first official acts was to push through a constitutional amendment to prohibit reelection, and Patterson bet John Roger that Don Porfirio would in some way or other circumvent his own law when the time came. But Charley died during Díaz's second year in office and so never knew the outcome of their bet. He had last been seen alive as he departed a malecón café where he had eaten a late supper and had a lot to drink. In the morning his body was floating facedown in the harbor. He bore no mark of violence and still had money in his pockets. It was assumed he had fallen in by accident and drowned.

He was old and tired and I suppose a lot lonelier than anybody knew, John Roger said. Except for Lizzie and my brother he was about the best friend I ever had. I wish I had let him know it.

My mother used to say that if wishes were horses no one would walk. It was the first reference Margarita had made in any way to her own past, a subject he had a few times before tried to broach and which she always artfully sidestepped. He asked what else her mother used to say.

She smiled at this attempt to steer the conversation toward herself. I think maybe your friend Charley knew how much you cared for him, she said. I bet he was laughing up in heaven because he did not have to pay the dollar.

John Roger said he wasn't so sure about the heaven part but she was probably right about the laughing. At the end of his four-year term Díaz had honored his own law against reelection and did not run again. But everyone knew that the newly elected president, Manuel González, was an old friend of Díaz's and would be his puppet until the next election, when Díaz would again be eligible to run.

❈

They had known each other four months when Margarita asked to know more about his sons, to whom he had made only cursory mention in earlier visits. So he told of 26-year-old John Samuel, who had proved to have John Roger's own gift for numbers and had been helping him with the hacienda's bookwork since he was sixteen. He was a decorous man, John Samuel, with a keen mind for business, but he tended to keep his own counsel and rarely expressed his opinion on any matter that did not bear upon hacienda operations. John Roger sometimes wondered if even John Samuel's wife knew him very well. Next week would be the third anniversary of his marriage to Victoria Clara Márquez, whose family raised the finest horses in the neighboring state of Hidalgo. They'd met when John Samuel went to her family's hacienda near Pachuca to buy a Justin Morgan colt from her father, a fine man named Sotero Márquez. John Samuel had always been somewhat shy around women, but sweet-natured Vicki Clara was not only fluent in English and his intellectual equal, having been schooled by Jesuits, but she loved horses too, and so they had a shared enthusiasm. Sotero Márquez had been as pleased by the match as John Roger.

Did John Samuel and Vicki Clara have children?

They did. Juan Sotero would be two in June and Roger Samuel was now eight months old.

Margarita smiled wider. "Pues, ya eres un abuelo, viejo."

A sad truth, John Roger said. A grandfather. Me. How is that possible?

"Háblame de los gemelos," she said. You speak so little of them.

He said he hardly knew the twins. It was a terrible admission for a man to make about his sons. To make it worse, he couldn't even tell which was which. They were eleven years old and he still couldn't do it. All twins as they grow older became distinct from each other to some degree, but not these two. Not yet, anyway. They were mirror images. Still, a father should be able to recognize his sons, for Christ's sake, no matter how alike they look.

Nobody can tell them apart?

Well, maybe the kitchen maids. A crone named Josefina and her helper, Marina. But then nobody else had spent as much time with them. He had thought about asking them how they knew one from the other, but that would be absurd. Shameful. Asking the kitchen help how to tell his sons apart.

Margarita regarded him without expression.

I know Blake's nickname is Blackie, I've overheard James call him that. The crone and Marina have picked it up. Can't say I much care for it. Too much of the thug in it. In English, anyway.

"Blackie. A mi me gusta ese nombre." Did Blackie have a nickname for James?

Jake. But lately it's more often Jeck. I suppose because it's how the maids say it.

"Jake," Margarita said, pronouncing it with care. She liked that name too. Did they look like their big brother?

No. Johnny had his mother's green eyes and the same reddish hair, but they—

Their hair is black and their eyes are brown with little dots of yellow, she said. Am I correct?

Well, my hair's not that black anymore, and judging by what I see in the mirror my eyes have picked up a lot of red.

I bet they look just like you.

I think they look more like my brother.

Margarita laughed. Don Juan the twin has made a joke! "Qué milagro!" He smiled and bowed his head in acknowledgement.

Were they close, the twins and their older brother?

John Roger sighed. Not in the least. And it had always bothered him that they weren't. He supposed it wasn't really so strange. As twins, they would naturally be much closer to each other than to him, or to anyone else, for that matter. Plus there was a huge difference of fifteen years between them. Still, there seemed to be more to it than that, he wished he knew what. For some reason they just didn't like each other.

But they are close to each other, the twins, no?

That, he said, was an understatement. He had thought he knew all there was to know about twinhood and had believed no brothers on earth could be closer than he and Sammy had been. But these two! They had a communion that was ... what to call it? Mystical would not be an exaggeration.

Margarita grinned. *Really*? So strange as that? Tell me, are they happy, these mystical twins?

They seemed to be. They liked to laugh. That was another difference between them and Johnny. He couldn't remember John Samuel ever laughing except for his first ride on a horse. The thing about the twins' laughter, though, is that it usually seemed to come from some private joke between them, some joke about you. They were like that about everything. They rarely spoke in anyone else's presence, even to each other. You might see them talking at a distance, but when you closed to within earshot they became clams. They were strange, there was no other word for it. They no sooner learned to walk than they were exploring every foot of the house and the patios and gardens. By the age of six they were climbing trees with the nimbleness of monkeys, they could scale rock walls like lizards. They were eight when they learned how to vanish within the house and not be found by the entire staff's most thorough search. Nobody ever saw them come out of hiding, either, so you never knew where they'd been. It spooked the hell out of the maids when they disappeared like that—except for the crone and Marina, who only got irked that the twins knew the house better than they did, who had lived in it so many years more. After each such vanishing act, John Roger would reproach them for upsetting the household and demand to know where they had been, but they would only shrug, their eyes full of amusement. He would lock them in their room as punishment. Then hear them in there, wrestling, laughing, reading aloud to each other.

Margarita grinned. How does the poem go? Stone walls do not make a prison? He said he was glad she found it all so amusing. She grinned at his sarcasm.

It didn't occur to him until a year ago that the only real punishment for them would be isolation from each other. So the next time they committed a serious infraction—he couldn't recall what—he locked them into separate third-floor rooms without any books or toys, and congratulated himself for his cleverness when he heard no laughter from within either room. But when he checked on them after a couple of hours, the rooms were vacant. They had gone out the windows and negotiated a six-inch ledge all the way along the side of the house and around the corner and then leaped onto a tree and climbed down and made away. For three hours the staff searched the entire casa grande enclave in vain, scouring the courtyards, the patios, the gardens, the stable, even the cemetery. John Roger concluded they must have somehow slipped out into the larger compound and was about to order a wider search when one of the housemaids reported that the boys had been found in their room. When he got there they were playing cards on the floor. They looked up at him and smiled.

The next time, he locked them in the armory. It was on the ground floor of the casa grande but had only one window, ten feet above the floor and with a hinged ironwork frame secured from inside by a padlock as big as a brick. The room was without furniture and the floor was of stone and he had the lamps removed. "Let's see how much you feel like smiling after a night in here without light or supper," he told them. He had a moment's qualm after locking the door but managed to suppress it. What father could permit such defiance to go unpunished? In the morning the barred window was open wide and the padlock dangling from it by its gaping shackle. The lock had been picked so deftly it didn't show a scratch. They had taken with them a pair of caplock pistols, a pouch of black powder and one of pistol balls, and two bayonets. It was five days before they were found in a forest clearing several miles upriver. They were slathered with mud against the mosquitoes and had built a lean-to of palm fronds and were maintaining a smokeless fire. With spears cut from saplings, they had killed birds and snakes and roasted them over the coals. Snake skins were drying on the sides of the lean-to and would be made into belts. They told the search party they could have fed on venison if they'd used the pistols but there wasn't much sport in shooting deer and the gunshots would have made it too easy for the trackers to find them. They were *ten years old*, for God's sake! They had never before been in the jungle. When they were brought back and I asked how they knew so much about living in the wild, they just shrugged, John Roger said, and smiled pretty much like you're smiling now.

Margarita laughed.

Josefina had overheard his interrogation of them, and later told him in private that the answer to his question was plain as the nose on his face. They know about the wild and all the other things they know, she said, because they have their parents' intelligence and you gave them the education to use it to learn things. The crone had a point, though he wasn't about to tell her so. He and Elizabeth Anne had naturally wanted their children to have the best education available, short of sending them to a boarding school, and as soon as the twins learned to talk he engaged tutors for them. It was no more than he and Lizzie had done for John Samuel, although in his case his mother had given him his earliest instruction herself. The twins' first teachers were brought from Veracruz, and by the age of five the boys could read and write in both English and Spanish.

They were six when he hired a tutor named James Dickert, who came with superlative recommendations from several prominent families in the capital. Educated in both his native South Carolina and in Mexico City, the bilingual Master Dickert was an eloquent man with a dulcet southern accent. For the next five years, until a windfall inheritance called him home to Charleston only a month before John Roger met Margarita, Master Dickert was the twins' sole tutor. It was an ideal match of teacher and students, and he educated them to rare degree. He every week showed John Roger the twins' compositions so that he could see for himself that their writing in both languages was cogent and lively and grammatically meticulous. Their recitations, Master Dickert reported, were fluent, their grasp of mathematics was sound. They were skeptical of history but they liked its stories and characters. They loved geography and were absorbed by the sciences, especially by the natural world and the workings of mechanisms. They learned that there was every kind of knowledge to be found in books and were quick to acquire the techniques for seeking it out in the vast library the Widow Montenegro had left behind, thousands of volumes, many of which had belonged to the Valledolids. Josefina sometimes thumbed through the books the boys kept piled by their bedside, and although she was illiterate the illustrations made clear enough what the books were about—guns, boats, the moon and stars, land and sea navigation, animal traps, rudimentary shelters, skinning and tanning, the human body. One anatomy text dog-eared at a graphic illustration of the female form. One book was all about locks.

Education is a good thing, Josefina had said to John Roger, but too much of it can lead to trouble. We must remember Adam and Eve. God warned them not to eat from the tree of knowledge because they already knew all they needed to know to be happy. But they ate the fruit anyway and we know what happened to them.

Yes, John Roger said, they gained the knowledge that it is unwise to disobey one's father, a lesson these two cannot seem to learn.

Maybe they have not learned that lesson, Josefina said, because of the way you have been trying to teach it to them.

And maybe, he said, *you* will some day learn how little interest I have in your opinion about anything outside of this kitchen.

Josefina shrugged. She told him the twins had taught Marina to read and write—in Spanish, of course. Marina is very smart, she said, but I believe the reason she learned so quickly is that they are good teachers. Some are, some are not. Then busied herself at the stove as if John Roger were no longer there.

He finished his coffee and left, keeping to himself his admiration for their tutorial achievement with a peon girl.

They had a facility for language, the twins, just as John Roger did, except that they used theirs mainly for mimicry. They sometimes spoke Spanish with the sing-song cadences of the crone's Chihuahuan inflections, at other times with the clipped diction of Marina's lowland dialect. In English they sometimes talked like Charley Patterson, who had died when they were eight, but they had known him long enough to emulate his locutions. It irked John Roger to hear them speak like Texan ranch hands, knowing they could exercise perfect grammar when they wished, and he had once admonished them for it. "Rightly or wrongly, others judge us by our mode of speech," he told them. "It therefore behooves a cultured man to speak in a cultured manner. Can you two understand that?" One said, "You betcha," and the other said, "Yessiree, good lingo's right important." They grinned—and he'd felt a sudden impulse to laugh, but managed to check himself and look away, shaking his head in disapproval.

"Son muy inteligentes," Margarita said. They have so many gifts.

They have so many gifts it's damned uncanny, John Roger said. In addition to their exceptional faculty for learning things from books, they had talents they were born with. Their skill with tools was something no one taught them. For the past three weeks they'd been building a little boat with no help but a manual, and what he had seen of it was an excellent job. And then there was their marksmanship. They had asked Reynaldo the mayordomo if they could use the armory pistols, and Reynaldo said he needed to think about it, then came to him. It displeased John Roger that they would not solicit his permission personally. As he had been aware for some time, they not only never asked him *for* anything, they never asked him anything at all. He had no idea why they had taken such a stance, but there was no mistaking they had. He was tempted to refuse them permission to use the guns until they came to him and asked directly, but the notion struck him as childish and he told Reynaldo to let them.

But Don Juan, Margarita said, even though it irritates that they will not ask anything of you, is it not commendable that they are of such strong independence? That they are of such strong will? Forgive my presumption, but perhaps you respect them more than you realize.

That they are of such hard heads would be nearer to the truth, he said. And you are indeed presumptuous, my dear. Have I ever told you how much you sometimes sound like the crone?

Margarita cackled.

The first time they fired the pistols, he heard them at it and went out on a balcony to watch. They were shooting at bottles they had set against the side of a dirt mound. So far as he knew, they had never held a gun except during their escape from the armory, and they had not fired them then. Yet they were scoring with every shot. At age eleven they were better shots than any man he knew. And come to think of it, better swimmers. Lizzie had been the best swimmer he'd ever seen until them. And what divers! Whenever they climbed a high riverside tree to make a dive, everyone in sight of the landing would stop to watch. He had often looked on from his window. From the highest branches they would execute perfect dives, plunging into the water with hardly more splash than a coconut. Sometimes they would not resurface for so long that some in the crowd would begin to cry out that *this* time they had surely drowned—and then their heads would pop up some thirty or forty yards up or down the river and the crowd would go wild with cheering. They are grand entertainers, John Roger said. Very popular with the folk.

Tell me, Don Juan, have you ever said to them that they are admirable swimmers? That their boat is a fine one? That they shoot well?

What for? They know what they're good at. And they don't lack pride about it, believe me. You can see it in their faces.

"Ay, hombre," she said with a reproving shake of her head.

When he first heard they were good fighters it had pleased him to know they could defend themselves. Then he heard disturbing things about one of their fights. They had seen some boys pouring lamp oil on a cat trapped in a fruit crate and they were going to set it on fire for fun. In preventing the cruelty, the twins badly beat up several of the boys, all of them bigger than the twins, according to Reynaldo. A nose was broken, a few teeth. Understandable things that could happen in a fight. But it troubled John Roger to learn that one boy had an ear ripped off, and that the twins' punishment of them didn't end with the beatings. They pinned the leader of the group facedown and soaked the backside of his pants with oil and set it aflame and then laughed to see him run howling for the nearest water trough with his ass on fire. Reynaldo had assured John Roger the burned boy would recover, although for the next few weeks he would eat standing up and sleep on his stomach. It bothers me, John Roger said, that they can be so vicious.

They were vicious only to punish the more vicious.

You and the crone, you just *have* to side with them don't you? Vicki Clara's the same way. I would think women had better sense.

You have a good heart, my darling, but you do not know women very well.

The simple fact was that the twins excelled at everything they took a liking to. They had begun riding at the age of six, just as John Samuel had. But while John Samuel had been obliged to train hard to make himself into the excellent horseman he now was, they could ride with an easy grace from the day they first sat on a pony. They did stunts no one else on the hacienda would even attempt. They would stand up on their galloping horses, riding side by side, and switch mounts in sidewise leaps. They would ride in pursuit of a chicken and position it between them and then one or the other would hang far down the side of his mount, clinging to the saddle with one hand, and snatch up the running bird by the head. John Samuel had witnessed some of these exhibitions and had been able to mask his resentment from everyone but his father. It's natural that he's a little jealous of their horsemanship, John Roger said, even if he'll never admit it. He loves horses, you see, but I think he believes the twins use them as only another way to show off.

Is that why he does not love them? Margarita asked. Because they are better horsemen? Because they are showoffs?

I didn't say he doesn't love them.

You did not have to.

Look, you have to understand something about John Samuel. It's hard for him to express his feelings. He loved his mother very dearly and her loss was very hard on him. They nearly died together when he was a baby. *Twice* they nearly died together. She used to sing to him at night—have I told you that? She sang him to sleep every night until he was eleven or twelve. She was his first teacher. He was fifteen when she died. I don't think anyone can know how terrible it was for him to lose her.

But the twins also lost her. That is terrible too.

It's not the same thing. They never knew her.

Maybe that is more terrible.

How could it be? You can't miss somebody you never knew as much as somebody you did.

"Pero que tontería, hombre!" she said. Of course you can! Even a child who never knew his mother knows what a mother is. To have no memory of her can be worse than to remember her at least a little.

He sighed. I don't know. If Lizzie had lived, then maybe all of them . . . ah hell.

She asked if he still locked them up for punishment.

Yes, sometimes. But he had reached an accord with them about it. If he put them in the same room they would stay there for as long as he decreed. He didn't even have to lock the door, not that a lock would have much effect. They had also come to an agreement about camping in the jungle. They could go for five days at a time but had to tell him or Josefina the direction they were going and about how far. It was an agreement made of air, since he couldn't enforce his conditions or even stop them from going short of chaining them to the cellar walls and posting guards at every portal—and even then he wouldn't be surprised if they escaped. And yet they had held to their end of the bargain. So far, anyway.

She wanted to hear more, but the hour was late and they were both tired, so they would have to wait until his next visit.

When he returned to El Castillo two weeks later the house mistress greeted him with a somber face and the news that Margarita was dead. Six days earlier, the afternoon post had included a letter for her, the only one she received in the four and a half months she'd been there. The house mistress recalled that the envelope bore no indication of the sender or the point of origin. She sent the letter upstairs to her, and some hours later, when Margarita still had not come down to begin her evening's duty, the house mistress went up to her room and found her on the bed, blue-faced and rigoring. On the bedside table was a nearly empty cup of tea and next to it the little vial of poison. A saucer held the letter's charred residue. She left no note. She was buried in the city cemetery.

The house mistress averted her eyes for a moment while John Roger regained his composure. He cleared his throat and asked if she knew why Margarita had done it. The woman shrugged. She said Margarita was not the first girl to work at El Castillo whose specific reason for being there or even her real name was known to no one in the house. She had shown up one day and said she sought employment. She gave her name as Margarita Damascos and admitted its falseness. It was obvious she was well-bred but she would reveal nothing of where she came from or even how she had learned of El Castillo de las Princesas. Then again, the house mistress said, it was not a profession that required the biographical facts of its practitioners.

John Roger wanted to know how it could possibly be that no one she had lived and worked with knew who she was. The house mistress said such a circumstance was far more common in this world more than he might think. She suggested the possibility that the person who wrote the letter was someone Margarita had never wanted to see again, almost certainly a man—a father, a husband, a lover. Someone who had somehow found out where she was and what name she was using and had written to tell her something she could not bear.

Like what? John Roger said.

Who knows? Maybe that he was coming for her.

If that were so, John Roger said, a lot of questions could be answered when that person showed up.

Possibly, the woman said. If that were so.

He went to her grave. The house mistress herself had paid to keep her remains out of the lowest ground in the cemetery—the mucky preserve of the criminal and the kinless and those without name—and had her buried in higher ground and under a simple stone tablet engraved with "Margarita Damascos" and "1880" below the name. He could not stop himself from imagining the unspeakable loneliness of the casket. The immutable darkness and silence of it. Her dead self within, so lovely and comforting and pleasurable in the warm living flesh and now but dark cold rot. He'd had similar thoughts and sensations at Elizabeth Anne's funeral, and now as then he was appalled by his rank perversity and did not believe that anyone of sound mind could have such macabre graveside imaginings.

He began calling at El Castillo once a week to see if anyone had come looking for Margarita Damascos. And was each time told that no one had. During the first weeks of this routine, he sometimes bought the services of a girl, but none of them was a listener such as Margarita had been and he soon gave up trying to talk to them as he had talked to her. Before long even his enjoyment of their flesh waned and he ceased patronizing them altogether, much to the annoyance of the house mistress. He persisted in his weekly inquiry for six months before concluding that no one was ever going to come in search of her—and whatever unendurable disclosure the letter had brought and she had put to the match would remain her eternal secret.

He would not return to El Castillo, and knew he would not again lay with a woman. And if his sexual memories of Elizabeth Anne would sometimes become too much to ignore and compel him to a weeping self-abuse . . . well, so be it.

DISCOVERIES

They made their first trip to the cove when they were fourteen years old, and they went there by running the rapids on a raft of their own making. They had by that time made numerous excursions into the jungle and were sometimes gone longer than a week. Josefina had scolded them for disobeying their father by never telling her which way they were going and for how long, and Blake Cortéz had said Well, if he asks, tell him we went north. She asked if that was the truth and he grinned and shrugged, then dodged the swat of her cane. If you two think I'll keep lying to your father for you, you're very wrong, Josefina said. Then tell him the truth, James Sebastian said. You forgot what we told you because you're too old to remember anything.

"Ay, que desgraciado sinvergüenza!" Josefina said, swinging her cane.

John Roger had never tried to enforce his provisos on the twins' jungle ventures. But the raft was a different matter. Reynaldo the mayordomo had thought so too. He was not one to relay to John Roger the twins' every peccadillo that came to his ear, but when his informants told him the twins were building a raft at the landing just above the start of the rapids and that it was nearly finished, he could guess what they intended to do, and he thought it his duty to tell their father. In all the collective lore of the hacienda, nobody had ever survived the rapids.

That evening at the dinner table John Roger told the twins he knew about the raft and forbade them from attempting the white water.

"Yes sir," one said, and the other nodded and said, "Whatever you say, sir."

He knew they were lying. They were going to try it no matter his prohibition or what punishments he might threaten. He had thought of putting men at the landing to prevent them from shoving off. Of having the raft destroyed in the night.

But if he did either of those things they would just build another raft in secrecy and on some other stretch of the river. He told himself he was a damned fool for even thinking of trying to stop them.

He had been feeling this sense of foolishness about the twins for some time. Since the day when he was just about to restrict them to their room yet again for some infraction or other but suddenly saw no point to it, not even as gesture. The punishment was an illusion, after all. They would stay in the room for no reason except they agreed to. They could escape whenever they wished and they knew he knew it. That's when it occurred to him that everybody knew it. Nothing of interest ever happened on Buenaventura that did not immediately become part of its circulation of gossip, and the twins' previous escapes from his efforts to punish them had surely been bruited through the compound and even out to the villages. The gist of such talk—as he learned from Reynaldo after insisting that the man be entirely candid with him—was an amused admiration for the twins' daring and resourcefulness, and a sincere sympathy for the patrón, a worthy man of great dignity except in contesting with his twin sons. John Roger had felt the embarrassment of it like a well-deserved slap. To be pitied by peons for his indignities with the twins— good Christ! Thus did he recognize the folly, the very ignominy, of trying to force them to his will.

He excused himself to Vicki Clara as he got up from his chair, then left.

John Samuel glared at them from across the table as Victoria Clara gave careful attention to her soup. Their brother's censorious scowls had become so familiar to the twins that between themselves they had taken to calling him Mister Sourmouth. One evening in the library they had referred to him by that name before remembering Vicki's presence, then saw her small smile even as she kept her eyes on the book in her lap.

They grinned at John Samuel's hard look. "What about you, hermano mayor?" one of them said. "Will you spare a tear when we are drowned?"

"I'll never understand why Father tolerates your insolence," John Samuel said, rising from his chair. "Were I in his shoes, I would have packed you off to a military school years ago."

The twins laughed, and one said, "Father's shoes would fit you like a pair of washtubs."

John Samuel reddened, then started for the door. Then stopped and looked back at Vicki Clara, who seemed unsure what to do. "Señora?" he said. She dabbed at her lips with her napkin and gave the twins a fleet commiserative smile as she got up and then accompanied her husband from the room.

Two days later they made the run, waiting till sunup before shoving off—the ride would be hazardous enough without attempting it in less than full light. They lashed their knapsacks tightly to the deck and checked and rechecked the tightness of the ropes engirdling the raft and once again rosined the pushpoles to ensure a good grip. They could faintly hear the rush of the white water where it began a half mile downriver. Each time they caught each other's eye they grinned.

When the sun was risen into the trees they threw off the lines and pushed off. They hadn't gone fifty yards before the current began a swift acceleration. They slid the pushpoles under the deck lashings and took off their hats and crammed them under the knapsacks and lay down side by side on their stomachs and took firm hold of the cross-deck rope lashed taut over the planks. The raft was going faster yet and swaying from side to side and the river ahead grew louder. Then they saw the white water directly before them and saw too there was a small drop just ahead of it and then the raft seemed to leap off the river before smashing down into a snarling torrent and they were pitching and bucking and the jungle was a green blur to either side of them as the raft rocketed downriver and was jarring off one cluster of jutting rocks after another and rearing skyward and plunging headlong and tilting sidewise and almost overturning and then banging off one steep bank to go spinning across the deranged river and bang off the other as the boys held on with all their might and bellowed in wild glee as they were slung about with arms twisting and legs flapping and at times they were in weightless detachment from the raft entirely but for their grip on the crossrope before again being slammed against the deck so hard that for days after they would be dappled with bruises. They sped along on the wild water, yawing and lofting and plunging and wheeling through a drenching tumult for some six miles, by their later estimate, that passed under them faster than they could believe before the river vanished and they were aloft—having arrived at a small falls they'd had no idea would be there, that nobody on the hacienda knew was there. The raft fell for what seemed to them an eternity of terrified elation—and was in fact a drop of almost twenty feet—before they collided with the water below in a foaming crash that clouted their heads against the deck and nearly banged them unconscious and loose of the deck rope.

They could not have said which fact was the more astonishing, that the raft was still right-side-up or that they were still on it.

The falls marked the end of the rapids. The twins lay dazed and gasping as the raft carried in a slow swirl away from the crashing water. Blake Cortéz said something but James Sebastian couldn't make it out and yelled, "*What?*"

"I *saaaaid*, goddammit . . . it's *goood* to be *aliiive!*"

"You can say that again! Man, I saw *stars!*"

They had knots under the hair plastered to their foreheads, and their mouths were bloody, but they had lost no teeth and their bones were intact. They hung over the side of the raft and slurped up water and rinsed out the blood, then looked at each other and started laughing again. And kept at it for a while for no reason but it felt so good to laugh.

"Say, friend, tell me something," James Sebastian said. "Who would you say are the best rivermen in the whole wide world?"

"Well sir," Blake said, "as it is contrary to my nature to engage in mendacity except when necessary to gain my objective or the plain damn fun of it, I'd say in no uncertain terms that it's them there inimitable Wolfe brothers."

"You mean them two that kinda look alike except the Jake one's better-looking?"

"No sir. I mean them other two that sorta look alike except the Blackie one is by far the handsomer as any mirror will attest."

"Oh *him*! The simple one with the poor eyesight who tries so hard to hide his ignorance behind a lot of fancy words. *That* poor fella."

"In point of actual fact, sir, the gent to whom you allude has got the visual acuity of a hawk and the intelligence of Aristotle, qualities so obvious to one and all that only the mentally deficient can fail to perceive them."

They carried on in this way even as they took up the pushpoles and steered the raft along the center of the current's easy glide. The trees down here were even taller and more densely leaved than above the falls, their shadows deeper. The light held a green haze. The boom of the falls began to fade as soon as they rounded the first meander, and soon the only sounds besides the twins' voices were bird cries and the high chatter of monkeys. The riverbanks here were of altered character. No longer blunt and lined with reeds like most of the banks above the falls but low-sloped with narrow beaches.

And roosting all along them, like a littering of dark and rough-barked logs, were crocodiles.

They could derive no explanation for them. Upriver of the rapids, a crocodile was a rarity, though alligators common. But no alligator that had ever been brought back to the compound landing had exceeded thirteen feet, while most of the crocodiles here were longer than that. They saw several that exceeded fifteen feet before Blake said, "Christ amighty, Jeck, lookee there!" He directed his brother's attention to the bank ahead where lay a monster of no less than seventeen feet. "That's a goddam *dragon*!" As the raft went gliding by, some of the crocs slid into the water and vanished but most remained still as stone on the narrow beaches. There were more of them around the next bend. The twins agreed they looked like money just waiting to be skinned off and rolled up.

They then began to notice skeletal fragments of sundry sorts littering the banks. A section of horned cow skull. Segments of ribcages large and small. "*That's* how come there's so many here," Blake said. "Everything that goes into the river up there ends up down here."

"That's right," James Sebastian said. "Think of all the guts and scraps the slaughterhouse sweeps into the river every damn day. And no telling how many cows and burros and pigs and dogs fall in and get washed down to all these waiting jaws."

"Falls in or gets thrown in, dead or alive," Blake said. And pointed at a portion of human cranium on the bank. "Whatever goes in alive is sure as hell dead by the time it gets here, and good thing, too."

"It's how come these fellas are so big and fat. They don't hardly have to work to eat their fill."

"Hacendados of the river," Blake said.

For most of the next hour of their slow downriver glide they saw no lack of crocodiles. But as the raft went farther downstream, where less and less of the river carrion carried, their number dwindled until there were no more to see. Then the raft went around yet another bend and they saw bright light ahead, where the trees gave way. And arrived at the cove.

They whooped as they cleared the trees and glided onto the sunlit water. "Ensenada de Isabel! We're there, brother!" Blake shouted. "You *smell* it? You smell that sea?"

James said he smelled it and heard it too, just beyond the palms across the way. They spied the house on the low bluff where they knew to look for it, and were surprised to see the dock still standing off its beachfront. Farther down the beach, at the south end of the cove where it had been landed by some great storm and who knew when, the *Lizzie* lay on its side, its broken mast angled awkwardly but not completely sheared.

As they poled toward the dock, they directed each other's attention to this or that part of the cove, to the clarity of the water and the green wall of jungle and the mouth of the inlet they were now at an angle to see. They eased up to the end of the dock and made the raft fast to the same posts on which the *Lizzie*'s snapped mooring lines still hung into the water. They leaped onto the dock and ran to the beach and raced around its south end and past the *Lizzie* and to the far side of the cove and through the stand of palm trees to the rocky shore and hollered in exultation at their first sight of the Gulf of Mexico.

"*Look* at it, Jake! Just *look* at it!" Blake yelled, hair tossing in the wind, arms spread wide as if he would embrace the entire sea. They stood there for a time, beholding the sunbright breadth of gulf, then went back through the trees to have a closer look at the rocky inlet.

They saw it was a tricky passage but told each other they could do it, they who had never yet sailed anything larger than a homemade twelve-foot pram on any water other than the nearly windless Río Perdido. Blake said the thing to do if you sailed up from southward was to go past this point a ways and *then* turn landward and run up just as close to shore as you could before heeling her over to come at the pass dead on.

"That's how I see it," James Sebastian said. "I'll man the tiller and you work the lines."

"That's exactly the opposite of how we'll do it."

"That so?"

They grappled and fell in the sand in a grunting tangle, and as usual neither was able to pin the other and they called it a draw. Blake then wondered how fast a fella could swim across the cove to the raft about eighty yards away. James grinned back at him and they threw off their clothes and crouched side by side on the bank and agreed to a count of three. In unison they counted "One"—and dove in. They cut through the water side by side with the smoothness of sharks homing on prey and did not slow down until they reached the raft and it was impossible to say which one's hand was the first to slap against it, the two slaps sounding like one. They argued in gasps about who had won and tried to dunk each other, then finally pulled themselves up on the planks and flopped onto their backs, chests heaving.

After a while they untied one of the two oilskin knapsacks lashed to the deck and took out a canteen and two of Josefina's cornhusk-wrapped tamales filled with bits of goat meat and red chile. They sat cross-legged and ate the tamales and passed the canteen between them and studied the house on the bluff. After fourteen years of neglect and the poundings of sun and rain and at least four hurricanes, its only visible damage from where they sat were a few missing shingles and a front shutter hanging askew and patches of peeling paint. Beside the house was a small stable with a collapsed roof.

After they ate they took ropes and machetes and went over to the *Lizzie* and examined her and found no holes or cracks in the hull. They hacked off the mast at the point where it was broken and dragged it out of the way, then attached one rope to the sloop's bow and one to the stern and then pulled in tandem, first on one rope and then on the other, now dragging the bow closer to the water and now dragging the stern, and in this bit-by-bit manner they worked the boat into the water. Once the sloop was afloat they climbed up into her and went below and inspected the interior hull and found only two minor leaks. Even as weathered as she was, the boat was free of serious defect other than the broken mast, which would be simple enough to replace. New sails and rigging, new fittings, some sanding, some oakum, a coat of paint, and she'd be ready for the open sea again.

Their confidence in the sloop's seaworthiness was founded on their study of boating manuals and the experience of having built a boat themselves, a little gaff-rigged pram. They named it for Marina, who fashioned its sail from flour sacks. It was a vessel of much mirth to the fishermen in their dugouts not only for its makeshift aspect but because the river breeze was frail at best and often nonexistent. A sailboat, even one this small, was simply out of place on the Río Perdido. Still, on its maiden try, the twins managed to sail it upriver for about a half mile with the weak breeze behind them before they came about and dropped the sail and rode the current back to the landing dock. The short trip took the better part of a day, and as they tied up at the dock they were aware of their father watching them from a high balcony of the house but did not let him know they had seen him. At that distance they could not see his smile nor anyway have known that he was recalling another small sailboat of another time and the young twins who often sailed it from Portsmouth Bay to the Isles of Shoals—and did so once in a squalling heaving sea.

They gained facility at sailing in the river's weak wind, but they hankered for the open sea they'd not yet laid eyes on and for a larger boat to sail upon it. When they learned of Ensenada de Isabel, their keenest interest wasn't in the cove itself or in its house but in the sloop their father kept moored at the cove pier. They wondered if the boat was there still, and if it was, if it might be in reparable condition. Very likely it was in ruin or long ago sunk. There was one way to know for sure. They had anyway been wanting to try the rapids everyone spoke of in such ominous voice. And so began to construct a suitable raft.

They were of course thrilled that the sloop was in reparable condition—and now that they'd seen the cove, were no less enthusiastic about the place itself, recognizing its manifold advantages. Its isolation and natural camouflage against detection. Its bounty of natural sustenance. And the house on the little bluff. They hauled the *Lizzie* out of the water again and up high on the beach, then went to retrieve their clothes and shook the sand from them and put them on. Then went back around the cove and up the bluff to have a closer look at the house.

The pilings looked like they would stand till the end of time. The gallery steps were solid, so too the gallery floor. The front door had swelled from the humidity and they had to shoulder it open. There was a smell of mold and decay and something else, some stink they could not identify, and they opened all the shutters to air the place. Spiderwebs everywhere, but the ceiling showed only a few water stains. An oil lamp lay in shatters on the floor. Some of the wicker furniture was overturned and one of the chairs was in shreds, but most of the furniture and lamps appeared functional. In the kitchen a window was missing its shutter and the floor held the dry mudprints of a young jaguar. In the pantry were a tattered sack of beans and a bag of salt hardened to rock, strings of jerky like sticks of black wood. The stink was coming from behind the bedroom door and when they opened it they startled a colony of roosting bats and they yelled and crouched down with their arms clasped over their heads as the creatures fled the house in a shrilling dark cyclone of beating wings. The reeking layer of guano on the floor made their eyes water.

They found the roof missing only a handful of shingles. The widow's walk was still securely in place and they marveled at the view from it. They checked the cisterns and saw they would need a thorough cleaning, but the piping system into the house was in good order. A shed behind the house held a variety of tools, most of them coated with rust. "He couldn't use much of this with just one hand," Blake said. "Momma had both hands," said James Sebastian.

They went back around to the front of the house and sat on the verandah steps and stared out at the cove and neither of them said anything for a time. They had reason to believe John Samuel's only time at the cove had been in his childhood and that their father had not been here since their mother's death. There was no sign of anyone else having been there in all those years, either, proof of how well the inlet was hidden from gulf view.

At length Blake said, "A fella could live out here real nice."

"Make himself a little money, too," James said. "What with all those hides just up the river."

They were there for three days, exploring the area around the house and clearing out the guano, shoveling several wheelbarrow loads before finishing the job on hands and knees with trowels and buckets, gagging even through the bandanas over their lower faces.

They slept on the verandah. The large hammock on which their parents had passed so many enjoyable nights was still suspended from the rafters, its craftsmanship and treated hemp resistant to the attritions of time and weather, and they took nightly turns sleeping on it and on a smaller hammock they hung beside it. They fed on coconut milk and mangos, on fish they caught on handlines and roasted over open fires, on oysters gathered from the shallows and pried open with their knives and eaten raw or after baking in the fire. And all the while, they talked about the enterprise they thought to operate from this place once they had fixed up the house and boat. They made a list of the materials they would need to make the repairs—the kegs of pitch and oakum and caulking and solvents, the buckets of paint, the shingles, the sails, the fittings, the special tools and so on.

There was of course a problem. One so obvious they had been skirting it and whose only solution was also so obvious that neither of them had to say it. A solution that held no appeal, requiring them as it would to renege on a vow of long standing. On the other hand, they told each other, things changed, and vows sometimes had to change with them. It was a matter of common sense.

"No matter how you cut it, it's gonna be double humiliating if the answer's no," Blake said.

"Yeah," James said. "I'd rather take an ass whipping. But there's no other way."

"Hell with it. He says no, we'll come anyway."

"And if some bunch comes after us, we'll go in the bush. Like to see them find us in there."

"And we'll re-mast that boat some kinda way and rig some kinda sail and—"

"—we'll start taking croc hides and—"

"—load em on the boat and—"

"Damn right."

⋙

They returned to the compound by way of the vestigial wagon track on which no one had passed since their father's last visit. Where it had not overgrown the track completely, the rampant foliage had narrowed it to an indefinite footpath and they had to hack their way through in some places. The jungle steamed, droned, shrieked as in some primeval madness. They daubed mud on their faces to fend the mosquitoes but the sweat kept washing it off and the bugs fed on them between applications. The brush slashed at their faces. At night they made a pair of small campfires on the trail and hung their hammocks low between them and under a drape of mosquito netting, and at every low growl from the surrounding darkness tightened their grips on their machetes.

They were two full days on that rugged track and arrived at the compound at a late hour of the second night. The guards opened the gates to admit them, and they crossed the plaza and vanished into the shadows and snuck around to the dark alamo grove adjacent to the casa grande's garden wall. In childhood they had dug various tunnels between the casa grande enclave and the main compound—and even one under the compound wall itself, running from the back of a stable stall out to a growth of brambles. Josefina and Marina had long suspected the existence of the tunnels and were sure that one of them ran under the garden wall, but the inner walls were lined with thorny shrubbery too dense for the women to search closely for the tunnel opening, and no telling where in the outer alamo grove the other end of the tunnel might be. It was a wonder to them the twins could pass through those thorns without a scratch.

They crawled through the tunnel and out into the shrubbery and then lay motionless, listening hard, making sure no one else was in the garden. Then crossed as silent as shadows to the kitchen door.

As soon as they entered the kitchen, where a lantern always burned through the night, Josefina came out of her room, belting her robe, her colorless hair hanging loose and her dark face pinched with sleep. She shook a finger at them and whispered reproofs for their rashness with the rapids. You're very lucky to be alive, she said. One of them made to hug her but she recoiled with a face of disgust and told them they stank to high heaven and their clothes looked like they were made of dirt. And your faces! You look like you've been trying to kiss cats!

"We have, but I'd rather kiss you, you temptress," James Sebastian said, reaching for her again.

She slapped him away with her skinny hand and said, "Cállate con ese inglés! Ya les dije mil veces!" She had never learned English nor cared to and had long since forbidden them from speaking it in her presence, yet they anyway sometimes did, either to keep her from knowing what they were saying or just to rile her for the fun of it.

Blake Cortéz said it had been easier to kiss the cats than to kiss her. She berated them for their disrespectful tongues and said not even to dream of sitting at her table without at least washing those filthy hands. Then she lit two more lamps and stirred up the oven fire and set about making tortillas and a skillet of eggs scrambled with grated sausage. Marina came from across the hall and made a small sound of dismay at the sight of their ravaged faces. She called them fools and hugged them, one with each arm. Then went upstairs with a lamp to inform their father, as he had instructed her to do if they should show up. He had been notified of their departure, the entire hacienda had known of it—the twins were trying the white water!—and had decided that if they were not back in ten days he would lead a party of men downriver along the old wagon trace to search for their bodies below the rapids.

He woke to Marina's light taps on the door and knew it was about them and he readied himself for the worst. "Abre," he said. She opened the door a few inches and he saw part of her face in the light of the lamp. "Dime," he said. She told him they were back and both of them unharmed. He thanked her and she said "De nada, Don Juan," and closed the door. He then lay awake for a time, staring out the window at the starry darkness. And thought, They did it, by damn. They *did it*!

❈

They were eating at the kitchen table when Marina returned. They asked what their father said and she told them he'd said nothing other than thank you but that she could tell by his voice he was glad they were all right. Josefina went into her room and returned with a small jar containing a salve of her own invention and gave it to Marina with instructions to apply the medicine to the cuts on the boys' faces after they bathed. She touched each twin on the head as if conferring a benediction and then returned to her room and shut the door.

When they finished eating, Marina picked up a lamp and ushered them into the patio and told them to fill the two tubs with well water and strip down and get into them and never mind complaining about the water being too cold. When they were babies she had bathed them in the kitchen, and then in the patio tubs when they were older. They had always liked to play with her breasts through her blouse at bath time and she never made objection. When they began to sprout erections in the tub she smiled at their pride in them, like young explorers who had made a grand discovery. They always giggled through the last stage of every bath when it was time to stand up so she could wash their legs and buttocks and little stiffies. Even after they were old enough to bathe themselves they would often ask her to do their backs, and though she would tease them for helpless children she usually complied. And always, as she attended to their backs, they would squirm around in the tub to face her and she'd return their sly grins and give their cocks a quick gentle squeeze. She was fearful that Josefina would discover them at this naughty play and always kept an eye on the kitchen door. She was startled the first time one of them—they were ten then—ejaculated as she was soaping him. He laughed and she joined in their grins, her hand at her mouth to hide the gaps in her teeth, an action that had become unconscious reflex. He boasted in low voice that they had both done it before with their own hands, and she called them nasty creatures and said they would go blind if they kept at it. In that case, the other one said, she should do for him what she had just done for his brother, not only in fairness but also because she would be helping to save his vision. You think you're very smart, don't you? she said, but was again covering her mouth. She glanced toward the kitchen door. Then put her hand to him too.

They were twelve when Josefina said they were too old to still be bathing in the patio and from then on they had to use a bathing room. They would give Marina a look each time they went off for a bath, and sometimes she ignored it and sometimes she would show up in the bathing room shortly afterward on pretext of making sure they had fresh towels and enough hot water. They would entreat her to wash their hair and scrub their backs, saying she could do it so much better than they could, and she would every time feign irritation and say they weren't children anymore and could bathe themselves quite well. Then position herself between the two tubs and oblige the rascals. While she washed their hair they would play with her breasts as always, and though they were now putting their hands inside her shirt she still did not chide them for it. But when they started trying to explore under her skirt she pushed their hands away and said, No you don't, little misters. They tried every time and she continued to rebuff them until one day—they were then thirteen—she thought Oh why not? And they touched her in ways that made obvious their familiarity with female anatomy—a familiarity they could have learned only by experience—and her own pleasure in the bathing games acquired new dimension.

One day as they were at this fondling game in the bathing room, a twin leaned forward and kissed her on the mouth and she flinched away in shock. She'd had willing sex with several men since the childhood rape that ruined her face but she had never had to question why none of them ever kissed her. The maiming had robbed her of all beauty above the neck except her hair, which at the time hung to the small of her back in a lustrous black spill, but she had refused to keep even that sole reminder of her former comeliness and cut it to a ragged crop barely covering her ears and kept it that way. When she recoiled from the kiss, the twins saw the stark self-revulsion in her eyes. They drew her to them and she made a small whimper as one of them kissed one side of her face while his brother kissed the other. Then they took turns placing soft kisses on her scarred lips. She broke into tears and clutched to them with an arm around each. One of them said they must be very bad kissers to make her cry and she laughed with them even as she wept. Then was kissing them and kissing them. And that day decided to let her hair grow long again.

On their fourteenth birthday, less than two months before they rode the rapids, she gave them the present of herself. Despite her brutal introduction to sex, she had learned to enjoy it in the years afterward but she had never imagined how fine it could be when appended to love. She had since made love with the twins many times, one snugged to either side of her in the sturdy little bed and caressing her as she alternated her attentions between them before coupling with one and then the other. Whenever they spent the night with her they always woke before dawn—Josefina the only one already risen at that hour and busy with the breakfast fires—and slipped up to their own room before the rest of the house came astir.

They finished filling the patio tubs and then stripped and eased into the water, protesting the chill of it, and she sneered and called them sissies. They sped through the washing and got out of the tubs and dried themselves and she made them wrap towels around their waists before going back into the kitchen to sit in the brighter light. She was tender in daubing Josefina's salve to their facial cuts, stopping at times to bat their hands away from her breasts and bottom, cutting looks toward Josefina's door and hissing at the twins to behave or she would give them even more bruises.

The salve was dark yellow and the twins made faces at the reek of it. "I bet she makes it from old dead dogs," one said and they both laughed. Marina asked what was so funny and one said, "Wouldn't you like to know?"

She said they had been told a thousand times it was impolite to speak English in front of her or Josefina and demanded to know what they had just said. The brothers grinned and one said in Spanish, We said wouldn't you like to know? They laughed as she swatted at them in feigned affront at the joke they were having on her and told them to hush before they woke the house.

She finished with the salve and they went across the little hall to her room and snuggled into her bed. But when they began to caress her she shrank from their touch. No, she said, not tonight.

Why not? one asked. What's wrong?

Affecting pique, she said, Wouldn't you like to know?

Then laughed at their expression and drew them to her.

<hr/>

John Roger was working at the big desk in his office the next morning when they appeared at the open door and asked if they could have a word with him. It was an effort to mask his surprise. They had never come to him unsummoned. He said to come in and pull a pair of chairs up to his desk. He took off his spectacles—he had needed them for reading these past two years and had long since become adept at opening them one-handed. He studied the twins' swollen and yellow-dappled faces. The only other time they had not looked identical was when their faces had been bruised in a fight defending some smaller boys against bullies. But, as then, the temporary difference in their facial markings in no wise let him know who was James and who Blake, and he felt his familiar guilt for not knowing.

"Guess you heard we rode the rapids," one said.

"I did," he said. "And yet here you are, still among the quick. No small feat."

"Yessir," the other said.

"Don't mistake my wonderment for admiration, and certainly not for approval."

"No sir," the same one said.

Such ready agreement was another surprise. He wasn't sure it wasn't ironical.

He gestured at their faces. "Vestiges of the saga, no doubt." He sniffed the air with a frown. "I take it that stuff is of the crone's making?"

"Yessir," one said.

"We just thought you ought to hear it from us, sir," the other said. "That we went on the rapids, I mean."

"I see. Am I to assume, then, you're here to receive your due punishment for disobedience?"

"Well, if you want to punish us, sir, you can," one said.

"I'm grateful for your consent."

"I didn't mean it like that, sir. Sorry."

And now apology! A dies mirabilis if ever there were one.

"So that's not why you're here."

"No sir," said the other. "Not actually."

The pendulum on the mantle clock sounded the passing seconds. "Are we waiting to see if I can guess?"

"Well sir," said one, "it's about that house on the beach."

"We went all the way down there, you see," said the other. "To that little, ah, bay, or cove I guess you'd call it."

There were footfalls in the hallway and they stopped at the office door. John Roger looked past the twins and raised his brow in question. The twins turned to see John Samuel gaping at them in manifest amazement. "I beg your pardon, Father," he said, "I didn't . . . I. . . ."

"Are those the shipment figures?"

John Samuel looked down at the papers in his hand. "Yes. Yes, they are."

"We'll review them in your office as soon as I'm finished here."

John Samuel seemed unsure what to do. The twins turned back to their father. "I'll be there presently," John Roger said.

"Yes sir, very well," John Samuel said. His footsteps receded down the hall.

"How did you know about the house?" John Roger asked.

They were ready for that question. "You mean before we saw it?" one said. "We didn't know about it before we saw it."

"We didn't even know about that little harbor," the other said. "We thought the river would take us straight into the gulf.

"When we got to the cove and saw the house, well, we figured you'd built it."

A quarter of a century ago, John Roger thought. Or near to it. A decade before they were born. The jungle at its back, the sea in its face. He had not been to the cove since Elizabeth Anne's death. The idea of being there without her was as lonely as a grave. "So it's still standing then?"

"Oh, yes sir, it sure is," one said. "You can tell nobody's been there in a long while, but it's in pretty good shape, all things considered."

"I shouldn't be surprised," John Roger said. "It was built by the best crew on the coast. You couldn't bring it down but with dynamite. You had to hike back, of course. I'll wager there's not much left of the wagon track."

"No sir, not more than a snake road," one said. "It's how come our faces took such a beating."

John Roger took a cigar from the humidor on the desk and cleanly bit off the smaller end and spat it into the cuspidor beside the desk and put the cigar in his mouth and patted his coat and then his vest in search of a match. One of the twins took a match from his shirt pocket and struck it on the rasp set into the lid of the cigar case and held the flame to his father's cigar and John Roger fired it to his satisfaction and nodded his thanks. He asked to hear more about the place, what it looked like now.

They told him in detail, and when they got to the part about the bats' panicked exodus from the bedroom—hunkering in their chairs with their arms covering their heads as they told it—his grin had a greater gusto than they had ever seen.

He was grinning as much at their theatrics and their capacity to laugh at themselves as at the tale itself. Grinning most of all in pleasure at the present moment, a moment he had thought past all possibility—his twin sons telling him things of their own volition, entertaining him. Their eyes showing the same light he'd seen in Elizabeth Anne's eyes when she first looked on the place and every time she spoke of the cove in the days thereafter. The too brief, too swift days thereafter.

They told him of the dock that still stood solid and of the sloop whose only major impairment was a sheared mast. Ah yes, he thought, the *Lizzie*. He could imagine their excitement at the discovery of it. They no doubt understood it was named for their mother, but they had never mentioned her in his presence and so it was unlikely they would allude to her even indirectly by saying the name of the boat. Their refusal to ask him about her, about himself, about anything, was as baffling to him as ever, but whatever their reason, he had to admire their tenacity in holding to it. Margarita had been right those years ago when she said he respected their will more than he knew.

He wasn't unaware of the sentimentality he was indulging, nor of his old guilt about them. Still, the moment they'd appeared at his door he'd known it was for no reason except they wanted something they could not have except through him. Wanted it dearly. And he now knew it was the cove. The cove with its sturdy house. And of course the boat—the boat for damned sure and maybe even more than the house. They would want to live there, naturally. In that wild isolation between the jungle and the sea. They had come to him in hope that he would grant their wish, even though they had little cause to believe he would. In addition to the gall they surely had to swallow to come to him, they were risking the ignominy of being refused. Such risk called for a different kind of courage from the physical sort they possessed without limit. He was impressed.

But he also knew they were not being fully forthright. As always with them, there were things they were not telling. Certain facts withheld. Secrets at work. He could sense it. He thought it likely they already had some use in mind for the place but he doubted they would tell him what it was. Then told himself, So what? He had come to fear that some day they would disappear into the jungle never to return and he would not know whether they had been killed or had kept on going to somewhere other without even a fare-thee-well. If he should give them what they wanted he would at least know where they were. Some of the time, anyway. Because once they repaired that boat their whereabouts would never be more specific than out on the gulf or someplace on its sizable coast, perhaps nearby, perhaps not. He knew that too.

They had been watching his eyes and had seen that they were going to get what they'd come for, and they restrained the urge to grin at each other.

He spared them even the need to ask. "Listen. That old house is just collecting mold. I don't know if you're interested, but if you want to fix it up so it's habitable, that's fine by me. If you're willing to do the labor, I'll underwrite the project."

The twins swapped a glance that to him seemed expressionless.

"Fix it up?" one said. "Well now, there's a thought."

"Yeah, it is," the other said. "Might be fun."

Their dissimulation struck him as more daring than artful, but he appreciated their quickness to employ it, given the opportunity. "It's a fine place for fishing," he said, "as I recall."

"Say now, we could maybe put a new mast on that little boat," one said to the other. "Do some fishing out on the gulf, sail around a little. I'm game. You?"

"Why not?" the other said. Then said to their father, "We'll be needing a bunch of materials, though. Supplies. Tools. There's tools there, but mostly in bad shape, as you can imagine."

"Get what you need from the compound store. Anything it doesn't have, tell Reynaldo and he'll order it from Veracruz."

"Firearms," one said.

John Roger stared at him.

"For meat."

"And protection," the other said. "As you know, sir, there's poisonous snakes and some awful big cats around there, to judge from some of the yowlings we heard."

"Yes there are," John Roger said. "Get what you need from the armory."

"Yessir, except, well, there's only those old muzzleloaders and caplock pistols. If we were in a tight spot and had to quick shoot at something more than once, well…"

"You want repeaters."

"Winchester's said to be dependable."

"Winchester," John Roger echoed.

"We understand they're hard to come by in Mexico, but we saw in a magazine that there's a place in New Orleans that—"

"I know a closer source," John Roger said. "I'll send word this afternoon and they'll be here in a few days. I assume .44-40s would meet with your satisfaction."

"Yessir," one said. "Forty-four forties be just fine." He rubbed at the edge of his eye as if to remove a speck as the other coughed lightly into his fist. John Roger almost smiled at their clumsy efforts to mask their pleasure. Whatever they had expected of this meeting it certainly wasn't that it would go in their favor—and for damn sure not as far as Winchesters.

"Reynaldo will get you the burros you need. And if you should ever improve that trail enough, you can have a wagon. Naturally, you'd need a labor gang to cut a proper wagon road, and that can be arranged."

"Well, sir," one said, "we'll probably hold off on that for a while, at least till we've taken care of everything else all good and proper."

John Roger understood him to mean they would never widen the trail. He should have known that. Why would they want to make it easier for others to get down there? They wanted to be hard to reach.

"Well, it's up to you. You're the ones who'll be using it. Anything else you want to ask for?"

They dropped their smiles. "We weren't asking, sir," one said. "Just stating the necessities."

"I see," he said. And thought, I'll be damned. They come hat in hand and I give them what they want without their having to ask and then they get proud about not asking. "There's one condition," he said. Until that moment he had not thought to impose a condition, but they were not, by damn, going to have it *all* their own way.

"Condition, sir?"

"You come home every, ah, two weeks, let us say. And you stay three days."

"But sir," one said, "why would . . . ?"

"If you want to make sure we're getting our proper nourishment," the other one said with a crooked smile, "well sir, we *can* feed ourselves."

He looked from one to the other. "That's the bargain, gentlemen. Feel free to turn it down."

"No sir, no, we're not turning it down," one said. "It's just that there's a lot of work to do and if we have to leave off from it for three days every couple of weeks, well, it'll take a whole lot longer to ever get done than if we can apply ourselves to it more, ah, consistently."

"Why don't we say . . . every three months?" the other said.

"Let's say at the end of every month," John Roger said, "and you stay two nights."

"Suppose we say—"

"Suppose we say it's settled."

They read his eyes. "Yessir."

He swept a pointing finger from one to the other. "Break the bargain and I'll send a crew down there with dynamite to blast that house to splinters and sink that boat a mile offshore. I hope you gents believe me."

"Yessir," one said. The other nodded.

He consulted the calendar on the wall. "We're already near the end of this month and you won't be ready to set off for a week or two. No sense in making you come right back at the end of June. You don't have to make the first visit till the end of July."

"All right, sir," one said.

"Well then," he said, "you had best get to it."

They were at the door when they turned to look at him, who was at the moment bent over a bottom drawer in search of a match to refire his cigar.

"Thank you, Father."

He was arrested. They had never thanked him, never called him anything other than "sir."

But when he sat up to look, they were gone.

-❦-

As they went out the casa grande's front doors, Blake said, "Any sonofabitches ever go down there and try to blow up that house—"

"Or sink that boat."

"Be the last damn thing they ever try."

"That's it."

They grinned at each other. Winchesters, by Jesus!

-❦-

The first thing John Samuel wanted to know when his father arrived at his office was what "they" had wanted.

John Roger told him of their intention to fix up the cove house and the *Lizzie*.

"I'm glad of it, frankly," John Roger said. "It'll give them something constructive to do."

"Will they be living out there from now on?"

John Roger sighed. "Most of the time, yes."

John Samuel looked out the window and smiled.

-❦-

That they had known about the cove and its house and boat before they ever went there was a truth they could not have admitted to their father without confessing to an act worse than their lie. A few months earlier, having just read about

167

the newest models of Colt revolvers, they recalled Josefina's description of the gun their mother had used to shoot the younger Montenegro. Josefina said it was the largest pistol she had ever seen. Shaped like a pig's hind leg, she said, and almost that big, and their mother had held it with both hands to shoot. James Sebastian was sure it was an old Walker, and Blake Cortéz said maybe, or a later Dragoon. They wondered if the gun might still be around.

The next time their father rode off to one of his all-day surveys of the coffee farm, they slipped into his bedroom and made a thorough search of it but did not find the pistol. They then went downstairs and sneaked into his office and Blake rummaged a wall cabinet while James Sebastian searched the desk.

"Not here," Blake said.

"Hey Black, look at this," James said. He was perusing a set of photographs he had found in the desk's middle drawer. They were old studio pictures, most of them of their mother, some of their mother and father together, a few of which included John Samuel, who was an infant in some of them.

"How young Father was," Blake said. "And Momma. She looks like a girl."

"This musta been made about the same time as the one Josefina's got."

They were tempted to take one of the pictures of their mother but thought their father might notice it was missing when he next looked through them, and they left the pictures as they found them. The Dragoon was in the top right drawer. James Sebastian took it out and saw that it was fully charged. He held it this way and that, aimed it at the map of Mexico affixed to the opposite wall, sighting on the heart of the country, on the Yucatán, at the rooster foot that was the Baja California territory. Then passed it to his brother, saying, "Feel the heft."

"Now this here's a damn *gun*," Blake said. He set it on half cock and with his other hand rotated the cylinder with a soft ticking. They had read much about the early Colts and if they had been obliged to load this weapon they had never set hand to before now they could have done so. Could have charged each chamber of the cylinder and seated a ball in it by means of the lever under the barrel and capped the nipple over each chamber for firing. "They say you can hammer ten-penny nails with this thing all day long and it'll still shoot straight as a sunray."

"Imagine what a .44 ball did to that boy's head Momma shot," James said. "About like a mallet would do a watermelon."

" Momma sure musta been something! Just imagine her shooting this thing."

"And good as she did."

"Like to shoot it myself, but we can't even ask Reynaldo to ask him. They'd want to know how we know about it."

They admired the Colt a while longer and then put it back in its drawer. Then thought to look in the others to see if they held anything of interest. The bottom right drawer and the top left one contained only business records. Then James Sebastian tried the bottom left drawer and said, "Say now." It was locked.

They examined the keyhole and recognized the kind of lock it contained and smiled at its simplicity. They had crafted skeleton keys that could open any sort of lock to be found in the casa grande, locks to doors and desks and trunks and such, but they liked to keep in practice with simpler implements. James opened his pocketknife and inserted the blade tip into the keyhole and made a careful probe and angled the blade just so and gave it a gentle turn and the lock disengaged.

The drawer held a leather-bound ledger and a document case. They took out the case and opened it and the first thing that came to hand was the framed daguerreotype of John Roger and Samuel Thomas on the day of their high school graduation. They stared at it for a time before James Sebastian said, "Do you believe *this*?"

"Cuates! Just like us."

"Not quite like us. One on the left's a little bigger in the shoulders, you can tell."

"Yeah. Doesn't tell us which one's Father though."

"Don't look to be much older than we are. And I thought he looked young in the ones with Momma."

"So that's Samuel, eh? Whichever one."

They had once asked Josefina if their father had any brothers or sisters and she had told them what their mother had told her, that John Roger had been orphaned with no sisters and only one brother, Samuel Thomas, an apprentice officer on a merchant vessel who was eighteen years old when his ship went down. Older or younger brother, they asked, and she said she didn't know.

"Why didn't she say they were twins, I wonder?"

"I expect she doesn't know or she would've."

"If Josefina doesn't know it's because Momma didn't know, either, and why wouldn't he have told *her*?"

James shrugged. "If Momma didn't know, she for sure never saw this picture. Bedamn if Father aint starting to seem like a secret-keeping man."

They laughed low. And now took from the case a rolled paper and unfurled it and saw that it was two papers—a letter with a bureaucratic heading, and rolled inside of it, an ink portrait.

"Looks like Father," Blake said of the sketch. "Except Father's name's not Roger Blake Wolfe and he aint dead yet, much less since 1829."

"Grandpap's my guess."

"Me too. Damn sure looks like Father, don't he?"

"It's how you'll look at his age."

"You too."

The letter was the one from the British Embassy to Mary Parham Wolfe. "Father's mam, must be," James said. They read it.

"Man was a goddam *pirate*."

"Begging your pardon, mister, he was a goddam *captain* of pirates. Says so right here, see? Captain."

"You suppose Momma knew *this?*"

"I'd wager she didn't."

They studied the letter again. "Says executed but not how," Blake said. "Hung for certain. It's what they did with pirates. And left them to rot on the rope. Our own granddaddy. Man, aint life just fulla surprise?"

"With a daddy like that, hardly a wonder Father's killed two fellas." James Sebastian said. Then grinned. "Two we know of, anyway."

"A grandpappy like that says something about a coupla other fellas I could name."

"We couldn't help it, Judge. It's in our blood."

They started to laugh and hushed each other lest they be heard by some passing maid. They extracted two packets of letters. Most of them were to their father from Richard Davison and to their mother from her mother, neither set of much interest to the twins except for the fact of their mother's maiden name—which they had thought was Barlet because of Josefina's pronunciation. Davison's letters were chockablock with details pertaining to the Trade Wind Company. Their Grandmother Bartlett's abounded with trivia about her family life. The brothers skimmed through them and arrived at the letters to their father from Sebastian Bartlett and James Bartlett, and after skimming these, they read them again.

"Who's he think he is, blaming Father for what happened to Momma?" Blake Cortéz said of Sebastian Bartlett's letter.

"A son of a bitch is who he is, grandpap or no. That goes for this James galoot too."

"Uncle James to you."

"I aint calling anybody uncle writes a letter like this to Father."

"Reckon he ever did come for Momma's bones?"

"Hell no. I think he was just blowing hard."

"Me too. If he'd come here to dig her up, Father would've stopped him cold."

"Hell yes, he would've. Would've done him like he did that soldier."

"Or like he did what's-his-name, the one Josefina said—"

"Montenegro."

"Yeah, that son of a bitch."

They opened the leatherbound book and saw what it was and Blake pulled up a chair so he could read along with James Sebastian. Its earliest parts had been inscribed at Dartmouth College and dealt mostly with fellow students and various academic notions. These entries meant little to them and they turned the pages swiftly, slowing only at their father's intermittent mentions of his mother and her father, Thomas Parham. They were interested most of all in his references to his brother, whose name they learned was Sammy and whom their father wished himself more like. "Our Physiognomies the same but Sammy's Spirit so much the more daring," their father wrote. They read of his desire to become a gentleman and of his fear that his classmates might learn the truth of his father's brigandage and about his brother's mysterious disappearance from Portsmouth.

"So he doesn't know what became of old Sammy," Blake said. "Or didn't when he wrote this, anyhow."

"Told Momma he was lost at sea."

"Maybe that's what he found out later, after he wrote this."

"Or maybe it was just another lie."

"Why lie about his brother? Think maybe he was a murderer too?"

"Who knows? But seeing how scared he was of his school chums finding out about his pa the pirate, I'll wager he never told Momma about Sammy either."

"That counts as a lie too. Lie of omission."

"Wooo, you're a hard judge, mister," James said.

"Hey, son, the law's the law, I always say. Law of the books, law of the truth."

There was an entry about his upcoming graduation and his disappointment at failing to qualify for valedictorian, and then the journal jumped forward by several months to a nearly illegible passage about his marriage engagement to "Lizzie"—his erratic penmanship occasioned perhaps by euphoria. Then a still greater leap in time to his first notation in Mexico, conveying his happiness over Lizzie's miraculous pregnancy. The next segment was five pages long and absorbed them above all others, detailing as it did what their father had learned about Roger Blake Wolfe from the Veracruz archives and the London genealogist.

"Well now," Blake said, "how about *this*?"

"Now we know. Firing squad."

"Girls fighting over him even when he's about to get shot."

"Buying drinks for his pals. Puffing a cigar. The man had aplomb, no question about it."

"Aplomb aplenty. How come shot, though? They always hanged pirates."

"Most likely offered the judge a little something to make it the muskets."

"You reckon? Hell of a note, having to pay to be shot."

"Beats hanging even for free."

"That's a point. They sure must've had it in for him to cut off his head after and stick it on a goddamn pike. Made his daddy and momma mighty mad about something too, to disown him like they did."

"Well, seeing as Grandpappy Roger was a pirate and his daddy was a navy man, I'd say they probably had different ways of looking at things."

"Roger's sure a right name for him, aint it? Man was a Jolly Roger in every way."

James Sebastian grinned. "A Jolly Roger and a Big Bad Wolfe."

"For damn sure! The Big Bad Wolfe of the family."

"The first one of it, anyhow." They muffled their laughter with their hands.

There was an entry about his great happiness over the birth of John Samuel, but the entries of the next five years consumed less than two pages, so terse and widely spaced in time were they. There were various mentions of Charley Patterson, whose mode of speech they liked so much, and references to "the company," and to people the twins had never heard of. Then came a lengthy segment about the house their father was building on the beach, and they learned of the cove he named Ensenada de Isabel and of their parents' great love of the place. There were a few pages of technical details pertaining to the construction of the house, then a passage about the fishing sloop he'd bought and named *Lizzie* and sailed from Veracruz to the cove with the skilled crewing of their mother. Interspersed through this section were brief references to John Samuel, including one about the only time he had been to the cove, when he was still a small boy, and his propensity to seasickness that had disappointed their father. The twins were tickled to learn their parents were such expert hands with a sailboat—and not in the least surprised their brother was no sailor at all.

The final inscription was dated a few days before their birth. It registered John Roger's great relief in Lizzie's easy term and their eager anticipation of another child.

The rest of the journal was blank.

"Not a word about Momma dying," Blake said. "Or about us. Or the other two."

"Well, he sure as hell wasn't gonna write down anything about *them*."

"I can understand that. But why not us?"

"Maybe we're . . . what's that word for something that's real hard to . . . ineffable."

Blake Cortéz grinned. "Yeah, I bet that's exactly why."

PART THREE

❀ HENRY MORGAN WOLFE *m* HEDDA JULIET BLAKE ❀

1 Roger Blake Wolfe ————————— *2* Harrison Augustus
   m Mary Margaret Parham
     1 John Roger ——————————————— *w/*Alma Rodríguez
       m Elizabeth Anne Bartlett   ↓ *1* Juana Merced
         1 John Samuel   *w/*Katrina Ávila
           m Victoria Clara Márquez   *1* Juan Lobo
              1 Juan Sotero
              2 Roger Samuel
          2 James Sebastian
          3 Blake Cortéz

   2 Samuel Thomas
     m María Palomina Blanco
       1 Gloria Tomasina
         m Louis Welch Little
           1 Luis Charón Little
       2 Bruno Tomás
       3 Sofía Reina
         m Melchor Cervantes
         m Arturo Villaseñor
           1 Francisco Villaseñor
         m Jorge Cabaza
           1 Pieto Tomás Cabaza
           2 Samuel Palomino Cabaza
         m Diego Guzmán

IN MEXICO CITY

Although John Roger and Elizabeth Anne had always wanted to visit Mexico City, they had for one reason or another still not done so when she died, and after that he no longer had any desire to go there. In all his years in Mexico he had made no trip farther than to Las Nevadas and a few other outlying haciendas of Veracruz state. And then in the fall of 1884, his thirtieth year in the country, he received an invitation from Amos Bentley—the invitation coming by wire directly to Buenaventura's newly installed telegraph station—to be his guest at a friend's party in honor of Porfirio Díaz, who two months earlier had been elected president for the second time. During the four years that Díaz's friend Manuel González had been president, Díaz's political organization had grown larger still, and his return to the presidency had been a foregone conclusion.

John Roger and Amos had been friends for twenty-five years, but they had seen less of each other ever since Amos got married and went to live with his wife at Las Nevadas. Although they neither one had much opportunity to make the long trip to visit the other at home, only managing to do so on a few special occasions— as when John Roger went to Las Nevadas to become godfather to Amos's first daughter—they always had dinner together whenever they were both in Veracruz. As Amos assumed greater responsibilities for the Nevada Mining Company, however, even their Veracruz reunions became more infrequent. During the early years of his marriage, while serving as Don Victor's chief accountant, Amos had taught himself everything about gold and silver, about their modes of mining and their practical as well as aesthetic uses, and he had acquired an exceptional faculty for assaying the worth of either metal in every form from ore to jewelry. In recognition of his talents—and because of the great advantages of his Yankee nationality and native facility with English—Don Victor had made him his principal agent with British and American buyers. The job obliged Amos to spend most of his time in Mexico City, and because his wife Teresa detested the capital and always chose to remain at home with their three daughters, he had in recent years seen less and less of his family. The simple and secret truth, as Amos would confide to John Roger, was that he no longer missed them very much. He loved his work and could imagine no place on earth as exciting as Mexico City. He had at first lived in a fine hotel, but before he had been there a year Don Victor deeded him a house in an exclusive neighborhood. A gift for his excellent service, Don Victor said, though, as Amos suspected, it was also the don's secret wish that the opulent residence would induce Teresa to join her husband in the capital. Don Victor's desire for a grandson had been thwarted by the birth of each granddaughter and his hope was that Amos and Teresa might again share a bed before she was fallowed by age. He could have reassigned Amos to Las Nevadas, of course, but his great value to the company was in Mexico City, and business, after all, was business. But Teresa remained adamant in her refusal to live in the capital, and that was fine with Amos. The mansion had a full staff of servants and he was ministered to with even greater solicitude than at the hotel. He had many times since invited John Roger to come for a visit, but John had always begged off with one or another plausible excuse. At the time of Amos's most recent invitation, they had not seen each other for nearly three years.

In his invitation Amos wrote, "You are long past due, old friend, to visit the Paris of the Western Hemisphere. The city is at its loveliest in November, and I can assure you an introduction to el presidente. I think you should find him most interesting."

Since the death of Elizabeth Anne, John Roger had ceased to attend parties. He took no pleasure in large company or loud gaiety. But in addition to wanting to see Amos after such a long time, he found the prospect of meeting Porfirio Díaz irresistible. He sent Amos a wire accepting the invitation and apprising him of his train's scheduled arrival in the capital.

John Samuel accompanied him on the hacienda train to the Veracruz depot. The twins, who had now been living at the cove for more than five months, had only two weeks before made their monthly visit to the compound. When John Roger told them of his upcoming trip they said it was about time he had a look at Mexico City. They themselves had never been to the capital or ever expressed the least interest in going there. The cove was their domain, and their contentment with it was ever evident in their obvious eagerness to get back to it. He did not like to admit it to himself, but it nettled him that, except for the family suppers, the twins spent most of their visits in the company of the crone and Marina Colmillo. Face it, he thought, you're jealous of the kitchen help. He had of course not asked the twins to accompany him to the train station and they had of course not offered to. Still, on arriving in Veracruz, he looked all about the station as he headed for the boarding platform. Then saw in John Samuel's annoyed aspect that he knew whom he sought.

Neither of them had seen the other off on a trip before, and at the coach steps there was a mutual uncertainty about how to proceed. They had not hugged one another since John Samuel's childhood—and in this awkward moment it occurred to John Roger that he and the twins had never hugged even once, never even shaken hands. Never touched. He moved to embrace his son just as John Samuel put out his hand, and then drew back and put out his hand as John Samuel raised his arms to receive him. They reddened at this clumsy dance, smiled stiffly for a moment, unsure what to do. Then John Samuel said, "Have a good trip" and again offered his hand and John Roger shook it and said he hoped to.

-◈-

That evening he detrained into the cacophonous swarm of the Mexico City terminal. Amos Bentley materialized from the crowd and came striding toward him with his arms open wide and a great grinning bellow of "John, old friend! Here at last!" His Southern accent as pronounced as on the day they first met. While he had always been stocky, Amos had over the years acquired a barrel of a belly, and John Roger felt the press of it between them as they embraced in the Mexican fashion with much patting of each other's back. Except for his greater girth, Amos, now in his late forties, seemed little changed. His round face was unlined, his sandy hair ungrayed but for traces at the sideburns. On their way out to the waiting carriage, John Roger gave him another clap on the shoulder for no reason but his great happiness to be with the last of his living friends.

Amos's house was on a tree-lined street along the north side of picturesque Alameda Park. The elite residential areas of the city had in recent years shifted from north and east of the zócalo to westward of it, to the Alameda and then along the imposing Avenida Reforma—broad and tree-lined, commissioned by Maximilian in imitation of the Champs Élysées—which went all the way to Chapultepec Park. In the residential style of the Mexican wealthy, Amos's property was shielded from the streets and his flanking neighbors by high walls whose tops were lined with embedded shards of glass. Amos gave him a cursory tour of the house before they sat to a light supper of fried eggs on white rice and a side dish of fried plantain slices sprinkled with sugar. They then repaired to the library until a late hour, smoking Cuban cigars and sipping French brandy and catching each other up on things.

Among the topics they discussed was the recent trouble at one of the silver mines at Las Nevadas. A few weeks before, nearly 300 miners had gone on strike in protest of working conditions. There were too many of them for Don Victor's gunmen to deal with, so he telegraphed to Mexico City for help. The next day there arrived an undermanned troop of twenty-seven Rurales—the Guardia Rural, an elite force of national mounted police, unmistakable in their distinct uniforms of big sombreros and charro suits of gray suede and silver conchos. In many parts of the country the Rurales were more feared than the army. They had been in existence since the time of Juárez, but it was Díaz who made them into a legendary force. He favored the recruitment of bandits into their ranks, believing that few men were as trustworthy as former criminals and that no one was better at hunting outlaws than a man who had been one himself. He gave them both incentive and license in the exercise of their duty. They were permitted to keep a portion of recovered loot, and in accord with Díaz's directive—Mátalos en caliente! was his standing order—to kill on the spot every bandit they caught. The Law of Flight sanctioned the shooting of a prisoner who tried to escape, and a dead man could not argue that he had made no such attempt. Díaz was lavish in his public praise of the Guardia Rural and hosted a sumptuous annual banquet in their honor. They were a source of national pride and the incarnate symbol of Díaz's personal might. And as loyal to him as dogs.

Don Victor offered the Rural captain the assistance of his thirty pistoleros but the captain politely declined, simply wanting to know where the strikers were. The Rurales then rode out to the mines and reined up in a line facing the protesters, their mounts stamping and snorting. Each man of them was armed with a saber, revolver, and Remington repeater carbine. They drew the rifles from their scabbards and held them braced on their hips, muzzle upward. The Rural captain took a watch from his pocket and called to the strikers that they had five minutes to get back to work. One of the mine leaders yelled We are not bandits! We only want fairness!

The captain made no reply nor even looked at the man but kept his attention on the watch while some of the strikers shouted their grievances and exhorted the Rurales to take the side of justice, for the love of God. As the minutes ticked away, at least a third of the men broke off from the crowd and hurried back to the mine, ignoring the curses and accusations of cowardice from those who stood fast and who told each other that no two dozen goddam Rurales were a match for 200 miners, even if the only weapons they had were picks and shovels and rocks. Then the five minutes were gone and the captain put away the watch. He raised his arm and the leverings of the carbines sounded like the cranking of some implacable machine. Some of the strikers shouted Get the fuckers! and started running at the lawmen with their picks and shovels raised and they were the first to die when the captain dropped his arm.

At the opening fusillade the rest of the strikers turned and ran in the other direction. But the carbines continued to fire and fire and powdersmoke billowed and drifted as running men cried out and flung up their arms and reeled and tumbled like drunken acrobats. The Rurales kept shooting until their magazines were emptied and then they re-sheathed the carbines and drew their sabers and put spurs to their horses and charged after the strikers still on the run, slashing at them to right and left and riding over the fallen, then reining their mounts around to make another pass at those still on their feet. In ten minutes it was done. Almost half of the strikers had made it back to the mine. Witnesses would tell of ground turned to red mud, of air laced with the smells of gunpowder and shit and blood. Of the wails of the wounded and the pistolshot to the head of every man of them who could not get up unassisted and walk back to work. Of having to beat away the buzzards and crows to gather the bodies for burial, more than a hundred of them. The following morning, Don Victor put out the word that he was hiring for the mines and by sundown he had replaced every man he'd lost and turned away even more.

Amos allowed to John Roger that the incident was awful, yes, but he had to agree with Don Victor that the miners' blood was on the miners' own hands. "It's a question of the national good," Amos said. "I don't have to remind *you*, John, how much a country depends on the orderly operations of its economy. A disruption of any those operations is harmful to everyone, to the entire body politic. It simply can't be tolerated. And if the malcontents won't yield to reason, well. . . ." He turned up his palms.

John Roger rolled his cigar between his fingers and studied its burning end. Of course workers could not be permitted to dictate to their employer the terms of their employment. But he was not sure the slaughter of a hundred unarmed men could be justified as a necessary measure to protect the national economy. It seemed to him the only economy that had been protected was that of Don Victor and others like him. But then, such men *were* the largest part of the nation's economy. There was also the question of whether a man warranted treatment as a brute simply because he was as ignorant as one, or, more to the point, simply because he could not stop someone from treating him that way. John Roger had heard much about the grueling work of mining and had seen a number of men who had been crippled by it, and he believed that Amos, having lived for years near the mines of Las Nevadas, must have seen even more. Reduced to mendicants, most of them. Becrutched or blind or otherwise maimed. Legless on a little square of wood mounted on metal rollers. All of them, crippled or not, marked with the brand of the mines, a thick pale welt across the forehead made by the tumplines of the endless baskets of ore hauled on their backs up ladder after ladder from the deep torchlit pits.

Still, the issue was hardly worth an argument with an old friend. "I suppose you're right," John Roger said. And held out his glass to Amos's offer of another dollop of the fine French brandy.

"Listen," Amos said, "a few days after that trouble at the mine, I was dining with some associates and I told them about it. One of them said thank God for the Rurales. And somebody else said no, thank Don Porfirio for the Rurales."

"Yes," John Roger said. "A nice point."

❦

After breakfast the next morning, Amos gave him a walking tour of the city's hub. They ambled along the wide sidewalk of Plateros Street, past fashionable shops and restaurants and theaters, the city's most exclusive clubs, the headquarters buildings of the country's most lucrative industries, including that of the Nevada Mining Company, and after a time arrived at the immense zócalo, where stood the Presidential Palace and the colossal Metropolitan Cathedral and all the main offices of the federal and municipal governments. John Roger was awed by the bluster and tempo of the city's core, the ceaseless clatterings of wagons and carriages, the ringing and rumblings of the railed mule trolleys, the press and babble of the sidewalk throngs in their mix of business suits and peón cottons and Indian ponchos. By the nattily uniformed policemen at every street corner. Not even the Boston of his memory had been so vital nor so loud nor so well-policed. Nor had its streets been cleaner than these.

"They weren't nearly so clean or safe before Don Porfirio became president, let me tell you," Amos said. "Law and order, John. To have clean streets and the safety to enjoy them you must first have law and order." He admitted that it was only the core of the city that was so well kept and secure. Many of the outer neighborhoods were still pestiferous and dangerous places.

"Nevertheless, you have to credit Don Porfirio for all the improvements to the city," Amos said. "The police, for example. He brought professionals from Europe to train them, did you know that? He dressed them in those French uniforms not only to give them a more professional look but also a sense of pride. You can bet that he'll now make the force even more efficient. The Rurales too, if you can imagine them any better at their work than they already are. It's a new age for Mexico, John. This country's always been a jackpot of resources, but these people, God love them, have never had what it takes to make use of their own riches. What this country needs is foreign capital and know-how and a good rail system, and it's getting them. In the next few years there won't be a corner of the country the rails haven't reached. But first you have to have order. That's what Don Porfirio's brought to this country, John, order. That's why outside investment's starting to pour in. And it's just the beginning, my friend. With Don Porfirio running things again, it's just the beginning."

John Roger grinned. "You speak as though the man can walk on water."

"You mock, sir, but much of what he's doing *is* almost miraculous. No other Mexican president ever managed to unify so many political camps."

"Ya lo sé," John Roger said. "Pan o palo."

"Exactamente, mi amigo. Share my bread or feel my club. A simple offer and a very effective one. And, if you ask me, a damned generous one to make to his enemies. The wise ones always choose the bread."

"I can understand why. His enemies have a tendency to vanish. Now and then one gets found out in the scrub with a bullet in the head or his throat cut."

"Oh come now, John," Amos said. "You can't be serious in that implication."

John Roger arched his brow and Amos looked away. Then looked back at him and then they burst out laughing. "Oh hell, let's eat," Amos said, and slapped him on the back. They lunched in a restaurant, then returned to the house for a siesta.

Just before he dozed off, John Roger reflected that his friend had found his rightful calling, and like every man's calling, it had its own credo and rationale.

-❦-

The party for Díaz that evening was in a mansion on a street adjoining the zócalo. John Roger would have preferred to walk there—the better for a close-up view of the city's center at night—but a light rain was falling and so they took a hired cab. The streets gleamed. The lamplights were nimbused with mist.

The cavernous ballroom was ablaze with chandeliers. Women sparkled with jewelry. Candles glimmering on the tables, glittering buckets of iced champagne. Ball gowns and tailcoats and military finery. The dance floor a colorful whirl of couples spinning to the orchestral strains of Strauss. John Roger was introduced by Amos to army officers and government officials and hacendados from all over central Mexico, but he would remember the names of none of them. The host had provided a number of unmarried girls as dance partners for men who had come without escort, and Amos took happy turns on the floor with all of them. John Roger claimed a bad knee and kept to the table. The closeness of the crowd oppressed him. The babble and laughter. The over-loud music. Only the expectation of meeting Díaz kept him from making an excuse to Amos and their host and taking his leave.

He had endured for two hours when the host mounted the dais to announce that he had just received a message bearing the president's sincere regrets that he would not be able to attend the festivities. Don Porfirio and Doña Carmen sent their deepest apologies to everyone present and urged them all to have a good time.

"Hard luck, chum," Amos said to John Roger, "but there'll be other chances."

John Roger said he hoped so. Then said he was tired and thought he might be catching cold and so was going to go back to the house and to bed. Amos said he would leave with him but John Roger knew he was enjoying himself and persuaded him to stay.

He intended to hire a hansom, but when he got outside and saw that the rain had stopped he chose to walk. The night was cold, the air sharp, the streetlights warmly bright. An evening so amenable he decided to alter his route and prolong the walk back, and he turned north at the first street corner he came to.

A few blocks farther on, the surroundings became distinctly less well tended and the people on the street louder. He came to a crowded little plaza of an unkempt, working-class neighborhood whose architecture testified to a more genteel past. The curbs were lined with litter but the square was gaily lit and piquant with spicy aromas, lively with chatter and laughter, with music from a pair of cantinas on opposite sides of the plaza. At a sidewalk cart he bought a pork tamal and ate it as he ambled. He paused at the open doors of one of the cantinas, in which someone was strumming a guitar and singing in tremulous nostalgia about his boyhood in Durango. He listened for a minute, then moved on, ready to head back to Amos's.

He was almost to the corner when he heard a different tune and from a different sort of instrument. Heard it but barely through the surrounding babble and other music, but heard it well enough to recognize it at once, and he halted in his tracks. He thought he might be having an aberrant mental episode. Maybe he was not really hearing the tune but only remembering it after so many years and for who-knew-what reason. He stood rooted, listening hard as passersby sidestepped around him. Now the tune was lost in the laughter of a group of men on the corner just ahead and then the laughter abated and he heard the tune more clearly now among the plaza's other sounds. And knew he was hearing it with his ears and not just in his head. The tweedle of a hornpipe. Playing "Good Jolly Roger."

The tune was coming from his left. From within the chocked-open doors of a small café not five yards away. A sign next to the door showed the name La Rosa Mariposa in ornate but faded lettering. He went to the door and kept to the shadow alongside it and peered into a dimly lighted room with a few small tables and only a single diner and no one at the little bar but a barman in a white apron. The barman was playing the pipe. He looked about thirty years old. Thick through the chest and shoulders, black hair combed back and parted in the center, short mustache. But even at this distance and despite the mustache, John Roger saw the likeness and knew who the man must be and how he had learned that tune.

For a moment, everything seemed unreal—the barman, the tune, the plaza, the people passing by, the fact that he was in Mexico City , the memory of a brother he had grown up with in a Portsmouth tavern. . . .

The sensation passed. And he thought, Maybe he taught it to somebody who taught it to this one.

No. Look at him. He could be my own. He learned it from his father and none other. From Sammy. Whom you have believed dead these many years but is not.

He is not dead.

But why has he never. . . ?

Who knows? But if that's not his son I never drew breath.

Well then?

He inhaled deeply. Exhaled slowly. Went inside.

The barman saw him approaching and set the hornpipe under the counter and wiped his hands on his apron. Good evening, sir. What is your pleasure?

Tell me, John Roger began, but heard the tight note in his voice and paused to clear his throat. Tell me, that tune you were playing just now. Where did you learn it?

The barman smiled. The little jig? You liked it, huh?

Did your father teach it to you?

The barman's smile went smaller. Yes, he said. How did you know?

I would like to speak with him.

With my *father*?

Yes, please. I'm . . . I know him. Listen, is he here? It's very important I see him.

But sir, my father . . . well, my father's dead. He's been dead for, ah, about ten years, I guess.

Dead? John Roger repeated the word as if he had never before heard it. In the midst of his stunning understanding that his brother had not died all those years ago, it had not crossed his mind that he might have died since.

You say you knew my father?

Yes. Yes, I . . . ten years?

Yeah, just about.

What did . . . how did he die?

Oh God, don't ask. It wasn't good. Listen, how do—?

How did he die? Tell me.

Jesus, man, if you *must* know, it was rabies.

John Roger stared at him. Then down at his hands on the bar top.

Yeah, see? Like I said, it wasn't good.

How did it happen?

How do you think? He got bit by a dog.

No, I mean *how*. What was the circumstance?

Christ, Mister, what is this? What—?

Please.

The barman sighed. Well, I didn't see it myself. I was in the army then. But the way Mother and my sister told me—the way Father told it to them—he was taking a walk and saw this little kid being threatened by a dog. A little kid scared really bad. There was nobody else around except a bunch of boys watching from across the street. Probably hoping to see the kid get all torn up—you know, for the entertainment, how kids are. So Father grabbed up the boy, but the dog bit him, bit Father I mean. Bit him on the leg and ran off. When he told Mother about it she got worried right away the dog might be rabid but Father told her he didn't think so, it didn't act like any rabid dog he'd ever seen, only like a mean one. He said he wouldn't have taken any chances with a mad dog, kid or no kid. Mother asked around the neighborhood if there had been any report of a mad dog, but nobody had heard anything. So anyhow, about three weeks later, Father started getting really sick in a way that everybody knew what it was. If you know about rabies I don't have to tell you what it was like after that. I saw a guy in the army die of it and I never want to see it again. The way Mother told it, it was the same way for Father. They had to get some of the neighborhood men to wrestle him onto the bed and tie him down and put a stick between his teeth and be damned careful not to let him bite them and so on, the whole awful business. Sófi—my little sister—she said he bucked so hard he nearly turned the bed over. He had horrible hallucinations. Pissed himself, shit himself, the whole neighborhood heard him screaming. They begged Mother to put him out of his agony. Stab him in the heart with an ice pick, they told her, for the love of God. Poison him, something. Sófi said Mother thought

183

about it. It nearly made her crazy to see him like he was, but she just couldn't do it. Anyway, he finally died. Jesus, I hate thinking about it. I should have told you to go to hell.

John Roger had seen the kind of terror inspired by a mad dog. Had twice seen rabid dogs shot in the streets of Veracruz to the great relief of everyone in the neighborhoods. He had never seen a rabies death but had heard the dreadful stories. He ran his hand over his face and was unaware of knocking off his hat.

Hey mister, you all right? The barman poured a drink and placed it in front of him and said, "Trágalo."

He took a sip of the tequila, then drank the rest in a gulp.

"So you knew my father, you say. Were you were his friend or. . . ?"

John Roger nodded. Then realized the barman had spoken in English. Accented but precise. "Yes," he said. "I knew him well. A long time ago."

The barman's gaze narrowed. "He did not have many friends, I can tell you that. He never went further than three blocks from here and that's no lie, not once in my whole life. Where do you know him from?"

"I'm his brother."

They held each other's eyes. The barman said "De veras?"

"De veras. We had just graduated from school the last time I saw him. In New Hampshire. That's up—"

"I know where it is."

"I never—" He paused to clear his throat. "I never knew what happened to him. I thought he was dead."

"Since you were just out of high school you thought he was dead?"

"Yes."

"Hombre! That was *how* many years ago?"

"Nearly forty."

"Jesucristo! Was he older or younger than you?"

John Roger hesitated, then said, "Older. He never told you he had a brother?"

"He told Mother he was an only child. He said his parents were dead." He narrowed his eyes. "I don't get it. Why would he lie about a brother?"

"I don't know. Why would I?"

The barman nodded. "Yes. Why would you? And Father, well . . . he had secrets, we all knew that."

"Now you know one of them."

"There are more of you? Brothers? Sisters?"

"Just me."

"Jesus. His brother."

"Yes."

"How did you find out where he was? I mean, after so long?"

"I heard the tune. I was passing by and I heard the hornpipe. Sammy and I—

your father and I—we made it up, that music you were playing. In New Hampshire when we were boys."

"You mean you . . . the reason you came in here is you were walking by and heard me playing the little pipe?"

John Roger nodded.

"If you had not heard it you would have passed by?"

"Yes."

"That is . . . that is just. . . ."

"Yes."

"We were so near to each other and we would never have known it."

John Roger nodded.

The barman stared. "So then you are my uncle."

John Roger managed a meager smile. "I suppose I am."

"Pues, como se llama, tío? Por supuesto su apellido es Wolfe."

"Sí, soy John Wolfe. Y usted?"

"Bruno. Bruno Tomás Blanco y Blanco. Muchísimo gusto, tío."

They shook hands across the bar with an awkward formality and then stood staring at each other a moment longer before Bruno came around from behind the counter to embrace him. They hugged hard and pounded each other on the back, John Roger tearful, his nephew grinning.

Bruno Tomás became aware of the solitary patron watching them. He told the man to get the hell out and then locked the door behind him and turned the little "Cerrado" sign in the door window. He poured another drink for each of them.

Bruno Tomás was eager to know what John Roger was doing in Mexico and where he was living. And was stunned to learn he had been in Mexico for thirty years. Which meant he and his brother had both been alive in Mexico for about twenty years without knowing of each other's presence in the country. Bruno was stunned all the more that this was the first time John Roger had been outside the state of Veracruz. It was a long story, John Roger said, one for later on, but he allowed that he'd been the Mexico agent for an American import company for a few years before an unexpected turn of fortune gained him the coffee hacienda where he now lived.

"Una hacienda!" Bruno Tomás said. "Jesucristo, tío! Pero que fortuna."

John Roger was puzzled by his nephew's surname, and Bruno Tomás told him the story he and his sisters had been told by their mother, the story of the brutal mistreatment by the American army that led his father and his friends to desert, of the cruelty they suffered after they were captured, of the hatred it had made him feel for his own country and the consequences of that hatred, including the change of his name from Wolfe.

John Roger had never before heard of the Saint Patricks, and he once again wept when Bruno told him of the punishments inflicted on his brother and the other captured ones who were not hanged. He now understood why Bruno Tomás could never have recognized him as Samuel Thomas's twin. The only face his brother's family had ever known was the one left to him by the war.

They had another drink, sipping and talking, shifting between English and Spanish, sometimes in the middle of a sentence. Bruno Tomás said his fluency in English had come naturally to him. When they were kids, he and his older sister Gloria had found an English grammar in a bookstore and taught themselves the basics from it. Whenever they heard Americans or Britons conversing on the street, they would eavesdrop. They sometimes bought an English-language newspaper from a zócalo kiosk and read to each other from it. Their younger sister Sófi could probably have learned the language as easily but, like their mother, she did not want to. It was a funny thing, but neither he nor his sisters ever heard their father speak English, not even once. Their mother had told them not to ask for his help in learning it, because he had renounced the language together with everything else American. Bruno thought that was why she and Sófi had never learned English. They felt it would somehow be a betrayal of him.

"Es muy curioso, tío," Bruno said, "but the older Father became, the more he hated the United States. Mother says it was because he began to miss it very much but he could not forgive it for what it had done to him and so he would not go back. The more he missed his country, the more he hated it for having made it impossible for him to go back. Seems a little mixed up to me, but that's what she thinks."

It pained John Roger that Sammy could have felt such rancor toward his own country. That he had renounced his American past so utterly that he would not even tell his own family he had a brother. So utterly he would not even let his brother know he was alive. It crossed his mind that maybe Sammy had not contacted him for fear that he would be ashamed of him for his desertion. Then dismissed the idea as ridiculous. Sammy knew better than that.

He asked Bruno if he knew why Samuel Thomas had enlisted in the army anyway. He had never wanted to be anything but a sailor. Bruno Tomás didn't know and said his mother didn't either. "She asked him once why he joined the army," Bruno Tomás said, "and he told her he didn't want to talk about it and so she never asked him again. She truly did not care where he had been or what he had done before she knew him. That's what she's always told us, me and my sisters. And he was never muy hablador. He never talked about himself."

They talked for more than an hour before Bruno Tomás said they should go upstairs so he could meet the Blanco women—two of them, anyway. He had not seen his older sister since she got married more than sixteen years ago. "Gloria se casó con un gringo," Bruno said. "You'll never believe how *that* marriage happened. She was always a wild one but lucky too. She lives with her husband's people in San Luis Potosí state."

They went up to the apartment and through the parlor and into the kitchen, where the two women sat drinking coffee. They looked at John Roger as much in suspicion as surprise—their eyes making swift appraisal of his expensive boots and fine suit and lingering for a moment on his folded coat sleeve before fixing on his face. They nodded and said "Mucho gusto, señor," when Bruno Tomás introduced them to him. The mother, María Palomina, was as darkhaired as the daughter and almost as lean. The daughter, Sofía Reina, called Sófi, was very pretty. John Roger guessed her age at around twenty. But when Bruno presented John Roger as "el señor John Wolfe, el hermano de papá," they looked confused, and then María Palomina glowered as if she thought they were playing a bad joke. Then she saw they were serious and her face changed.

"Es la verdad?" she said.

"Sí," John Roger said. "Éra mi hermano."

"Ay, dios mío," she said softly.

She stood up and went to him and hugged him hard, and then Sófi had her turn at embracing him. Sófi then brewed a fresh pot of coffee and they all sat at the table to talk.

TURNS OF FORTUNE

So then. This reunited family that for almost forty years had not known it was disunited and had in the interim produced a second generation and gained a second surname—this family that on the night they discovered each other was represented by all the living Blancos save the elder daughter Gloria and by a sole Wolfe, but he the patriarch—this mutually discovered clan passed the rest of that night in a long conversation of acquaintance and revelation. John Roger and Bruno Tomás would at times lapse into English when addressing each other, and María Palomina or Sofía Reina would each time clear her throat to make them aware of it and bring them back to Spanish. It was a conversation marked by interrogations and explanations, expositions and clarifications, interspersed with tears and chuckles and sudden crescendos of everyone talking at once and sudden silences that as abruptly gave way to laughter and still more questions and more explications and more expressions of awe at their having found each other as they had. What if Bruno had not played the tune when he did or if John Roger had not been walking by and heard it when he did or even been in Mexico City when he was and so on and so forth. Only Sofía Reina was unmoved by the chain of coincidence. Everything had to happen in some way, she said, so why not the way it did? But then, as John Roger would learn, Sofía Reina had already known so many fantastic turns of fortune in her own life that nothing that happened to her or to anyone else, however improbable or even bizarre, could surprise her anymore.

By dawn they had addressed the most pressing particulars and learned much about each other that it was of greatest importance to know. They would become still better acquainted over the next few days, but on that gray dawn in that upstairs residence of that rundown café in that ramshackle neighborhood near the center of

189

Mexico City, the only important question remaining was what they should do now.

For John Roger the answer was simple. The three Blancos should go to live at Buenaventura. The family would be united and the Blancos would be relieved of the burden of the café, which by their own admission was barely earning enough to maintain them. More to the point, they would be relieved of financial concern for the rest of their lives. There are worse fates, John Roger said with a benign smile, than to have a rich relative with a fondness for his kin.

Bruno Tomás was agog at the prospect of life at the hacienda. He felt he was being liberated from a living death, although, in deference to his mother's feelings, he did not say so aloud. Downstairs at the bar, however, he had confided to John Roger that he hated working in the café and always had. His calling, as he had discovered in the army, was in working with horses. His father hadn't been pleased when he enlisted. He had come to view all armies as nothing other than the powerful weapons of the greedy privileged in their contentions with each other, and he did not want his son to risk his life in the cause of such sons of bitches, as Bruno Tomás would surely have to do because there was always a war. But he also believed Bruno was old enough to decide for himself, and so did not forbid him from enlisting. And although there had in fact always been war during Bruno Tomás's time in the ranks—one rebellion or another always breaking out in one part of the country or another—he had not had to fight in any of it. During his basic military training he and the army had found out that he had a natural talent for working with horses, and he had been made a wrangler whose main duty was to care for the cavalry mounts. He was never near enough to the fighting to have to shoot at anyone or for anyone to shoot at him. He would have been content to make a career as a breaker of horses in the army, but after his father's death he felt honor-bound to care for his mother and help her to manage the café. "After all," he said to John Roger, "lo primero es lo primero." And so he came home when his enlistment expired. But he had not forgotten the great pleasure of working with horses and had clung to the hope that he might one day do so again.

John Roger told him he wouldn't have to work at all at Buenaventura if he chose not to, but if he wished to work on Rancho Isabela—the hacienda's horse ranch—he certainly could. His eldest son, John Samuel, had created the ranch and had always been the one to manage it. But he was spending more and more of his time helping with the operation of the hacienda and would soon need a foreman to run the ranch. If Bruno Tomás was as good with horses as he claimed, and if he could manage the other wranglers—a pretty rowdy bunch, it had to be said—John Roger thought there was a good chance John Samuel would give him the job.

Bruno Tomás was confident on both counts. He had been a sergeant in the army and was seasoned in command. But what about the guy expecting to be the next foreman? There was always a guy expecting to be the next foreman, and sometimes the guy had good reason to feel that way. "What of it?" John Roger said. "You're my nephew. And as somebody just said, 'lo primero es lo primero.' Of course, if you'd rather step aside for whoever it is that expects to be the next foreman, well. . . ."

"No," Bruno said, "I wouldn't."

"Didn't think so," John Roger said, and both of them grinned.

But María Palomina would not part from Mexico City. She told John Roger she appreciated his sense of paternal obligation toward his brother's family and she was sure that Buenaventura was as beautiful as he described it and she thanked him very much for his generous invitation to live there, but the capital was her home. She had been born in this city and lived in it all her life and she had met Samuel Thomas here and married him here and lived with him here and buried him here, and she would not abandon it.

John Roger could not sway her. But that evening, after he'd returned to Amos's house and relieved his friend's worry about what had become of him—and after everyone had a much needed siesta—he took the Blancos to dine in a restaurant and during the meal was able to persuade María Palomina to at least let him sell the café for her and provide her with a house in a better neighborhood. A house with a cook and a cleaning maid and a monthly stipend to support herself and Sofía Reina, who had made it clear she would not leave her mother alone in the city.

The next morning he sent a telegram to John Samuel to let him know he would be staying in the capital a while longer but wasn't sure yet how long that would be. He said he had a grand surprise for everyone when he got home but gave no further details. Bruno Tomás then took him to the cemetery and John Roger placed flowers on Samuel Thomas's grave. And again wept for his dead brother, whose reasons for ending up in this plot of ground so far from New England and so foreign to it he would never know. When he had told Amos the story, Amos said, "Good Christ, John, that's some tale. I can't imagine the odds against finding them as you did. Say now, what other secrets have you been keeping from me, you sly man of mystery?"

Among Amos's many friends of influence was one of the city's most successful real estate dealers. John Roger retained the man's services in the morning and by that evening the café was sold. The day after that, the broker showed John Roger and the Blancos an available residence he thought might be what they were looking for, a fine little red-brick house on a lush high-walled property in an upper-class neighborhood two blocks off the elegant Avenida Reforma. María Palomina loved it. Loved especially its garden in the rear. She had always wanted a garden but the café residence did not have even a patio, and her flowers had always been nurtured in window pots.

John Roger bought the house and put the deed in her name and hired a crew of movers to transport the Blanco belongings from the café. Then hired painters to repaint every room to María Palomina's preferences, excepting Sofía Reina's room, whose walls Sófi would have no color but purple even in the face of her mother's objections to it as a hideous contrast with the pale yellow walls of the rest of the house.

Amos stopped by to see how things were going, and when John Roger introduced him to the Blancos, they all grinned at the blushing smile he gave Sófi. Disregarding his aversion for physical labor, Amos took off his coat and rolled his sleeves and helped John Roger and Bruno to arrange and rearrange the new furniture until it was all positioned precisely to María Palomina's liking. The corpulent Amos was soaked with sweat when they were done but he took no offense at the others' gentle teasing of him, and his smiles for Sófi were incessant.

They had a fine time, John Roger and the Blancos, getting to know each other during those days of working together to make the new house a home. In the evenings after dinner they sat in the parlor with glasses of wine and conversed until a late hour. The Blancos wanted to know everything about the childhood he had shared with Samuel Thomas. He told them about Portsmouth and their mother and their Grandfather John Parham. They were not surprised to hear of Samuel Thomas's propensity for fighting with his fists, but they had not known of his love for sailing, or that he had hoped to make his life at sea, or that he had been a superior student and could have excelled as a scholar if he'd but had the inclination. For reasons of decorum John Roger refrained from telling some things about his brother, such as his larks in the Blue Mermaid tavern. Nor did he reveal to the Blancos—as he had not revealed to anyone save the late Margarita Damascos—the fact of their father's piracy. A secret he was now sure that Sammy had kept from them.

In answering their questions about himself, he tried to be self-effacing and perfunctory, but the facts were the facts, and the Blancos were impressed by his university education, his legal profession in New England, his management of the Trade Wind Company. They of course wanted to know how he'd lost his arm, and were enthralled by his account of the duel with Montenegro, and deeply moved by Elizabeth Anne's action in saving his life. They could not hear enough about Elizabeth Anne and asserted that she seemed "muy simpática," a characterization John Roger had heard from every Mexican who ever met her. He showed them her photograph set into the inner lid of his pocketwatch, and they cooed in admiration of her beauty. Then became tearful when he told the details of her death. Then smiled again on learning that the younger two of his three sons were identical twins.

Not until then did it occur to John Roger that he had not told any of them that he and Sammy were twins. He thought to say so now, but decided against it. What difference did it make? They had not been physical twins since Sammy's disfigurement by the army, which occurred before María Palomina met him. He supposed they might like to know that he was a good approximation of what Sammy would have looked like but for the war. But still he did not tell them. He wanted to keep something of Sammy for himself alone.

I have always thought it would be wonderful to be the mother of twins, María

Palomina said. Now I can only hope to have twin grandchildren. Imagine how fabulous it would be to have a set of twins in every generation! She gestured toward Bruno Tomás and said, Maybe this one will father twins someday, if he should ever find some fool of a woman to marry him.

Bruno grinned. Don't lose hope, Mother. I've heard there are plenty of foolish women in this world.

Only Sófi did not join in the chortling. She tended to reticence on the subject of children, and John Roger had come to know why. She was thirty-one years old, a decade older than he'd thought when he'd first seen her, a fact the more startling in light of a history of marriage and motherhood that struck him as nothing less than tragic. No less awesome to him than Sófi's chronicle itself was the matter-of-fact manner in which she had related it to him. He had long suspected that the female heart was stronger than the male's in almost every way, and her account left him doubtless.

⚜

She had just turned sixteen when she wed Melchor Cervantes, two years after her sister Gloria had married and gone. Melchor was twenty years old and newly graduated from military college. María Palomina had warned both daughters since their early childhood never to fall in love with a soldier, especially a young officer with dreams of glory, and how many young officers did not have such dreams? Few young men of that sort lived to be old men, she told the girls, and told them too of her own passionate betrothal when she was seventeen to just such a young soldier who was killed before they could marry. She anyhow thought Sófi too young to marry anyone. She pleaded with her and Melchor to wait at least another year, but she was arguing with a wildfire. Forbid them, she beseeched Samuel Thomas, make them wait. But he would not. They would only run away, he said, and you would regret that even more. María Palomina was in tight-lipped vexation for three days before she finally admitted defeat, and Sófi and Melchor were married three weeks later.

They lived in a little house next to the army post, just outside the city. He was permitted to come home on most nights and they were very happy. They had been married almost four months when his battalion was sent to quell an insurgency in the hills near Pachuca, some fifty miles from Mexico City. Rebels. There were always rebels. Melchor was eager for his first combat and promised Sófi he would earn a medal of bravery in her honor. He rode off like a prince of war in his pristine lancer uniform, his high boots gleaming, his shako affixed with a proud black plume. The following week he was killed in an ambush. His comrade and best friend later told Sófi that Melchor had been shot in the head by a ragged and shoeless boy barely big enough to hold the antique musket. For lack of proper ammunition the boy used a stone for a bullet. The friend wanted to tell her what they did to the captured boy but she did not want to hear it. She lit a candle for Melchor's soul three times a day and prayed to the Blessed Mother to please, please let his seed from their last lovemaking take root in her womb. Then awoke one morning to the death of that hope, its blood staining her bed sheet. She thought she would never stop crying. But of course did.

She went back to live with her mother and father. She dressed in black for a year and wore her hair loose in the mourning mode and passed her days working in the café. She grew to understand that you can mourn someone for a long time, even for the rest of your life, but you cannot grieve forever. Besides, she dearly wanted children.

Almost as soon as she put away her black dress she began to be courted by Arturo Villaseñor, a thirty-three-year-old city policeman whose beat took him past La Rosa Mariposa three times a day and where he often stopped in for a cup of coffee. Arturo had known many women and received much pleasure from them, but he had never wanted to be married until he met Sófi. She let him woo her for three months before she said yes to his proposal, and they married the month after that. She was yet only seventeen.

They say you can never love anyone else as much as you love the first, Sófi had told John Roger, but I disagree. I think you can love somebody else as much or even more than the first one. What you cannot do again is be in love for the first time. The sadness of that knowledge is why the first one seems so special.

But there is only one first time for anything we do in life, John Roger said, from birth to death.

Exactly so, Sofía Reina said.

He did not want to distract from her story and so did not pursue the theme. But he believed that what made memorable first times so special was that most of them happened to us in youth. What made us sad when we later recalled them was that we were no longer young. Then again, he thought he might be chasing his tail.

Arturo Villaseñor was a good man and Sófi loved him for his goodness, but not until their wedding night did she realize how much she had been missing the enjoyments of the bed. And because Arturo was more experienced than Melchor while no less passionate, her conjugal enjoyments were keener than ever. They lived in his top-floor apartment in a six-story building only three blocks from La Rosa Mariposa. Their son, Francisco, was born in December. María Palomina was jubilant to be a grandmother, and though less effusive, Samuel Thomas too was pleased by his grandson.

Arturo was overwhelmed by his own joy in fatherhood. More, my dearest treasure, he said to Sófi, we must make more of these amazing creatures! We must make dozens! She was dazed with happiness and eager to give him all the children he wished. But three months later and two days after their first anniversary, she had not yet conceived again when Arturo tried to break up a street fight on his beat and one of the combatants stabbed him in the heart. The murderer got away, and while

Sófi hoped he would be caught and punished, she could not muster the energy for a righteous vengeance. Whatever became of his killer, Arturo would still be dead.

For the next two months she hardly spoke except to coo endearments to baby Francisco as she tended him. But for the baby, she might have passed her days in bed and staring at the ceiling. María Palomina brought meals every day and gave the apartment a quick cleaning and made sure the child was not being neglected. Then Arturo's long-widowed mother, Eufemia, arrived from Guadalajara to stay with Sófi for a time and help with the baby and the housekeeping. By late summer, six months after Arturo's death, Sófi was doing well, even smiling on occasion, and Eufemia made plans to return home at the end of September.

The sixteenth of that month was the nation's Independence Day, when Mexico City became a cacophony of marching bands and skiffle bands and street dancing and church bells and firecrackers and military rifle volleys of tribute, a daylong celebration culminating after dark with firework exhibitions all over town. That evening, Eufemia sat in a rear bedroom, holding the baby and crooning to him to allay his fears of the blasts in the outer dark, while at the other end of the apartment Sófi stood out on the balcony and watched the fireworks lighting up the sky. The nearest show was taking place in the open ground of a park but two blocks away. It featured Catherine wheels and sun wheels, Roman candles and pastilles, elaborate displays of every sort—and of course skyrockets, some of them four feet long and as big around as a man's arm, one after another arcing up into the night in a streak of fire and detonating into a dazzling spray of colors high over the city. The air was hazed and acrid with powdersmoke.

Sófi thought she would watch one more rocket and then go back inside and close the balcony doors against the noise in hope that the baby could get to sleep. But the next rocket did not fire off like the others, did not zoom off the ground in a streaking blaze but rose in a struggling, sluggish, spark-sputtering wobble as if improperly fused. It had barely cleared the rooftops when it stopped rising and for a second simply hung suspended and shedding sparks. And then, just as it tilted and started to fall, its tail flared and the rocket whipped around in a quick bright-yellow circle and came streaking directly toward Sófi where she stood seized. Before she could think to move, the rocket shot by within inches of her, singeing her hair and scorching her cheek, and blazed down the hall and into the bedroom and found the embraced grandmother and child and blew them asunder, bespattering the walls and setting the bedclothes afire.

Who could explain such a thing? Terrible firework accidents were commonplace and firework deaths no rarity, but a fatality in this manner gave new dimension to the idea of freak misfortune. The disaster was publicized in the most purple prose and the most lurid illustrations of the city's penny broadsides. But nothing in those newssheets was as outrageous to Sófi as the witless blather of the priest at the funeral mass, his pious pronouncements about God's mysterious ways and our need to accept them on faith and so on. Had she not got up and walked out of the church midway through the service—wholly indifferent to the stares and whispers she provoked—she might have thrown her shoe at the man and cursed him for a shithead fool.

She again returned to La Rosa Mariposa. And this time did take to her bed and stare at the ceiling. She could not rid herself of the idea that the rocket had sought out Eufemia and Francisco, but she shared this thought with no one, fearing she would be thought insane. It came as a dull surprise to her that she could not abide her inertness for more than a week before getting cleaned up and assisting in the operation of the café. María Palomina and Samuel Thomas were relieved to see her at work so soon after the catastrophe and thought it only natural that for weeks to come she would yet seem remote and have little to say. The loss of two husbands in a span of two years and three months, followed hard upon by the death of her only child, was a sizable downpour of misery by any measure and especially so for someone only nineteen. Still, she knew as well as anyone that there was nothing to be done about it but to bear it, and she bore it well. And bore well too her father's rabid death less than two years after the loss of baby Francisco.

Samuel Thomas had been dead a year, and Bruno Tomás had since returned from the army to help María Palomina manage the café, when Sófi married Jorge Cabaza. He was twenty-five, only three years her senior, and worked in his father's bakery, from which La Rosa Mariposa bought its bread. Jorge was plain and, as Sófi found out on their wedding night, lacked imagination as a lover. But he worshipped her and he was industrious and wanted to have many children, and it was of no small importance to her that a baker was far removed from the mortal risks faced by soldiers and policemen. And because he would do whatever she asked of him, she was able to teach him—gradually and in a spirit of shy curiosity, lest he think her wanton—a number of her favorite things in bed. And so did this marriage, too, come to provide her dearest pleasure.

Jorge's only remaining family was his father, Pieto, who had taught him the baker's trade and who adored Sófi from the moment they met, and she reciprocated his affection. The three of them lived in quarters at the rear of the bakery, which was on a street fronting a canal and near enough to La Rosa Mariposa that Sófi and her mother were able to visit each other often.

Pieto had been a widower for seventeen years. Before his wife was taken by a typhoid epidemic she had borne six children, but only Jorge had survived to adulthood, and Pieto's great wish was for a grandson to keep alive the family line. When Sófi gave birth to a husky boy whom she and Jorge called Pieto Tomás, the elder Pieto's tearful joy was compounded by his namesake honor. The year after that, Samuel Palomino was born, as lusty of health as his brother, and it was María Palomina's turn to feel honored in addition to her elation at another grandson. We are truly blessed, Jorge said in his half-drunk happiness during the celebration party attended by everyone in the neighborhood. His father, no less happy and no less drunk, raised his glass high and said, A man cannot have better luck than mine. The dispute that ensued between father and son over which of them was the luckier man was about to come to blows when a woman's plea for somebody to *do* something was followed by a loud and prolonged fart and the room erupted with laughter. Later that evening while dancing with Sófi, Pieto tripped over his own feet and fell and broke his arm, and so the following day they hired a neighborhood girl named Prudencia to care for the babies during working hours while Sófi tended to Pieto's duties in the bakery until he could resume them. Under his instruction she learned the work quickly and well, and even after Pieto was able to work again she kept working too, and the bakery increased both its output and profits.

Neither child had ever evinced any sign of illness until Pieto Tomás was eighteen months old and his forehead one morning seemed a little warm to Prudencia's palm. She feared he might be taking fever. The child did not feel feverish to Sófi's touch but old Pieto had seen enough of his children die of illness and he would not abide even the smallest risk to his grandsons. He insisted that Jorge take the child to the doctor and take six-month-old Samuel Palomino to be looked at too, just in case. Prudencia held the well-bundled babies securely against her as Jorge hupped the mule forward and the wagon went rumbling away over the wooden canal bridge.

Sófi would later learn that the doctor had found both boys to be in perfect health. She would imagine Jorge's relief on hearing this and his eagerness to share it with her as he headed back home. Of the various eyewitnesses, several would agree that he had been smiling and saying something to Prudencia as the wagon drew near to home, that the maid had been smiling also, that the babies in her embrace had been waving their arms for the sheer pleasure such action gives to children of that age. Then the wagon turned onto the bridge and its weight bore upon a piling that must have been rotting for many years without any sign of its weakening until that moment, when it gave a loud groan and abruptly buckled. There was an enormous cracking and twisting of planks as that end of the bridge gave way in a sudden tilt and the wagon turned over as it fell, taking the shrieking mule with it. It crashed into the brown water upside down and on top of all four occupants and sank from sight to settle into the silty bottom ten feet down. There was a great rush of bubbles to the agitated surface and then only the diminishing ripples.

Sófi and Pieto were in the rear of the store, working at the ovens, and so didn't know of the accident until a neighbor rushed in to tell them. They ran out to the collapsed bridge where a large crowd had gathered, and several men had to restrain old Pieto by force to keep him from jumping in. A work crew had been summoned and was quick to arrive but it took them several dives to free the wagon of the mule carcass and then several dives more to lash lines to the wagon so that a winch could pull it over on its side and the bodies be retrieved. Pieto was half crazy with grief and keening like a dog. Sófi stood on the bank the whole while with her arms crossed and a hand to her mouth, staring down at the dirty water with no thought that she would later remember. The first bodies recovered were of Jorge and Prudencia, sodden and muddy and lank in that unreal way that only the dead can be. Finally a diver came bursting to the surface, gasping for air, and handed up to workers on the bank the two small and ill-formed effigies of mud that had been her children. She nearly screamed. Nearly vomited. Nearly fainted. Nearly turned her face up to heaven to bellow maledictions. Nearly threw herself into the water to inhale a great fatal draught of it. Nearly did all of those things but finally only put her face in her hands and wept.

Late that night, as she lay sleepless, she heard Pieto pacing in the other room and then after a while heard him go out the front door. In the morning his body was in the canal, floating facedown. That afternoon she moved back to La Rosa Mariposa.

This time there was no lying in bed for two weeks and staring at the ceiling. She simply put an apron on over her black dress and set to work. Her mother and brother did not know what to say to her, how to conduct themselves around her. It was hard enough to express an adequate condolence to someone who had all at once lost her husband and two children, but what could you say to someone for whom such a catastrophe was only one more in a series of disastrous losses?

Sófi could hardly bear their solicitude. Their strenuous efforts at casual conversation in her company only made her as self-conscious and tense as they were. She stood it for two weeks before telling them to stop treating her as if she were made of glass. She was heartbroken, yes, and so what that she was? She would sooner or later get over it. She always sooner or later got over it. What else was there to do except sooner or later get over it, what else? What that old fool Pieto did? Yes, *fool*! Only a fool could have lived so long and not known that there is nothing you cannot sooner or later get over.

Maybe he did know that, María Palomina said softly, but could not endure the wait. Sófi stared at her mother. Then went back to work.

For weeks her eyes were red and dark circled, and her lean frame contracted to the skeletal for her lack of interest in eating. But the weeks did pass, and she did, as she knew she would, get over it. Did regain an interest in her meals and the table talk of her mother and brother and the news of the neighborhood and sometimes even that of the larger world.

It was during that period of getting over it that she began to wonder if perhaps she were cursed. She had always prided herself on her rational mind and had disdained superstitions of all stripes, but the sum of her misfortunes by the age of twenty-four defied rational understanding. But even when, solely for the purpose of self-argument, she allowed for the possibility she was cursed, she could not think why she should be, neither by God nor witch nor someone of the Evil Eye. Had she transgressed against any such agent of fortune, she felt sure she would have known it, and hence would know whose forgiveness to ask, what penance to perform, what atonement she must make. She refused to believe she could be cursed and not know why or by whom, and so was left with no explanation for her misfortunes except random bad luck. Bad luck could befall anybody anytime anywhere for no particular reason, just as good luck could. Everybody knew that too. Her bad luck, she told herself, was only bad luck, no matter its tenacity, no matter its accumulated heft. The idea was devoid of self-pity, an emotion she had abhorred since childhood and would recoil from whenever she sensed its encroachment. She told herself that her bad luck would change, as luck always did, bad or good, and there was nothing to do about it except hope for the change to come sooner rather than later.

She was five years into her third widowhood when Diego Guzmán proposed to her in October of 1882. He was a shoemaker without any family, his shop just two streets from La Rosa Mariposa. A handsome, courtly, well-spoken man of thirty-eight whose hair and mustaches had early gone white. Better than anyone else, he understood Sófi's sad history, himself having lost two wives, one to the cholera and one to the unbelievable failure of her twenty-year-old heart as they were dancing at a fiesta. Both marriages had produced a child, a son each one, but the first died of some mysterious illness a few days after his first birthday, and the second somehow got tangled in the bedclothes and smothered at the age of five months. Diego had been wifeless for more than eight years when he began courting Sofía Reina.

Until they met each other they had both been sure they would not marry again, unwilling to risk having to bury yet another spouse, or worse, another child. But now Diego mocked himself for having been so fearful. It was easy to say never again when I was forlorn and had no one to love, he said. But now I am in love with you, my dearest Sófi, and now I know that love is stronger than fear. Let us be brave, Sófi! Let us be brave and marry.

She found it hard to share his bravado. She consulted with her mother, who said, I understand your worry, Sofita, but you mustn't let it rule the rest of your life. I agree with Diego. Love is worth the risk. Besides, be reasonable. It is not very likely, is it, that the two of you together would have more of the same bad luck each of you has had so much of in the past?

Sófi wasn't so sure about that, either. She thought very hard about it. But the more she thought, the more her focus sidled away from the risks involved and toward visions of herself and Diego in bed. Oh, how she missed *that* benefit of marriage! He was tall and lean, Diego was, and had long beautiful fingers. The thought of those fingers on her naked flesh deepened her breath and made her blush at her shameless reveries.

They were married in February in the little church of their neighborhood, the ceremony attended by their few friends who afterward joined in a party at La Rosa Mariposa that carried on until late in the evening. And when the last of the guests had left, the bride and groom went upstairs to Sófi's room, which María Palomina had adorned with vases of fresh flowers and whose sheets she had sprinkled with perfume. The room was softly lighted with aromatic candles of all colors, and on a small table was an iced bucket of champagne and a platter of treats—spiced crackers, stuffed olives, shelled nuts—so the newlyweds wouldn't lack for sustenance in the night.

Diego poured two glasses of the sparkling wine and said, To us, my darling, and all the life ahead.

They drank to their happy future. Then she made him sit in the armchair beside the refreshments and told him to stay put and just watch.

He sat back and sipped champagne and popped stuffed olives into his mouth, watching with bright eyes as she slowly began to undress. When she was down to her filmy underthings, she turned her back to him and slowly peeled off her undershirt—and smiled to hear his sudden gasp. She tossed the garment over her shoulder without a backward glance and then in a slow, teasing writhe began pushing down her underpants. She giggled as he began grunting and snorting like some aroused beast, thumping the floor with his feet. Oooh, she said in a small voice, I think I hear a big bad bull behind me. Is the big bad bull going to get me?

She turned and saw him slumped in the armchair with his hands at his throat and his face gone dark, eyes huge and bloodshot, mouth open and working with a soft gagging, legs atwitch. She was speechless with cold horror as she thought that this could not be happening and that of course this was happening. Of course. Then his gagging ceased and his feet went still and his hands slid away from his throat. He lay in an awkward slump, his wide eyes suggesting great surprise that all the sudden losses of his loved ones in the past had not in the least prepared him for his own abrupt end.

An hour later the summoned doctor held up for them to see—Sófi and María Palomina and Bruno Tomás—the stuffed olive he had dislodged from Diego's windpipe.

I had been crying and crying, Sófi told John Roger, but when he held up that olive, well, you might not believe this, dear uncle, but I nearly laughed. I just barely caught myself. For a moment I was aghast. I was ashamed of myself for such a disrespectful impulse. And then in the next moment I was petrified. Because I realized the urge was insane and I knew that if I started to laugh I would never be able to stop, I would go forever crazy. It took all my will to keep from laughing.

You are too hard on yourself, John Roger said. The loss of a loved one can cause great emotional confusion. I think the impulse to laugh at such times is not so unusual as one might think.

And I think, she said, I was this close—she held up her hand, thumb and forefinger almost touching—to losing my mind. And I was very aware, Uncle John, that my mind was the only thing I had left to lose. So I refused to laugh. Otherwise, you would have known me only as your pitiful little niece in the crazyhouse.

What she had not told John Roger was that she could not regard Diego's death as one more instance of bad luck by chance. However randomly bad luck might strike, she could no longer believe that it would by accident strike the same person again and again to such degree as it had struck her. The death of Diego not only revived her suspicion she was cursed, it convinced her she was. Once she accepted that explanation for her cumulative misfortunes, she felt the relief that comes from an end to perplexity. But she still could think of no reason for any supernatural force to place the curse on her, and hence had to believe its cause was in herself, that some dark personal fault was the source of her sorrowful calamities. Something in her blood. And when she thought of her father's ordeals and those of her Uncle John, she had to wonder if maybe the curse was in the blood of the whole damned family.

On their last night together in Mexico City, they were joined for dinner by Amos Bentley. Sófi prepared chicken enchiladas with her special sauce seasoned with roasted garlic and minced green chile, and Amos was effusive in his praise of the meal. María Palomina complimented Amos on his Spanish and said that he and John Roger spoke the language better than most Mexicans she knew. Samuel Thomas had also spoken it well, she said, but with an accent all his own. She mimicked her husband's enunciations, pretending to be him lauding Sófi for her enchiladas and asking for a second helping, and they all laughed, Bruno Tomás saying, That's him! That's exactly how he talked!

None laughed at his brother's accent so hard as John Roger. He laughed until he was gasping, aware that the laughter was his first full-bellied guffawing since Elizabeth Anne was alive. And the others laughed with him, happy for him, understanding why his enjoyment was so great and why it came with tears. He wiped his eyes and blew his nose and said, Well now, that felt better than a thorn in the butt. And set off another round of laughter.

The following morning, he and Bruno Tomás took breakfast with the Blanco women and assured them they would return for a visit before long. The women promised in turn they would soon visit Buenaventura. There was much hugging and kissing at the front gate and then the men boarded a hack for the train station and the women cast kisses after them until they rounded the corner and were gone.

TWO WEDDINGS

Unlike her sister Sofía Reina, Gloria Tomasina had married only once, a marriage that was into its seventeenth year at the time John Roger heard about it from the Blancos in Mexico City. But it was a marriage more inconceivable in its making than any of Sofía Reina's. It was but one extraordinary aspect of it that the man Gloria had been engaged to for five months when she awoke on the morning of July thirteenth, 1867, was not the man she married that night.

The fiancé of five months was a cavalry officer named Julián Salgado. María Palomina disliked him for a preening peacock but would have been displeased regardless by Gloria's betrothal to a soldier. Sófi shared her mother's dislike of Julián's haughtiness but could not deny that he cut a handsome figure. She secretly believed that her sister—who well knew how much their parents detested all things military—had accepted the lieutenant's proposal less out of love for him than for the dual satisfactions of spiting them and getting out from under their roof.

Gloria had always been an unpredictable puzzle to her family. She was always at odds with her parents, and if she rarely quarreled with her brother it was only because they were content to ignore each other. Only with Sófi did Gloria ever converse or join in genuine laughter, share a confidence or a pleasurable opinion. When she was fourteen she had refused to speak to her father for almost three months because he had not permitted a man nearly ten years her senior to escort her to a dance. Samuel Thomas was protecting a virginity the girl cheerfully granted a few months later to a shy army recruit headed for a post in distant Sonora. By sixteen she'd known three other lovers. Her mother, who had been to bed with but two men in her life, dared not share with Samuel Thomas her suspicion that their daughter was not only no longer a maiden but was not even chaste.

Gloria had just turned seventeen when she announced her intention to marry Lieutenant Salgado, who had been courting her for three months. Knowing that to argue against the marriage would only reinforce the girl's determination to go through with it, and hoping Gloria would change her mind of her own accord, María Palomina told her that if she truly wanted to marry the lieutenant, well then, she wished her the best. But Gloria had long been able to perceive her mother's true feelings in any situation, and her smirk at the counterfeit good wishes made María Palomina want to snatch her by the hair and shake some proper respect into her. Samuel Thomas was a different matter, as Gloria had never been able to read her father's mutilated face very well, and so when Julián made formal request for her hand and Samuel Thomas granted it with a smile and handshake and hearty congratulations, Gloria's satisfaction derived entirely from her conviction that he did not mean a word of it. But Samuel Thomas's blessing was sincere. As he confided to María Palomina, his dislike of Gloria's marriage to a soldier was much outweighed by his relief that their daughter would soon be her husband's problem and no longer theirs. The wedding was scheduled for the first Saturday in August.

It so happened that Raquel Aguilera, Gloria's friend since childhood, was to be married three weeks before then, on the second Saturday in July. Gloria would serve as her maid of honor, and Sófi, who was almost fourteen and had also known Raquel most of her life, would be a bridesmaid—though she would be unescorted, as the boy who was to go with her would be taken ill at the last moment. Because of his refusal to venture farther than a few blocks from home, Samuel Thomas would not attend Raquel's wedding, which would take place in a neighborhood at the far end of Avenida Reforma. The truth, as everyone in the family knew, was that he had never liked Raquel Aguilera and would probably not have attended her wedding if it had been held in the next room. But because Samuel Thomas did not go, María Palomina did not go either. And so, when Gloria left for the church on Raquel's wedding day—on the arm of Julián Salgado and with Sófi in tow—it was the last time in their lives her parents ever saw her.

❈

Raquel was marrying an American she had met at the end of the war against Maximilian and had known less than a month. She was working as a nurse in the central hospital when the Yankee was brought in with a chest wound he'd received a week earlier and which had become badly infected. His arrival caused a stir because he was accompanied by the military hero, General Porfirio Díaz, who made it clear to the hospital administrators that the American was a dear friend and ordered that he be attended by the best surgeons in the place. It was said the two men were of the same age and had saved each other's lives, but nobody knew any of the details. It was a friendship even more unusual than anyone could have guessed, given how few true friends either man had or ever would. In the gringo's case, only a brother already dead, his own first son, and a great-granddaughter not yet born. And while Díaz had called many men his friend and would so call many more—often with a patent irony that would chill them to the bone—the truth was that he had never had a true friend in his life, not even his own brother, save this gringo.

Raquel Aguilera was one of the nurses assigned to the American, who spoke fluent Spanish, and she told Gloria and Sófi of Díaz's daily visits to him. The gringo's only other visitor was his grown son, Louis, who understood Spanish much better than he spoke it. A rough-looking but handsome young man with a short blond beard and long hair to his shoulders in the fashion of American frontiersmen.

It was toward the end of the gringo's stay in the hospital that he proposed marriage to Raquel and she accepted, even though she had known him so briefly and though he was more than twice her age. And even though, as everyone who saw him would attest, he was a man of grisly aspect. After seeing him at the wedding, Sófi would describe him as having a face scarred even worse than her father's. The gringo had also lost an ear but hid the nub of it under long side hair. Worst of all, he had sometime in his youth been scalped by Indians—or so it was said. After seeing the tight black skullcap the man wore at his wedding, Sófi was sure it was true. She could tell that he was hairless under the cap and it made her shudder to imagine what the crown of his head must look like. Raquel Aguilera herself had never seen him without the cap.

That Raquel would marry a man she hardly knew, a foreigner—a gringo!—a man so physically repellent and so much older than herself, was baffling to her family and friends and every young man who had ever wooed her. Some believed she was marrying the Yankee because he was a man of secret wealth and she had somehow found out. Others said she was probably attracted to his power—if only because of his closeness to Díaz, the gringo was clearly a man to reckon with, and power was an attribute many women found even more alluring than wealth. But some only shrugged and said maybe there was no reasonable explanation for Raquel's decision to marry him, maybe she was just in love. Which was in fact the case. The man's name was Edward Little.

⁂

The wedding was performed in a church within sight of Chapultepec Castle. Attending from the bride's side were Raquel's few relatives and friends, but the groom had no family other than his son, who was not present at the start of the ceremony, and no friend but Díaz, who was his best man. To give the occasion a greater size and sense of festivity, Díaz had invited three dozen army officers and their female companions, plus a handful of stags to serve as extra dance partners at the reception. The officers were in full dress uniform, including their sabers.

It was Sófi's first look at Díaz in person and she thought him even more striking in the flesh than in the photographs she had seen. He was tall and lean, with intense black eyes, unkempt short black hair, the downturned mustache of a pirate. He radiated ready quickness. But his manners were of the field camp. He was chatting with some officers just outside the church doors as Sófi was about to enter, and she saw him turn and spit into a bush behind him. And not until he was in the church and the ceremony had begun did he think to remove the toothpick from his mouth.

Díaz himself was recently wed, married but two months to a pretty mestiza named Delfina Ortega, who was sitting in the front pew on the groom's side of the aisle. At age twenty, she too was much younger than her husband, and hardly better versed in the ways of polite society. She was also, Sófi had heard it whispered, her husband's niece.

The ceremony was near conclusion when Sófi saw a black-suited young gringo come down a side aisle and take a seat at the far end of the pew where Díaz and his wife sat. By his long yellow hair and short beard Sófi knew him for Louis Little. During the final minutes of the mass, she looked his way again and saw him staring at Gloria where she stood at her post as maid of honor. Just then, as if she'd felt his gaze on her, Gloria turned her head and their eyes met. And he winked at her. The indiscretion was so shocking Sófi could hardly believe it. And even more incredible was the smile Gloria gave him in return. Sófi cut a look at Julián Salgado at the far end of the adjacent pew and saw that he was staring out the nearest window, his boredom with the ceremony as obvious as his unawareness of the exchange between Gloria and the gringo.

Then the service was over and everyone—including Father Benedicto, the old priest who had performed the ceremony and was known to have an affection for tequila—set off to the reception, which was being held in a mansion only a block away and owned by a friend of Díaz. On the walk there in the fading light of early evening, Sófi looked about for Louis Little but didn't see him anywhere. Nor did she see him in the ballroom. She kept an eye out for him even as she waltzed with one young officer or another. During respites from dancing, she sat at a table reserved for the bridesmaids and their escorts, next to the dais on which the bridal couple shared a table with General Díaz and his wife. Sófi wanted to ask Gloria about the byplay with Louis Little in the church, but with all the other people at the table and all the coming and going between the table and the dance floor and Julián Salgado almost constantly at Gloria's side, there was no opportunity for such private talk.

When the reception was in its second hour and there was still no sign of Louis Little, Sófi concluded that, for whatever reason, he wasn't coming. Then an officer came to their table and told Julián there was a civilian in the parlor who wished to speak with him. Julián asked who it was but the officer said he didn't know, he was just delivering his message. Sófi watched Julián heading toward the parlor hallway on the other side of the room, then turned to her sister, thinking she at last had a chance to talk to her—and was startled to see Louis Little standing at the table and

Gloria smiling up at him. His eyes were dark blue, Sófi saw, his face sunbrowned, his smile confident. In his fractured Spanish he asked Gloria if she would honor him with a dance. She said it would be her pleasure, and he took her offered hand and escorted her onto the floor.

A few minutes later Julián was back and looked annoyed. Sófi asked what was wrong and he said there hadn't been anyone in the parlor waiting to see him. He asked where Gloria was and Sófi pursed her lips and shrugged. He scanned the other tables. Then the dance floor. Then spied them. Talking and laughing as they waltzed round and round. He caught Sófi looking at them too and asked who the gringo was. She said she didn't know. He sat down and poured a glass of champagne and watched them until the waltz concluded. But they remained on the floor, talking in evident earnestness, and then another number struck up and they again began to dance. Julián stood and Sófi's heart jumped as he started toward them, sidestepping dancing couples as he went.

Gloria saw him approaching and said something to Louis Little. They stopped dancing as Julián came up, his face tight with anger. Louis Little looked at him without interest, and then in his faulty Spanish thanked Gloria for the dance.

"It was my pleasure," she said. Her use of English was as galling to Julián, who did not speak the language, as the smile she was giving the man.

As Louis started to walk away, Julián said, Hey, gringo. Louis stopped and turned. Don't bother to ask her for another dance, Julián said. I won't permit my fiancée to take any further risk of contracting fleas.

"Julián!" Gloria said.

"The only fleas I ever had," Louis Little said in his soft southern English, "I got from your mama."

Julián needed no translator to comprehend "mama" and that he had been insulted.

Watching from the edge of the dance floor, Sófi saw him give Louis Little a hard shove rearward—and a woman cried out as he unsheathed his saber faster than Sófi would have thought possible. Just as suddenly, Louis Little was brandishing a massive knife drawn from under his coat. There were startled squeals and the couples nearest the two men backed away from them as they began to circle each other with weapons ready. Some of the officers shouted bets on Lieutenant Salgado but could get no takers. A Bowie knife was no match for a saber in the hands of a cavalry officer and they all expected the lieutenant to drop the gringo with his first sally.

Díaz stepped between the two men and they froze.

Put up your blades and come with me, he said. They traded hard looks as they followed him to a side door, where Díaz paused before a clutch of officers and said, "Pistolas." Several ranking officers beckoned their aides, who came at a trot from their posts near the doors, each of them with a revolver on his belt. The guns were unholstered and held out butt first for Díaz's inspection. He took one and unbuttoned his tunic and slipped the pistol into his waistband and then selected two more, one in each hand. He told the officers at the door to make sure everyone else stayed inside and then ushered Lieutenant Salgado and Louis Little out into a large lamplit garden. An officer shut the door behind them. Up on the dais, Edward Little stood with his hands behind him and his eyes on the garden door. Only the two young women at the table could see he was holding a gun.

The orchestra was told to resume playing but nobody wanted to dance— they were all too tense about the imminent duel. There was loud debate about its outcome, a flurry of wagers offered and accepted. The odds were in heavy favor of Lieutenant Salgado not only for reasons of partisanship but because he was known to be a good shot, while no one knew how well the gringo could handle a gun. It was said he had fought in the American Civil War, but even if true, that fact revealed nothing about his ability with a pistol. Some of the older officers, more experienced with the ways of duels, bet that there would be no winner. The combatants would either kill each other or, as in most duels, both be wounded but neither fatally.

Sófi sat with her sister and found out what had been said in the confrontation. Gloria's eyes were as bright as when boys had fought over her in girlhood. Sófi could not have denied that her own dread was laced with a strange elation. It wasn't every day a pair of men fought a duel over your sister.

Out in the garden Díaz picked a spot that would put the two men in equal illumination at a distance of some thirty paces and where an errant bullet was unlikely to hit anything other than a tree or a wall. He asked if either of them wanted to end the contention with an apology. Neither one did.

Very well, Díaz said. He showed them that both revolvers were fully-loaded Kerr single-action five-shooters. Then made them stand back to back and handed each of them a pistol. He told them to begin pacing when he began to count. When the count reached fifteen they could turn and fire at will.

If either of you turns before I call fifteen, Díaz said, drawing his own pistol, *I'll* shoot you. Understood? He backed up a few feet from the line of fire and began a measured counting.

The two men paced away from each other until Díaz called "Quince!" and then they whirled and fired. But even as he spun around, Louis Little—who had been a guerrilla fighter with Bloody Bill Anderson's wildwood Missourians in the war of the American states and thereby learned everything on earth there was to know about pistol fighting—dropped to one knee and Salgado's bullet passed above and to the left of his head as his own round hit the lieutenant in the chest and staggered him rearward into a tree. Julián collapsed to a sitting position with his back against the tree trunk and the revolver yet in his hand, and Louis Little, still crouched, shot him three times more, cocking and firing as fast as he could, the first of these bullets passing through Julián's head and pasting the tree with blood and the next two striking his unbeating heart even as he was toppling onto his side.

Captain Anderson had always said to make sure they were finished, that he'd seen more than one man killed by another assumed to be dead.

Louis Little stood up, the revolver cocked on the remaining round, and he studied Julián's still form. Satisfied the man was dead, he uncocked the Kerr and went to Díaz and handed it to him. The general tucked it and his own pistol into his pants.

Your father tells me you are from Louisiana, Díaz said.

Yes.

They must have some interesting duels in Louisiana. Here the rule is that a man must stand his ground during the exchange of fire and the rule is understood to mean that he should stand it upright. You stood your ground, yes, but somewhat, well, gymnastically, let us say.

Louis Little stared at him. He had not known Díaz very long and wondered if he was one of those bossmen who purposely didn't tell you all of the rules just so he could have the pleasure of charging you with breaking one that you didn't know about. He'd had a bossman like that in a timber camp when he was sixteen years old, his first job after leaving home following his mother's death. The bossman had not liked him for some reason and made things hard for him at every turn. One day the man upbraided him loudly in front of a crew of witnessing timberjacks for breaking some rule Louis hadn't heard of. The bossman said ignorance was no excuse, that Louis would have to pay him a fine of a day's wages and if he argued about it he'd give him a hiding to boot. The contretemps concluded with the bossman on his back and his head in bloody mud with Louis's timber axe wedged in his skull to the sinuses. Louis then mounted the bossman's horse and galloped off to places unknown.

The War Between the States was then in its second year and he was soon riding with William Clarke Quantrill and his confederate guerrillas, whom many regarded less as military irregulars than as a band of outlaws using the war as pretext for their depredations. When dissension broke up Quantrill's company, Louis chose to ride with Bloody Bill. Then the war was lost and so he went west and roamed without purpose and here and there took employment as a marshal and once as a train guard and on various occasions killed men either for the bounty to be collected or over an insult of some sort or, most often, in some drunken argument whose particulars he would not remember. Finally he did as a few other die-hard rebels had done and went to Mexico. The republicans were still at war with Maximilian and there was no shortage of opportunity for a man of Louis's skills. Because the imperialists were invaders, he saw them as akin to Yankees, and he hired on with Juárez. But he had got there at the tail end of things and had been in Mexico but six weeks when the war ended.

One afternoon, shortly after the liberation of Mexico City, he was drinking in a cantina and wondering what he might do next when he overheard the name of Edward Little mentioned in a group of American roughnecks at a nearby table. He bought a round for the bunch and asked about Edward Little and learned that he was General Díaz's chief scout and was at present in the central hospital with a bad chest wound.

An hour later he was at Edward Little's bedside. He introduced himself as Louis Welch and asked if he remembered a woman in Louisiana named Sharon Welch. "It was a long time ago," Louis said. "Momma said you were on your way to Texas and yall didn't know each other but the one night, so you might not recall. She told me about it when I was twelve. Said she wanted me to know who my daddy was, even if she didn't hardly know more than your name. She said she liked you an awful lot."

Edward Little remembered young Sharon Welch. She was sixteen, as was he, on the cold evening she sneaked out of the house and into the barn where her daddy had permitted him to spend the night. In the years since, he had at times thought of her. He was sorry to learn she was dead but was glad to make the acquaintance of the son he had not known they created. He offered his hand and the young man accepted it. The next day he introduced Louis to Porfirio Díaz, who seemed more amused than surprised to learn Edward had a son. That had been two weeks ago.

Don't worry, kid, Díaz said. I didn't specify what the rules were, did I? You were free to use the rules of Louisiana. And I have to say, you handle a pistol very well.

Louis smiled back. Thank you, general.

Díaz went over to Julián and retrieved the other revolver. I feel sorry for this one's fiancée, he said. A widow before she was even a wife.

In his bad Spanish, Louis Little said he intended to make things right for her.

Really? Díaz said. Tell me. I would like to hear about this intention.

Louis told him, not sure if the way Díaz smiled as he listened was because of what he was hearing or the way it was being said. But he listened carefully, and when Louis finished explaining what he had in mind, Díaz said, I have only one question. Do you want to do this because you feel guilty for killing her man? Louis assured him it wasn't guilt. It was what he wanted the minute he saw her. He gestured at Julián Salgado and said maybe now what he wanted would be easier or maybe impossible. Díaz clapped him on the shoulder and laughed. There's only one way to find out, my friend. Goddammit, I should have known by the way you looked at her when you were dancing. "Pero que cosa fantástica es el amor, no?"

In the ballroom, the first two shots—which all of the women and even some of the officers in the room had taken for one, so closely together did they sound—had stopped the music and hushed all talk, and Gloria squeezed Sófi's hand so hard it would ache the next day. Almost immediately behind those first shots, there came three more reports in rapid sequence, and one of the officers said, Well, I'll bet somebody just killed the hell out of somebody.

There followed long minutes of buzzing speculation before the garden door finally opened and Díaz and Louis Little reentered the room. There were low groans from the bet losers and chuckling from those few who had backed the gringo. No one saw Edward Little return his gun to its holster under his coat.

Díaz handed the guns to one of the officers and gave low-voiced instructions to some others and they nodded and went out to the garden.

As Louis Little headed for the bridesmaids' table where Gloria sat and watched him approach, Díaz gestured at the others sitting there and they all got up and moved away—except for Sófi, until Gloria hissed, "Vete," and she sighed and left too. Then Louis was at the table and asked Gloria's permission to sit beside her and she nodded. He sat down and leaned toward her and spoke in a voice so low she had to lean towards him too, their heads almost touching, and to every eye in the room they looked like longtime intimates. Louis Little spoke without pause for about a minute and was done. Gloria stared at him a moment more and then smiled and said something in response and he grinned and took her hand and turned to look at his father, who smiled in his own maimed fashion and raised his glass in salute.

"Bravo!" Díaz said. He leaped up to the dais and called for everyone's attention and proclaimed the impending marriage of Louis Little and Gloria Blanco.

The room erupted with applause and cheers and copious wisecracking about the ball-and-chain and the poor gringo's excessive punishment for the simple crime of shooting á man, and so on. The smiling couple stood with their arms around each other and Louis Little bent to Gloria's ear and said something and her smile widened. She was beaming.

Díaz called for Father Benedicto and someone shouted that the old padre was passed out in the bar adjoining the ballroom. Díaz joined in the laughter and said to rouse him and bring him up there, to carry him if they had to. While the revived priest was being assisted in making his unsteady way across the room, Díaz announced that the funeral for Lieutenant Julián Salgado Ordoñez would be held in the garrison cemetery tomorrow afternoon. He expected every officer in the room to attend. Lieutenant Salgado was an honorable soldier who fell in an honorable contest and he would be shown every respect.

Sófi stood bewildered. Julián Salgado was lying dead in the garden while in this boisterous ballroom her sister was smiling in the arms of the man who'd killed him. A man she had only just met and would marry in the next few minutes.

Father Benedicto was hoisted up to the dais and an officer held him upright by one arm. White hair disheveled and eyes a red glaze, his collar awry, the old priest protested to Díaz that it would be an offense before God to perform a sacred office in such shameful condition as he was in. Don't worry, Father, Díaz said. God and I are old comrades. I'll square you with Him in my prayers tonight. Just keep it short and simple. You ask if they want to be married, they say yes, and you say all right you're married.

The priest swayed and the officer holding to him said, Easy does it. Another said, The old boy needs a bracer, that's all. He handed a bottle to the priest and said, Here you go, Moses. Father Benedicto took a deep drink, paused for breath, then took another big swallow. He smacked his lips and gave a contented sigh. The color rose in his cheeks. Díaz grinned and said, Father, you'll outlive us all.

Sófi pushed her way through the crowd to get to Gloria's side at the foot of the dais stairs. Gloria smiled to see her and said Hey, girl, I was wondering where you were.

What are you *doing*? Sófi said.

Getting married, sweetie, what's it look like?

It looks like you've lost your mind.

Gloria laughed and gave Sófi's cheek an affectionate pat.

The old priest took another drink before Díaz gently detached the bottle from him. Let's hold off on that for just a minute, Father, he said, and beckoned Louis Little.

"Come on, darlin," Louis said, "before the old coot passes out again."

A minute later Gloria was Louis Little's wife. And by legal definition had also become daughter-in-law to her lifelong friend Raquel Aguilera de Little, who was in fact two months younger than Gloria and herself only three hours a bride. The band struck up a lively tune and the brides each kissed Díaz in turn, and the bridegrooms, father and son, shook his hand, and then both couples headed for the door. As Gloria was being hurried along on Louis Little's arm, Sófi trotted up beside her and said, Where are you going? What do I tell Mother and Father? What about your clothes? What about—?

Gloria blew her a kiss. I'll write you, sweetie, I promise! And was gone.

When Sófi got home and told her parents what happened, María Palomina said, Oh my dear Jesus, and sat at the table and put her head in her hands. She had not liked Julián Salgado, true, but to lose his life in a stupid duel over her impetuous daughter! Nothing Gloria Tomasina ever did could surprise her, but María Palomina had to wonder about the girl's mental condition. To marry a man she had not known an hour—and even more unbelievable, whose hands were still dripping with the blood of her betrothed!

How could it be, María Palomina said, addressing the room at large, that I gave birth to such a one?

She looked at Samuel Thomas, who sat sipping brandy at the other end of the table, scowling at some vision in his head.

I guess we know which side of the family she takes after, María Palomina said. *My* people never produced anybody even a little bit like her.

Samuel Thomas ignored the gibe. He did not care about what happened to Julián Salgado, but he was incensed that Gloria had married an American. A goddam gringo, he said. That stupid girl.

He persisted in his bitter mutterings about it until María Palomina, in her irritation with the whole matter, said that if he was so strongly opposed to marriage between Mexicans and Americans, maybe they should have their own holy union annulled. She asked what he was anyway so mad about. He had wanted Gloria gone and she was gone. What did he care who she was gone with?

You know what? Samuel Thomas said. You're right. You're absolutely right. To hell with it. Her punishment for marrying an American will be that she's married to an American.

To which María Palomina said, Tell me something I don't know, Mister Yankee. How long has it been? Eighteen years?

He fixed her with a thin look and she returned it in mock fashion. Then put the back of her hand to her forehead in a theatrical gesture of long-suffering and sighed loudly and said, Eighteen years. *Eighteeeen lonnnng yeeears.* And cut a sidelong look at him. He tried to hold to his indignation, but then she grinned at him and they both laughed.

Well, I'll tell you what, Samuel Thomas said, raising his glass. Here's to eighteen more. Because I can take it, woman, you hear me? I can *take* it. I've taken other punishment almost this bad.

They laughed harder still and Sófi joined in. She had never before heard her father jest and rarely heard him laugh and never with such gusto. He laughed and pounded the table with his fist. María Palomina laughed so hard she nearly slipped off her chair, which made them all laugh harder.

They had just got themselves under control when Bruno Tomás came up after closing for the night and said, Hey, everybody, what's new?

And flinched at the explosion of renewed laughter.

GLORIA LITTLE

Gloria kept her promise to write to Sófi, but her letters were infrequent and most of them brief. In the first seventeen years of her marriage she wrote only eleven letters to her sister, the first of them not until almost a year after her wedding, by which time Bruno Tomás was in the army and Sófi had given up hope of ever hearing from her. Sófi wrote back right away, eight pages, front and back. She would write two more letters to Gloria in the eight months before receiving a second one from her. Such would be the pattern of their correspondence for the rest of Gloria's life—Sófi writing two or three letters for each one she got from her sister, who would sometimes let more than a year go by between writing one letter and writing the next, and at one point three years would pass without her sending Sófi a line. Even when Sofia sent the news of each of her marriages, of the bereaving loss of each husband, of the wonderful births of her children and of the unbearable deaths of them, there was no telling how long it would be before Gloria wrote back. But respond she always sooner or later did, with buoyant good wishes for each marriage, with high joy at the birth of each child, with deep commiseration at the death of every husband, and, in the two most wrenching letters Sófi ever received in her life, with such keening anguish over the deaths of her infant nephews—whom she never even had a chance to see, to hold in her arms—that Sófi was both times reduced to sobs of renewed grief for her children even as she felt a great swell of love for her sister.

Gloria never wrote to her parents and they never wrote to her, but Sófi always relayed regards between the parties, even when, as was always the case, no actual regards had been tendered.

215

While infrequent and brief, Gloria's letters to Sofía Reina provided a sketchy chronicle of her life with Louis Little. For the first four of those years, she and Louis—as well as Raquel and Edward Little—lived at La Noria, a hacienda Díaz received as a gift from his home state of Oaxaca, whose governor happened to be his brother, Félix. Having fallen out with Juárez after the defeat of the French and then losing to him in the presidential election, Díaz had resigned his commission and repaired to La Noria, taking with him thirty hand-picked men of his most formidable cavalry company. Juárez may be the president of Mexico, Díaz would say, but in Oaxaca *I* am the law. Félix Díaz would grin at this and say it was true. I am the governor, yes, he said, but he is my big brother and our mother always told me I must do as my big brother says. Gloria described Félix to Sófi as shorter and darker than Porfirio, but as handsome, though in a more menacing mode. Félix is as full of shadows, Gloria wrote, as the strange mountains of this place.

Edward and Louis—the younger Little's Spanish having much improved—were part of Díaz's small cadre of personal guards that accompanied him whenever he left La Noria, which was usually to Mexico City and sometimes for as long as several weeks. Unlike Díaz's military guards, who were uniformed and always stayed close to him, the Littles dressed like ranch hands with big sombreros to shadow their faces and with ponchos to hide the pair of revolvers each of them wore on his belt, and they worked at a distance from Díaz, melding into the throngs and moving along the fringes of wherever he might be. Díaz himself sometimes would not know where they were but Edward and Louis always knew where he was and never let him out of sight of both of them at the same time.

In private Díaz had told his military guards that as much as he liked the Littles and found their bilingualism useful to him, he preferred his nearest protectors to be fellow Mexicans. The soldiers had smiled to hear it. But the fact of the matter, as Díaz confided to the Littles, was that he did not trust his army guards, and he wanted Edward and Louis in a position to keep an eye on them as well as on everybody else. It is a sad truth about my countrymen, Díaz told the Littles, that not one in ten would hesitate to kill his best friend for two pesos, though you can be sure he would attend the funeral and shed the loudest and most heartfelt tears. It is the natural perfidy of their Indian blood. I tell you, my friends, the Aztecs were conquered not by Cortéz but by the treachery of the other Indians.

Between themselves, the Littles remarked on Díaz's increasing penchant for speaking of Indians and mixed-bloods as if he himself were not of them. "I expect the day's coming when Pórfi will be talking about his daddy the Spanish grandee," Edward Little said to Louis, who grinned along with him.

❦

The four years at La Noria were rife with joyful births and piteous early deaths. Gloria's son, Luis Charón, was born in the tenth month of her marriage, the only child she would ever have. He had his father's dark blue eyes and his mother's ebony hair. She had liked the name Charón on having heard it only once, from a boy calling to a friend in the street. Louis liked it too because of its similarity to his mother's name of Sharon.

In the fall of the following year Raquel gave birth to a robust son as dusky as herself whom Edward named Zachary Jackson Little. Porfirio and Delfina were the most fecund of the couples, producing two sons and a daughter. But shortly after the birth of the second son both boys were taken by typhoid, and the parents were still grieving for them when the baby girl died in her sleep for no knowable reason.

⁂

There came a spring day in their fourth year at La Noria when Díaz and the Littles left their families at the hacienda and went to live in Mexico City in preparation for that summer's presidential election, in which Díaz once again ran against Juárez. And once again lost. This time Díaz had no doubt that the government had engaged in electoral fraud and that Juárez was absolutely set on perpetuating himself in office for life by any crooked means necessary. In public Díaz said that no law was more vital to Mexico's future than one to prohibit presidential reelection. In private he said, I won't lose to that fucking Indian dwarf again. Then went back to La Noria to plan his revolt.

The Littles told their wives to pack for a long trip, that they and the children would be going to the border along with Delfina Díaz to be well removed from danger during the coming trouble. Gloria asked Louis how long they would have to be gone and he said he didn't know.

On a morning of drizzling rain the women and children boarded a coach guarded by a detachment of Díaz's cavalry and set off on a journey that was supposed to take ten days but because of bad weather and battered roads took seventeen. The trip was especially hard on Raquel, who was midway through another pregnancy. They were met in Matamoros by friends of Díaz and then ferried across the Río Bravo to Brownsville, where they would be safer still. They took residence in a rented two-story house at the west end of Elizabeth Street.

⁂

In January, Raquel delivered John Louis Little, the only American in their party. His complexion caramel as her own but his auburn hair and green eyes would remind Edward Little of his own mother's. They hired a young maid named Silvania to help with the housework and the care of the children. Díaz's rebellion was then in its fourth month and faring badly. Much of the support he had counted on had failed to muster, and his forces were no match for Juárez's federals. Not Delfina nor either Little wife had heard from her husband since the uprising or knew if he was dead or alive. Their fears grew greater with every report from Mexico of another federal victory.

It was not until spring, when a dapper man named Ramos came to them with a note written in Díaz's recognizable though barely legible hand, that they learned all three men were still alive. The note did not say where they were, only that they were in hiding from the Juaristas but would soon begin making their way to the border.

There followed another two months without any word from their husbands before Ramos reappeared early one morning with another terse note from Díaz. It instructed the women to pack up and go with Ramos. He had brought a team and wagon and the women helped him to load it. That afternoon they ferried across to Matamoros and then began heading southwestward. Their husbands, Ramos told them, were awaiting them at a ranch about ten miles away.

Their route took them through an encampment of a few hundred haggard insurgents where the air was smoky with cookfires and stank of shit. The soldiers smiled at the women, and a few of the officers hailed Ramos in recognition. Then they were on the ranch and rattling past a herd of bony cattle gnawing at the ragged pasture and then a herd of bleating goats thriving on the same spare feed. And then the ranch house came into view.

Their husbands had seen them coming and were waiting on the gallery when Ramos halted the wagon at the front steps. Díaz's head was bandaged and he had a splint on one hand, Edward carried an arm in a sling, and Louis was hobbling on a cane. Leaving the children to Silvania the maid, the women scrambled down from the wagon and ran up to the porch and threw themselves on the men, who protested the rough treatment of their wounds by such happy affections but could not quit their own grins at the women's happiness to see them. Through most of that night there were small yelps and sweet moanings from all the bedrooms except the one at the rear of the house, where amid children sleeping like the deaf, Silvania the maid lay awake on her little cot, smiling at the sounds of the happy couplings and feeling so left out she wanted to cry.

Not until after breakfast the next morning did the women find out that Félix Díaz was dead. He had been killed in a little village called Juchitán. Murdered by Oaxacans, Díaz said. His own people. Treacherous bastards. Díaz gave no details, but that night, in the privacy of their bed, Louis told Gloria the story they'd heard from the witness who brought the bad news. Díaz had rewarded the man with a purse of silver for bringing the details—and then shot him in the foot for not having tried to defend Félix, no matter that the man would have been killed too had he tried.

What happened was that Félix had gone to Juchitán to give its men hell for not having joined Porfirio in his fight against Juárez. It was a typically rash thing for Félix to do. Not long before, while he was governor, he'd personally led a troop of militia to Juchitán and hanged five of its residents because of a rumor that they belonged to a local bandit gang. The villagers had all sworn to him the men weren't bandits but he executed them anyway, saying it was better to be safe than sorry. Then this time Félix went there alone and apparently without a thought to the bitterness he had created on his previous visit. When they saw him ride in alone the Juchitanos could scarcely believe it. They swarmed into the street and pulled him off his horse and punched and clawed him bloody. They gouged out one of his eyes and knocked out his teeth and fried his tongue with a hot iron to put an end to his cursing of them. They sliced off the soles of his feet and paraded him through the village at the end of a rope noosed round his neck, children trotting alongside him and hitting him with sticks and laughing at each other's mimicry of his seared tongue's cries of agony. They slung the rope over a tree limb and repeatedly hauled him up off the ground and let him drop and in this way broke both his legs and other bones. As is the way with mobs, the more they did to him the more they wanted to do, became frenzied to do, until they finally lost all control and tore him apart as a dog pack does a hare. Then gathered his remains in a bean sack and buried them.

"Porfirio cried like a child when he heard what they did to Félix," Louis said. "I'd say that little town's got a real bad day in its future."

It did for a fact. Four years hence would come a summer morning when a party of twenty armed riders led by a man the surviving women and children would be able to describe only as having the devil's own hideous face would descend on Juchitán and drag the mayor from his house without heed of his sworn protests that he had not been the mayor four years ago and they would make him dig up the sack containing Félix's disjointed and discolored bones and broken skull and then take the mayor to the public square and there behead him and quarter his corpse and hang the five segments of him each from a different tree and then shoot every male who looked above the age of fifteen and shoot too all the livestock and set fire to every hut and cornfield and then ride out again a bare hour after they rode in. Taking with them Félix's desiccated remnants to receive a respectful interment in a lush Mexico City cemetery.

⁂

The three men were not yet fully recovered from their wounds when they got the news of Juárez's death and Lerdo's succession to the presidency. Then came word of Lerdo's proclamation of amnesty to all rebels who would quit the fight. Díaz suspected a ruse. Over the next weeks, he made inquiries via couriers until he was finally convinced Lerdo was sincere. Then notified Lerdo of his acceptance of the amnesty, and the insurrection was formally ended.

The women were very happy to be going home. In the year since they had left La Noria, Gloria had written to Sófi twice—about three months after Raquel gave birth to John Louis and just before they left the Matamoros ranch to go back to La Noria. In the first letter she complained at length about Brownsville as a dirty, smelly town infested with mosquitoes and overrun with the mangiest dogs and least civilized men on earth. The distance between heaven and hell, Gloria wrote, was not so great as that between Brownsville, Texas, and Mexico City. Sófi smiled at her sister's propensity for dramatic exaggeration. Gloria missed the high country and its fresher, drier air. Brownsville's humidity pasted your clothes to your skin and your skin to the bedsheets and it bred mold everywhere. Thank God for the trees that made a shady refuge of the rear patio where one could spend an almost pleasant hour or two with a good book. The four months at the Matamoros ranch had been no better. They had gone into town a few times and she found it to be even worse than Brownsville. A town of pelados and rateros and every sort of border trash you could imagine. The gringos liked to joke about its name and said that you didn't have to be a Moor to get killed there, that the town ought to be called Matatodos. More and more, Gloria felt like she was imprisoned at the very edge of the world, and her fear of suddenly falling off the earth was sometimes so great she could barely resist the impulse to clutch tight to a tree. As you can see, she wrote, this place has abused my sanity no less than my flesh. We are going back home none too soon.

❊

When they got back to La Noria it was not there anymore. Only black ruin and a landscape strewn with the carcasses of stock shot dead and fed on by scavengers and decayed to bone and withered hide. Nothing remained of the buildings but sooted stone walls. The cane fields had been burned and sown with salt for good measure. All the wells were poisoned.

This grim report came to Sófi in Gloria's first letter since departing Brownsville more than a year before. It was written at a sugar plantation called La Candelaria, in the south of Veracruz state, where Díaz and the Littles were residing as guests of yet another friend of Don Porfirio. Gloria was thankful to be back in Mexico—the borderland around Matamoros was neither truly Mexican nor American, she said, but a bastard offspring of both countries. But she had expected to return to the Oaxacan highlands, not be brought to this steamy plantation with cane fields on every side and nothing but jungle beyond them. She lived for the day Porfirio took over the country and they could again live in Mexico City, a day she believed would not be long in coming. Many mysterious visitors had been coming and going in recent weeks, Porfirio receiving them in private, and it was her feeling that he was planning another revolt and this time taking much greater care in his preparations. When he wasn't busy with his plans and secret conferences, he was often doting on his newborn son, Deodato, whom everyone called Porfirito. The child was healthy and strong as a colt, and they felt certain that, unlike the unfortunate siblings who preceded him, he would survive infancy.

When Sófi sent Gloria the news of their father's death, she told her only that he had died of illness, wanting to spare her the awful detail of the rabies. But in her reply of months later, all Gloria said about Samuel Thomas's passing was that she could not feel very much about the death of someone she had hardly known, who had kept himself a stranger to his own children. Sófi was appalled by her sister's attitude toward their father and would not hurt their mother with it. She told María Palomina that Gloria had sent condolences. And her mother smiled and nodded as though she believed it.

❈

The year after Samuel Thomas died, Graciela María was born to Edward and Raquel Little. Edward said he felt himself a lucky man to have a daughter. But later in that same year the region was struck by yet another rage of yellow fever and both Raquel and Graci contracted the disease. The mother died a day after the child.

Edward dug their grave himself in a stifling heat and a haze of mosquitoes, laboring shirtless and hatless, a black bandanna capping his head. The low snifflings of Gloria and Delfina mingled with his huffing and the sound of his spade. Besides the two women and the priest Delfina had summoned, the only ones present were Díaz and Louis Little, and Edward had refused their offers of help with the digging.

None of them knew that Raquel and Graci were not the first beloveds he had buried in this country. None knew he'd had a younger sister and an older brother and when he was sixteen the three had been separated by fell straits in their homeland American South. Two years later during the war with Mexico he had by chance met with both of them again, each in turn, and in both instances had soon after had to bury them. First interring young Maggie in the plains of Tamaulipas, where he discovered her among a wagonload of American whores chasing after General Taylor's army and where she died of the nameless disease that had been killing her for weeks. And then some months later burying nineteen-year-old John in the sierras north of Mexico City after cutting him down from the tavern rafters from which he'd been hanged by American soldiers who found him out for an escaped San Patricio. Edward had sat beside John's grave and bawled his desolation into the wilderness and had been certain of nothing on earth save that he could never in his remaining life know a greater sorrow. He had persisted in that belief for almost thirty years, until at work digging these newer graves he finally comprehended that the sole impossibility regarding human sorrow is to arrive at some unsurpassable limit to it. There was no such thing as sorrow that could not be exceeded. With every spadeful of dirt he flung from the deepening grave he raged the more at his stupidity for ever having believed otherwise.

He forwent a coffin for the woman and child because he would have needed help to set it in the grave. He had shrouded them in a blanket, the infant enfolded in the mother's arms, then sewn the blanket closed and lain them beside the spot where he dug. When the grave was ready he dragged them into his arms and set them at his feet. Then climbed out and picked up his spade and covered them over with the earth from which they'd come. He tamped firm the grave mound with the flat of his spade and then put on his shirt and picked up his tools and walked away without a word. Not until he was beyond earshot did the priest, who had seen the mad fury in his eyes, recite the requiem prayer.

The letter that brought the sorrowful news of Raquel and her baby was the last Sófi received from her sister for almost three years.

-⊛-

Díaz was in his second year as president and Lerdo was in exile in New York when she next heard from Gloria, who was then living at Patria Chica, Edward Little's hacienda some 200 miles northwest of Mexico City.

Edward and Díaz had first seen the place during the war against Lerdo. The surrounding terrain was mostly dry and rocky but a river ran through the eastern range of the estate, and for a few miles along its length it was flanked to either side by lush pastureland. A good road spanned the fifty miles between the estate and the rail line at San Luis Potosí, the nearest town of appreciable size. Edward admired the hacienda for its rugged beauty and geographical isolation, but Díaz said, Hell, man, it's so far into nowhere you'd go crazy out here in a month. You may not want to admit it, Lalo, but you've become a man of the capital like me. Edward said maybe so, but he still liked the place an awful lot.

The estate belonged to a staunch Lerdo supporter named Delacruz who had willingly let Lerdo's federals use it as an outpost and had regularly supplied them with beef. He was put under arrest when Díaz's troops drove the federals off. Díaz had the man brought before him and gave him the choice of deeding the hacienda to Edward Little and then leaving the country forever, or being hanged as a conspirator against the constitutional government—after which his hacienda would be confiscated as rightful reparation and then deeded to Edward Little in reward for his service to Mexico.

So you see, my fucked friend, Díaz told Delacruz, either way Mr Little will own this place. But if you sign it over to him you will save your life and you will save my soldiers the bullets they would use to kill you and you will save my clerks the extra paperwork and above all you will save Mr Little the bother of having to wait longer than he wishes to for legal ownership of the property. You will do much saving. Delacruz signed it over. Díaz said it was always a pleasure to witness a man doing the reasonable thing. There you are, Don Eduardo, he told Edward. Now you'll have a home to go to and rest your weary bones when you retire.

The phrase "patria chica" was a common Mexican reference to one's village or town or home province—one's "little country"—and Edward Little thought it a perfect name for his hacienda.

But even after Díaz was elected president, Edward continued in his employ and so spent most of his time in Mexico City, where one of his perquisites was a fine residence on Bucareli Street, near the zócalo. Díaz had wanted Louis to keep working for him also, but Louis preferred a rancher's life and was happy to manage Patria Chica in his father's stead. His boyhood dream had been to have a ranch of his own one day, but not even in dreams had he imagined himself in charge of a place so grand as Patria Chica.

According to Gloria, Edward Little had become even more distant from everyone since the death of Raquel. From everyone except Díaz. He seemed to have no interest in anything but his work for Don Porfirio—work he never spoke about to anyone in the family. Not even Louis knew what his father's job was. Edward didn't visit the hacienda often, and nobody would see much of him when he did. He would spend most of his time riding by himself to the far reaches of the estate. The visits were always brief, never more than a few days, and he was away for so long between them that each time he came he was more of a stranger to his young sons Zack Jack and John Louis. Their half-brother Louis Welch was more of a father to them than Edward was, Gloria told Sófi. They called him Uncle Louis and called her Aunt Gloria, though she was in fact their sister-in-law, and they were growing up as brothers to her own Luis Charón, who was actually their nephew. Sófi smiled at her sister's sardonic observation that the family tree had grown some very strange branches.

Gloria missed Mexico City very much, but she knew now that Louis did not care for cities and least of all for cities the size of the capital. She had given up all hope that they would ever live there or even go for a visit. This knowledge was a daily sadness. It was peculiar, she wrote, but even though she was now geographically much closer to Mexico City than she had been while in Brownsville, she felt no nearer to it, and in some ways felt even more isolated. Not that she was unhappy with life at Patria Chica, because she wasn't, though she did wish there were more trees. Except for the cottonwoods along the river and a scattering of mesquite stands, there was no outdoor shade to be had and nothing to block the wind that sometimes raised dust storms to imprison her in the house for days. She confessed she felt silly for making these petty complaints, given the luxury of her life. "En verdad estoy encantada," she wrote. After all, little sister, I'm the wife of a hacendado. Lady of the Manor. Doña Gloria. How could I *not* be happy?

EL PRESIDENTE

In that November when John Roger and the Blancos discovered each other in Mexico City, Gloria had been at Patria Chica for eight years and had known Porfirio Díaz for nine years before that—while John Roger had never even seen the man in person. And Díaz, who only two months earlier had been elected to his second presidential term, was celebrating the third anniversary of his marriage to Carmen Romero, daughter to Manuel Romero Rubio, a rich and politically influential man who owned the Jockey Club, the most luxurious gambling establishment in the city and the favored gathering place of the capital's most influential figures. Díaz's first wife, Delfina, had died in the delivery of a stillborn child, and the following year Don Porfirio married Carmen. On the day of their wedding he was fifty-one years old and she was nineteen.

The most surprising thing about their marriage—even more so than their genuine love of each other—was the change that the young Creole bride was able to effect in her much older mestizo husband. Díaz had always exuded a charismatic authority, but even by the end of his first presidency he remained a provincial in both appearance and manner. His hair was an untamed thatch, his drooping mustache a wild thing, his collars unbuttoned more often than not. His speech was shot with profanity and slang and his grammar was egregious. He was prone to broad gestures and loud laughter, to slumping in his chair with his legs outstretched and boots crossed at the ankles. He walked in a habitual haste and took the stairs three at a time. His way with knife and fork in polite company provoked furtive smirks. There was ever a toothpick in a corner of his mouth. While Carmen's father had been proud to see her married to such a powerful man, he had nonetheless felt an inward cringe at the mating of his aristocratic daughter with a mestizo roughneck.

But Díaz was neither too proud to admit his social shortcomings nor to accept instruction from his wife, and he was a swift study. Under her tutelage he learned to comport himself with the poise of a patrician. Carmen taught him how to dress for every occasion. She directed the styling of his hair and mustache in the close-cropped military fashion of European royals. She taught him dining etiquette, taught him how to sit in a chair in gentleman fashion, even how to walk with a stateliness befitting a national leader. She improved his grammar, bettered his diction, refined his speech and gestures. She elevated his entire social demeanor. She was teaching him to speak English and instructing him in world history. Those who had seen him at the inaugural ball of his first presidency could hardly believe it was the same man at his second.

His transformation was greater than they knew. To many of Díaz's most powerful political allies, the four-year wait for his return to office had been a frustration they did not wish to go through again. As they saw it, Don Porfirio was Mexico's best hope for raising the country into the company of the world's great nations, and such a man should not be hindered by restrictions intended to keep lesser men from perpetuating themselves in the presidency.

Díaz was effusive in thanking his supporters for their faith in him. And although, with all due modesty, he had to agree that he was the man best-suited to lead his country to a brighter future, he reminded his stalwarts that the hallmark of a great nation was its respect for the law, and he, for one, would always respect it. The constitution is the primal law, he said, the very core of civilized progress, and we must never abuse it, never violate it in letter or spirit. He proclaimed reverence for the patriots who wrote that glorious document and for those who recognized that it must never be amended for any reason other than the noble one of doing what is best for Mexico.

His followers understood. Before the next election, the constitution would be amended—by a congress composed largely of Díaz cronies and acting under the sanction of doing what was best for Mexico—to permit a president to succeed himself once. And Díaz would easily win election to his second consecutive term. And before the end of *that* period, the constitution would again be amended to remove all restrictions on reelection. So would it come to pass that Porfirio Díaz, that vehement opponent of presidential reelection, would be president of Mexico for thirty years, the last twenty-six of them in uninterrupted sequence.

⚜

As in the case of all great leaders, there were many dark rumors about Don Porfirio, and early in his second presidency one of the darkest pertained to a secret police force that answered only to him and whose headquarters were said to be in Chapultepec Castle, the official presidential residence.

His supporters didn't care if there was such a force. After all, a secret police was the most effective means for uncovering plots against the government and defending the president from assassins. Who but a fool or an enemy of Mexico could argue otherwise? Yet rumors persisted that Díaz's secret agency was more than a means of defense against threats to his person and to the republic. There were whispers that the foremost assassins in the country were carrying federal badges. And that the head of the organization was Díaz's mysterious Yankee friend, Edward Little.

Government officials neither affirmed nor denied the existence of a secret police force. After all, they said, how secret would it be if they admitted to it? On the other hand, even if it did not exist, to permit the suspicion that it did would help to deter subversives. The president did of course have a small corps of bodyguards. What head of state did not? It was a sad fact of life that national leaders had ever to be on guard against violent personal attack. As for the American, Mr Edward Little, yes, he was in the employ of the president, but solely as his personal translator of English.

⚜

On one of Edward Little's visits to Patria Chica, Louis asked him outright if there really was a federal secret police.

"Secret police?" his father said with a perplexed expression.

And they burst into laughter.

PART FOUR

✎ HENRY MORGAN WOLFE *m* HEDDA JULIET BLAKE ✎

1 Roger Blake Wolfe ———————— *2* Harrison Augustus
    m Mary Margaret Parham
      1 John Roger ———————————— *w*/Alma Rodríguez
        m Elizabeth Anne Bartlett   ↓ *1* Juana Merced
          1 John Samuel   *w*/Katrina Ávila
            m Victoria Clara Márquez   *1* Juan Lobo
              1 Juan Sotero
              2 Roger Samuel
          2 James Sebastian
          3 Blake Cortéz

      2 Samuel Thomas
        m María Palomina Blanco
          1 Gloria Tomasina
            m Louis Welch Little
              1 Luis Charón Little *m* Rosario Monte DeLeón
                  1 Eduardo Luis Little
                  2 Sandra Rosario Little
                  3 Catalina Luisiana Little
          2 Bruno Tomás
            m Felicia Flor Méndez
              1 Javier Tomás
              2 Joaquín Félix
          3 Sofía Reina
            m Melchor Cervantes
            m Arturo Villaseñor
              1 Francisco Villaseñor
            m Jorge Cabaza
              1 Pieto Tomás Cabaza
              2 Samuel Palomino Cabaza
            m Diego Guzmán

TALES FROM THE COVE

When they made the first of their promised visits, after six long weeks at the cove, they were brown as Indians and it seemed to John Roger they had grown noticeably taller. God, were they growing! They were stronger too. He saw it in the sinews of their hands, in the new tightness of their coats across their shoulders when they dressed for dinner. He had thought much about them during their absence. About how near they were to full manhood and the ways in which they were already more capable than most men of his acquaintance. Their "Thank you, Father" had come to mind many times since. He regretted his mistakes with them. Regretted having kept himself a stranger to them for so long, no matter they had as much kept themselves strangers to him. As the father, he had the greater obligation to wisdom and fairness, and it was neither wise nor fair—quite the contrary—to defend one's conduct toward one's children on the basis of tit for tat. He could not recall ever having addressed them as "sons."

That they had honored their agreement to make the visit was far less surprising to him than the size of his gladness to see them. Victoria Clara, too, was happy to have them home. In her six years at Buenaventura she had watched them grow from precocious and cocky identical children to handsome and cocky identical young men and had become very fond of them. She had lost her mother to a disease of the throat four years before, and a year later her father to a pulmonary infection. Her two brothers, who had inherited everything, were both much older than she and had always been strangers to her. She'd had no true sense of sisterhood until she came to know the twins, and it didn't bother her at all that she couldn't differentiate between them. John Roger never saw her so animated as at dinnertimes in their company. Neither, to his unspoken chagrin, did John Samuel.

The greatest surprise of that first visit was their unprecedented loquacity at the dinner table, the conversation shifting at whim between English and Spanish. John Roger grinned and Vicki Clara laughed at their amusing account of journeying to the cove with the six burros that on hearing a jaguar growl in the bush went so crazy with fright and thrashed so wildly it took the twins two hours to calm them and repack the scattered pack goods. And because the stable at the cove was too small for six burros and anyway too dilapidated to afford protection, the twins had tethered the animals on the verandah every evening.

On the verandah! Vicki Clara said. Like a little hotel for donkeys!

You including a couple who walk on their hind legs? a twin said with a wry grin, and Vicki laughed with them even as she protested that she did not mean any such thing.

They told about the work they had done on the house and on the sloop, and confessed that they had devoted themselves to the full repair of the boat before they even began to work on the house. "We just couldn't wait to start sailing her," one said. It did not escape John Roger's notice that they still did not refer to the *Lizzie* by name.

Once the sloop was seaworthy they had spent the mornings working on the house and the afternoons teaching themselves to handle the boat out on the gulf—which dazzled them with its vastness. It gave them a strange feeling of being awful small and awful free at the same time.

John Roger said he knew what they meant. "I always had that same feeling out there." Their zest for the open sea had made him recall his own youthful passion for sailing. But it shocked him to realize he had spoken in the past tense. That he had not been aboard a boat since before they were born. He had a moment's banal curiosity about where the years had gone.

He mentioned the inlet's tricky passage, and they said it was tricky, all right, but that was what made it so much fun, and they had gotten pretty good at zipping through it, if they did say so themselves. Because they did not want to seem braggarts, they did not tell him they had already become expert at navigating by the stars. Or that they were keeping track of the lunar cycle so they could at any time of day or night predict the turns of the tide within a quarter hour's accuracy. It was their objective—and they would achieve it—to be able to negotiate the inlet even on a moonless night.

Vicki Clara asked what they planned on doing out there once they finished repairing the house, and they said there would never be a problem keeping busy, as the house and boat would always be in need of some kind of upkeep. When they weren't busy working they'd go fishing or hunting, or catch up on their reading.

John Roger admired the shrewdness of their answer. It was the truth as far as it went but it was hardly the whole truth. They had some plan in mind, some enterprise. He had sensed it when they came to him those weeks ago and he was even more certain of it now. But whatever they intended to do—were perhaps already doing—it would remain their secret until they chose to reveal it, if ever.

Vicki said it sounded like a very simple life. But I think there is one problem with it, she said.

The twins smiled, knowing some tease was coming. And what is that? one said.

I do not believe you will meet very many girls out there.

The twins laughed with her. "Dang it!" one said. "I knew there was something we forgot to account for." And the other said all they could do was hope to get lucky and meet a few mermaids.

John Roger smiled at the laughter of his daughter-in-law and twin sons. He could not remember the last loud mirth at the table. Not since Lizzie was there. He wanted to contribute to it, to add to the banter by saying . . . what? . . . that the trouble with mermaids was that they were such terrible dancers? But he feared his joke would seem a lame effort and any smiles they might show would be mere politeness. He recognized the silliness of this qualm, but now the moment for the quip had passed, and he refrained from making it for fear of seeming slow witted. Good Lord, he thought, I'm thinking like an old man. Then had the melancholy apprehension that a man of fifty-six *was* old.

John Samuel did not join in the table conversation nor show the least interest in anything the twins had to say. He had avoided them since their arrival from the cove. They did not see each other until dinnertime, when they were all in the dining room and John Roger said to his eldest son, "Look who's here." John Samuel stared at them without word. The twins smiled at him, then looked at each other and made puckered faces of sourness and laughed and took their places at the table. They and John Samuel then ignored each other for the rest of the evening, as they would on all of the twins' subsequent visits.

The disregard between his older and younger sons had become so familiar to John Roger, and to Vicki Clara too, that it hardly bore the notice of either of them anymore. Still, John Roger had hoped that when the twins grew to adolescence and the difference in age between them and John Samuel mattered less, they might all begin to appreciate the fact of their brotherhood and accord each other some degree of respect. But it hadn't turned out that way, and it saddened him that their mutual dislike was more pointed than ever. He had several times in recent years thought to ask John Samuel directly why he and the twins could not get along. But he had each time held back, telling himself it was not the right moment to bring up the subject. And then one day he knew it was too late to discuss it at all. Knew that whatever the reason for the rancor between his sons it was past all possibility of being reconciled or even rationally explained.

John Samuel finished eating before everyone else and forwent dessert and coffee, excusing himself to his wife and father, saying he had work to do. After he'd gone, Vicki Clara asked the twins if they would like to go upstairs with her after dinner and see the boys, who as always had taken supper with the maids. You won't believe how much they've grown since you saw them last, she said.

The twins had never indicated more than passing interest in their young nephews, and John Roger assumed they were only being polite to Vicki when they followed her upstairs. But later that evening, when she joined John Roger in the library, Vicki reported that the twins had greeted their nephews, five-year-old Juanito Sotero and soon-to-be-four Roger Samuel, with man-to-man handshakes, and not two minutes later were on all fours and letting the boys ride them like rodeo broncos, neighing and snorting and tossing their heads while the boys clutched tight to their uncles' shirt collars with one hand and used their free arm to keep their balance, waving it about and as they had seen the bronc-breakers at the horse ranch do, whooping like them. When Roger Samuel lost his grip and tumbled off his uncle and knocked his head hard on the floor, Vicki jumped up from her chair in alarm but Rogerito quickly got up, laughing and rubbing his head, and said, "Don't come in the corral, Mother, you might get kicked by that mean mustang." He remounted his uncle's back and got a firm grip on his collar and dug his heels into his ribs and ya-hooed as the uncle resumed bucking.

John Roger said it was hard for him to imagine the twins playing with children. Vicki laughed and said, I *know*, Papá Juan, but I saw it with my own eyes.

⁂

They would never lack for dinnertable tales about the cove. They would tell of storms that rose out of the sea faster and blacker and with stronger rain than any they had ever known at the compound. Rain that struck the house like stones and sometimes left the beach and even the verandah littered with fish. Would tell of a black jaguar that every day for more than a week had shown up at the edge of the jungle and there sat and studied the house for a time before baring its fangs in a gigantic pink yawn—it did that every time—and then padding back into the bush in no hurry at all. Then one day it did not show up and they had not seen it again, which of course did not mean that *it* had not seen *them* many times since. They would tell of a gargantuan sawfish that found its way into the cove and spent an entire day and night circling within it. It was near to seventeen feet long and terrified the other fish, which again and again broke from the water in fleeing silvery schools by day and fiery ones by night until the monster finally swam back out to the open sea.

And always, in a custom established on their first visit, they would bid their father goodnight after dinner and accompany Vicki upstairs to their nephews' room for a quick session of the bucking-horse game. And after saying goodnight to them and Vicki too, they would go down to the kitchen, where Josefina and Marina would be awaiting them with fresh coffee and pastries in case they weren't full from dinner. They would all four sit at the table and the women would regale them with the latest hacienda gossip and the twins would in turn tell them mostly the same things they had related at the dinner table.

Then came a visit when they confided their business enterprises to Josefina and Marina and told of their monthly trips to Veracruz. Josefina said she had known they had to be doing *something* besides lazing on the beach. She loved hearing about Veracruz, where she had lived for so many years, and Marina, who had spent her whole life on Buenaventura, could not imagine some of the city sights the twins described.

But they would not tell their father about their business. They thought it better to keep him uninformed than to risk some objection from him that might jeopardize their residency at the cove. Nor would they tell him of having renamed the sloop, not wanting him to misconstrue the change as disrespectful to their mother. But the *Lizzie* had been his boat and they felt that it could not truly be theirs unless it had a name bestowed by them. The little sailboat they had plied on the river when they were twelve had been the *Marina*, and so the sloop became the *Marina Dos.*

Finally, at the end of every evening of the twins' every visit, after Josefina said goodnight and retired to her room, the twins would go with Marina to hers, and just as soon as they closed the door they would all three race each other in getting out of their clothes.

When they arrived for their visit at the end of November and learned they had a cousin from Mexico City now living at the hacienda, Bruno Tomás had already been there two weeks. He looked to them about the same age as John Samuel, but unlike their older brother he bore resemblance to their father and hence to themselves. John Samuel wasn't present. He had already made Bruno's acquaintance and heard John Roger's account of the fortuitous discovery of his brother's family in Mexico City. Elizabeth Anne had told John Samuel in boyhood about his Uncle Sammy who'd been lost at sea and in whose honor he was middle-named, but he had not since given his uncle a thought. He listened to his father's tale with a polite avidity but was not really interested in a man he'd never met and who'd been dead ten years.

In conversing with Bruno, however, John Samuel was impressed with his cousin's knowledge of horses. And just as John Roger had predicted, when Bruno said he'd like to work at the horse ranch, John Samuel said it so happened the ranch was in need of a foreman and gave him the job.

In introducing Bruno to the twins, John Roger presented him first, then said, "And these two are Blake and James," gesturing at them without indicating which was which. Bruno had been gawking at them from the moment they'd arrived at John Roger's office. Christ, he said, how does anybody tell you guys apart? He turned to John Roger. "How do you do it?"

"It's not easy," John Roger said. "Sometimes I have a hard time." He smiled but the twins saw the embarrassment rising in his eyes. They had always known he didn't know one of them from the other but this was the nearest he had ever come to being forced to admit it—in their presence, anyhow.

"Sometimes *you* can't tell them apart?" Bruno said. "I don't believe you, tío. Come on, tell me how you do it."

"Don't tell him, Father," James Sebastian said. He smiled and put his hand out to Bruno and said, "Yo soy Blake. Mucho gusto, primo. But listen, if you want to know how to tell us apart you have to figure it out for yourself. That's a rule of the house. Father's not allowed to help you."

Bruno laughed. Oh, that's a rule, is it?

"That's it," Blake Cortéz said, offering his hand. "I'm James."

John Roger suspected they were probably lying about who was who, as they liked to do for fun. But they had deliberately extricated him from an awkward moment—and done so in a way to prevent its recurrence—and he smiled his gratitude at them. Then told them of his brother whom he'd thought dead at seventeen, and yet again related his account of chancing on Sammy's family by means of a hornpipe tune he and his brother had composed as boys. Told them of their Aunt María and cousin Sófi who lived in Mexico City and their cousin Gloria, who lived near San Luis Potosí.

The twins said it was some story, all right, and that they looked forward to meeting their Mexico City kin some day. They said all the things they intuited they were expected to say and again welcomed Bruno to Buenaventura, then excused themselves to go clean up before dinner.

On the way downstairs they agreed in low voices that the addition of Cousin Bruno to the family could in no way affect their life at the cove and hence he was no cause for concern. Then they were in the kitchen and the embraces of Josefina and Marina.

As for Bruno Tomás, he was determined to fit in at Buenaventura, to accept its ways without qualm or question. When John Roger told him on the train trip from the capital that the twins lived by themselves at the hacienda's seaside and made a two-day visit to the casa grande every month, Bruno had thought it odd but could not think of even how to ask why that was so. But from the first few minutes of his first dinner with the twins he was quite aware of the mutual snubbing between them and John Samuel. He had hoped John Samuel might sometime volunteer to clarify the situation for him but he did not, and Bruno had a feeling it would be best not to broach the subject with him. Nor with the twins, whom he would see but infrequently and who, he'd known from the moment he met them, were not ones to explain themselves. And because Uncle John and Victoria Clara seemed oblivious to the way his sons ignored each other, Bruno would not ask either of them about it either. A strange bunch, these Wolfes. If not exactly secretive toward each other, for damned sure not much inclined to forthrightness. It had not escaped his notice that Uncle John did not tell his sons that the family Gloria married into was close to President Díaz. Or of his discovery that his brother had been a San Patricio. Did he wish to spare them shame in their turncoat uncle? Did he expect *him*, Bruno, to keep it secret as well? It would be simple enough to do, as neither John Samuel nor the twins seemed very curious about their Blanco brethren. He wondered if their lack of interest was a matter of station, the Wolfes being hacendados, the Blancos café keepers. Well, what matter? If this was how it was with them, fine by him. He did not have to understand anything except horses to be content here. He would do as his uncle and cousin Vicki did and speak only of what they spoke of and ignore the antagonism between the brothers. And would refrain from mention of his own family unless directly asked about them, a prospect of little likelihood.

He would, however, write periodic letters to Sófi and his mother and tell about life at Buenaventura among these odd blood kin. In their return letters to him they would rarely ask about John Samuel but always remark on the twins and ask to hear more about them.

⁂

They were as skilled at taking crocodile hides as at everything else they undertook. They had determined a procedure that proved effective on their first try, and so held to it every time after. They started out at dawn, poling the raft against a current that was much stronger than it had seemed when it had so gently carried them downstream from the falls. They poled hard around the first meanders and around the last of the mangroves and then came the first beaches and then the first few crocodiles. And still they poled on. And then poled past the first large bunch of them and around the next meander and past the next bunch too. They kept poling until late in the afternoon, when they arrived at a point within a mile of the falls and there they moored to a tree. They supped on jerky and spent the night on the raft. After breakfast the next morning, they began drifting downriver on the current, scanning both banks as they went. The first crocodile they saw that was at least twelve feet long and not too close to any others was the one they started with.

They tied up to the nearest bankside tree that afforded a clear shot from the raft. Sometimes they were able to tie up so close to their target they could have hit it with a flung brick and it was no problem for one or the other of them to shoot it squarely in the vital spot directly back of the eye and destroy the creature's meager brain. But sometimes the nearest tree that offered a shot at the croc was at some distance and then it was a test of marksmanship to hit that vital spot no bigger than a silver dollar. It was a harder shot still whenever the crocodile lay facing the raft so that they could not see the spot back of the eye and instead had to shoot the creature

237

through the eye itself. For these more challenging shots, one of the twins would stuff his ears with little wads of cloth and lean forward with his hands on his knees so his brother could use his shoulder to steady the rifle.

It was imperative to kill the croc instantly. If it were only wounded, it could go into the river in a bloody thrashing that would clear both banks of other crocodiles to come feed on it. The ensuing tumult—in which some of them even tore into each other—ended all chance of taking a hide from that part of the river the rest of that day, and they would have to drift farther down. But if the croc were killed cleanly with a single shot, the others on the banks might stir at the rifle report and a few might slide into the river and vanish, but most would stay as they were, still as paintings. The twins then went ashore with their sack of gear to skin the kill, first severing the croc's spine with a hatchet chop just behind the head to ensure it was dead. They had read of croc hunters who thought their prey was dead and had begun to skin it when the creature suddenly revived in a murderous rage.

From the larger crocs they took only the belly hide—the flat, as it was called in the trade—which was not only easier to remove than the hornback, or top hide, but also fetched a better price, being softer and easier to fashion into boots and holsters and belts and hatbands, however the skin might end up. Only a small croc had hornback supple enough to be worth as much as a flat and hence warrant the taking. They would alternate between killing three large crocodiles for the belly hides and then a small one for the whole skin. In either instance, after they removed the hide they fleshed it on the spot, scraping as much meat and fat off it as they could, then rolled it and put it in one of the tubs of brine they had affixed to the raft deck. The skinned crocs were left on the bank for its fellows to gorge on. Then they drifted around the next bend to where the crocs were still placid and there they tied up again and repeated the process.

They would be on the river for five or six days before reaching the last of the downstream beaches where they would take the last hides of the trip. Then came the stretch of mangroves and then they were back in the cove, tired, crusted with gore, singing, though they yet had to give the hides another scraping and salt them and hang them up to dry. Only then would they rest.

Sometimes it rained for most of a hunting trip and they did their killing and skinning in a dripping, green-gray gloom. If it was raining when they got back to the cove, there could be days of waiting for it to pass. But once the clouds broke, the sun made short work of drying the skins. The twins then stacked them in bundles and lashed them with cord and loaded them in the hold of the *Marina Dos*. And set sail for Veracruz.

LOS CUATES BLANCOS

At the time they took their first hides to Veracruz the town had but a single tannery. It stood on the far side of the harbor, on a slight rise back in the woods and out of view of the city, in a clearing next to a creek that carried the tannery detritus to the bay. It was owned and operated by the Carrasco brothers, of whom there were four, the oldest and head of the family being Moisés, a large man of around forty-five. They were a clannish lot with no friends or family except each other, and with a few employees who lived in a bunkhouse behind the tannery. They rarely went into town except for supplies and an occasional night of roistering. Now and again one of their bar fights ended with somebody dead on the floor but their standard claim of self-defense had never been refuted by any witness. They had long been a womanless bunch. Only two of the brothers, Genaro and Chuy, had ever married, but in her fourth month of pregnancy Genaro's wife had hanged herself, and barely six months later and five days after their wedding, Chuy's wife had run away.

When the Carrascos arrived in Veracruz, there had been two tanneries in town, one larger than the other. The Carrascos persuaded the owner of the larger one to sell it to them, and the seller and his family then packed up their possessions and left town without a parting word to anyone. A week later the smaller tannery somehow caught on fire late one night and its owner and his wife and his only son all perished in the flames. In the thirty years since, the Carrascos had held a monopoly of the Veracruz hide trade. For the past two years, there had been a rumor of a tannery in the Chinese quarter, but even if true it meant nothing to the Carrascos, as the Chinese were a world unto themselves and no one would anyway do business with a Chinaman except another Chinaman.

The only challenge to the Carrasco monopoly had occurred seven years prior to the twins' arrival with their first load of skins. Franco Carrasco, the brothers' father, was still alive then, though already shitting blood from the cancer that was eating his guts and would kill him the following year. The competition was a family of tanners named Montemayor, newly landed from Cuba. They bought a property further inland than the Carrascos's but on the same creek. The construction of their tannery was near completion when the Montemayor patriarch called on Franco Carrasco to introduce himself and say that he was sure the local hide trade could support two tanneries. Besides, Mr Montemayor said, everyone knew that a little competition always inspired a business to its best effort, didn't he agree? Old Franco said he certainly did. And the two men shook hands and wished each other well. Because Old Franco smiled throughout their conversation, Mr Montemayor took him for an amiable man, not knowing a Cuban accent was ever a dependable amusement to a Mexican.

Late one night, just two days before it was scheduled to begin operation, the Montemayor tannery went up in flames—and with it the family residence and the workers' quarters and the stable. The blaze was soon visible from the malecón, and everyone knew it was one of the tanneries, but as far removed as it was, there was no help for it. At sunrise all that was left of the place were smoking ruins and the charred bones of the entire family—five men and two women, three young girls and an infant boy—and of three employees and two mules. The family's horses were gone.

Franco Carrasco would attest that on seeing the fire's glow he had roused his sons and workers and rushed over to help, but it was too late, the fire too intense, they could only watch it consume the buildings and the luckless souls within. Because only three of the employees were among the dead, Old Franco said it seemed obvious to him that the missing workers had murdered everyone and then set the place afire to try to cover their crime before riding away on the horses. Who could say why they committed this terrible act? Robbery? A grievance? A drunken wrath? Who could understand the minds of such brutes? He said he had met Mr Montemayor and thought him a fine man of admirable competitive spirit. It is a great tragedy, Old Franco said. Everyone agreed—though some whispered to each other that the real tragedy lay in the Montemayors' misbegotten belief that they could cut into the Carrascos' trade.

❧

The twins knew nothing of all this the first time they sailed into the Veracruz harbor on a bright fall afternoon. They called to a passing turtle boat for directions to the tannery, and a crewman pointed out the Carrasco dock that ran alongside the bank on the far side of the bay. They tacked to it and dropped the sails and tied up near another sloop moored there, a sleek red-hulled craft about four feet longer than the *Marina Dos*, the name *Bruja Roja* on its stern. It too was a fishing boat, but though bigger than theirs, its wider beam gave it a draft almost as shallow. "Pretty thing," James Sebastian said.

A path led from the dock up a slight rise and into the trees. They could not see the tannery but they could smell it. And too the stink of the copper-colored creek debouching into the bay beyond one end of the dock. Blake Cortéz went into the hold and came out with two rolled hides, a flat and a hornback. "Who are we?" he said. "Rivera," James said, the first name that came to him. "I'm Tavo and you're, ah, Lucio." Blake said, "Got it," and headed up the path to the tannery while James stayed with the boat.

He returned in the company of three men, one pulling a two-wheeled cart with slatted sides. The three looked from one twin to the other, registering their likeness. Two of them were bareheaded and obviously younger than the other, who wore a straw hat and carried a knife on his hip and a money bag on his belt. This elder said his name was Moisés Carrasco and introduced the others as his brothers Genaro and Crispín. The Genaro one was missing the outer two fingers of his left hand. James Sebastian said he was Tavo Rivera and was pleased to meet them.

Mr Carrasco likes the two hides and wants to see more, Blake said. Of course, James said, and went into the hold. Blake hopped onto the deck and James handed a stack of hides up to him and he set the stack on the dock. The Genaro one began picking out hides at random, examining each in turn, bringing it to his nose, pressing a thumbnail into it in different spots.

Moisés asked where they were from. The Lucio one flapped a hand to northward and said, Little place on the coast. Moisés asked if this little place had a name. The Lucio said of course it did, Puerto de Lobos. Moisés said he'd never heard of it. The Lucio one said he wasn't surprised, it was a very small place. Moisés smiled and spat in the water. He asked if it was their first time in Veracruz and the Lucio one said it was. They were going to take a look around town after they finished with business.

So you won't heading back to, ah, Puerto de Lobos tonight? Moisés said.

No sir. Not till tomorrow after breakfast.

I see. Tell me, where did you get these hides?

From the river, the Tavo one said.

Moisés looked at him. Let me guess. The Puerto de Lobos River.

Yes! How did you know?

Lucky guess.

Genaro told Moisés the hides looked pretty good. But they picked them out, Moi, he said. Let me go down and pick some myself.

Oh, these boys look pretty honest to me, Moisés said. I don't think they would try to sneak any bad hides in with the good ones. The Lucio one assured him they would do no such thing.

Moisés had all the hides unloaded onto the dock. As the younger Carrascos were counting them he told the twins his rate.

The Tavo one asked if he paid the same rate for all hides.

Why? Do you think I would cheat you?

No sir. It's just that if these hides are better than most, they should get a better rate than most.

Moisés smiled and said, So young but such shrewd men of business. Well, it so happens, these hides *are* better than most. He quoted a higher rate and said it was more than he had ever paid. Genaro called out the total number of hides and Moisés did the computation in his head and told the twins his price. They had done the mental arithmetic too and arrived at the same figure. They exchanged a look, and told Moisés it was a deal.

As the younger Carrascos began loading the hides on the cart, Moisés took the purse from his belt and shook some gold coins into his palm and handed them to the Lucio twin. Here you are, boys. I hope you'll bring me some more of these good hides.

We'll do that, the Lucio twin said. He sprang up to the dock and loosed the mooring lines and tossed them into the sloop and then hopped onto the foredeck and shoved the bow from the dock. The raised mainsail tautened in the breeze and the *Marina Dos* began to move away.

Be careful, boys! Moisés Carrasco called after them. That town is full of bad people! Guard your money well! And your backs! The twins waved, and one shouted, Thanks for the warning!

As they made their way across the harbor in the gold light of late afternoon, they saw Moisés and one of his brothers lugging the hide cart up the path toward the tannery. The other brother was seated on the dock and watching the *Marina Dos*.

"You see what I saw in all those eyes?" Blake Cortéz said.

"Plain as a wall poster. I'd bet they used to collect hides themselves and that's how that one lost those fingers. Likely got a crew to do it now. A lot cheaper than buying them from a middleman like us. All they need to know is where to send the crew."

"Reckon they'll follow us?"

"Give odds on it," James Sebastian said.

"Well, *Marina*'s no tub but she can't outrun that red thing, not even with an empty hold. We could head back tonight, make it harder for them."

"Not hard enough. Moon's about three-quarters waxed. They'll see us plain as day from a long way off."

They were silent for a moment. Then Blake said, "What in hell we talking about? Even if we lost them this time, they'd only try again the next."

"Right you are, Brother Black. I say if they want to follow us, well, let them. Let's see them run that red thing where we run *Marina*."

Blake laughed. "Goddam right. Let's just see them do that."

The one on the dock watched them all the way across the harbor. He was still there, a small indistinct shape, when they tied up at the malecón, then padlocked the hatch of the boat's cuddy cabin and headed for the zócalo.

They had a Veracruzano supper of grilled red snapper on white rice slathered with fried green peppers and tomatoes, then ambled around the zócalo. The night was loud with laughter and music, the flanking streets with the ringing and rumbling of streetcars. After a while they went into a cantina called Las Sirenas and ordered mugs of beer. There was naturally much remarking by the other patrons about the boys' youth and their twinhood, much jesting about being drunk and seeing double. There was a tense moment when a drunk turtler—a large mulatto accompanied by a zambo crewmate—wisecracked that such babies should be asking for their mama's teat rather than a mug of beer. But he smiled when he said it, and so the twins treated the gibe as good-natured, and they retorted that, to them, beer *was* mother's milk. The turtlers joined in the laughter, and the Cuates Blancos—as they would come to be called by the other patrons—bought a round for the bar. A little later, when the White Twins made the casual remark that they were crocodile hunters, there was no lack of curiosity about their trade. The ensuing talk about the hunting and skinning of crocodiles naturally expanded to include the topic of the tannery across the harbor and the family that ran it.

They did not get back to the *Marina Dos* until almost midnight, but the harbor operated round the clock and was brightly lighted and loud as ever with the work of loading and unloading ships. The far side of the bay was in darkness.

"Think they're still watching?" Blake Cortéz said. "They can sure see *Marina* easy enough in this light."

"They're watching. They aint gonna chance us slipping out of here without them knowing."

They heard much about the Carrascos while in the cantina. About the barfight killings and the rumors regarding the Montemayors and about the various hide hunters who had been known to sell to the Carrasco tannery just once and then were never seen in Veracruz again. They learned that the Carrascos did have skinners in hire—a trio of Mayans, short and neckless like the rest of their race, strong and stoic as mules. It was said the three were escapees from a henequen prison plantation in Yucatán. They never came into town but had many times been seen to depart from the Carrasco dock in the red sloop and then a week or two later seen to return, every time with a store of hides to unload at the dock. It was all of interest to the twins—including the rumor of a tannery in the Chinese quarter, said to be owned by a man named Sing.

They unlocked the cuddy hatch and ducked inside and keyed open the heavy padlocks on the lockers beneath the bunks on either side of the little cabin. They were careful of the inch-high razor strips they had embedded along the top edge of the lockers' front panels to slice the hands of thieves. They took out the Winchesters and checked their loads and set them in easy reach in the J-racks above the bunks, then curled up and went to sleep.

They ate an early breakfast on the patio of a harbor café from which they could see the Carrasco dock and the man sitting on it and looking their way. A half hour later, as they cast off, the sun was risen to the rooftops and the lookout was hurrying up the path to the tannery.

The clouds were few and scattered, the wind steady. They were a mile north of Veracruz, and beginning to think maybe they'd been wrong about the Carrascos, when James Sebastian, keeping watch behind them with binoculars, said, "There they be." At the tiller, Blake Cortez looked back and made out the red dot that was the *Bruja Roja*. "You tell how many?" James said they were too far yet. He lowered the glasses and smiled. "Could be an interesting day."

As they had surmised, the *Bruja Roja* was the faster boat. She fast closed the gap between them to about four hundred yards and then loosened her sails to maintain that distance. James could now make out that the boat held four men.

In early afternoon they came abreast of where they knew the cove inlet to be. The red boat had held its distance behind them as precisely as if they were towing it on 400 yards of line. Blake held course for another fifty yards, then said, "Now we'll see just how good they are." And tillered the sloop toward shore.

"They're trimming sail," James said. "Here they come!"

The twins had timed the tide well. There was a good foot and a half of water between the keel and the rocky bottom when Blake turned the sloop to port again, and the boat bore toward the inlet mouth that as yet wasn't visible to the men in the red boat. They laughed at the certain confusion of their pursuers, who had to be wondering what the hell the twins were doing, first running in so dangerously close to the rocky coast and then turning back to southward. Not until the *Marina Dos* vanished would they realize there was a pass there.

As soon as they entered the inlet and were behind the stand of palms and out of sight of the *Bruja Roja*, James Sebastian dropped the mainsail and handed his brother the line to the jib. He grabbed up the oilskin sack containing the Winchesters rolled up in clothes for protective padding and threw it out onto the portside bank and waited till the boat was past the rocky stretch before he sprang from the deck to land in a rolling tumble on the sand. Blake continued steering the boat toward the south beach—and just before running aground he let the small sail drop and heaved the anchor over the stern. Then swung himself over the port side and dropped into water up to his chest and slogged out onto the beach and ran back to where his brother was crouched in the palms, a position affording clear view of the approach to the inlet. James handed him a carbine and Blake levered a cartridge into the chamber.

The red boat came in view and turned toward the inlet, following the same route as the *Marina Dos*. But its unsteady weave bespoke the pilot's lack of confidence in steering at that speed toward a passage so narrow. One man was working the mainsail and another the jib. The fourth was crouched at the starboard side, leaning out and serving as lookout, a rifle in one hand.

The pilot's attention was fixed on the tip of the inlet's rocky tongue, but in his fear of the point he was holding the boat too far to the right to suit the lookout, who thought they were going to rake against the inlet's inner bank and began flapping his left arm and yelling That way, that way! Thinking the lookout had spotted some obstacle within the inlet and was waving him away to open water, the pilot panicked and heeled the sloop to port so sharply that the lookout lost his balance and went overboard. But they were already too close to the inlet to clear the tongue and the boat struck the rocks at a point near the starboard bow. The arresting jar sent the other two crewmen hurtling out onto the rocks as the pilot slammed face first into the roof of the open cuddy hatch and dropped into the cabin. For a moment the swaying boat held in place on the point, its loosed sails flailing and popping in the wind, and then the inlet's outgoing current shoved the stern to seaward and the boat detached from the rocks with a loud cracking shudder. It carried away in a slow rotation as the bow went under and the stern lifted and it sank in fifteen feet of water.

The twins came out of the palms, the Winchesters dangling from their hands. The two who landed on the rocks were Mayans. One lay on his belly, eyes closed, the top of his head a bloody mesh of hair and bone. One hand kept opening and closing on the stony ground as if were trying to hold to the earth itself. The other Mayan was on his back with a leg turned inward at an unnatural angle and nothing of him moving but his heaving chest and his eyes, which fixed on the twins as they loomed over him. Blake Cortéz nudged him with a foot and said, What's the matter, friend? Bust your back? The Mayan blinked but did not speak.

"Lookee here," James Sebastian said.

The one who had fallen overboard was climbing out of the water. Genaro. Of the missing fingers. He no longer had the rifle. He saw the twins and halted in water to his shins, dripping, clothes sagging. He slicked his hair back and smiled and said, That did not go very well.

What were you planning for us? James Sebastian said. Same as with the others who sold you good hides?

Genaro Carrasco coughed and spat and affected puzzlement. I do not know what you mean, he said. He started to come out of the water and then stood fast when James Sebastian raised the carbine like a pistol at his hip.

"You see the lie in this fella's eyes, Brother Black?" James said.

"In great big old capital letters, Brother Jake."

"Como?" Genaro said.

My brother says you are a bad liar, James said. And cocked the carbine's hammer.

Genaro Carrasco raised a cautioning hand. Be careful with that nice rifle, boy. I know you don't want—

The crack of the Winchester spooked an eruption of birds from the trees as the impact of the bullet to his heart knocked Genaro back into the water with a flat splash. He floated supine, spread-eagled and bobbing, eyes wide to the sun. The twins watched the current wheel him around the point and out into the gulf and take him under.

"Well hell," Blake said. He went over to the paralyzed one and shot him. Then shot the one with the broken skull. "The tillerman?" he asked his brother.

"Never come up," James Sebastian said. "Way he hit that cabin, probly busted his neck like a stick."

"Or got knocked cold and drowned. Either way."

They put the rifles aside and picked up one of the dead Mayans by the hands and feet and slung the body into the outgoing current and it was gone by the time they did the same with the other.

Those were their first three—the tillerman not counting. It came to them as easily as all else they ever determined to do.

"They won't be expecting them back for a while," James Sebastian said. "Few days at soonest. Gives us the advantage."

"Let's get to it," Blake said.

❈

That night, Crispín Carrasco had just finished tending to the animals in the stable and blown out the lantern wick and started out the door to go back to the house when he was grabbed from behind. An arm closed hard around the lower part of his face and over his mouth even as it tugged his head back and the edge of a knife blade sliced deeply into the left side of his throat and in a single smooth action carved through it all the way over to his right ear. He could then not have called out even if his mouth were uncovered. His eyes swelled at the pain and he felt the heat of his blood sopping his chest and his whimper was a wet gurgle as he tried with both hands to detach the iron arm and felt the killer's breath warm and easy at his ear. They held in that posture like perverse lovers for a moment and then Crispín felt an abrupt sleepiness and his hands fell away from the arm. Then the man behind him was not there and Crispín saw the stars tumbling toward his feet as he thought, This is not so bad. And was past all thought and feeling when he struck the earth.

They dragged the body into an empty stall and covered it with straw and kicked dirt over the blood trail. Then went to the bunkhouse and slipped into its darkness. James Sebastian struck a match and a couple of the workers stirred but didn't wake up and he saw where the lantern hung on a post and went to it and lighted the wick. Blake Cortéz tapped the muzzle of his carbine on the wall until all six workers had come awake and were sitting up in their bunks. One of them had started to say, What the hell is—? But went mute at the sound of a rifle being cocked.

Don't speak except to answer my questions, Blake told them.

The workers informed them there were four Carrasco brothers but one had gone away in the red boat with the Mayans. There were no women in the house, no children.

James Sebastian told them they could have all the animals in the stable but to get them immediately and then get out of Veracruz and never come back.

The workers moved fast, and the ones that got the best animals were those who did not even take the time to dress but hurried to the stable with their clothes under their arms.

Moisés and Chuy Carrasco were at the table playing cards when the front door opened and one of the twins who called themselves Rivera and whom they had never expected to see again came in and stepped off to the side so he would not be an easy target in the doorway. He held an old musket with a cavernous .60-caliber muzzle on a barrel sawed down to about ten inches. Moisés Carrasco had seen other makeshift shotguns and he wondered what dread load this one carried. He could only assume the Mayans were dead. So too Genaro and Crispín. So too his workers, unless they had fled. A pair of Spencer carbines were propped against the wall behind him next to the kitchen door but they may as well have been on the moon.

Listen to me, son, Moisés said, let's talk about this. He heard the other one entering the room through the kitchen door. Chuy turned to look, then started to stand, saying, Hey, wait a—

The rifleshot was ear stopping. Blood jumped from Chuy's head and he fell against the table and then slumped back into the chair and slid off it to the floor. Moisés looked down at him. The one who'd shot him went over to stand beside his brother.

Kids, for Christ's sake! Moisés thought. In the instant before the shotgun's charge of coral nuggets removed the top half of his head.

Those were their fourth and fifth and sixth.

-◈-

When they docked at the malecón, it was jammed with people staring at the fire's bright flickering through the trees across the bay. Everyone knew it was the tannery but the twins detected little distress among the spectators. And actually heard somebody say something about reaping what one sowed.

-◈-

The next afternoon, when the Carrascos' blackened bones were excavated from the smoking ashes and it was seen that there were only three sets of skeletal remains and one of them was absent half its head, it was largely assumed that the missing skeleton was still in service of the missing brother, whichever one it might be, and further assumed that the missing brother had become estranged from the other three in the most serious of ways. But in a certain waterfront bar, a few seamen and a bartender would among themselves recall the young crocodile hunters they called the White Twins who two days earlier had stopped in for mugs of beer and had been so interested in hearing everything anyone had to say about the Carrascos. And a certain zambo turtler would say that, all in all, it was probably a good thing for his mulatto friend that those boys had taken his joke about mother's milk with such good humor.

OTHER CROCODILES, OTHER SHARKS

On the trip back to the cove they drank beer from large green bottles and when the bottles were empty lobbed them over the side and pulled up the netful of beer they kept cool by trailing it in the water on a stern line. James Sebastian extracted two more bottles and lowered the rest back into the water. He unsnapped the metal clamps on the corks and worked the corks out with a pop and handed one of the foaming bottles to his brother. It was another fine day on the gulf and though they had not had much sleep the previous night they felt in fresh good humor and passed the time singing ranchero songs learned from Josefina in their childhood.

The night before, while the malecón crowd was still gaping at the distant blaze across the harbor, the twins had gone into the Chinese quarter and wandered the narrow winding streets of that alien world whose border was but a block from the beach road. The streets were crowded and smoky, pungent with strange smells, and the twins felt the lack of enough eyes to see all there was to look at. They began asking after Mr Sing, asking various pedestrians and cart vendors, and were each time ignored or dismissed with no more than a glance.

They chanced on the place by smell, a stink like the one at the Carrasco tannery, detecting it even in the tangle of the quarter's outlandish odors. It came from a brick warehouse with boarded windows. They entered into a haze of smoke and steam in the amber light of oil lamps. There were rows of wooden frames with hides stretched on them. Most of the skins looked to be of jaguar and deer and snake, though here and there they spied one of an alligator or a crocodile, none of them very large. The place was shrill with Chinese babble, the churning of wash vats, the rattlings of carts trundling over a cement floor.

A man no taller than their collarbone was suddenly before them, shouting at them, pointing them back toward the door. In English and then in Spanish they told him they wanted to talk to Mr Sing, but the little man persisted in his angry demands that they get out. Abruptly the man's eyes cut past them and he went silent and took a step back and made a small bow. The twins turned to see a man almost as tall as themselves, wearing a cream linen suit and dark-tinted spectacles. In English he said, "Good evening, young gentlemen. May I be of assistance?"

One twin said they wanted to speak to Mr Sing, and the man said, "He stands before you." His expression was such that he might be smiling but it was hard to tell.

"Well sir, we came to talk to you about hides," the same one said. "Crocodile hides. As many as you want."

"I see," said Mr Sing.

"Big ones," the other twin said. "Bigger than any in here. Superior in every respect."

"I see. I admire your directness, young gentlemen. You are American?"

"Mexican."

"Ah. Most interesting." He waited a moment to allow them to expand on the disclosure, but they didn't, and he said, "You will follow me, please."

They went to the rear of the tannery and into a room bare of furniture but for a few chairs and a desk, where they sat across from him. There was nothing on the desktop but a thick ledger and an abacus. Mr Sing said it was very unusual for someone not Chinese to come to him with hides, but he was not surprised they had, as he was aware of the terrible fire at the Carrasco tannery that was still burning at that moment, an event that had quite suddenly made his tannery the only one in town, at least for the time being. He asked if they had ever done business with the Carrascos, and the twins admitted they had sold hides to them earlier that day for the first and last time.

Ah, Mr Sing said. He said he himself was acquainted with the Carrascos only by reputation. "But if some of the things I have heard are true," he said, "well, what has befallen them this evening seems to me less shocking, let us say, than . . . inevitable. What no one seems to know as yet is whether there are survivors."

"There aren't," one twin said. Mr Sing looked from one twin to the other, face impassive, eyes inscrutable behind the tinted lenses. He had not commented on their twinhood and never would. "I see," he said. And seemed to smile. "Well then. Shall we attend to business? Dime, jóvenes—hablaremos en inlgés o español?"

"English is better for business," a twin said.

Mr Sing told them he had a ready buyer of crocodile hides in Puebla, a Chinese maker of footwear and other clothing who shipped his products from Salina Cruz, but he had been unable to provide the man with as much hide as he wanted because Mexican hide hunters were violently intolerant of Chinese competition. Mr Sing's hide collectors could venture only where the Mexicans did not, where the hides to be had were few and generally smaller. "As you young gentlemen surely know," he said, "the common Mexican opinion of Chinese is not a kindly one. I intend no disrespect to yourselves."

"None taken," said a twin. "And we obviously don't share the common opinion about Chinks. No offense."

"I take none," Mr Sing said, almost with a smile. He told them how many belly hides of no less than seven feet the Puebla buyer wanted and how many hornbacks of no more than four feet. A delivery of those quantities every two months would be sufficient for the buyer's production schedule and quotas. The twins grinned and Blake said they could easily get him that many flats and hornbacks *every* month. Mr Sing said that was very impressive, but his buyer needed only as much hide as specified. Any more than that would create a storage problem and increase his risk of theft. "Whatever you want," a twin said.

How much, Mr Sing asked, would they charge to fill such an order? A twin quoted a figure that was double what Moisés Carrasco had paid them. Mr Sing said that was acceptable but their agreement would naturally be contingent on his approval of the hides. "I am certain they are as fine as you say, but with all due respect, young sirs, I of course must see them before I oblige myself to buy."

Of course. Each twin in turn shook his hand across the desk. They were satisfied with the arrangement, but told Mr Sing they wished he needed more hides. In less than a month they'd be back with a boatload of all he wanted, but then they wouldn't have much to do for the month after that. Did he know any other hide buyers they might sell to?

"Pardon me, young gentlemen," Mr Sing said. "You say you have a boat? I had assumed you brought the hides overland."

"No sir. We get them from near the seaside and so we bring them in the boat. It's an old fishing sloop but in good shape."

"A fishing boat. Most excellent."

The twins brightened. "You in the market for fish?"

"Not fish," Mr Sing said. "Fins."

"Fins?"

"Shark fins. For making soup." He said the Chinese markets and restaurants in Mexico City were always in need of shark fins, and because he had the means for processing the fins into readiness for soup—skinning and trimming and drying them before shipping them to the capital—he could get top price for them. As with crocodile hides, however, he had been unable to meet the demand, and for the same reason, the enmity of the Mexicans. Mexican fishing crews wouldn't tolerate Chinese working the same waters, not even if the Chinese were after nothing more than sharks.

The twins knew it was so. Mexican crews were infuriated by the sight of a Chinese junk—a boat widely disparaged as requiring no more skill to sail than to operate a set of Venetian blinds—and if the Chinks fished from a sloop the Mexies were even more enraged by the attempt to fool them. It was commonplace for Mexican crews to shoot at Chinese boats to drive them from a fishing ground, and sometimes they got even rougher, boarding the Chink boat and throwing the crew overboard and setting the vessel on fire. There were stories, too, of Chink crews being trussed and left in the hold when their boat was put to the torch.

"But as you are not Chinese," Mr Sing said, "you should have no trouble." Would they be interested in collecting shark fins for him? He assured them they would earn at least as much from that enterprise as from crocodile hides, perhaps more. The twins said they were very much interested.

Over the next few hours Mr Sing taught them everything they needed to know to begin taking shark fins. He had them draw a diagram of the deck of the *Marina Dos* and then used it to show them where to position the tackle. He told them the sort of line and leader chains and hooks to get, the kinds of baitfish to use. He drew illustrations of how best to secure these elements one to the other, and of the best pattern for scattering chum—bloody fish or the waste parts of butchered animals—over a range of water to attract the sharks. He took them down the alley to a restaurant he owned, where a small bull shark, a four-footer, was retrieved from the cooler and laid on a butchering table in the kitchen. It had been caught before dawn that day by a pair of thirteen-year-old boys fishing with handlines from the malecón. The best way to kill a shark, Mr Sing instructed, was to shoot it at the intersection of an imaginary line down the middle of its head and a line from one eye to the other. He traced the lines on the bull shark's head with his finger and put his fingertip at the intersecting point. Right there, he said. Using a knife with a serrated nine-inch blade and a double-edged, slightly upcurved point, he showed them how to cut off a shark's dorsal fin and two pectoral fins. The fins were then to be stored in brine barrels until delivered to him. His buyer wanted at least ten dozen fins every other month. Twelve dozen would be preferable. "If you bring hides to me one month and fins the next—"

"We can fin forty-eight sharks every other month," a twin said.

"Most excellent," said Mr Sing. He presented them each with a knife like his own, and asked if there was anything else they might need. There was, they said. And two weeks later, the Colts were in their hands. Mr Sing did not reveal his source and they did not ask to know it, but he had got the guns at a good price, and the twins paid him a bit extra for his fine service. The revolvers were Colt .44 Frontier models and used the same ammunition as the Winchesters.

From the first, they liked sharking more than crocking, as they referred to their two trades. Shark fishing was the more exciting, and they anyway preferred working on the open sea—in the wind and under the sun and away from mosquitoes—rather than in the shadowy upriver jungle. They liked working shirtless, wearing only hats, trousers cut off at the knees, and canvas shoes with hard rubber soles. They simply sailed out and netted a load of fish to hack into bloody pieces and then picked a spot and chummed the water and baited the hooks and set out the lines.

It had not taken long to refit the boat. Bolted to the reinforced deck were four short chairs made of ironwork, two on each side of the boat and each equipped with foot braces for leverage in reeling and a center ring brace to hold the rod butt. The rods had been made for Mr Sing by a Chinese craftsman using a special dark wood from China. They were six feet long from butt to tip, about as thick as a pretty woman's arm and as barely tapered. The strongest man could brace his knee against the middle of one of these rods and pull on both sides of it with all his might and not bend it even a little. But according to Mr Sing—and as the twins would find was true—the rods would flex without breaking under the force of the biggest sharks in the gulf. The reels were the size of a gallon cask and had crank handles long enough to work with both hands if necessary and were fitted with a drag mechanism to lessen or increase the force required to pull line off the spool.

There were days of disbelief when they raised not a single shark, not with the bloodiest chum. Days when it seemed every shark in the gulf had departed for other seas. Sometimes two and even three such days in sequence. More often, however, they no sooner began to tack back and forth over the red-chummed water than the first dark dorsals cut the surface and one of the lines began running off a reel. One twin then lowered the sails and dropped the anchor while the other began to reel in the shark. Even a small one could make a fight of it and the largest ones could take more than an hour to bring in. The exhilaration of catching a shark far surpassed that of shooting a crocodile. It was thrilling to pit your strength against it, to feel the power of it in the quiver of line and rod, in the sway of the boat, to reel the beast in until it was alongside the boat and feel its furious thrashing against the hull and stare into those eyes as black and indifferent as gun bores, into those jagged jaws. The twin working the rod then locked the drag on the reel and got a gaff and hooked the shark through the jaw and wrested its head around to present his brother a clear shot at the kill spot with the Colt. The dead shark was then hauled into the boat and the fins cut off and put in the brine cask and the carcass dumped over the side for the other sharks to feed on.

The first time they had sharks on four hooks at once was the last time they tried to land them all. The boat was tossing and shuddering so violently it seemed about to come apart and the lines became so entangled that finally there was nothing to do but cut them all. They understood then why Mr Sing had advised them to carry plenty of extra line. It became their practice, whenever they had two sharks hooked at once, to cut free the other two lines before sharks were on them as well. Still, there were days when they spent as much time replacing line as they did fishing.

※

Some months after the destruction of the Carrasco tannery, a new one was raised on the same ground by a businessman from Orizaba, but the twins continued to deal exclusively with Mr Sing. The Orizaban had been told of the Chinese tannery and of the twin Creole youths who supplied it with crocodile hides of superb quality, but he was not by nature an aggressive man and took a live-and-let-live outlook toward the white boys and their Chinese buyer.

Some of the Veracruz fishermen were another matter. The twins had been seen unloading casks at the dock and carting them into the Chinese district, and everybody could guess what must be in those casks if they were going to a Chinaman. Most of the fishermen didn't care about it. They saw sharks as a nuisance that damaged their nets and sometimes scared away the other fish. The fewer sharks in the sea the better. Yes, some people liked to eat them, but there was not much demand from restaurants, and yes, a few curanderos and even doctors sometimes wanted a shark liver for whatever it was they used it for, but overall there weren't enough buyers of the meat or livers of sharks to make them worth the great effort of catching them. If the White Twins were selling fins to a Chink, so what? Every shark they killed was a favor to all fishermen. But others were of a different temper. As they saw it, if the White Twins were catching sharks for a Chinaman it was the same as if the Chinaman himself was catching them, and they would be goddammed if they were going to let a fucking Chink poach Mexican sharks.

One afternoon in the early spring, anchored off a reef so far offshore that the coast was but a thin dark line on the horizon, the twins spied a large sloop bearing toward them from the north. It had been one of those rare mornings when they had not raised any sharks in any of the usual areas. So they had tried farther out but remained luckless until mid-afternoon when they happened on this reef, and the last of their chum raised a horde of shark fins. To lessen the chance of entangled lines in such a rich lode of sharks, they reeled in two of them and left only one on each side of the boat. They had landed and finned one shark and were reeling in the second one when they saw the coming sloop.

They knew of the bitterness some of the fishermen felt toward them and had been wondering how long it would be before some crew tried to do something about it. They brought in the shark, a nine-foot mako, and shot it and hauled it onto the deck. Then made ready for the approaching boat. When they were all set they turned back to the mako and finned it. They waited till the other vessel was close enough to see what they were doing before pitching the carcass over the side.

The other boat was half again as big as theirs. A man at the bow raised a hand and hollered, "Qué tal, amigos!" The twins stood at either end of the little cuddy and grinned widely and returned his wave and kept their hands in sight of the other crew. The Colts were tucked into their waistbands at the small of their backs, and the Winchesters, with bullets chambered and hammers cocked, were leaning against the cabin side where the other crew couldn't see them.

The boat dropped its sails and came abeam of the *Marina Dos* with about fifteen feet between them, the two vessels bobbing on the gentle swells. The pilot worked the rudder to keep the boat in place. Fishnets hung gathered on their upraised beams, dripping silver in the sun.

"Hola, jóvenes," called the man at the bow. The twins took him for the captain. He looked down at the sharks tearing up the carcass in the churning red water, then looked at the twins, his smile brilliant against his dark face. "Tiburoneros, eh?"

That's right, one twin said. Shark is all we go after. "Y ustedes?"

Oh hell, the captain said, anything we can catch. Sometimes this, sometimes that, sometimes something else. We saw your boat and we thought maybe there are fish here and we catch some too, so we take up the nets and get here quick, but . . . shark? He made a face of disgust and shook his head.

There were four of them, including the pilot and captain, the other two standing amidship at the near side—and the twins were sure they'd seen still another two duck behind the cabin as the boat closed in. Low-voiced and without looking at his brother or losing his smile, James Sebastian said the two at the near side likely had weapons at the ready below the gunwales. "Sneaky sonofabitches," Blake Cortéz whispered through his own smile.

We heard a shot, the captain said. You shoot the shark, eh? I don't see no gun. What kind of gun you have?

An old beat-up thing. We keep it in the cabin except for when we need it so it doesn't get any rustier than it is.

Very smart, the man said. And then in a voice of different sort said, Tell me, do you take only the fins?

That was the signal. The captain ducked below the gunwale as the pilot reached behind a high coil of mooring line and the two men at the near side stooped to take up their muskets and the two behind the cabin rose up with their muskets ready and fired the first shots. One ball bit nothing but the sea on the far side of the *Marina Dos* and the other glanced off the cabin roof in a spray of splinters and passed so close to James Sebastian's ear he heard its hum as he and Blake snatched up the Winchesters. Then the twins were shooting and shooting as fast as they could work the levers. They shot the two men at the near side before they could raise their muskets and shot the pilot—whose pistol discharged into the deck as he staggered backward and went heels over head into the water—and they shot one of the men on the other side of the cabin in the face and he spun into the gunwale and lost his balance and screamed as he too fell overboard and they shot the other one in the neck and he slumped against the cabin roof and Blake shot him in the crown this time and the man spasmed off the cabin and onto the deck.

The twins stopped firing but still held the carbines ready. Not ten seconds had elapsed between the first shot and the last. The powdersmoke carried away on the breeze. The only sounds were the swashings of the ravening sharks, the flappings of loose sails, someone moaning. An open hand showed itself above the rail near the bow and the captain called out that he was unarmed, he swore it, he wanted to surrender. All right then, James Sebastian said, stand up. Don't shoot me, for the love of God! the captain cried. We won't, James said, now get up. The man raised himself just high enough to peek over the rail and James Sebastian shot him through the eye.

The boat began to drift from them, and they saw now its name was *Marta*. Somebody on it yet moaning. Blake set down his rifle and picked up a grapple line and whirled the end of it over his head like a lasso and sent the grapple lofting onto the other deck and quickly took up the slack until the hooks snagged the gunwale. James Sebastian helped him pull the other boat toward theirs, which was held fast on her anchor. When the *Marta* was within a few feet of them, Blake made the grapple line fast to a cleat. James Sebastian retrieved their axes from the cabin and tossed them into the other boat, and with Colts in hand they jumped over onto it.

The moaning man was one of two still alive, the two who'd been standing at the rail. Please, the man said, please. He'd been shot in the arm and the thigh. The thigh wound was streaming blood he was trying to stem with his good hand. This wasn't my idea, he said, believe me. I didn't want anything to—Blake Cortéz shot him square in the heart.

The other one had been hit in the stomach. His hands were tight on the wound and his face clenched against the pain. Bastards, he said. Sons of whores. Blake Cortéz smiled and cocked the Colt but James Sebastian said, "Hold on, Black." Then said to the wounded man, You should not speak of our mother that way.

Oh yeah? What are you going to do, you bastard, shoot me? The man gasped through his grimace. Well, do it, you son of a whore! Go on! Shoot me, whoreson!

Shoot you? James Sebastian said. He grinned. Then yanked the man up by his shirtfront and propelled him toward the rail, the man screaming in pain and the horror of what was happening—and then he was in the air and falling in a flail of arms and legs into the riot of jaws.

They took the axes below decks and applied them to the hull. The in-rushing water was to their waists before they clambered topside and slung the axes into the *Marina Dos* and freed the grapple and leapt back onto their deck. The *Marta* sank stern first in five fathoms and settled on the reef to become roost to all manner of marine life.

They knew the boat had encountered them by chance. There was no way its crew could have known beforehand where the *Marina Dos* would be working—the twins themselves rarely knew where they would go to fish for shark until they were under sail. Whatever suspicions about the *Marta*'s disappearance might obtain among the crew's friends and family, there was no evidence whatever to implicate them, the White Twins. Oh yes, they were aware of the name they were known by. Los Cuates Blancos. They liked it.

How many now? They did not know nor care. They had decided it was silly to keep count of men killed. Nor did they feel misgiving. In their view, any man who intended harm to them was simply another kind of crocodile, another kind of shark.

So would they pass two years. One month collecting crocodile hides for Mr Sing, the next collecting fins. They never failed to meet their quota and rarely required more than two weeks to do it. They took care of business during the first half of each month, spent a few days in Veracruz, then returned to Ensenada de Isabel. As they requested, Mr Sing always paid them half in gold specie, half in currency—paper money the Díaz banking system had made as sound as the bullion and silver that backed it. Because they had few expenses, they each month added a large portion of their earnings to the strongbox they kept wrapped in a tarpaulin and buried at the jungle's edge behind the house. They spent their time at the cove exercising their talents with guns and knives, practicing hand-to-hand fighting techniques. They grew so skilled at silent movement through the forest they could close to within ten feet of a deer before it was aware of them. In the evenings, they talked, played cards, drank beer of their own brewing. They read. And always, during the last days of every month, they made the promised visits to their father. It was a simple and regimented life, and had it lasted to the end of their days it would have been fine with them. But they well understood that the only certainty in life other than their faith in each other was that things could change with profound suddenness. Hence their practiced arts.

BRUNO AND FELICIA

In June Sofía Reina received a letter from Gloria telling of Luis Charón's enlistment in the army on his seventeenth birthday. *My God!* Gloria wrote. *One day they're eight years old and playing at being soldiers with stick rifles and the next they're big enough to join a real army! Where do the years* go!

Luis's true ambition was the Guardia Rural, but he would not do other than as his Grandfather Edward advised, which was to serve two years in the army—the first year as a private in an infantry company to acquire understanding of life in the ranks, the second as an officer, to learn leadership—before transferring to the Rurales.

❧

Came the dog days. August marked nine months since John Roger's only trip to Mexico City and Bruno Tomás's move to Buenaventura. They had both maintained a correspondence with María Palomina and Sofía Reina, and in his most recent letter John Roger had again apologized to them for not having made a return visit. That the Blanco women had failed to keep their own promise to visit Buenaventura was understandable in view of the handicap that had befallen María Palomina. She had been demonstrating a lively dance step to Sófi and Amos one evening when a loose tile gave way under her foot and she fractured the ankle. At first she insisted it wasn't broken, just badly sprained, and there was no need for a doctor. She bound it herself and hobbled about for more than a week until the foot was so darkly swollen that the pain of it pounded with every heartbeat. By which time surgery was necessary. The doctor told her that had she waited another day she would certainly have lost the foot. As it was, even after a lengthy recuperation, she could not walk, or even stand, on the foot for very long before the pain became unbearable, and she cursed the incompetency of the medical profession. She wanted to make a trip to Buenaventura anyway, but Sófi would not agree to it, not until her mother could walk with her cane at least one block without limp or grimace. Unable to pass that test after many efforts, María Palomina had to accept that the foot would never get better and she would not be making a long trip anywhere.

John Roger had been unable to return to the capital because of Buenaventura's demands on his time. The coffee farm had produced yet another record yield, requiring still more bookkeeping and more correspondence, and more meetings than ever with buyers. And as with María Palomina, a broken bone figured in his circumstance, though it was not his bone but that of his venerable mayordomo. Now sixty years old, Reynaldo had some months before fractured a leg in a fall from a horse, and the next seven weeks had been the busiest of John Roger's life on the hacienda as he attended to the mayordomo's duties as well as his own. He might have been overwhelmed but for John Samuel's help—and that of Bruno Tomás. Since appointing Bruno foreman of the horse ranch, John Samuel had devoted most of his time to assisting John Roger with Buenaventura business.

Nevertheless, John Roger wrote, ten months without making a visit to his Mexico City kin was unforgivable, and he promised María Palomina that he and Bruno would go for a visit in October for sure. In closing, he said Bruno had something interesting to tell her and Sófi in his own accompanying letter. And he thus left it to Bruno to break the news of his imminent marriage, which was so soon to take place it would be an accomplished fact before the Blanco women's letters of response arrived at the hacienda.

The girl was Felicia Flor Méndez, seventeen-year-old sister to Rogelio Méndez, who was eleven years her senior and a longtime wrangler at the hacienda. Like Rogelio, Felicia was born and raised on Buenaventura, and he had been her only immediate family since she was thirteen. She had worked in the seamstress shop until the previous October, when their uncle in Córdoba died and she went there to live with her invalid widowed aunt, who had no one else to care for her. Felicia loved Buenaventura and did not like having to be away from it, much less indefinitely, but neither was she one to shirk an obligation to family. She had been at Córdoba a month when Bruno Tomás arrived at Buenaventura—and three weeks later he had a memorable fistfight with her brother.

Bruno had known that some of the wranglers would resent him for an interloper who'd got the foreman's job by dint of being nephew to the patrón, and they did. But once they saw how well he knew horses and that he was willing to work as hard and get as sweaty and filthy as any man of them—unlike Don Juanito, whom they respected, yes, but who but rarely got his clothes dirty—they began to grant him a due respect. But Rogelio Méndez remained unimpressed and persisted in his recalcitrance. He had been a wrangler at the hacienda since age fourteen and was the best breaker of mustangs on the place, excluding perhaps the twins, who in the estimation of many had no equal in the handling of horses. Rogelio had been Don Juanito's segundo since the inception of Rancho Isabela, and he had been confident that he would be named foreman if Don Juanito should ever give up the job. But then this cousin from Mexico City comes along, this fucking Bruno—who wasn't even a Creole like his Wolfe kin, for Christ's sake!—and just like that, *he's* the foreman.

Bruno heard the gossip about Rogelio's resentment and understood how he felt. But after three weeks of giving deaf ear to the man's snide mutterings and enduring his insolent attitude in hope that he would soon enough adjust to the situation, he knew he had to do something about it or lose the other wranglers' respect.

It happened the next day. One minute they were walking past each other just outside the main corral, and the next they were down in the dirt and punching and then up on their feet and punching harder. They fought for half an hour and not a man looking on had seen a better fistfight or one more evenly matched. Finally, wheezing like asthmatics, clothes ripped, lacerated faces smeared with blood and snot and dirt, eyes and lips and ears bloated red and purple, fists swollen, they stood teetering in front of each other. Rogelio somehow mustered the strength to swing one more time and Bruno somehow managed to sidestep without falling and the punch missed and Rogelio's momentum carried him in a sideways stutter step for a few feet before he collapsed. He managed to sit up but could not stand.

Bruno dropped his hands to his sides. Chest heaving, knees trembling. Rogelio looked up at him and gasped, Fuck. Bruno nodded and huffed, Yeah. He hawked bloody snot and spat off to the side, then asked Rogelio if the fight was over or if he just wanted time to catch his breath.

Rogelio's forearms rested on his upraised knees. He stared at the ground and made a dismissive gesture with one hand. "No más. Ya me ganaste."

Thank Christ, Bruno thought. He did not think he could have raised his hands again. Knew he could not have reformed them into fists. I hope, he said, still panting, you will continue to be the segundo.

Rogelio grunted with the effort of looking up again. All right, he said. But I still think I should be the foreman.

I know. But you're not. I am. Oh man, I hope we don't have to do this again.

Nah, hell. You hit too fucking hard.

I hit too fucking hard?

Their grotesque smiles were the best their mauled mouths could muster. Bruno put a hand down to help Rogelio to his feet. They groaned at the effort and Rogelio did not make it halfway up before they both went sprawling—and they joined in the wranglers' laughter, their bruised ribs aching.

By day's end the news of the fight had carried to every corner of the hacienda. It had already circulated throughout the casa grande when Bruno arrived at the dining room that evening, his neat suit and tie in ludicrous contrast to his bruised and tinctured misshapen face. Vicki Clara cooed over him with solicitude, but John Samuel was angered by the whole thing. He had worked with Rogelio and thought him a fine segundo, but for the man to start a fight with the new foreman—the patrón's nephew, no less!—was a transgression that had to be punished.

Bruno said the fight had been his own doing as much as Rogelio's, and that Rogelio *had* been punished. If you think I look bad, he said, you should see him.

John Roger smiled and Vicki Clara shook her head in exasperation with the ways of men. John Samuel sighed and half-raised his hands and said, Very well, you're the foreman who has to work with him.

—⋘—

The Córdoban aunt proved to be an interesting companion and was valiant and good-humored to her last breath, which she exhaled on an early morning in July. Though saddened by the old woman's passing, Felicia Flor Méndez was happy to return to Buenaventura. She had been home a week when her brother invited Bruno to supper and introduced him to her as his foreman, Bruno Tomás Wolfe y Blanco—a name change Bruno and his sister Sófi had decided on as more accurate to their parentage.

Like many a brother with a little sister both pretty and unafraid of men, Rogelio had been fretful for Felicia Flor's virtue from the day her breasts began to bloom. The whole time she had been away at their aunt's he lived in apprehension that she would succumb to some charming son of a bitch. He wanted nothing for her so much as the safety of marriage and motherhood. Various young wranglers had courted her from the time she turned fifteen but none had struck her fancy. She was too damned choosy was her problem. What do you want, Rogelio asked her, some guy in shining armor like in a goddammed fairy tale? Of course not, she said. A suit of armor would rust very fast in this climate. That was another thing, her sassy tongue. His hope that she and Bruno might like each other and that something might come of it was rooted more in desperation than in reason. It was crazy to think she would give serious thought to a man thirty-four years old or that a man of thirty-four would put up with her impudence. Rogelio could not have imagined the mutual smiting that took place within minutes of their meeting.

Two weeks later, despite his great fear that she would reject him as an infatuated, impulsive, middle-aged fool, Bruno Tomás asked Felicia Flor to marry him. She gave him a gaping, wide-eyed stare and said, My God, Mr Wolfe—she who had been calling him Bruno, even Brunito, these two weeks—are you truly *serious*? She was able to sustain her aspect of incredulity for several long seconds as his face sagged with disappointment and regret before she grinned and said, I was afraid you'd never ask. Twenty minutes later they rushed in on Rogelio as he was eating supper and Bruno petitioned him for his sister's hand. Rogelio swabbed chili sauce from his mouth and stared as if confronted by crazyhouse escapees. And said Yeah, sure, of course. *Jesus*, you two!

That was two days before Bruno's letter to his mother, which he wrote six days before the wedding. He told María Palomina that the minute he'd seen Felicia he knew she was the one for him. Anticipating María Palomina's desire for him to be married in Mexico City so that she and Sófi could attend the ceremony, he told her he wished he could be married in the capital but to do that he would have to wait until such time as the ranch was not so busy as it was now, but he loved Felicia so much he didn't want to wait a minute longer than necessary to make her his wife. He said Felicia felt the same way and they both hoped very much that she understood and would not be too angry with them. Not until the end of the letter did he make known that Felicia Flor was seventeen years old, and yes, that made him twice her age, but she was a very wise girl and she was really not too young for him.

When Sófi read Bruno's letter to their mother—who refused to get spectacles though her eyes were no longer what they used to be—and got to the part about the difference in their ages, María Palomina said, Too *young* for him? Listen, I know my son, and if she's seventeen she's way too *old* for him! A *twelve*-year-old is too old for him!

In truth, María Palomina was delighted at the news of Bruno's marriage, which took place on the same day she received his letter. Delighted in spite of her immediate suspicion that the real reason for their haste to marry was the age-old one of having put the cart before the donkey by starting the family before the wedding. In which case, his claim of knowing the girl less than a month was of course a lie too, intended to keep her from having the suspicion she was having. What a silly boy he was, she told Sófi, to think he could fool his mother. Or think that the reason for his hasty marriage could mean as much to her as the fact that he had finally taken a wife.

In her letter of response, dictated to Sófi, María Palomina told Bruno that she was of course very vexed that he did not get married in Mexico City, but she understood and she forgave him. She asked to know everything about Felicia. Bruno wrote back that his bride was petite and beautiful and smart and beautiful and such a wonderful dancer that she had even been able to teach him to dance—him! with his three left feet! And did he mention how beautiful she was? You will see for yourself very soon, my dearest Mother, Bruno wrote. Uncle John and I and Felicia will be there sometime in early October.

⚜

Sofia Reina too sent Bruno a letter of congratulations. And hoped in secret that their mother was correct in her suspicion about the marriage. Because otherwise Bruno was telling the truth and couldn't wait to marry Felicia. Perhaps out of love, as he claimed, but also, perhaps, because of his great desire to get the girl into bed as soon as he could. It might be that he was at least as much in thrall to his lust for the girl as to his love of her. This possibility made Sófi uneasy, convinced as she now was that the family was cursed by twin passions. Some in the family—herself chief among them, maybe her brother too—were in thrall to the passions of the flesh. And some—her father a prime example and her uncle perhaps another—to a passion for risks of blood. She prayed for God to have mercy on them all, but especially on those of them who might be damned by both.

BLACK HORSE

Only a month after Bruno's wedding, the hacienda celebrated Roger Samuel's fifth birthday. The fiesta was held at the Rancho Isabela, and John Roger provided wagon transport for everyone from the compound and both villages. There were the usual fiesta delectations of roasted sides of meats and tablefuls of food and vats of beer chilled in mountain ice, the usual fireworks and music and dancing. The dance floor was a wide clearing of packed dirt, and boys with sprinkler cans of water were charged with keeping down the dust. A large piñata, shaped like a horse and covered with colorful paper and filled with wrapped candies, hung from a tree branch. Each child in turn would be blindfolded and allowed five swings with a wooden pole—one swing for each year of Rogerito's life—to try to break the piñata as it was made to jounce about on the end of its rope. By custom the birthday boy was allowed to go first and have a few extra swings, as it was deemed good luck for everyone present if he were the one to break the piñata. Felicia Flor and Vicki Clara stood side by side and gave Rogerito loud cheers of encouragement but the best he could manage was to snap off one of the horse's legs, which contained only filler paper. Then his brother, next in line, with his first swing shattered the piñata and set the other children scrambling after the shower of treats.

The twins too had come to the party, and after the piñata ritual they clapped Juan Sotero on the shoulder and praised the power of his swing. They told Felicia Flor—whom they had first met on her wedding day—that marriage certainly agreed with her, as she looked even prettier than a month ago. She blushed and kissed them. Vicki Clara hugged Juanito and congratulated him for his smash of the piñata, then curtsied to Roger Samuel and said, "Most excellent sir, may I have the honor of a dance on this glorious day?" The boy smiled and said, "Yes, mam," and took her hand and they headed for the dancing ground. "Your next dance is with me, Victoria!" Blake Cortéz called after them, and Vicki looked over her shoulder and blew a kiss at him.

John Roger and John Samuel were surveying the proceedings from up on the ranch house porch, sitting side by side and sipping bourbon newly arrived from Louisiana. Now the twins and Juan Sotero were making their way toward the main corral, and John Roger was aware of John Samuel's attention on them. He had been unsure the twins would be here today, on John Samuel's domain, but their distaste for their older brother was outweighed by their fondness for their nephews. It nettled John Samuel, John Roger knew, to see their easy camaraderie with his sons. Only last week Vicki Clara had confided to John Roger that, although she had no doubt of her husband's love for their sons and theirs for him, they never seemed at true ease with each other. She believed it troubled all three of them that this was so, but the obligation to do something about it rested with John Samuel, who was after all the father. Yet he seemed incapable of making the correct gestures, of saying to them the things a father should say. Her disclosure had discomfited John Roger more than she knew, reminding him too well of his own paternal failings.

Among the horses trotting in circles in the main corral—the lot of them nervous from the crack and bang of the fireworks—was a splendid appaloosa John Samuel had bought the week before and given to his son for his birthday. Roger Samuel was elated by the horse. John Roger thought it a fine gift, though the appaloosa was as yet too much mount for the boy, who had only recently learned to ride. "I know that," John Samuel said. "I want him to have that horse to look forward to. At the rate his riding's improving he'll be astride that beauty long before his next birthday, you'll see."

But no horse in the corral drew more attention than a black Arabian stallion John Samuel had acquired at the same time as the appaloosa, buying both horses from a dealer he'd met through Vicki's father. He got an especially good price on the Arab because the dealer, who had a reputation for honesty and no wish to be later accused of foisting bad horseflesh, said the animal was prone to outbreaks of mean temper and he himself had been duped when he bought it. They were a demanding breed, Arabs, but a mean one was a rarity unless the horse had been mistreated as a colt, and perhaps this one had been. Whatever the case, the dealer said, it was the strangest Arabian he'd ever set eyes on. When it got in a temper it turned ornery as a mustang. It was a change that had to be witnessed to be believed, much like a gentleman of good breeding all of a sudden carrying on like a drunken dockworker. But John Samuel had seen no indication of bad disposition in the horse, and he anyway believed that, even if the Arab was ill-tempered, the trait was an acquired one and would not be transmitted in breeding, and so the horse still had great stud value. Maybe yes, maybe no, the dealer had said. Just don't say I didn't warn you.

Everybody on the hacienda had since heard what followed. The first man at

Rancho Isabela to try to saddle him was Bruno Tomás—and the black rammed him into the stable wall so hard Bruno thought he'd never be able to draw breath again. Rogelio Méndez was the next to approach the black with a saddle and it bit him in the shoulder so hard he still couldn't lift his arm over his head these four days later. When they finally did manage to get a saddle on the Arab, it threw off one rider one after another and each time tried to stomp the man while he was crawling away for his life. None of the wranglers had ever seen an Arabian exhibit such wild-horse malice. One try on it was enough for most of them—the rest wouldn't try the horse even once. "According to Bruno, that black nearly wiped out the ranch roster," John Samuel told his father. Not a man who had tried to ride the horse was unbruised or unsprained, at the least. When John Samuel heard that Bruno had put the Arab in the main corral with the other horses rather than isolate it in a smaller corral, he thought his cousin was foolhardy to put the other mounts at such risk. But when he rode out to the ranch he was stunned to see the Arab in easy mingle with the other horses, docile as a cart pony. Watch this, Bruno said, and went into the corral and saddled the black without meeting resistance and mounted it and hupped it out the gate. Bruno rode the Arab two miles out and back and reported that the horse had been a model of Arabian conduct. The problem seemed solved. Keep the black with the other horses and its demon was pacified.

That was two days ago. Then yesterday one of the other hands had tried to saddle it in the corral and the Arab knocked him down and started stamping on him as the other horses formed a circle around the action like spectators at a street fight. The bloodied wrangler was barely conscious when some of his fellows at last managed to drag him out of the corral. Somebody suggested that maybe Bruno was the only one the black would abide. But when Bruno entered the corral and picked up the saddle, the Arab bared its teeth at him and growled like a guard dog, and Bruno quick-stepped out of there. That settled it for John Samuel. No more trying to ride the black, not by anybody. The horse would be strictly for stud.

At the corral, the twins were talking with Bruno and Rogelio, who by turns gesticulated toward the Arab, no doubt relating the whole calamitous tale. Then one of the twins—not John Roger nor even anyone at the corral could know it was James Sebastian—took a hackamore bridle off a post and swung himself over the top rail into the corral.

John Samuel leaned forward in his chair. "What's he think he's doing?" John Roger was wondering the same thing.

The other horses shied from the twin as he went up to the Arab with his hand raised to it. The black lowered its head to his hand and he stroked its nose. Then ran the hand along the horse's flank and then rubbed himself against the horse and patted its neck and spoke into its ear. He slipped the hackamore over its muzzle and sprang onto its back as lightly as a cat. Jesus, John Roger thought. The other twin opened the gate and the rider hupped the Arab out and went loping toward the open country. Then heeled the horse into a gallop and bore directly for a rise some five hundred yards from the corral and vanished over it. Now everyone was aware that one of the twins was riding the crazy black and they were all giving their attention to the distant rise. John Roger saw Vicki Clara and Roger Samuel join the other twin by the corral gate. The twin picked up Roger Samuel and stood him on the top rail for a better view.

John Samuel was slumped in his chair. "If he harms that stud. . . ."

"He won't," John Roger said. "You know that."

They could track the horse by the dust plume, which widened and thinned as the horse drew farther away. And then the plume began to regain form and density and they all knew the horse was heading back. When it came galloping over the rise, James Sebastian was standing on its back. Standing with his hands in his pockets and his hat flapping behind him on its chin thong. Standing on that speeding horse with the ease of a man on a rocking railcar platform. The witnessing crowd raised a great cheer. James Sebastian dropped astride the horse and took up the rein and slowed the animal to a canter, then to a trot as they approached the corral. The ranch hands gathered around him, yelling congratulations while being careful not to get behind the horse or within biting lunge of it.

John Roger saw Vicki Clara blow the rider a kiss. Saw Juanito Sotero push through the men to run up beside the horse and hop up and down, his hands raised to his uncle. The twin reached down and took the boy's hand and hauled him up to sit astraddle before him.

John Samuel stood up. "God *damn* it."

"Oh come, John," John Roger said. "You were no older the first time I took you for a fast ride."

"You're my father. And it wasn't bareback."

Now little Roger Samuel was tugging at the rider's leg. And now Vicki Clara was speaking to the mounted twin. The rider said something to Juan Sotero and then eased him down off the horse and pulled Rogerito up to replace him. Holding the boy against his chest with one arm, his other hand on the rein, the twin hupped the Arab into a canter and headed off. And again roused the horse to a gallop before going over the rise. As before, they were gone for some minutes before booming back into view and still at full stride. It would hardly have been a wonder to anybody in the crowd if the rider had again been standing on the horse and this time with the child on his shoulders—but they were seated as before, though even at this distance they could see the boy pumping his arms in the air like an exulting Comanche. They could not hear, as could James Sebastian, the boy whooping like an Indian too. James was just about to rein the horse down from its gallop when it dropped from under them.

He felt himself airborne in a slow somersault. Felt the boy detach from him as weightless as if they were underwater. Lost sight of him. Saw his own feet against the sky. His next awareness was of lying on his back in the settling dust and staring at bright thin clouds. He felt himself breathing but had no pain. Then tried to sit up and pain exploded in his right forearm. He cursed and gasped and struggled one-armed to his feet.

The Arab was on its side and trying to get up on broken front legs, its head lunging up repeatedly as if it could will the rest of its body up after it, shrilling its agony with every try. Beyond the horse lay the boy. A wee form huddled on his side as if in nap. Unaware of the rider bearing toward him at full gallop and the others far behind him, James went over to the boy. He saw blood in his ear. Hooves came pounding and a cloud of dust rolled over him—and then John Samuel was screeching, "Get away from him!" and slammed both hands into James Sebastian's chest, staggering him and jarring such pain through his arm he nearly threw up.

John Samuel knelt beside his son. He gingerly raised him to a sitting position and James Sebastian saw the unnatural tilt of Rogerito's head. John Samuel pushed the hair from the boy's eyes and then eased him back down. Then stood up and looked at James Sebastian with tears coursing from eyes gone mad. He stalked stiffly to his horse, which sensed his rage and shied, but he lunged and caught the reins and pulled himself to the horse and drew the carbine from the saddle sheath. James Sebastian had no defense but to run at him, holding his broken arm to his chest, thinking to ram him with a shoulder and somehow grab the rifle. But John Samuel sidestepped and James struck him only a glancing blow and fell down on his arm and bellowed. He struggled to regain his feet, hearing more horses closing fast but keeping his eyes on John Samuel, who thumbed back the rifle's hammer and aimed squarely into his face. And even as their father's voice carried through the rumble of hooves—"*Noooooo!*"—John Samuel pulled the trigger.

The hammer dropped on an empty chamber. John Samuel howled his rage and ran at James Sebastian, swinging the carbine one-handed from side to side like a cumbersome sword amid another upheaval of dust, screaming "You kill everything! You *kill everything!*" He swung and swung and James Sebastian kept back-stepping and dodging. Then Blake Cortéz had John Samuel in a headlock from behind and James snatched the carbine from him.

Blake threw John Samuel to the ground and kicked him in the face, ripping his cheek to the bone. He dropped astraddle of him and grabbed him by the hair and began punching him in the face like he was driving nails. A clutch of men converged on him and grabbed him by the arms and collar and wrested him off John Samuel and dragged him well away and would not release him till he swore not to resume the attack. But still kept themselves between them.

John Roger saw none of that. He had gone straight to the boy and sat down and gathered him up with his arm and rocked him and wept. James Sebastian stared at his father's hunched figure. Then over at the black horse, still bawling with every effort to rise. With a one-handed flick he worked the lever to open the breech and saw the empty chamber and the ready bullet levered into the breech from the magazine. He worked the lever again, inserting the bullet in the chamber, and walked over to the crippled horse. The black saw who it was and ceased its agonized struggle. It watched him and snuffled hard. James Sebastian set the rifle muzzle between its eyes and said, "You're a damn fine horse." And shot it. Then dropped the rifle beside the horse.

Blake Cortéz rode up, leading John Samuel's mount by the reins. "You manage?" he said. James nodded and took hold of the mount's saddle horn with his left hand and put his left foot in the stirrup and with a loud grunt and an awkward move pulled himself up onto the saddle.

Their father yet sat rocking the dead boy in his arms. He had not turned at the rifleshot. Seemed not even to have heard it. John Samuel yet lay supine, being attended to. They hupped their mounts and rode away, bearing wide around the ranch house.

They did not go back to the casa grande but to the compound stable, where they always left their rucksacks on arriving from the cove. Blake Cortéz told the stableman to fetch a couple of short wooden slats to serve for a forearm splint and some cloth strips to bind it. The man was quick to do it and then Blake told him and his helper sons to go outside. He would brook no witness to his brother's pain as he doctored his arm. Both bones of it were broken and the top one dislocated and it took Blake several tries to align it properly. His own right hand was swollen thick as a mitten from punching John Samuel and was clumsy in its working. But it wasn't broken and he knew his pain was picayune in comparison to James Sebastian's. At Blake's every effort to set the bones, James groaned through clenched teeth, his face pale and dripping sweat. When Blake at last judged by feel that the bone was set right he splinted the arm and bound it and fashioned a sling for it. He helped James Sebastian to get his rucksack slung across his chest and then shouldered his own and they headed for the river trail and the long hike home to Ensenada de Isabel. The stableman and his boys waited until they were into the trees and out of sight before going back into the stable.

—※—

Excepting John Samuel, who would for the rest of his life blame the twins for what happened, everybody who was there agreed that it was an accident. Some would say it must have been that the horse was frighted by a snake, though it might have been a rabbit, a turtle, an armadillo. But most would ridicule the idea of any such thing scaring a horse that was moving at a gallop. Besides, the horse didn't try to veer, it had gone straight down, so it had to have stepped in a hole, a gopher hole, turtle hole, or on a large rock that gave way under its hoof. Some few others would say that the horse may have seen a snake or stepped in a hole or slipped on a rock, but given the horse they were talking about, the snake or the hole or the rock may have existed only in the crazy horse's head. Who could know what really caused the black to fall? The only thing they all knew for sure was that, to the dead boy's family, it could hardly matter. And that, had John Samuel not bought the crazy horse, his son could not have been killed by it.

⚓

The dark news came to María Palomina and Sofía Reina in a letter from Bruno Tomás. Mother and daughter cried together over the loss of a young kinsman they never had the chance to meet. John Roger's own letter was later in coming and its sorrow even heavier and the more pathetic for being that of the boy's grandfather. When Amos Bentley arrived for his regular visit and heard the news, he sat with the women for the rest of the day, listening without interruption when they wanted to unburden themselves to him, holding silent with them when they had nothing to say.

DISTANCES

Even as he began to accommodate his grief, John Roger remained deep in dejection. He was given to morbid fancies and memories. Lying awake one night, he recalled a circus bear he and Sammy had seen at a traveling show one Portsmouth summer. The bear was old and mangy and sat in a wagon cage. It had a red fez strapped to its head and a tin drum strapped to its belly and its dull eyes seemed to stare at nothing as it beat and beat on the drum in unceasing monotony. Sammy had been disdainful of the bear, saying it should refuse to play the fool and instead grab the first man it could get hold of through the bars and tear his throat out before somebody could shoot it. But John Roger's heart had felt a secret pity for the animal. Unlike Sammy, the bear could not reason nor entertain choices but only go on beating and beating the drum simply because, as with a living heart, there was nothing else for it to do.

John Roger well understood the pain of John Samuel's loss, but he could imagine too how the twins felt about being the agent of the boy's death. And could understand the protective imperative the one must have felt on seeing John Samuel pointing a rifle at the other. Could understand the rage of all three, but that his sons had tried to kill each other was an iron weight in his heart.

He knew why the twins were staying away, but as the months passed, he missed the boys more and more. He thought of going to Ensenada de Isabel to see them but could not bring himself to do it. It would be hard enough to talk to them without the distraction of being reminded of Elizabeth Anne every minute he was there. Besides, what if they weren't there? What if they'd gone away, perhaps forever? The thought of being at the cove absent both her and them infused him with such cold loneliness he had an urge to weep—and the impulse in turn made him angry.

His lachrymose feelings of late had more and more confused him. You have become an old fool, he told himself. The worst kind of all.

He had not seen them in almost six months when he decided to send Bruno Tomás to the cove to see if they were there, and told him what to tell them if they were.

When Bruno informed Felicia of his mission, she gave him a Saint Christopher medal to give to the twins. Tell them to share it, she said. He took a load of supplies for the cove house and two men to assist him, a pair of wranglers named Mongo and Stefán. They rode out on burros and trailed a pack donkey, each man armed with a revolver.

⁂

Bruno had thought the forest flanking the compound and Santa Rosalba was as dense as forest could be—until they made their slow way along the narrow jungle track leading to the cove. They spent the night on the trail, making an in-line camp between a pair of lanterns they let burn all night, but they slept very little for the burros' braying nervousness. The following day, about two hundred yards from the cove—though they did not know yet how much farther it was—the trail was blocked by a felled tree nearly four feet thick.

How long you suppose it took them to chop down *this* goddammed thing? Mongo said. They relieved the pack burro of the tarp-covered load and set it aside and tethered the burros to the barrier tree and climbed over it and trudged on. Over the last part of the trail, they twice tripped wires that in turn set off a great jangling of bells in the overhead branches. For damn sure nobody's gonna sneak up, Stefán said.

Then there the house was, and beyond it the cove. The pier stood boatless. The twins were away.

They found a store of food in the house and a cabinet with casks of beer and shelves lined with green quart bottles sealed with clipped corks. The men grinned. In a shed in back of the house they found the brewing vats. John Roger had left it up to Bruno, if he found the twins gone, whether to wait a few days in case they came back. The place was so pleasant, and with beer at hand besides, he decided to wait.

They had been asleep but two hours that night when they were awakened by a frantic braying from the jungle. "Los burros!" Mongo shouted. The braying was so loud it seemed the donkeys were not a hundred feet from the house.

They had left a verandah lamp burning low, and were quick to light another and yank on their pants and boots. Holding the lamps high and with pistols in hand they ran down the steps and around the house and entered the solid blackness before them. They hied along the narrow trail, the brush slapping at their arms and faces, their shadows disjointed in the wavering lantern light, and arrived gasping at the barrier tree, where the burros were still honking in terror and jerking against their tethers and kicking out behind them, white-eyed in the sudden light of the lamps.

One burro was gone. Its broken tether like a rent umbilical in a swath of blood vanishing into the underbrush where the animal had been dragged off.

Jesus Christ, Stefán said. You know how *big* that fucking tiger must be to carry off a *burro*?

And even as they all had the same thought at the same moment—that the beast could not be very far away—there came from the blackness a reverberant roar to seize the heart and all three of them flinched and cried out , and the burros went into another mad fit of shrieking and kicking. The men huddled close, guns cocked, swinging the lanterns to right and left.

It was several long minutes before the burros began to calm a little, and only then did the men become conscious of a telltale reek on the air. Someone had shat himself. For a minute no one said anything, none being certain he wasn't the guilty party. When Bruno realized with no small relief that it wasn't himself, he said, Christ almighty! Which of you guys—?

Not me, boss, said Mongo, who'd made a furtive probe of his pants to be sure.

They glared at Stefán, who stared down at his feet.

Goddam this fucking place! Bruno said. He said they would stay out there through the night to keep guard over the burros and head for home at dawn.

God bless you, boss, Mongo said.

They hung a lantern from an overhead branch, and while Mongo and Stefán soothed the burros, Bruno took the other lantern and with his gun still in hand went back to the house.

He wrote the twins a letter summarizing what he had come to tell them, then folded it once and wrote "para ustedes" on it and left it on the table. Then remembered the Saint Christopher medal and on another piece of paper wrote, Felicia sends this with her love, and lay the medal on it.

He appropriated a pair of his nephews' pants for Stefán and had the presence of mind to take back three bottles of beer as well.

--- ❋ ---

Some days later the twins returned to the cove from Veracruz and smiled on finding the medal from the darling Felicia. Bruno's letter told them there had been a requiem mass for Roger Samuel and he had been buried in the casa grande cemetery, the funeral attended by family members only. Their father had of course understood the twins' absence. So too had Vicki Clara. She had asked Bruno to tell her brothers (her very words, Bruno emphasized, *my brothers*) that she knew Roger Samuel's death was an accident and it did not even matter which of them had taken Rogerito on the horse. She'd had a long talk with Juan Sotero. He was only six but was a wise and sympathetic child, and it had added to his sorrow these past months that his uncles might think they were at fault for what happened to his brother. As for John Samuel, his jaw and cheekbone had been badly broken and his nose would never look the same. He hadn't been able to talk very clearly for weeks, but even after his jaw was healed he didn't say much, and if he had spoken to anyone about the accident, Bruno wasn't aware of it. Their father wanted them to know that he was sure that John Samuel's grief these past months had only been compounded by the realization of what he had almost done in those first mad moments, having so nearly committed an act for which he could never have atoned. But it had been nearly six months now, time enough for everyone's emotions to ease, and he wanted the twins to resume their monthly visits. The end of the letter informed them of the supply of staples next to the barrier tree.

"You believe Mr Sourmouth's sorry?" Blake said.

"Sure do. I believe he's sorry you busted his face and sorry as all hell he was so crazy mad he didn't think to jack a bullet in the chamber before trying to shoot me."

◆

They did visit the casa grande the following month but didn't let their father know they were there. Did not let anyone know but Josefina and Marina. They sneaked into the compound late at night by way of one of their secret passages and then, through another, into the casa grande garden. Josefina woke to their soft tread in the kitchen and rushed from her room to hug them each in turn even as she hissed reproaches at them for being such rude and thoughtless brutes that they had not once let her know these past six months that they were alive. James Sebastian said, Dance with me, my beauty—and turned her in a waltz step before she pulled away and slapped at his arm and called him a good-for-nothing. Then Marina was there too, crying without sound and kissing first one and then the other and then the first again, until Josefina said, "Ya, mija, ya. Déjalos respirar, por amor de Dios."

Only a few weeks past their sixteenth birthday, they were yet lean but grown even thicker of shoulder and had the arms of timber men and were now taller than their father and their older brother. And yet remained indistinguishable, so selfsame of feature, of stride and stance and voice and gesture, that only Josefina and Marina could tell them apart, though only up close, knowing as they did that Blake's left little finger had a pronounced crook and that James Sebastian's right eye had a green flaw at the upper rim of the iris. In time they would note too a little node just above the fore part of James's right wrist where the broken bone had mended unevenly. But the twins were also aware of these differences and knew how to camouflage them by means of a partial squint and by keeping their fingers slightly flexed and hands turned just so.

They sat at the kitchen table over coffee and conversed in low voices. The women confirmed everything Bruno had said in the letter. It is a horrible and unnatural thing for a child to precede a parent to the grave, Josefina said, but to precede a grandparent was too horrible for words. Marina said their father would be very happy to see them, but they said they did not want to see him, that it was too soon yet. If they talked to him now he would insist that they resume their visits as before, which meant sitting to dinner with the family, but they didn't think John Samuel was ready for that. "Ay, ese pobre Juanito," Josefina said. She gestured at her face and said that the doctor had tried to correct his nose but. . . . And the scar on his cheek, ay! Then she caught herself and said to Marina, Forgive me, child, I am old and stupid. Marina took her hand and said there was nothing to forgive, that she had years ago stopped feeling shame about her scars. Josefina patted her hand and stood up with a soft groan and put a hand to each twin's head in turn as if in benediction, then retired to her room. Minutes afterward they were in bed as well, Marina between them.

❋

They returned to the kitchen six weeks later, again surprising Josefina and Marina, who again were the only ones to know they were on the grounds. Until the following evening, when just as they were about to depart, Vicki Clara happened into the kitchen.

She had not seen them in eight months, and she rushed to them and hugged them and kissed them, asked again and again if they were all right, said, My God, how you've grown! She wanted them to sit and talk, but they explained they did not want to chance an encounter with their father because it could mean having to see John Samuel too. She said they had no reason to fear John Samuel. Blake Cortéz said, *Fear* him? Are you joking? and James Sebastian said, *Us* afraid of *him*? She saw the umbrage in their faces and said she did not mean to imply they were afraid of him, that she knew they were not, that she meant no insult, please forgive her. She was near tears. "Ah Christ," James said in English, and took her in his arms. Blake apologized for their tone and asked her to please forgive *them*. She brushed at her eyes and caressed their faces and said she would forgive them if they would forgive her, and they said it was a deal.

She told them Juan Sotero's First Holy Communion was to take place in the hacienda church in two months and asked if they would please attend. It will make Juanito so happy if you are there, she said. He has been worried about you and has so many times told me how much he misses you. And of course it will please your father. He has missed you more than you can imagine. He will be hurt to know you have been here without seeing him, but he would be very happy if you are at the ceremony. Please?

The twins looked at each other, and Blake said they would be there. Did they promise? They promised. The twenty-fifth of July, she said. Without fail, they said. Josefina and Marina smiling too.

THE ESPINOSA LEGACY

In 1590 Carlos Mercadio Valledolid Jurado, a Spanish nobleman whose grandfather had landed in the New World with Cortéz, established La Hacienda de la Sombra Verde and appointed his longtime friend José María Espinosa de la Cruz as its mayordomo. For the next 296 years every mayordomo of La Sombra Verde would be an Espinosa, each of them the oldest living son of the mayordomo he replaced. Most of them tended to longevity of service—José María himself would serve for twenty-two years—and Reynaldo, the twenty-first mayordomo, had held the post for a decade at the time that John Roger Wolfe became owner of the hacienda and changed its name to La Buenaventura de la Espada. By the summer of 1886 Reynaldo's tenure had lasted thirty-seven years, far longer than that of the longest-serving of his predecessors. He was sixty-three years old but had all his life been blessed with good health. Except for a few weeks of the previous year when he had been incapacitated by a broken leg, he had never missed a day's work.

Reynaldo had married at twenty-one and over the next sixteen years sired twelve children, all of them born in consecutive years but the last one, Alfredo, whose conception was something of a surprise to Reynaldo and his wife after a barren three-year period. Four of his children were girls, all strong and pretty and all of them married and gone by the age of seventeen. Of the eight boys, three died at birth and three others before they were six years old. The only two who made it to adulthood were his oldest child, Mauricio, and Alfredo. But Alfredo's birth was a difficult one, and his mother, worn old at thirty-seven, never afterward regained her strength and died a few months later.

The following year Reynaldo married a seventeen-year-old girl for no reason but the want of more sons. The girl's mother had borne twelve children, a fact bespeaking strong odds for the bride's own fertility. But after a year of his efforts, the young wife had not conceived, and he was forced to accept the sad truth that his seed had lost all vitality. His spirited wife secretly rejoiced in their failure. She had no desire to share her mother's fate as a lifelong maker of babies. When she absconded one night in the company of a theatrical troupe that had entertained at the hacienda, Reynaldo made no effort to seek after her and hoped she would fare well.

His wish for more sons was prompted by Mauricio's lack of interest in replacing him as mayordomo. From early boyhood, Mauricio had liked to fight and yearned for adventure and to see places beyond Buenaventura and he believed the life of a soldier would satisfy all his cravings. Reynaldo had hoped the boy would outgrow this fancy and accept his calling as the next mayordomo, but whenever he spoke to him about the honor and prestige of the position, Mauricio's boredom was obvious. Not for him the rooted and routine life of a hacienda manager. He desired to be a cavalryman. Not long after his mother died he turned seventeen and on that day enlisted in the army. Reynaldo was crestfallen, but could only accept it. One could not force a son to love the same life as the father's. If it's what you truly want, he said of Mauricio's choice of the army. Mauricio said it was. At their parting at the train station Reynaldo said, Remember, son, if you ever change your mind, the position will be yours.

The military life was everything Mauricio had anticipated and he flourished in it. He distinguished himself in the war against the French and soon became a sergeant. He displayed a gift for leadership and at the end of the war was selected for officer training. On the day before his twenty-second birthday he was made a lieutenant. He fought Yaquis in Sonora for a time and then saw combat against the rebels of Porfirio Díaz and was promoted to captain. He later became an adherent of General Díaz and joined him in the uprising against Lerdo and greatly impressed Díaz with his leadership and tactical expertise. He was made a major and was awarded a medal of valor that Díaz himself, the new president, pinned on him in a ceremony at the National Palace. Over the following years he earned a colonelcy and even more decorations for heroism against various military insurrectionists and marauding Indians. In 1885, at the age of forty, he was made a general and was given command of the military district headquartered just outside of Durango City.

Because so much of his duty had been in the faraway north—and because his Durango post was more than 500 miles from Mexico City and over 800 miles from Veracruz—Mauricio had only rarely had opportunity to visit his father and brother. He might have requested assignment to some post closer to Buenaventura, but he had come to prefer the dry heat and the sun-bright immensity of the desert to the looming shadowy forests and muggy wetlands of his boyhood. In the summer of 1886 it had been five years since his last visit home.

On his last visit, Mauricio had been the patrón's dinner guest in the casa grande. John Roger was impressed by the young general's intelligence and bearing, and he shared Reynaldo's faint hope that Mauricio might yet choose to become mayordomo. It was this hope, more than anything else, that had kept Reynaldo from retiring and ceding his post to his younger son, Alfredo, now twenty-five, who was avid to become the mayordomo. Alfredo was not unintelligent, but he lacked his older brother's skills, his acumen, his natural authority. Lacked above all Mauricio's self-discipline and sense of order. As a boy he'd been taught by Mauricio to shoot and to handle a knife, to fight with his fists, but had always been prone to pick on those smaller than himself. He had a liking for spirits but was not a good drinker, was loud and belligerent when drunk. No less troublesome was his penchant for young girls. On four occasions to date Reynaldo had been obliged to make monetary compensation to an outraged father for Alfredo's violation of his daughter's virtue. It was as demeaning to Reynaldo to have to make such payment as it was to the aggrieved fathers to have to accept it, but what else could be done? Except what the father of a pregnant fourteen-year-old did in flinging the bag of silver back in Reynaldo's face and rushing around him to grab Alfredo by the throat and very nearly throttle him before several stewards pulled him off. Despite a bloody mouth, Reynaldo admired the man for doing as he did. John Roger did too, and he got the man a job at a ranch in Jalapa and made arrangement for the girl to be married to a young cowboy who promised never to mistreat her.

Nevertheless, if Mauricio did not claim his right to be the next mayordomo, Alfredo, as the only remaining Espinosa son, would perforce be entitled to the post. And though John Roger was aware of Alfredo's shortcomings, Reynaldo had no doubt the patrón would grant him the appointment. Don Juan had too much respect for the Espinosa tradition—and for the honorable service he, Reynaldo, had rendered to Buenaventura for so many years—to dishonor the family's name by denying the post to the only Espinosa left to assume it. The fact remained, however, that Alfredo would certainly prove a failure and Don Juan would sooner or later have to dismiss him, and thus would the last of the Espinosa mayordomos be the first ever to be fired for incompetence, a turn hardly less dishonorable than if he were denied the job in the first place.

Reynaldo gave the dilemma much thought. And late one evening a resolution occurred to him. It was so simple he felt doltish for not having thought of it long before. When Don Juan offered him the job, Alfredo would turn it down. He would do so in a formal letter thanking Don Juan for the offer but expressing his regrets that, for reasons he wished to remain personal, he could not accept it. The letter would be notarized, would be historical proof that he had turned down the post, not been denied it. Thus would the Espinosa name be spared dishonor and the hacienda spared the harm of even the brief tenure of an incapable mayordomo. Don Juan would surely be pleased by this decision—and no doubt appoint Don Juanito the new mayordomo. Alfredo would of course be unhappy, but that was of no import. If he should be obstinate and refuse to write the letter, Reynaldo would write it himself and append his son's signature to it and present it to the patrón with a truthful explanation.

Having settled on this course of action, Reynaldo felt both relief and the full weight of his years. In the past few months he'd had recurrent episodes of breathlessness. Of nausea. He sometimes felt a tingling semi-numbness in his arm, a feeling similar to when he awoke from sleeping on it the wrong way. It was without question long past time for him to retire. All right then, when? Why not tomorrow? Just like that? Yes, just like that. He felt himself grinning. Tomorrow, at the end of the day. Don't tell Alfredo till then. Best not give him too much time to dwell on it. Tomorrow afternoon you tell him, have him write the letter—or write it yourself, if need be—then have it notarized and go to Don Juan.

He fell asleep smiling.

—❊—

Alfredo was aware of his father's perception of him as unsuitable to be mayordomo, and he could tell that the patrón felt the same way. But he knew he could do the job and that Mauricio thought so too. Alfredo had last seen his brother five years prior, on which occasion Mauricio had told their father once again that he was not interested in managing the hacienda and did not intend to leave the army until it forced him to retire. Let Alfredo have the job, Mauricio said, and gave his brother a wink.

Alfredo had always idolized Mauricio. He believed his brother was the only one who saw the truth of him and respected him and recognized that he would make a fine mayordomo. The great desire of his father and Don Juan for Mauricio to manage the hacienda was of course understandable, Mauricio was so talented in so many ways. What galled Alfredo wasn't that they so badly wanted Mauricio for the job, but that they didn't want *him* for it at all. His father's poor opinion of him had become more evident in recent years. Alfredo saw it in his face every time his father delivered the same tired lecture on the importance of how a mayordomo should conduct himself, in his every harping on the dangers of drink. Good Christ! As if he were one of those hopeless rummies who needed help getting home from the cantina every night! Yes, he took a drink now and then—what man did not? And what man didn't get a little tipsy sometimes, for God's sake? Or have some fun with a girl? What was more natural than *that*? Did they think Mauricio never took a drink? Never put his hand under a girl's skirt? Like hell he didn't!

Well, they could think what they liked, his father and the patrón. The simple fact was that Mauricio was never going to take the job and his father couldn't keep at it forever—or even much longer. Very soon he would have to retire and they would have no choice but to give it to *him*, of whom they thought so little. Then, father mine, Alfredo thought, *then* you'll see. Mauricio and I will have the last laughs on you and the patrón when you see the kind of mayordomo I am.

—❊—

On Friday the sixteenth of July, Reynaldo awoke before dawn as always—and smiled once again for having found a satisfactory solution to a long-vexing problem. He would put in this last day of work and at the end of it go to Alfredo and then to Don Juan and it would be done with.

There was a peculiar aura to the day. The sunlight itself seemed somehow different, its cast softer than usual. But he felt an ease of mind such as he had not known for years, and the workday glided by. And then it was over and he became melancholic. He felt a vague ache in his chest. He was halfway across the casa grande courtyard on the way home to talk to Alfredo when his arm began to tingle in the familiar way of recent months. And again he felt faint nausea. This time the arm pain did not abate after a minute or so but began to intensify. Then his chest was seized by a band of pain so tight he felt his entire body constrict and he doubled over, hugging himself, breathless, his cry stoppered in his throat. And saw the flagstone rising to meet his face as the world came to an end.

❦

As soon as John Samuel heard the news he went to see his father and found him already informed. John Roger was saddened by the old mayordomo's death—and not unaware that his sadness contained more than a touch of self-pity for his own dwindled life. He poured drinks and they raised their glasses to Reynaldo. John Samuel said he knew that his father and Reynaldo had been very close and had shared a great respect for each other. John Roger nodded and sensed what was coming. But there were shows of respect to the living, John Samuel said, that were of no worth at all to the dead. And now that the noble Reynaldo was gone—God rest his soul—there was really no obligation to subject Buenaventura to even a brief period of mismanagement, was there? John Roger said he supposed not. He had been thinking the same thing before John Samuel arrived.

"Well then," John Samuel said.

❦

On Saturday morning Alfredo telegraphed the news to his brother. Mauricio wired back his commiseration, but it was needless to say he could not make it to the Sunday funeral, as far away as he was. Alfredo was disappointed that Mauricio did not offer congratulations to him on becoming the new mayordomo, then realized his brother would have thought it unseemly to do that in the same telegram devoted to the sadness of their father's death. Such congratulations would anyhow have been premature, as he had not yet received official appointment as his father's successor. The patrón would of course want to wait—also as a gesture of respect—until after the funeral before naming him the new mayordomo.

And, as he expected, immediately after the funeral he was invited by the patrón to come to his office the next afternoon. For a talk, as Don Juan put it. Alfredo was a long time falling asleep that night, so keen was he for tomorrow.

❦

He sat down across the desk from Don Juan, and John Samuel sat off to the side. The patrón again tendered his condolences and again said that Reynaldo had been like a father to him, who had never known his own father. And I know, John Roger said, that your father was very happy about what I am about to tell you. Happy and very proud.

Alfredo beamed.

John Roger told him that the volume of shipping through the hacienda's rail depot had become so great that there was a need for someone to be in charge of it all, a depot manager, a man with the intelligence and skill to insure that all the necessary documents pertaining to goods passing through the depot were in proper order and recorded accurately. It was a most important position and would of course fetch a salary commensurate with its responsibilities. It also came with an assistant, a young man well-trained in every facet of accounting and who was already on the job. It is my very great pleasure, Fredo, John Roger said, to appoint you the first depot manager in the history of Buenaventura de la Espada. I am confident, as was your father, that you are the right man for this vital responsibility.

Alfredo sat stunned before Don Juan's smile. Don Juanito simply stared. His face had always been hard for Alfredo to read and had become more so after its alteration in the fight with the twins. Alfredo cleared his throat twice. I don't understand, he said. I was the next in line. To be the mayordomo, I was next.

Mayordomo? John Roger said. But son, didn't your father tell you? We discussed that matter, he and I, when he told me he was ready to retire. Just two days before . . . no, the very *day* before he, ah, was so suddenly taken from us. He said he would tell you.

Tell me what? Alfredo said. Confusion stark on his face.

John Roger leaned forward in an attitude of earnest sincerity. Look, Fredo, he said, I have three sons and already one grandson, and when Don Reynaldo told me he was ready to retire, he understood completely my intention to begin a line of mayordomos from my own family. Johnny here, my eldest, will be the first of them, of course. But let me tell you, Fredo, your father was very happy about the position I have just given to you. He was concerned, of course, that you might be disappointed not to be his replacement, but he was sure that, when he explained the new job to you, you would be as pleased with it as he. I thought he was going to tell you that night, but, well, he obviously delayed for some reason. Perhaps he intended to tell you the next evening. Ah well, may his soul rest in peace. In any case, I'm sorry this comes as a surprise to you, Fredo, but as I said, I am very confident, as was your father, that you will like the job very much and will excel at it.

Alfredo could not think what to say.

There was no hurry about starting on the new job, the patrón told him. His new salary was effective that very day, but of course he would still need time to mourn his father. Take all the time you need, John Roger said. The job will be there waiting for you when you feel ready.

John Roger stood up and offered his hand. Alfredo stood and shook it, looking like a man waked from a dream and not yet sure of where he is. Then shook John Samuel's extended hand. John Samuel saw him to the door and closed it after him and turned to John Roger and smiled. "I think that went rather well," he said. "You know, Father, you have a gift for diplomacy."

John Roger sighed.

❧

Liar!

His principal thought as he made his way home.

He told the cleaning maid and the cook to go away and not return until next week. The cook had just prepared dinner and she left everything in covered cookware on the stove to stay warm. There was an open bottle of mescal with a single swallow left in it and he gulped it down. Then opened a fresh bottle and poured a proper drink and sat in the parlor and thought things over. The room grew dark but he did not light a lamp. He slept in the chair and woke and had another drink and then slept again. The next time he woke the windows were gray with dawn and his head pained him pinch-eyed until he assuaged it with mescal.

Over the following days he rose from the chair only to urinate or to eat a few spoonfuls of food from one of the cold pots on the stove or to open another bottle each time he emptied one. When there was nothing more to drink in the house he went to a window and called to a couple of boys practicing rope tricks and gave them some money to fetch him six bottles of mescal from the store. The neighbors were aware that he was keeping to his house and drinking by himself and they sympathized. Poor Alfredo, they said. How he grieves for his father.

Thus did he pass six days and nights. By the fifth night he had determined a course of action and by the sixth he was committed to it. He wanted to send a telegram to his brother to tell him what he was going to do but he knew better than to let a telegrapher read it. In ten minutes the whole hacienda would know his plan, including the patrón. He couldn't tell his brother about it until he saw him in Durango. Just as well. If Mauricio knew what this gringo had done he would want to be the one to make him pay for dishonoring the family. For violating 300 years of tradition. And for what? So his own son could become the mayordomo. Rich gringo whoresons! No respect for honor, for tradition, custom, for anything! His father in his grave barely a week and they didn't have enough respect to postpone their kid's communion fiesta! Well that was fine, just fine. Let's see how much they enjoy their fucking fiesta.

He made his preparations. Then slept a few hours and woke at first light. A sunbright Sunday morning. His throbbing head soon assuaged by a swallow or two of mescal. The clock was chiming eight when he stood before a mirror, freshly shaven and wearing a clean black suit. A .36 two-shot derringer in one coat pocket and a full flask in the other. His grandfather's military scout knife with its honed seven-inch double-edged blade in its soft leather sheath snugged between pants and belt. The saddlebags over his shoulder held a change of clothes and his father's packed money belt and a loaded five-shot Ehlers Colt. He took a final look around the house in which he had been born and had lived all his life. Then left the house and went out the main gate of the casa grande enclave and into the compound where preparations were underway for the fiesta to follow the mass.

He went to the stable and saddled his horse and tied the saddlebags down tight behind the cantle and led the horse outside and tethered it at a hitching post in the shade of an alamo tree. Then stood leaning against the tree and watching the courtyard gate of the casa grande. Waiting for the patrón.

25 JULY 1886

The church bells are clanging the imminence of the ten o'clock mass at which Juan Sotero Wolfe—being raised in his mother's Roman Catholic faith without objection from his agnostic father—will make his first Holy Communion. The Bishop of Pachuca, a long-time familiar of Victoria Clara's parents before they passed away, has come to administer the sacrament himself. The mood of the hacienda is loud with merriment in anticipation of the fiesta to follow the mass. The great double doors of the compound's main gate will be open wide all day to ease the coming and going of villagers from both Santa Rosalba and Agua Negra. A pair of marimba bands are setting up on far opposite sides of the plaza fountain. Sides of beef and kid are roasting over open fire pits, and the aromas carry across the plaza and into the cool dimness of the church to mingle with the fragrances of incense and flowers and women's perfumes. The church hums with low-voiced conversations as the pews fill. The front center pew is reserved for the patrón and his family but the only ones to have arrived are John Samuel and Victoria Clara and Juan Sotero.

❧

In the kitchen of the casa grande, Josefina hobbles about on her cane, alternately scolding the scouring technique of the young maid laboring on that morning's breakfast cookware and harrying a boy in the adjoining patio who is charged with keeping the water hot in a pair of large bathing tubs. The scrub maid is a pretty seventeen-year-old named Concha who was promoted to the kitchen from the laundry only days earlier.

Marina Colmillo tends the fire in the stove, then consults the small clock on the wall and extracts two handfuls of sugar lumps from a tin container and places them on the end of the wall counter in readiness for John Roger. It is his habit to go to the stable every morning and give the sugar to his horses. She then sets to work at the center counter, carving raw chickens for a stew. Most of the household will be dining on the fiesta's offerings, but the twins will be here today and their favorite meal is her chicken-and-chiles stew and so she will have it ready for them. It has been two months since she last saw them, and she cannot stop smiling in her eagerness.

John Roger appears in the doorway between kitchen and dining room. He wears an immaculate white suit, one sleeve folded and pinned by the upstairs maid who also knots his ties. In the ten months since the loss of his grandson he looks to have aged a decade, and the suit hangs loose on his gaunt frame. His nose webbed with red veins. His hair and short beard the color of ash. His eyes dark pouched.

"Todavía no han llegado?" he says.

Not yet, Josefina says. But they will be here any minute.

They promised Doña Victoria they would be here, John Roger says. And feels foolish for saying it. For whining like a petulant child.

Don't worry, Don Juan, Josefina says, they wouldn't disappoint their little nephew. Their baths are hot and their suits are ready. It won't take them a minute to clean up and be dressed.

Tell them I want them in that church, I don't care how late they are. You understand?

She blinks at his peremptory tone. "Sí, señor, a sus ordenes. Le entiendo perfectamente."

He is familiar with her trick of formal address and blank look whenever she takes offense at his tone. Coming from her, such formality has always suggested more of impertinence than respect. He feels his vexation on his face and is the more irritated for letting the crone see she has succeeded in riling him.

In case I don't see them before the mass, John Roger says, I want you to tell them to see me afterwards. *Immediately* afterwards. In my office.

"Muy bien, señor."

I mean it, madam. He points a finger at her. Be very sure you tell them what I said.

"Claro que sí, señor." And adds that she is sure they will be along any minute now, but if they should be late it will be for reasons that could not be helped.

He turns and goes. Yet once again irked by her defense of them, whom she has ever and always defended against him in every case of contention, large or small, however right he might be, however wrong they. He has already left the house before Marina notices the sugar lumps still on the counter.

❖

He had lain awake through most of the night, reviewing the decision of which he intended to apprise the three of them today. The twins would resume their monthly visits as before, and during those visits they and John Samuel would sit to dinner with the rest of the family. And if, as before, they couldn't do it except by not saying a word to each other or even looking at each other, fine, very well, so be it. But they were going to do it for as long as he, their father, was still alive. He had by Jesus had enough of this rift. Whoever of them could not agree to the terms could leave Buenaventura—yes, leave! The family could hardly be more fractured for the departure of one or two of them than it was at present. *But* . . . whoever chose to leave would surrender his inheritance. *That* should get their attention. They all knew John Samuel would by dint of primogeniture inherit Buenaventura, but, as they would be informed today, his inheritance would not include that portion of the estate from just below the rapids all the way to the coast. He would bequeath that region to the twins. The deed to it had already been drawn and signed and needed only registration to become official. He would within the week submit it to his Veracruz legal firm, together with his will, specifying that the deed be officially registered immediately upon his death. But he wasn't dead yet, and a will could easily enough be changed, an unregistered deed easily enough torn up. Simple as that. So would he tell the three of them in his office right after this church thing. His decision would go down hard with John Samuel, but there was no chance that he would pack his trunks, not him, to whom nothing on earth mattered more than becoming the next patrón, even of a hacienda made smaller by the bequeathal to the twins. The twins, John Roger knew, were the question. They loved Ensenada de Isabel and would of course love to own it. Yet he wasn't sure they wouldn't give it up rather than yield to what they might view as an ultimatum. The trick would be in the manner of his appeal. You boys want that place for yourselves? Free of your brother's authority over it? Resume the visits. It's no surrender, gentlemen, just a recommencement of our agreement, a matter of honoring your word. So he would say to them before sending for John Samuel. He hadn't seen them in ten months, for Christ's sake! Enough was enough.

⚜

Barely ten minutes after John Roger departs, Josefina's attention turns toward the garden door and she says, "Hay están." She calls to the boy tending the tubs that he can go now, and the boy waves and scoots away through the patio gate. Marina has to listen hard for a moment more before she too hears the boys' faint laughter from the garden, and she smiles at Josefina. Nobody knows the old woman's age—it is a household joke of long standing that she was the cook on Noah's Ark—but she still has the hearing of a fox.

That the twins have chosen to come in by their garden route makes it clear they know how late they are and that they don't want to run into their father before getting to the church. The young maid, Concha, is alight with excitement. She has never met the twins and has seen them only from a distance, but she has heard much about them from the women in the laundry, most of it scandalous and therefore enticing.

The garden door bangs open and they come stomping in, still laughing over some shared joke, charging the room with masculine energy and infusing the air with the effluvia of the sweat and blood caked on their clothes and seasoned with the smell of campfire smoke. They are hatless and their hair dusty. For the last two weeks they have been taking crocodile hides on the river, the skins now drying at the cove.

"Pues, al fin llegan estos brutos desgraciados!" Josefina says. She whacks at the boys with her cane, berating them for their lateness and their filthy stinking state and the trouble they have caused her with their father.

They laugh and fend her blows, and then Blake Cortéz snatches her to him and pins her skinny arms against her sides and kisses her full on the mouth. He says he's damned glad a crocodile isn't as tough as she is or they wouldn't have collected a single hide. Marina has often marveled at the blush only the twins can raise in the brown wither of Josefina's face.

Let go of me, Blackie, you good-for-nothing, Josefina says, trying to wriggle free. He kisses her again, then hops back from her with his fists raised like a pugilist, exhibiting a fancy footwork and feinting with lefts and rights, saying, "Come on, you old warhorse, I'm ready for you. This one's for the championship."

She swats at his arms with the cane and calls him a wicked child and says she's told him a thousand times not to talk that gringo talk to her. She drives him rearward toward the patio door, ordering him to get into the bathtub this minute, they are late enough as it is.

"Oye! Pero quién es esa hermosa?" James Sebastian says, taking notice of Concha at the other end of the room.

Never mind that, Marina says. Get in those tubs and clean up, there's no time for foolishness. As she pushes James toward the patio door, he grins and fondles her bottom and whispers in her ear that he has missed her terribly and how about sneaking into the tub with him. Marina slaps his hand away and calls him a donkey and cuts a look at Josefina, whose attention is still fixed on driving Blackie toward the patio with jabs of her cane. It frets Marina that James could be so indiscreet. But she knows how he feels. When the twins entered the kitchen it had been all she could do to keep from running to them and kissing them with all her might. She had done that once, after not having seen them for six months. Had come into the kitchen and seen them standing there, just arrived, and even in Josefina's presence she could not refrain from kissing them each in turn with all her heart until Josefina said, Enough, girl, for God's sake, let the poor boys catch their breath. She had felt her face flush and expected Josefina to be shocked, but the old woman simply busied herself at making the boys something to eat. She and the twins have now been lovers for more than two years and she cannot believe Josefina is still unaware of it.

Her incredulity is well-founded, for Josefina has in fact been aware of her sexual relation with the twins since it began. She had at first been dismayed by the realization that Marina had accepted the boys as lovers, but the more she turned it over in her mind the less it troubled her, until at last she felt obliged to ask the Holy Mother's forgiveness for her lack of moral affront. Where, after all, was the sin? The boys' cheekiness with Marina was but a flimsy veil over their adoration of her, and Marina was still a fairly young woman with a young woman's natural appetites and she loved them too and knew how to guard against conception. Who could have taught them better than she what they should know most about women? And who else has ever given her the respect and protection she deserves? Who else has ever defended her honor as they did last summer when they accompanied her to the hacienda market to carry back a side of beef and that fool of a muleskinner called out that if she would place a sack over her head he'd be willing to play with her body? He was a very large man of rough repute but no match for the two of them. They went at him from opposite flanks like a pair of boar dogs and got him down fast and began beating him in the face with a cobblestone and surely would have killed him if Marina had not managed to make them desist. Even so, they pounded the man's face to a ruination worse than hers, fracturing it so severely he would for the rest of his life have to breathe through his mouth and have trouble making himself understood. They had already acquired a reputation as ferocious fighters but after the public maiming of the muleskinner there were few men who weren't at least a little bit afraid of them—and they were only fifteen at the time. When their father heard about the fight he said nothing of it to them or to Marina but summoned Josefina to get the details, and she had sensed both Don Juan's pride in their gallantry and his dismay at their viciousness. Like their father, Josefina fears for the twins' future. Fears it because of the men they are becoming and cannot be prevented from becoming and the dangers such men seem naturally to attract and those they seem naturally to seek out. And yet she cannot but admire them for their bravery and love them the more for their devotion to Marina. In a girlhood of so long ago it seems more like some tale she once heard told than an actual part of her past, Josefina had learned that the only man of worth to a woman was one who was willing to kill for her, a truth that was proved in her own marriage to a man who was not of that sort. In her prayers to the Holy Mother she has allowed that, if there is sin in the love between the twins and Marina, then she herself, Josefina María Cortéz de Quito, must be held to a share of that sin, because she cannot condemn it.

Marina is trying to shove James out the door, but he laughs and braces himself against his brother, who has also become aware of Concha and stands fast in the doorway, grinning at her. Despite herself, blushing Concha is smiling back.

Get *into* those baths, you little pigs! says Josefina, half their size, flailing at them with her walking stick.

The twins yip in mock pain and affect to flinch at the blows as they stumble rearward into the patio, holding to each other as if to keep from falling. They trade a grinning look—and then swiftly unbuckle their belts and drop their pants and grab their cocks and wag them at the women.

Concha squeals and whirls about with her back to them as Josefina screeches, You'll burn in *hell*, both of you! You *filthy evil* things!

Marina slams the door shut on the boys' wild laughter and slumps against it in a caricature of slack-jawed exhaustion.

Josefina issues a groaning sigh as she eases into a chair. "Jesucristo," she says, "que par de bárbaros!"

Concha looks from one woman to the other, her hands at her mouth, her brown face darker yet with embarrassment.

And then all three of them break into a cackling laughter louder than the boys outside.

⁂

From the shade of the alamo tree, he keeps intent watch on the casa grande's courtyard gate. The steeple bells in their final clangoring summons to the ceremonial mass. He is familiar with the patrón's habits and knows that before he does anything else he will come to the horses to give them their treat. He takes the flask from his coat and uncorks it and has a drink and re-seals it and tucks it away.

His heart jumps when he sees the white-suited patrón come out the casa grande gate. Unaccompanied, as usual. Excellent. He puts his hand inside his coat and fingers the haft of the knife snug in its sheath under the heavy money belt. The derringer in his coat will have no part in this. To be done as it should, the act calls for the blade. Face to face. So the gringo will see who is doing it, and seeing who, will die knowing why.

But now the patrón stops and pats at his coat pockets, then tosses his head in irritation and looks back toward the casa grande. He takes his watch from a vest fob and checks the time, then puts away the watch and heads for the other end of the plaza and the church.

The circumstance is clear enough. The old bastard forgot the sugar. What to do? To ride after him would put him on his guard. With that damned pistol everybody knows about. A revolver with the barrel cut short for easier carry under his coat. There is nothing to do except stay put and wait until after the mass. Then he thinks, Idiot! Why will he come to the stable afterward? He will go straight back to the house is what he will do. While you stand here with your thumb up your ass.

Damn it. To kill him at the stable would have made it all so simple. No one else nearby. A horse and out the gate before anyone even thought to give chase. A back trail into the mountains and then a mule track he knows of, unused for years. He would be in Jalapa before sundown and on a train for Mexico City and from there a train to Durango and the protection of his brother. But now what? If you do it at the church you've got a lot of people around and you're a whole lot farther from the main gate. Wait until tomorrow and do it here at the stable like you planned. Be smart. And there'll be fewer people tomorrow.

No! Today! You're ready *today*. And you don't want fewer people. You want as many as possible to see it. To see what happens to this gringo who spat on your family's honor!

All right, then. Take the horse over there. You can still mount up fast and get out quick. Goddammit, man, where are your balls?

He leads the horse across the plaza to the church and tethers it to a tree a few yards from the wide breadth of church steps. Then positions himself at the periphery of the crowd assembled outside the doors, hat low over his eyes. And now has only to wait for the end of the mass. Engrossed in his thoughts, he is heedless of late arrivals.

—❦—

The mass is in progress when the black-suited twins ease through the crowd listening at the open doors. The people grouped at the back of the room make way so that the brothers can stand at the forefront with a clear view of the altar. As those in the rearmost pews become aware of their presence, they make gestures of offering their seats to them, but the twins decline the tenders with their own hand signals.

They see their father in the front pew, his shoulders slumped as never before. To one side of him are John Samuel and Vicki and Juanito Sotero, and next to them Bruno Tomás and his wife Felicia Flor, great with their first child, due in a few weeks. The empty space to the other side of their father is where the twins would be sitting if they had arrived in time. Not until Juan Sotero goes to the altar to receive the communion wafer from the bishop does their father turn to look toward the back of the church and see them. His gaze is tired but reproachful at their lateness. The twins acknowledge him with respectful nods and he nods in turn. Then gives his attention back to Juan Sotero as the boy returns to the pew, hands together in a prayerful attitude contrasting with his wide smile. He sits down and Vicki Clara puts an arm around him and whispers in his ear.

Josefina has told them of their father's directive to go to his office after the mass. They cannot guess what he wishes to see them about, but have a hunch it will entail John Samuel in some way and that he will be there too, and so the session cannot possibly be anything but unpleasant. As the mass nears its end, Blake says, "Let's go."

—❦—

He freezes at the sight of them emerging from the throng at the doors. They had not been seen in the compound since the business with the horse—almost a year now—and he'd had no reason whatever to think they might be here today. They are walking in his direction and for a petrifying moment he thinks they have already seen him, then realizes they haven't and he averts his face just as one looks his way. They stride past, almost close enough to touch. He feels a tremor in his fingers and stills it with his fists.

And sees the patrón come out of the church, flanked by family.

-❧-

They are halfway to the casa grande when Blake Cortéz stops and looks back toward the church, where the crowd is just beginning to exit. James Sebastian looks back at him. "What?"

"I don't know. Something."

James looks toward the church. "Good-looking, huh?"

"Not that. Something else. Just barely saw it. Goddammit, what was it?"

"Harm?"

"Has that feel."

"See Father?"

"Not in that crowd."

They head back to the church.

-❧-

As they surge from the church, people are laughing, speaking in shouts to be heard above the clangor of the bells. Children race off toward the far end of the plaza, toward the music and the tables of food. John Roger begins to descend the steps—John Samuel and his family to one side of him, Bruno Tomás and Felicia Flor to the other—and then, directly before him, two steps below, is Alfredo Espinosa, his expression such that for a second John Roger doesn't recognize him, and then he does, and he smiles and halts, wondering what he might want. Alfredo now smiles too and steps up and places a hand on John Roger's arm in unseemly familiarity—then locks his hand on the arm and brings up the knife and stabs him with terrific force three fast times. In the abdomen, the stomach, the chest.

The others have already descended another three steps before they are aware John Roger has halted behind them, and when they turn to look he is on the seat of his pants and falling onto his side, hat tumbling, face clenched and teeth bared, hand splayed against his chest. The people to either side of him are agape with shock. John Samuel says "Oh God" and backs down another step. A woman shrieks. Bruno sees the bloom of blood on his uncle's white coat and sees Alfredo with knife in hand as he is starting to move away. He lunges and grabs him by the collar and Alfredo twists about and slashes Bruno's arm and face and Bruno lets go as Felicia Flor pulls him to her and gives her back to Alfredo, who slashes again and the blade opens her sleeve without touching flesh. More screams now as others see what's happening, but most of the churchgoers are still oblivious or in confusion, and Alfredo vanishes among them.

The twins come shouldering through the crowd and see their fallen father, his head cradled in Vicki Clara's lap and his coat opened to expose a shirtfront sodden with blood so bright they know he will be dead within the minute. Don't die, Papá, Vicki Clara pleads, don't die! John Roger's eyes are wide and keep moving from one looming twin to the other. He wants to say "Sons" but manages only what sound like gasping exhalations. Then his eyes go still and their light is gone.

James Sebastian takes the shortened Colt from his father's shoulder holster and Blake Cortéz shouts "Pa donde fue?" Hands point and wave in the same direction amid a chorus of strident babblings and the twins charge through the throng, knocking aside men and women and children alike.

In all the turmoil, no one has tried to stop Alfredo before he reaches his mount. He swings up into the saddle, knife still in hand, and heels the horse hard, heading toward the main gate at the other end of the plaza. The twins break through the crowd and spot him. James Sebastian assumes a shooting stance and sights just above the distancing rider to allow for the truncated trajectory of a short-barreled handgun and squeezes off three rounds in measured succession, adjusting his sight after each shot. The first bullet falls short and ricochets up into the horse's thigh but the animal barely flinches and doesn't break stride. The people at the far end of the plaza flee for cover. The next round strikes the horse in the hindquarter and it staggers but keeps its feet and Alfredo heels it hard and presses himself low against its neck. The third bullet hits the horse behind the ear and it plunges headfirst and Alfredo hears its neck break like a tree branch as he sails forward and onto the cobbles and goes tumbling to a stop. Blackie would later praise the shot and James would confess he had been trying to hit the rider.

Alfredo scrabbles to his feet, incredulous that he has broken no bone, his heart ramming against his ribs as though trying to make its own getaway. His knife is gone. The twins are coming at a jog and the crowd trotting behind at a distance. He bolts down a narrow alleyway between worker row houses and turns into a wider alley behind the residences, this one lined with animal enclosures—chicken houses and cattle corrals, goat pens and pig sties. He sees another alleyway junction up ahead and runs toward it and then stops short when the twin with the gun comes sprinting out of its shadowed mouth and sees him and turns toward him at a walk. Alfredo whirls around and sees the other twin advancing on him too, Alfredo's knife in his hand. Onlookers stream out from each of the flanking alleyways but each bunch keeps well back of the twin ahead of it. Alfredo remembers the derringer in his pocket but is too afraid to make a move for it.

It occurs to him that surrender will resolve everything. Surrender, yes! Let them lock him up! What else can they do in the eyes of so many witnesses? He raises his hands high and yells, "Me rendiro! Me rendiro!" He'll have someone send a telegram to his brother. To General Mauricio Espinosa de la Santa Cruz. Who will speed down here. Then let's see how long he stays locked up! Then these two sonsofbitches'll see what's what!

Look! he yells. All of you, *look*! He shakes his raised hands. I am surrendering! You see! He keeps shifting his attention from one twin to the other as they approach him from either side. And then they are near enough for him to see their eyes. I surrender! he yells, voice breaking. I *surrenderrrrr*!

Blake Cortéz stabs him just below the ribs and with a lateral yank slices him open. The pain exceeds any Alfredo could have imagined. He clamps his hands over his exposed viscera and his face contorts but the pain constricts his voice to a rasp. The front of his pants darkens with blood and urine. He falls down, knees drawn up, and moans low. They are next to a pig sty loud with snortings, and a row of little furious eyes peer between the slat rails. The twins look at each other—and then James Sebastian puts his boot against Alfredo's shoulder and pushes him onto his back and shoots him through each elbow to render his arms useless and Alfredo finds his voice and screams. And then screams higher still as the twins pick him up by the wrists and ankles and sling him over the top rail of the pen. He smacks down into the muck—and then everyone hears the clamorous raven of the pigs. The excruciations of his final minutes.

They take the Dragoon from the top right drawer and then from the middle drawer take a handful of the photographs of their mother and two of their father and one of their parents together. They pick the lock of the lower left drawer and take the ledger and the document case and put the ledger into the case with its other contents. They ignore the other drawers. They have already been to see their father where he is laid out. In deference everyone else left the room. When it was just him and the two of them, they touched him for the first time in their lives. His hand, his hair. Touched his face.

As they head for the office door James Sebastian says, "Hold on" and goes over to the big map of Mexico on the wall. Blake Cortéz comes up beside him.

"Where'll it be?" James says. Veracruz was out of the question. It was the first place their seekers would look.

"I don't care as long as it's near the gulf. I'd rather not live anywhere other."

"Me neither. North or south?"

"Nothing south but Indians who mostly can't even speak Spanish."

"Well then, that just about leaves only here," James taps a fingertip on the map. "Fine by me."

They are midway down the stairs when John Samuel comes through the tall front doors and across the great room at a quick stride, heading for the staircase. As he nears the foot of it he looks up and sees them and stops short. The twins pause a few steps below the middle landing to regard him. They had not seen his face since the horse accident and see now what Bruno meant about his nose and that Josefina was not exaggerating the scar on his cheek. His eyes move from one of them to the other. Linger a moment on the gun each has tucked into the front of his pants. One of them puts a hand on his gun and says, "You aint got a rifle hid on you, do you?"

John Samuel reddens. The twin grins and takes his hand off the Colt.

"I want to talk to you," John Samuel says. His voice has deepened, no doubt because of the nose.

"Make it quick," says one.

"I mean in private, not out here in—"

"You have something to say, say it," says the other.

He seems unsure how to proceed. Then gestures in the direction of the plaza and says, "What you did to that man was . . . was. . . ."

"Discourteous?" one offers. "Ill-mannered?"

"Good God! You two are just—"

"He murdered our father," says the other. "Yours too, I guess."

"*Yes!* Yes, he did! And he deserved to be punished for it. By the *courts*! Not the way you two—"

"We punished him no more than he deserved."

"*Punished*, you say? Christ, you *defiled* him. What do you think Mauricio . . . do you fools not know who his brother is?"

"Ah, quit your mewling," says one. "We know about his brother and we aint about to fight his army. We're leaving. When he gets here you tell him we're gone and you don't know where."

"He'll know you're at the cove. He'll find out and he'll go there. People talk, especially if they're afraid. Somebody will tell him."

"No doubt," says one. "But don't worry about us, big brother, we won't be there for long."

John Samuel's surprise is more apparent than he knows. "Where are you going?"

"China. The moon. We aint decided."

John Samuel glares. "Fine. That's fine. I don't care a damn. But don't ever come back here. I mean it. This place is far more important than you two and I won't put it at hazard just to protect you from—"

"Protect us?" one says. They laugh and start down the stairs and he steps aside to give them berth. As they pass, he notes the document case and says, "What do you have there? If that's Father's it stays here!"

They stop and turn and stare at him. Then grin at the look on his face. Then go off to the kitchen.

❦

Josefina hugs them each in turn. Her withered face looks older than ever. Of course you must go, she says, of course, go quickly. She has never cried in front of them and will not do so now. But her red eyes tell them she has been weeping for their father. When she'd seen the pistols in their pants she'd said, "Ay, Dios." Said it like a sigh. The Concha girl stands mute at the wash sink, her arms soapy, staring at the twins, at the set of their faces. So different from this morning.

Marina Colmillo had fled the room as soon as they said they were leaving. Both she and Josefina had known at once that they did not simply mean they were going back to the cove but were departing Buenaventura for somewhere else—and with small likelihood of coming back.

Now Marina returns, a little breathless, a sack of clothing in one hand and in the other a small straw case with a handle. Her worldly goods.

Where are *you* going? says Blake Cortéz.

With you.

No you're not.

Yes I am.

You can't come, says James Sebastian.

Why not?

You just can't.

I'll follow you.

Don't be foolish, James says. We'd leave you way behind quick. Lose you easy.

I'll follow the trail.

We're not going to stay at the cove, Blake says.

I know.

We'll be gone before you get there.

Maybe.

You'll just have to turn around and come all the way back.

I won't.

Oh? What'll you do?

Wait.

Wait? You mean there?

Yes.

For what?

For you to come back.

You don't seem to understand, James says. We may never come back.

Then I will wait there until then.

Until *when*?

Until you never come back.

The twins stare at her. James turns to Josefina and says, Tell her she can't come.

It is not for me to tell her, she says.

He blows out a long breath and cuts a look at Blake, who shrugs and says, "Hell man, *I* don't know. Maybe."

Josefina swats at Blake and says, No gringo talk!

James Sebastian points a finger at Marina. The minute you complain, the minute you cause any kind of trouble, we'll put you on a train right back here. You understand?

Of course I do, she says. *I* am not sixteen years old.

Josefina smiles at Marina's rebuke of them for addressing her as if she were the child among them, she who is nearly twice their age.

Yeah, well . . . just so you know, James says.

The boys give Josefina a last quick kiss and put on their hats and take up the food sacks she has prepared for them and head for the door. Where they stop and look back at the two women hugging hard and murmuring endearments to each other.

You coming or not, for Christ's sake? says Blake.

Josefina watches Marina go to them, the burlap bag over a shoulder, the basket hanging from the crook of an elbow and bumping against her hip.

You're already slowing us down, James says, taking the basket from her.

All your blah-blah-blah is slowing us down, Marina says. Then turns and mouths a kiss at Josefina, who makes a benedictory sign of the cross at them.

And they are gone.

—※—

After his father's body is taken away to be washed and dressed for that night's vigil and tomorrow's funeral, when he will be buried beside Elizabeth Anne in the casa grande graveyard, John Samuel goes to the telegraph office. Everyone within but the telegrapher steps outside to grant him privacy while he dictates a wire to General Mauricio Espinosa, informing him of the morning's violence. Still shaken by his witness of his father's killing and the reports of what his brothers did to Alfredo, he cannot bring himself to relate the grislier details, and he tells Mauricio only the bare facts of John Roger's being stabbed to death by Alfredo who in turn was stabbed to death by the twins.

He sends for Bruno Tomás and Rogelio Méndez to meet with him in his office and is somewhat better composed by the time they arrive. He is brief and to the point. Bruno is now the mayordomo of Buenaventura and Rogelio the foreman of Rancho Isabela.

As they make their way back across the plaza, Rogelio says, Didn't waste a minute, did he?

—※—

John Samuel goes into his father's office and closes the door and seats himself behind the desk. He feels his father's absence like a sudden, unseasonable change in weather. But at the same time it feels right to him to be sitting where he is. He opens the middle drawer and passes the next twenty minutes studying the photographs he had not known existed. His childhood pictures seem those of someone he never knew, some boy stranger. The ones he looks at longest are of his mother. He feels a mix of peculiar sensations and the oddest of them is very near to an urge to cry.

He remembers the day they collected seashells on the Cove's gulfside beach and the wind blew up her skirt and he saw her underwear. He wishes he had a picture of that moment. Then feels a hot shame on his face and glances about as if someone may have been watching him and known what he was thinking. And puts the pictures away.

The next drawer he tries is the top left and in it he finds John Roger's will and an attached document. He scans the will and smiles. Then examines the other document and his smile falls away. It is a prepared deed for the entire eastern tract of Buenaventura, including all of its coast. It is made out in his brothers' names and ready for legal registration.

Good Christ, he thinks. This almost was.

His hand trembles as he puts the match flame to the paper.

❦

John Samuel's telegram about the killings does not come as news to Mauricio Espinosa. The general has already received several telegraphed accounts of the bloody morning from other residents of Buenaventura. His father dead but a week and now his brother dead too. The Espinosa de la Cruz family reduced to himself alone.

That stupid kid. Twenty-something years old and still a stupid kid. Witless. Killing the patrón because of a damned job. In front of his family! In front of a hundred witnesses! Based on his own acquaintance with John Wolfe, Mauricio regarded him a good man. His own father, who had known the patrón for more than twenty-five years, had always had high opinion of Don Juan.

Stupid kid.

He pours another drink. He feels partly at fault, having encouraged Alfredo to believe he would make a capable mayordomo. He had done it solely in hope that it might make Alfredo work harder to better himself, so when the time came for him to take over the job he might prove adequate to it. It was less a hope than wishful thinking. You could sooner alter the configuration of the stars than change a man's character, and Alfredo's character was not the stuff of a mayordomo. Simple as that. Had he been in the patrón's place he would not have given the job to Alfredo either.

But the denial of the job to Alfredo was not the point. The whole thing seemed clear enough. The patrón denied Alfredo the job and gave it to his own son, so Alfredo killed the patrón for wronging him—as Alfredo saw it, anyway—and then the patrón's twin sons killed Alfredo. That Alfredo committed a wrong is without question. And who could argue that the twins were not justified in avenging their father?

However. That they killed Alfredo was also not the point. John Samuel Wolfe's telegraphed report said of the killings only that Alfredo had killed the patrón with a knife and the twins then knifed Alfredo. But as others of the hacienda have reported to him, that wasn't all there was to it. For one thing, it was said that Alfredo had surrendered. It was said he was yelling that he surrendered and that everyone in the crowd heard him and that his hands were up. But they killed him anyway. Injustice? Some would so argue. But not he, a cavalry officer who has seen more than his share of killing in hot blood and understands the power of its compulsion. No, injustice was not the point.

However. They stabbed him and shot him and fed him to the pigs—while, it was said, he was still alive. But even if true that he was still alive, that they added to his final suffering, that they prolonged it, well, that was not the point, either. He himself has ordered men burned alive, buried alive.

But in feeding him to the pigs what they were truly doing was making him into pig shit. They had made pig shit of his brother.

That was the fucking point.

The new patrón must've thought he could protect his brothers by keeping those details from him. Well, hell, that's what a big brother's supposed to do, isn't it? Can't really blame the man for that. If he's ever met John Samuel Wolfe, Mauricio has no recollection of it.

He had mulled whether to send for the body and decided against it. Let them bury him. Except in cases when you really had no choice but to make some public display of honor or respect or suffering or some such thing, the dead were the dead and it didn't make a bean's worth of difference who buried them or where or even whether they were buried at all. If a lifetime of soldiering had taught him anything, it was the unsurpassable indifference of the dead. Dust to dust was absolutely right. The only truth ever to come from the mouth of a priest.

He is told they are sixteen years old. Christ. He had seen them only twice on his rare visits to Buenaventura, had first met when they were around eight and seen them again the last time he had been to the hacienda, when they must have been eleven or so. He remembers them as the only truly identical twins he has ever set eyes on. Polite but close-mouthed. With a way of looking at you as if they were studying a picture on a wall. His own father had liked them very much, though he said they could at times be devils. Good. They would feel at home when he sent them to hell.

For many years General Mauricio Espinosa has maintained close at hand a small corps of civilian hirelings for employment in missions outside of official sanction. He now sends for the most reliable of them. Esmeraldo Lopez, a man of wide experience in various forms of warfare, with particular skill in the jungle. He arrives within the hour, saying, Yes, my general.

Mauricio briefs him about the events at Buenaventura and then acquaints him with a rough map he has drawn of the hacienda and instructs him in his mission. He answers Lopez's few questions, then provides him with money and dispatches him to Veracruz via private train.

Alfredo Espinosa has been dead for eleven hours.

THE HARROWING

Esmeraldo Lopez took with him a party of twenty men, all of them former soldiers, all of whom had worked for him before. The train carried their mounts as well. They arrived in Veracruz early the following evening. As instructed by the general, Lopez rented a room in the Hotel de las Palmas, which had a telegraph office through which the general could contact him. He posted a man there to serve as a message runner if necessary and he and the others then rode north in the light of the moon through most of the remaining night. The Veracruz road on which they arrived at the boundary to Buenaventura—marked by an arched gateway of lime rock—was one of the two roads into and out of the hacienda. The other, the road to Jalapa, was fifteen miles farther inland. Two miles west of the Veracruz road ran the hacienda rail track.

Lopez divided his force into two groups and sent one bunch to encamp within sight of the Jalapa road entrance and himself stayed with the group near the hacienda's Veracruz gateway. He unpacked his tailored black suit and sprinkled it with water and hung it with care on a tree to smooth out the wrinkles. He slept for an hour and woke at daybreak. Then bathed in a creek and gave his nails a quick cleaning, then shaved his neck, then put on the suit. He had recently been to a Durango barber and his hair and beard were close-cropped and neat. Then he mounted up and rode to the hacienda compound to call on its new patrón.

✦

By Sunday evening John Samuel was berating himself for having omitted the graphic details from his cable to Mauricio. It was now very important that Mauricio know the particulars of what the twins did to Alfredo. So he went again to the telegrapher's office, intending to send Mauricio a wire explaining his oversight and his view that it would be dishonest to keep the full facts from him, repugnant as they were. When the young telegrapher read the message, he told John Samuel that several other persons had already provided the particulars to General Espinosa. I see, said John Samuel. Very well then. He thanked the telegrapher for saving him the needless transmission and returned to the casa grande.

Sipping a glass of brandy before bed, he regarded the wastebasket holding the ashes of the unregistered deed. After its burning he'd had the alarming thought that there might be some other record of it somewhere, some mention of it in his father's papers, maybe, or in a letter he sent to someone. Maybe more than a mention. Maybe a specific statement of his bequeathal. They had taken a document case with them and what looked like a ledger. What information did those contain? The possibility was unbearable. This place was *his*. All of it. His by right. He was the eldest, goddammit! It was unjust—*unjust!*—that his father should have wanted to give a share of it to those two, who had never given him anything but trouble. Those insolent, arrogant, reckless killers of his mother! Of his child!

Unjust, yes! A fact plain and simple. It could not be permitted any chance to happen.

John Samuel did not know Mauricio Espinosa personally. He was eight years old when Mauricio left for the army, and he had been away at the Rancho Isabela on each of the rare occasions when Mauricio came to visit his family at the compound. But he had all his life heard much about him. The man had supped with Father in the casa grande and Father had thought highly of him. Mauricio was by all accounts a man of principles and honor, and was said to be very fond of his little brother. He would doubtless be enraged by the twins' degradation of him. Sufficiently enraged, it was John Samuel's hope, to seek retribution. A retribution that would incidentally remove all possibility of the twins ever returning to Buenaventura with some legal paper in hand to claim a portion of the estate. *His* estate.

His hope was well-founded, John Samuel believed, but in order for the hope to be realized, Mauricio's response would have to be swift. The man was hundreds of miles away and the twins had said they would not be at the cove for long. What did that mean? A few days? A week? Surely no longer than that. If they were to leave the cove before Mauricio got there it would most likely be on that boat they so often prattled about at the dinner table. And once they were out on the open sea, who was going to find them?

❖

John Roger was interred at sunrise. The rest of Monday passed without word from Mauricio. And then early Tuesday morning Lopez arrived.

He presented himself at the compound gate as a courier from Durango with an important and confidential message for the patrón, John Samuel Wolfe. When

John Samuel was told of him, he was certain that he was from Mauricio. He had the man brought to his office.

Lopez settled into a chair across the desk from John Samuel, his smile warm. The only incongruities with his grooming and good manners were a white jag of scar that bisected an eyebrow, and the absent little finger of his left hand, severed just below the top joint. On the ring finger of the same hand he wore a thin band of gold. Despite the man's articulate and polite demeanor John Samuel had no difficulty envisioning him in an army uniform or the rough clothes of a guerrilla.

Because John Samuel had introduced himself by his American name, Lopez addressed him as Don John and seemed somewhat amused by the intonation of the title. He said he was in the employ of General Mauricio Espinosa, who had directed him to present his deepest sympathies to Don John on the death of his father, a man the general had greatly respected.

I thank the general, John Samuel said. Please convey my appreciation to him.

Lopez said he certainly would. Then said the general wanted to meet with Don John's brothers, who by all accounts were the ones most familiar with the facts pertaining to the deaths of their father and his brother. He has engaged me, Lopez said, to escort your brothers to him. And then of course to escort them back.

Lopez's manner was pleasant, his smile unchanged. But it was clear enough to John Samuel that Mauricio's desire to have the twins brought to him was less request than directive. He had to restrain himself from smiling. He could not have arranged the whole thing better himself.

Well, John Samuel said, I quite understand the general's wish to hear from my brothers whatever they can tell him about the, ah, tragic occurrence. I regret to inform you, however, that they are not here. I mean, not *here* at the compound. They left immediately after the, ah, the terrible event. They went to the coast. The hacienda extends to the coast, you see. There is a little cove there. And a house. It's where they live.

Perhaps, Lopez said, you can send a man to retrieve them.

John Samuel cleared his throat. To be quite frank, Mr Lopez, if I send for them, I do not think they will come. You see, my brothers and I are not, ah, very close. That is one of the reasons they live at the coast house rather than here at the casa grande. In fact, now that my father has, ah, passed away, they really have nothing to keep them on the hacienda. They told me they would not be staying at the cove for very long. They have a boat there, you see.

Oh? Lopez said. He studied John Samuel's eyes. And did they say where they would be going when they left this cove?

No. I asked but they wouldn't tell me. I don't believe they have told anybody.

I see. Tell me, how far is this cove?

Fifteen miles or so, I would guess.

And the terrain is jungle, is it not?

That's correct. But there's a trail, you see. A little rough, I'm told, but still, a trail.

Let me see if I have a proper understanding of the situation, Don John. Your brothers confided to you that they were going to a residence at the seaside. Yet they pay you no heed and so they will not come at your summons. Therefore I myself must collect them from a place more than fifteen miles away and on the other side of the jungle. A trip that I estimate will consume most of a day. *And* I must leave for that place at once, because, as they also confided to you, they may soon be gone from there. Gone for good. *And* if they are gone, nobody knows where to. Is that an accurate assessment? Tell me. Lopez smiled as if he had just told John Samuel a quirky anecdote.

Yes, John Samuel said. And began to sense how the man might be interpreting things.

I wonder, Don John. Is it possible your brothers told you that they were going somewhere *other* than this cove, but for the moment it has slipped your mind?

No, that's not possible.

But Don John, you lost your father just two days ago. Your fortitude is admirable, but it is only natural that such a terrible loss should be distracting. That it might interfere with an accurate recollection of other details. It can happen to any man.

No, that's not . . . no.

Perhaps you need a little time to think about it. To make a careful mental review of events and conversations. Maybe they did mention where they would go when they left the hacienda, and maybe it will come to you.

John Samuel was now convinced that Lopez thought he was trying to mislead him in order to protect his brothers. That he was misdirecting him to the cove to give the twins a chance to escape from wherever they were really hiding. That the business about them soon sailing off was meant to make him go there at once and then later to explain why he did not find them.

Are you unwell, Don John?

John Samuel shook a hand dismissively. I'm fine. A moment's vertigo.

You see? It is as I say. Grief is very hard on both body and mind.

Listen, Mr Lopez. Between you and me, I don't care at all about my brothers, I truly do not. To be blunt, I detest them. Believe me, I hope they're still at the cove when you get there.

Lopez smiled. My big brother used to say he hated me too, he said. He was always beating the hell out of me. But let somebody else pick on me and, oh man, my brother would beat hell out of *him*. My brother could beat me, you see, but he would not stand for anyone else harming me. One time a man kicked me and my brother chopped off half his foot, and then later the same day beat the hell out of me again. That is how it is with many big brothers.

That's not how it is with me.

Lopez smiled and said, I see. He consulted his pocket watch. I suppose I should leave for the seaside at once in the hope I get there before they depart to . . . well, wherever they may be departing to. I thank you for your time, Don John. And I apologize for taking up so much of it when you are under such distress.

Lopez took a small card from his coat and placed it on the desk. It bore the name of the Hotel de las Palmas and a telegraphic address. He said he had a messenger service there if Don John should want to contact him. In case you remember something that might be of help in locating your brothers, he said. Something that had slipped your mind during this conversation.

As soon as the man was out the door John Samuel went upstairs and to a window facing the plaza. He spotted him talking to a group of men seated along the verandah of the hacienda store. Lopez then went to the marketplace to converse with some of its vendors and buyers. In every clutch of men he spoke with, some among them pointed eastward toward the sea. Toward Ensenada de Isabel. John Samuel smiled. If others told him of the place, who could say it had been their older brother who revealed where to find them?

Lopez went to his horse and mounted and started for the main gate at a trot. And John Samuel thought, Go, damn you. *Move.*

❈

At mid-morning Bruno showed up at John Samuel's office. The bandage covering his cheek was stained a rusty red where blood had seeped from the stitches. His engauzed arm was in a sling. He asked John Samuel if he knew about the man named Lopez who had been telling everyone that Mauricio Espinosa sent him to fetch the twins so he could talk with them about what happened. Asking where the boys might be. Everybody was talking about him. The general opinion was that the twins should stay in hiding, wherever they were.

He was here and asked if I knew where they were, John Samuel said. I said I didn't know, but somebody told him about the cove, because he asked me if I thought they might be there. I said maybe. What else could I say?

Are they there? Bruno said.

I don't know. Maybe.

He saw Bruno looking at the hotel card on the desktop and told him Lopez said he could be contacted there.

"Maybe they sailed off already," Bruno said, turning the card for a better look. "But if they're not there he won't know if they're gone or hiding on the hacienda. He could make things hard till he knows for sure one way or the other."

"He made no secret of working for Mauricio."

"Why should he? Lets everybody know who they're dealing with. Mauricio probably told him to collect the twins and kill them on the road. Shoot them and claim that they were killed in a bandit ambush or something. Who could prove different?"

❈

From John Roger's office Bruno headed for the telegraph station. He was hoping the line had not yet been cut, as it no doubt soon would be. On Sunday he had wired his mother and sister the news of Uncle John's murder by Alfredo Espinosa, the mayordomo's younger son, and that the twins had then killed Alfredo. Not wanting to add worry to the pain of this news, he omitted all other detail, including that of his own wounds. The next afternoon he'd got a wire from Sófi conveying her and María Palomina's great sympathy for all of the family at Buenaventura and expressing their great grief at the loss of John Roger, whom they had known for much too short a time.

Now Bruno sent another wire to Sófi, telling her that Alfredo's brother Mauricio was an army general and had sent a man named Esmeraldo Lopez to find the twins, who had fled. Nobody knew if the boys were still on the hacienda, but there was fear for them, and fear of the harm Lopez might do to Buenaventura in his effort to find them. He told Sófi he did not mean to alarm her but it was important for somebody outside the hacienda to know these details in case some disaster should occur. He remembered the card of the Hotel de las Palmas in Veracruz and told her it was where Lopez was staying.

The telegrapher read the message with evident interest. Bruno told him that if he knew what was good for him he would be true to his sworn oath to preserve the confidence of all information that went through him. If I find out you've told anyone about this, I'll cut off your fingers and your tongue. The telegrapher had never before heard him in any humor but pleasant. Yes, Don Bruno, he said, yes, of course.

⚜

Ten minutes later the hacienda's line was inoperative. A repair team was sent out, and two miles down the road they found where it had been severed. But even after they fixed the break the line was still dead. Another mile farther along they spied another cut. They were heading toward it when rifleshots came from the shadows of the trees. Warning rounds that struck no closer than a few yards from the wagon. The crew turned around and sped back to the compound.

The incident confirmed John Samuel's suspicion that Lopez had not come alone. John Samuel had never before given a thought to the hacienda's lack of hired protectors, but how he now wished his father had kept a party of pistoleros on the payroll. He believed that the men of the compound, armed with muskets and pistols from the armory, could defend the walls, should things come to a fight. But they were not trained combatants, and even if they outnumbered Lopez's men they would stand no chance against professional gunmen in a fight outside the walls. If Lopez so chose, he could hold the compound under siege while he destroyed everything outside of it. Never had John Samuel been more aware of the hacienda's isolation and of his lack of friends to whom he might send for help.

⚜

Two hours before Wednesday's dawn a faint orange glow was reflecting off the low hang of clouds to the distant east. Those who saw it first woke others to look at it. What could it be but the cove house on fire? They wondered if the twins had been there when Lopez arrived. If they had been killed. If they were at that moment burning in the flames casting that distant glimmer.

Looking from his window John Samuel was wondering the same things. And hoping hard. By daybreak they could barely descry the smoke cloud of the fire steaming itself out against the wetness of the jungle.

Later that morning came word that Buenaventura's daily outbound train had derailed. The sabotaged tracks had come apart under its wheels before it even got off the estate. A crew went out to repair the rails—but as before, rifles opened fire from the trees and the workers retreated to the compound.

The destruction of the tracks was strong implication that the twins were still at large, else Lopez would have no reason to persist. But what if Lopez had given the order to uncouple the rails before he went to the cove in search of the boys?

Then at midafternoon came a report that both of the main entrances to the hacienda had been blocked by felled trees and that a labor crew had again been warned off by rifleshots—and the proof that the twins were still unfound seemed irrefutable. But had they sailed off before their hunters arrived at the cove, or were they in hiding in the jungle, or somewhere else on the hacienda? And if they had got away and Lopez wasn't sure of it, how much longer would the man persist in his afflictions of Buenaventura before he gave up?

As if those two haven't caused enough misery, John Samuel thought. Now they bring this on me.

That night a fire broke out at one of the coffee warehouses and its entire store was lost. A few hours later the slaughterhouse was in flames and the damage was extensive. In the last hour and a half of darkness, one of the stables at Rancho Isabela was set ablaze. The hands were able to rescue the horses but the stable would be reduced to ashes.

When Amos Bentley arrived for his usual Sunday supper with Sofía Reina and María Palomina he found them in red-eyed sorrow. They told him the news of John Roger's murder and he said Oh my God and slumped onto a sofa and cried like a child. Sófi and María Palomina sat to either side of him and crooned consolations and stroked his head even as they brushed at their own tears. They all three stayed up most of the night, talking of John Roger and bemoaning the loss of him. Next morning Sófi went to the nearest telegraph station and sent a wire of commiseration to her brother and the rest of the family at Buenaventura.

On Tuesday came the telegram from Bruno about General Espinosa and the man named Lopez whom he'd sent in search of the twins and about Bruno's fear that disaster might ensue. And now, atop their bereavement, Sófi and María Palomina were afraid too.

Think of poor Felicia, María Palomina said. So near to giving birth. Imagine her worry! Who *is* this man, this damned general, to cause such fear to everyone?

Gloria! Sófi said.

What? her mother said, confused.

Gloria! We have to tell Gloria! Sófi said. Gloria's husband was a friend of President Díaz. Her husband's father still worked for him. Maybe Gloria could get one or the other of them to speak to him about this and maybe he would do something to help Buenaventura.

María Palomina's face was bald disbelief. Maybe *who* would? The president? The *president*, Sofita? She bit her lower lip and regarded her daughter as if the girl had lost her mind.

The idea suddenly seemed to Sófi as preposterous as it did to her mother. But what else was there to try?

Rather than use a public telegraph for such a sensitive message, Sófi went to Amos, who himself knew Morse code and whose office in the Nevada Mining Company building was equipped with its own telegraph apparatus for private correspondence with far-flung clients. She showed him Bruno's latest wire and he shared her concern and of course would do what he could to help. Addressing the transmission to Gloria Wolfe y Blanco de Little at the station of the Hacienda Patria Chica, Amos tapped out Sófi's message, informing Gloria of their Uncle John's killing and all else that Bruno had said and asking if her husband or father-in-law could in any way be of assistance to Buenaventura.

Sófi then wanted Amos to send a message to Bruno to let him know she had told everything to their sister, who might be able to help. Amos tried, but Buenaventura was not receiving. The line must be down, he told Sófi.

❦

Sófi had been home three hours when a messenger arrived from the Nevada Mining Company with a sealed envelope for her from Mr Amos Bentley. It contained a wire from Gloria that said, The matter is being attended to. Be brave.

CREEDS OF FRATERNITY

A few days before Gloria received Sófi's telegram, she and Louis had quarreled about his dalliance with one of the girls in the hacienda laundry. I won't be like those stupid Creole wives who pretend never to know what's going on behind their backs, Gloria said. Not me, mister! And because he was no more bred to the role of a hacendado than she was to that of a hacendado's wife, Louis could not muster the lordliness to ignore her protests and by a cold stare and utter silence make clear that he would do as he damned well pleased. Rather, he chose to profess outrage at the allegation and demanded to know who had told her such a malicious falsehood. She would not reveal that the information had come from her devoted personal maid Leila, who had wept in telling her of seeing Louis and the girl coming out of his office just off the main courtyard, the girl still straightening her clothes. Besides, Gloria knew her husband well and she could see the lie in his eyes. I'm warning you, she said. I won't be humiliated. *Warning* me? Louis said. He had an urge to slap her, and that he didn't was not entirely due to gallantry. Whenever she was truly angry, the look in her eyes gave him pause, it always had. In the four days since the argument, they had not said more than a few words to each other. Edward Little had meanwhile arrived for a visit and was aware of the tension between them, but he never intervened in their marital disputes nor even commented on them.

When Gloria read her sister's telegram she put aside her resentment and went to Louis and said, "I need your help," and handed him the wire. He read it, and then together they went to the library to see his father.

Edward put aside his volume of *Our Mutual Friend* and read the message. He asked Gloria how old her twin cousins were. She wasn't sure but believed it was about two years younger than her Luis Charón, which would make them sixteen.

"The fella deviling the place aint the problem, it's the general he works for, that Espinosa," Louis said. "Find out for me where he is and I'll do the rest."

Edward affected to study the wire as he deliberated the situation. He knew that Gloria had never met her Uncle John Wolfe, the American hacendado her family in Mexico City had not known of until a chance meeting between him and her brother a couple of years ago. Gloria had got the story from her little sister Sófi and in turn related it at the supper table one night while Edward was visiting. She also announced that, as her sister and brother had done, she had added Wolfe to her name, which was now Gloria Tomasina Wolfe y Blanco de Little. Louis joked that he had to take a deep breath just to say it. The Littles had thought it an interesting story, but both men—as well as Gloria herself—had known too much happenchance in their own lives to be awed by the coincidence of her family's reunion. Gloria told them how much better her Uncle John had made the lives of her mother and sister and how happy her brother had been to go live at the uncle's hacienda. It seemed unfair, she said, that the only sad part about the reunion fell to Uncle John, who'd made everyone else so happy. According to her sister, Uncle John had thought his brother—Gloria's father—had been dead for many years before he actually was, and did not learn the truth until many years after he actually died.

Poor Uncle John, Gloria said. Bruno said he cried when he heard of his brother's terrible punishments as a San Patricio.

Anyone observing Edward Little at the moment Gloria disclosed the detail of the San Patricios would have seen no sign of the jolt it gave him, so helpful was his disfigured face in disguising his emotions. He busied himself with his pipe as Louis said, "Whoa there, girl. Your pa was a Saint Paddy? I never even knew he'd been in that war."

Edward's younger sons, Zachary Jack and John Louis, were listening hard. Now sixteen and fourteen years old, respectively, they were hard-muscled ranch hands but versed in social etiquette by their Aunt Gloria, as they called her, and they knew not to intrude on the conversation of their elders.

That Gloria had revealed something she had not intended to was obvious from her sudden flush. She looked down at her plate and stirred the lamb stew with her fork. "No. I mean yes," she said. "Yes he was a San Patricio, and no I never told you."

"How come?"

She looked at Edward, who sat puffing his pipe with an affected casualness. Then said to her husband, "I did not tell you because you and your father are Americans. I was afraid you would both be disgusted by my father as a traitor to your country." She hesitated a second before adding, "And that you would think less of me. For being daughter to him."

For a second, Louis Little fixed her with a blank stare—then chuckled as if she'd made a witticism and he had just caught on to it. He looked at his father, who showed a small smile. The two boys were smiling too. They'd never heard of a

Saint Paddy but they were amused by Louis's amusement. They would soon enough investigate the subject and learn about the Patricios.

"Listen darlin," Louis said, "first of all, it wouldn't matter to me who your daddy was. If he was a damned horse thief or even worse, a preacher, or a damned politician"—that got a smile from his father and a laugh from the boys—"it wouldn't have a thing to do with how I see *you*. What I don't understand is how you could think I'd be disgusted by a man who turned his coat against the United States government when you damn well know I did too. I quit the Union, didn't I? Quit it and fought against it. On account of it quit me, or it anyway quit the bargain it was supposed to keep with the state of Louisiana. I don't believe I'm a traitor, though. How can you betray a country that's already betrayed you? For all I know, your daddy felt the same way. My daddy speaks for himself, but I expect he'd agree there's all kinds of reasons a man might side against his country and some of them can be right ones." He turned to Edward. "You told me once you rode with a bunch of Mexicans scouting for the U.S. of A. in that war back then. Did they disgust you, the traitor Mexicans you rode with?"

"They did not," Edward said. "They were doing what they believed right."

"See?" Louis said to Gloria.

Edward had not, however, told Louis that the Mexicans he had ridden with had been convicted of numerous acts of banditry and murder before and during the war, and that he himself and another gringo, the only two non-Mexicans in the gang, had been sentenced to be hanged along with them. The entire bunch was spared from the gallows only because General Winfield Scott, commander of the American invaders, was desperate for scouts who knew the country between Veracruz and Mexico City, and every man of the gang agreed to so serve him. They became General Scott's so-called Spy Company—a foolish name, given that they were not spies but scouts. They were outfitted in distinctive uniforms and provided with fine mounts and armed with the best of American cavalry weapons. The Mexicans of the Spy Company had felt no qualms about fighting against their country. Had in fact exulted at the chance to get even with any number of Mexican enemies, especially the authorities who had wanted to hang them. In siding with the Americans, they had saved themselves from execution, which seemed to Edward as right a reason as any for turning one's coat. Every man's first obedience was to the law of self-preservation, and anybody who said different was a damned fool or a damned liar. In full fact, Edward's association with men of tenuous allegiances had begun even before his membership in the Mexican gang—though no one of his family knew that, either. At the age of seventeen he had ridden with a band of scalp hunters, most of them Americans but some from who-knew-where and who spoke languages Edward had not heard before or since, plus a handful of Shawnee trackers. A company of men with the common purpose of killing Indians for the bounty on their scalps but with no abiding loyalty save each man to himself. Yet

313

Edward believed that each of them must have felt as he did—that in such a company of friendless isolates and outcast wanderers he was among his true breed. A breed bound to the fate that befell them on a hellish afternoon in Mexico's northern wildlands when they were set upon by a host of Comanches and every man of them slaughtered save for Edward, who survived despite wounds whose scars would stay with him to the grave. And absent his scalp.

"I am glad neither of you hate me for my father," Gloria said.

"You coulda been glad about it a lot sooner if you hadn't kept it a secret all this time," Louis said.

Yes, she said. Now she knew that.

"What other secrets you been keeping from me?" Louis said, smiling.

Well, if you must know, Gloria said, I'm really Chinese.

Even Edward joined in the laughter.

It was yet another of his lifelong secrets that he too was kin to a captured and convicted, flogged and branded San Patricio—his brother, John. Unlike Gloria's father, however, John had escaped from captivity after his punishment. His liberation was planned by Edward and effected by a wealthy Mexican woman, a devoted champion of the San Patricios, assisted by a few men in her employ. The woman and three of the men, posing as lawyers she had retained to assist the Patricios, made an evening visit to the prison and were very clever about disguising John Little so that he could leave with her in the place of one of her men, who would stay behind. They were out the prison gate and almost to her carriage when the plan came undone. There was a gunfight on the street and the carriage driver and the two men with the woman were killed, the woman herself arrested, but John Little escaped into the night. Edward had witnessed the fight from a few blocks down the street where he had been waiting for his brother to be brought to him, a saddled horse ready. He was searching the streets for John when he saw a crowd of men fleeing a back-alley cantina. In that deserted tavern he found his brother hanging from the rafters. Lynched by American soldiers who'd known him for a Saint Patrick by the brand on his face. Johnny. Murdered at nineteen.

He had kept John a secret not because he felt shamed by him but because of his own shame in having failed to protect him, no matter John was his elder by a year. They had somehow got lost of each other in New Orleans in the year before the Mexican War, on their way from Florida to Texas to make their fortune. He did not see John again until almost two years later when the American army assaulted the Mexican force making a desperate stand at the gates to Mexico City. The Spy Company had been with the attackers, the Saint Patricks with the defenders, and amid the pandemonium of the battle's culminating hand-to-hand carnage came the bewildering instant when he and John recognized each other among the berserkers—and then both of them went down with bad wounds. Edward had healed sufficiently to be in the crowd of spectating American soldiers when the surviving Saint Patricks were punished. For almost forty years now he had carried the guilt of his helpless witness to John's flogging and branding along with the other Patricios who had been spared the noose. He did not know how his brother had come to be with the turncoats, but knew without doubt that Johnny must have found some breed of fellowship among them, a brotherhood of sorts, else he would not have sided with them, for sure not to the end. Edward could not help but feel included in that fraternity. The brothers of his brother were his brothers too. Hence did he feel bound to defend the family of his daughter-in-law, she who was daughter to a San Patricio.

He had never met General Espinosa but he had heard Díaz speak of him. He was young for a general and a favorite of Porfirio, who was going to be unhappy about this. Which was why Edward would not assign the job to any of his agents. He would not place any of them at direct risk of the president's wrath. He could not be sure that Porfirio would forgive even Louis.

He set aside Sofia's telegram and said, "I'll take care of it."

"I can do it," Louis said.

"I know you can, but it has to be me."

"Why's that? Because he's a friend of Porfirio's? Hell, Pórfi don't have to know it had anything to do with us."

"Of course he does, son."

Louis held his father's gaze. "Yeah, well. Even so. I'm willing to take my chances with him."

"I said I'll do it."

He turned to Gloria. You may tell your sister the matter is being attended to, but do not mention my name. Not now or later.

"Muy bien, Papá Eduardo," Gloria said.

THE POWER
HIS SISTER MARRIED

In addition to Patria Chica's general telegraph line, there was a private one in Edward's study. For the rest of that evening he swapped messages with his agency's main office at Chapultepec Castle and studied topographic maps. The agency office was belowground, in a stone room that had once served as a dungeon and a section of which still did. Stored there were files on every member of the federal government, every state governor and important political chief in the country, every general officer in the Mexican military. By two in the morning he knew all he needed to know about General Mauricio Espinosa de la Santa Cruz and his residence near Durango City. He then slept three hours and woke refreshed.

The dawn horizon was a hazy pink when his train left the Patria Chica depot. The train consisted of two cars behind the locomotive, one for himself and one carrying his horse. That afternoon it halted in the high country a few miles outside of Durango City. The umber landscape isolate and hardrock. Mountain peaks looming and dark with timber, low ranges brown as old bone in the arid distance. Edward saddled the horse, a sturdy pony bred for just such country, and tied on his saddlebags and then the deerskin sheath containing his rifle—a Sharps chambered to fire a 550-grain bullet a half inch in diameter powered by a cartridge with ninety grains of black powder. With just such a rifle had buffalo killers been able to fell their quarry from as far away as a mile. He hupped the pony onto an old timber trail that led to the other side of the mountain. The train went ahead to the city's station, there to await him.

⁕

General Mauricio Espinosa's manorial estate was set on a tableland projecting off a mountainside and overlooking a gorge several hundred feet deep, at the bottom

317

of which a swift river ran through a misty dell. An hour before sundown Edward settled into position behind a small boulder flanked by a pair of larger ones on a shadowed outcrop of the mountain directly across the gorge from the general's residence. There was heavy pine and scrub growth all about and the horse was tethered on the track back among the trees.

Edward's spot afforded a clear high-angled view of the rear courtyard, awash in the last of the day's sunlight. It was the general's habit to observe the sun's setting behind the western ridge, as often as not in the company of his paramour of the moment. Edward took off his hat and put it aside. He pushed forward the Sharps's trigger guard to drop open the Sharps's breech and then slid a cartridge into the chamber and reclosed the breech by snapping the trigger guard back into place. Attached to the tang was a folding vernier peep sight and he unfolded it and peered through it at the courtyard across the way. He adjusted the little calibration knob with the finesse of a scientist at a laboratory instrument. Then sat back and waited with the rifle across his lap.

He had been there half an hour when a trio of figures came out of the house. Two of them walked very close together and the third trailed behind. The couple came all the way to the low rock wall overlooking the gorge. There was a table a few feet behind them and the other figure paused there a moment and then headed back to the house. A servant, Edward surmised, who'd carried out a tray of refreshments for the lovebirds. He had judged the distance to the couple at a stone's throw beyond eight hundred yards. They were specks hardly bigger than birdseed but he would not look at them through a field scope because he believed a telescopic lens dulled the aim of his naked eye. Even if he had not already known whom he was looking at he would have known the two figures at the wall for man and woman, so closely were they standing, no doubt with an arm around each other. And as far away as they were, he still could discern their difference in size and so knew which was the man and which the woman. More likely a girl. It was said the general had a preference for young ones. Who did not? He saw no one else in the patio. He rested the rifle's forebarrel on the small boulder to steady the weapon and made a final gauging of the light breeze. Then put his eye to the vernier peep and cocked the hammer.

<hr />

As always at this hour Mauricio pronounced on the beauty of the sunset sky along the jagged crest, and the girl, whose own loveliness would have been evident even without the face paint and powder, said yes, it was truly beautiful. It made one very happy to be alive. They turned to each other and embraced and were in the midst of the kiss when all in the same instant she felt him flinch and without knowing what she was hearing—the sequence so fast it seemed a single erratic sound—heard the thuck of the bullet striking at the base of his neck and the snaps of bone as it passed through vertebra and rib and the shatter of the wine bottle and the thunk through the tabletop and the ricochet whine off the flagstone. Then heard the rifleshot itself and the resounding echoes of it all along the gorge. The dead weight of him slipped from her grasp to an awkward crumple at her feet and she saw the bright spreading blood of his destroyed heart and lungs and even as she began to scream soldiers were coming on the run.

—❈—

Before boarding his train at the Durango depot that night, his horse already in its car and being tended, Edward sent a telegram to Esmeraldo Lopez in care of the Hotel de las Palmas in Veracruz—Your chief is dead. Leave there and live.

Then sent one to Gloria that said, Tell sis all is well.

—❈—

As soon as she received Edward's wire, Gloria had the hacienda's telegrapher send one to Sófi by way of Amos Bentley that said, Am told all is well.

She then went to Louis's room to tell him of the developments.

"That's good," he said. "I knew Daddy could take care of it. I could've done it, you know, if he'd let me."

"I know," she said.

When she remained standing there and looking at him, he knew she was giving him the chance to set things right between them. "Listen," he said. "I feel bad that, ah, that *you* feel bad on account of . . . things."

She stared at him.

He cleared his throat. "I mean, I *want* everything to be all right between us."

Her eyes narrowed a little.

"I mean, I don't want to make you, ah, feel bad anymore."

He got the smile he was hoping for. Well, it was an odd smile, true, with a sort of sadness in it, he had to admit, and for sure not as big a smile as he'd hoped for. But very much better than no smile at all.

—❈—

When Amos arrived at his office on Thursday morning and read Gloria's message, he immediately sent a runner to take it to Sófi and María Palomina.

That afternoon Sófi came to his office to send a wire to Bruno. But the Buenaventura line was still down.

—❈—

Esmeraldo Lopez was sitting his horse in the darkness of the trees and watching the ranch hands rescue the horses from the burning stable when his man from the hotel arrived with the telegram, his mount lathered and sonorous and near to foundered. Another man struck a match and held it close so Lopez could read the wire. Lopez asked the messenger if he had contacted the Durango army post to check the truth of the message, and the man said he had and it was true. The general had been killed by an assassin. That was all the post dispatcher could tell him.

Lopez nodded. Of course an assassin. A leading cause of death among powerful men in Mexico. And almost always, whoever the shooter, there was someone else behind him, some schemer, and usually more than one. In this case too, no doubt. Somebody who wanted to protect this goddam place for whatever goddam reason. Somebody who knew Espinosa was a threat to it and who had been very quick and efficient about removing that threat. Worst of all, somebody who was unknown to him, Lopez, but who knew that he was Espinosa's man and even where to send him the news of the general's death. Goddammit, he should've had the boys cut the lines while he was talking to that fucking gringo patrón and not waited until afterward.

Leave there and live.

It was Esmeraldo Lopez's belief that when somebody with an advantage on you gave you a chance to walk away it was generally best to walk away, especially if there was little to be gained by risking otherwise. It was a lesson worth the learning, not to let pride prevail over reason. Many died young because they had not yet gained that knowledge. Reason was best. Maybe next time you would be the one with the advantage and deciding whether to give the other fellow a chance to walk away. His regret was for the lost money. The agreement with Espinosa had as always been for half the fee in advance and the rest on completion of the assignment. Now there would be no rest of the fee. He would nevertheless pay his men the full wages they had coming. Never shortchange the men. Another rule he learned long ago. Anyway, what the hell. There was plenty more work out there. Always plenty of Espinosas in want of his service.

That's it, boys, he said. Job's over.

❈

The people of Buenaventura had expected to wake that Thursday morning to the smoke of some new fire but there was none. The wranglers who remained at the ranch while the stable burned down had been busy with calming the spooked horses and fearful of being shot at from the shadows, but there had been no further attack, and at first light they drove the horses to the compound corrals. When the church bells rang at noon there still had been no new destruction visited on the hacienda. The apprehensive afternoon was slow in passing. Maybe the bastards were waiting till dark to resume the harrowing. As evening closed in, people spoke in lower voice and kept an ear cocked for more trouble. But the nervous night passed without disturbance and at daybreak everyone was sure the raiders were gone. It was a bittersweet conclusion because its only justification was that Lopez had found the twins.

John Samuel thought so too. Either Lopez had captured them and taken them away to be killed on the road, as he and Bruno had conjectured, or he had killed them where he found them. Somewhere in the jungle, most likely. Where scavengers and insects would devour the last earthly trace of them.

Well. They brought it on themselves, didn't they?

Bruno dispatched work gangs to find and repair the breaks in the telegraph line, reconnect the train tracks, clear away the felled trees blocking the entrance roads. The crews were armed with muskets and pistols but were under Bruno's order to speed back to the compound at the first sign of Lopez men. A superfluous directive. But none of them saw any sign of the raiders. For whatever reason, they were gone.

No sooner were the lines repaired than a wire arrived for Bruno—the message from Sófi that Amos had been trying to send since the day before. The telegram said, I told Gloria. She says all is well now. True?

Gloria? Bruno was puzzled. What did Gloria have to do with any of this? Unlike his affectionate tie to Sófi, he and Gloria had never been very close. Except for the brief period in childhood when they helped each other to learn English, the only times they were even in each other's company was at family meals, where Gloria rarely joined in the conversation except to argue with their parents about one thing or another. During his years in the army he had corresponded with Sófi and his mother, and through them with his father, but he and Gloria had never exchanged a letter. They were not estranged but simply strangers. The last time they had spoken to each other was just before she went to Raquel Aguilera's wedding and never came back. But Sófi had given him periodic reports on their sister's life, and he recalled now that Gloria and her husband—Louis? yes, Louis—and Louis's father and his wife had all lived with Porfirio Díaz back before he was president. And that the hacienda where Gloria now lived had been a gift from Díaz to her husband's father, but her husband managed it because the father had kept on working for Díaz in Mexico City. Did he still?

The whole thing was suddenly clear to him. Sófi had sent word to Gloria and Gloria had spoken to her husband and her husband had spoken to his father and the father had spoken to Díaz. Yes! Spoke to the president of Mexico about Buenaventura's troubles! El presidente then sent word to Mauricio who then sent word to Lopez who then ceased his offensive on Buenaventura. That was what happened—Bruno was sure of it.

Sweet Jesus! What power his sister married!

He was now also certain that the twins had not been caught. They had escaped by their own device or with Gloria's assistance, but they had escaped, he was sure of it. But how would they find out Mauricio had called off his search for them? And when they did find out, would they return? To what? Their father was dead and John Samuel was the patrón, and they sure as hell would not live under his authority.

He thought about sharing his thoughts with John Samuel but decided against it. Let him believe they were dead. Imagine his face should they some day return.

He sent Sófi a wire telling her that all was well at Buenaventura and thanking her for contacting Gloria. The two of you saved the place, kid, he said. Nobody knew where the twins had gone but he believed they were all right, wherever they were. He asked for Gloria's telegraph address so that he could thank her personally. Sófi wired back that he should not thank her via telegram but with a proper letter. He could send it to her at Patria Chica by way of the San Luis Potosí post office.

He went through several false starts before settling for the short and simple. Dear Big Sister, Thank you. And thank whoever else who had a hand in it. Love from your little brother.

He drew a tiny heart under his signature and then felt embarrassed about it and thought about scribbling over it, but doing so would only make a mess and make her wonder what it was he'd had second thoughts about, so he left it as it was.

Gloria wrote back. My Dear Little Brother, You are most welcome. I am very happy you are well. A hug and kiss from your big sister who loves you. Beneath the large looping letters of her name, she appended a small heart drawn in replication of his.

The exchange would inspire them to maintain a regular correspondence for years to come. Bit by bit they would acquaint each other with their lives. And if some of their letters were hardly a page long and said little more than they were doing well and hoped the other was too, that was enough for both. What mattered most were the affectionate salutations and the inscribed hearts at the close.

OR EVEN EVER GROW OLD

When Edward Little got back to the capital he told Díaz what he'd done. He gave as his reason the need to protect his daughter-in-law's family from Espinosa's retribution. He had thought about telling him the full truth, of explaining his sense of obligation to the San Patricios, but he had never told Porfirio of his brother John and did not want to tell him now. To do so would raise questions about the rest of his family. About his murderous father and lunatic mother and tragic little sister, none of whom he wanted to talk about to anyone ever.

Díaz banged his palm on the desk. Goddammit, Lalo! Espinosa was a good general. A *loyal* general. You know how hard it is to find a loyal general?

Yes.

You should have come to me. I would have talked to him and that would have ended it.

Edward could see Díaz was trying to keep his anger in check. He had granted Edward license to take care of certain problems without first consulting with him, but Edward had never before dealt with a general, much less one who stood in Díaz's favor.

I didn't think that would resolve it, Edward said.

Oh really? You didn't think that would *resolve* it. So you now decide whether I, who am only the president, will be permitted to *resolve* things my way, is that it?

No, my president.

No, my president, Díaz mimicked. That's right—*your* president! President of the whole damned country! That's who *I* am. *You* are not the president of anybody, not even those crazy fuckers who work for you. You're their boss but *I'm* their president!

Like everyone else, Edward had been amazed by the changes young Doña Carmen had wrought in her husband. In public today Don Porfirio was ever the patrician, the terse but precise speaker, the sagacious man of noble bearing who seemed to have been born to the purple. In private, however—at least in private with Edward Little—he could still revert in an instant to the profane cavalry officer of his youth.

I understand that, my president.

Goddammit, this wasn't some bandit. Some fucking politician. He was a *general*. You don't shoot a general without my say-so. What the hell's wrong with you?

His men were setting fires at the place. They cut the telegraph lines, they blocked the roads. I had to move fast.

Goddammit! You—

I didn't come to you, Porfirio, because no matter what you said to him it wouldn't have stopped him from trying to get even for his brother. He would've—

He would've heard *me* tell him don't do it and he wouldn't have done it!

If *God* told you don't do it, would that have stopped you from getting even for Félix?

Díaz's face stiffened.

A whole town, Porfirio. We did away with a whole town. Chopped up the mayor and shot every man and most of the boys too. Burned the place to the ground. And you remember what you said when I got back and handed you what was left of your brother? I wish there'd been a thousand more of them for you to kill, Lalo. I wish there'd been a thousand more of their filthy huts for you to burn.

He saw Díaz remembering behind stone eyes.

Espinosa was loyal, Porfirio, because he was an honorable man. But because he was an honorable man, no order you gave him or threat you made would've stopped him from trying to get revenge. Somebody killed his brother and fed him to the pigs—he *had* to do something about it. If you told him don't do it he'd say, Very well, my president, as you wish, my president. But he'd say it only so he would still get the chance to kill those boys and the hell with the consequences or whoever else he killed along with them.

They fed him to pigs?

They did.

You didn't tell me that.

No? Well. Nevertheless. Edward had deliberately withheld that detail for the most opportune moment to introduce it.

These boys. How old are they?

I'm told they are sixteen.

Sixteen. Your cousins?

Cousins to Gloria.

Ah yes, Gloria. Gloria of the unforgettable wedding. This wasn't the first of my officers to get shot because of her. A dangerous woman, your son's wife.

Aren't they all?

Díaz almost smiled. Then scowled and said, You should have come to me anyway, goddammit.

You would have said no.

And if I had?

Edward said nothing.

You would have done it anyway.

Edward said nothing.

And then *I* would've had to do something about it. You know that.

Edward said nothing.

And don't think for a minute I wouldn't have, goddammit, friend or no friend. I let you get away with disobeying my orders and then what? Everybody'll think he can get away with it. No, sir. No.

Edward said nothing.

Díaz stared at him.

That's why you didn't come to me, isn't it? If I didn't say no, you weren't disobeying.

Edward looked off to the side.

Very clever, Lalo. Very fucking clever. You should've been a goddam lawyer.

Edward's smile was small and crooked.

Díaz rubbed his face hard with both hands. All right, let's settle this. Now listen to me. Listen good. You listening? No more shooting generals without my permission. That's an order, Mr Little. Understood?

Understood, my president.

I mean it.

I understand.

You fucking better.

I said I understand.

All right then. Good.

Díaz gazed out the window at the darkness. Edward waited.

You say he was kissing the girl?

It looked like it.

Did he have a hand on her ass?

That I can't say. I was pretty far off.

Díaz turned to him. Spare me the bragging. He probably had a hand on her ass, don't you think? I would have had a hand on her ass.

He probably did.

One shot, right, Mister Deadeye? Quick kill?

Probably dead on the way to the ground.

Just can't keep from bragging, can you?

Edward returned his smile.

Kissing a woman. Hand on her ass. There are worse ways to go.

Plenty of them.

Goddammit, Lalo. I liked him.

I know.

He wasn't a son of a bitch, not that one.

I believe you.

Well thank you so much for your belief and go fuck yourself.

Edward grinned.

Christ, the older you get the scarier that smile. I bet mothers point you out to their kids on the street. *There*, you see him? Right *there's* the man who comes to take away bad little boys who disobey their mamas. Kids probably piss their pants and can't sleep for a week.

They both laughed.

Díaz consulted his gold pocketwatch, a gift from Doña Carmen. Let's go to Lagrimas. What do you say?

Las Lagrimas de Nuestras Madres was a brothel in a derelict neighborhood a dozen blocks from Chapultepec. Díaz had discovered the place the year before and he and Edward would two or three times a month slip away from the bodyguards and go there for a few hours of fun. They did not go there to fuck the whores but only to drink and dance with them. Like Díaz, the madam and most of her girls were from the state of Oaxaca, and the music and dances of that house were those of his boyhood. Dances that Edward himself had learned back when he first met Colonel Díaz in Oaxaca during the war against the French. They always went to Lagrimas after dark and always walked there rather than rode because it was a district of dangerous reputation and Díaz always hoped to be accosted by robbers. He had often complained to Edward that the worst thing about being president was the lack of action. He missed the action of his army days. They had run into thugs only once. Five of them suddenly blocking the sidewalk and showing their teeth in the light of a streetlamp, pleased by the easy pickings of two graying men with gold-hilt canes and fine clothes that bespoke fat purses. Young toughs so ignorant of the world outside themselves that even in full daylight they would not have recognized the president of their country. They produced knives and demanded money. Díaz laughed and ignored the pistol holstered under his coat and drew his cane sword. Edward too. In less than half a minute three rateros were down and the other two fled bloodied. Díaz examined the fallen ones and determined that two were not mortally wounded but advised the third to make his peace with God as quickly as he could. When they would pass by here again on their way back from Lagrimas long after midnight, only the dead one would still be there, rolled into the gutter and absent his shoes. The fight so invigorated Díaz that he danced that night with even greater gusto than usual and till a later hour. He drank with keener pleasure and sang in louder voice and tipped the girls with a freer hand. And as always in that dingy malodorous cathouse called The Tears of Our Mothers he and Edward danced and danced with every girl in the place. Danced as if they were yet young men who would never die or even ever grow old.

I say let's, said Edward.

NOOSES

A month after John Roger's death, Javier Tomás Wolfe y Blanco Méndez was born to Bruno and Felicia. At the insistence of Vicki Clara they had brought a doctor from Veracruz to make the delivery. Old Josefina waited in the kitchen, ready to be of assistance, but although the birth was difficult no one thought to summon her. Bruno and Felicia were delighted by Javier Tomás but sick at heart when the doctor told them they could not have more children. It wasn't that Felicia could no longer conceive—how much better, the doctor said, if that were the case—but that she had an irregularity in her womb. Another pregnancy would place her at grave risk, regardless of her youth. Abstinence was the only sure protection, but the doctor was a cosmopolitan young Creole who shared their lack of enthusiasm for that solution and knew as well as they there would be times it could not hold. With a casual frankness—We are sophisticated adults, are we not?—and with Bruno blushing no less than Felicia even as they smiled, the doctor discussed various ways other than intercourse by which they might pleasure each other. And for the inevitable occasions when coitus was simply not to be denied, he informed them of the latest English condoms, in his opinion the finest in the world. He would send them a supply from Veracruz. He warned, however, that although condoms were quite effective, they were known to fail, and he recommended the additional safeguard of withdrawal. A less satisfying climax, to be sure, he said, but a much safer one. I cannot stress strongly enough the importance of safety in this regard. The passions are pleasurable but must never be permitted to overrule reason.

Bruno wrote to Sófi and María Palomina with the good news of the baby's arrival but did not tell them of the doctor's warning, only of his pronouncement that they could not have more children and of their sadness about it, for they had wanted to have many of them. Sófi wrote back that they should consider themselves lucky to have even one child, and a healthy son, at that. There was no need to remind him of her own sad history with husbands and children. Bruno had told Felicia about it, and Sófi's letter was of great help to them in shunning self-pity.

Javier Tomás was baptized at three months. His godparents were John Samuel and Victoria Clara. The celebration party in the compound plaza produced the first loud gaiety heard at Buenaventura since John Roger's death. The fiesta dispelled the gloom of the last five months and the hacienda began to revive.

The baby was ten months old when Bruno and Felicia took him to Mexico City so his Grandmother María and Aunt Sófi could meet him—and at last meet Felicia Flor too. The two women doted on Javier Tomás and lavished Felicia with affection. It was Bruno's first return to the capital since moving to Buenaventura, and the weeklong visit was a happy one for them all. His mother and sister several times told him he was luckier than he deserved, and he each time smiled back at them and said he knew it. Just before they left for the train to return to Buenaventura, Bruno said his wife had something to tell them, and Felicia announced she was three months pregnant. They had deliberately saved this news for a goodbye present. María Palomina and Sófi whooped and hugged Felicia yet again and told her over and over to be careful. Sófi shook a finger in Bruno's face and said, You *see*? What do doctors know?

It had happened on the night of her brother Rogelio's wedding party. The evening of dancing and drinking had so heated their blood that when they got home they did not even get all their clothes off before they were at each other, her skirts gathered at her breasts and his trousers bunched atop the boot yet on one foot. It was the only time they did it without a prophylactic since the doctor's warning. They afterward lay in close embrace and made effusive apologies to each other for their lack of caution. They agreed that a single instance was not a great risk but also agreed they would not take another such gamble. While alarmed by their rashness they were stirred by their abandon, by their own wild crave for each other. They joked about crossing the high wire without a net. Then two months passed without her menses and they knew.

The young doctor confirmed the consequence of their lapse. He told them that of their two choices abortion presented the lesser danger. Not to the baby it doesn't, Felicia said, and began to cry. Bruno and the doctor exchanged glum looks. The doctor then said that he was sometimes not so assured in his opinions as he might seem. That some of his prognoses had proved wrong. That it would not astound him if everything went well. For the next five months and sixteen days Felicia Flor told Bruno daily she believed everything would be fine, that she felt strong, that she knew, just knew, she and the baby would both fare well. Bruno each time said yes, yes, of course, he felt sure of it. And for much of every night lay in a sleepless dread.

On the last night in October, Felicia went into labor and five hours later their second son—whom they had already decided to name Joaquín Félix—was born dead. And twenty minutes afterward Felicia Flor too was dead. When Bruno learned the baby had strangled on the umbilical, he had a momentary vision of the infant hanging from a gallows. Sentenced to death by his father's brute lust. As was his mother.

Sofía Reina and María Palomina were stricken by the news. Only three months after completion of a year's mourning for John Roger they again dressed in black. Six weeks later little Javier Tomás contracted an intestinal illness, then seemed to be improving, then took an abrupt turn and died. And Sófi and María began the mourning period all over again.

It was not until some months after Javier's death, when he at last went to visit his mother and sister—who were shocked by his skeletal aspect—that Bruno Tomás told Sófi about the doctor's caveat. It was late and he'd had much to drink. Amos Bentley had said good night and left for home and María Palomina had retired to bed. In a voice so low Sófi had to lean forward to make out what he was saying, he told of the doctor's dire prediction and of the stupid chance he had taken for no reason but sexual urgency. I was supposed to protect her, he said, but I couldn't protect her from my own stupid cock.

And Sófi thought, I knew it. I *knew* it.

She went over and sat beside him on the sofa and held him close and said that what happened was not his fault, nor Felicia's, nor anyone's. Things sometimes just happened and were nobody's fault. She knew he did not believe her but she knew too she was right. How, after all, could he be at fault for a wild curse in his blood? A curse like a ready noose around the neck of every Wolfe.

NOTICIAS
DE PATRIA CHICA

On a cold Sunday afternoon a few weeks after Sófi and her mother had once again put away their mourning clothes, the lower-floor maid announced that a neatly groomed young gentleman who gave his name as Luis Charón Little Wolfe y Blanco was at the front gate and wished to see them. There followed joyous introductions between Luis Charón and his grandmother and aunt, who said he must join them for dinner. Luis grinned and said his timing had worked out as he'd hoped. He was a lean young man just turned twenty-one, poised and well-mannered, jet-haired, with eyes so dark blue they were nearly violet. His mustache was cropped in the military mode made popular by President Díaz.

Amos Bentley was present, as he always was for Sunday dinner, and was very pleased to meet the young officer. Luis had at this time been in the Rurales for more than a year. He had been promoted to captain on his reassignment from the army to the Rurales' Eighth Corps at Aguascalientes, where he'd been an adjutant to the corps commander. Now he was in command of his own company in the Fifth Corps—the youngest commander in the Guardia—at the outskirt of the capital. He cut an urbane figure in his pinstriped suit. The Guardia uniform was strictly for duty, and the only time Sófi and María Palomina would ever see him in it was in parades when he and his comrades passed by on their prancing horses.

At his first bite of Sófi's chicken enchiladas Luis Charón pronounced the dish every bit as savory as his mother had alleged. The women invited him to be their dinner guest every Sunday but the best he would be able to do was every six weeks or so. Not only did he alternate Sunday command of the detachment with another captain but there would be times when his company would be out on a mission. And too there was a young lady back at Patria Chica whom he went to see whenever he could. This last bit of information intrigued the women. Was marriage a possibility, they wanted to know. If she will have me, he said, and everyone laughed.

As they would on his every visit thereafter, the women told Luis Charón stories of the family and of his mother's girlhood, giving many of the episodes about Gloria a comic aspect they had lacked at the time. They would prevail on Amos to relate some of their favorite anecdotes of his days as an assistant at the American consulate in Veracruz and of his experiences with the Trade Wind Company before the firm's demise in the American Civil War. In turn Luis Charón told of his childhood on Patria Chica and of his parents. He depicted his American father Louis as a hardworking man who enjoyed his life as manager of the hacienda—and much enjoyed being addressed as "patrón" in his own father's long absences—though he much preferred being in the saddle and working with the ranch hands to dealing with the estate paperwork. To his mother Gloria he attributed an affectionate nature that Sófi and María Palomina could scarcely relate to the querulous girl of their memory. He told them of his uncles, Zachary Jackson and John Louis, now young men of nineteen and seventeen and being groomed by his father, Louis—their older brother—to manage the hacienda on his retirement. It amused the women that Luis Charón's uncles were younger than himself, one of them by nearly three years. He told too of his Grandfather Edward, though he was sorry to admit he did not know him very well. In boyhood he had seen his grandfather only on the man's brief visits from Mexico City, and even though he was now posted so near to him, their respective duties were such that it was unlikely they would ever see each other in the capital.

He would volunteer little about his life in the Guardia Rural and always responded to the women's questions about it with general details of camp routines and training and amusing anecdotes about some of his comrades. But whenever he and Amos were alone while the women were busy in the kitchen, Luis would tell him in low-voiced enthusiasm of his company's most recent skirmishes with bandit gangs and of executing captives on the spot. Amos an avid audience.

Because Patria Chica was a train ride of only a few hours from his post at the northern outskirt of Mexico City, Luis Charón was able to make frequent, if brief, visits home. The main reason for these trips was Rosario Monte DeLeón, daughter of the Creole foreman of the hacienda cattle ranch. Luis had known her since childhood, a soft-spoken girl who after accepting his proposal confessed she had been in love with him since she was six years old.

They were married in the summer of 1891 and their three children were born on Patria Chica. Eduardo Luis in winter of 1893, Sandra Rosario a year later, and on New Year's Day of 1895, Catalina Luisiana, blackhaired like the others but the only one with the blue eyes of their father and grandfather. Rosario bore all three with ease, but after delivering Catalina she did not stop bleeding and died the next day. Luis Charón made no public show of grief save for a black armband. The upbringing of the children fell to their Grandmother Gloria and a trio of maids.

Catalina's middle name was meant to be Louisiana. Luis Charón had heard his father speak of the natural beauty of that place and both he and Rosario thought the name a pretty one and decided they would so name the next child if it was a girl. The church recorder, however, having never heard of Louisiana, assumed the name was a variant of "Luisa" and entered it as "Luisiana." The misspelling appealed to Luis Charón and he left it that way.

❦

The year after Rosario's death, twenty-four-year-old John Louis Little was introduced to seventeen-year-old Úrsula Filomena Bos at a quinceañera fiesta hosted by a mutual friend at an estate in San Luis Potosí. From the moment of their meeting they had eyes for none but each other. She had been educated at an academy in Monterrey and spoke English very well. Her parents were present and when she introduced him to them they saw at once that their only daughter was smitten as she had not been before. They had one surviving son, Gaspar, but Úrsula had been their only girl and besides was the baby of the family—the jocoyote—and hence their favorite. They called her Sulita. Her father, Don Hector, owned a large hacienda, containing a cattle ranch, just south of Matamoros, and in addition owned a horse ranch a few miles west of town. He was a man without social pretense and had fretted to his wife that the men who aspired to woo young Úrsula were either too old for her or were spoiled brats who had not done a day of manual labor in their lives, a failing in Don Hector's view that more than offset their wealth and station. But he liked John Louis at once. So what if he was a gringo with red hair and green eyes? He had his mestizo mother's brown skin, and in most of Mexico that made him more Mexican than any Creole, even one of long lineage such as Don Hector himself. Besides, the young man had grown up in Mexico and spoke Spanish and had fine manners and was well educated and knew much about ranching and, thank God, had calluses on his hands. Úrsula's mother, Doña Martina, herself mestiza, also approved of him. The owner of the hacienda invited Úrsula to remain as his family's guest for as long as she wished, giving John Louis the opportunity to court her, and Don Hector granted his permission for her to do so, knowing she would be properly chaperoned.

Only four months later, John Louis and Úrsula Filomena were married at Patria Chica. Don Hector had no qualms about the speed of the courtship but wanted the couple to hold to tradition and be wed in the home of the bride, which would have been fine with John Louis, but Úrsula, who could be sweetly headstrong, insisted that she preferred to be married in her new home of Patria Chica. Her parents' mild annoyance at this breach was forgotten the moment they found that President Díaz was among the wedding guests. They were awed when introduced to him. Úrsula had wanted to surprise them with the revelation that the president was a longtime friend of the Wolfe family. Don Porfirio did not stay long, however, not wanting to further detract attention from the newlyweds.

Edward Little was gracious toward Don Hector and Doña Martina but tended to reticence, and they found it difficult not to stare at his disfigured face. They met Luis Charón—an officer in the Guardia Rural!—and expressed condolences when informed he was a widower, then offered congratulations on learning he had three young children, ages one through three. They also made the acquaintance of Louis Welch Little, Don Eduardo's eldest son, and his wife Gloria. If Doña Martina had not discreetly directed his attention to it later in the evening, Don Hector would not have noticed that Gloria and Louis Welch rarely looked at each other and almost never at the same time, and that the few looks they did exchange were without evident affection. She tries not to show it, Doña Martina said, but she is very angry with him. Don Hector said Don Louis himself did not seem troubled. That is because he does not pay very good attention, Doña Martina said.

Úrsula's parents would return to Patria Chica in February of the following year to dote upon their newborn grandchild, Hector Louis Little Bos. Then visit again in January to cuddle their first granddaughter, Luisa Raquel. She was named in honor of Luis Charón and John Louis's mother, Raquel. Four months later, however, Don Hector and Doña Martina would be back yet again, this time to attend the baby girl's funeral after her death by a swift-acting sickness of the lungs.

In the summer of 1899 Luis Charón's children, motherless for four years, became orphans when his company engaged with bandits a few miles outside of Coyoacán and a bullet shattered his jaw and ricocheted up through his brain. His body was conveyed to Patria Chica for burial and the funeral was attended by several army generals and the highest officers of the Guardia Rural. Standing at the side of a stone-faced Edward Little, Porfirio Díaz wept as Louis Welch Little delivered the eulogy.

Louis and Gloria endured in their separate ways the sorrow of losing their only child. Gloria devoted herself to helping the maids with the grandchildren. Louis devoted himself to drink. He could afford the indulgence, having relinquished the management of the hacienda—with Edward Little's sanction—to his half-brothers, Zack Jack, now thirty years old and well-trained to the duties of a manager, and John Louis, a most capable segundo.

Edward Little would not remonstrate with his eldest son about his drinking. Louis was a grown man and responsible for himself. But Edward did not know that Louis had also reverted to his former penchant for occasional dalliances. Louis told himself he was simply seeking solace against the pain of his son's death. A kind of solace unattainable from his wife, who could not help it that her body was almost fifty years old and had lost all allure. They had years ago taken to separate bedrooms on the mutually accepted pretext that his snoring interfered with her sleep. In truth he no longer wanted even to lie beside her and she knew it—and she preferred to sleep alone than in the heartbreaking company of a husband who could no longer bear to touch her.

A fact Louis chose to ignore was that he had resumed his infidelities prior to the death of his son. Moreover, he believed himself a master of discretion, and for good measure always threatened the woman of the moment with severe punishment if she should say a word of their assignation to anyone. But although he had been an able patrón in his father's stead, Louis had never really understood the society of a hacienda and was ignorant of the impossibility of keeping such secrets within it.

PLEASURES
OF A LATER HOUR

By the fourth year of Amos and Sófi's acquaintance, it had become their custom, as soon as María Palomina retired for the night and left them alone in the parlor, to move from their separate chairs and sit together on the sofa and hold hands as they talked to a late hour before at last saying goodnight. One night he dared to kiss the inside of her wrist, an act that caught her by surprise and seemed so sensual—so long had it been since she'd had any intimate touch from a man—that her breath caught. He said he felt her pulse quicken in the vein under his lips. Don't, she said. You mustn't. We mustn't. But made no effort to withdraw her hand. It was another year more before he ventured to kiss her on the lips, to which she reacted by yielding to the kiss for a moment before drawing back and saying, This is not right. But did not stop him from kissing her again. And then one night kissed him in return. Another year passed before the first touch of their tongues left her breathless and wondering how she had managed for so long to do without such delectation. In time they were kissing as if seeking to remove each other's mouth, and by the end of still another year she had ceased pushing his hand away and left it to its playful explorations of her clothed breast. Not until the ninth year of this relationship of steamy restraint did he finally summon the courage to confess he had loved her since the day they met. She had of course known that for many years but she said he must not say such things. You have a wife, she said, you have children. It is terrible enough, what we do, without saying such a thing. He said he was only saying what was true and she should not prohibit him from saying it to her in their private moments. She hushed him with a kiss.

The following year he said he would get a divorce. His daughters had grown up as strangers to him, and the last of them had got married within the past year without inviting him to the wedding. It had been almost five years since he had seen his wife, Teresa, and they had not written to each other in the past two. His father-in-law, Don Victor, now white haired and in tenuous health, had years ago come to accept that his daughter's marriage had been drained of all affection and there was no hope at all of a grandson. But Sófi would not hear of a divorce. You cannot do that, she said. No matter your daughters are grown, no matter how small your feeling for Teresa, they are still your family and you cannot do that to them. She had, however, confided to him her terrible history with marriage and children and had even told him of her fear of being cursed, and he was sure that her opposition to his divorce was more a matter of that lingering superstition than of concern for the sentiments of Teresa and his daughters.

And, all the while, their amorous diversions grew bolder. She had at last granted his hand entry into her dress top, and his fingers at her nipple made her bite her lips to keep from crying out and waking her mother. Soon her own hand was on him through his trousers and she had to shush him too. For many months thereafter she would not allow him any greater liberties, and then one night she relented and let him delve under the hem of her dress as she loosed his buttons and took him in hand. They bit each other's clothes to stifle their moans—and then had to muffle the gasping laughter of their pleasure.

So did it go for yet another year. Until the winter day a pair of attorneys presented themselves in Amos's office to inform him that Teresa Serafina Nevada de Bentley wished to be divorced. She was offering a substantial settlement in hope that the matter could be concluded with dispatch.

Amos conjured an aspect of Deep Concern even as his spirit soared and wheeled. A double windfall—his freedom *and* a trove of cash! And however much she was offering, when he was done with these fellows it would be a fortune for sure.

He propped his elbows on the desk and steepled his fingers in an attitude suggestive of prayer. She's fallen in love with someone else, has she? His voice quivered with injury. His eyes shone with heartbreak. She wants my daughters to call another man Father, is that it?

The lawyers smiled with no hint of humor. They knew the man's daughters were married and had children of their own, and according to Doña Teresa they had not even mentioned their father in years. One of the men said the amount of the offer had been determined by Doña Teresa herself, and despite their advice that it was too high she would not reduce it. However, the doña wanted it understood that it was the only offer she would make and she would tender it but this once. Either Mr Bentley agreed to it here and now or she would employ every legal means necessary to effect the divorce without his cooperation and at the same time see to it that he received not one cent.

I'm not sure she can do that, Amos said. Either legally or, ah, morally, I suppose is the word.

The lawyers smiled their mirthless smiles and began replacing papers in their cases. Well now, gentlemen, Amos said, let's not be hasty.

He signed every paper they put in front of him. The settlement was not insignificant. Just before they left they handed him a letter from Don Victor. It expressed the don's deep regrets at his daughter's decision, assured Amos of his position with the Nevada Mining Company, and awarded him a raise in pay.

He went straight to Sófi and told her what happened and asked her to marry him. She said no. He was stunned and asked why not. She said he knew why not and that he could think her as foolish as he liked but she would not be persuaded otherwise and if he should persist in so trying to persuade her she would no longer see him at all. On the other hand, she said, we are now truly free to disport ourselves, are we not?

Amos accepted her terms—and disport themselves they did. They established the routine of her visit to his house every Wednesday afternoon for several hours. "El miércoles magnífico," they called the weekly tryst. The residents of his neighborhood were so private in their ways he never saw them but for glimpses as they came or went in their coaches. There was no need for Sófi to worry about what they might think of her visits, on each of which they would get naked and indulge in every sort of pleasure they could devise short of copulation, as she would take no risk at all of pregnancy. She was still a lean beauty at forty-five, and he apologized for his own lack of physical attraction, for his gray hair and the size of his belly. She said not to be silly, that she liked having so much of him to hug. Besides, she said with a wicked smile, the size of *this* is just right.

And María Palomina? She had for years been aware of the intimacies they thought she was unaware of, and she had no doubt about what took place on Sófi's visits to Amos's house. But she believed that if anyone deserved a little happiness it was Sofía Reina, and if all the happiness her daughter needed was no more than the sort to be had in nakedness with a man who loved her, well, what of it? It wasn't as if she were some blushing maiden, for God's sake. She was four times widowed. Which fact reminded María Palomina that she herself was now on the very cusp of seventy. And how in the world, she would have liked to know, had *that* happened?

UNDER THE PORFIRIATO

Under the rule of Porfirio Díaz, Mexico boomed. He assembled a singular group of technical and financial advisors, highly educated and worldly men who approached their national objectives with the rational and clinical dispassion of scientists, which was in fact the collective name they were known by—Los Científicos. Even as Díaz established the civil order necessary to the protection of capital interests, he brought economic order to the country. He made good on Mexico's foreign debt. He reformed the banking system. Most important to Mexican progress, he attracted a steady influx of foreign investment through every sort of incentive—tax breaks, mineral rights, long-term leases, railroad and telegraph rights-of-way, autonomy of operation, whatever was wanted. American and European entrepreneurs mined copper and silver and gold, operated plantations of henequen and tobacco and coffee, raised cattle on the lushest and largest pasturelands, and— as Amos Bentley had predicted to John Roger Wolfe only a few years before— expanded the railroad like a great steel web to every profitable pocket of the country. And when the old century would give way to the new, there would arrive the first seekers after petroleum, a commodity whose worth was heralded by the horseless carriages already puttering over Yankee roadways.

Besides the raw riches of the Mexican earth, the greatest boon to foreign investors was the inexhaustible supply of peón labor so cheap it was almost costless. And on those inevitable occasions when some insubordinate bunch should go on strike or otherwise impede the orderly operation of a business, well, there were the army and the Rurales—the Rules, as the gringo bosses called that vaunted organization of law enforcement—to set things aright.

This singular era, known as the Porfiriato, would be the most industrially ascendant and most economically prosperous in Mexican history—and there would be much international trumpeting of Porfirio Díaz for his intrepid transformation of a lawless wilderness into one of the most progressive of nations.

At the same time, barely audible through all the fanfare, came the rumblings of a swelling fury in the hopeless impoverished. The distant thunder of a forming storm.

TAMPICO

The town stood some six miles inland from the Gulf of Mexico, on the north bank of the Río Pánuco, in the southeast corner of Tamaulipas state. Smaller than Veracruz City, Tampico was even hotter for being those few miles removed from the coast. When they arrived in that late July the air was like steam. The country about was swampland, all marsh and hammocks and shallow lakes. The swamps sometimes pulsed in the night with strange glowings said to be restless spirits of the dead. Because the city had once been a haven for pirates, some of the locals believed the lights were the ghosts of those damned to remain forever at the site of their buried booty. There were countless stories of men who had gone into the night swamp in search of treasure marked by the eerie lights and had not come out again. The first time the twins found themselves on the edge of the swamp at night rise and caught a glimpse of such a light, one of them wondered aloud if Roger Blake Wolfe had ever been in Tampico, and the other said he would wager that he had. They stood a long while in the closing darkness, now losing sight of the spectral light and now seeing its glow again, fainter each time, as if, as it receded into the deeper shadows, it was daring them to follow.

⚜

They claimed to be Thomas and Timothy Clayton, American sons of Irish parents and fishermen by trade. Marina was María Sotí. They did not explain her relation to them and no one asked to know it. They rented a three-story house on Calle Aduana. A tall narrow structure overlooking the Plaza de Libertad and only a short walk from the river port, where they moored the *Marina Dos*. The neighborhood featured numerous balconies and galleries of lace ironwork such as

345

the twins had seen in Veracruz and in pictures of New Orleans. Part of the house roof was peaked and part was flat and on the flat part there was a ramada and a table and chairs and it was a good place to eat supper and from which to observe the plaza and listen to its nightly music. On the hottest evenings they all three slept up there where the river breeze could reach them and on cloudless nights the stars looked close enough to touch. They liked hearing the trains at the loading docks, the ship whistles and bells in the night.

All her life Marina had lived within twenty miles of the Gulf of Mexico without ever having seen it until she went to the cove with the twins. And as happened to them before her, she loved the sea at first sight. She was sorry they did not spend more than one night there. The twins had dug up the strongbox containing their savings in coin and paper of high denomination and transferred the contents into several money belts they would wear to Tampico, joking that if they fell overboard they would sink like bricks. Marina had more reason than they to fear drowning, as she had not yet learned to swim, but she was never truly afraid of anything when she was with them. They hated having to abandon their books but did take with them an atlas of the world and one of North America. On the way to Tampico they began teaching her the rudiments of seamanship and by the time they entered the mouth of the Pánuco she was an able hand with sheets and tiller.

—❈—

They could not know how much effort Mauricio Espinosa might put into searching for them, but their seekers would for sure be looking for twins, so James Sebastian had Marina crop his hair very short and he remained clean shaven and took to wearing plain-lensed, wire-rimmed eyeglasses in public. Blake Cortéz let his hair grow to his collar and cultivated a sparse goatee. The physical distinctions made Marina feel for the first time as if she were sharing a bed with two different men.

And? said James.

Woo-woo, she said.

They would not go unarmed in public, but the Colts were too cumbersome to carry in concealment, so they made inquiries and were directed to a small, signless shop next to the docks where they bought a pair of .36-caliber two-shot derringers. Easy to hide on their persons even when coatless.

—❈—

They had plenty of money and passed their days at play and at familiarizing themselves with the city and its surrounding world. The Plaza de Armas was but a short walk from the Plaza de Libertad, and some nights they went dancing at one square and some nights at the other and some nights at both. They bought nautical charts and books of all sorts, including volumes of poetry and stories, and on some evenings took turns reading to each other. Marina at last grew tired of telling them

346

to speak only Spanish in her presence and asked to be taught English. They said of course—though Blake affected disgruntlement and said, Well hell, no more telling secrets in front of you.

They bought a canoe and three paddles and began to explore the outlying swamps and on occasion took the pistols with them for target shooting. They tried to teach Marina to shoot, but she could not overcome her fear of guns and fired only a single round with a derringer, flinching at the report, and then would shoot no more.

They took coach trips to Mante, to Victoria, and when the railroad arrived from Monterrey they went for extended visits to that large and rowdy city. They kept the *Marina Dos* in ready trim and sometimes went cruising for weeks at a time, acquainting themselves with the shoreline for more than a hundred miles in either direction, putting in at seaside hamlets not to be found on any map. They entered rocky passes and navigated lagoon waterways where the only sign of people was the pluming smoke of steamships out on the gulf.

—❈—

They took her to a dentist who was able to fit her with front teeth. When the job was finally done she could hardly believe the woman grinning from the mirror was herself. It was all she could do to keep her hand from her mouth, so ingrained was the action whenever she smiled, and she would be a long time undoing it.

Do I look . . . better? she asked.

Prettier than ever, James Sebastian said. Blake Cortéz said she'd always had pretty hair and pretty eyes and now had a pretty smile too.

It was not just sweet talk. She had in truth acquired a kind of prettiness in spite of the facial scars. Since joining herself to the twins, she had known danger and uncertainty and yet, paradoxically, had at the same time felt more secure than ever before. She loved them very much and felt very much loved by them, and in that strange way that happiness in love can affect a face, her scars seemed somehow less stark, the misalignment of her cheekbones almost beguiling.

Speaking of pretty, Blake said, we don't even have to mention this lovely thing. He patted her bottom and she slapped away his hand. Then was laughing as she hugged them to her, one in each arm.

—❈—

They liked to go to the beach just north of the river mouth. They rode out on the public mule-carriage and took a picnic basket and a sheet to spread on the sand and stayed all day and came back on the last coach. They would have preferred to frolic naked as they did at the cove but there were always at least a few other people in view, often with children, and so the twins wore pants cut short above the knees and Marina wore a swimming suit of her own creation, made of cotton and hemmed at mid-thigh and its halter top thin-strapped and low in the back. The costume sufficed to meet the proprieties of a sparsely populated Mexican beach but would have gotten her arrested at any American seaside resort. Her dusky skin became so much darker they began calling her Negrita. They taught her to swim, and the sensation of propelling herself through the water became one of the joys of her life. The three of them would swim out to where the waves formed, and when a big one began to build they would start stroking hard atop it and side by side ride the wave's accelerating forward roll all the way in to shore where it broke in a great crash of foam and sent them tumbling over the sand.

It became her habit to have a long solo swim on every visit to the beach. On one such swim a trio of dolphins suddenly appeared beside her, and she trod water as they circled her, rolling under and up again, blowing spray. She laughed and stroked them as they passed. Then one came up under her and with its face against her bottom raised her out of the water entirely and dropped her with a splash. The twins were watching from down the beach and heard her happy shriek. Far up the beach in the other direction a small party of people was watching too and they cheered when the dolphin tossed her. Then the dolphins vanished and she swam to shore and the other people waved to her and she waved back and came sprinting toward the twins, grinning wide, no hand at her mouth, shouting, Did you see! Did you *see*!

They practiced their fighting techniques on the beach and it pleased her to watch them at it, to witness their dance-like spins and torsions as they threw and dodged open-hand punches fast as snake strikes, never hitting each other in the face with more than a brush of fingertips but exercising no such reserve with blows to the body, and she cringed at each loud smack of palm to belly or ribs. At the end of every session, both of them sported large red blotches on their stomachs and chests.

Their social world contained the three of them alone and they were content within it. They sometimes spoke of Vicki Clara and hoped she was doing well, and of young Juan Sotero. But they would not chance a letter to her lest John Samuel somehow get hold of it and know by the postmark where they were and pass the information to Mauricio Espinosa. What if they wrote to their cousin Bruno, Marina said. They didn't really know him, they said, not enough to trust him. Josefina they missed dearly. To her they might have chanced a letter had she known how to read— but they would trust no one to read it to her.

In their fourth year they began to run low on money but they were unworried. There was always money to be made, always someone willing to pay you to provide them with something they could not get for themselves. In fact the twins were eager to return to work, though they would not go back to the hide business. The swamps teemed with alligators but there was no shortage of hunters or buyers and the market was glutted. As in Veracruz, however, there was a Chinese quarter, and as in Veracruz the Chinese did not dare to fish in the open gulf for fear of attack by Mexican boats. The twins found their way to a man named Chu, the quarter's chief broker in various enterprises. As they had hoped, he was in the market for shark fins. Like Mr Sing, he had inland buyers who were always in short supply of fins—and of shark livers, to which some of the local Chinese attributed medicinal and aphrodisiacal power. Mr Chu agreed to the twins' rate for fins and they agreed to his for livers. And they were back in the shark trade. They had thought that, as in Veracruz, they might have trouble when the local crews found out they were selling to a Chinaman. But unlike the Veracruzanos, the twins learned, the Tampiqueños didn't care who caught fish for the Chinese so long as it wasn't the Chinks themselves.

They eventually yielded to Marina's entreaties and let her go sharking with them—and she loved it from the first and fast proved an able hand. She was awed by the sharks, exhilarated by the process of catching and killing them. She could soon do every job the twins could except reel in a big one by herself, or—for her fear of guns—shoot one dead. But she was very good with the shark knife and became so adept at extracting livers and excising fins that the twins soon left those tasks entirely to her.

—❈—

Over time they came to believe that Mauricio Espinosa was either no longer looking for them or was never going to look for them in Tampico. It was of course also possible that his men had come to Tampico and made inquiries and then reported to Mauricio that no one here had seen any twins of the Wolfes' description.

Marina believed it would be best for the twins to retain their distinct appearances. "It is better to be in safety," she said, "than to be in sadness." Her English was improving, though she would never gain command of its grammar or solid footing with its idioms.

And if they kept themselves looking different, Blake Cortéz said, it would be better for whoever might prefer the excitement of two different-looking men in bed with her than the boredom of twins.

She blushed and stuck her tongue out at them.

—❈—

Her thirty-fifth birthday was notable in that nobody else in her family had ever lived that long. So far as she knew, only her Uncle Brito had made it to the age of thirty-four, in which year he was killed trying to stop a fight between his two best friends. I have become *old*, she said. You two are in company with a hag. A few weeks shy of twenty-one, the twins grinned and ran their eyes over her with exaggeriaced leers. Some hag, one said. She smiled and mouthed kisses at them.

They insisted that such a significant birthday called for a significant celebration.

They bought her a finer dress than she had ever aspired to wear and new suits for themselves. They had always been disinclined toward settings that called for formal clothes, but on this occasion they insisted on taking her to El Palacio, the city's most elegant establishment. Owned by an American from Memphis, it contained a restaurant and ballroom and casino. The staff was Mexican but every waiter spoke English, and it pleased Marina to give her dinner order in that language. She had been afraid she might make a fool of herself in such a refined place, but the twins had tutored her in etiquette, and midway through the meal she was no longer uneasy. After dinner they went into the ballroom and each twin took a turn on the floor with her. Vicki Clara had taught them to waltz and they taught Marina. Then they went upstairs to the casino and there were informed it was restricted to members only.

The manager was summoned, a man named Murtaugh. He inspected the cut of their clothes and asked in English who they were and they said the Clayton brothers out of New Orleans, where they owned a fishing company called The Gulf Bounty. They were thinking about setting up a small company in Tampico too. Murtaugh shook their hands and smiled at Marina and approved them for club membership. He apologized for the interrogation, but membership was the best way to keep out undesirables. The twins said they understood the need and approved of the policy.

They had enjoyed gambling ever since boyhood games of dice and cards in the hacienda stables and in the cantina of Santa Rosalba. On their first few visits to Veracruz they had played in most of the gambling halls, but they were all strident places of rough patronage and prone to sudden violence, usually incited by allegations of cheating. The twins had made a careful study of methods for cheating and they thought about using their own dexterous chicanery to counter that of the Veracruz halls, but decided not to. If they were caught at it, or even only accused, it would not be worth the consequences—the certain brawl to follow, the possible killing, the intervention of summoned police who were sure to be in league with the establishment. They liked Veracruz and dealing with Mr Sing and did not want to risk having to exile themselves from the city for doing injury or worse to any of its policemen. So they quit the Veracruz halls. And on finding that the public gambling houses in Tampico were no less crooked, they had shunned them too.

But the handsomely appointed casino at El Palacio was a far remove from the public halls. There were roulette wheels, tables for dicing, tables for cards. With Marina between them, the twins strolled about the floor, pausing at one table and then another to scrutinize the play, and they detected no sign of underhandedness. The casino seemed satisfied with the profits ordained to it by the iron law of percentages. They were also pleased to see that at most of the card tables the game was jackpot draw poker, their favorite. There was no betting limit and both Mexican and American money was acceptable. Moreover, property could be wagered in lieu of cash, contingent on the consent of the players still in the hand. Such bets were not uncommon among these men with large holdings in real estate, and most of the regular players always brought a deed or two to the tables. The casino kept a contract lawyer on hand to certify bills of sale and transfers of title. After being assured Marina would be properly safeguarded by Palacio personnel at a side gallery reserved for the women of the players, Blake Cortéz accepted the floor manager's offer of an open chair at one poker table and James Sebastian was seated at another. They were cordially received by the other players—a mix of Americans, Britishers, and Mexicans.

Both twins fared very well that first night. In addition to cash, Blake won the deed to a small orange grove a few miles upriver and would two days later sell it for twice as much as the bet it had covered. Their fellow players grumbled good-naturedly about a chance to regain some of their losses, and each twin smiled and promised to return.

⚜

For almost two years they went after shark in the first half of every month and played poker at the casino in the latter half. Sometimes Marina would put on her fine dress and go to El Palacio with them. They would have dinner together and then a few dances before going up to the casino where she would sit in the ladies' gallery while they played at the tables. Most of the time, however, she chose to stay at home and they didn't fault her, knowing how bored she must get in the gallery. On the nights she stayed home they would on their return find her dozing on the parlor sofa in wait of them, fresh coffee on the stove, pastries in the warmer.

Sometimes one twin would lose more money than his brother won and sometimes they both lost, but far more often they both ended the night as winners, usually by sizable amounts. They won more property too—agricultural acreage, a bean farm, a dairy, a tannery, a brickworks. They had no interest in operating any of the businesses or developing any of the land, but most of the properties were close to town and easy to sell at a good price within days of winning them. At first, they had accepted in wager even property in other regions of the country and at one time or another held title to land and other assets as far north as Sonora and as far south as Oaxaca. Such distant holdings, however, were harder to sell, some only at giveaway prices, and they soon stopped accepting bets of any real asset sited more than twenty miles from town.

Of all the properties they won title to, they held on to only one—an expansive tract of Texas acreage snugged midway between Brownsville and the Gulf of Mexico. Blake Cortéz had won it from an American named Walthers who had never seen the property and himself had won it in a San Antonio dice game from a Texan named Mizzell. The deed carried the imprint of the Cameron County land company that originally prepared it, and the legal transfer of ownership to Walthers in San Antonio had been recorded on the back. Just underneath that record, the Palacio's lawyer certified Walthers's grant of ownership to Thomas Clayton. Another man at the table said he had once been to Brownsville and that it was mostly cattle country around there except for between town and the gulf, which was nothing but marsh and scrubland. On hearing that, Walthers smiled like a man who had won the bet even though he'd lost the hand.

The twins had nautical charts of the gulf coast all the way from Coatzacoalcos up to Corpus Christi, and the chart for the region flanking the Río Bravo showed but a single settlement east of Brownsville, a hamlet called Point Isabel, nestled in a lagoon a few miles above the mouth of the river. Point *Isabel*! They took the name for an auspicious omen. Even if the property was in fact swampland and scrub, so what? It was on a river and practically on the gulf and by damn in the United States. It gave them a certain satisfaction to own land in the country of their parents, even if the place was as far south from their parents' patria chica of New England as you could get and still be in the USA. They went to a lawyer in the Plaza de Libertad, introduced themselves as cousins, and had the title transferred from Thomas Clayton to James S Wolfe.

On average they earned well more from the poker tables than from shark fins, but they liked working on the gulf too much to give it up. They lived off the sharking income and kept the casino winnings in money belts they sealed in oilskin and put in a sack and hid in one of the rain barrels behind the house. And if some of the other players had over the past year begun to grumble about the Clayton brothers' consistency at winning, well, the twins thought that was to be expected. There would always be some men who could not understand that you should not gamble if you could not bear to lose.

❋

Their time in Tampico was not without violent event. There were various brief punch-ups in the street, mainly with men who groped Marina in passing or hissed some vileness to her, but also with men who were simply looking for a fight and had the bad judgment to pick it with the Wolfes. The damage the twins inflicted in these affrays was rarely worse than broken teeth or bones but there were some rougher occasions too. As on the evening they were walking with Marina along the levee and spied a pair of men beside a boathouse trying to force themselves on a drunk but unwilling woman. The fight ended with both men in the river, one with his back likely broken and who therefore likely drowned—the twins made no effort to find out. Marina was also with them the afternoon they came upon a drayman whipping his emaciated mule with a length of bamboo because the animal could not pull the overloaded wagon any further. James Sebastian snatched the man's stick from him and began beating him with it, and when the man pulled a knife James brought the fool's arm down hard over his knee and disjointed it at the elbow. He would have cut off the man's nose for good measure but for Marina's plea not to. They flung money at the man and unharnessed the mule and took it to the edge of town where there was plenty of wild grass for it to feed on and there set loose the animal and wished it luck.

Still, they were in Tampico for almost six and a half years without serious trouble until one night just after Christmas. Marina had gone with them to the casino and the twins had again done well at the tables and they had come home just before midnight—the plaza fronting their street still loud with music and aswirl with dancers—and found three men waiting for them in the parlor. Two held five-shooters and one a shotgun with a shortened double-barrel with bores you could have fit your thumb into and both hammers cocked. At the sight of the men Marina made a small sound, then went mute, and the one with the shotgun said, Shut the fucking door.

The men looked angry and were sweat-soaked and the room was sour with the smell of them. One of them made a quick search of the twins and relieved them of the derringers. The one with the shotgun ordered them all three to sit on the floor with their hands under their ass.

The parlor had been laid to waste. Picks and axes and pry bars were scattered about. Every stuffed chair lay overturned and slashed open and its stuffing strewn. Various holes had been axed in the walls, in the floor. The twins knew the upper rooms would be in similar wreckage.

Where is it? the one with the shotgun said, looking at Blake Cortéz.

Where's what? Blake said.

Say that again and I'll kill you.

In a rain barrel, James Sebastian said.

What?

It's in one of the rain barrels in back of the house. In a bag. Wrapped in oilskin.

The robbers looked at each other—and in that moment so did the twins.

The one with the shotgun said, Show me, and told the other two to stay with the girl and the brother.

James Sebastian led him through the kitchen to the back door and saw that they had axed an opening through its thick wood and then reached in and shoved the door's heavy bolt up and out of its slot. Not much finesse but fast and effective. They could not have breached the iron grillwork embedded in the windows except with a long day's work of sawing and prying, and the front door was in plain view of the plaza. With the man right behind him, James went out the door and onto a small porch and down a short set of steps.

Stop, the man said.

The patio was in deep darkness under the cover of the trees. They could hear the music from the plaza on the other side of the house. The man pressed the muzzle of the shotgun against James Sebastian's back and said that if he even thought about jumping off into the blackness he would blow him apart. Not me, mister, James said. I can get more money but I only have one life. Smart boy, the man said, and prodded him with the gun. Now show me.

They eased through the gloom to the corner of the house where four big rain barrels, barely discernible, were aligned along the wall beneath the gutter drains. The barrels stood chest high and had wirescreen covers. James Sebastian went to the barrel at the far end. In here, he said. The bag's tied to a cord hanging over the other side.

Well get it, the man said.

James removed the screen cover and reached across the barrel for the cord. The shotgun muzzle pressed into his spine as he started taking the cord up hand over hand. Christ, it gets heavier every time, he said. Which was true—the sack now held nine fat money belts and a partially filled tenth. Glad to hear it, the man said.

As he got the sack to the surface James Sebastian cursed low and hunched forward against the rim of the barrel. *What?* the man said. Gashed my hand on the edge of this goddam thing, James said. He held the sack against the inner rim of the barrel with his left hand and with the right slid the shark knife out from between the sack and the cord wrapped around it. It was a principle of his and Blackie's to keep a weapon wherever they kept money. Fuck your hand, the man said. Get it out here.

Holding the knife close against his chest as he would an injured hand, James grunted and raised the heavy dripping sack out of the barrel with his left hand. As he turned toward the man he felt the shotgun muzzle slide off his back. Take it, quick, James said, it's slipping.

As the man's hand closed on the sack, James brought the knife up as quick as a punch and skewered his neck and grabbed his shirtfront to support the instant dead weight of him—the hilt wedged under the jaw and the blade angling out the back of the skull, the brain stem severed so he could not have pulled the trigger even in reflex.

He had feared the shotgun would discharge when it hit the ground but it didn't. The blood was hot on his knife hand. He yanked out the blade and let the man drop. He rinsed his hands and the knife in the water barrel and slipped the knife into his belt and picked up the shotgun and opened the breech to ensure both chambers were loaded and then snapped the breech shut again. He took up the money sack and went to the kitchen porch and set the sack under the steps. He recocked both hammers and went up to the door and eased into the kitchen as noiseless as shadow. He stood still and listened hard a moment. Then crossed the kitchen to the parlor door.

The two men were standing with their backs to him, facing Blake and Marina, who still sat on their hands. One of the men was saying something to Marina in low voice and the other was giggling. She was staring at the floor, her face stiff and dark with fury and embarrassment. Blake looked past the men and saw James, who nodded and entered the room, raising the shotgun as he advanced toward the two men and said "Oye."

As the men turned, Blake pushed Marina down and threw himself atop her—and in the next instant and from a distance of five feet James Sebastian shot one man in the side of the head and the other square in the face with blasts that shook the room and slathered large portions of both heads onto the wall behind the sofa.

The air stung with gunsmoke. James's ears felt plugged. Blake got off Marina and she scrambled to her feet in a rage and glared down at what remained of the one who had been talking to her. "Pinche puerco!" she said, and spat on him and kicked him. Then cursed at the blood on her shoe and wiped it off on the man's pants.

She saw the twins staring at her. *What?* she said, her look defiant. You heard what this *asshole* said to me. She rarely used profanity, and when she did, it had bite. Like Blake, she was flexing her fingers to regain circulation.

Blake raised his palms to her. "I didn't say anything."

Then stop looking at me like that. Both of you.

"Yes mam." The twins exchanged an arched-brow look, then Blake said, "I take it the other's down too."

"Yep." James Sebastian picked up the two revolvers—.38 Smith & Wesson double-action top-breaks—and passed them to Blake. As he retrieved the derringers from the coat of the one who'd taken them, the coat flap fell open to reveal a badge. Policía de Tampico.

"Ah Christ," Blake said. "Is that real?"

"Looks it. Doesn't mean it's really his."

Now Marina saw it. "Es un *policía*? Ay, dios mío."

James flipped open the other man's coat and exposed his badge too.

"Son of a bitch," Blake said. "And the one out there?"

"I didn't look but I'd bet on it. He was the bossman."

"Well, Brother Jeck, I'd say it's time we mosey."

"For damn sure, Brother Black. They probly didn't hear the shots in the plaza but the neighbors might've. Could be they sent for police."

"For the rest of them, you mean."

❖

In five minutes they were out of there. They left by the kitchen door and out the rear gate of the dark patio and made their back-alley way to the river. The twins each wore a full money belt and were armed with the derringers and the cops' revolvers. In one hand Blake carried a valise of clothes and in the other the shotgun and a smaller valise containing only money and a Colt revolver. James Sebastian carried identical valises with identical contents. Marina carried a bag of clothes too—including her lovely dress—and tucked under her other arm was the document case, which in addition to their father's papers held their mother's Dragoon and the deed to the Rio Grande property. Another fifteen minutes and they had the sails up on the *Marina Dos* and were pulling away from the dock.

As they headed downriver they speculated that some sore loser at the casino who was friends with the crooked policemen had tipped them about the Anglo brothers who had been winning too much for too long. Probably made a deal with them for a cut of the recovered money. The police had likely watched them for a time and came to know they never went to the bank and so the money had to be in the house.

Maybe it wasn't like that. There were various other possibilities. But however it really was didn't matter. They had been after the money, that was the simple fact of it. So the only thing that really mattered was in Marina's question that wasn't a question at all—If they had intended to let us live they would have worn masks, wouldn't they?

Nor was there any question about which way to go when they cleared the mouth of the Pánuco. They bore north.

PART FIVE

❧ HENRY MORGAN WOLFE *m* HEDDA JULIET BLAKE ❧

1 Roger Blake Wolfe ───────── *2* Harrison Augustus
  m Mary Margaret Parham
    1 John Roger ─────────────── w/Alma Rodríguez
      m Elizabeth Anne Bartlett   ↓*1* Juana Merced
        1 John Samuel   w/Katrina Ávila
          m Victoria Clara Márquez   *1* Juan Lobo
            1 Juan Sotero *m* Estér Leticia Hernandez
              1 Juan Román
              2 Carlos Sebastián
            2 Roger Samuel
          2 James Sebastian *m* Marina Colmillo
            1 Morgan James
            2 Harry Sebastian
        3 Blake Cortéz
          m Remedios Marisól Delgallo
            1 Jackson Ríos
            2 César Augusto
            3 Victoria Angélica
  2 Samuel Thomas
    m María Palomina Blanco
      1 Gloria Tomasina
        m Louis Welch Little
          1 Luis Charón Little *m* Rosario Monte DeLeón
            1 Eduardo Luis Little
            2 Sandra Rosario Little
            3 Catalina Luisiana Little
      2 Bruno Tomás
        m Felicia Flor Méndez
          1 Javier Tomás
          2 Joaquín Félix
      3 Sofía Reina
        m Melchor Cervantes
        m Arturo Villaseñor
          1 Francisco Villaseñor
        m Jorge Cabaza
          1 Pieto Tomás Cabaza
          2 Samuel Palomino Cabaza
        m Diego Guzmán
        m Amos Bentley

HIS MOTHER SAID

that his father was a very rich man, richer even than Don Máximo. Look here, she said, right here, her fingertip tapping the map. The hacienda is there. That is where we were born, I and then you. Where we were *born*. Our *home*. The home we were banished from. Remember it. . . .

that his father had other sons. Your brothers, she said. White brothers born of a white mother. He was married to that one and he loved her and loved them. But he was not married to me and I was not white and he did not love me and so he does not love you. That he does not love you for such a reason is unjust. *Unjust!* Never forget it. . . .

that she had no right to anything from his father. But *you* do, she said. You have as much right as the other ones to a place in his house. You have the same right by blood. By *blood*, do you understand? You have as much of his blood in your veins as the white ones have in theirs. Remember that, Juanito. You have his blood. Remember. . . .

that he had no reason to feel shame about himself. His father was the shameful one. A father who turns away his son, who sends his son away from his true home, who refuses to grant his son what is his right by blood, is a dishonorable father. He has spit on you. He is worthy only of your hate. It pains me to speak of him to you this way, my son, but it is the truth. It is important that you know the truth about him. He is an unjust man and a coward in his heart. Do not forget it. . . .

the world is full of injustice, and more so for the poor of course. But anyone, rich or poor, who was a victim of injustice and then had a chance to right that injustice should do so. It is a matter of honor that he do so, she said. A poor man can have as much honor as one who is rich. Never forget, my son, never. . . .

His mother said all this and more about his father, reiterating it through his boyhood like a catechesis.

Feeding him of her own bitter creed.

❦

They had always been outlanders on this hacienda, among these Poblanos, these people of Puebla state, whom all the rest of Mexico knew to be the most duplicitous and treacherous people in the country. By the age of fifteen he had been in many fights because of her. Because of the things other boys said about the shameless Veracruzana widow who pleasured the patrón under his own roof even as Doña Alicia was at mass. About the whore whose son's obvious gringo blood testified to a bastardy doubly disgraceful. He fought like a berserker and broke the bones of some and bit the nose off one and beat another to stuttering imbecility. Some said his lunatic temper made him a menace and he should be locked away. Even older boys who were too big for him to defeat with his fists did not come out of the fights undamaged, and when word went around that he now carried a knife, even the bigger ones grew careful with their talk in his presence.

It was said that Doña Alicia had feigned ignorance of the Veracruzana's bewitchment of her husband for as long as she could, until the day the maids heard her voice through the heavy bedchamber door, shouting at Don Máximo that if the whore ever set foot in her house again she would have her killed.

After that, the patrón came to her, to their house in the workers' quarter. The boy would hear him arrive late in the night and hear his mother admit him. Then hear them in her adjoining room, sounding as if in struggle. Then hear him leave before dawn. On the mornings after those nights he would refuse to meet her eyes. One day she made him look at her and said he should not think of her what he was thinking or be disturbed by what others might think. You are old enough now to understand, she said. I do what I do by my choice. No one forces me to do anything. I am only a laundress, yes, but I am nobody's plaything against my will. It is *I* who decided this thing. Not Don Máximo. *I.* Do you understand?

He saw that she believed what she was saying and that she felt no shame in it. And so he ceased to feel shame for her and said yes he understood. He became so familiar with the sounds of the don's visits that after a time he did not wake to them anymore.

Then came the night he was roused by her shrieks. He leaped out of bed with the knife in his hand and ran to her door and crashed through it to find not the patrón but the patrón's son crouched over her, twenty-year-old Vicente, wild-eyed and pantsless and erect, her shift ripped open and breasts exposed, her blurred face bloody. Vicente was strong and bigger than the boy but the boy was strong too and very quick with the knife, and when Vicente fell with a number of wounds the boy continued to attack him, oblivious to his mother's screams. Then the room was full of shouting men and he was subdued.

❦

That he lived to stand trial in a Puebla courtroom was testament to the fairness of Don Máximo, who even in his grief would not violate his principles of justice. He would not yield to Doña Alicia's mad cries for the blood of her son's assassin, nor capitulate to the impassioned exhortations of his son's many friends that he hang the son of a whore in the hacienda's main square. Nor to the woman's pleas to him to let her son escape in the night. You know they will kill him, she said, no matter the truth. Don Máximo had seen for himself her torn nightclothes and the bruises on her face, her broken nose, her lacerated mouth. He believed her account of what happened. That Vicente had entered her house with such stealth she did not waken until he touched her. That he had refused to leave and attempted to have her by force. That she resisted and he began hitting her and she cried out and the boy came running.

Many believed she was lying to save her son's life. They believed she had invited Vicente to her bed and that the son discovered them together and flew into a fiendish rage. He had slashed Vicente's face beyond even Doña Alicia's recognition and severed his private parts. Then beat his mother for being a whore. Then saw that Vicente was not yet dead and resumed his mutilations of him, so insane in his fury he might still be at it had he not been stopped. The whore mother, they said, was the cause of it all and should be hanged alongside the murderer son.

But Don Máximo had known that Vicente wanted the woman. Like everyone else, Vicente had heard the talk of the father's relations with her, and as father and son had always been frank with each other Vicente had told him he thought the woman was very beautiful and he envied him. And instead of telling Vicente never again to speak of her that way and never to go near her, Don Máximo had only smiled. I was a fool, he said in the courtroom, an old man gloating over his son's jealousy of him for his mistress. Now my son is dead for my stupidity.

Because Don Máximo had the courage to make such public testament—to admit his relations with the woman and reveal his son's lust for her and profess his certainty that Vicente had tried to violate her—the boy was spared a death sentence. And Doña Alicia would never speak to her husband again.

However, said the judge. Although the defendant was justified in protecting his mother, he was not justified in killing Don Vicente once the don was too severely wounded to be a threat or even to defend himself. For the defendant to have given Don Vicente forty-one distinct wounds—forty-one!—was to go far beyond a defense of his mother to an act of arrant savagery. Considering also the extensive testimony regarding the defendant's violent nature since childhood, it was the judge's opinion that the boy presented a great danger to the public and should be removed from it. He sentenced fifteen-year-old Juan Lobo Ávila to the Puebla penitentiary for fifty years.

❧

He had been in prison only two months when he was informed of her death. Someone who either sneaked into her house or was there by invitation had throttled her. He could imagine the hands at her throat. Whose hands? There were so many who hated her and wanted her dead. And him too. The only thing he knew for sure was that the agent of their misfortunes was the man who had made use of her but had not loved her because she was not white and therefore had not loved the son she bore him. The man who banished them, mother and child, from their patria chica and to a place where they would be detested strangers. Where she would be strangled and he locked away.

He might have hanged himself rather than grow old and rot to death in that prison—and to deprive them of the pleasure of keeping him caged—but his hatred would not permit it. His hatred was the very sustenance of his continued existence. It burned in his heart like a fire in a cave that was each day murkier with smoke, its rock walls each day blacker. Day after day and year after year in that cage of iron and stone he reveled in the waking dream of his hands at the man's throat. His father's throat. And then, each in his turn, at the throats of the man's other sons. The loved sons. His white brothers. Two of them twins who from the day they took their first steps had walked like they owned the earth. So his mother said.

A COUNTRY ALL ITS OWN

The sloop's low draft would have permitted easy crossing of the sandbars at the mouth of the Rio Grande, but they sensed it was no river for a sailboat. Unlike the Pánuco, whose route from Tampico to the gulf was a single smooth curve, the Rio Grande, as shown on their map, was as loopy as a cast-off string. It meandered in every direction of the compass and doubled back on itself in so many places that they estimated the distance to Brownsville by boat might be three or four times farther than by foot. The windward side of the boat would be in constant shift in such meanders—provided there was enough upriver breeze to even produce a windward side. They would have given odds they could walk to town *and* back to the coast faster than the *Marina Dos* could get them to Brownsville, if it could get them there at all.

So they sailed past the river mouth and Blake Cortéz intoned, "Lady and gent, be apprised that we are now in the territorial water of the United States of America."

"Gringolandia," Marina said, "ya llegamos."

The twins had heard the USA called Gringolandia by one of the Mexican card players at the Palacio. They thought it a clever coinage and told it to Marina, who liked it a lot.

A few miles north of the river they went through an inlet called Boca Chica, then across a small bay, then through another short pass to enter the south end of the Laguna Madre. The lagoon extended more than a hundred miles up to Corpus Christi. Their charts showed that it was no more than four feet deep in most places and had an average width of about five miles. The Point Isabel lighthouse gleamed white two miles to northeast. As they made for it they saw a stingray gliding along the bottom and estimated its wingspan at near to six feet. Further on, a school of mullet burst from the water in a great silvery rush and Marina yelled, "Mira!" and pointed at the dark shape of the hammerhead closing behind the fish.

-⊛-

Point Isabel was a compact village with a busy quay and with a small train depot on a narrow-gauge track. They leased a moorage for the sloop and were told that the daily train to Brownsville had already made its run. They registered at the little hotel and went up to their room and cleaned up and the twins unpacked their suits and hung them up to air. They took the money valises with them when they went to eat at a café. They afterward took a turn around the village and watched a merchant ship come in off the gulf through the Brazos de Santiago pass. It was already furling its sails, the Point Isabel harbor lacking the depth for vessels of such size. It anchored in the bay and lighters went out to it to transfer the cargo to the wharf.

The next day was graced with perfect December weather for the region, cloudless and almost cool. The Brownsville train arrived shortly before noon, bringing the mail and a handful of passengers and a load of Mexican imports for shipping to Galveston and New Orleans. The train then took on the Brownsville mail and all cargo bound for the Mexican ferry. It was early afternoon when its whistle blew and the last of the passengers for Brownsville got aboard and the train chugged away from the depot. The twins wore suits and each carried a money valise and under their coats an S&W five-shooter, less powerful than the Frontier Colt but also less obtrusive. Marina's bag held a change of clothes for each of them. The rest of their belongings were padlocked in the boat cabin's razor-tricked lockers. The harbormaster assured them the quay was under guard around the clock and they need not worry about their boat being thieved.

The rail line to Brownsville was less than twenty-five miles long but spanned a number of short bridges in traversing the marshiest regions. The wagon road alongside the track was intermittently corduroyed with logs. But there were wide expanses of drier ground too, vast pale sand flats, here and there clustered with prickly pear cactus and stands of mesquite. In some places the thorny brush was so dense it seemed to them not man nor beast could penetrate it. Chaparral, the locals called such countryside, sometimes el monte. The twins liked its roughness. Marina thought it was an ugly place, but she agreed the immense sky was dazzling.

-⊛-

The track terminated at the freight platforms at the east end of Levee Street. A clamorous place where goods for Mexico were loaded onto carts and conveyed to the ferry landings on the river. From a clerk in the freight office they got directions to the White Star Land & Title Company. It was only a few blocks distant, mostly by way of Elizabeth Street, the town's main thoroughfare. *Elizabeth* Street! The trio grinned at each other. They asked the clerk which was the best hotel in town and he directed them a block north to the Miller. He said they could be assured of fairly clean sheets and practically no bedbugs and of being mostly among Americans, but, as close as it was to the ferry landings, it could get pretty noisy. "Then again," the man said, "who ever heard of a quiet border town?"

They went to the hotel and James and Marina sat in the lobby while Blake registered, and then they set out again. On this market Saturday afternoon the town was loud with traffic and a babble of Spanish and English. Elizabeth Street was a graded dirt thoroughfare teeming with wagons and carts and buggies and horsemen, its sidewalks with pedestrians. Many of its buildings were two-storied and had verandahs, and most of the single-floor structures had wooden awnings to shade the sidewalk. There was a thin haze of dust. Odors of horse droppings and aromas of Mexican cooking at once familiar and yet of somewhat different piquancy. The muddy smell of the river. There was no shortage of saloons.

How strange it was, Marina said. Mexico was just across the river but it seemed so very far away. And although she was walking on a street in the United States, there were so many Mexicans around her she did not feel like she was in the United States.

"I'll wager it's the same way all along the border from here to California," James Sebastian said. "Like a country all its own."

Blake agreed. It's all that English and Spanish being spoken at the same time, he said. And so much of it mixed together. "What's the word that . . . patois. You hear those fellas we just went by? Hey Juan, the jefe's looquiándo for you."

James laughed. "Looking and buscando. Border lingo. It's what happens when one language gets in bed with another."

"You have a much dirty mind," Marina said.

"It's what you love about me," James said.

She punched his arm. "Sinvergüenza."

They stopped in at a bank. Its air of decorum a contrast to the boisterousness of the street. While James Sebastian conferred with a bank officer named Fredricks about opening a joint account in his and his brother's name—speaking in easy emulation of Charley Patterson's East Texas accent and using his real name—it was Blake's turn to sit with Marina in the lobby. The banker's smile widened as James took bundles of currency from the valise and placed them on the desktop and then emptied the bags of gold and silver specie. Fredricks made quick work of arranging the bundles and coins into neat stacks. Nearly half the money was in Mexican pesos but he was glad to convert it to dollars at the official exchange rate. It was a deposit of uncommon size and the man could not stop smiling. James beckoned Blackie to the desk to cosign the account form. Fredricks asked where they hailed from and James said they were born in Galveston and lived there till they were nine, when they moved with their parents to Veracruz, where their father had been posted as an assistant to the American consul. The banker was impressed—then tendered his condolences when James added that they had lost both parents to yellow fever the previous summer. They had come to the border with an eye to investing part of their inheritance in some promising enterprise, but they wanted to take their time about it and first get acquainted with the region and its economy, with the character of the town and the local ways, before deciding where to place the funds. "Very sage," said Mr Fredricks. He kept glancing at the valise in Blake's hand. It was exactly like the one James had emptied of its money and the man was obvious in his hope that there was more to come. But they ignored his pointed looks at it. It held their operating money. Once they took up residence somewhere they would decide where to keep it cached. They shook the banker's hand and departed with Marina between them.

Where Elizabeth Street met the perimeter of Fort Brown they turned north and at the next corner found the White Star office. They presented the deed to an agent named Ben Watson, an agreeable man of middle years. When James told him he won the property in a card game in Mexico, Watson nodded as if it were a commonplace occurrence. They gave him the same brief sketch of themselves they had given banker Fredricks, and he too was impressed and commiserative by turn. They saw his curiosity about Marina and introduced her. He shook her proffered hand, said in accented Spanish he was charmed, and thenceforth addressed her as Señora Wolfe, assuming she was married to one or the other, and nobody corrected him. In his presence they addressed her only in Spanish, and he said they surely spoke it well for Americans.

He examined the deed to make sure the two transfers recorded on the back of it were in order, then got out the ledger in which the original title was recorded and found no liens entered against it. According to the record, Watson told them, their property had once upon a time been part of a Spanish land grant. Much of South Texas had once been part of one grant or another. Who could say why the Spaniard who held the grant had measured off the portion of it described in their deed, or why in 1875 the deed was transferred to a man named Mizzell. "Could be the Mizzell fella bought it," Watson said, "or could be he won it in a bet, same as you did. Or could be he somehow hornswoggled the Spaniard's descendants out of it through the courts. There's been plenty of that sort of thing in South Texas with regard to land grants, I can tell you." At James's request he drew up a new deed in the name of both brothers, then Marina and one of the office clerks signed as witnesses and Watson entered the transaction in the company ledger. He would also record the new deed with the county clerk.

There was a map of Cameron County on the wall and he showed them where the property was. It was bounded on the south by the Rio Grande and on the north by a creek that ran about a mile below the Point Isabel rail line and roughly parallel to it. The creek had never received an official name and so had been called Nameless Creek for as long as anybody could remember. Traversing the twins' property was a road with state right-of-way from Brownsville to Boca Chica Pass. The property was six miles long, somewhat less than three miles wide at its west end and somewhat more than three along its east side. But owing to the river's meanders, the width between the north and south boundaries varied from barely a mile in some places to almost four miles at others, and so the area of their land was at best a loose estimate.

"An average of two and a half miles between the creek and the river is as good a guess as any," Watson said. "That would give you roughly fifteen square miles. Good-sized piece of land, but if you'll pardon me for saying so, fellas, it aint really much good for anything. Most of it's too mucky for raising cattle and it's way too risky for farming. Even if you cleared it for planting—and there's parts of it I don't believe you could clear in a lifetime—that region floods over so often you couldn't hardly count on a crop. Brownsville's got a levee, but out there the river comes over the banks just about every time there's a big storm or even a steady spell of hard rain."

"Yeah, well," James Sebastian said, "we aint thinking to farm it, Mr Watson. Could be we'll just use it for picnics and such. For going out to look at the birds."

Watson's smile was wry. "Every man to his own pleasures, I always say."

"This a lake?" Blake Cortéz said, putting his finger to a crescent figure near a sharp bend in the river along their property.

"Oxbow," Watson said. "What around here they call a resaca. That's a good-sized one." He pointed to an S-shape and said, "Here's another, see? Another over here. There's so many around these parts no map can show them all. This whole tip of Texas is delta country, boys. Low and mostly soggy. River floods over pretty regular and a resaca is what sometimes gets left behind when the river draws back. Others of them get made where the river loops around real tight on itself so there's a coupla bends close together and then one day the current breaks across from one bend to the other, takes a sort of shortcut, you might say. The cutoff loop left behind pretty soon gets plugged up at both ends with silt and such and presto, you got another resaca."

The north and south boundaries—a creek and a river, respectively—were as definite as boundaries could be, but Watson didn't know if the property lines along the west and east side had ever been staked out. Because they were direct north-south lines, they were simple enough to establish on paper, but at the actual site the line could be hard to stake out if there was a lot of brush or trees in the way of it. Like all the company's agents he was a licensed surveyor, and he proposed to take the brothers out to the property the next day. If the boundaries had not been staked, he would sight and stake them for the standard fee. The twins said that would be just fine.

They went back to Elizabeth Street and had supper in a café near the Miller Hotel. When they came out the city lamplighter was making his rounds from post to post, lifting the glass globes and lighting the kerosene wicks. They had bought a county map like Watson's and were up late that night, poring over it, until Marina prevailed on them to come to bed.

Watson collected them at the appointed eight o'clock hour in a dual-seat buggy powered by a brace of husky mules. Blake Cortéz sat beside him, Marina and James Sebastian in the rear. Tucked behind the back seat was Watson's instrument case and a basket lunch Mrs Watson had packed for him and his clients. The twins had tried to dissuade Marina from coming, saying it was likely to be a long day of tracking around in the dirt, but she had insisted on going and said she would not hold them at fault if she got bored. The day promised to be another fine one that would get warm but not hot. Steeple bells pealing. Except for the church-bound, traffic was sparse, and once they were out of town they saw not another soul.

The Boca Chica road was little more than a rugged trail through the same marsh and sand flats and chaparral they'd seen along the rail line. But in the distance to their right, all along the river bottoms, the landscape was thick with trees— ebonies and acacias and cottonwoods, and above all, tall shaggy palm trees, wide groves of them, one after another, sporadically interspersed with stretches of high brush or grassy flats that afforded brief views of the river.

"You'll find bunches of them palms all the way down the river to the gulf," Watson said. "It's how come the first Spanish to land here called it Río de las Palmas. Used to be they grew for miles upriver too, way up past Brownsville. The farmers and ranchers thought they were a nuisance and cleared them out."

About ten miles from town Watson turned the mules north, the buggy rocking and swaying over the uneven ground, and they soon arrived at the creek and reined up. He unfurled a map and checked the coordinates on the deed once more, then opened up his instrument case and got out the tripod and transit. He was good at his work and it took him but a few minutes to locate the northwest corner of the property and he marked it with a wooden stake. They saw that the western property line would run straight to southward without encountering any trees or heavy brush. "The Spaniard who laid out this boundary sure picked the right spot to do it," Watson said. "I'll wager the east line won't have no more obstruction than this one."

He took a due-south sighting with one twin holding the marking pole for him about seventy yards away, moving the pole right or left as Watson indicated with an upraised arm while peering through the scope. When the marking pole was in line with the sighting, Watson snapped his hand down at the wrist and the other twin drove a stake in the ground. In this manner did they advance southward on foot, setting a stake every hundred yards. The twins were within twenty yards of the river when they set the last stake but they still couldn't see the water for the high barrier of carrizo cane along the bank. When they went closer, however, they heard the current's rush in the reeds.

They returned to the buggy and ate the basket lunch. Marina was uncomplaining but the twins sensed she was wishing she had stayed at the hotel. Blake unfurled the map and he and James studied it as they ate their boiled eggs and beef sandwiches.

They intermittently looked up from it and off to southeastward. "Say, Mr Watson, this shading along the river," James said, running a finger over that part of the map, "is it all palms?"

"That it is," Watson said. "You fellas got the biggest bunch of em in the county." His mien was commiserative. "Too bad there aint much you can do with the things. No good for lumber. Makes a poor firewood, so smoky. It's a job just to make your way through them palms, what with hardwoods and shrub all mixed in with them. I tell you, boys, there's probly places in there nobody's ever set foot. Me, I don't go tracking around in any such jungle, not if I got a choice. Give me streets and sidewalks."

After lunch they drove eastward along the creek until by Watson's estimate they were near the corner of the property, and he again found the spot with no difficulty. They repeated the process for staking out the property line—and Watson won the bet with himself that it would be as free of tree obstruction as the west line.

As they headed back to Brownsville the sun was more than halfway down the sky and reddening. Watson looked tired but satisfied with his day's work. Marina dozed in her seat, the brim of her hat pulled low over her face. The twins kept looking back down the road and grinning at each other. Plan forming.

ROOTS

They were eager to begin exploring the palm groves along the river, an area Watson had estimated at about six square miles. As they had expected, Marina did not want to go with them and slog around in the mud and live in a tent the whole while. But they did not want to leave her alone in the Miller Hotel. Even in the middle of the night it was as loud as they had been warned, and it housed a number of rough men. The twins would not put her at risk of being accosted or harassed in their absence. They spent the next days looking for a house to rent but there were few available and they had to settle for an old weathered clapboard on Adams Street and near the Market Square. Its outhouse was falling apart and the roof needed repair and the house demanded a thorough cleansing, but Marina agreed it was better than the Miller.

Over the next two weeks, while Marina gave the interior of the house a good scrubbing, the twins repaired the privy and reshingled the roof and replaced the broken windows. By then they were into the new year. They had strolled down Elizabeth Street on New Year's Eve, beholding the arrival of 1893 in a din of fireworks and gunshots and high howlings in the streets. Though smaller than Tampico, Brownsville was rougher, and not only on festive occasions. In their first weeks in town they would witness a number of fistfights in the street, a group of raucous spectators always looking on until police arrived. Sometimes knives came into play and someone got badly cut. There were nights they heard gunfire near or far. It was an uncommon week the newspaper lacked a report of at least one killing.

They took Marina around town to buy household items and cookware. A market stood handy at the street corner. They bought a wagon and a brace of mules, and while she was arranging the house to her satisfaction they drove to Point

371

Isabel to check on the *Marina Dos*. They retrieved the Colts and shotgun and the rest of their clothes and the document case, locked up the sloop and drove back to Brownsville. That night there was a heavy rainstorm and in the morning they discovered the roof still had a leak and they had to reset a few shingles. Water had run down a closet wall and got into the document case, but the contents were sealed in oilpaper packets and undamaged. Except for one packet with a tear through which the water had seeped and smeared unrecognizable the ink portrait their father had labeled as that of Roger Blake Wolfe.

They went to a barbershop where Blake had his beard shaved off and they had their hair shorn in the same short style. The customers waiting their turn were as awed as the barber by the brothers' transformation into an indistinguishable pair but for one's lower face being paler than the other's, and three days of outdoor work would remove that difference so that even Marina would again find it hard to tell who was who from more than a few feet away. The twins told her there was no need to hide their twinship on this side of the border. They had expected some sardonic remark about reverting to the dullness of twins in her bed, but she made none. She seemed out of sorts and avoided their eyes. They told each other she was just uneasy about their going away for a while, that she wasn't yet very comfortable in this borderland world.

They bought camp bedding and tools and supplies. She was not going with them so they saw no need of a tent. Early one morning they gave her a sum of money and one of the derringers, though she protested she did not want it. Then kissed her each in turn and said they would be back in two weeks or so.

⊷⊷⊷

They explored from west to east and in a week arrived at the largest of the property's palm groves. There were yet a few more groves to the east of this one, but from out on the road they could see that those palms were neither as tall nor as dense as these. They left the wagon and the tethered mules in a high growth of scrub in the chaparral and out of view of anyone who might pass by on the road—a remote likelihood, as in all the time they had been there they had not seen a single wagon or horseman pass in either direction. There was a stream where the mules could water and grass for them to feed on. They waited till the sun was well up before they entered the grove, machetes in hand and their bedrolls and rucksacks slung on their shoulders. This was the thickest grove yet and some of the palms looked to be forty feet high. They had to hack their way through much of the underbrush and were often in mud to the shins. Past midday they were in a segment of grove so dense it was in twilight, and after another few hours they began to suspect they might be going in a circle. Then they saw light through the trees ahead and as they drew closer to it they felt a slight incline under their feet. They came out of the palms and into a large sunlit clearing—a rectangular expanse about seventy yards west to east and forty yards north to south, the south side abutting the gray-green river, which they could see through gaps in the reeds and cane.

The clearing was high and flat and dry, some three feet above the surrounding ground. It contained moss-hung oaks and cottonwoods, patches of lush grass to their knees. They thought somebody must have axed out the clearing and raised it with a mix of rock and river dredge, a formidable undertaking. But they found not a single stump nor any other sign that the clearing was man-made or even that anyone else had ever been there. The only explanation they could think for the clearing was geographical quirk. Such high and solid ground should not naturally exist in a marshy palm grove, yet here it was. The river at this point was a hundred feet across and they saw that on the Mexican side there was no similar high ground or clearing.

They built a campfire and caught small frogs to use for bait on handlines and in quick order landed four fat catfish, which they filleted and peppered and fried in a pan with lard. They divided the fillets into two tin plates and sat beside the fire with the map spread between them and studied it as they ate. They figured where the clearing was and penciled it on the map and reckoned a distance of five miles from there to the Point Isabel road—though they would have to build a wagon bridge over Nameless Creek—then about twelve miles to Point Isabel itself.

They knew the unexplored groves to the east could not provide such privacy as this, nor, they were certain, a clearing of such good ground. This was the place for a house. A big one on heavy pilings ten feet above ground, high enough to protect it from any flood lesser than Noah's. With a verandah. It was no Ensenada de Isabel, of course, but it was on a river and the gulf was but eight miles downstream and it was far from town and its people and its noise and its afflictions. The problem was Marina. She had made it plain she didn't like it out here.

They talked of her recent remoteness and wondered if she might never adapt to this region. What if she hated it even more than they knew? She dearly loved Tampico and would have been very happy had they stayed there forever. Would she prefer to return there, even without them? They had known her all their life and had lived in her company for so long now that they did not like to think of being without her. But they would not have her think she was obliged to remain with them, and they of course would never alter their plans to suit somebody else, not even her. They decided they would tell her quite frankly what she should already know—that she was free to choose her own course. If she wanted to live in town, fine. Go back to Tampico? Very well. To Buenaventura? All right. They would fund her. Whatever her choice.

Vapor rose off the river as the night closed around them. The air heavy with the odors of dank earth and muddy water. They unrolled their bedding next to the fire and settled themselves and talked a while longer. And determined, among other things, to name the clearing Wolfe Landing and their entire property Tierra Wolfe.

As expected, she said she would not live out there, no matter how nice the house they would build. I don't like it there, she said. They said they understood, and gave her their prepared talk. Told her she could live in town, if that's what she wanted, but if she did not want to live in Brownsville, well, she could go wherever she chose. They would always see to it she had plenty of money to live on.

Her eyes brimmed. I will not go live somewhere else, she said. I do not want to go away from you. They smiled. They had been almost sure she would say that. That she loved them too much to go away. All right then, Blake said, so you'll live here and—

Besides, she said, a child should not be apart from his father.

They stared at her.

She said she had suspected her condition for a few weeks before they left Tampico but hadn't said anything because she wasn't sure. Now she was sure. Her great fear, she said, was that they would think it had been deliberate. It was not. She would never do that. She was anyway thirty-six years old, for the love of God. Too old for this. She had never wanted to be a mother. It is hard enough tending to you two children, she said with a weak smile. She had always taken precaution, always, but they knew as well as she that there could never be absolute certainty. Now that it happened, she said, the wonder was that it had not happened long before.

They stared at her. I know the question in your mind, she said.

Well? Blake Cortéz said.

She looked from one to the other. How is it possible to know whose?

They nodded. They had another question in mind too but they would not ask it. If she had said she wanted to go to a curandera to resolve the matter, they would have said all right, and would have looked somber in saying it—and would secretly have been relieved. But she did not suggest a curandera, as they knew she would not, even if she really did think she was too old for motherhood.

I have to take the laundry from the clothesline, she said. Before it rains. They watched her go out the back door. The day was nearly cloudless.

"After all these years," Blake said. "I never expected this. I sure as hell never wanted *this*."

"Hell no, you never wanted it. Neither did I. Neither did *she*. But here it is."

"I know, I know. So what do we do?"

" I don't know. Hell."

They stood silent a long few seconds.

"Aint but one thing *to* do. Unless you got another idea," James said.

Blake shook his head. "Dammit."

"Yeah."

"Well hell, then, let's get it over with."

James Sebastian took a coin from his pocket. "Call," he said, and thumbed it spinning in the air. Blake called tails. James caught the coin and slapped it to the back of his other hand and uncovered it for Blake to see. Tails. Blake looked at it without expression. Then looked at his brother. James nodded and sighed.

When Marina Colmillo came back in the house James Sebastian asked her if she would marry him. But even at such a moment they could not resist deviling her. They had their hands in their pockets so she could not see who had the crooked little finger or node on the wrist. They were dressed differently but had not called each other by name since arriving. She gave them a chiding look and then stepped closer to the one who had asked her and told him to stop squinting. And saw the green flaw in his eye.

Yes, James, she said, I will.

Two hours later, on that bright January afternoon, they stood before a justice of the peace and were wed.

❈

The marriage did not change their plan for a river house, but first they had to provide a home for her. They looked at different lots around town before buying a large one on the west end of Levee Street. While they were building a sturdy clapboard house of three bedrooms and a small room in the rear as a servant's quarters, they continued living in the Adams Street rental. Most days were cool and bright and favorable for hard work but they had not imagined a South Texas winter could some days be so cold. Some mornings the bushes were sheeted with ice. The occasional blue norther burned their faces raw and had them exhaling on their fingers every few minutes.

They finished the house near the end of March, including the privy and fencing and cistern, everything. They insisted Marina should have a live-in maid while they were working at the landing. She felt she could manage well enough by herself but did not want to argue, and so interviewed several applicants before hiring a bilingual seventeen-year-old named Remedios Marisól Delgallo. The girl had grown up in a San Antonio orphanage run by Irish nuns, then went out on her own at fifteen and made her way to Brownsville to see what it was like. She stayed because she liked the spirited border life and had supported herself with intermittent jobs as a housemaid and as occasional assistant to a midwife. The twins had hoped Marina would choose someone older, but she insisted on Remedios, to whom she had taken an immediate liking. She said the girl would not only be of great help with the birth but also in improving her English. When Remedios was introduced to them she was captivated by their identicalness. She did not ask how to tell them apart but she was sharp-eyed and attentive and within two days could address them by name when they were close enough for her to see the telltale little finger and the wrist node.

The house was furnished, the pantry stocked. With a wagonload of tools and kegs of beer, the twins set out for the river property.

❈

To transport materials to the clearing, they first had to make a wagon road through the grove, a process that would take almost as long as all the construction to follow. The shortest distances between the grove perimeter and the clearing traversed the boggiest ground and presented the most obstacles. The best route they could chart ran parallel to the river and was almost a mile long, and still required cutting through scrub and trees. With machetes and axes they hacked and hewed their way through the grove, using the trunks of felled trees to form a corduroy surface which they then graded by shoveling mud and dirt over the logs and packing it down. It was an arduous process and the early stage of it even more difficult for the advent of the rainy season. All in all it took eight months to complete the road, which they finished on a freezing day in December. Then began the long and strenuous months of cutting the pilings and raising them in place in the corner of the clearing where the house was to stand. Once the pilings were in place they would lay the floor across them and then finally begin to build the house itself. After which they would build a dock, then a stable and some sheds. A seasoned construction crew might have finished the entire project, from first to last, in less than a year, less than half the time it would take the two of them. There would be times, as they labored in the clearing, when they would almost decide to hire a crew to finish the job, but they had reckoned their expenses from first to last and the budget would not allow for it. In truth, they were glad they had no choice but to do it all themselves. Because even if they'd had a choice, they would do it themselves. And that, they told each other, would be perverse.

-❖-

The twins had been baffled when Marina, on marrying James Sebastian, no longer permitted Blake Cortéz to join them in bed. Things are different now, she said. They did not understand. They argued to her that nothing was different except that one of them had married her to give the forthcoming child legitimacy, but for all any of them knew, the child was really Blake's and she was refusing to make love with the true father. No-no-no, Marina said. When they decided that James would be her husband, they had also decided that James would be the father. She was now the father's wife and was pledged in faithfulness to him and could make love to no other man. It's not some other man, James said, it's Blackie! Besides, what if I say it's all right? She said it wasn't up to him to decide that. She admitted that the three of them had always done things by their own rules and lived very free of the world's opinion, but there were some rules in the world that were greater than their own. Why did one of those rules, Blake said, have to be one about no more me? It just did, she said, and kissed him on the cheek. You have always been my darling Blackie, but now you are my darling *brother* Blackie.

"Goddammit," Blake said, "I didn't know it was gonna mean *this*." He turned to James. "Let's make it two out of three."

What galled Blake most was not the loss of sex with her. There had always had other girls, in Tampico as well as Buenaventura, none of whom meant anything more to them than an occasional treat of carnal variety, and none of whom, they were certain, Marina had ever been aware of. For sure there were girls in Brownsville and Matamoros as easily to be had. But with Marina, sex was the least of it. It had always been fun with her, yes, but the best thing about it was their sharing of a woman they had loved all their life. James felt the same way. It seemed to them a cruel twist that she should become the first thing in their life they could not share. But if they could not be husband to the same woman or father to the same child, they could at least share the experiences of marriage and fatherhood. Experiences that, on the day Remedios Marisól entered their lives, Blake Cortéz began inclining toward before he was even aware of it.

From the beginning of their project in the palm grove, it was the twins' custom to go into Brownsville every Saturday to get supplies and visit with Marina and Remedios. The first few times they did not stay until nightfall. They had lunch with the women and then late in the afternoon headed back to the palm grove so they could resume work on the wagon road at daybreak. From the first visit, however, it became James's and Marina's ritual to retire to their bedroom after lunch—and to give them more privacy Blake and Remedios would take a walk around town, a routine by which they came to know each other well. Besides being pretty, Remedios was an intelligent and astute girl with a wonderful laugh it pleased Blake to provoke. And too, she had a sassiness much like Marina's, peppery but never mean. Probably the main reason, the twins believed, Marina had taken such immediate liking to her.

Blake found himself thinking about her during the week's work on the grove road, and he looked forward to seeing her on Saturdays. She always seemed pleased to see him too. They had known each other a month when he discovered she was even more akin to Marina than he'd thought—in that she had the same bohemian attitude about sex. From then on, when James and Marina went off to one bedroom, Blake and Remedios went off to another, and they stayed with the women overnight, though it cost them half a morning's work at the clearing on Sundays.

Remedios soon intuited that Blake was falling in love with her, which pleased her very much because she was already enamored of him. But she had early in life acquired the valuable defense of keeping her true feelings out of her eyes, and she did that with him until she could be sure how he felt about her. Marina had confided to her the relationship she'd had with the twins and how sad it had made her to turn away Blackie when she and James married. Remedios thought it exciting that the trio had been able to share themselves as they had, but she secretly fretted that Blake might never feel toward her as he did about Marina. She did not have to fret very long. They had known each other almost four months on the evening in July when he told her he loved her. She saw the truth of it in his eyes and told him she loved him too—and they grinned at each other like fools. Well then, he said, seeing as they loved each other, and knowing that sooner or later she was sure to get pregnant, they might as well get married now as wait until later. Well, she said, it certainly seemed the practical thing to do, all right, and they laughed at themselves for such talk of practicality. But listen, she said. You must ask me. Of course I must, he said. And did. And she said yes. And when they learned of it, James Sebastian and Marina were overjoyed.

The wedding took place on the last Saturday of July. Outside the church after the ceremony, James Sebastian took Blake aside and said that in all fairness he should be permitted to join him in bed with Remedios Marisól until she conceived. After all, they had shared in the making of the child Marina was carrying and it seemed to him only fair they do the same with Remedios's first. Blake said it sounded fair to him, but he wasn't sure what Remedios would say. They looked over at her where she stood outside the church doors, talking with the priest and Marina and Mr and Mrs Flores, the good neighbors she had invited to the nuptials.

Large-bellied in her eighth month, Marina caught sight of the twins and studied their faces. Then excused herself from the group and went to James and hugged him and gave him a kiss. And whispered to him, Don't even dream about it, sonny.

❦

A month later Morgan James Wolfe Colmillo was born in the house on Levee Street during a late-night rainstorm. A healthy bellowing boy of more than eleven pounds. Remedios Marisól did a commendable job of midwifery. The labor had so exhausted Marina that she slept for fourteen hours. The next day, with the baby at her breast, she was not unmindful of the circumstance of suckling a son she had borne to a man she had suckled in his infancy. When she asked James Sebastian why he wanted to name him Morgan, he skirted explication about his great-grandfather and simply said it was a name he had always admired and he hoped it was all right with her. Of course, she said. She liked it, it had a sound of strength. But she would in the first year of his life more often call him Gringito.

With the twins in Brownsville only one day a week, Marina and Remedios became even closer friends and confidantes. Given the twenty-year difference in their ages, it was only natural the relation between them had a strong semblance of mother and daughter, a bond that became the more pronounced when, a month after Morgan James's birth, Remedios found she was three months pregnant.

Remedios loved to hear Marina tell of life at Buenaventura. She was hardly able to imagine such grandeur. She was gripped by Marina's account of the bloody Sunday when they'd had to flee the hacienda before the army arrived to kill the twins. Many of Marina's recollections of course involved old Josefina, and in speaking of her she sometimes missed her so much she couldn't hold back her tears. In October she asked the twins if she might now write to Josefina. It had been more than seven years. Maybe Mauricio Espinosa had quit his search for them. Maybe John Samuel was no longer on the watch for a letter that might reveal their whereabouts so that he could inform Mauricio. Josefina would anyhow certainly choose someone worthy of her trust to read the letter to her and write her response.

She had expected refusal but the twins said yes. What did it matter anyway if Mauricio found out they were in the United States? If he came after them over here, he couldn't bring a company of soldiers with him, and they weren't afraid of just him and a few henchmen. Marina bolted from her chair to hug and kiss them in gratitude. But there was no reason to make it too easy for Mauricio, the twins said, so she should not put her name or a return address on the envelope, only in the letter.

The next day Marina wrote Josefina a long letter recounting everything that had happened to them since their flight from Buenaventura.

CORRESPONDENCE

The reply that came some weeks later was not from Josefina but from Bruno Tomás. It arrived on a Thursday but Marina did not open it until the twins arrived for their weekend visit—then read it aloud to them and Remedios.

Bruno explained at the outset that as mayordomo he had been given her letter by the hacienda postal clerk because its addressee, Josefina Cortéz de Quito, was deceased, and had been for almost two years. Bruno wrote that although he and Marina had not been well acquainted, he knew of her close friendship with Josefina, and he wanted her to know that her death was the sort everyone hoped for himself—of painless old age and in her sleep.

Though this news should hardly have been unexpected—Josefina had been old since before the twins were born—Marina lay the letter on her lap and wept into her hands. Remedios shifted her chair closer and placed an arm around her, her own eyes tearful. The twins gazed at the floor. After a minute Marina dried her tears on her skirt hem and Remedios gave her a handkerchief to blow her nose. She loved the two of you with all her heart, Marina said.

The twins nodded, aspects solemn. Then Blake Cortéz said, "It's a lowdown shame. Had her whole life ahead of her." He tried to restrain his grin but failed. James Sebastian snickered.

Marina was incredulous. You think this is *amusing*?

The twins struggled to contain themselves but broke out laughing. The women gaped. Then looked at each other in horrified perplexity at their own sudden urge to laugh. And then they too were guffawing.

Oh my dear God, we are terrible, Marina gasped, her hands on her face. *Terrible.* James said they probably could have got a good price for her from a museum. You are so *evil*, Marina said, both of you.

They all laughed until they were gasping and their ribs could stand no more. And Marina once again had to dry her eyes and blow her nose before she could resume reading the letter.

Bruno apologized for violating the privacy of the letter, but the envelope had borne no identification of a sender nor address to which it could be returned, and Josefina had no known next-of-kin to whom he could pass it on. The postal clerk told him it was the first letter ever to come for Josefina Cortéz in all his years at the job. It made Bruno even more curious that the postmark was of Brownsville, Texas, as many years ago his older sister had lived there for a few months. Even before he read the letter, he had a strange feeling it might be news from or about the twins, and he nearly shouted when he found he was right. He was very happy to know, after all these years, that the twins had escaped the gunmen Espinosa had sent after them. And of course very happy to learn of their marriages.

My most sincere felicitations to you, my dear new cousin Marina, Bruno wrote, and of course to James Sebastian. And my congratulations on the birth of Morgan James. Please convey my warmest wishes also to Blake Cortéz and his bride Remedios and for their coming child.

"The man sent pistoleros to get us?" Blake said. "*Damn*."

It was clear from Marina's letter, Bruno wrote, that the twins did not know Mauricio Espinosa was dead, and it was a pleasure to be the one to inform them that Mauricio had been assassinated only three days after his brother's murder of John Roger. No one had ever learned who the assassin was.

Marina looked up from the letter. Three *days*, she said.

All this time we've been hiding from a dead man, Blake said.

How were you to know? Remedios said. How was anyone to tell you? You hid so well nobody could find you.

"Yeah," said James Sebastian. "Joke's on us."

Bruno said Marina's letter also implied their great trust in Josefina to keep all information about the twins in confidence, and he promised he would keep their confidence too. He said he liked his life as mayordomo and admitted that he and John Samuel had a good rapport in attending to hacienda business. But apart from business they spent little time in each other's company and he did not feel it his duty to inform him about his brothers. He told of the brief siege of Buenaventura by the Espinosa gunmen and of John Samuel's conviction that his brothers had been captured and killed. But neither he—Bruno—nor Vicki Clara had ever believed the twins were caught. After the siege, Bruno had gone with some men to the cove and found that the house had been burned down to the piling foundations. The dock too had been destroyed. But they found no bodies or parts of bodies nor any sign of a grave and so were pretty sure the twins had not been there when the place was razed.

The cove house, James said. Bastards.

As for Vicki, Bruno was sorry to report that for the past three years she had been in poor health more often than not. She slept little. She lacked appetite and had lost much weight. Her vision troubled her and she now wore thick spectacles to read. As they knew, she was not one to complain, but she had mentioned she sometimes got severe headaches that seemed rooted at the back of her eyes. John Samuel had at last persuaded her to have a medical examination. The doctor said her nerves were exhausted and prescribed a nightly soporific and a diet of dried fruit and boiled eggs. That was a year ago. The regimen seemed to have had no effect.

About Juan Sotero the news was cheerier. The boy at fourteen was as smart as they come and an excellent athlete. For the past year he had been set on becoming an army engineer, an aspiration prompted by a book he'd read about the road-making ingenuity of Yankee engineers under Captain Robert E Lee during Mexico's war with the United States. John Samuel had of course been opposed to a military career for his son. He wanted Juanito to succeed him as patrón of the hacienda. It was fine with him, John Samuel had said, if the boy wanted to become an engineer, but why must he be one in the army? He could get his education at the university in Mexico City, and if he wanted to build roads he could build them at Buenaventura—God knew the place could use them. But in Juanito's view the only thing better than being an engineer was being an engineer *and* an army officer. Vicki Clara was insistent that her son would choose his own vocation, though she had in private told Bruno of her own disappointment in Juanito's choice of the army. Ever since the horse accident, Bruno wrote, things had changed between Vicki Clara and John Samuel. She was no longer reluctant to express differences of opinion with him and could be firm in defending them, and he seemed determined not to argue with her. In any case, and no matter what else one could say of him, John Samuel was not a stupid man. He understood he could neither force nor persuade Juanito to devote himself to a vocation he did not want, and so next fall Juan Sotero would attend a military school at Veracruz.

Not until near the end of his letter did Bruno tell them—in a single sentence that looked to have been scrawled in such haste it was nearly illegible—of the deaths some years earlier of Felicia Flor and his baby sons. And in the next sentence asked the twins' permission to show Marina's letter to Vicki, who would be greatly relieved to know they were alive and well. She was a far better writer than he and he was certain she would be happy to do all the letter writing for both of them in the future. Besides, the correspondence would be good for her spirits. He also asked if he could share the information with his sisters. Gloria Tomasina, he told them, lived with her husband Louis Little on his father's hacienda near San Luis Potosí, and it was by means of the Littles' close friendship with Porfirio Díaz that she had been able to end the siege of Buenaventura. His younger sister Sofía Reina still lived with their mother in Mexico City, but she had always had a keen interest in the Wolfe family and would be eager to learn what had become of the twins and that they were well. He closed with, My love to you all. Your most affectionate cousin, Bruno Tomás Wolfe y Blanco.

"We got a cousin whose in-laws are friends with *Díaz*?" James said. "That's some friend to have." Díaz had first become president when the twins were six years old.

Marina wanted to know if they would return to Ensenada de Isabel, now they knew Mauricio was dead. The twins said no. When their father died, the whole place, cove and all, became the property of she-knew-who. It wasn't home anymore.

Well, what of Bruno's request to share the letter with Vicki? Of course he can, James Sebastian said. And he can tell his sisters as much as he wants to, Blake said. They neither one cared whether anybody told John Samuel anything. But nobody would.

-⊱⊰-

None of them could know Josefina's death had not been so serene as Bruno supposed. For a great many years she had believed that life could produce no more surprises to someone her age, and then Marina and the twins were gone and she was astonished to discover that even an ancient relic such as herself—who had known every variety of loss and believed she had learned to endure them—could miss anyone so much. She was lonelier than she had thought it possible to be. There was a great stone weight in her withered breast that every day grew heavier until she felt it would crush her heart. As, finally, one night, it did.

-⊱⊰-

In her letter to Bruno, Marina tendered everyone's condolences on the loss of his family, and their regret at not having had the chance for better acquaintance with Felicia and the boys. She conveyed the twins' gratitude for his informing them of Mauricio Espinosa's death, and told him he could share her letters with Vicki Clara and tell his sisters all he wanted about the twins. But, knowing Vicki would read the letter, she made no reference to Bruno's concern about her frail health. She reported that Remedios was doing very well in her pregnancy and the child was due in the spring. She described the house the twins had built in Brownsville and told of the one they were building in the wild palms downriver at the place they called Wolfe Landing. She told about Brownsville, about its residents, an almost equal mix of Mexicans and Anglos and all of them inclined to public conversation in bellows. Though smaller than Tampico it was louder and had even more cantinas. And more dogs. She had never seen so many dogs at large. Sometimes she heard parrots in the trees and sometimes saw a flock of them streak over the patio in a colorful flash, and in such moments she missed Tampico terribly. And of course Buenaventura.

Bruno passed Marina's two letters to Vicki, who was ecstatic about them. She was in the library reading the letter to Josefina yet again when John Samuel happened by and asked who it was from, and she said an old school friend. As she saw it, if the twins wanted John Samuel to know anything about them they would ask her to tell him or they would tell him themselves. As Bruno had expected, she was delighted to correspond for both of them with their kin across the border. She addressed her letter to Marina but directed it to all of them. She said how happy she was to know they were unharmed. How wonderful it was that Marina and James Sebastian were married and had a son! And Blake married too and also to soon be a father! She knew Remedios must be very lovely and precious and she could hardly wait to meet her. How good to know the family was still growing—but dear God, how the years were flying! She made no reference to the medical troubles Bruno had mentioned, but she wrote at length about Juanito Sotero. Told how handsome he was and how strong, how accomplished in his studies. About his excitement to be going to military school in the coming fall. Her only concern about him was that his attitude had become so serious. Oh, he enjoyed his sports and he had friends, yes, but to be frank, she rarely heard him laugh. She did not mean to suggest he was solemn, because he was not—his smile was lovely and not infrequent. It was only that he seemed less a child than a very young and purposeful adult. As though the death of his brother had ended his own childhood. How silly she must sound, she wrote, to have such concern about a son so healthy and intelligent. He had been thrilled when she told him his uncles were alive and well. In the years since the twins' departure, she and Juanito had sometimes made a game of imagining where they might be and what they might be doing. Juanito asked if she were going to tell his father what they had learned about Uncle James and Uncle Blake, and she said she wasn't. She gave no explanation and he did not ask for one, but only said he wasn't going to tell either. In closing, she wrote, With love to you all, my dear sisters and brothers, including my baby nephew and the niece or nephew soon to join you. Vicki Clara.

Marina wrote Vicki in March with the news that she was again pregnant and had been for about four months. This one was no accident. James Sebastian was so pleased with Morgan James that he wanted another son. She had told him they could try but she wasn't sure she could conceive again, and even if she did he should keep in mind that it might be a girl. He said that would be all right with him. And, just like that, she was pregnant. What in heaven was going on? Who would have thought another seed could sprout in this old pot? As for Remedios, her baby was due any day. And Vicki should see the twins now! Twenty-three years old and handsomer than ever. At the end of the letter, the twins had added a few lines of their own to Vicki, each penning an affectionate greeting and lamenting the eternity since they'd last had the pleasure of her dear company. They were pleased Juan Sotero was doing so well and asked her to convey their proud salutations to him. They invited her and Juanito, together or when each might have the chance, to come and visit them in Brownsville. Nobody mentioned John Samuel.

In that first letter to Vicki, Marina addressed her as she always had, as Doña Victoria, and was chided for it in Vicki's next letter. Sisters, Vicki wrote, are never so formal with each other. Marina loved her for her graciousness.

That spring they received their first letter from Sofia Reina Wolfe y Blanco, addressed, at Bruno's suggestion, to Marina Colmillo de Wolfe. It was a brief and affectionate missive conveying Sófi's admiration for the twins, having heard so much about them from her brother. Marina wrote back that they were all very happy to make her acquaintance, if only by way of letter, and told her of their great fondness for Bruno. This correspondence would continue for seventeen years, during which time Sófi and María Palomina would learn much about their relatives at the border and the Wolfes would come to know a good deal about their kin in Mexico City. But some things, of course—such as the history of Sófi's marriages—could not be told in a letter and would have to wait those seventeen years before becoming known to the whole family.

❦

Came the fall and Juan Sotero kissed his mother goodbye and shook his father's hand and entered the gates of El Colegio Militario de Veracruz. By which time there had been two more additions to the Wolfe family across the Río Bravo. Remedios Marisól had borne Jackson Ríos at the end of April, and then a little more than three months later Marina brought Harry Sebastian into the world. Now Remedios was pregnant again. Mother of God, Marina wrote to Vicki, we are like a bakery of little Americans!

But Harry Sebastian's birth, like his brother Morgan James's, had been hard on Marina, and because the danger of another pregnancy would be graver yet for a woman of nearly forty, she and James Sebastian had agreed to have no more children. She would resume taking precautions, but if there should be an accident she would certainly seek the help of a curandera, a choice that of course had its own hazards. In all honesty, Marina confided to Vicki, I will be so very happy when I am dried-up and no longer have to be so careful. May it happen soon soon *soon*.

❦

They finished the river house two weeks before the new year of 1895. A large single-story with four bedrooms, a big kitchen and spacious central room, a wide verandah all around. When they brought the wives out to see it, Marina said it was pretty and she would live in it if it were in town. Remedios liked the house too but if Marina would not live there neither would she. They were amenable, however, to occasional visits. After taking the wives back to town, the twins allotted themselves a rare day of leisure. They went to Point Isabel and took the *Marina Dos* out for a sail. They had missed the sea very much, and by that day's end they were decided that one way or another they would again have a beach house.

There was still much work to do at Wolfe Landing. They would next build a stable for the mules and some horses and maybe a dairy cow, and then assume the harder job of constructing a dock along the bank. And there was still a bridge to build over Nameless Creek. They reckoned they could finish it all by April but it would actually take them until July. They had months ago used up the money in the valise and had since then been making regular withdrawals from the bank. By their estimation, those funds would be nearly depleted by the end of the year. They hadn't even had time to explore the several other of their palm groves east of the clearing, about three square miles of them, by their reckoning.

—⧈—

One night as they sat by the campfire at Wolfe Landing—an evening nearly silent but for a soft soughing in the palms—they heard a faint but distinctive sound they had not heard since their days on the Río Perdido. A sequence of low rasping grunts, coming from the darkness beyond the northeast corner of the clearing. James Sebastian said if it wasn't a bull alligator he would eat every hat in Cameron County. "Let's go see," Blake said.

They tucked the Colts in their belts and took up firebrands and went into the palms. It was a dense stand and the firelight was bright against the trunks as the twins wound their way through them. They had gone about twenty yards and almost walked into the resaca before they knew it was there, catching themselves short at its bank. They could not make out the other side, which in the light of the next day they would see was some forty yards distant—and see too that the resaca was crescent-shaped and they were near one of its ends, the other end out of view behind a stand of palms. But standing there in the darkness, they saw the red glowings of alligator eyes on the surface of the black-glass water. They had read that there were alligators in the region—and no crocodiles—but they would give no thought at all to taking hides. They'd had enough of that trade. Yet they liked knowing the alligators were there in that big nearby resaca, and thereafter always listened for their gruntings in the hushed darkness of still nights.

Some weeks later they found a dead man floating in the river reeds where they were constructing the dock. A young mestizo, shirtless and shoeless. Brought down by the current from who knew where, though it could not have been very far, as he had not been long in the water, the eyes not yet eaten, the lips yet intact. There was a small bullet hole above his ear. His pockets were empty but he was no peón—the pants were part of a suit, the hands unscarred, two fingers showed pale bands where rings had been.

The only adequate ground for a grave in that lowland was Wolfe Landing, but they were not about to bury anyone there not family to them. But they had an idea. They bore the body to the resaca and looped one end of a rope around its ankle and lashed the other end securely to a tree and set the corpse in the water. The next day the rope was slack and the dead man gone.

—⧈—

Blake and Remedios's second child, César Augusto Wolfe Delgallo, was born on the thirtieth of April, exactly one year, to the day, after his brother Jackson Ríos. Marina wrote the news to Vicki Clara, from whom there had been no word in nearly six months. When the first four months had passed without response to two of her letters, Marina had written to Bruno Tomás to ask if anything was wrong with Vicki. But in the two months since, that letter too had gone unanswered.

In May came a letter of bleak tidings from Bruno. Vicki Clara had kept secret the worsening condition of her vision until it became apparent to everyone that she could barely see at all. John Samuel had taken her to four different doctors, including two in Mexico City said to be the best eye surgeons in the country. They all agreed there was nothing that could be done to arrest her vision's accelerating degeneration and predicted she would be blind by spring. And she was. Bruno had not informed the twins and their wives of Vicki's trouble before now because he had been hoping for some miraculous recovery to report. Juan Sotero had wanted to withdraw from the Veracruz academy and come home to care for his mother, but Vicki dictated a stern telegram forbidding him from doing so. She had asked Bruno to convey her apologies to their Texas kin but she could not bring herself to dictate a letter. She felt it was too unnatural, Bruno wrote, to tell someone what to write for her, felt it was too contrary to the personal nature of a letter, and she simply could not do it. She said she would understand if they should feel the same way about someone else having to read their personal words to her, and she absolved them from any obligation they might feel to continue writing to her. She had excellent caretakers who were never beyond range of her summon. Her great regret was that she had not learned to play a musical instrument and so could not entertain herself that way. She passed her mornings listening to the player piano, her afternoons sitting in the patio shade and, as she liked to say, letting the sensations of the world come to her, its smells and sounds, its feel under her feet and to her hands and face. In the evenings after dinner Bruno read to her. Poetry, novels, and—in much lower voice, lest John Samuel venture into the room while he was at it—letters from their Texas family. John Samuel had offered to read to her and Vicki thanked him but said she preferred Bruno to do it and gave no explanation. In private Bruno told John Samuel he hoped he was not in any way intruding on his prerogatives by reading to Vicki Clara. John Samuel assured him he was not, that he appreciated Bruno's help in making his wife comfortable as possible. He was unaware how clearly Bruno perceived his relief that he did not have to do it himself. Except when being read to, Vicki preferred solitude, even at mealtimes. She had joked to Bruno that what she needed was a blind friend, then wept and apologized to him for her self-pity. John Samuel would sit with her for an hour every evening before dinner, but if they ever had a conversation Bruno never heard them at it.

"God *damn* it," said James Sebastian.

"I agree," Blake Cortéz said.

CORRESPONDENCE

Marina continued to write Vicki a monthly letter with bits of family news, and the twins added a few words at the end of each one. Bruno would read the letters to her as many times as she wished to hear them. He kept his promise to her never to tell Marina or the twins of the tears the letters prompted from her blind eyes. If they find out they make me cry, she said, they may think it a kindness to stop writing.

—❦—

What neither the Mexico City doctors nor John Samuel told her was that the blindness had been caused by a cancer in her head. They believed the information would only add to her dejection. But as the severity of her headaches worsened, she knew—everyone knew—she was in a grave way. Her power of speech began to falter, then failed altogether, and she was reduced to communicating with chalk and slate until she lost the capacity to spell even the simplest words. She had trouble remembering things. The pain worsened by the day. She locked her jaws against the impulse to scream. Laudanum had been of help for a time and she took larger and more frequent doses of it until it was of help no more. The anguish of her final weeks beggared description. Her sightless eyes were monstrous bulges for the pressure of the growth behind them. Bruno would spare his Texas kin this detail and others even worse. At last, on a bright November afternoon, in answer to her prayers and to the blessed relief of everyone in the casa grande—as the open window admitted birdsong, the faint laughter of children playing beyond the patio walls, the insistent barking of a distant dog—she died. The entire hacienda turned out for the funeral. Not even at John Roger's requiem service, Bruno wrote in a letter, had he witnessed such an outpouring of grief. Looking every inch a grown man in his cadet uniform, Juan Sotero gave the eulogy for his mother and then returned to Veracruz that evening. John Samuel placed a floral wreath atop the coffin before it was lowered in the ground but did not speak during the entire ceremony.

TRESPASSERS

During the final months of that year they were living off the last of the dwindled bank funds and were unsure what their next move would be. But they at last had the chance to investigate the smaller groves on their property east of Wolfe Landing. They discovered several more resacas, but saw no alligators in them. By the waning days of December they had explored all the groves but the east-most one.

Their map showed that this grove followed the river on a northward curve to about two hundred yards from the Boca Chica road before the river looped southeastward again. They set out at first light with their rolled bedding and camp gear on their backs and machetes in their hands. By mid-afternoon they had advanced through most of the curving length of the grove and could see daylight between the trees ahead, indicating a clearing at the river bend. Then they heard voices—and they stopped and stood fast.

They listened hard. Men laughing. Speaking in Spanish. Somebody telling of a fight in a Matamoros cantina and involving a woman named Carla. They set their packs down and eased forward as soundless as cats to the edge of the clearing. Some ten yards away a mule-drawn wagon stood near the riverbank and three men were taking wooden cases from it and stacking them on a raft with railed sides and moored by a line to a stake in the bank. A large tarp lay heaped beside the wagon and there were only a few cases left to unload. The logos on the cases identified their contents as bottles of James E. Pepper bourbon whiskey. On the far bank was another wagon and three more men, one of them holding a rope that slacked into the water and reappeared near the outer end of the raft, where it was attached. The men loading the raft were mestizos, one of them bigger than the twins. He and another one had holstered pistols on their hips and the third man looked to be unarmed. The twins looked at each other and nodded.

They came out of the palms in quick soft stride, Colts in one hand and machetes in the other, and closed to within twenty feet of the men before someone on the other bank shouted a warning and the three on this side turned and saw them. One of the armed men threw off the mooring line and jumped onto the raft and ducked behind the stacks of cases. The big man grabbed for his pistol—and in a move he had practiced a hundred times, Blake Cortéz flung his machete overhand and it flew in a lateral blur and transfixed the man's lower torso, several inches of the pointed end jutting from his back just below the ribs. The man grunted and his half-drawn gun tumbled from its holster and he clutched both hands around the machete blade and fell to his knees and then onto his side, cursing through his teeth. James Sebastian pointed his Colt at the unarmed one, who already had his arms straight up and now yelled "No me mates! No tengo arma!" James told him to sit on the ground with his hands under his ass, palms down. He jabbed his machete into the ground and picked up the fallen man's revolver and slipped it into his waistband.

Blake stood on the bank, holding the Colt down at his side, and watched the raft being pulled across by two of the men while the third held a rifle half raised and kept his eyes on him. The man on the raft was watching him too, still crouched behind the cases and peering over them. Blake tucked the Colt into his pants and the man on the raft stood up and holstered his pistol too and the one on the bank lowered the rifle. The raft was almost to the other side when Blake turned to the fallen man. He seemed smaller than before and his curses had thinned to a low muttering. The machete had severed an artery and the ground under him was red muck. Blake stood over him and the man stared back, eyes wide, breathing in shallow gasps, brown face paled from the loss of blood. He tried to speak but could not. Then died. Blake sat beside him and took hold of the machete handle with both hands and placed his feet against the man's chest and to either side of the blade and with a hard yank extracted it, falling on his back. He sat up and wiped the blade on the man's pants and lobbed the machete to James, who stuck it in the ground beside his own. Blake searched the man's pockets, rolling the body to one side and then the other, and found a fold of American currency. He stood up and counted it and smiled. Across the river the raft was mooring, the three men making haste to transfer its cargo to their wagon.

Blake went over and stood beside James Sebastian. The prisoner looked from one to the other the way everyone did at the first close sight of them. "He know English?" Blake said. James said he didn't think so but he might fake that he didn't. Blake smiled at the man and brandished the money and said, "Para el whiskey, no?" The prisoner nodded. He asked if they were going to kill him. Blake put the money in his pocket and said, Let's start with *our* questions.

The man told them everything they asked to know and more. His name was Anselmo Xocoto. He was twenty years old. For the past eight months he had been working for Evaristo Dória, a smuggler who took things across the river in either direction. Mostly liquor, whiskey to Mexico, tequila and mescal to the United States. This was one of the best spots for smuggling between Brownsville and the gulf because it was close to the Boca Chica road but well-hidden from it and the ground here was much firmer than almost anywhere else along the lower part of the river. There was a curving gap through the palms, a sort of natural trail wide enough for a wagon. Everybody called the place the Horseshoe because of the shape of the river's loop here. Evaristo had won control of it about a year ago after a war with some other smugglers, but he himself no longer came out on any of the jobs. He had a couple of men who took turns making the actual transactions. Well, only one now, Anselmo said, glancing at the dead man. Anselmo was the helper. There was no regular schedule for the transactions. Sometimes they did two or three in a month, but once they went two months without doing any. Almost all of Evaristo's dealings were with the Goya brothers in Matamoros. If there were others, Anselmo didn't know who they were. He described Evaristo as dark-skinned, about forty years old, tall for a Mexican and on the skinny side, with a thick mustache to the corners of his chin. He had a wife and children and lived at the west end of town.

They told him he could bring his hands out from under his ass, and Anselmo rubbed them to help restore the blood flow. Blake informed him that this spot he called the Horseshoe was now part of their property and if Evaristo wanted to keep using it for his business he would have to come to some arrangement with them. He and his brother would like to meet with him to discuss it. Would Anselmo be seeing him tonight? Yes, yes, Anselmo said, breathless with relief that they were not going to kill him. After every job he had to take Evaristo the money received for the goods. Remembering the money, Anselmo again looked fearful. He will want his money, he said. Tell him we'll talk about the money when we meet, Blake said. Tell him Berta's Café in the Market Square, tomorrow morning, eight o'clock. Lots of people around, no place for trouble. Yes, Anselmo said, yes, he would tell him. They said he could go and James Sebastian helped him to his feet. Anselmo stared at the dead man and Blake said, We'll take care of that. Anselmo nodded and went to the wagon and climbed up onto the driver's seat. There were still four cases of whiskey in the wagon bed and he looked at them and then at the twins. You keep them, Blake Cortéz said. Anselmo smiled for the first time since the twins had come into his life. "Gracias, jefes," he said, and took up the reins and raised a hand in farewell, then hupped the mules into motion and the wagon clattered away.

They thought of dropping the body in the river but decided against it. Best not to chance anyone finding it, not with a living witness who knew how it came to be dead. They fashioned a carrying pole and ripped the sleeves off the dead man's shirt to tie his hands to one end of the pole and his feet to the other and bore him to Wolfe Landing as they would a killed deer. It was full night when they got there. They built a campfire and lighted a torch and then shouldered the carrying pole again and conveyed the body to the resaca. And there did as before and tied the body to the rope attached to a tree and set it in the water and gave it a shove away from the bank. The rope would let them know if it were taken.

And when they checked at first light the next morning before mounting up and leaving for town, they found it had been.

MISTER WELLS

Berta's was crowded and loud, as on every morning. The café was owned and operated by a family named Hauptmann. It was the most popular breakfast place with the town's Anglos, but a number of Mexican businessmen and ranchers were regular patrons too, men who had more in common with Anglo ranchers and merchants than with Mexican laborers. The twins wore suits and ties, and like other men in the room they carried guns under their coats. They had made it a point to arrive early so they could have the rear corner table. It afforded good views of both the front door and the passageway to the kitchen, where the back door was.

At five minutes before eight, there entered a stocky Anglo of middle years with a big broom mustache and wearing a cattleman's hat. He paused by the front wall and scanned the room as he received a chorus of greetings, some hailing him as Jim and some few addressing him as Mr Wells.

The twins knew who he was. It was Marina's custom to save the daily newspaper for them to read on the weekends and they had seen Jim Wells's picture in its pages many times. On some Saturdays they had seen him driving his cabriolet along Elizabeth as he commuted between home and law office, trading waves with friends as he went. The basic facts about his life were well and widely known. He'd been born and raised on a ranch near Corpus Christi and earned his law degree in Virginia. He came back to Texas and settled in Brownsville and became law partner to a man twenty-six years his senior and with the fitting name of Powers. An easterner with a New York law degree who once served as an American consul to Switzerland and had a gift for languages and for making and keeping friends, Stephen Powers had been living in Brownsville since right after the Mexican War. He had at various times been mayor of the town, a Cameron County judge, a district judge, a member of the Democratic state central committee, a state representative, and a state senator. To say he was the most powerful man in Cameron County was akin to saying the sky was blue, and if Jim Wells could not have had a more suitable mentor in the four years of their partnership before Powers's death, Stephen Powers could not have had a more brilliant protégé. Moreover, when Wells married Powers's niece, Pauline Kleiber, he joined an august circle of prominent families into which Powers himself had wed.

Powers's specialty was real estate law, and Wells fast became as expert as his partner in land grant litigation. Their firm's clients included Mifflin Kenedy and Richard King, who owned the largest cattle ranches in the state and were part of a coalition Powers had formed of the region's most important ranchers, fewer than a hundred of whom owned almost all of Cameron County—which in that day stretched a hundred miles from the mouth of the Rio Grande up to Baffin Bay. This alliance of ranchmen was the core of Powers's political strength. Each ranch employed hundreds of mestizos who would in any election cast their votes as their bosses directed. Like all mestizos in South Texas, regardless of their actual nationality, the ranch workers were all of a category and called Mexicans—"my Mexicans" by the ranchers who employed them—and if some or even most of them who voted were not American citizens, well, who could prove it in a rural world largely devoid of birth certificates? On their arrival in Texas the twins had recognized that the relationship between a rancher and his mestizos was not much different from that of a Mexican hacendado and his peons. A relationship that had developed, after all, from the same cultural traditions.

In return for Powers's protection and promotion of their interests in the state capital, the ranchers delivered their workers' votes to whichever candidates he pointed. It was a form of political brokering as old as the republic, and Powers was a master of it. And Jim Wells became a wizard. He was as affable as his partner, but having grown up on a cattle ranch he was one of the ranchers' own and hence even more adept at dealing with them. He knew their ways, talked like they did, was given to the same gestures. But in his rapport with the peons he had no Anglo equal. Like Powers he was fluent in Spanish and familiar with Mexican culture and respectful of Mexican traditions, and having converted to his wife's Catholic faith, he shared the peons' religion. More than any other Anglo of authority, Jim Wells had a genuine concern for the local Mexicans, and they recognized his sincerity and repaid it with steadfast personal loyalty. He knew hundreds of them by name, and in times of want provided for them from his own pocket. He defended them in court for a nominal fee, when he charged them anything at all. He got them out of jail with reduced fines and sentences. He visited with them in their homes and played with their children and was a godfather many times over. Many a Mexican child had been named in his honor—Santiago or Jaime or Diego. The peons venerated Wells as a patron saint and not even their employers had greater sway with them. When Señor

Wells—or Don Santiago, as he was widely known—said he would be grateful if they would vote for a particular political candidate, so did they vote. In the thirteen years since Stephen Powers's death, Jim Wells, who had never held public office except for a brief stint as Brownsville city attorney, had expanded the political machine he inherited from his partner and enhanced its operation. His influence now reached not only to the Texas capitol but to the Washington offices of Texas congressmen he had helped to get elected. El jefe de los jefes, the Mexicans called him.

But to see him standing by the café wall and surveying the room, his hat pushed back and his hands in his pockets, you might have taken him for a grocer or a hardware dealer—albeit a popular one, to judge by all the invitations he received to join one or another table. He declined them every one with a smile and small wave. Then his gaze fixed on the twins across the room and he started toward them, still swapping hellos as he went. "Well now, what's this?" Blake Cortéz whispered.

Some of the other patrons turned to see who Mr Wells was headed for and saw it was those Wolfe twins nobody could tell apart and who you hardly ever saw in town but on the week's end. Been building a house in that downriver palm swamp for well-nigh three years on account of they were doing it all themselves, if you could believe that, which was about as crazy as building a house out there in the first place. Said to be from Galveston. Their daddy some kind of bigwig diplomat down in Mexico till him and their momma got took by the yellow jack. Elmer at the bank said they come with scads of money but had near spent the last dollar of it, what with their Mex wives and children and a house in town to support besides building the one in the swamp. Oh, they were finelooking young fellas, no disputing that, and always good to return a howdy and a smile. But you had to admit that none of them—meaning their wives too—were given to passing the time of day. Pleasant and all if you ran into them at the market or the bank but always ready to move along. Odd clan, truth to tell. What would old Jim want to see *them* about?

"Howdy boys," Wells said as he got to their table. He looked from one to the other. "Had to see for myself if you the spittin images I been told. Begosh if you aint. About as hard to believe as we never met in all the time you been here." He put his hand out. "Name's Jim Wells." They each shook his hand in turn and said their names. He asked if he could join them and they both glanced at the wall clock. In a voice that couldn't be heard at the nearest tables, Jim Wells said, "Evaristo aint coming, boys. I'd be obliged if yall could spare me a minute."

The twins looked at each other and then back at him and said of course and pardon their manners and asked him to join them. Wells hung his hat on the ladderback chair and sat himself so that he could easily shift his attention between them. "I mean to say, you fellas are the twinnest twins I ever saw." A few of the curious were still eyeing them, but when Wells glanced their way they cut their attention elsewhere. "I take it you know who I am?" Wells said, again pitching his voice not to carry beyond their table.

"Yessir," Blake Cortéz said, muting his own voice. "Doesn't everybody in here?"

Wells's mustache widened. "I suppose they do." His eyes were bright with bonhomie and crafty intelligence. "I know about you boys too. Leastways I know what-all you've told folk and what they have to say about you. Speak good Spanish, they say, on account of you grew up in Mexico. I can see I was told true about your proper manners."

In fluent Spanish with only a trace of accent, he said, But I don't believe there are many people who know that at least one of you might—I emphasize *might*—be able to throw a machete through a man some twenty feet off. It's something I heard tell, but it's mighty hard to believe. His smile and manner did not alter. To anyone glancing their way he could have been relating an amusing anecdote.

The twins wondered whether he had talked to Anselmo, or to Evaristo after *he'd* talked to Anselmo.

Well sir, Blake said, I don't fault you for finding it hard to believe. Because *if* such a thing actually happened, it would probably have been more like ten feet.

If such a thing actually happened, James Sebastian said.

"I see," Wells said. "Well, let me just say that *if* such a thing actually happened, even at ten feet, I'd be mighty doggone impressed." As they would soon come to realize, Jim Wells almost never used profanity in either language—and, like themselves, he could shift from folksy vernacular to formal diction whenever it suited him. He again reverted to Spanish. Of course, if anybody wanted to try to prove such a thing actually happened, first thing he'd have to do is produce a body, or at least a witness more reliable than, oh, the employee of a smuggler, say. But I would bet that *if* such a thing actually did happen, the body would probably already be somewhere beyond all possibility of recovery.

That would be my bet too, James said. He and Blake smiled back at him. He was as genial as they'd heard. He piqued their curiosity.

"Look here, boys, I hope you'll pardon my bluntness, but there's something I have to know and I want you to tell me true. You on the run from the law? I mean real law, American law." They would have smiled to learn that his curiosity had already prompted him to make telegraphic inquiries of sheriffs' offices all over the state, seeking to know if they had warrants on either James S or Blake C Wolfe.

"No sir, we aint," James said.

Wells nodded. "Good, good. Well now, let me just say, I never take long to make up my mind about somebody, and I have a feeling that neither do yall. I'd like us to speak frankly, so what say we quit being coy about that riverside business and let's agree that whatever gets said between us stays between us. You have *my* word on it. I got yours?"

Again the twins swapped a quick look. Then Blake Cortéz said, You do, sir. Despite the man's casual fostering of trust, they had read his eyes and knew he was not one to ever tell anybody anything incriminating, not in any way that didn't allow for easy legal refutation should that need later arise. But then of course they would as always keep their own secrets and they sensed that Wells knew it. And sensed too that what mattered to him wasn't whether a man kept secrets but that he knew which secrets to keep.

"I'd say call me Jim," Wells said, "but my momma raised me to respect my elders and I expect yours did likewise."

He did all the talking for the next quarter hour. He told them Evaristo wasn't coming because he hadn't received their invitation. Rather than go to Evaristo after leaving the twins, Anselmo had gone to Wells. He had once worked for Wells as a stable groom, and though they hadn't seen much of each other since then, Anselmo believed Don Santiago was the only one who could help him. He told Wells what happened at a smuggling site called the Horseshoe and that he was sure Evaristo would kill him for not bringing him the money for the whiskey. He was willing to be arrested and put in jail where he might be safe. Wells said that wouldn't be necessary and let Anselmo take refuge in his carriage house. But what to do about Evaristo? Anselmo hadn't told them Evaristo was a lawman, had he? Well he was. A constable. A constable who had become a problem. "And there's nobody to blame for that but myself," Jim Wells said, "since I was the one to recommend him for the job." A constable was an elected office but a Wells recommendation so surely determined an election it was tantamount to an appointment, and his deputy recommendations were routine hires. The legion of law officers who owed their jobs to Jim Wells included sheriffs, police chiefs, and even Texas Rangers.

But in South Texas a constable had a special duty. Wells said that, loosely speaking, the Cameron County sheriff took care of trouble on the ranches, the police took care of trouble in the towns, and it fell to a relative handful of constables to take care of trouble among the countryside Mexicans—most of whom lived in squalid little settlements called colonias, places you'd never find on any map on account of they weren't official settlements. What's more, few colonia residents could speak English, and most Texas lawmen, like most Texans, didn't know more than a few words of Spanish, a lack that was of major hindrance in dealing with trouble in the colonias. Which was exactly why almost everybody Jim Wells ever recommended for a constable's post was Mexican—because next to the necessary sand for the job, the chief requisite was Spanish. It was a hard job but it had its advantages. For one thing, because a constable had to work so far out in the brush so much of the time, so far from towns and courtroom, he had a lot of leeway in how he operated. It was no secret that for most crimes short of murder a constable was a lot less likely to arrest a bad-acting Mexican than to fine him and send him on his way with a warning, and then pocket the fine. If the man didn't have enough money for the fine, he might pay with something else of worth. Because a bad actor would usually rather pay a constable than go to jail, it worked out for both of them, and for the county too, since it didn't have to cram its jail full of Mexican troublemakers and burden its courtroom with their cases. Of course, if a fella did something just *too* wrong to be let off with a fine, the constable would bring him in. Unless of course the hardcase was too drunk or too ornery or too stupid to know not to make a fight of it and left the constable no choice but to shoot him. That happened now and again and everybody knew it did. But there was hardly ever any to-do about it.

Evaristo had been a constable for four months now, and Jim Wells said the mistake he'd made in getting the man a badge had nothing to do with his being a smuggler. Along the southern Rio Grande a smuggler was about as commonplace as a carpenter and at least as beneficial to the community, and the only real difference between the smuggling business and most others was the rather more serious consequences of rival competition. No, the problem with Evaristo was that he was a rank bully with the people he was supposed to protect. Since Evaristo's appointment, Wells had received a load of complaints from various colonias about Evaristo beating up fellas for no good reason and taking gross liberties with women and stealing stock and so on. The folk were begging Wells to make him stop.

"Why not just take back his badge?" James Sebastian said.

"I could see to that," Wells said. "But then he'd like as not be meaner than ever with the folk on account of they complained on him. And it's not just him. Anselmo mention the two sidekicks? Evaristo calls them his deputies although they got no more legal standing as deputies than I do as brother-in-law to the Pope. One's named El Loco and the other Bruto, to give you some idea the kinda fellas we're talking about. Besides being his so-called deputies, they do most the smuggling jobs for him, one or the other usually working with Anselmo. The fella who got the machete throwed through him—*if* such a thing actually happened—that was Bruto. I'm told he's Evaristo's cousin."

Blake said, "This is interesting, sir, but, well, what's it got to do with us?" But they had been studying his eyes and were pretty sure what it might have to do with them.

"Why, son, I thought it might behoove you to know something about the fella you wanted to meet with this morning to, ah—how did Anselmo put it?—to try and make an arrangement with him about his using your land. And, as Anselmo says, to talk about the money you took off his recently deceased cousin. Have I been misinformed?"

"No, sir," said Blake. "We wanted to let him know that if he wants to keep doing business on our land, we think it only fair he give us a certain percentage of his profits."

"And to let him know the money from yesterday would be a sort of good-faith binder," James Sebastian said.

Wells smiled at one of them and then the other. "You don't believe for a minute he'd agree?"

"Well, sir, that'd be up to him," James said.

"I see. What will you do when he tells you to give him his money and go jump in the lake?"

"Tell him it's not his money anymore and we'd ruther stay dry," Blake said.

"I see." Wells beamed. "I have to say, you boys aint lacking in self-confidence."

In that moment, the Wolfe brothers and Jim Wells recognized in each other something they would none of them have known what to call except perhaps an affinity of outlook. An understanding that prompted James Sebastian to say, "If you don't mind my saying so, Mr Wells, it seems like the best solution to your problem with this Evaristo would be if he decided to light out to a new life somewhere else."

"Oh you're right, son, that'd be a blessing for sure."

"Well, it's the sorta thing happens all the time," James said. "A man just up and goes one day. Without so much as an hasta la vista to anybody."

"I've heard that some men do that, yes," Wells said.

"And of course if Evaristo lit out, he'd be taking leave of his river business," Blake said. "Be an opportunity for somebody who was looking to get into the trade."

Wells smiled at them. "I have to tell you, boys, I admire your, ah, eye for opportunity."

"When do you reckon Evaristo might head out in the brush again?" James said.

"Can't say. But if I was him and neither of my smugglers come back last night, first thing I'd do today is go to their house to see if they're there. If they weren't, and neither was the wagon—which it isn't, since it's at my house where Anselmo brung it—then I'd likely go out to that Horseshoe place to see what I might find there." Wells consulted his pocketwatch. "It's my guess he's probly already been to their houses and is on the way to the Horseshoe this minute."

-⧓-

They met them coming back on the Boca Chica road, less than a mile from the turn-off that led to the Horseshoe. They saw each other from a long way off on that open road and both parties reined their mounts from a lope to a trot as they advanced on each other. The short shotgun was slung muzzle down on James Sebastian's saddle horn and he had removed his coat and hung it from the saddle horn too so that it covered the gun. He patted his horse's neck and then slipped his hand under the coat and cocked both hammers. Blake's revolver was in his waistband and covered by the flap of his open coat. When the two parties closed to twenty yards, the twins slowed their horses to a walk and the other riders did the same and they reined up with less than ten yards between them. Evaristo was easy to recognize by Anselmo's description of his leanness and the droop of his mustache. The other wore his hat pushed back on his head and his grin seemed more permanent state than response and his eyes spoke of some restless eagerness. El Loco. Both men with revolvers on their hips. His eyes bespoke his recognition of them, los gringos cuates. And he had surely heard too of the house they had built somewhere out here.

"Buenos días, señor," Blake said. "Que bonito tiempo, verdad?"

Evaristo grinned to hear his Spanish. Yes, he said. The pity about fine weather, however, is that it never lasts long enough.

"Lo mismo como la vida," James said, reaching to pat his mount's neck and then sliding his hand under the coat.

Evaristo saw the move and reached for his own gun but before his hand could close on it the hung coat flung up in the shotgun's blast and the charge hit him high in the chest and batted him from the saddle. His horse was hit too and shrieked as it bolted. El Loco was raising his revolver when Blake Cortéz shot him above the eye and his hat jumped as he slung rearward, stirrups flinging, and landed facedown in an attitude of listening to some secret of the earth. Now Evaristo was raising himself on an elbow, red holes in one cheek and chest blood-sopped, again reaching for his gun. James reined his mount steady with one hand and with the other pointed the shotgun like an outsized pistol and with the second barrel of buckshot removed much of the man's head. At almost the same instant, Blake shot El Loco again, to be certain.

They calmed their horses and studied the road in both directions and saw that it lay empty to the horizons. They collected the men's guns and took the money from their pockets and then rounded up their horses and were glad to see that the wounds on Evaristo's mount were not so serious they would have to kill it. They draped the bodies over the horses and put the animals on a lead rope and rode back to westward for a distance before turning off toward the river and then onto the trail that took them through the palms to Wolfe Landing. There they put both bodies on El Loco's horse and took with them another rope and led the horse to the resaca.

IN THE GETTING

When the news got around that Evaristo Dória was missing, everyone who knew him was sure he was dead. Most likely in consequence of some dispute with a smuggling rival. You watch, people said, sooner or later he'll be found in the river reeds, or what's left of him by the fish and the turtles, unless he floated all the way out to the gulf.

For weeks after Evaristo's disappearance a gringo in a suit would show up at his house every Saturday to give Mrs Dória an envelope containing Evaristo's weekly salary. The man said his name was Smith and he worked for Mr Jim Wells, who had said to tell her he hoped her husband soon returned home and to please let him know if she needed anything. The whole neighborhood witnessed Mr Smith's Saturday visits, and Mrs Dória made it known who he was. They all knew that the county did not pay anybody for not working, and so the money had to be coming from Mr Wells's pocket, and they all said thankful prayers to God for putting them in the care of Don Santiago.

After three months went by without a word from Evaristo, Jim Wells himself called on Mrs Dória. He told her he was sorry but it was probably best to assume her husband wouldn't be coming back. He informed her that a bank account had been opened in her name and would receive a monthly deposit sufficient for her to take care of her children until they were of age or she remarried.

❦

"I have to say, she didn't seem all that distressed by the idea her husband might be gone for good," Wells told the twins. "Her only concern was the means to feed her kids, and now that's took care of. Anyhow, she's a right goodlookin woman, so I don't expect her children will be without a daddy too long."

It was a chill March evening and Wells and the twins were sitting with drinks and cigars before a low fire in his den. In the parlor, his wife Pauline and their thirteen-year-old daughter Zoe were entertaining the twins' wives and young sons while the family cook was preparing supper. In the three months of their acquaintance, the twins and Jim Wells and their families had supped together at the Wells' home several times, and there would be many more such evenings over the years to come. Suppers and small parties in the company of their families and occasionally with other guests as well. And there would be meetings too of just the three of them, at an hour when their families were abed, when the men would converse in muted voices and dim lamplight about topics privileged to themselves alone.

Only two weeks earlier, Wells had told the twins that his boyhood dream had been to become a man of influence and respect, and if he did say so himself he had achieved that aspiration and was proud of it. They knew he was mildly drunk—his drawl a little more pronounced—and enjoying the bourbon's liberation of sentiments he rarely voiced. "But I'll tell you the truth, boys," he said. "I'd give it all up in a minute if I could just be your age again. And I mean without a nickel in my pocket. All the money on earth aint worth spit compared to bein young and havin a dream to chase after. It's nice to arrive at it, no denyin that, but the real fun's in the gettin there. The *gettin there*. I cannot say how much I envy you. I expect you fellas have some dream of your own and I surely hope you attain it."

Blake Cortéz said that, for one thing, they wanted a house by the sea.

"Well heck, that's simple enough," Wells said. "Just build yourself one. Around Point Isabel probly the best place. Then you'll only have three houses—excuse me, I mean four. *That* your big aim? Own more and more houses?"

They had bought the lot next to the Levee Street house and were nearly finished with the house they were raising on it. Enlarged as their two families had become, and with Remedios Marisól expecting her third child in the summer, the house they shared had become much too small and they decided that each family would have its own, side by side.

The seaside house wasn't their big dream, they told Wells, but in thinking about a beach house they had come to understand what they really wanted. Instead of acquiring a separate gulfside property, the thing to do was to extend Tierra Wolfe to the gulfside.

"You mean to buy up all the land in between?"

"Yessir," James said. "The coast aint but about eight miles from our eastmost line as the crow flies."

"Make it sound like a stone toss," Wells said. "How far up you thinkin to go?"

"Nameless Creek. We figure it'd be best to keep the same north boundary."

Wells smiled from one of them to the other. "That's a smart of property, boys."

"A hankering for a little more land aint anything needs explaining to a cattleman," Blake said.

"Well, you're right about that, though I know dang well you aint about to raise cows out there. Fact is, a hankerin for more land don't need explainin to nobody. Some men know what they want it for before they get it and some don't know till after and some just want it to have it."

"That's right," Blake said. "And like a fella once said, it's the getting that's the fun."

Wells grinned. "Well, that aint *exactly* what the fella said but it's close enough. Tell me true, boys, you got a reason for wantin all that ground?"

"Well sir," James said, "I guess we'd just like to keep the world from crowding us too close."

Wells nodded. "Good reason as any." They could see he knew it wasn't the only reason or even the main one. But he'd come to know them well enough to understand they never explained anything to anyone until they were ready to, if ever they should be.

The cost of all that land would of course be great, and they had been forced into debt in order to buy the second Levee Street lot and the building materials. But their financial circumstance had very much brightened since they had taken up the smuggling trade. They'd gone to Matamoros with Anselmo and had him introduce them to the Goya brothers with whom Evaristo had done most of his business. The Goyas expressed no surprise that Evaristo was gone and did not ask to know the circumstances but were pleased to learn the twins would continue his trade at the Horseshoe. Two weeks later the Wolfes made their first transaction, receiving a wagonload of tequila at the Horseshoe and paying the Goyas for it with money they'd received for the *Marina Dos*. It had made them heartsick to sell the sloop but there would be other boats. Anselmo suggested a buyer he knew in Harlingen, thirty miles north. The proceeds exceeded what they'd received for the boat and, even minus Anselmo's share, were sufficient to let them pay off part of their debt and provide their wives with household money for the next several months.

They were confident they would succeed at the "river trade"—Jim Wells's preferred term for smuggling—though they knew it was a volatile business and could not be counted on for steady revenue. Their plan was to use most of the money from each smuggling deal to buy some of the land they wanted, even if they had to mortgage the more expensive parcels. They had spoken with Ben Watson at the White Star Company and he had been able to ascertain the titleholders to some of the land to either side of theirs, but legal ownership of other parcels was tangled up in land-grant disputes that had been in the courts for decades, and he was not optimistic about any of those cases being resolved soon.

When they told him of Watson's outlook, Jim Wells said, "Well, gents, in all modesty, I remind you that you are in the presence of the foremost legal mind in Texas with regard to land-grant law. If you'd like, I'll be proud to see what can be done to speed things up a bit and get them properties available."

"We were hoping you'd say that," Blake Cortéz said. They understood that he couldn't guarantee a quick resolution to every case. "However long it takes is how long it takes," James Sebastian said.

Jim Wells's smile was rueful. "Of course. No press for time when you're young."

Now, two weeks later, Pauline Wells called to them in the den that supper would be on the table in ten minutes. Jim Wells called back they would be there with bells on. Then said to the twins, "Listen, fellas, we all know how chancy the river trade can be. It wouldn't hurt if you also had a regular income of some sort you could count on for at least family money."

He took something from his coat pocket and placed it on the low table between their chairs. A pair of badges emblazoned with "Deputy Constable" along the top curve and "Cameron County" along the bottom.

"I spoke with the county bigwigs, and in their wisdom they have seen fit to offer you boys the job of special deputy constables. What's so special is you wouldn't be reporting to the constables' office but to me. Your reports would all be word of mouth and if I thought anything you told me warranted the attention of the sheriff's office, I'd let them know. Nothing else in your reports would go further than me. Now before you get any grinnier about it, I want you to hear me out. I been getting a lot of stories from the country folk about roughneck gangs. Seems all South Texas is crawling with little bands of bad actors. Fellas too dang lazy to work for a living and who think they're pretty tough because they can push around a lot of poor folk with no means of defending themselves. The folk say the constables are scared of the gangs, being outnumbered like they are. For sure they aint been getting the job done. I could ask the Rangers to help out, of course. They'll do me about any favor and they love shooting Mexican bad actors and bringing the bodies into town and laying them out in the market square to be gawped at. However, the Rangers aint kindly disposed to Mexicans of any kind, bad actors or not, and the poor folk got good reason to be as scared of them as of the gangs. I want somebody helping them folk they know is their friend. Somebody who's gonna protect them and attend to any meanness done them, and I do believe you boys might just be the fellas for it. You'll be responsible for all of the colonias in the county—all of them. From now on, the other constables will stick to dealing with the town Mexicans. Another thing is rustlers. They're actually the sheriff's job but if you run into them they're yours. Mexican rustlers were pretty bad all along the border till General Díaz took over down there and his Rurales pretty well put the boot to them, but not even the Rurales can stop them all. Anyhow, as for how you do the job and what profit you make off it besides your salary, that's your business. My only rule is to do right by the poor folk." He smiled. "So. Interested?"

They picked up the badges and pinned them under their coats. They all three chuckled. "Ought be fun," James Sebastian said. "Yeah," Jim Wells sighed. "It's one more reason I envy you." And they went to join their families at the table.

The residents of the colonias trusted them from the start, having learned that Don Santiago himself had assigned these indistinguishable twins to protect them. The twins of the gringo name and the gringo skin but who spoke borderland Spanish and carried themselves like Mexicans. Los Puños de Don Santiago, the colonia Mexicans called them. The name got around and before long even some of the Anglos were calling them the Fists of Mr Jim.

They spent much of their time in the saddle, riding a circuit of the colonias. The residents of a colonia could take care of most of their own troubles but not against gangs or even the armed hardcase or two who sometimes showed up and lingered among them and ruled the place by brute force. Until the twins showed up. Any hardcase who brandished a gun at them the twins killed on the spot. Those who were smart enough to submit to arrest were divested of whatever money they had and the twins returned to its owners any portion of it that had been stolen and declared the rest of it a fine. They ordered the bad actors to leave Cameron County with the caveat that if they saw them again they would shoot off a kneecap. Of all those they banished in the early years, only four returned and all four suffered the promised punishment and were warned that next time they would be shot in the other knee and both elbows as well. Word of these punishments got around fast and not a man thereafter returned to Cameron County after being banished from it.

The kneecap punishment was part of a draconian code they devised for certain crimes and would be rigorous in prosecuting through all their years as backcountry lawmen. Any man who deliberately harmed someone weaker than himself—a woman, a child, an old man, a cripple—would be maimed in one foot and told that next time it would be the other. Thieves were ordered to make restitution and in addition their thumb was cut off. A second conviction cost them the rest of the hand. A third—and there would never be a single case of a third—would cost them both eyes. Captured rapists were brought back to the colonia and turned over to the family of the victim so it could extract its own rough justice without condition except for the obligation to bury the remains. Accused murderers were made to stand trial in the particular colonia where the killing had occurred. The twins sat as judges. If the evidence was insufficient to convict but the accused was nevertheless perceived as a threat, the twins exiled him under penalty of being shot if he came back to Cameron County. The guilty were hanged from the nearest suitable gibbet.

When a colonia reported a raid by a passing gang, the twins went in pursuit. Once they caught sight of the bunch they would keep their distance and hold to the chaparral to keep from being spotted. When the men stopped to make camp the twins moved up closer on foot. If the bunch was a small one of five or six men, the twins took positions with a clear view of the camp and in the last light of day opened fire with the Winchesters and dropped the lot of them before they even knew where the shots were coming from. Larger gangs—few had more than a dozen men—were the more fun for being the more challenging. The twins would trail them too until they stopped for the night. At a wee hour they would sneak up to the camp and throttle the sentry and make swift work of cutting the throats of the sleeping men—each man waking in turn to the apprehension of his death underway but incapable of voicing his horror or crying an alarm. It pleased the twins to prove to themselves time and again that they yet had the skillful stealth they acquired as boys. Each time they put down a gang they would take whatever money and valuables they found on the bodies, whatever weapons were in good condition, whatever horses and saddles they deemed of salable worth. They sometimes trailed a gang into an adjoining county before it stopped for the night. Local lawmen who followed the black flocks of birds to the remnant carnage always had a good idea of whose work they were looking at but took no umbrage at the jurisdictional trespass. Less work for us, they said. On occasion the twins would track a gang even into Mexico and deal with it down there. As they were leaving the scene of one such incursion, they were set upon by a squad of Rurales and had to outrun them back to the border, riding double the last two hundred yards to the river after Blackie's mount was shot from under him.

In their earliest years on the circuit they did not meet with any rustlers despite Jim Wells's warning that they might. But they heard much about them in the colonias. And about their favored routes to the river and their special fords in the wildest riverside regions of Cameron County and its neighbor county of Hidalgo. So the twins expanded their circuit to include these isolate fords—and began to have run-ins with bands of cattle thieves. The best situation was when the rustlers simply abandoned the animals and sped away. The twins then took the herd across the river themselves and sold it and nobody on the Texas side was the wiser. When they met with thieves less willing to give up the cows but who preferred to avoid a fight if they could, the twins would offer to let them take the herd across in exchange for payment of half its worth. Some agreed and the twins made a tidy profit with no effort at all. But some objected to the rate as exorbitant, whereupon the twins would affect to negotiate, and then, at a practiced signal, pulled their revolvers and started shooting, and in moments the issue was settled. They hated to do it that way because it meant having to round up the cattle spooked and scattered by the gunfire. And because it obliged them to return some of the stolen steers to their owners in order to cover themselves in case the gunfight had been witnessed, or the bodies were discovered, as they often were. They would sell half the herd in Mexico and return the rest to the rancher who owned it. They would tell the man they had run into the rustlers at a ford and got in a fight and dropped most of them, but, sorry to say, a few made it to the other side and got away with some of the herd. They would apologize for their failure to recover all the cows, but the ranchers were always grateful to have even some of them back and were profuse in their gratitude. And they spread the word of the twins' fine work.

❈

They were often away from home for weeks at a time. But as the years went by and the incidence of crime in the colonias fell off they were able to return to their families more often and stay for longer periods. Marina and Remedios Marisól were always as relieved to see that they were unhurt as they were glad to have them home, and the children were always happy as pups at their return.

In June of 1896 Remedios Marisól added the first daughter to the two families, Victoria Angélica, and her father and uncle doted on her. She was three and a half years old when the world entered the twentieth century. Jim Wells was by then Judge Wells, having accepted a gubernatorial appointment to serve out the term of a state district judge who'd been obliged to resign. On the last night of 1899 he hosted a New Year's Eve party for a hundred friends and their families. The celebration took place in a large rented hall and on its lantern-lit surrounding grounds arrayed with picnic tables and bandstands and dance floors. Morgan James was a month shy of seven years old and attending the best school in the county—a Catholic school run by nuns—where the other boys would also be enrolled when they were of age. Harry Sebastian and Jackson Ríos were now five, César Augusto four. The boys wore suits and ties and everyone smiled to see them dancing with their mothers.

On each of the twins' respites with their families, the Wolfes always took supper at least once or twice with the Wells. And too, in the course of every visit home, there would be a stag barbecue at one ranch or another with some of Jim Wells's friends, most of them ranchers, but always a few politicians in attendance as well, plus the Brownsville marshal and the chief of police and a Texas Ranger or two. From one year to the next, more of Jim Wells's friends—men of power and experience and not easily impressed—became the twins' friends too.

❧

For his varied efforts on the twins' behalf, Jim Wells of course received something of great value from them in return, something more than their protection of the countryside peons, whose votes were the core of his political influence. Something he did not in fact ever actually *ask* for, not in so many words, but which they never failed to grasp as a request and never failed to fulfill. And for which service they always received an appreciative and generous remuneration. After each circuit of the colonias, they would as always meet with Wells in private and give him their report and usually that was that. Sometimes, however—not often, rarely more than three or four times in the course of a year—he would tell them about someone or other who was causing a problem for the regional party or for the coalition of ranchers or for some other association important to South Texas. Someone who had persistently rejected Jim Wells's every effort to arrive at some reasonable resolution to the problem, some sensible accommodation. "I tell you, boys," he said, "being reasonable is all the means we've got for getting along with each other in this world. A fella who won't be reasonable, who aint willing to compromise the least little bit, is about the biggest liability on God's green earth. Fellas like that, well, sometimes they don't leave you much choice about things, sad to say." In terms that no law court could ever construe as directive, Wells would say that a number of important people were of the same mind as his in wishing this person would cease and desist in the difficulty he was causing. Wells was never specific about the problem presented by the man under discussion, but the details were in any case irrelevant to the twins. They never said anything in response to his account of the troublemaker but only listened and nodded. Some days or weeks later, the man in question might be found expired in his bed with not a mark on him and hence presumed the victim of heart failure or stroke. Or sprawled neckbroken on the floor of his barn after a fall from his loft. Or drowned in a creek or the river after being thrown from his horse, which would be grazing nearby. And every time some such gadfly succumbed to some such natural cause and ceased to present a problem to Jim Wells and his associates, a thick sealed envelope bearing no mark at all would sometime in the night be left at the front door of one or the other twin's Levee Street home. Marina or Remedios was usually the one to find it and would pass it to her husband without remark. If the women intuited what was in the envelope or what it was for, they never said so, not even to each other.

⚜

Their constable duties left them scant time to attend to their smuggling business, so they hired Anselmo Xocoto to run it for them. Anselmo in turn hired as his assistants his younger brother Pepe and Licho Frentes, Pepe's best friend. The twins permitted the trio to build cabins at Wolfe Landing for their personal quarters, and in Anselmo's name they opened a bank account to be used strictly for the business. They bought such great quantities of whiskey at cut rates from suppliers in Corpus Christi that Anselmo and the boys were obliged to build a large separate shed for the storage of it. Their main buyers of Mexican liquor were also in Corpus Christi, buyers who in turn sold to clients in Galveston, Houston, New Orleans. The twins permitted Anselmo to arrange transactions with the Goya brothers and let him keep twenty-five percent of the profits and pay Pepe and Licho twelve and a half percent each. The remaining fifty percent was reserved to the twins, a share justified by their financing of the business and their ownership of the land on which it was conducted and, not least of all, by their readiness to defend their employees against any trouble, legal or otherwise. Each time they were home from a backcountry patrol they would go to Wolfe Landing for at least one night to consult with Anselmo about the river trade. Anselmo would review with them all the transactions that had taken place since their last visit and apprise them of pending deals. He would show them the account books and the inventory lists. All in all, he did a fine job, his helpers too, for which the twins would reward them with a bonus every year.

CULMINATION

The fifteenth of August, 1903.

She has been lying awake for hours when the first faint dawnlight shows in the window. She knows where he is. Knows that this one is not a one-time thing but that he has been seeing her for many weeks. Bad enough to be pitied for a wife whose husband hops from this one to that one to still another. But when he begins repeat visits to one, well, then it's no longer a matter of wanting to bed others but of wanting to share another's bed. That makes it something different. Something worse. Something she can no longer endure.

She cannot think anything she has not already thought many times before. Well, enough of thinking. She supposes she should write a letter to the grandchildren but the thought of explication is more tiring than she can stand. He has exhausted her. Let him explain.

She gets out of bed and strips and washes with thoroughness at the basin, avoiding even a glance at her slack breasts in early wither. Then puts on a black dress and her best shoes and sits before her mirror and brushes her hair to a fine loose hang and leaves it that way. Her flaccid flesh evidence of her fifty-three years but her hair yet the lustrous ebony of a girl's. She goes to the closet in his room and there finds the holstered revolver he long ago taught her to shoot. A single-action, .36-caliber Navy Colt he used in the days of the American Civil War. She checks the chambers and sees all six are charged. Then goes to his neatly made bed and lies down on her back. Legs straight, feet together, head on pillow, eyes on ceiling. She cocks the Colt and holds it in awkward fashion with the muzzle positioned against her breast and over her heart, her fingers around the back of the butt and one thumb against the trigger guard and the other on the trigger. She feels her pulse thumping up through the gun.

Wait a minute. Wait just a goddam minute. This isn't right.

She removes the gun from her breast and sits up. Sits motionless, pondering. Then gets up and straightens her dress and gives her hair another quick brush and drapes a shawl over her shoulders and takes up the gun and goes downstairs, holding the pistol under the shawl, her arms crossed as if against the morning chill. She leaves the house and goes across the main courtyard and out the gate into the larger compound that even at this early hour is already bustling.

She has rarely ventured into the workers' quarter, and she receives respectful but puzzled greetings as she passes. Induces whispers about her all-black attire and unpainted face and loose uncovered hair. She has been told where the woman lives and as she turns onto that street she is thinking that she will have to wait for a time before he comes out. And then almost laughs aloud when she spies the woman's house and sees her door come open and him step out. What timing. As though it had all been planned somewhere sometime long before now and she doesn't even have to think what to do but only let herself do it. She stops on this side of the street and watches as he turns to give the bitch a parting kiss. Then the door shuts and he starts in her direction. Smiling. His thoughts yet inside the house.

Now he sees her and halts in the middle of the street. Sees her raising the Colt—is that *his Navy?*—as others on the street are scattering, having seen the gun too. He raises his palms as if he might push away this entire circumstance or at the least fend the bullet and he has no idea what he is about to say and then is on the ground and breathless, the report of the pistolshot still in his ears. A numbness in his chest. He manages to get to one knee, regaining his breath in gasps, and feels a great inflating pain under his ribs. Dark blotches of blood forming in the dust below him, his hat on the ground. He leans back on a haunch, hand to his hot wound and sees her aiming even as she comes toward him. The next bullet smashes his shoulder and swats him half-about and onto his side.

She stands over him and says, "Mírame." He looks up and sees the small smile above the gun. Does he see the bullet emerge from the bore in the infinitesimal instant before it stains the ground under his head with the ruby ruin of his brain? She shoots him in the face three times more, until the hammer falls on an empty shell. Then drops the gun and looks about. Then in swift sure strides makes for a well at the end of the street and without hesitation goes into it headfirst.

At the corner of the nearest building, Catalina Luisiana Little, eight years old and given to roaming the compound in the early gray hours, witness to the whole thing, hears the deep resonant splash.

❈

By the time Zack Jack and John Louis have been summoned from the ranch, Gloria has been hooked out of the well and taken to the casa grande. Don Louis there too. The two bodies washed and covered with sheets to their chins. On adjacent tables in a room aglow with the amber light of scores of arrayed candles. Ancient women of dark fissured faces and dressed all in black are seated against the walls and loud in their ritual lamentations. Zack Jack and John Louis stand there for a time, looking on their elder brother. His face with four black holes. He whom they called Uncle Louis and who had taught them so many things in their boyhood. And who, as Gloria once told her sister, was more of a father to them than Edward Little had ever been. They regard too their sister-in-law who was Aunt Gloria and the only mother they'd known. Like everyone else of the hacienda except for their father, the brothers knew of Louis Welch's infidelities and that Aunt Gloria was pained by them. The outcome is no shock.

They send telegraphic notice to their father at Chapultepec but he is at his work somewhere else when the wire arrives and three days will pass before he reads it. By then his eldest son is buried. He tells Porfirio, who weeps. That evening they go to Las Lagrimas de Nuestras Madres but do not dance, only drink to the memory of Louis Welch Little and recount tales of him, begat fifty-eight years ago in Louisiana of a sixteen-year-old girl named Sharon.

The Little brothers also inform Bruno Tomás at Buenaventura, and Sofía Reina and María Palomina in Mexico City, none of whom have seen Gloria since the day of her precipitate marriage to Louis Welch Little thirty-six years before, nor ever met her husband. Bruno mourns for the sister with whom he had at last become familiar through their affectionate correspondence. Sófi and María Palomina are grieved to the bone. And yet, at the same time, Gloria having for years confided to Sófi—and thereby to María Palomina—the infidelities of Louis Welch, they cannot help but feel a guilty pleasure in her remedy of those injuries. From the day they met, María Palomina says, that gringo should have known that she was not a woman to mistreat. Well, Sófi says, he at least should have known it by the time they got married. And they laugh louder than they cried.

BRANCHINGS

For more than a decade the twins would smuggle only liquor and conduct transactions with no one but the Goya brothers in Matamoros and their regular suppliers and buyers in Corpus Christi. Contrary to their expectations, the river trade never slackened for more than a few weeks at a time, and there was never a period of as long as two months that it did not turn a profit. Together with their income from the intermittent cattle sales in Mexico and the sums in the occasional envelopes left at the door, it gave them more than enough money to buy the properties they wanted as they became available, no mortgages necessary.

They of course began their acquisitions with those parcels that already had clear title. Most of those were in the wilder country, eastward of Tierra Wolfe, and the owners were so glad to be rid of the worthless grounds that the twins were able to buy them at a bargain. Came a summer day in 1905 when they bought a tract that ran northward from the river mouth up to Boca Chica Pass and then along the east coast of South Bay up to Nameless Creek. The property was mostly a mix of marsh and scrubland, but its stretch of beach between the river and the pass was broad and dense with dunes along the higher ground, and the sea wind was a bracing contrast to the stifling humidity of Brownsville. Scattered about the riverside just off the beach were the weather-eaten foundations of former structures, the remains of a one-time boomtown port called Clarksville. According to Ben Watson it had been the wildest place on the border with the possible exception of Bagdad, a Mexican port directly across the river. Both towns had teemed with smugglers, bootleggers, fugitives, runagates, outlaws of every stripe, and so of course attracted gamblers and whores as well—and both had long since been obliterated by economic turns of fortune and a series of hurricanes. Marina and Remedios and the kids were agog when the twins showed them where the house would stand with its grand view of the gulf and the enormous gulf sky.

On each visit home during the next two months the twins spent time with a Brownsville architect, discussing with him exactly the sort of house they wanted. A two-story on twelve-foot pilings and large enough for both families, with roofed upper and lower porches in front and an unroofed lower porch in back. When the architect's plan at last met with their approval they went to the best builder in Brownsville and hired him to construct the house. Their plan was to live there in the summers while the kids were out of school and then move back into town during the school year and come to the beach house on weekends. While the house was being built, they hired another crew to excavate a horseshoe cove into the bank about fifty yards upstream from the river mouth and there built a dock large enough for several small boats.

They named the place Playa Blanca and moved into the house in the early summer of '06. The eldest child, Morgan James, was almost thirteen, and the youngest, Vicki Angel, had just turned ten. The youngsters all took to the sea like dolphins. Just beyond the small whitecaps, the water was a placid undulation, shallow and clear pale green all the way out to the sand bars. Any shark that crossed the bar could be seen while it was still a long way out. Marina had taught the children and Remedios Marisól how to swim in a resaca, but swimming in the gulf was far more fun, though it was a vexation to the boys that Vicki Angel was the fastest of them. When the twins said they weren't sure Vicki should be swimming naked with the boys, their wives laughed and hooted at them and called them evil-minded Yankee hypocrites, and the twins sheepishly retreated and said no more about it.

But then one day when the twins and Remedios were running errands in town, Marina went out on the porch and saw the children about fifty yards down the beach, standing in a group in water to their thighs, and she looked through the powerful telescope mounted on the porch rail and saw that the boys were exposing erections to Vicki, who sat in the water to her shoulders and looked both amused and uncertain. As Marina stalked down the beach toward them, the boys saw her coming and lowered themselves in the water, then came out at her beckon with not an erection in evidence. She told them there would be no more naked swimming when Vicki was with them and that if any of them ever did that again to her or any other girl, she, Marina, would tie their thing in a knot they'd never be able to undo.

She did not tell the twins about the incident but later asked Vicki if they had done that before, and the girl said no. Marina suspected she wasn't being truthful but did not question her further, not wanting to force her to lie. She knew that although Vicki would not let them boss her about, she loved them dearly and would never betray them.

In truth, the boys had displayed erections to Vicki a few other times, making a game of it they called Look at This. They almost always dared her to touch them, and she once did, a quick two-finger feel of César Augusto's, which was the smallest and least daunting. She had affected to be repulsed but was secretly fascinated. Still, there was something in their eyes when they played Look at This that scared her, and she had not touched one again.

❦

The twins bought a twenty-two foot sloop and named it *Gringa* and taught the boys and Vicki Angel how to sail it. They also instructed them in building their own boat, which they did, a fifteen-foot modified catboat with a centerboard. They named it *Remerina* in honor of both mothers. The twins taught them how to read the clouds and the wind and the different colors of the sea. How to fish for shark. And the beach was a good place for teaching them to shoot and for lessons in how to defend themselves with hands and feet. Marina and Remedios would sometimes sit on the shaded porch and watch the self-defense sessions with narrowed nervous eyes. Though the boys were of course bigger and stronger than Vicki Angel, she was the quickest and very nimble and was sometimes able to trip one of them down. One day she tripped Morgan James, who was the oldest and biggest, and when the others laughed he was furious with embarrassment. He pinned Vicki on the ground with a knee on her chest and tried to force a handful of sand in her mouth but she flung sand in his eyes and broke free and outran him down the beach until he gave up the chase.

❦

When Morgan James turned fourteen, the twins started teaching all their sons the river business. The ways and means of it, the finances and accounting methods, the recording codes, all of which the boys were quick to absorb. They began taking the boys in pairs and by turns on some of the smuggling transactions, instructing them to watch everything very carefully and questioning them afterward to see how well they had observed. They introduced them to the Goyas and to the buyers in Corpus Christi.

The twins never spoke to their wives about this training process, and the boys never said anything of it to their mothers. But Marina and Remedios of course knew it was taking place, as it had to, and if they thought the boys too young to be learning such things, they did not say so.

❦

The following summer the Goyas sent word to the twins that there were two men who wanted to talk to them and it might prove profitable if they did. At the Goya estate the twins were introduced to a pair of well-groomed mestizos who said their names were Yadier and Elizondo and their last names did not matter. They wore good suits in which they did not seem comfortable but they spoke well and were quick to the point. They wanted guns. Rifles. And ammunition of course. As many and as much as possible. The twins smiled. Blake Cortéz said it sounded like somebody was thinking of going to war. Against who, I wonder, James said grinning. The two men neither smiled nor answered the question. The word of late from across the river was that Porfirio Díaz's political enemies were still in mortal fear of him and keeping to the shadows, but there was a growing and bolder discontent in the countryside. Two years ago, Díaz had won reelection for the sixth time and had now been president for twenty-four consecutive years and twenty-eight of the last thirty-two. He was seventy-six years old but not about to step down—or stop using his club on those who rejected his bread.

The Yadier one said they knew the Wolfes had an excellent smuggling point on their property that permitted them to operate in great safety. The question, said the Elizondo one, was whether the Wolfes could get the guns and ammunition. Blake asked what kind of rifles they wanted. They said the new Springfields. Those could be a little hard to get, James Sebastian said. Of course, the Elizondo one said. That is why we will pay well for them. But naturally, we do not want to be cheated on the price. Naturally, James Sebastian said. The twins said they would see what they could arrange. They agreed to meet at the Goya estate again in ten days.

The twins made inquiries that led them to a Fort Brown master sergeant named Leonard Richardson, the NCO in charge of the post armory. Silverhaired and beefy, he was dressed like a rancher when they met at a corner table in a loud and crowded Matamoros cantina. Richardson knew about the twin constables by reputation. He'd heard of their law enforcement methods in the outland and the rumors of their sideline as liquor smugglers. He told them he had been dealing in army weapons for ten years and had suppliers from various army forts and other military installations throughout Texas and all over the gulf coast, every man of them an expert at reworking inventory ledgers to disguise the thefts. He could easily get them Mausers or Krags. The Springfield M1903 was of course a more difficult acquisition but he could do it for the right price.

"Which is?" James Sebastian asked.

Richardson told him—and was quick to admit it was steep, but then he was the most dependable provider they could hope to do business with. "Every delivery I ever said I'd make got made," he said, "when and where promised." He let them confer privately for the time it took him to go to the bar to get three more mugs of beer.

When he returned to the table they told him they had a different price in mind. Richardson sighed and started to say the price wasn't negotiable, but then heard one of them offer to pay ten percent more than what he'd asked—on condition that from then on he would sell Springfields to nobody but them. Richardson grinned and said they had a deal.

"You understand that if we should find out you're selling Springfields to somebody else, we'll look on it as a breach of contract," James Sebastian said.

"Such a breach would be unjust," Blake said, "and we have a strong belief in justice."

Richardson looked from one to the other. He had dealt with many dangerous men and was no fool. "I understand you very well, gentlemen," he said. "I have the same view of justice."

There were handshakes all around, a surreptitious exchange of money.

Six days later a pair of heavily laden wagons were turned over to them at two o'clock in the morning at the northern city limit. By daybreak the contents of the wagons were cached in the shed at Wolfe Landing.

The next time they met with Yadier and Elizondo the twins brought one of the Springfields for them to examine. The Mexicans were pleased, and they understood that, as a matter of precaution, the twins' supplier—Mr Jones, the twins called him—would never deliver more than one wagonload at a time but could deliver as often as every two weeks.

The twins would continue their traffic in booze but their main trade henceforth was guns, a far more lucrative commodity. Most of their arms transactions would be with Yadier and Elizondo, but there would be some with other parties too, few of whom had any political principle in common with each other besides antagonism to Porfirio Díaz.

❦

In the fall of '08, John Louis Little and his family arrived on the border. A yellow fever epidemic had struck Matamoros earlier in the year—Brownsville had been quarantined—and one of its victims was Úrsula's father. Úrsula and John Louis attended Don Hector's funeral and were afterward informed that he had bequeathed the cattle hacienda, Las Lomas, to his son Gaspar, and that Doña Martina would continue to live there. To Úrsula and John Louis, Don Hector had willed his sprawling horse ranch to the west of Matamoros. It was a fine place, its rich pasturelands nourished by a wide web of creeks, its large house well shaded by cottonwoods.

It was not easy for John Louis to take leave of Patria Chica. He had lived there all his life and for the past eight years had been his brother's segundo. But he was very happy to have his own ranch. Zack Jack said he hated to see him go but he understood why he must. Zack had an able man in mind to serve as segundo in John's place until young Eduardo Luis—Luis Charón's son—was seasoned enough to assume the job. Eduardo was only thirteen but already eager to start learning the estate's operations. Edward Little, too, told John Louis he would miss him, never mind the infrequence of their time together through the years. They promised to visit each other as often as they could, and Edward wished him luck with the Tamaulipas ranch.

For both Úrsula and John Louis it was a return to the region of their birth, though he was less than a year old the last time he'd been there. They named the ranch Cielo Largo. It was managed so well by the foreman and his segundo that there would never be much for John Louis to do except attend to its finances.

He knew he had kin in Brownsville—his Aunt Gloria's twin cousins, Blake and James Wolfe. Although she had never met them she had learned much about them from her brother, Bruno, who had been living at the Wolfe hacienda in Veracruz for twenty years. She had in turn told John Louis and Zack all about the twins, including the story of their killing the man who killed their father and escaping the assassin's vengeful brother, an army general.

One Saturday, just a few weeks after their arrival at Cielo Largo, John Louis and Úrsula went into Matamoros and ferried across the river and asked after the Wolfe brothers at the city clerk's office. They were directed to the two Levee Street addresses. As it happened, the Wolfe families were at Playa Blanca that weekend—except for the twins, who had remained in town for a meeting with Jim Wells. In shirtsleeves rolled to the elbows and with a cigar in hand, James Sebastian answered the knock at the door and saw a neatly dressed couple standing there, the man rugged-looking, brownskinned but green-eyed, the woman a striking mestiza. John Louis introduced himself and Úrsula in English and said he was looking for James and Blake Wolfe, who were first cousins to his sister-in-law Gloria Wolfe y Blanco de Little.

Two hours later, sitting at the kitchen table over their second pot of coffee, they were as easy with each other as if they'd been acquainted for years. The twins liked the Littles but were habitually chary about revealing very much of themselves. They were so artful about it that not until later would the Littles realize they had not really learned much about them beyond what Gloria had already told John Louis. Only that they were county constables and real estate investors and had homes in Brownsville and at the seaside, where their families were passing the weekend.

The twins, on the other hand, had learned a great deal not only about the Littles and their kin but even about their own. Such as their Uncle Samuel having been a San Patricio, one more detail their father had withheld from them. And about the death of their cousin Gloria and the circumstance of it, which evoked a smile from Blake Cortéz both sympathetic and admiring. "Wish I'd known *her*," he said.

James Sebastian wanted to know if it was true the Little family was friends with Porfirio Díaz, as they'd been informed. John Louis said it was.

"You know him yourself?" Blake said.

"Only all my life," John Louis said. His father had known Díaz for some forty years and still worked for him.

"Doing what?" Blake asked.

John Louis shrugged and said that was something known only to his father and Porfirio Díaz.

"Sounds mighty damn mysterious," James Sebastian said with a grin. And quickly added, "Pardon my language, Miss Úrsula."

She smiled and said, "Please, no more Miss Úrsula. I am Úrsula or Sulita, as you prefer. And you are damn well pardoned." Evoking laughter from them all.

⸺❀⸺

They were quick to grow close, these border branches of the families Little and Wolfe. Marina and Remedios welcomed Úrsula with sisterly camaraderie, and their children regarded Hector Louis as one more brother in the bunch. Persuaded that the school the Wolfe boys attended was the best in the region, John Louis and Úrsula decided that Hector should also go there, and to make it easier they bought a house in Brownsville, a brick two-story on a large corner lot on Palm Boulevard and only a three-block walk to the Wolfe homes. The first time the Wolfes visited the Littles in their new residence, Hector Louis and César Augusto got into a fight in the backyard, the cause of which was never made clear. The adults came out of the house to see what was happening and found the other boys yelling fight strategies now to one combatant and now to the other, Vicki Angel looking on with them and with as much avidity. César was nearly two years older than Hector Louis and much better versed in fighting, but Hector was slightly larger and had no lack of courage or verve. Úrsula wanted to stop them but Marina put a hand on her arm and restrained her with a shake of the head. The men let them punch and grapple in the dirt for a minute longer before James Sebastian pulled them apart by the collars, declaring César the winner but telling battered Hector he had no cause for shame. The two boys thereafter became best friends, and César taught him how to fight but then was sorry he did, realizing too late that if they should ever fight again, bigger Hector would surely get the best of him.

The families made frequent visits between their Brownsville homes and between Playa Blanca and Cielo Largo, and the Wolfes greatly enjoyed the barbecues and rodeos at the Littles' ranch. The twins admired the excellent breed of John Louis's herds and introduced him to several serious buyers of horseflesh. As for the Littles, their first visit to Playa Blanca was their first view of the sea. They learned to swim there, all three of them, and to sail.

⸺❀⸺

Eventually the twins took John Louis to Wolfe Landing, their arrival heralded by the yappings of Anselmo's dogs, and introduced him to Anselmo and Pepe and Licho. Anselmo had now been married for three years and he and his wife Lupita had a two-year-old son named Costo, and Licho Fuentes was engaged to a girl named Selma. The twins showed him through the large house they had not used much over the years but that was well-kept by a crew of maids Pepe Xocoto transported from town once a week.

The twins and John Louis were seated on the verandah and finishing their third drink when they told him they thought he should know they sometimes did a little smuggling.

"Oh hell," John Louis said, "Suli and I have known that since our first meal in a Brownsville café. People talk, you know."

-◈-

The railroad had come to Brownsville in 1904, and with it a greater influx of Anglos, most of them in search of good cropland. More and more of the countryside continued to be cleared for agriculture, and small mestizo farms continued to give way to larger Anglo operations. More so than in any other part of the state, the mix of Mexicans and Anglos in the delta had long been harmonious, but few of the newcomers had any interest in local customs or in learning Spanish, and most of them disdained all things Mexican. Racial resentments had begun to simmer, then to boil.

In addition to these alterations to the natural landscape and the social fabric, there had come the inevitable transformations of technology. The telephone. Electric lighting. A sewer system. A waterworks. A trolley line. The changes came and came.

And the world spun ever faster.

-◈-

Over time, the twins had gradually reduced their colonia circuit rides to twice a year, which sufficed to maintain order in them, though sometimes a colonia would send a plea for help to Jim Wells who'd get the word to them and they would at once ride out to attend to the matter. Now they didn't want to do it anymore. They liked being with their families at the beach and they liked taking part in the gun transactions at the Horseshoe, as they had begun doing.

They tried to give their badges back to Jim Wells but he refused to accept them. He said they would no longer be required to ride the circuit, he would have other constables assigned to it. But he wanted them to remain special constables with no specific duty other than to be his "confidantes," as he called it, to be available whenever he should need to talk about somebody who was causing him a problem and refusing to be reasonable in settling it.

They said being his confidantes was the least they could do for him.

"Good," Wells said. "So keep the badges. They're a mighty handy thing for confidantes to have."

-◈-

The profits from arms smuggling dwarfed what they earned from liquor. They had been smuggling guns for more than a year when they bought the last of the parcels extricated by Jim Wells from the welter of land-grant litigation and achieved their goal of owning all the land—minus the state right-of-way to the gulf—east of the city and between the river and Nameless Creek. An area of some fifty square miles, depending on the Rio Grande's unpredictable and ever-shifting meanders.

Shortly after that final deed came into their hands, they told Jim Wells they wanted one more thing.

"A *town*?" Jim Wells said. He grinned from one of them to the other. They were puffing cigars and sipping whiskey in his den and waiting to be called to Christmas Eve dinner with their families, after which Wells and his wife and children would attend the midnight mass at the Immaculate Conception Church, as they did every Christmas.

"Yessir," Blake Cortéz said. "You always wanted to know what our big plan was. Well, that's it."

The three had been talking of the state's intention to form several new counties in South Texas in the next few years, and Blake asked if it was true that one of the new counties was going to be named Jim Wells. "I've heard that rumor," Wells said, as though he had no inkling at all. "If it happens, it'll be an honor." They all laughed and had another drink. Then the twins told him of wanting to make Wolfe Landing a town.

"Let me get this straight," Wells said. "You want Wolfe Landing to be a bona fide *town*. A state-chartered town. Out there in the middle of that godforsaken land nobody owns but you?"

"Yessir," James Sebastian said.

"And of course the state would get the right-of-way for a road to it from off the Boca Chica Road," Blake said. "Can't have a town without a public road to it, naturally."

Wells looked at them as if not quite sure they weren't joking.

"You know we've always wanted to keep the world from crowding in too close," James said. "What better way than live in a town in the middle of your own land?"

"Which would pretty much make it *your* town," Wells said.

"Well, I suppose you could say it's our town in the sense that we're its founders, yessir," Blake said.

"Every town had to be founded by *somebody*," James said.

"Your town with *your* laws."

"Well naturally there's got to be laws, same as in any town," Blake said. "Municipal ordinances and the like. For the protection of the community. For the sake of economic progress. Heck, Judge, nobody knows that better'n you."

"You already got the petition papers all writ up, aint you?"

Blake tapped his coat pocket. "Every i dotted and t crossed, yessir."

Wells laughed. "You boys. You make it sound so goldang easy."

"It will be, sir," James Sebastian said. "If *you* push for it, it'll be easy as pie."

"Especially when the state's about to charter all these counties," Blake said, "and one of them to be named in your honor's honor." He grinned.

"I mean, how much trouble would it be to throw in a charter for one little-bitty town?" James said. "At the request of the esteemed James B Wells?"

"If anybody can do it, Judge, you can," said Blake.

"You two think way too much of me."

"Now don't be getting all modest on us, your honor," James Sebastian said. "We known each other too long."

Wells smiled and stared into his nearly empty glass.

"What say, Judge?" Blake said.

"You're aware that there will be, ah, some requisite political contributions? To certain personnel on certain state committees."

"Of course," James Sebastian said. "Just let us know how much and when."

Wells emptied his glass and smacked his lips. "Well heck," he said. "I suppose I could talk to some people, see what happens."

Pauline had to come to the door and rap hard on it more than once to get their attention and tell them to hush all that whooping and braying laughter before the neighbors thought they were drunk as coots on the Good Lord's birthday.

⁂

It took almost a year but Wells did it. He received the official decision shortly after Thanksgiving but he kept it to himself till Christmas Eve because it seemed fitting to him that they should be notified exactly a year to the day after making the proposal. And in the same setting and circumstance—his den, waiting to be called to dinner. As their families socialized in the parlor and kitchen, Wells poured drinks for the twins, but when they raised their glasses to him he said, "Just a second, boys. I got something here yall might want to drink to." He took a bound copy of the charter out of the top drawer and placed it on the desktop. "Merry Christmas, muchachos."

They saw the bureaucratic insignia and the embossed image of the lone star and knew what the packet was. They looked at each other and then grinned at Wells.

"This aint the end of it, is it?" Wells said. "You think I don't know what all you got in mind for down the road?"

"Why, Judge, whatever do you mean?" Blake Cortéz said in mock bafflement.

"What you aiming to call it? Something modest, no doubt. Wolfe County, maybe."

"Whoa there, your honor, now don't go getting too far ahead of us," James Sebastian said.

"Ahead of you two?"

They all laughed. The twins raised their glasses and James Sebastian said, "Muchísimas gracias, your honor."

"De nada, fellas," Wells said. "Here's to the newest town in Texas and its whole handful of residents!"

"A handful for now," Blake Cortéz said. They drank to Wolfe Landing, to their health and long lives.

The charter for the township of Wolfe Landing would go into effect in the coming May, two months after the birth of Jim Wells County.

CRIES OF LIBERTY

They have been careful to spare his tongue, his power of speech, though his screams have abraded his voice to a raw rasp. No tooth remaining in his head. Only one eye. Two fingers left to each hand and not a bone unbroken in either foot. His crotch is red pulp. Edward Little arrives. Despite his eighty-one years he is erect and easy in his carriage and his lean frame and white suit imbue him with a ghostly aspect in the low light of the oil lamps. As always, he pauses just inside the door for the necessary moment to adjust to the smell. A fetor no man of them ever gets used to. He then goes to the table where the rebel lies strapped in his mutilated nakedness. The man's chest heaves. His wild red eye fixes on Edward Little looming over him. In a low, expressionless voice, Edward assures him that the pains yet in store for him will exceed everything he has so far known of pain, but it will still not kill him. That freedom will be a long time coming, Edward says. But I will promise it to you much sooner if you tell me where your associates may be found.

The man's lips work, his breath quickens the more. Edward bends closer to hear what he has to say, then nods and steps back. Now, the man gasps, kill me... for the love of God. Edward smiles at the expression. First I must assure that you have told me the truth, he says. He turns and goes, ignoring the man's rasping cry of *KIILLLL meee*!

He finds Díaz in his chamber and tells him what he learned. Very good, Díaz says. Have you assigned somebody? Edward says he has.

That same evening eight men are seated at a table in the basement of a house at the western edge of the capital, attending to the final details of their plot, when the door abruptly sunders and a clutch of men rush in with shotguns booming in yellow flares—and in seconds every man of the insurgents lies in a rent sprawl on the blood-sheeting floor.

On the night of the fifteenth of September of 1910, his eightieth birthday and the eve of the one hundredth anniversary of Mexico's declaration of independence, President Porfirio Díaz, uniformed in full splendor and having been reelected for the seventh consecutive time just three months earlier, stands on the balcony of the National Palace overlooking the gigantic zócalo blazing with electric lights and packed with two hundred thousand cheering capitalinos. Mexican flags everywhere, bunting of red, green, and white. Díaz clutches a pull rope attached to an overhead bell—the same bell rung in the village of Dolores by Father Miguel Hidalgo in 1810 and since moved to the National Palace by order of Díaz. At eleven o'clock Díaz yanks the pull rope and the bell's tolls reverberate throughout the center of the city, and in emulation of the cry of independence raised by the great Hidalgo, Díaz shouts "Viva Mexico! *Viva Mexico!* VIVA MEXICO!" And the zócalo resounds with the crowd's echoing bellows of "Viva! *Viva!* VIVA!" There follows a staccato eruption of colorful fireworks and then a frenzy of music, and the national celebration proceeds in full timbre.

Among the company with Díaz on the palace balcony are a number of federal officials and army generals and an elite squad of bodyguards under the command of Lieutenant Colonel Juan Sotero Wolfe Márquez. Some nine years earlier, Gloria Tomasina had shared with the Littles the news from her brother Bruno that her cousin Juan Sotero Wolfe, an artillery officer, had just received his degree from the army engineering college. Edward Little recalled the name a few years afterward when he and Díaz attended the army's annual fencing competition and were much impressed with the daring swordplay of one Captain Juan Wolfe, who was barely defeated in the championship match by a cavalry major who won for the third year in a row. A little *too* daring, that Wolfe fellow, Díaz said, but I admire his style. When Edward told him the Wolfe fellow was Gloria's cousin, Díaz chuckled and said, Well hell, no wonder he fights the way he does, he said, with the same blood as Gloria's. Then remembered the deaths at Patria Chica the year before and added, No disrespect to Louis. I know that, Edward said. After pinning the victor's medal on the cavalry major, Díaz congratulated Captain Wolfe on his fine showing and asked him to come see him the next day. The interview lasted half an hour and concluded with Juan Sotero's acceptance of Díaz's offer to join his squad of personal guards. He's an engineer and likes it, Díaz told Edward, but he's a good man who puts duty first. Edward wasn't sure an engineer was a good choice for a bodyguard, but then the military guards were mostly for show, while the president's real protectors were plainclothes secret policemen under Edward's authority. Two months later, at the annual dinner Díaz hosted for the Rurales in the best restaurant in the capital, a drunk Rurales colonel walked up to Díaz's table saying, My president, I have something for you—and reached for a pistol on his hip. Edward's agents had their guns only halfway drawn before Juan Sotero materialized like a magic trick between the colonel and the president's table with his saber brandished and its tip at the colonel's throat. The colonel froze, white-eyed, as Juan Sotero relieved him of a pearl-handled Peacemaker. It turned out the colonel had taken the gun from a bandit chief and simply wanted to give it to the president as a gift. Díaz thanked him for it and everyone had a good laugh and the party resumed. And Díaz looked sidelong at Edward and said, Some engineer, and Edward smiled and nodded.

Now six years since, Juan Sotero Wolfe is a colonel and has been commander of the president's military bodyguards for the past three years. His wife of two years, Estér Leticia Hernandez, is a striking Creole poet with eyes as black as her hair, and her charged romantic verse has been published in the capital's most distinguished literary journal—to the chagrin of her straitlaced parents. The young Wolfe couple resides in a fine house near the south end of Avenida Reforma. Their first child, Juan Román Wolfe Hernandez, was born in July. Their second, Carlos Sebastián, will be born next March.

-❀-

The month-long celebration of the centennial of Mexican independence includes sumptuous dinner parties at the National Palace and lavish balls at Chapultepec Castle. Parades upon parades. The celebration is no less a tribute to Porfirio Díaz, whose presidency has now encompassed thirty of the past thirty-four years and in which time he and Mexico have become inseparable concepts. The festivities are attended by international dignitaries bearing gifts and declaiming encomia. The consensus of civilized opinion is that Mexico's ascendancy to the ranks of the world's rich and orderly nations could not have come to pass but for Porfirio Díaz. Leo Tolstoy has declared him a "prodigy of nature." Theodore Roosevelt has extolled him as the greatest statesman of his time, a man who "has done for his country what no other living man has done for any country." Andrew Carnegie has deemed him "the Moses and Joshua of his people." U.S. senator and former Secretary of State Elihu Root has called him one of the great men of the world and said he should "be held up to the hero-worship of mankind." Britain has made him a member of the Order of the Bath. Indeed, his very complexion now differs little from that of the European leaders who lionize him, extensive medical treatment having made his face and hands as pale as any Spaniard's. His house on the Calle Cadena is decorated entirely in European fashion and staffed exclusively with Caucasian servants. The Man of Stone, his countrymen call him, the Strong Man— though in private many have nicknamed him El Llorón for his easy shed of tears on a variety of occasions. A rendition of the national anthem. A student recitation of a patriotic poem. A funeral for a fellow soldier. A futile personal plea from a mother to spare her son from the firing squad.

-❀-

As a man grows older, Díaz more than once said to Edward Little, he may or may not become any wiser but he damn sure better become more careful.

But even a sly and careful old man can make a bad mistake, and Díaz had made his in an interview for an American magazine early in 1908 when he said he welcomed the formation of an opposition party to replace him in the next election. He claimed he had no desire to continue as president and that at the age of seventy-seven he was satisfied. The truth was that he did and he wasn't. Perhaps his assertions were intended only to persuade the magazine's American readers of his democratic outlook and his tolerance for divergent political opinion. But how could he not have foreseen the repercussions? The interview was reprinted all over Mexico and set off a frenzy of maneuvering by a number of presidential aspirants.

Chief among them was Francisco Madero, who came from a wealthy Coahuila family. Barely five feet tall and high-pitched of voice, Madero had been educated in Europe and the United States and had become an apostle of democracy. In 1909 he published a book advocating an orderly transition from the Porfiriato to a truly democratic republic. The two central principles of his newly formed Anti-Reelection Party were no reelection—obviously—and effective suffrage.

As Madero gave speeches throughout the country, Díaz was at first amused by him and referred to him as El Loquito, sometimes El Enano. But by the time the two men met in person in the early spring of 1910, Madero's following had grown impressively, and Díaz was no longer laughing about the Little Lunatic. He had supposed Madero just another power-hungry hacendado, but in their meeting he perceived the ardent sincerity of his views. Listen, Díaz told him, a man needs a lot more than honesty to govern Mexico, don't you know that? He afterward told Edward Little it was unfair of God to force him to deal with more than one troublesome dwarf in his lifetime. First that fucking Indian Juárez and now this half-pint hidalgo son of a bitch.

The following month Halley's Comet blazed across the Mexican sky and the fearful peón populace saw it as an omen of imminent catastrophe.

By June of 1910, Díaz had had enough of Madero's public agitations and ordered him arrested on charges of inciting rebellion and insulting the president. Madero was still in jail when the election took place in July. It was officially declared that Díaz had won ninety-nine percent of the vote. After the election Madero was permitted to post bail to get out from behind bars but was kept under house arrest. He escaped in October and fled to El Paso.

He called for a revolution to begin on the twentieth of November—he who knew nothing of leadership, nothing of warfare, who had no personal experience with violence. But his egalitarian ideals attracted a motley multitude of followers, among them a swelling horde of bitter impoverished illiterates who were ignorant about the workings of democracy and of government but who knew a very great deal about violence. And who were burning with hatred. A hatred bred by the legally sanctioned thefts of their ancestral lands. By unjust imprisonments and brutal whippings. By violations to their women and countless humiliations endured in the witnessing eyes of their sons. A hatred that for the first time since the great uprising of Padre Hidalgo was set loose to exact its retribution in blood.

By early spring the Revolution was in flaming riot. More and more men with nothing to lose but their lives flocked to the insurgents, turning their machetes against the bosses, the Rurales, the army, against anybody wearing a uniform or a suit. Sacking haciendas. Plundering towns. Breaking open prisons. Wrecking trains. And too, more and more bandits pillaging under the sanction of The Revolution and crying of liberty. Liberty from the law. From every restraint.

It's the *truth*, man, I'm telling you—they busted open Tehuacán! Everybody says so! Killed every goddam guard. Hung the fucking warden from the front gate! Like in Cuernavaca, man, like in Morelia! Let anybody ride with them who wanted to. Gave them horses and guns! *Guns*, man! Tehuacán, Christ! That's just down the tracks. Everybody says they're headed this way. Headed *here*, Juanito!

He tries very hard not to expect it. To keep from thinking it even likely. Barely able to breathe for the effort of his restraint. . . .

CATALINA

Many years later Catalina would tell her children that their great-great-grandfather had been feared by many men who never even met him and by every man who ever did. Except for Don Porfirio, I suppose, she would say. But then, your great-great-grandfather was probably the only man in Mexico not afraid of Don Porfirio.

To say she had always been Edward Little's favorite would be misleading in its implication that he was simply fonder of her than of his own children and other grandchildren. In fact, she was the only one whose company he looked forward to on his visits to Patria Chica. All the things she would love best in life she would learn to love from him. She alone called him Buelito. While she was yet an infant he had carried her about the casa grande courtyard, naming for her the trees and birds, the types of clouds above. She was four when he began taking her for long saddle rides over the hacienda's expanse, holding her to his chest and teaching her now of the larger world. The language of the land. The secrets of the wind. On long walks at night he instructed her on the nature of the moon, on the stars and their turnings and the unerring maps they provided to those who knew how to read them. He gave her a pony when she was six. When she began wearing Eduardo Luis's outgrown pants and boots, Gloria objected on the grounds that it was unfeminine, that she was turning into a cowboy, but Edward spoke to Gloria in private and the matter was closed. He took Catalina to the hacienda store and bought her several pairs of pants and had her fitted for boots, and bought her too some pretty dresses to wear when occasion demanded. Though you are much more, he told her, you are also a lady. By the age of eight she had learned from him how to track anything—horses, game, a man afoot. No one else in the family knew of her witness to her grandmother's murder of her grandfather, but she told Edward all she had seen and described for him even the expressions on their faces in the moment before the first shot—his of a man in nightmare and hers of an amused sleepwalker—and the way her grandmother's feet slung up as she went into the well. He taught her to shoot when she was twelve and a year later she killed her first deer, dropping it with a head shot from a hundred yards and then dressing it herself under his supervision. At her quinceañera on New Year's day of 1910 she was beautiful in white finery, and her first dance of the occasion was with him. His gift to her, bestowed in private, was a bone-handled scalping knife he had taken from an Apache warrior he'd killed sixty-four years before.

Edward Little never explained his predilection for Catalina to anyone—he explained nothing of himself to anyone—and no one of the family, not even her father or grandfather, ever mentioned it. Catalina was Don Eduardo's darling and that was that. It had occurred to Gloria, who kept the thought to herself, that her father-in-law's partiality for the girl might be rooted in the loss of his only daughter when she was still a baby. But if that were so, why choose Catalina over Sandra Rosario who had been born first? Gloria had a notion about that too. Sandi was a sensitive child who wept for the injured and the helpless and the all alone, while Catalina . . . well, Gloria had never seen nor heard Catalina cry, not in pain or for any other reason, not even as an infant.

❈

Given Patria Chica's isolation and proximity to the railroad, its safety was unsure. In early March when rebel action was reported only fifty miles from San Luis Potosí, Díaz had a company of infantry posted on the outskirts of the hacienda. But still Edward wanted to send Catalina someplace safer, and so of course would send Sandra Rosario too. He put the girls on an army train bound for Monterrey, where the next afternoon they would transfer to another military train and arrive in Matamoros around midnight. He assigned Eduardo Luis to go along as his sisters' protector until he turned them over to John Louis at the Matamoros station. John Louis would take the girls across the river to his Brownsville home and Eduardo Luis would return to Patria Chica. Catalina asked how long they would have to be away. Until things settle down here, Edward said. He gave her a roll of American currency and hugged her hard and kissed her. Then patted tearful Sandra Rosario on the head and was gone.

In Monterrey there was a mechanical problem with the train they were supposed to transfer onto. Wanting to deliver the children on schedule, the officer in charge had a sleeping coach added to a special train about to leave for the Matamoros garrison—a train of only two other cars, one packed with munitions and the other carrying a guard detail of two rifle squads. The train chugged off through a sunset-reddened countryside and then into a desert night made ghostly by an incandescent moon. Catalina lay awake for a time, staring out the window at the night sky and wondering what the border would be like.

She came awake to a thundering clash of iron as the coach yawed and shuddered and came to a jarring halt. Her head struck the wall and she was unconscious for a moment before becoming aware of her brother shaking her by the shoulder and shouting "*Cat! Come on!*" Gunfire blasting outside. Men bellowing, howling. Crying out in pain. She found it hard to sit up and then realized the coach was at a sideward tilt. The little amber lights just inside the doors were still on but the air was hazed with dust and smelled of steaming oil. Eduardo Luis wore only pants and boots. She saw the fear in his eyes, the pistol in his hand. Sandra Rosario shrieked from the other end of the coach where men with big hats and wild dark faces had rushed in and one had his arms around Sandi from behind and was dragging her out. As Eduardo Luis started to raise his pistol somebody shot him and he fell to the floor on his back with his eyes rolled up and a red–black hole in his forehead. Catalina tried to get her knife from under the pillow but was grabbed by her gown and yanked rearward. She twisted and tried to wrest free and the gown ripped away and she fell on the floor, naked but for underpants. The man holding the gown stared down at her, grinning under a huge mustache. Then was on her.

She would not know how many took a turn. Five? Six? The coach windows were gray when the last of them was done. He was the only one of them still in the coach and was having trouble rebuckling his pants belt. He paid no attention to her as she sat up. The floor under her sticky with blood and semen, the pain between her legs like a raw wound. She heard the snortings and stampings of horses, the clatter of heavy wagons. She pulled herself up against the bunk and slid her hand under the pillow. Somebody hollered for the laggard to hurry up, what the hell was he doing, courting her? There was laughter. Without looking up from his struggle with the buckle the man yelled back for them to fuck themselves. She turned to face him and said softly, "Oye, bruto." The man raised his face to look at her and she backhanded the blade through his neck all the way to the bone. Blood jumped and spattered her breasts. The man staggered, hands to his throat as if trying to hold his head in place as much as stanch the blood throbbing through his fingers and cascading onto his shirt. He tried to cry out but could not. Then tripped over Eduardo Luis and fell facedown and let a gurgling groan and in a moment more went still, blood widening on the floor under his face. There was another shout for him to come on, goddammit. She stood next to the door with the knife ready for whoever came in first. To hell with him, somebody said, he can catch up. She heard them leaving, horsemen and wagons.

She found her clothes and got dressed, nearly falling once from a sudden swirl of dizziness. The floor viscid under her feet. She knelt beside Eduardo Luis and cleaned off his face with her gown and then covered him with it. She had to think hard for a moment to remember he was eighteen. His gun was gone. But the dead man's gun belt was still on the chair where he'd placed it and she went to it and took the Remington revolver from the holster and emptied the cylinder and saw that all the cartridges had been spent. She reloaded the chambers with bullets from the belt loops and then with the point of her knife made another hole in the belt for the buckle tongue so the belt would fit her. Then put it on and slid her knife under it but had the revolver in hand as she went outside into the light of the risen sun.

The locomotive was canted to one side on the ground beyond the disjointed tracks with its great iron wheels buried to the hubs and a thin haze of steam still rising off the engine. Dead men in every attitude. Some of the attackers and all of the soldiers. Ants already at work on the faces. She did not find Sandra Rosario among the dead but found several canteens of water. In every direction the horizon ran to distant ranges except to the northeast which lay flat all the way to the sky. There was a low dust cloud in the southwest she took to be that of the departed raiders. She had to assume they had Sandi with them. She tried various hats before finding one that wasn't too big. She had no idea how far she was from Matamoros but knew that the tracks would take her there. She slung a pair of canteens across her chest and started walking.

Near midday a billow of dust rose in the northwest and began to enlarge. She had the Remington in her hand when they came riding up, a band of men of the same breed and aspects as those of the night before. Teeth bright against faces black in the shadow of their sombreros. Every man of them draped with bandoleers and guns and knives, their horses hung with rifles and machetes. They reined up around her, grinning and joking about the pretty soldadera so ready to shoot them all. The leader said he was Tomás Urbina and asked what happened. She told him about the train attack. He asked if she had been violated and when she didn't answer he cursed her attackers with such artful vileness she nearly smiled. He told two men to take her to Matamoros. She hesitated but a second before clasping the hand reaching down to her and being swung up behind the rider.

———※———

It was late in the afternoon when they deposited her at the Matamoros depot. The stationmaster immediately sent a wire to John Louis at Cielo Largo to let him know. John Louis had been informed the evening before of the change in trains and the reason for it, but when the train had still not arrived by morning he was frantic. He had exchanged a half-dozen wires with the Monterrey garrison before finally going back to Cielo Largo and maintaining telegraphic communications from there. When he got to the station it was the first time he and Catalina had seen each other in the five years since he'd left Patria Chica, and he nearly stopped her breath with the force of his embrace. When she told him Eduardo Luis had been killed and Sandi Rosario taken, he said, Oh dear God, and hugged her again to hide his face. She did not tell him of her assault nor of the man she killed, would for years not tell anyone, though she'd have told Buelito if she'd had the chance and pleaded with him to take her along when he set out to hunt them down. John Louis composed himself and then sent a wire to Edward Little.

The entirety of Edward's responding telegram said, Send Eduardo to Patria Chica. Attend well to the Cat.

-❦-

Edward Little assigned his best agents, each with his own crew, to search the border in hunt of the train attackers, especially in the towns where most of the trade in guns and munitions took place. Over the following weeks every man of the gang but three was captured and interrogated to the bloody bones before he was granted the mercy of death. Most were in agreement that the girl was taken from the train by Berto González and Chato Ruíz, two of the three who remained unfound. After receiving their shares from the sale of the munitions in Reynosa, González and Ruíz had left the gang, taking the girl with them. Maybe to sell her, maybe for their own fun, nobody knew. Or knew where they'd gone. Some thought Monterrey, some Nuevo Laredo, some Chihuahua City, but nobody knew. Edward's men would follow every tenuous lead but find no trace of either man nor of Sandra Rosario.

-❦-

Úrsula had known Catalina since the girl was a baby and she was very happy to have her living with them. Hector Louis had been eight the last time he'd seen her and was now a little shy around his sixteen-year-old cousin who seemed somehow to have grown more than just two years older than he. Though the house was large by Brownsville standards, she had never lived in a place so small, but she didn't mind. Her room looked out on a backyard full of trees and abutting a small resaca and she marveled at the variety of birds that watered there. She was in a secret apprehension for the first few weeks and formed a contingent plan to sneak off to town and find a curandera—and then was profoundly relieved when her menses came, and she felt as much delivered by chance as injured by it.

The Littles held a fiesta at Cielo Largo to introduce her to the Wolfes, her kin by way of her Grandmother Gloria. They came in a pair of new Model T Ford touring cars, the twins relinquishing most of the driving to the boys, and Jacky Ríos and César Augusto protested to no avail when Blake Cortéz also allotted Vicki Angel a turn behind the wheel. That evening at the banquet table there was much loud discussion about family lineage and Catalina's relation to the Wolfes. Beyond the solid facts that Samuel Thomas Wolfe was her great-grandfather and John Roger Wolfe her great-granduncle there was much debate about great-uncles and great-aunts and degrees of cousinship until everybody was laughing at the genealogical tangle. It was finally resolved that although they were technically her granduncles and grandaunts, John Louis and the twins would simply be her uncles, Úrsula and

Marina and Remedios her aunts, and all their children her cousins. It was only natural that they would abbreviate her name to Cat and that the nickname would carry over into Spanish as La Gata.

She was one more Little who had never seen the ocean until her first time at Playa Blanca. They could now drive there in the Fords, the twins having reinforced the wagon trail from the Boca Chica road to the house and there built a garage to protect the cars from windblown sand. Catalina had learned to swim in the river at Patria Chica but shared her cousins' preference for swimming in the gulf rather than in a river or resaca. All the boys were in a stir over their long-legged, blue-eyed cousin and vied with each other to teach her how to sail. Jacky Ríos and César Augusto nearly got into a fistfight about it, which seemed to amuse her. She chose Vicki Angel to be her instructor and by the end of that weekend she was sailing like an old hand. A year and a half Catalina's junior, Vicki Angel adored her cousin and was elated to have another girl in the family, an ally at last in a tribe overrun with rough boys. She took to wearing pants and boots too, whenever Catalina did, and none of the adults objected, so long as the girls never failed to dress properly for mealtimes and social outings. They enrolled Catalina in the same Catholic school for girls that Vicki attended and the two of them walked there together every day in their blue-and-white uniforms. The women were pleased by the novelty of two girls among them, girls at the threshold of womanhood but who still in the way of girls could communicate with each other through mysterious smiling glances that sometimes led to outbursts of laughter for reasons they shared with no one else. The twins too were taken with Catalina. They admired her refusal to give up her Remington revolver to John Louis. He had offered to keep it for her in his gun case, he told the twins, but she preferred to keep it in her room and he could think of no argument by which to deny her. That she knew how to use the gun was evident the first time she took a turn at a family target shooting session and outshot all her cousins except Harry Sebastian, the deadeye of the bunch. And the day she slipped the bonehandled knife from its hip sheath and threw it whirling to pinion a four-foot rattlesnake still writhing after Jacky Ríos had shot it was one more proof she'd been well-trained in self-defense and the arts of weaponry. She learned everything from Don Eduardo, Úrsula told the twins. Catalina herself never spoke of her great-grandfather to anyone other than Vicki Angel, who would not have betrayed her confidences even under torture.

And if in those first months with the border families Catalina sometimes withdrew into silence or went for long solitary walks at the ranch or on the beach or kept to her room for an afternoon of staring out the window, it was understandable to Marina and Remedios. Just think of what that poor girl had been through! She had seen her brother killed and her sister taken away and God alone knew how frightened she must have been for her own life. Naturally she would sometimes remember that terrible experience and be sad. Give her time. She was young and would learn to live with the pains of the past as we all must. Úrsula agreed, but said that even as a child Catalina had always had a reclusive side to her, some secret part of herself she never shared with anyone. Except probably Don Eduardo. And now Vicki Angel, to whom she seemed even closer than she had been to her own sister. It is a very right name for her, Úrsula said, the Cat.

Hector Louis told his cousins much the same thing. Catalina had always been a little odd, he said. She never asked if she could play with you, you always had to ask her, and sometimes she would and sometimes she wouldn't. It was like she didn't really care if anybody asked her to play or not. I always liked her anyway, Hector said, even though she was odd.

"Well she's not any odder than any of *you* all, that's damn for sure!" Vicki Angel said, and stomped off as the boys all laughed at her clumsy profanity.

Harry Sebastian said the really strange thing about the Cat was how well she could shoot and throw that knife. Jacky Ríos said he'd sure like to get his hands on that knife of hers. "There are lots of things of hers *I'd* like to get my hands on," Morgan James said with a lascivious smile. All the boys had by this time disposed of their virginity, fourteen-year-old Hector Louis just a couple of months before, when Morgan James, the eldest at seventeen and the most experienced, took him to one of his compliant Mexican girlfriends in Brownsville.

Jacky Ríos told Morgan he better not try anything with the Cat, not only on account of she might gut him with that knife but you weren't supposed to do such things with your cousin, he'd heard you could go to jail for it.

"Ah hell," Harry Sebastian said, "she's so far out on a limb of the family tree she hardly counts as a cousin."

César Augusto said for them to quit talking about her that way.

"What's biting your ass?" Morgan said.

"Just don't talk about her that way, that's all," César said.

"Why not?" Jacky Ríos said, winking at the others. "You sweet on her? You gonna *marry* her?"

And César said, "Yeah, as a matter of fact I am." And grinned at their laughter.

THE MATRIARCH

In the final days of 1910, some years after finally accepting that she was past all possibility of conception and at last acquiescing to sexual intercourse with Amos Bentley—berating herself for her long abstention even as she thrilled to the act as much as she had the first time in her life, at sixteen with her young soldier husband Melchor—Sofía Reina, age fifty-seven, at last also accepted as fact seventy-two-year-old Amos's insistence that she was in no way cursed and they should get married before they were too old to even remember each other's names. Six years earlier, after Victor Nevada died of a stroke, Amos had become an independent assayer and had been making more money than ever. Theirs would be a very comfortable old age, he promised Sófi.

When they told María Palomina they were going to marry, all she said was, It's about time. They set the date for March.

❧

A few weeks before the wedding, María Palomina awoke early one morning from a pleasant dream of walking hand in hand with Samuel Thomas in Chapultepec Park, both of them yet very young and Samuel Thomas scarless of face and walking without limp. They had never actually gone for such a walk, Samuel Thomas never having gone anywhere beyond a three-block radius of home, and she had not been to Chapultepec since girlhood. But the dream was so real it seemed more remembrance than imagination. Just before she woke from it, Samuel Thomas kissed her hands, first one and then the other, and remarked that they had always been the prettiest he'd ever seen. Then she was awake and looking at her hands. Crippled with arthritis, the knotty fingers as twisted as scrub roots and the gnarled knuckles seized like rusted bearings, they had not been free of pain in years. She suddenly realized that tomorrow was the second of February, her eighty-first birthday. No, no, no, she thought. That's just *too* damn old.

And closed her eyes and took a deep breath and released it in a slow settling sigh.

The funeral was three days later and was attended by a handful of neighborhood friends. Sófi's grief was absolute but when Amos suggested she might want to set back the wedding date she said certainly not and that not even her mother would have wanted them to.

They married as planned on the first Sunday in March. As they were leaving the church, Amos said, "This is the happiest day of my life." And took three more strides before stopping short and turning to her in disbelief as he clutched his chest. And fell dead.

She shed a few tears and wore black for two weeks, and if her neighbors thought her show of mourning altogether perfunctory and disrespectful, what did she care? She was a lifelong intimate of grief, a practiced expert at mourning, and no longer felt need to make public display of her feelings. And only once did she say, speaking to herself as much as to the sheepish spirit of Amos, I *told* you, you idiot!

-※-

She telegraphed the news to her border kin, and, with no family left to her in Mexico City, asked if she might go to live near them. Marina's return wire expressed everyone's condolences and said they would all love to have her with them and that she could take her choice of which family to live with. But Sófi would not burden anyone and insisted on a house of her own. Amos had left her a large inheritance and she sent money to the Wolfes and asked them to please buy a small house for her not too far from theirs. Her friends said she was being rash. Mexico City was the only home she'd ever known and she would wither in the primitive country of the border. Maybe, Sófi said, maybe not. In April she sold her house and moved to Brownsville in the only border crossing she would ever make.

-※-

The families received her with an outpouring of felicitous affection. She had for so long looked forward to meeting them all, and was especially effusive toward the twins, who even at the age of forty-one were indistinguishable except to those who knew the identifiers to look for. She was pleased with the little frame house they had selected for her, a block north of the Wolfe homes. She had never lived anywhere but Mexico City but was acquainted with dramatic change and would easily adapt to Brownsville and its ways.

Two years older than Marina, she was by tradition of age entitled to be the new family matriarch—the Mamá Grande. But she protested that Marina was the true matriarch because she had known the twins since their birth and was wife to one of the family's two heads. For her part, Marina deferred to Sófi as the rightful matriarch because she was not only first cousin to the family heads but was also the daughter of John Roger's brother and hence the only one in the borderland family to have known both brothers. The twins settled the dispute by decreeing that both women would be accorded the title and respect of Mamá Grande and would be addressed by everyone in the family as Mamá Marina and Mamá Sófi.

But it was Sófi's singular distinction to have been born and raised in Mexico City, where nobody else in the border families had ever been. They loved to hear her descriptions of the capital, her reminiscences of the Wolfe y Blanco family and her account of how it came to have that surname. They were enrapt by her epic tale of Gloria's wedding to Louis Welch Little. Were awed by the sad saga of her own marriages and the lamentable outcomes of them all.

It would be years yet, however, before she would tell any of them of her conviction that the family was cursed by its own blood.

—❦—

She had been in Brownsville two months when the twins came to her with a document case and told her it contained information she might find interesting. Then opened the case and she saw the banded bunch of photographs, the various packets of letters and other documents, the leatherbound ledger. It was all in English, which she did not know, but they promised to translate it all as time permitted. What was important, they told her, was that *she* know everything about the family. That she be the keeper of its history. The one to pass it down.

Sofía Reina looked from one to the other of them, her eyes shining. She reached across the table and took each one by a hand. "Gracias, mijos," she said. "Con todo mi corazón. Gracias."

THE UNCAGED

They broke through the gate, howling like fiends. The guards stood no chance. Many of them threw down their weapons and surrendered, pleading for mercy. And were eviscerated, pulped, quartered, decapitated. Screams of agony and of exultation. The warden was dragged out into the main yard and doused with oil and strung up by his feet and set afire. Everything of wood in flame, everything of paper. Among the first to reach the armory were Juan Lobo and his henchmen—Fat Pori, Sarmiento One-Eye, Ugly Dax, the three with whom he had ruled a prison block for the last nine years. With rifles in hand they ran out to the main yard where he and Sarmiento caught riderless mounts and Pori and Dax shot men out of the saddle for their horses. They rode away with the attackers and camped with them that night, but the rebels were going in the wrong direction, and in the morning he and his trio and ten others recruited to his party reversed to eastward. They plundered as they went. He taught himself to shoot by shooting people. There were challengers to his leadership and he fought and killed them each in turn in front of the spectating others. They crossed the sierras, descended to the valley roads, dodged army patrols and the Guardia Rural. Their number increased. He did not know the country they passed through nor the names of the villages they left smoldering behind them. But he knew where he was going, and every man of them, now almost fifty strong, believed his promise of ample and easy pickings. He had his mother's map branded in his brain. Could yet see her finger tapping the spot as she said, Right there, Juanito, right *there*! And as surely as a raptor winging for home he bore toward Buenaventura.

And arrived on a warm June morning.

John Samuel wakes to blastings of gunfire, cries of panic and anguish, lunatic howling. He fumbles for his spectacles and goes to the window and opens the shutters to a daybreak vision of apocalypse. Horsemen amok in the plaza, shooting people, hacking them, throwing torches through windows, onto rooftops. Sees more of them in the courtyard below. The bloody bodies of casa grande servants. There are crashings downstairs, gunshots, terrified cries. Hard thumpings of boots in the hallway. His door bangs open and he stands stricken as men of wild aspect rush in, one hollering, Don't *kill* the fucker, don't kill him, the chief said! He is grabbed by each arm and propelled from the room unshod and in his nightshirt, pulled stumbling down the stairs, his thin gray hair disheveled, skinny legs flashing with each flap of his nightshirt. He sees draperies afire, broken furniture burning, white-eyed mounts stamping through the salon and down the hallways. Then out into the burning compound hazed with smoke and strident with the cries of the dying, the maimed. Women wailing over the dead and in desperate attendance to the wounded. The shooting now reducing to sporadic reports. He is yanked along to the plaza fountain where Bruno Tomás sits on the ground, bareheaded and in shirtsleeves, a man with an eye patch standing over him, pistol in hand. Three years older than John Samuel, sixty-year-old Bruno yet has thick hair more black than gray, but his face is now bloody, one eye purple and swollen shut, nose obviously broken.

They jerk John Samuel to a halt in front of a man sitting on the rim of the fountain and eating a mango. He is flanked by two men, one fat and smiling, the other with hideous burn scars on one side of his face. At their feet are three strongboxes. John Samuel recognizes the one from the rear room of the main kitchen and the two that had been locked in the armory, but he does not see the two boxes kept cached under the stone floor of his office, which is at that moment pouring smoke from its windows. The man eating the mango tosses the half-eaten fruit into the fountain and wipes his mouth and fingers with his shirt and stands up. "Yo soy Juan Lobo," he says. "Mi mamá se llamó Katrina Ávila. ¿Te acuerdas de ella?"

John Samuel sees the madness in the man's eyes. "Katrina Ávila?" he says.

Juan Lobo punches him hard in the mouth, jarring the spectacles off his face and knocking him down. Two men haul him back up to his feet. He tastes blood and feels the sudden bloating of his lips and chokes on a dislodged front tooth and tries to cough it up but swallows it.

Juan Lobo picks up the spectacles and puts them on and looks all about, squinting. Then takes them off and snaps the lenses out of the rims and sets the frame back on his face and grins at his men. Then turns back to John Samuel and says, Your father fucked my mother for his fun, and then when he became *my* father he sent us away. *But.* I am now here to say—he spreads his arms wide and grins with great exaggeration—*Helllooo*, brother!

Certain that he is going to be killed, John Samuel is crying now, gasping, mucus streaming from his nose, blood from his mouth.

Lobo gestures about the plaza and says, These, ah, *people* tell me somebody gutted your father a long time ago. They tell me the twin ones were killed for something to do with the same thing. Have I been told the truth?

John Samuel stutters, gags on snot, manages to say, Yes, it's the truth, yes.

Aaaah Christ, Juan Lobo says, shaking his head. I knew it was too much to hope for that the old cocksucker would still be alive, but, goddammit, the twin ones dead *too*? He smiles at John Samuel in the manner of a commiserative friend and says, I feel *soooo* cheated, you know what I mean? But what the hell, my brother— and he again makes the open-armed gesture—there's still *you*! Then loses his smile and snatches John Samuel by the hair and shoves his head back and draws his knife and puts it to his throat.

John Samuel whimpers and pisses in his pants.

Somebody shouts, Don't do it! Listen, *listen*! I know where they are! They're not dead!

Juan Lobo looks over at Bruno Tomás. He steps back from John Samuel and gestures for the guard to help the mayordomo get up, and then beckons Bruno to him. Bruno comes limping. His only hope to save John Samuel is in giving Juan Lobo what he wants. The twins can look out for themselves.

He stands before Lobo, who says, You're a very helpful man, Mr Old Mayordomo. It was helpful to show us where the money was, though of course you only did that to save your hide. But nevertheless it was helpful. And now you want to tell me where the twin ones are. That would also be very helpful. He taps the knifepoint on Bruno's chest and says, *But*. Everybody else, you see, says the twin ones have been dead as long as their fucking father. *Soooo*. What can I think except you want to lie to me to try to save this son of a whore? He runs the knife up to Bruno's throat and the point forms a dimple in the skin. You have fucked yourself out of our deal, Mr Mayordomo.

I'm not lying. They're at the Río Bravo. I have letters to prove it. Letters that tell about them. With addresses, with postmarks.

Oh? Where are they, these letters?

I'll tell you if you won't kill the patrón.

It's a deal. Where are the letters?

How do I know you won't kill the patrón anyway? Bruno says—and glances at John Samuel, who is squinting at him as if trying to comprehend some alien language.

Very good question, says Juan Lobo. But your bigger worry should be whether I'll kill *you* anyway.

Yes. How do I know you won't do that?

Juan Lobo issues a loud mock sigh and lowers the knife and calls for two saddled mounts. The horses are brought and he has John Samuel—still dazed with fear, confused by the proceedings—helped up onto one. He tells Bruno the other horse is for him. But listen, Lobo says. A man's word is the only thing in this world worth more than gold, don't you agree? Well, I give you my word—*my* word!—that if the letters prove what you say, you and this cocksucker can ride out of here. But if they don't, I'll kill you both. You have my word on that too.

Bruno points to his quarters and specifies where the letters are stashed within it. Juan Lobo sends a man to retrieve them—fast, as the fire is by now already consuming the roof of that building.

The man is not long about it, panting on his return. He hands the packet of letters to Juan Lobo, who cannot read and passes them to Dax, he of the half-burned face. Dax scans several of them and says they all mention twins named Blake and James and also their wives and children.

Ah, they have *families*, how excellent, Juan Lobo says, and smiles wide.

All the letters show the same addresses, Dax tells him. In Brownsville, Texas. Across the Bravo from Matamoros.

"Muy bien," Lobo says. He gestures toward the ready horse and tells Bruno he can go.

Bruno struggles up onto the horse and takes up the reins. "Let's go, John," he says.

Before John Samuel can hup his horse forward Juan Lobo grabs him by the nightshirt and yanks him down and sends him sprawling onto his hands and knees. Bruno yells *Noooo!* as Lobo takes a machete from one of his men and steps over to John Samuel and with one swing beheads him. A thick jet of blood lays a bright red stripe six feet long on the cobbles as the head tumbles and stops with a wondering stare at nothing at all.

You gave your worrrrd! Bruno screeches.

Juan Lobo turns to Fat Pori and says, Count to five and if he's still here shoot him.

Bruno heels the horse and gallops away.

Juan Lobo picks up the head and sets it on the rim of the fountain and transfers the lensless spectacles from his own face to the head's. How's that, patrón? he says. Can you see more clearly how things are, my brother?

❖

He hid in the bush off the hacienda road and waited. And envisioned again and again the wanton slaughter. John Samuel's severed head. Rogelio Méndez hacked to pieces. He wept. He was there for half an hour before Juan Lobo and three others rode past at a canter. It was another hour more before the others came by, riding at a trot, singing and laughing, most of them drunk. Trailed by three mule-driven wagons creaking under their loads of booty. Bruno would never know it but two days hence the larger band of bandits would encounter a company of Rurales who would kill every man of them and divide the loot among themselves.

❖

When he got back to the charred and smoking compound, corpses were being carted to the Santa Rosalba graveyard. A crowd gathered around him and he

446

was helped down from the horse. They brought him water and tended his wounds and an old woman kissed his hands and murmured a prayer to the Holy Mother. They told him John Samuel had been taken for burial in the village and begged his forgiveness for not waiting until the fire died out and then burying him in the casa grande graveyard. Bruno said it was all right. Then one among them, weeping, told him Lobo took the head with him in a sack. Bruno could think of nothing to say to that, did not know whether to nod or shake his head. They told him Lobo and three companions filled their saddlebags with all the money from one of the strongboxes and left the other two boxes to the gang. There was nothing else to tell him that he had not seen for himself.

Then someone asked, What will we do now, patrón?

Patrón. Bruno Tomás Wolfe y Blanco, battered, and feeling very old, held the word in his mind for a moment. He looked about at the wreckage of Buenaventura. And said, Recover, what else? Then collapsed into a feverish unconsciousness from which he would not fully recover for two weeks.

He would babble in his sleep, hallucinate, intermittently come half-awake and be given water and broth, more than once be thought to have died. And when he would at last regain his senses, among his first clear thoughts would be that he must send a telegram to his border kin to warn them of what was coming. Though by then it had already arrived.

⸎

When the end came it came fast. Madero's forces took Ciudad Juárez on the tenth of May—one of the leaders of that major victory being a bandit-turned-revolutionary who called himself Pancho Villa. Then in quick order fell Durango, Hermosillo, Torreón, Saltillo, many smaller towns. As Emiliano Zapata and his Indians were taking Cuernavaca on the twenty-first of May, representatives of Díaz and Madero reached an accord on a peace pact in the desert outside of Juárez, signing the papers by the light of automobile headlamps. Among other provisions, the treaty called for Díaz's resignation before the end of May. Three nights later—as the wind whipped stinging dust through the Mexico City streets and thunderheads were massing—Díaz sat before his drafted but yet unsigned letter of resignation. An ulcerated molar had been tormenting him for days and his jaw was now so swollen it was an effort even to speak. He could not believe only eight months had passed since international heads of state were lavishing him with gifts and admiration during Mexico's commemorative centennial. The agony of yielding his presidency to that little lunatic dwarf, of surrendering to an army of ignorant peons, was hardly less than that of his jaw. Advisors had been coming and going all evening but Doña Carmen never left his side except when he conferred with Edward Little. Edward reported that all the arrangements had been made for his departure. You sign that damn thing and we get you to Veracruz and then you're off to Europe and to hell with all this. Díaz said that nothing in his life had ever been harder than writing the resignation. Except signing it. Every time I pick up the pen to do it, he said, all I really want to do is ram it in Madero's heart. You'd have to hunker way down to do that, Edward said—and Díaz laughed in spite of his pain. There was a rumor he would be resigning that very night, Edward told him, and the zócalo was packed with fools waiting to cheer the news. Díaz glanced at the door to be sure it was closed, then said, Well fuck them. For damn sure I won't sign it tonight. And he didn't. The zócalo multitude was by then chanting for his resignation and menacing the palace guards. Mounted police were sent out to disperse them, swinging clubs and trampling the fallen. The crowd fought back with stones and banner staves, but when they started pulling policemen off their mounts, the soldiers on the rooftops opened fire. And still the enraged mob fought on. At which point the looming storm at last detonated into thunderclaps and lightning bolts and loosed a torrent of slashing rain that sent the crowd running for cover off the open square, taking their dead and wounded with them. And the battle of the zócalo was done.

In the morning, Díaz resigned.

On the last day of May, Porfirio Díaz sails from Veracruz on the German ship *Ypiranga*, accompanied by his family—his wife and daughter and wastrel of a son, an army officer via nepotism alone—and a cadre of guards under the command of Juan Sotero Wolfe. Juan Sotero's wife and two sons, baby Carlos Sebastián only two months old, will remain in Mexico City until his return on some uncertain date that will prove to be more than four years hence. Díaz has appointed Edward Little to attend to a few details that will keep him in the capital perhaps another week. After which, Edward means to return to Patria Chica for good. In his valediction to a group of reporters on the dock, Díaz says of Madero, He has let the tiger out of its cage, now let's see him tame it. He weeps when he and Edward hug hard at the foot of the gangplank. Two old men, friends of fifty years. It isn't death that defeats us, he whispers in Edward's ear, it's fucking *old age*! He wipes his tears and says, Come see me in Paris. We'll find another Lagrimas and dance with the girls all night. Edward tells him to plan on it.

Then the Man of Stone is gone. He will travel throughout Europe and be royally received wherever he goes, then settle in Paris, the Champs Élysées evermore reminding him of the Avenida Reforma. On the second day of July of 1915, lying on silk sheets and listening to a raspy phonograph recording of ranchero music, he will remember the Mexico City night when he and Lalo, already old, were on their way to Las Lagrimas de Nuestras Madres and with their cane swords fought off a gang of rateros. And have his last laugh.

Eight days after Díaz's departure from Mexico, Edward Little, eighty-one years old and uneasy in his bones, wakes to darkness but needs no clock to know it is his hour of rising. He has never had much use for sleep and in the past forty years has rarely retired before midnight or failed to rise before dawn. More recently he has come to regard a night's sleep with a vague dread, as the surrender of one more of his remaining days, and so he has been waking earlier still. As if even in sleep he senses the waning of time and cannot abide being unconscious in its passing.

Madero is to arrive in the capital today but Edward plans to be gone by then. Yet there is time enough to indulge, in the single instance of his life, a brief lingering in bed. He will miss this city, though he knows he will be missing a place that no longer exists, that has already become someplace other. A truth of our lives, he thinks. All the places we have loved in the past have become someplace other. There is no place to go back to, not for any man. Nothing endures but the beauty of the natural world, and so he will retire to the beauty surrounding Patria Chica. It is a wonder the place was spared. So many rebel gangs in the region and yet none attacked it. No need after all to have sent the children to the border. But you make a decision and live with its consequences. Eduardo Luis dead. Sandra Rosario vanished. But Catalina alive—and what was of greater import? When he gets to Patria Chica he will send for her, first thing.

As he starts to get up he feels the bed quiver queerly. And then the entire house shudders violently and there is a great shattering downpour of glass in every room. The bed tilts and he falls back onto it. The house begins convulsing. The walls shedding scales of plaster, breaking open, falling. Ceiling beams cracking and buckling, sections of roof crashing down. There is a great groan from the earth below and the entire house sways and he is flung to the floor from which he cannot rise for the antic undulations of it. And then the floor itself gives way and he plunges into the roaring black maw of the rent world. And the ruins of his Mexican home follow after and bury him.

—❈—

It is the worst earthquake in the capital since Mexico's independence, lasting nearly fifteen minutes and killing several hundred and reducing much of the city to rubble. And still, only hours later, Francisco Madero enters the capital at the head of a long parade of blaring bands and rowdy celebrants. Bands blare and the crowds lining the broken streets weep and cheer in the joy of their deliverance, crying Viva Madero! again and again. Viva Madero! Whom a cabal of army generals led by Victoriano Huerta will assassinate in February of 1913. The ensuing civil war will be the most protracted and most savage in the country's bloody history—and the onlooking nations of the civilized world will be appalled by Mexico's brute regression from the pinnacle of the Porfiriato.

SINS OF THE FATHERS

On an early Saturday afternoon they ford the river a few miles west of town and then ride into Brownsville. Four red-eyed horsemen as gray with dust as their mounts, each man of them wearing pistol and knife, each horse hung with rifle and machete, one saddle horn with a stinking gray sack of black-stained bottom attended by a drone of flies. The fighting has made chaos of rail travel, but they managed to bribe their way onto a flatcar of one military transport train after another, moving northward stretch by stretch—to Jalapa, to Tampico, to Ciudad Victoria, where the northward rail line had been destroyed and they bought horses to carry them the last two hundred miles to the border.

Market day. The town abustle. Their horses bare their teeth at honking puttering automobiles amid the wagon traffic. None of the four men speak English but through casual queries of an assortment of Mexican locals they learn everything they need to know. Learn of the Wolfe properties and residences and that the twins are longtime constables of celebrated feats who in the course of doing their duty have killed many bad men. Of course they would be lawmen, Juan Lobo thinks. Of course they would have a home on the seashore and own a great tract of land and call it Tierra Wolfe. Of course.

❦

A Ford touring car is parked alongside one of the Levee Street houses, Marina having come to town earlier today, driven by Harry Sebastian, to have an aching tooth attended by a dentist. They plan to return to the beach in the morning. No neighbors are in sight as the men dismount and lead their horses to the car and tether them to it. Dax and Sarmiento go around to the back and Juan Lobo and Pori to the front.

Harry Sebastian answers the knock at the door. A fat man in dirty clothes, hat in hand, says he is sorry to disturb anyone but he has an important message for Blake and James Wolfe. Harry says neither of them is in town at the moment and there is no telephone where they are, but he will be seeing them tomorrow and will be glad to take the message. Fat Pori brings a revolver up from behind the hat and cocks it as he puts the muzzle to Harry's forehead and backs him into the parlor. Juan Lobo follows them inside and closes the door. Marina enters from the kitchen, drying her hands with a dishcloth and asking who it was, then freezes, seeing the strangers and the gun to her son's head.

Go back in the kitchen, Mother, Harry Sebastian says, thinking of his folded knife in his pocket, his pistol in the other room.

Juan Lobo tells her to stay where she is. Then takes a look into the bedrooms and returns with Harry's gun in his belt and goes into the kitchen and says something to someone at the rear door. Then is back and standing before Marina. She meets his eyes and it is all she can do to hide her fear. Listen, she says. I am Marina Wolfe. You better leave right now and go somewhere far away before my husband hears of this. Juan Lobo grins and says, Which one is he? James Sebastián Wolfe, she says. Poor bastard, Juan Lobo says, married to such a hag.

Don't talk to her like that, you son of a bitch, Harry Sebastian says. Pori drives a knee into Harry's crotch and the boy falls down and clutches himself and vomits. Marina starts to scream but Lobo clamps a hand over her mouth and seizes her to him from behind. He nods at Pori who draws his knife and goes down on one knee and thrusts the blade into Harry's heart.

Marina is wild-eyed, her horrified cries muffled under Lobo's stifling hand as she fights to free herself. And then her struggle slackens and she can make no cry at all for her slashed throat. Lobo lets her fall and puts up his knife and he and Pori leave.

She crawls through her blood to Harry and puts a stoppering hand to his wound as though the force of her love might save the dead boy before her own slowing heart's last stumble.

<hr/>

There is a sign, small and low to the ground, the letters carved into it and burned black—Wolfe Landing. An arrow under the name points down a winding road leading through the high grass and mesquite stands into a riverside palm grove and the town within it, its charter not two months old, with a resident population of eight. Only the tops of the tallest trees are still touched by sunlight at this late afternoon hour as the four horsemen turn onto the narrow road. The sky has gone strange, with clouds bunching overhead and to westward but not in the east, out over the sea.

The road takes them into a large clearing amid the palms and moss-hung trees. The place is but a hamlet, comprising a large two-story house and a few smaller residences, some outbuildings, a stable and corral holding horses and mules. There are several dray wagons. A pier with a moored pair of rowboats. The men ignore the barking dogs that have converged around them, but the irritated horses snap down at them.

Beside a house, Anselmo and Pepe pause at their work of planing a board on sawbucks and watch the horsemen approach. Lupita comes in view at a window, drying her just-washed hair with a towel. The horsemen rein up and Anselmo says, "Buenas tardes, caballeros. A su servicio." Beside him, Pepe orders the dogs to shut up but they persist in their commotion.

Juan Lobo smiles and says he wishes to speak to James and Blake Wolfe.

I am sorry to say neither one is here, Anselmo says. His rifle is leaning against the side of the house ten feet away and he curses himself for not having retrieved it as soon as these men came in view. Up close the stink of them is terrific and he sees now the flyblown sack dangling from the saddle horn and feels a stir in his stomach. He tells the man the brothers have gone into town and he should look for them there.

Juan Lobo looks at the woman in the window and she moves out of sight. He had known the twins would not be here, that they are at the beach house as he had been told is their weekend custom, but this place, this so-called town, is theirs, a part of them, as were these people, and he would not pass it by.

A dog nips at his mount's leg and dodges the horse's kick that jostles Lobo in the saddle. Lobo draws his pistol and shoots the dog in the eye and its head hits the ground ahead of the rest of its body.

The gunshot frights the birds from the trees and the other dogs sprint away into the brush as Anselmo yells, You son of a—and the next bullet passes through his head.

—※—

By the time they are back on the Boca Chica road and heading east again, the night is fully risen and its only light is from the flaming hamlet. The glow is visible for miles but the only witnesses in range of it are the four horsemen themselves and a trio of Mexican shepherds a half mile south of the river, and even the shepherds cannot see the smoke against a sky so black with clouds. The gunshots and screamings have carried unheard into the uninhabited countryside. The horsemen feel invigorated, two of them having taken their pleasure with Lupita Xocoto, the other two with Selma Fuentes. The remains of the entire population of Wolfe Landing—all eight residents, including two boys, ages six and three, and an infant girl but seven months old—are charring in the flames.

—※—

They ride to the end of the Boca Chica road and onto the beach, the enormous dark undulation of the gulf before them. In the eastern sky the clouds have broken and the lowest of the stars demarcate a vague horizon. The men head south along the smooth beach, the breeze briny, the swash of the breakers muting the jinglings of harness. After a time they see small glowings of light in the distance ahead. The house. When they close to within a hundred yards, they can tell by the lights that it is a two-story on the crest of the sloping beach. They ride up into the dunes and out of sight of the house and then turn south again. Their horses strain for footing in the soft sand and the men dismount and lead them by the reins. They traverse a road of logs packed over with a mixture of gravel and dirt, the trail to the Boca Chica road, the turnoff onto which they could never have found in the dark. When they reckon they are near the house they hobble the horses and crawl over two low dunes and reach the crest of a taller one. And there the house is, fifteen yards from them. Atop the dune they are still below the level of the roofless porch and the windows of the lower floor are much too high for them to see into the house. But the breeze carries to them the sound of laughter. They can make out the garage just south of the house, and a few yards behind it a shed. Lobo and Dax scurry to the shed in a low crouch. By matchlight they find the store of lamp oil for the house—three barrels, one tapped. On a shelf are several empty paint cans, and they fill three of them with oil. Then they roll the three barrels, each in turn, from the shed to the house, setting one against a piling at the rear southwest corner and the other two against the pilings at the east side front corners. They retrieve the open cans of oil and set one beside each of the barrels. Then rejoin Sarmiento and Pori on the dune. And wait for the moon to come up.

❖

Although Juan Lobo has imagined the pleasure of presenting the twins with their brother's head just before he kills them, the fact of the matter is that such a moment cannot be had without first capturing them, and to try to capture them is to give them more of a chance to make a fight of it. No. Not these two. The least chance possible for them. If they die without knowing who is killing them and why, so what? Even if they knew, they would no longer know it when they're dead, would they? The dead are without memory and so have no regret. Lobo well understands that the great failing of revenge is that the moment you kill a man you deliver him from pain and regret and can no longer get even with him. But. You can remember the occasion of getting even with him. You can remember it for the rest of your life. So. The thing of importance, Juan Lobo has told himself, the thing to keep in mind, is that these Wolfe twins will die because *he*, Juan Lobo, wills it. He who will know he was the instrument of their death and will take pleasure from that knowledge for as long as he has left to live.

❖

By eleven o'clock the house is quiet and its windows dark. At midnight a cusp of moon shows at the far end of the gulf. A fat bright crescent just entering its last quarter, it silvers the water surface as it ascends, brings the beach into pale form, shapes the house in distinct silhouette.

The moon is almost detached from the gulf when Lobo sends Fat Pori to his assigned post. They lose sight of him in the dunes until some minutes later when he appears on the beach about forty yards north of the house. He lies belly down and pushes sand into a mound in front of him for some modicum of concealment. From there he has an unobstructed and moonlit view of both the front of the house and its north side. He settles himself with rifle ready.

Now Lobo and Sarmiento and Dax scurry down to the house, Dax with his rifle slung on his shoulder. Each of them goes to one of the oil barrels and with his machete hacks a gash into it, the blades whunking loud through the metal. Each man then picks up a paint can of oil and pours a track of it from the pool forming around the barrel as he backs up, Lobo and Sarmiento moving toward the rear of the house, Dax toward its front. They strike matches and put them to the oil tracks. As the flames rush along the ground toward the barrels, Lobo and Sarmiento race back to the dune behind the house while Dax sprints out to a spot on the beach from which he can cover the dark south side of the house and, like Pori, the front as well. As he runs, the barrels boom into spheres of fire.

—◈—

The hackings into the oil barrels wake the twins. All the bedrooms are on the second floor and theirs are the last two at the north end of the rear of the house. Blake Cortéz lies still a moment, listening hard, a hand on the revolver under his pillow. When he gets up and goes to the window, Remedios wakes. What is it? she says. He shushes her and stares hard into the blackness directly behind the house. Reviews a quick mental roster of who is in the house. César and Hector are away on the *Remerina*, night fishing in the Laguna Madre. And then come the booms of the barrels bursting into flame—and in the glare of orange light from under the house, he glimpses two men ducking behind opposite ends of the nearest dune. At the same moment, James Sebastian, at the north window of his room and scanning the area without, spies the low mound of sand on the beach and the man lying prone behind it.

—◈—

Laced with distilled coal tar as protection against the elements, the pilings burn like oversized matchsticks. The fire sheets the underside of the house in less than a minute. It flares through the plank seams and leaps up from the floor inside, combusting the rugs and drapes, igniting the furniture. It scales the walls, finds the hallways. . . .

—◈—

The twins are in a hallway murky with smoke, James Sebastian with a Winchester, Blake Cortéz a double-barreled shotgun. Remedios has a wet cloth to her face, red eyes great with terror. Morgan and Jacky Ríos join them, revolvers in hand. "Las muchachas!" Remedios cries. James and Morgan start for the other side of the house where the girls' room is, the hallway ahead already churning in flames and smoke. They are about to run through the fire when a portion of the floor before them collapses in a downpour of burning wood and a swirling uprush of sparks. They hurry back to the others and James Sebastian says, "No way to them! They'll use the window!" His throat feels flayed. As they hasten down the burning stairway Blake says there are two behind the house and James says he spotted one on the beach. At the foot of the stairs part of a wall falls on Morgan, and his father and Jacky pull him out fast and beat at his clothes and hair and he hollers when they strike his broken arm. Blake is already heading with Remedios toward the back of the house and yelling at James to take the others out by the front.

❋

The sound of the machetes does not reach the room Catalina shares with Vicki Angel midway along the south side of the house and so she does not wake until she smells the smoke. She shouts for Vicki to wake up and flies into her clothes in the dark, the knife as always already on her belt. Vicki is confused in the darkness, terrified by the smoke and Catalina's urgency. She can't find her pants. Smoke is rising off the floor, their bare feet near to burning. The door shows a wavering band of light along its bottom edge and Catalina senses that to open the door is to admit hell. The window, she says, and pulls Vicki, still in her shift, over to it. This side of the house is away from the moon and still in darkness but for the glow of the fire from under the house, and they can barely see the ground thirty feet below. Catalina tells Vicki she'll lower her as far as she can before letting her drop, that it's soft sand, that she won't get hurt. As Vicki begins to ease out the window with Cat gripping her wrists, the door behind them erupts into flame and a searing blaze fills the room.

❋

Even at some forty yards from the house, their angles of vision and the forward projection of the porch permit Dax and Pori to see only the upper part of the front door. If the fuckers come out standing up, how convenient, but even if they crawl out on the porch and can't be seen, they'll soon enough have to come off the burning porch and into the light. Now an upper window on the dark side of the house comes aglow with fire and Dax sees a pair of vague silhouettes in it, one of them climbing out and holding to the other. He aims and shoots and hears a cry and the one partway out falls into the darkness below. He works the rifle bolt as the other scrabbles through the window and he shoots as that one too drops out of the frame of light. He works the bolt again and peers hard, but the uneven ground on that side of the house is all flickering shadows in the firelight and he cannot distinguish the forms of the two who dropped from the window. He hears nothing but the waves breaking on the sand, the crackling of the fire. Then rifleshots resound from the house and he returns his attention to the front porch.

—✥—

They're now in the kitchen and Remedios is suffocating. She lunges for the back door but Blake restrains her, forces her to the floor. Her hands are burning and she screams. He hunkers beside her and kicks the door open and lunges out onto the porch, pulling her with him—and the two men start shooting from either end of the dune. Keeping below their angle of sight and holding Remedios to him, Blake flings his shotgun over the porch's south rail, then drags Remedios to the rail and scoops her up and stands up and is shot in the back and shoulder as he heaves her over and then falls wheeling after her. He lands hard on the sand, jarred almost breathless. Remedios lies sprawled and still. He grabs the shotgun and is shot in the back yet again as he rolls under the porch and behind the steps. He lies prone, fighting for breath, then rises on his elbows and looks out between the porch steps and sees a muzzle flash at the near end of the dune, the bullet striking a step and deflecting into his side. He fires one barrel at a point just below where the flash was and the buckshot blows through the top of the dune and he glimpses a man pitching backward.

—✥—

A figure appears at the front door, visible only from the chest up, silhouetted by the firelight within. He stands just inside the door and to the left, as though aware of Pori and staying out of his view but unaware of Dax—who smiles as he shoots him. The man falls forward onto the porch and out of sight. Pori too sees the man fall and has the same thought as Dax—that whoever else comes onto the porch will do it in a crouch. But the fire is gobbling up the porch and the fuckers will have to come off it or be cooked.

—✥—

Embers fall into Blake's hair and burn into his scalp and he brushes them away. His clothes are smoking, his hands and face blistering. Through the flaming porch steps he watches the dune. The second man behind it has not fired again and Blake guesses he is positioning for a better shot. Maybe he's waiting till I have to move out from under here, he thinks. That's what I'd do. Then sees him on the dune crest, directly in front of the steps, looking at him, rising on his knees and raising a rifle. They both shoot.

—✥—

Juan Lobo is enraged. He knows he hit the son of a bitch twice—and he's still alive. Maybe Sarmiento hit him too before the fucker cut loose with that shotgun and probably nailed him. *Goddammit!* Shot up and roasting and he still nails the One-Eye! Lobo flings off his hat and slogs through the soft sand along the foot of the dune, moving to a better angle of fire. Right about here, he thinks, and crawls up the slope and peeks over the crest. The underside of the house is roiling with red-yellow fire and the glare of it makes him squint. He scans the flaming stairway. Sees him. Face framed between two of the lower steps and looking right at him like a devil peering out of hell. He rises to his knees as he brings up the rifle and he pulls the trigger at the same instant that the buckshot charge hits him. He feels himself floating rearward. Then is staring up at the whirling starry sky. Whirling and whirling and fading and gone.

—⚜—

Jacky Ríos and Morgan crawl out beside James Sebastian on the porch floor as the gunfire continues on the rear side of the house. The planks under them are crackling and smoking, the fire closing on them from every direction but ahead. A shotgun resounds and the shooting behind the house abruptly ceases. There's two out here, James Sebastian says, wheezing. The one that hit me's somewhere to the right but the other's at ten o'clock. Jacky picks up James Sebastian's Winchester, scorching his hand, and crawls forward to the porch rails and peers between them. He scans the beach slightly to his left. Sees nothing. Wipes at his streaming eyes and looks again. Sees the slight mound and what could be a head peering over it. He aims between the rail slats. Shoots. The head jerks and drops forward. Now Jacky drags James Sebastian down the steps and Morgan James comes tumbling behind them and cries out at the pain of his arm, all of them ready to take a fatal bullet rather than burn to death—as a shotgun and rifle fire together from the back of the house.

—⚜—

"No te mueres, querido! No te mueres!" Blake is hazily aware of being dragged by fits and starts, of gruntings and profanity and crying. He tastes blood, smells burned flesh. Now recognizes Remedios's voice. Pleading with him not to die as she drags him, tug by tug, away from the flaming house.

—⚜—

In the firelight shadows alongside the house, Catalina crawls to Vicki and finds her unconscious but breathing. She searches by feel for a wound and finds it on her left buttock. Entry and exit without hitting bone. Bloody but not bad. Vicki moans at her probe of it and Cat claps a hand over her mouth, shushes her, tells her to be very quiet. She can see the prone form of the shooter on the moonlit beach and knows he's looking their way but can't make them out among the gyrating shadows. Lock your teeth, she tells Vicki. Then drags her away from the growing heat of the burning house, their gaspings inaudible over the breaking waves. About ten yards from the edge of the house's shadow is a grassy sand dune, but the man is still looking this way. Catalina is sure she will be shot as she runs across that moonlit span but she cannot lie there and do nothing. Stay here and don't move, she tells Vicki. Just then there's riflefire at the house and the man's head turns in that direction, and Cat dashes out of the shadows and over the open ground, expecting a bullet at every stride. But she reaches the dune without drawing fire and keeps on running. There's a rifleshot from the beach and she nearly yells in rage that the man may have shot Vicki. She estimates her position as she runs, and when she's sure she is south of him she starts scrabbling up the dune. A shotgun fires somewhere. She reaches the crest and sees him to her left, a prone stark figure on the moonbright beach. She comes down the dune in a crouch, thinking, Don't turn, don't turn, don't turn. And then she's on the beach and twenty feet behind him and starts closing fast, knife in hand, her footfalls muted by the breakers. At the house a rifle fires, and the man on the beach raises his head slightly, the better to see as three men come stumbling down the porch steps and into the light of the moon. The man lowers his face to take aim.

And Cat plunges onto him and he is dead before he can know his neck is skewered to the rifle stock.

REMAINS OF NIGHT

Each twin asks about the other and learns he yet lives. As familiar as they are with mortal wounds, they refuse Jacky Ríos's plea to drive them to the hospital in town, not wanting to die in such a place or in a car on the way to it. With broken-armed Morgan following, Jacky and Catalina and Remedios carry Blake Cortéz down to the edge of the beach where his brother sits. They ease him down beside James, facing the moonbright sea.

"Dame un beso, mujer . . . y déjanos," Blake says. Remedios kisses him and then hurries away with tears coursing.

James beckons Morgan, who says "Yessir" and crouches before him.

"It's on . . . you now," James says. "See to things. Kiss . . . your momma for me."

Morgan cannot speak. He grips his father's hand and nods. Then goes.

After a minute, James says, "Who the hell . . . those guys?"

Blake tries to shrug. "Bastards . . . mad about . . . *something.*"

James grins and makes a sound like a small hiccup. "Took it awful . . . *personal.*"

A long minute passes.

"I'd rather . . . firing squad . . . than this," James says.

Blake chokes on his chuckle. "Puffing . . . cigar."

"Girls fighting . . . over us."

"That old . . . Bad Wolfe."

"Jolly Roger."

They groan their laughter.

The day breaks. The sky at the end of the gulf graduates from gray to pink, a thin shred of orange, a welter of reds. The house reduced to a great black rectangle of smoking embers. The tide now rolling to within a few feet of the twins. Morgan

James and Jacky Ríos sit together at the top of the beach slope, watching their fathers. Remedios too, holding Vicki Angel to her, the girl on her side, keeping the weight off her wound. Catalina sits apart. The twins have not moved in almost an hour, but they all know. Not yet.

The sun flares up from the gulf as the *Remerina* comes in sight to the north, its sail white as a seabird.

"So damn … *grand*," Blackie breathes. And his head descends to his brother's shoulder.

"Yessss. . . ." Jake manages as his head lowers.

And their family—their blood—comes down to collect them.

EPILOGUE

They find the four horses. The gold and silver in the saddlebags. Find the moldering head, a pair of lensless spectacles affixed to it with a strip of wire, and bury it, bespectacled, by the roadside. Later in the morning they find the horror at Wolfe Landing amid the smoking grove. The roasted bones in the embers. And that afternoon find the staggering heartbreak at the Levee house, where the Wolfe sons weep for the first time since infancy.

They report to the county sheriff and the chief of police the savagery visited on them by a gang of killers. Inform them that the bastards' bodies are in the brush a half mile inland from Playa Blanca. Feeding the scavengers.

❀

The next day, after telling Mamá Sófi and Remedios of their intention, the three sons go to the Davis & Sons Mortuary and retrieve their fathers' bodies and convey them by wagon to the mouth of the river. There, with no witnesses save themselves, holding to the promise their fathers asked of them some time before, the sons bury the twins on a grassy rise with a fine view of the gulf.

❀

Two days after that, there is a funeral service for ten at once in the Brownsville cemetery. For the five Xocotos, the three Fuentes, the two Wolfes. When Wolfe Landing is raised anew, as it will be—just as the house at Playa Blanca will be—Marina Colmillo and Harry Sebastian Wolfe will be reburied there, the first to be interred in the town's graveyard. The Brownsville funeral is restricted to the families of the deceased, with the exception of James and Pauline Wells. Following the ceremony, the judge has a few quiet words with the three young Wolfe men. They accept his invitation to supper on Sunday next. There are matters he wishes to discuss with them. Propositions. Constable badges.

❖

That night they have supper in the Levee Street house of Remedios Marisól, all of them, every surviving borderland Wolfe—Mamá Sofía, Remedios and her sons Jacky Ríos and César Augusto, her daughter Vicki Angel, the orphaned and now brotherless Morgan James. Also present are the Littles, John Louis and Úrsula, Hector Louis, Catalina. Two tables have been pushed together to accommodate the ten of them and the many platters of food. There are tubs of iced beer, a phonograph player issuing ranchero music. They have all had several rounds of beer when Morgan James recounts the time Marina caught them exposing themselves to Vicki Angel on the beach and threatened to tie their things in a permanent knot, an episode that comes as news to Mamá Sófi and Remedios, who belatedly berate the boys for their nastiness—and then a minute later and despite their blushes they are laughing along with everyone else, including Vicki and Catalina.

So does it go the rest of the night. They eat and drink and dance and tell funny story after funny story about their lost beloveds. In the middle of a dance with Catalina, César Augusto asks her to marry him, and she laughs at that too and says maybe she will, maybe she won't. He asks what the hell kind of answer that is and she says it's the kind he gets for now, and he goes out on the porch and sulks. A short time later she goes out to him and gives him the best kiss of his young life and he beams his happiness and asks if that means yes and she says no, it only means maybe she will, maybe she won't. In that moment he senses the sort of marriage ahead of him if she should finally say yes, which he also senses she has decided to say but in her own good time.

The neighbors shake their heads at the loud music and raucous laughter from the Wolfe house. They regard as most unseemly such a party only hours after burying two of their own and eight friends besides. They should be mourning, the neighbors tell each other. They should be grieving.

The Wolfes *are* mourning, of course, they *are* grieving. But grief cannot restrain the shared laughter at their reminiscences of Marina, and of Harry Sebastian, and of the twins. The twins, above all. Who founded this borderland family and who are already the stuff of legend. And whose graves will be forced opened by the next hurricane and their bones borne away to the sea.

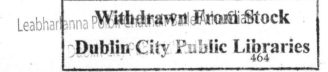